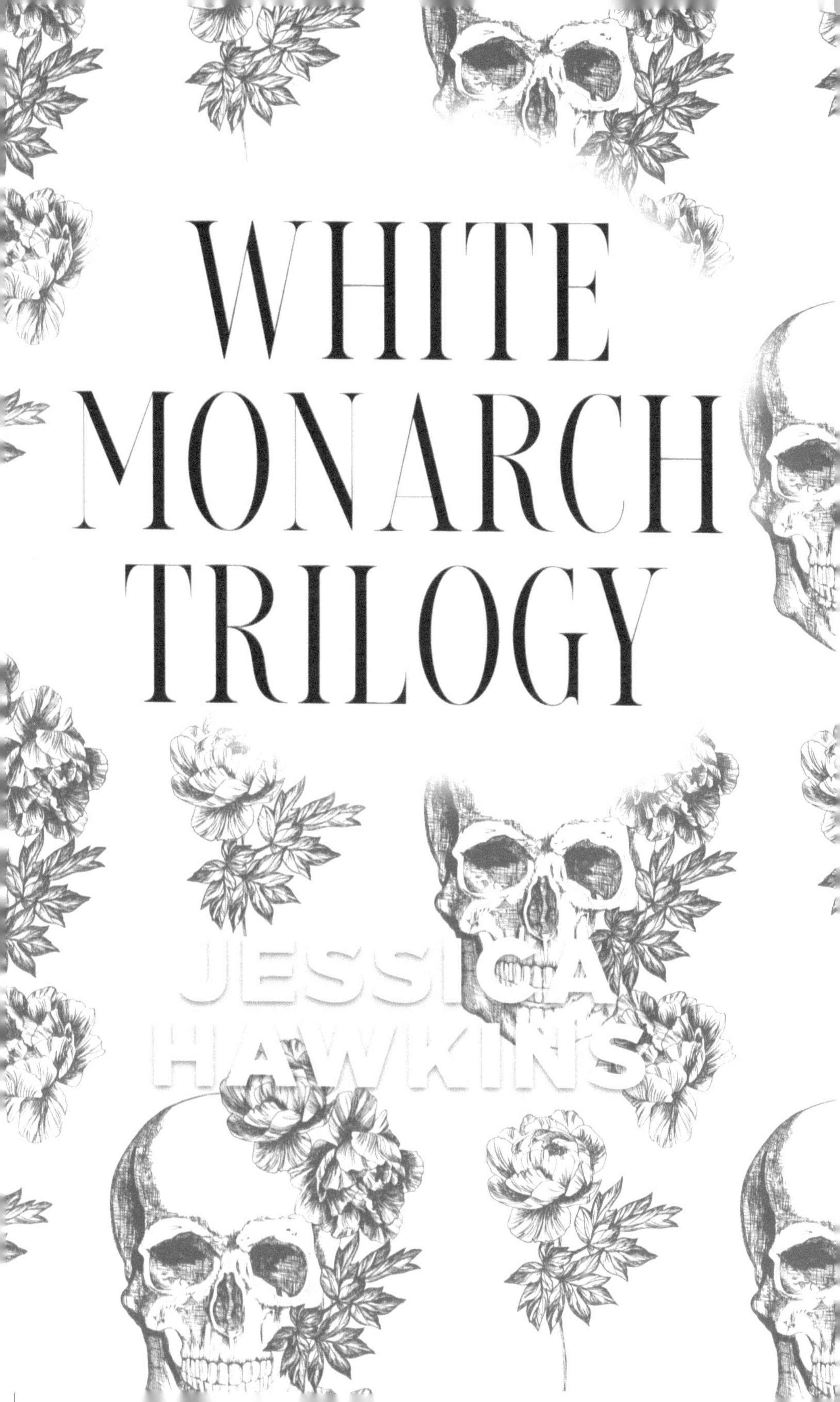
WHITE
MONARCH
TRILOGY
JESSICA
HAWKINS

## PRAISE FOR JESSICA HAWKINS

Twisty, chaotic, sexy, smart, and well written . . . An absolute must read.

— ANGIE'S DREAMY READS

Cristiano steals the show. This man. I am next level obsessed. For a Cartel leader who shows no emotions, **this man was fierce, lethal, and without even trying, completely romantic**.

— BOOKSANDBANDANAS, GOODREADS

Exciting and suspenseful and sexy and breathtaking.

— LAUREN ROWE, *USA TODAY* BESTSELLING AUTHOR

**Kindle-melting hot.** I laughed, I gasped, I chewed all my nails off. This author is proving herself to be a ruiner of my heart because she played with it so masterfully.

— AMAZON REVIEWER

Jessica Hawkins has **raised the bar where sexual tension and anticipation is concerned**. At this point in the game, no one writes it better.

— ROX, GOODREADS

[Hawkins] writing is so sophisticated, and kept me on the edge of my seat the whole time. I literally couldn't put the book down for two days—I lost sleep over it.

— VICTORIA, AMAZON

**Addictive and deliciously promising.**

— RS GREY, *USA TODAY* BESTSELLING AUTHOR

*The White Monarch Trilogy* is available in:
Ebook
Audiobook
Paperback
Hardcover



Editing by Elizabeth London Editing

Beta by Underline This Editing

Proofreading by Paige Maroney Smith

Cover Designed by Najla Qamber Designs

# VIOLENT DELIGHTS

## BOOK ONE

I was born a princess among criminals. An untouchable among thieves. Heiress to a life others have killed for, and one I'd do anything to escape. I vowed not to leave without Diego, my first love and best friend, but if his ruthless brother has his way, I won't leave at all.

Cristiano de la Rosa is a man as big and bold as his legend. Once upon a time, he was our cartel's best soldier . . . until he became my family's worst enemy. And a man like Cristiano will bend fate to his will to get what he wants—even if it means tearing me from another's arms.

Because in the de la Rosa family, old grudges run deeper than loyalty, and betrayal is a three-letter word: war. But his feud isn't between enemies—it's between brothers. And I'm the prize.

PROLOGUE

# NATALIA

On my bedroom balcony, I danced to the upbeat mariachi music coming from the parade in town. Street fireworks popped and crackled to a soundtrack of trumpets and violins, but I couldn't see much beyond the fortress of olive trees surrounding our compound. They'd been planted after my first birthday party, when my father had been shot at in the backyard while holding me. The *sicario* had hit an inflatable bouncy castle instead, trapping kids inside and inciting a mob of screaming parents. That was what my best friend had told me years later, anyway, and Diego would know, since his parents had ordered the hit.

I waved to one of the guards, who tipped his AK-47 to me. I was supposed to be at the Day of the Dead parade now, honoring the deceased. Diego had promised me two slices of sugar skull cake if I went early and got a good spot, but since Papá was out of town with half his security, my mother didn't want me leaving the premises without her. And as important as every man around here acted, she was the neck that turned the head of the Cruz cartel.

I returned inside to see why she was taking so long, twirling through the maze of hallways so the colorful, floral embroidery of my floor-length skirt ran together. Almost an hour ago, my mother had been nearly ready in an off-the-shoulder, white, green, and yellow dress with a red ruffle along the bottom. She'd pulled her hair back with silk, orange marigolds, and I'd stood on a stepstool to clasp her necklace, a starburst with gilded chains heavy enough to sink a small ship.

"We're missing the parade," I called as I skipped down the corridor, my woven leather sandals clicking on the tile. I rounded the corner into my parents' sunny bedroom, tripped, and landed in a puddle.

A pair of combat boots stopped in front of me. I raised my eyes to meet the cold, distant gaze of a man dressed in all black—Cristiano de la Rosa, a high-level member of my father's security team.

"Get out of here," he ordered. "Now."

Cristiano was all brawn, beast, and towering height with opaque eyes to match his hair. Based on the stories Diego had told me, people feared his older brother, but I had no real reason to. Though their parents had been enemies of ours once, Cristiano and Diego had been on our side for eight of the nine years I'd been alive.

Plus, Mamá had always told me—go to Cristiano in an emergency. He would protect me.

But something was off. He didn't like me being here.

In one of his large, powerful hands, he held an army-green duffel bag. In the other, a solid black gun. Then, there was the blood—on his pants, splattered on his shoes and hands.

And on mine. Warm and sticky between my fingers, soaking through my fancy skirt. Not even its metallic smell could mask my mother's signature perfume.

I looked over my shoulder. I hadn't tripped over my own two feet, but hers. Mamá was lying on her back. Sunlight glinted off the large, gold necklace she'd bought for the parade. Her gleaming black hair was coming loose from its bun after she'd spent all that time pinning flowers in it. She shouldn't be on the ground in her expensive new dress—it was already ripped at the neckline. The vibrant design almost hid what seeped through its fabric, pooling on the terra-cotta tile underneath her body.

*Blood.*

Goose bumps started at my scalp and spread to my fingers and toes. *No.*

Gasping for air, I scrambled to her side. "Mamá."

Her lids eased open as she struggled to focus. "Natalia," she managed.

My chin wobbled as I fought back tears and grasped her still-warm hand. A bruise formed on her cheek.

"*Mija.*" She fought to keep her eyes open, but they went glassy as her gaze shifted over my head. "Please, Cristiano," she begged, her voice strangled. "Please don't . . ." She shuddered with the effort. "My daughter . . ."

"I'm here," I whispered, but she wasn't talking to me.

I looked up at Cristiano. His jaw sharpened as he clenched it and turned his face away. "*Sueña con los angelitos.*"

*Dream with little angels.* When I turned back, she'd gone still.

"No," I whispered.

Cristiano tossed the bag and gun onto the cloud-like comforter and reached for me. On instinct, I dove under the bed, knowing he'd be too big to follow—and came face to face with *la Monarca Blanca.* I wrapped my hand around the cold, hard metal of my father's two-tone silver-and-gold-plated 9mm. Time slowed as I ran my thumb over the pearl grip where the name was engraved into the side.

*White Monarch.*

I choked back a sob. This was the kind of emergency I was supposed to go to Cristiano for, but *he* was the one standing over my mother's dead body as she begged him for mercy.

He grabbed my ankles and slid me out from under the bed. I screamed in a way I never had before, ear-splitting, throat-shredding, as I tried to kick him off.

He clamped a hand over my mouth as his other arm circled my body and pinned my arms to my sides. "Natalia, *hush,*" he said in his chillingly deep voice as he lifted me off the ground. "Let me handle this."

I wailed against his hand, thrashing and trying to hit him with the gun, but my arms were trapped. I slammed my heels into his thigh and groin.

But Cristiano was the cartel's most lethal soldier for a reason. It wouldn't have mattered who I was—nobody could match his strength, which had to be that of two men. By the age of twenty-three, he had more kills under his belt than most in the cartel.

He'd been raised as a weapon.

His hands had taken the lives of our family's enemies—but never any of our own.

Until now.

Footsteps sounded in the hall, and Diego rushed into the room with his gun drawn. He stopped short and sucked in a breath as he noticed the body. He shut his lids briefly. I tried to call for my best friend, but Cristiano's hand muffled my words.

Diego's eyes flew open and darted over Cristiano and me. He was dressed for the parade in a loose, white button-down and jeans. He scanned the room, his gaze shrewd as he tucked some loose strands of his brown hair behind his ear. "What the hell is this? What happened?"

"I don't know," Cristiano said. "I got here right before you did."

*Liar.* I inhaled smoke and gunpowder as I squirmed against Cristiano's hand, trying to convey to Diego what I'd seen.

Diego turned his attention on me, his forehead wrinkling as if he was trying to read my mind. *He did this,* I tried to tell him. *Cristiano shot her.*

After a moment, Diego swallowed. "Put Natalia down."

"Holster the gun, and I will," Cristiano answered.

Diego looked at his pistol as if he hadn't realized he'd been holding it. He was no saint, either—he'd done things I wasn't supposed to hear about at my age, according to Papá—but that didn't make Diego anything like his brother. Diego was a lover, not a fighter. He was only sixteen, and he still had a chance to make something of his life. His eyes drifted from the firearm to my mother, then across the room. His expression eased as realization seemed to dawn on him. He turned back to Cristiano.

"After everything they've done for us?" Diego asked and gestured the gun toward my parents' walk-in closet. "This is how you repay them?"

The safe lay open and empty except for scattered paperwork. The White Monarch had been in there, along with cash and my mother's jewels. I tried to nod at the duffel bag but couldn't move my head.

"Careful what you say, Diego," Cristiano said evenly. "You *know* I didn't do this."

"Then who?" Diego asked. "The house is surrounded by security. Who else could get in here? In the safe?"

"It was already open," Cristiano said in an increasingly frustrated voice. "As I said, I walked in right before you."

Diego shoved his fingers through his hair, then spotted the duffel. "What's that?" Diego would never hurt me, but when he raised his gun at us, my heartbeat quickened. He kept the weapon and his eyes on Cristiano as he moved toward the bed. With his free hand, Diego slid the bag across the comforter and glanced inside. "Cash and jewelry from the safe, but not much."

"I know." Cristiano readjusted his grip around my torso. "I found it discarded by the bed."

"Where's the rest of it?"

Cristiano hesitated. "Someone must've been here—"

"Impossible," Diego said, and he was right. My father took no risks when it came to his family's safety. "There are two ways in—through the guards out front or the guards at the tunnels."

Diego took a two-way radio from his back pocket.

"Diego," Cristiano said, warning clear in his voice. "Don't."

He pressed a button and spoke into the device. "*Doña* Bianca has been shot. By Cristiano. I need security in here now."

Cristiano noticeably stiffened behind me. "*Vete a la chingada*," he cursed. "You're going to tell Costa I did this? I'm your blood, Diego."

"And Bianca was just as much my family." The anguish in Diego's eyes conveyed what my mother meant to him. At her urging, my family had taken him in when he was only eight and Cristiano was fifteen. Tears leaked from my eyes and onto Cristiano's hand as I looked anywhere but at her body.

"She was family to *me*, too," Cristiano said through his teeth. He was so angry, his voice broke, and he forgot to keep my mouth covered. "You can't accuse me of hurting her."

"All you do is hurt people," I screamed. "You're a—"

He slapped his hand over my mouth just as the front door slammed downstairs. "*Fuck*," Cristiano said. "Tell them I didn't do this, Diego, or they'll kill me on the spot."

"Release Natalia," Diego begged. "Please. Try to remember who you were before all of this—you wouldn't have hurt an innocent girl."

Cristiano started left then shifted to go right, as if trapped. Finally, he released my mouth but kept me against him like a shield as he one-handedly wrestled the White Monarch from my grip.

He was going to kill Diego next.

*Diego*.

The boy who'd not only watched me grow up, but had protected me like an older brother. Who'd never treated me like a little girl despite a seven-year age difference. Who brought me stinky marigolds when I was sad and never complained that we could only ride our horses up to and along the fence Papá had built to keep me in, even though *Diego* could go anywhere he wanted.

Diego's eyes widened as Cristiano got the gun from me. It would devastate Diego to kill his own brother, but for Cristiano to shoot Diego, it would mean nothing. Cristiano took lives all the time.

"You're caught, brother," Diego said. His nostrils flared as his anger finally seemed to override his confusion. "Don't make this worse than it is. Put her down and face them."

Boots pounded up the staircase with a chorus of shouting men. Cristiano carried me toward the door, his back to the wall, eyes on Diego. He switched the gun to his other hand to lock the door.

In that split second, Diego lunged forward.

Cristiano whipped around and pulled the trigger.

I screamed when the shot rang through the air, covering my ears as I hit the ground. Diego crumpled, clutching his bloodied thigh.

Men pounded at the bullet-resistant door Papá had specially

installed. Fists hammered the wood, followed by what sounded like the butts of their rifles.

Cristiano picked up Diego's gun, stuck it in his waistband, and leveled the White Monarch on his brother's writhing body. "You left me no choice. Loyalty is king around here, but look how quickly it's broken."

"Don't shoot—I know a way out," I exclaimed through my sobs. Cristiano towered over me, looking like the Grim Reaper himself. "I can help you escape," I said.

Cristiano stilled. "It's not possible."

"I know a secret way." My voice shook. I wasn't helping my mother's killer, I told myself, but protecting Diego and me.

"Natalia, no," Diego said, huffing as he made an effort to sit up. "He—he has to pay for this."

"Where is it?" Cristiano asked.

Diego was getting unnaturally pale as if he might pass out any second. I got to my feet and started to go to him, but Cristiano grabbed my arm and yanked me back against his hip. "They'll get in before he dies. Show me the way out."

Diego groaned and closed his eyes, and I inhaled a quick, stuttering breath to keep my panic at bay. "The c-closet," I managed.

Cristiano marched me back across the room and into my old nursery. Once I'd outgrown the space, my mother had converted it into a sizeable walk-in closet that held much more than just clothing. There were walls of shoes, purses, drawers, and mirrors, as well as an island in the center for her costume jewelry and Papá's ties.

Cristiano took a chair from my mother's vanity dresser, wedged it under the closet's door handle, and turned to look at me. "Now what?"

I couldn't think. There was a bullet in my mother's stomach and one in my best friend's leg. My bloodied skirt stuck to my knees. I was going to be sick. "The . . . the dresses."

Cristiano walked to me. He put the chilled metal barrel of the gun under my chin and tilted back my head to get me to look him in the eye. "If they get in here before I get out, I can't promise we'll both make it out alive. Show me the escape, or tell your father I didn't do this. Those are your options."

I tried to swallow, but I couldn't even breathe. I'd never been so sure I would die if I made one wrong move. I shook my head hard. "I won't lie for you."

"Look what loyalty got me, Natalia." He raised the gun higher and I glanced down the barrel. The silver nearly sparkled under the closet's lamp. "Whether I did or didn't do this, I'm dead. If they don't get me here, they'll hunt me down. That isn't loyalty, and there is no justice."

"*Loyalty?*" I was shaking now, but there was no quiver in Cristiano's voice, no tremble in his hand. "You killed my mother. Why? She cared about you—she treated you like a *son*."

His Adam's apple bobbed as we stared at each other. "Show me the way out," he commanded.

"I'll help you, but only to save Diego," I said. "Promise you'll never come back here."

"I can't." His expression hardened as his voice dropped. "Consider this a lesson—never trade your life for someone else's."

I backed away slowly, turned, and went to the safe. Amongst the papers, I found the small metal box I needed. I popped it open, took out a key, and stilled with a *bang* from the next room. If security was breaking down the door, then Diego must not have been able to let them in. I quickly prayed he was still alive.

I hurried to the closet that held my mother's party dresses. They were heavy enough that I had to use both hands to push them apart so I could crawl through them. "In here," I said.

Against the closet's back wall, I felt around for a keyhole. It was dark, but my father had walked me through this plenty of times. There were tunnels under the house all the security knew about, including Cristiano, but *this* secret passageway was only for my parents and me. When I'd pointed out to Papá that the men who'd built it must've known about it, he'd exchanged a grim look with my mother and changed the subject.

I put the key into the hole, but it was already unlocked. I slid the wall open to reveal a dark, dank room. "There."

If Cristiano was surprised, he didn't show it. "There what?"

I pointed to a trapdoor inside. "Go down that hole. There are no lights; you'll have to feel your way."

He stared into the dark. "How do I know this isn't a trap?"

"It's your only choice."

He got closer, his presence looming tall. "Open it for me."

It wasn't a request. Fortunately, my father had ensured that I knew the escape drill well, so entering the small space wasn't foreign to me.

I squatted down to unlatch the trapdoor that led to the one passageway nobody else knew about. Cristiano closed and bolted the door behind himself, extinguishing everything but a sliver of the closet's warm light.

I hoisted open the hatch and it fell with a hard *thud* against the ground. I concentrated on keeping my voice steady. "This also connects to the tunnels the mules use," I explained. "But if you stay to the left, that's a way nobody else knows about. It will take you south."

"To where?"

I glanced back at him. "That's all my parents told me."

The dark turned him into a shadow as he stalked toward me. "I'll have to take you with me."

"What?"

"We're going down there together."

I backed away, but since he blocked the door, there wasn't anywhere to go. "Why?"

He tucked the White Monarch into his waistband with his other gun, grabbed my arm, and yanked me toward the entrance of the tunnel. I flew forward, no match for his strength. My heart leapt into my throat as everything happened in a flash. He couldn't take me. He wouldn't. Nobody dared cross my father—but Cristiano already had, and now, he had nothing left to lose. If he got me into that tunnel, I'd never return. Never see Diego again. My father. I wouldn't attend my mother's funeral.

"I *helped* you," I said as more sobs bubbled up into my throat. I looked down the ladder. Since we were on the second floor, one push would send me flying some five meters down into the pitch dark. "Why are you doing this?"

"To show you that you can't trust anyone. Not me, not Diego, maybe not even your parents. Just because you help someone doesn't mean they won't betray you." He turned toward the ladder. "And because I need a head start. Get on my back."

Once he released me, I switched into high gear. Perhaps he was known for his ruthlessness, but I'd spent my short life sneaking into places I shouldn't, surprising even the stealthiest of my father's guards. I grasped the White Monarch from his pants and stumbled back, leveling the pistol on him with both hands.

With the light at my back, I saw a hint of amusement flash in his eyes. "You don't know true fear, little girl. It puts you in danger."

I *did* know fear. I was staring at my mother's murderer. I couldn't swallow. Couldn't hear over the deafening pounding of my heart.

Wherever Cristiano surfaced, my father would kill him.

Or I could save Papá the trouble and do it myself.

For the first time since before I'd tripped over my mother's dying body, calmness fell over me. Nobody had been able to stop Cristiano —not my mother or father, not Diego, and not security. I could, though. He deserved to die for his sins.

I urged myself to act, but something Cristiano had said stopped me. *There is no justice*. Was I sure, down to my very core, that he had done this? What if he hadn't? I didn't know him nearly as well as I did Diego. Cristiano was fourteen years older than me—a man. Despite his reputation as a killer, he had always treated me with kindness.

And my mother, too.

But as he'd said—you couldn't trust anyone in this world. Not even your own blood.

"Do it," he invited.

Based on what I'd seen, I was pretty sure in order to shoot, I first had to slide the top of the gun toward me. But the firearm itself was so heavy, I needed both hands to keep it steady. I glanced at the top part to determine the best way to do this.

"Never hesitate, Natalia." Cristiano snatched the pistol from me and pressed the muzzle to my forehead. "See? *Bang*. You're dead."

My breath caught in my throat. *I was dead*. Defenseless. Shivering like the little girl I was.

"And *never* draw a weapon you can't operate. When you aim, kill." He flicked a switch on the side, stuck the gun back in his pants, and grabbed me.

"Stop," I cried and pushed against him as he hugged me to his chest with his arm.

"Hold on." One-handedly, he quickly descended the ladder.

I wrapped my arms around his neck. He was the furthest thing from a safe place, but in that moment, I was no longer concerned with being brave. I was trapped. I gave into my fear, submitting to the warmth of his body, sobbing into his neck as he descended into the dark.

"Is there another key to the secret door?" he asked.

I sniffled. "My father keeps it on him."

"He's probably already on his way," Cristiano said, almost consolingly. "They'll find you eventually, Natalia. This is the only way I'll be able to put enough distance between them and me."

It was cold and black at the bottom. I shivered uncontrollably as he reached the final rung of the ladder and jumped the rest of the way. *Never go down if you don't have to,* Father had said. *You won't be able to reach the ladder to get back up.*

This was it. I was at Cristiano's mercy now.

On solid ground, he took a few slow steps, feeling for a wall. When he found one, he squatted. "Sit here," he said. "Don't move until they come for you."

I didn't let go of his neck. The scent of his sweat and my tears mixed with the soil around us. I'd never been worried about the dark before, but I couldn't even see my own hand.

"What if nobody comes?" I asked.

"They will. And by that time, I'll be long gone." He pulled at my arms. "You're brave. Let go."

I released him. The next thing I heard was his retreating footsteps.

I sat against the wall, wrapped my arms around my knees, and held my breath. Tears flooded my eyes, overflowing onto my cheeks.

I'd always known the love and protection of my parents and their titles. Being the daughter of one of the most powerful drug lords in Mexico meant I'd been in danger since the day I was born—and also sheltered from everything.

No longer.

As the threat of Cristiano receded, I was left alone in the dark with the realization that my mother had kissed my cheek and tucked me in for the last time. Her lyrical voice would never again lull me to sleep and end each night with, *"Te quiero mucho, mariposita."* There would be no more of her famous homemade "Talia taffy" for the rest of my birthdays, no more riding horses into town to shop for fabric or spices.

That morning, impatient to go, I'd hugged her waist and asked her to hurry up as she'd done her makeup. Now, I wished only to stay with her a little longer. I wished for more time.

But the parade was over.

Death's day had come.

# CHAPTER 1

## ELEVEN YEARS LATER

# NATALIA

I ducked out of the helicopter and into dry desert air as the blades whipped wind through my hair. My father's head of security offered a hand and helped me down. "*Bienvenida a casa, señorita,*" Barto called over the whir of the rotors.

*Welcome home.*

The pilot carried my bags to a black Suburban waiting on the tarmac. Somehow, the Mexican heat felt stronger than in California, the sun intense and unforgiving. I slipped my sunglasses into place and followed Barto to the car.

"How's it feel to be back?" he asked.

No words could properly convey it. Leaving home for a boarding school in the United States had been my choice, but Father would've shipped me off even if it wasn't. I both dreaded and anticipated coming here. California was safe, clean, easy. Nothing like this place, where danger haunted the streets. It was the thought of seeing Diego that lifted any sense of dread that came with getting into a car headed for home.

Barto glanced at me in the rearview mirror. "If I can say so, you look more and more like *señora* Cruz each time I see you."

I had my mother's light eyes, and her small, sharp nose, but our physical similarities stopped there. "I'm more like my father," I said.

"But you have her grace."

I swallowed. *Regal* was how my father often described her.

"And that determined look she often wore," Barto added.

I didn't doubt that. I wasn't only home to spend time with my dad, catch up with friends, and celebrate Easter. I was here for Diego—my best friend and my love. The boy who knew all my secrets because he'd been there for many of them, if not physically, then a phone call away. But with the distance between us, we'd done enough talking for a lifetime. I couldn't wait to just be close to him for the first time in a year.

Next summer, I'd be graduating, and I was dead set on having Diego in Santa Clara with me by then—permanently. But since my dad wanted the opposite, it would take some convincing.

Barto steered us up the long, winding drive lined with imported banana leaf trees. Men with AR-15s stood along the side of the dirt road, waving us on, smiling at me through the blacked-out windows.

Barto handled my luggage and sent me straight upstairs to see my father. At the threshold to Papá's study at the south end of the mansion, I stopped when I heard his raised voice. "Do you have any *idea* the magnitude of what you've committed us to?"

"We can handle it." When Diego spoke, a kaleidoscope of butterflies erupted in my stomach. "We've been refining our operation for over a decade, and it's as close to perfect as it gets."

"'Close to perfect' is not perfect," came my father's grave response.

"Nevertheless, we're ready. With this partnership, we take things to the next level."

I should've made my presence known. I'd found out at a young age that sneaking around was the only way to get information. Back then, it'd been exciting. Now, information was both powerful and burdensome. People who knew too much were targets. Witnesses. Leverage. The more you knew, the harder it was to escape this life.

And the more dangerous you became.

But my curiosity continued to burn the brightest flame, no matter how I tried to extinguish it. I resisted the old habit of removing my shoes to mute my steps, but I still peeked into the light-filled room, finally laying my eyes on Diego. He was as beautiful as ever. His normally silken brown hair had been kissed by the sun and was long enough to tuck behind his ears. He'd been working outdoors more, and it showed, not just in his skin tone and hair color, but in his broad, muscular shoulders. He stood straight and tall to address my father. I wanted to run and throw my arms around his neck, but Papá wouldn't stand for it.

*Patience*, Diego had told me a million times before.

It had never been my strong suit.

"This is not a *partnership*." Deep lines slatted across Papá's tanned face. Each time I saw him, he appeared older, but his voice boomed, and his clear, molten brown eyes painted him as more youthful than his fifty years. He was as astute as ever, and his overbearing height defied how the bags under his eyes sometimes made him seem tired. "The Maldonado cartel is not a partner but a master," he said. "With this deal, they'll own us."

I considered entering the room and cutting off the conversation, but the name stopped me short. Even *I* knew—and I made it my business not to know much anymore—doing business with the Maldonados was dangerous.

"Times have changed, Costa," Diego said. "Eleven years ago, you reevaluated your business model, trading risk for security and violence for a quiet life—not that such a thing exists in this world. It's time to adapt again."

With my mother's death, much had changed, and not just in the obvious ways. Father had scaled back his business as newer, more bloodthirsty cartels like the Maldonados had come up the ranks.

"My father would roll in his grave to know we're not as feared as we once were," my dad said, glancing out the window of his second-floor office.

Diego put a hand on his shoulder. "We're still here, and we're just as powerful, but in different ways."

Diego spoke earnestly and with his hands. It was hard *not* to see his passion, intelligence, and charm, but that still wasn't enough to convince Papá that Diego was the man for me. Nobody was good enough in my father's eyes—especially not someone who belonged in this world. My father cared about Diego in his own way; he'd practically raised him. But unless I could convince him otherwise, Diego would always be a soldier, a right-hand man, a cartel member . . . and a threat to my safety.

"Many leaders of the old order have either been captured, killed, or forced out," Diego continued. "Who of your former enemies remains? Not many. I'm going to ensure the Cruz cartel—and the de la Rosas—don't fall to the same fate. We do that by moving forward with the times."

"The de la Rosas don't exist," Father said, warning in his voice as he regarded Diego with heavy eyebrows. "You're a Cruz. And while I know our success is as important to you as it is to me, there's risk in wanting more. There's much to be said for stability."

"With new technology hitting the market each day, there's more risk in staying still. We're number one in shipping and logistics now, but that can always change."

I leaned on the doorjamb, worried Diego was into something he shouldn't be. If I asked either of them why they'd taken a meeting with the Maldonados in the first place, I'd get the same answer I always did.

*Don't worry.* Todo bien. *Everything's fine.*

My father rubbed his forehead as he frowned. "And making a risky deal is moving forward?"

"We'll deliver," Diego said, crossing his arms with a shrug. "Their requirements are no different than any of our other arrangements. They have a valuable shipment to get across the border. As the premier transportation option in México, we can make that happen. Simple."

"The difference is who we're dealing with. How much product are we moving?"

"More than we're used to," Diego admitted. "But I'm not concerned. As other cartels distract themselves battling each other, we've solidified a nearly flawless, strategic network. I've assured them an eighty-seven percent success rate."

"Eighty-seven, eh?" Papá asked, slipping on his glasses to bend over and read his computer screen.

"Lower than our stellar average," Diego said, pulling back his shoulders. "We've delivered better results countless times, and in less than the twenty-one days they've given us."

"And after that?"

"We make a more permanent arrangement," Diego said. "With the rate they're growing, their business could take us to the next level."

"I've been at that level," Dad said. "It's dangerous up there."

"But those who were once your competitors are now your customers. You've neutralized." Diego stuck his hands in his pockets and glanced out one of the study's wide windows. "We'll use the income the Maldonado deal generates to expand."

Papá grunted. "You didn't say how much we have to move."

"Two-hundred million in product in three weeks."

My father straightened up. "That's almost four times what we normally do."

"The amount doesn't matter as much as—"

Papá held up a hand for Diego to stop when he saw me leaning in the doorway. "*Mija,*" he called, removing his glasses and opening his arms. "*Ven aquí.*"

He shut his laptop as I went to him, then surrounded me in a strong, protective embrace.

Over his shoulder, I met Diego's gaze. His face had been pinched, but it eased as his eyes cleared to emerald green. Neither video chatting nor photos did the color of them justice. "Welcome home," he mouthed.

*Home.* It had been once, but I found no comfort in the word now. Diego schooled his expression for my dad, but I knew him well enough to read his happiness to see me.

"What's wrong?" I asked, reluctantly tearing my eyes from Diego to look up at Papá. "You were arguing."

"Not at all. Don't worry." He kissed the top of my head, then turned to Diego. "Leave us."

Diego didn't flinch, though I knew the dismissal hurt. He yearned for my dad's respect, but I could see age and experience had not fully earned him it. *Yet*. I didn't doubt my father would one day see what I did, but I also knew it pained Diego that the approval he'd so desperately sought since his own father's death continued to elude him.

I hoped during this trip I'd be able to open my dad's eyes to who Diego really was—a sensitive, creative man who'd been trapped by circumstance. My father wanted me out of this life, and I wanted that too, but to Papá, Diego *was* this life. I had to show him the potential Diego had outside of it.

With a short bow and a brief, promising wink in my direction, Diego exited the room.

My father took my shoulders and held me at arm's length. "Let me look at you. *Qué bella*. Turn for me."

"Papá." I blushed. "Please."

"I don't get to see you often enough and want to commit every visit to memory."

"We were together at Christmas."

"But that was in California, not here, where I watched you grow up. Indulge your old man."

Rolling my eyes playfully, I turned in a circle. "All my limbs intact as previously reported," I said. "Fingers and toes too."

"Your hair has grown. Do they not have salons in Santa Clara?"

I smiled. "Of course, but long hair is always in style."

"You're taller too, no? You get that from me."

I had taken after my father's side of the family and was the tallest of my girlfriends at five-foot-seven. He was a sturdy six-foot-two, my grandpa even taller, which had suited his far more menacing temperament.

Father liked to tell the story of an eighteen-year-old girl named Bianca who'd flown down from northern Mexico "like a migrating butterfly." She'd come for a cousin's *quinceañera* and stayed for love, caught in my father's net by the time dessert was served.

As romantic as it was, sometimes I wondered why she'd been stupid enough to trade a safe and happy life as a farmer's daughter for this. It'd been foolish and risky, and it had gotten her killed. I wouldn't share her fate, and neither would Diego.

I had to find a way to free him from the chains of the cartel so he could come to the States and start a life with me. I would convince my dad to let us go and live in peace rather than war, looking over the Pacific instead of over our shoulders.

Diego had been in my father's grip too long, and I was the only one who could ask a favor like this.

Father sat back behind his desk. "Tonight, we celebrate. What're your plans while home?"

"I thought maybe you, me, and Diego could have dinner tonight," I said.

He picked up his folded glasses and tapped them against his temple. "I've already arranged a feast in your honor."

"Tomorrow then, or sometime this week."

"What for? I'd rather just the two of us," he said. "Anyway, my annual party is Thursday night as you know. I'll have my hands full with that, and so will Diego." He frowned. "Why don't you visit the stables? It's been so long since you've ridden."

Eleven years to be exact. I would go see the horses, but I hadn't gotten on one since my mother's death. It'd been our thing, an activity we'd done together almost every day. I nodded so as not to start off my visit with an argument. "Maybe, but it's hotter than Hades here. I'll go to the beach, no doubt."

"No doubt." He patted my hip. "How was the trip?"

"Barto took great care as always. No attempted murders."

"A joke," he said. "I'm glad you see the humor. I don't."

It was important to remember to laugh when traveling with three guards and in bulletproof transportation.

"I need to get back to work," he said, opening his laptop. "Dress well for dinner."

I stooped to kiss his cheek. Out of habit, I glanced at the computer screen for clues as to what he and Diego had been discussing, but I forced my eyes away. I didn't want trouble. I just wanted to get Diego and myself the hell out of there before someone else I cared about got killed.

On my way out, Papá called me back. "One more thing. Don't let me catch you trying to sneak into the ballroom again this year. It's no place for a young girl."

"I know many girls who've been to your parties."

"None of which is my only daughter."

My mom had hosted a legendary annual affair for clients and friends of the Cruz cartel in a ballroom on the property. I'd never made it into a party and had been forced to settle for hearing the music from my bedroom across the lawn, followed by weeks of gossip and folklore. Papá had tried his best to keep me isolated from this world since birth, but that'd bred curiosity.

Now that I knew better, I appreciated his intent. But it hadn't saved me from witnessing my mother's murder.

"I'm not a young girl anymore," I said with a shrug. "I'm twenty."

I left the room and tried not to think about the party. I'd once harbored a morbid curiosity about the life my parents led—until I'd learned firsthand the senseless violence, corruption, and evil that came with it. Since then, I'd been trying to tame the little girl in me who'd been fearless enough to draw a weapon on a man three times her size. The girl who'd equated danger with fun. The one who'd listened to the devil whispering in my ear that there was no escaping this life, not now, not ever.

I had run away from all this, but the devil still tempted that stupid little girl. She knew better than most what could come of that.

After all, she'd ended up locked in a pitch-dark hole for hours, senseless and defenseless, covered in her own mother's blood.

## CHAPTER 2

# NATALIA

In the corridor on my way to the library, a figure sprang from the shadows and seized me from behind. I gasped, but the moment I caught Diego's familiar scent, I relaxed in his arms.

"*Buenas, princesa*," he murmured in my ear, stealing me toward the library.

As children, Diego and I had scoured almost every inch of the house with the exception of my parents' bedroom. We knew it better than any member of the security team, likely better than my father himself, as he couldn't fit in some of the spaces Diego and I had been known for folding ourselves into back then.

The library was one of the only surveillance-free spots. Papá had built it for my mother's ever-curious mind, but hardly anyone went in it anymore. My dad claimed he wasn't intelligent like my mother and had no use for books, but it was simply too painful for him to spend time in here.

My father was smart in other ways.

Diego left the door open behind us. Since we'd spent so much time together growing up, it wouldn't be unusual for a guard or even my dad to find us alone together. But with the door closed? That would raise red flags.

He spun me around and pressed his lips to mine for a hasty kiss. "Are you really here?"

"I am." I put my hands to the chiseled, lean jaw and high cheekbones of a face worthy of being immortalized on a statue. "Every time I see you, you're less the boy I knew and more the man I love."

He took my wrists and kissed the inside of one palm. "I was a man back then, Tali. I had to be."

"I know." His bravery in a world of danger and a life of loss continued to awe me. "Are you happy to see me?"

"You have no idea." He went to the long window overlooking the grounds, then turned and perched on the sill. His eyes lingered on me. "Every time I see you, you're less the girl I knew and more an alluring creature with wiles that could possess the devil."

"You'd call me a creature?" I asked, smiling as I formed claws with my hands and stalked toward him in my leopard-print flats.

He held up his hands to form a square, looking at me through it. "When you're back at school, I'll remember you this way—a lioness."

"You won't have to remember," I said. "You'll be able to look up and see me with your own eyes."

"I want that more than you know." When I neared, he put his hands on my hips and drew me to him. "I just don't want you to get your hopes up."

"He'll understand once I tell him how much you mean to me. How much you've *always* meant to me," I said, smoothing away dark, golden strands that fell right back over his forehead. "My father adores you."

"Adores?" He arched an eyebrow. "He adores two things in this world—you, and the memory of your mother. The rest of us hope for his respect and his mercy."

I wrinkled my nose. "You're exaggerating. These days, he's more forgiving than most. At least, more than my grandpa ever was. Papá is a fair man."

"Fairest in all the land," Diego agreed. "But nothing about the land is fair. Except for his daughter. She's both her mother and her father, darkly beautiful with cunning eyes."

My beloved was a poet—a side he only showed to me. I wanted to melt into him, but I could sense the tension in his forearms, the restraint in his touch. Diego followed my father's example, though, and rarely volunteered when something was wrong. I would've happily ignored any problems, except that I didn't want my time with Diego encumbered by the stresses of business. "What was your argument about?" I asked.

"Nothing, nothing, *está bien*." He slid a hand under the hem of my top. I arched into the warmth of his skin on mine while acutely aware of the open door behind me. His green eyes danced as he looked up at me. "Tali?"

"Diego."

"We have to talk about our future."

I grinned. "That's why I'm here."

"I want nothing more than to be with you." He sighed. "This town is a jail cell. A death sentence, even. I'm only alive today. Tomorrow is never guaranteed."

When he talked like that, it hit too close to the truth. So many nights, I'd stared up at the ceiling of my dorm room waiting to hear from Diego, both craving and fearing news. Keeping in touch with someone whose life depended on staying under the radar hadn't been easy. "It won't be for much longer," I said. "You'll see."

"But how can I leave?" He inched his fingertips a little higher. "I have responsibilities here."

I bit my bottom lip as he approached the underwire of my bra. "You'll get out of them."

"This isn't a job I can just quit. Your father took me in when he didn't have to." He removed his hand from my top to rest it on the outside of my thigh. "Costa brought me into this business and gave me a chance."

I didn't want him to stop touching me, but even though our self-control continued to hold, it was thin. "That doesn't mean you're indebted to him forever."

"I'll never be able to leave without your father's blessing, and he won't give me that."

"He brought you and your brother in at my mother's urging, out of a sense of duty for what he did to your parents." I slipped my hand in his and squeezed. "And yes, he could've left you behind, or worse, killed both of you. But he's also the reason you're an orphan in the first place."

Diego's eyebrows knitted. "I've never heard you put it like that. Are you suggesting I hold that against him?"

"No," I said. "He won't feel any guilt. He did what he had to. If he hadn't gone after your parents, they would've come for him. And I don't think the de la Rosas would've taken *me* in if the situation had been reversed."

"They wouldn't have. I miss my mom and dad, but you're right—they weren't so merciful." He glanced away. "Perhaps it would've ended up worse for you than death."

What was worse for a young girl than death, I didn't have to ask. Though our families had been rivals, they'd still abided by a code. Back then, the de la Rosas had trafficked weapons, and the Cruzes had dealt in narcotics. My father and grandfather had imposed a strict pact that neither family would enter into the vile space of human trafficking. And when Papá had discovered Diego's parents had broken that pact, the de la Rosas had needed to be dealt with.

But it was plotting against my father that'd ultimately gotten them killed.

I sighed. "Maybe we should just smuggle you across the border like a brick of cocaine." I leaned in conspiratorially. "After all, that's what the Cruz cartel is known for, right? Our unusually high success rate at getting illegal goods into North America?"

The corner of Diego's mouth quirked. "Where'd you hear that?"

"It's true, isn't it? My father's instinct is unrivaled, but you're the brains behind this business."

"I'm hardly that," he said, but deep dimples appeared with his smile. Once I'd been old enough to notice how sexy they were, they'd proven irresistible. "I just want him to see me as . . ."

"As?"

"More than the others." He kissed the back of my hand. "Someone worthy of being part of his family."

"You *are* worthy. I know that, and so does he."

"But I can't blame him for doubting me after the way my parents conspired against him."

I refrained from pointing out what he already knew. Yes, Papá *had* agreed to take in both boys, but on one condition—that they wouldn't follow in their father's footsteps. In order to ensure the boys never made a move against Costa Cruz, my dad had made them watch as he'd put bullets in their parents—a warning.

"My father knows you'd never go against him," I said. "Their murder ended a decades-long feud between our families—"

"Until Cristiano," Diego said.

I shivered, a natural response to hearing the devil called by his name.

Mamá's hospitality had come with a price—her life. But it had also brought Diego into mine.

*He'd* understood that my father and *abuelo* had had no choice but to stop his parents.

Cristiano, on the other hand, hadn't.

Eleven years later, he should've been a distant memory. I tried not to think of his tight grip on my arm, his gun tipping up my chin, or the shadowed, divine face of a godless man. But how could I not look over my shoulder? Cristiano de la Rosa still inspired dread, even from the grave. At least, I hoped that's where he was. Despite rumors that he'd been running an underground drug empire in Russia, or that he owned a freighting company in Bolivia, or had become an arms trafficker between America and the Philippines—I'd convinced myself he was six feet under. I didn't sleep well most nights, but assuming he was dead helped a little.

"My father knows you aren't your father, and he *definitely* doesn't think you're anything like your brother," I said.

Diego stuck his hands in the back pockets of my jeans and pulled me closer. We were tempting fate by being affectionate out in the open, but it excited me that Diego couldn't resist touching me. "Your parents treated Cristiano like a son, and he *still* turned on them," Diego said. "No matter how I prove myself, your father keeps me at arm's length—even before the betrayal, I was just another worker to him. I sometimes question whether Costa would've taken me in without my brother."

Even though it hurt to hear that, I understood why Diego felt that way. Both boys had been tossed into the Cruz cartel army right away. Cristiano had taken to it like a child to sweets, while sensitive, creative Diego had struggled to adapt.

"You've shown him almost twenty years of loyalty," I said. "You're now one of the cartel's most trusted advisors. You've helped make this business what it is—one with an average success rate above eighty-seven percent."

Diego's mouth fell open as he scoff-laughed. "How long were you listening at the door?" He narrowed his eyes, playfully scolding me. "You little snoop."

"I just didn't want to interrupt," I said. "But is eighty-seven percent good?"

"The best. Our competitors don't even touch us. Cartels come to us when they need the absolute best chance of getting their shipment over the border." He winked. "That's how we can charge so much."

"See?" I said. "You could never be just another worker. Papá knows that."

"Let's get back to the topic of our future." He squeezed my ass cheeks. "In the States, will we be royalty like we are now?"

Not if I could help it. To be royalty was to put a target on our backs. We already had that here; I wanted to escape it. There was much more to life than wealth and status. "How does a bungalow near the Pacific Ocean sound?" I asked. "Fresh fish, fruits, and vegetables every day. No guns in sight. And California has great schools."

"Schools?"

"For the children."

He chuckled. "We have children, do we? Do they have names?"

"I'm serious," I said. "Once I graduate and start my career, we'll marry in a small, cozy ceremony. Although, the churches there are big and tacky, not like the ones here." Regretfully. Our little Roman Catholic church in the town center was beautifully maintained thanks to my family. Father lavished millions every year on our small *pueblo* nestled between arid desert lowlands and lush mountainside on the west side of the country—a business investment more than charity, as it secured him the loyalty of the townspeople and local law enforcement.

"But how will I show off such a beautiful princess if we have a cozy ceremony?" he teased.

"Oh, my whole family will be there. Show off what you like, but I don't care about being fancy—I just want you and the people I love around." Diego made good money here, and had been saving instead of blowing it like a lot of his friends, but it wouldn't last forever where we were going. California was expensive, and Diego would struggle to find work without experience. I wanted to make sure he knew I didn't need money to be happy. I cupped his cheek, impatient to feel his lips on mine again. "We can throw a party that would blow all other weddings away if that's what you want, but all I need is you."

He leaned into my palm. "If I could, I'd make you mine tomorrow."

Excitement fluttered in my tummy. I'd pictured our nuptials many times. Whether the affair was big or small, blessed by my father or forbidden, the core of it remained the same. Diego was my soul mate. He'd seen me through the dark months after my mother's death, checking on me whenever he could get away from the ranch, making sure I'd slept and eaten and gotten fresh air when I'd only wanted to give up. It wasn't hard to conjure the image of promising to care for *him* too in sickness and in health.

But would my father be there to walk me down the aisle?

Papá was a fair and decent man, but he'd been ruthless once. He didn't value anyone's innocence but mine. He'd tried to awaken more in Diego, to turn him into the killer his brother was, but Diego remained pure. A peaceful soul trapped in a fight for survival. He wasn't made for this world, but there was no way out—except, maybe, through me.

Diego frowned. "I should go check on things at home before anyone notices my absence."

I sighed, but sulking wouldn't change anything. "When will I see you next?"

"I wish I knew. I have to show my face at the costume party and do some networking. Then this weekend, I'm trapped at the house to oversee some things."

"I've still never seen your place," I hinted. Diego had told me enough about it over the phone that I could picture it clearly. "What if I come over?"

Diego rose from the windowsill and lifted my chin with his knuckle. "You know I'd love that if it wasn't too dangerous. It's a hub. Men come and go from my house all day. And if I know your dad, he'll have security detail on you the next two weeks. They'd never let you come over, and you can't be there without them."

"But *you'll* be there." Everyone loved to remind me how dangerous this life was as if I didn't know. And though staying in the dark felt safer, I also knew ignorance could expose me to danger.

"I'll be preoccupied, though," he said.

"Then what about the party?" I asked. "I promised my dad I wouldn't show up, but if you think about it, isn't it really the *safest* place to be? With all the important people in attendance, there'll be a guard every meter."

"He's not keeping you from the ballroom for safety reasons, Natalia Lourdes." Diego only used my full name when he was serious. "His parties are a cesspool."

"They're attended by the highest government officials in the country."

"My point exactly. Those people are deadlier, greedier, and more corrupt than anyone. They've ruined countless lives and families without ever dirtying their hands." He thumbed my bottom lip. "Promise me you'll stay home. I have no doubt you've already mapped a route inside."

"I don't care about the party. I have no interest in what goes on there." That wasn't entirely true, but the only thing stronger than my curiosity was my desire to disassociate myself from this life. Then again, what trumped *all* of that—was Diego. "I don't have much time here," I said. "I only want to spend it with you."

"I want that too, *princesa*, but not if it puts you at risk." He glanced over my head, then pecked the bridge of my nose. "I'll see if I can steal away for a kiss after the party, all right?"

"You expect me to sit home and wait on the small chance you'll be able to meet me?"

"No, my angel straight from heaven. My Aphrodite incarnate. I don't expect it, but I hope for it." He took me in his arms and brushed his lips over my cheek, then the corner of my mouth. "Promise me you'll stay home," he said in my ear, "and in exchange, I'll tell you a secret."

I was getting exactly what I wanted—a clear divide between myself and this life. But I wasn't getting what I needed—Diego. Maybe the party was wild, but it would also be safe. Security would be tight. If I found the right costume, nobody would even recognize me. "I'll stay home," I said. It wasn't exactly a lie—the ballroom was on our property. "What's the secret?"

"I wrote you something."

"A poem?" I melted against his hard chest. "Let's hear it."

"Not so much a poem as a love letter. A tribute to my princess." He half-smiled. "It's in my pocket, but it's not ready."

I reached for it. "Give it to me."

He laughed, catching my wrists and pulling me close. "If you put your hands in there, I can't promise I'll let them out."

I blushed, at a loss for a response. We'd been best friends a long time, and we were still a little new at the intimate parts. I laced our hands together, admiring his long fingers and the tattoo on the inside of one—a sketch of roses he'd done with his family name and the date of his parents' death.

And inked on his inner ring finger, small enough so nobody like my father would notice, were our initials in black ink. I brushed my lips over his knuckles.

"God, I've dreamed of your mouth on me since your last visit." His voice dropped. "Tell me you're still my girl, Talia."

I knew what he was asking, and although I'd assured him many times that I'd kept my virginity intact at school, there was always an edge to his voice when he asked. I put my cheek to his. It was easier to talk about sex without looking at him. "I'm still your girl."

"Good." The word came out on a growl. "I worry about those fraternity sharks circling someone as sweet as you."

"Sharks don't eat sweets," I said with a smile. "The sharks are *here* —out for blood. Americans are boys compared to you. I've no interest in them." I put my arms around him and nuzzled his neck. "I only think of you."

He sighed. "How have we lasted this long?"

Even though most of my friends, both here and in the States, had lost their virginity, it was easy to save myself knowing I'd only ever give myself to one man—my best friend. As scary as my father's grief had been after Mamá's death, I still wanted what they'd had—an all-consuming devotion to each other, even now. As far as I knew, Papá had never so much as been on a date with another woman in the last decade. "Because it's important to me," I said. "I want to commit myself to you in every way once it's time."

He kissed my forehead. "It's important to me too."

I arched a brow at him. "Only because you're afraid my father will find out we didn't wait."

He laughed lightly. "It's true—I value my life. Luckily, even if we were tempted, the guards keep you in and me out." He ran his fingers through the ends of my hair. "Our first time will be special, *mi sol*."

I smiled quizzically. He hadn't called me that before. "Your sun?"

"You're always alight. That, and you hate the night."

"Mmm. It rhymes. You *are* a poet."

Diego knew me well, but then, he'd heard firsthand accounts of my night terrors until I'd left for boarding school. The shadows that tried to catch me, the lingering memories of a nine-year-old watching her mother take her last breath . . . and then there was his brother.

*"Promise you'll never come back here," I said.*

*"I can't."*

It was hard to believe Cristiano had once been the hero of my nightmares. Like the time, as a girl, I'd woken up screaming, and my mother had come running. She'd smoothed sweat-sticky hair off my face and asked me what I'd dreamed about.

"Monsters," I'd told her.

I hadn't noticed Cristiano, who'd been patrolling the property, standing in the dark doorway, until my mother had turned to him. "Are there monsters here, Cristiano?" she'd asked.

"Yes," he'd said gravely. "But they'll never hurt Natalia."

My little heart had raced as fresh tears had filled my eyes. "How do you know?" I'd asked him.

"Because I'm here to protect you," he'd answered. "And I'm scarier than any monster."

Cristiano had chased away the monsters under the bed until he'd become one.

And Diego was the light.

"Will your nightmares return?" Diego asked.

Not wanting to worry him, I'd told him I didn't have them while at school since they were less frequent and less frightening. Now that I was home, I expected they'd return, but there was nothing he could do about that, so I shook my head.

If I had my way, I'd be on a plane back to California before my nightmares could even catch up with me.

But I knew from experience—I could never completely outrun them.

## CHAPTER 3

# NATALIA

Under a starry sky, I walked away from the house, crossing our damp back lawn in heels. Lit from within, my father's ballroom shimmered like a golden paradise to welcome the state's elite. Town cars and limos lined the curved driveway, inching forward to meet the valet. Fountains out front glowed sky-blue, the water shimmering as it reflected hundreds of strung lights. It was how I imagined the gates of heaven—down to the large men in suits and earpieces guarding the entrance and scrutinizing invitations.

Unfortunately, I had to use heaven's back door. Security was heaviest at events like these. Armed men patrolled the perimeter of the property, keeping certain criminals out and others in. The main house was off-limits.

I took cover in the garden between the house and ballroom, crouching behind a fountain with a statue of Poseidon.

*Your curiosity is an affliction,* my father had often said to me. *And there's no cure,* I'd teased him. Being forbidden from the party was like being sent from the dinner table as a girl when conversations had turned to business. Or like when my father had put up a fence in our backyard to keep me from exploring the grounds beyond the trees.

Most of the time, finding ways around the blockades was more fun than whatever lay on the other side.

Once one of the guards had turned back the way he'd come, I hurried through the courtyard. Intricate, lifelike butterfly wings, strapped over a black bodysuit, flapped at my back. My best friend, Pilar, had been too skittish to sneak in with me, but I'd convinced her to help me make an elaborate black-and-orange eye mask with feathers and glitter before streaking blonde extensions through my hair. She'd then clipped handmade, delicate monarch butterflies throughout my curls.

*Full costume required*. It'd been printed there on the invitation, and from what I'd heard and glimpsed of these parties, anything less than an extravagant, costly costume, and I'd stick out.

"*Alto*," I heard behind me. I stopped and turned as a guard approached. "*¿Qué hace?*"

I swallowed and disguised my voice with my best North American accent. "*¿Hablas inglés?*"

"You are not permitted here," he said in broken English. "*¿Invitación?*"

I pulled a sharp-cornered card from my pocket and handed it over. I'd looked at the guest list earlier to forge an invite with the names of one of the few attending couples from the States.

"*Señor* Matthewson?" the guard asked.

"Husband." I flashed a small diamond ring one of my uncles had gifted me at my *quinceañera*. "Inside. Waiting."

He picked up his two-way radio, but as he was about to speak, a voice came through asking for security at the front. He handed me back the invitation. "*Adelante. Quédate en la fiesta*."

*Stay in the party*. I continued around the side of the house. A Playboy bunny with red lipstick and a cigarette held open the door for me on her way out, and I entered the hall to "Walk Like an Egyptian." As my eyes adjusted to the glittering affair, waiters circled with trays, passing between rooms. To my right, disco music vibrated the chandeliers that looked as if they'd been dipped in gold and crystals and hung to dry.

Belly dancers rippled through the crowd. Walking toward the main hall, I crossed the imported Moroccan tile Mamá had bought on a trip to Africa, hypnotized as a heavyset man took the stage for an emotional aria.

Partygoers showed off their costumes—a black vinyl catsuit that hugged every curve. Cleopatra in a metallic leotard with layers upon layers of necklaces over her breasts, her nipples poking through. A bare-chested Tarzan with nothing but a cloth covering his genitals. Marie Antoinette walked in on the arm of Two-Face. Even some of the security guards wore painted masks or had gold-plated machine guns.

A waiter stopped and lowered his tray for me. It wasn't canapes or mini quiche as I would've thought but an assortment of pills and powder. Growing up in the world of drugs, I had little interest in them, so I opted for a fizzing drink instead. With a sip, bubbles tickled my mouth and made me smile.

This wasn't the ballroom in which I'd grown up playing hide-and-seek or had taken piano lessons, but an opulent show come to life. I walked into the next room, my heels solid on the floor even as music muted them. On a balconette overlooking a dancefloor, a row of women in lace corsets, bejeweled thigh-high stockings, and vibrant feather boas kicked slender legs for the can-can. A man in an open-collared suit and gold chains stood beneath them, likely hoping for a glimpse of heaven. I turned in a circle, taking in the spinning dancers. Men wore women's clothing, ladies dressed as animals, and caged birds sang. In one corner, a tiger paced its gilded pen for partygoers' amusement. Nearby, a woman in black leather also wore a leash.

The affair lived up to its tales of opulence and extravagance. I could hardly believe all this had been happening a hundred meters from my bedroom.

Glancing up, I spotted Diego in a long-sleeved denim shirt, a brown suede vest, and a cowboy hat. He surveyed the room from behind a second-floor railing. When our eyes met, he narrowed his. I bit my bottom lip as recognition crossed his features. He shook his head at me to signal his disapproval but tipped his hat with a small smile. After a quick scan of the room, he started down to the ground floor, but a security guard stopped him to speak in his ear. Diego looked at me, checked his watch, then turned back up the stairs.

I walked toward a pair of fire dancers twirling on the patio, their flames making shapes against the backdrop of night, but my attention snagged on a scribbled *Fortune Teller* sign. One corner of the room had been sectioned off with hung purple fabric. *How strange.* My father became more devout in his faith the older he got and held nothing but contempt for the occult.

I heard Papá's booming voice before I saw him. I craned my neck, but he was a head taller than most and easy to find. He shook hands with a governor. If Diego recognized me, my father probably would too, and I'd be banished back to the house.

I ducked behind the fortune teller's curtains to watch through a sliver. Papá carried an ornamental staff and wore a heavy looking jeweled crown that flattened out his black and gray hair. A ruby-red velvet cape with ermine trim weighed on his big frame.

"All these riches will be yours one day," said a craggy female voice.

Startled, I turned around. The partitioned area was shrouded in crimson light, but a glowing purple crystal ball illuminated the deep-set wrinkles and dark eyes of a woman at a small table. On the exotic tapestry, a stack of tarot cards sat by her slender, veiny hand. A convincing actress, she certainly looked the part. "I'm sorry?"

"You will inherit all of this. Not just material things."

"I don't want my fortune read," I said, peeking back through the curtains.

"You don't believe in it?"

"No."

"Then what's the harm?"

*Damn.* I'd lost sight of my father.

"It's no use hiding. He'll find you." She spoke unevenly, her words jagged.

I glanced over my shoulder. "Who?"

She stared at me from under thick black lashes and a shimmering gold headdress. "I see a man . . ." She tapped one nail on the table, squinting. "The man of the rose."

*De la Rosa*. It wasn't unusual that she'd have heard Diego's name somewhere—he was well-known around here. "You're wrong," I said. "I'm not hiding from him."

"I'm rarely wrong, *muñeca*." She gestured for me, calling me a doll and treating me as one, too. "Come. *Siéntate*. The monarch wills it."

I turned to face her completely as chills covered my shoulders. It occurred to me that up until my mother's death, she'd planned every detail of these parties. Maybe she'd known this woman. "What?"

She said nothing more, waiting. Father would never have a true oracle here, if such a thing existed. As she'd said, what harm could it do? I took the cushioned folding chair across from her. In the light, her eyes were as ultraviolet as they appeared shrewd. One look told me she had seen things, knew things, but that didn't scare me. The past was the past. It was impossible to tell the future.

"Did you know Bianca King Cruz?" I asked.

"Only from afar." The woman lifted up and fixed the pillow on her chair. "*Perdón*. My achy back."

"I'm sorry," I said, unsure of the appropriate response. Her musky, floral perfume wafted across the table. When she didn't offer anything else, I held out my palm. "Well? Are you going to read it?"

"You're a young girl," she said.

"That's obvious to anyone with eyes." My gaze drifted to the deck of cards. "Aren't you going to tell my fortune?"

"I don't need to. It's clear as day." She reached out, her bracelets jangling as she took my hand in hers. She wore rings upon rings on each finger—amethyst gemstones set in gold, a silver snake coiled to the knuckle of her right thumb, a pearl cradled by a tiny pair of intricately carved, pewter hands. "With so few years behind you, you've already met your true love."

"Yes, I have."

"You know who he is?" she asked. "He's close by."

I nodded. "He's here tonight."

"I see great love for you."

Diego had taken a bullet for me all those years ago, and he'd saved my life many times since as he'd seen me through brutal pre-teen years without a mom. We already possessed a deep devotion to each other, and we hadn't even been intimate yet. I nodded. "It is a great love."

"I see pain," she said in the same flat tone.

I shifted in my seat. That was a given considering the circles my father moved in. He and I had already gone through tragedy—that was, if there was such a thing as going through it. Grief ebbed and flowed, but it never truly receded. Now, he ran a more respectable operation, but for those who dealt in vice and contraband, risk would always be present. The fortune teller saw pain? She could've been speaking to anyone in the room.

"I see betrayal and violence," she continued. "And much death."

The grandfather clock in the main ballroom chimed. How long had I been sitting there? "I've already experienced all of those."

"And at such a young age," she said, clucking. "There's more to come, I'm afraid."

Whether I believed in her powers or not, that wasn't what I'd hoped to hear. I took my hand back to put it in my lap. "Whose death?" I asked, touching the diamond on my finger.

Her rings clinked against the glass ball as she palmed it, but she didn't bother to look, as if that was just the most convenient place to rest her hands. "You will die for him, your love," she said.

"I would, yes."

"No. You *will* die for him."

Goose bumps pebbled my skin. I thought of the barrel of Cristiano's gun pressed to my forehead. *"Bang. You're dead."*

The dark came next. The pitch black, my cries, and the scurrying rodents, the smell and feel of blood that didn't leave me for weeks. A shadow, the same one that often haunted my dreams, rose in me.

My heart raced. In the warm glow of the red and purple light, I couldn't tell if the woman looked on with sympathy or delight. Either way, I didn't like her face just then, or any of this. It was silly. Child's play. She was wrong to hide behind a costume for a night and play with people's lives.

"This is stupid," I said and stood to return to my post at the curtains. I willed my heart rate to slow so I could focus on finding Diego. I spotted him standing in the entrance hall. He looked like he belonged in an old Western in his cowboy getup, yet blended perfectly amongst Mexico's upper echelon. At the same time, he was utterly out of place. I could give him an escape. I could give him everything.

Was *I going to die for him?*

I slipped out from the make-believe lair, and like a hawk to a mouse, his eyes set on me. The worry in them eased, replaced with the same longing surely reflected in my eyes. The soothsayer's dark words lifted, and I saw them for what they were—generic, baseless, fearmongering sentiments, a one-size-fits-all likelihood that more than the majority of this room would encounter death, pain, violence—and *riches*. That was the point of all of this, anyway.

As if plotting his route to me, Diego rubbed his jaw. He'd be blamed if we were caught together. That didn't stop my craving to feel his lips on mine. He started toward me, but after only a few steps, my father appeared, slapped him on the back, and pulled him away to introduce him to a couple.

I moved through the crowd, catching and losing Diego's gaze as people passed between us. He shook the hand of an Elvis impersonator as I ducked by a man in a toga. He kissed Catwoman's cheek but winked at *me*. I touched my neck in mock-offense and stopped short of face-planting into a wall of a security guard.

"*Perdón*," I said as I went to go around the man.

The guard moved to block me, and in an instant, the energy around me shifted. I tilted my head back until I was looking straight up at a monster of a man and into the face of a ghoulish black-and-white skull. The blackened eye sockets, rimmed in deep red, didn't hide the menacing way his eyes focused on me. Nor did the drawn-on teeth, shaped in a sinister grin, disguise his frown—or the flawless bone structure beneath his veneer. Raven-black hair had been slicked back, as stark against the chalky face paint as his tie cutting down the center of a pressed white dress shirt.

Standing as still and straight-backed as a mannequin, and looking as polished as one too, he inclined his head toward me. “May I have this dance?”

## CHAPTER 4

# NATALIA

It wasn't a request.

The stranger costumed as a brooding *calavera* sugar skull wasn't *asking* for a dance. There was more than simple bass and gravel weighing down his words—he spoke the way a lion growled, with a snarl and a gaze as powerful as the muscles rippling under what appeared to be an expensive custom suit.

*May I have this dance?*

*No*. Neither my gut nor my brain left any room for argument, but my body drew toward his, as if he were the sun pulling me into its orbit. I forced myself to step back. He wasn't security; he wasn't here to protect me, but the opposite. He was the danger my father had warned me of. This was a man who walked into a room and left with what he wanted—revenge, money, women . . .

Me.

No one in the room matched his obvious strength. It would take a bullet to stop him.

He'd asked my permission, and though I declined in a whisper, he put a large hand on my waist anyway, drawing me in, towering over me like a threat.

The dancers gave him a wide berth, staying just outside the span of his long arms—as if he might reach out and snatch one of them. He placed my hand on his solid bicep and engulfed my other with a gentleness that contradicted his hold on my side and the severity of his costume.

"I don't know how to tango," I said as a Gotan Project song started.

"You've been away from Latin men too long," he said. "Follow my lead, *mariposa*."

What made him think I'd been away at all? I'd lived in North America eight years, but the Latina in me would never fade. I did, in fact, have some basic knowledge of the dance and fell into step with him.

"We're a match," he said, his eyes drifting over the butterflies in my hair.

"I'm sorry?"

"Our costumes."

There was no obvious correlation between a sugar skull and a butterfly, but I didn't dare contradict him.

"Why the monarch?" he asked.

I turned my cheek. Beside us, a minotaur and a French maid danced a beat faster. I wasn't going to tell this calavera what monarchs meant to me, so I resorted to facts. "It feeds on poison."

"Milkweed—to render itself unpalatable to predators," he said, sliding his hand to the center of my back where my leotard dipped. I stiffened as he dug his fingertips under the straps of my wings, into my exposed flesh. "One bitter taste, and the hunter backs off."

His skin touched mine and stole my focus, just like that. It had taken Diego years to make his first move. Against my will, my nipples hardened between us. "I—I think it's clever that they do that."

"It's just nature," he said. "Monarchs also represent the souls of the departed. Like me."

I looked up at him, unnerved at the way his black eyes drank me in. "You're very much alive."

Leaning in, he lowered his voice. "It's said if you whisper your desire to one, it can deliver your wish to the gods on quick and soundless wings."

I realized he was dancing me farther from the other partygoers. "I should get back," I said.

"To?"

"My . . . fiancé," I said, hoping it would fizzle his interest in me.

He stopped dancing. "Your fiancé? What about California?"

My mouth fell open, but I quickly closed it. I should've known better than to look caught off guard, having been raised by masters of schooling their emotions. "Do I know you?"

He hesitated before resuming our tango. He danced with precision and a peculiar grace, like a hunting lion. "I detect an American accent."

Somehow, that didn't give me any relief. "I have to go," I said, trying to pull away.

He tightened his grip on me, and with what I suspected was hardly any effort on his part, kept me where I was. "But I haven't whispered my wish in your ear yet."

I swallowed dryly, wondering where Diego had gone. Surely, he wouldn't like to find me pressed against another man. "People are waiting for me."

His roughened hand constricted around mine. I followed his gaze to the diamond ring on my finger. "Which people?" he asked.

Would my father's wrath be safer than where I stood now? The mystery around this man stopped me from telling him who I was. "People who would not like me to go missing."

"Then perhaps they shouldn't have left you all alone, *mariposita*."

"Don't call me that." Sometimes, my parents had called me their little butterfly. Even my father knew better than to use that nickname anymore. I looked around the man, panic rising the more tightly he held me.

He drew me flush to him, the warmth of his body contradicting his cold stare. "Then what should I call you?"

My gaze locked onto Diego as he separated from my father and scanned the room.

"And nobody left me alone," I said, ignoring the man's question. "I can take care of myself."

"Is that so?" he asked. "Regardless, I wouldn't take the chance if you were mine."

*If I was his.* My chest rose and fell a little faster, but this time, it wasn't in fear. His tight, possessive hold made it feel as if he already thought I belonged to him. For a split second, the thought of being at his mercy both scared and excited me. "But I'm not yours," I said to gauge his reaction.

"Are you suggesting I remedy that?"

How bold. Nobody in this world had ever come on to me like this. "You could try," I said, "but I can promise it wouldn't go well for you."

"I like a challenge. Because it doesn't sound to me as if your *fiancé* deserves you. He'd be wise to recognize that someone else might come along and show you that."

I didn't know many men around here who would speak so shamelessly about another man's fiancée. "You're worse than that hag of a fortune teller," I bit out.

One dark eyebrow rose, his interest obviously piqued. "What'd she tell you?"

I looked around his shoulder and saw Diego wipe his temple as he started toward the dancefloor. He still hadn't spotted me, but his movements became agitated. I tried frantically to make eye contact. "She told me not to dance with masked strangers."

The man moved so I could see nothing but him. He had tangoed us into a dark corner, away from anyone else, and my heart started to thump. He lowered his mouth to my ear. "What if I'm not a stranger?"

He was playing games. As he isolated me from the crowd, all I heard was Cristiano de la Rosa's threats to my nine-year-old self. *You don't know true fear.*

"What are you doing?" I asked, trying to see around him.

"Tell me. Are you willing to die for your fiancé?"

The eerie echo of the soothsayer's words made my face heat with anger. "Are *you* willing to die for *me*?"

"Excuse me?"

"If you don't let me go," I said, searching for the most menacing threat I could, "I'll scream."

"I thought you could take care of yourself."

"I'm no match for your size. I wouldn't scream to be rescued, but as the fastest means to get a gun in your face."

"I see. Do you think they'll hear you over the music?" he asked, sounding amused.

"I'll scream as loud as I can, for as long as I can, until my vocal cords give out or I can no longer keep my mouth open."

A disarmingly slow smile moved over his face, the teeth of his disguise spreading ear to ear. "I admit, I *am* curious to see how long you can keep your mouth open."

I shivered at the insinuation and pulled back, this time unable to hide my shock. "You've threatened the wrong person. I can have you killed in seconds without lifting a finger."

"Then I'd like to change my order. Please tell the heavens it is my dying wish to hear you scream."

He spoke with a rumble so deep, I felt his voice between my legs. And I was sure, by the way his eyes bore into mine, he'd meant me to. He wanted my screams, and to scare me, but it didn't come from a place of menace. I couldn't put my finger on his intention, but it was something much more carnal.

We were no longer dancing, but his hand still clenched mine as his fingers buried into the skin of my back. He held me like I was an instrument to be played, one he would snap in half before he gave it up. Not even Diego held me so greedily.

"Then I'll grant you your wish," I threatened.

"Your loyalty to him is admirable if not baffling." He checked over his shoulder, then released me with a bow. "We've been discovered anyway. If you'll excuse me, I'll have to take you with me."

*I'll have to take you with me.*

I'd heard those words in my nightmares and any place I was alone in the dark too long. "What?" I asked, my throat suddenly dry as I was transported back to the tunnel.

"I said, I'll have to take my leave. Excuse me."

He walked away, leaving me in darkness as I hung on his words, torn between never wanting to see him again and a temptation to call him back—in a way that felt all too familiar.

Diego pushed his way through the crowd. "Who was that?" he asked when he finally reached me.

"I don't know," I said, hugging myself. "I told him I didn't want to dance."

"And the bastard put his hands on you anyway? I should get Barto so we can hunt that *cabrón* down and teach him some manners." Diego searched the space around us. "I told you not to come."

"You knew I would anyway."

He paused, then glanced over my costume, and his expression relaxed. "In a mask that didn't fool me for a second. You make a liar of an innocent butterfly, Natalia."

"I didn't lie," I said, cozying up to him, pulling gently on his bolo tie. The braided leather was held together by a metal shield with his family name in decorative script. "I said I'd stay home, and I did. This is my home."

He drew his brows together, something unfamiliar sparking in his eyes, but then he glanced away.

"What is it?" I asked.

"Nothing."

I ducked my head to get him to look at me. "No, it's something. Tell me."

"I promise, it was a passing thought."

I crossed my arms. "Diego."

He took my shoulders and brought me close to kiss my forehead. "It's nothing bad. I just had this weird . . . sense of joy hearing you call this place home again."

His sense of joy was my sinking feeling. Diego's attachment to this town was stronger than mine; he'd never lived anywhere else. There were times I questioned how devoted he was to leaving here. He said he wanted a life in California with me, yet he continued to embed himself in the cartel and ingratiate himself with my father.

"This place will always be part of me," I said, "but I can't call this home again. Not knowing that every day I'm here, every day *you're* here, death is a possibility."

"I know, and of course, I'm in complete agreement that the U.S. is where we belong." He pecked me briefly and ghosted his thumb over my bottom lip. "Let's not argue about something we both agree on. We should move before someone recognizes you."

I ran my fingertip over the curling, cursive letters of the *de la Rosa* engraved on his metal tie. "You won't make me go back to the house, will you?"

"Not if you swear you'll stay by my side every moment."

"An easy promise to make." I smiled as he guided me through the crowd by my shoulders until a friend waved at us from the main room.

"There's an announcement coming," Tepic called. Dressed in a Hawaiian shirt, fanny pack, and aviators, Tepic was as wild as the curls on his head and only as tall as me, but compact and mighty nonetheless. As we approached, he took an entire tray out of a waiter's hands. "Come one, come all," he said, showing us an assortment of narcotics. "What kind of night do you wish to have?"

"A sober one." Diego waved a hand. "None for us, *compa*."

I glanced around the room for the skull-faced stranger. There was something about him my mind tried to grasp on to, like a word at the tip of my tongue.

"Aren't you going to introduce me?" Tepic eyed me when I looked back at him. "I'm Tepic, like the city I come from."

"You don't say." I laughed and shook his hand. "*Mucho gusto*."

"You must've missed the gossip," Diego said, sliding an arm around my shoulders and looking into my eyes. "Should we let him in on our secret?"

Tepic lowered his sunglasses, gaping. "Talia? I didn't recognize you in that mask."

"That was the plan."

"Costa will be happy to have you here for Easter," he said, looking up as the music lowered. "Speak of the devil."

On a large, wide balcony overlooking the main room, dancers

stopped the can-can and parted, gathering on both sides of the gallery. My dad appeared through red velvet curtains and came to the railing, scanning the crowd and waving as his staff herded everyone into the same room. I moved behind Diego but kept my eyes on Papá, who looked almost cherubic with a cheeky grin, red face, and his crown tilted to one side. He tapped his scepter against the tile to get everyone's attention, but the effect was muffled by a clear tarp on the ground. Soon, silence fell over his audience.

"Thank you all for coming to celebrate tonight," he said almost drunkenly yet maintaining the sense of calm and composure he'd become known for in a world of chaos. "I know you're all eager to get back to the party and to the drinking,"—he paused for some laughs —"as am I. But there's a quick matter I want to resolve while all my closest friends and colleagues are in one place."

Diego glanced over his shoulder at me, his eyebrows drawn in question. I shrugged.

A waiter handed Papá a champagne glass. "On this day, the Cruz cartel welcomes back an old friend."

A murmur moved through the crowd as Tepic whispered to Diego, "*¿Qué está pasando?*"

Diego kept his eyes up and shook his head to say he didn't know what was happening. "*No sé.*"

If Diego didn't know about this, I wasn't sure who would. I slipped my hand into his and squeezed.

"Years ago, a wrongdoing was committed, and I intend to make it right before all of you tonight." Papá looked over his shoulder, into the wings. "Let it be known that a Cruz doesn't cower from his mistakes or turn his back on *familia*."

What family did he speak of? I looked to Diego, but his gaze was still trained on my father.

Papá turned forward again, and any belligerence vanished as he fell serious. "And that in the Cruz cartel, no betrayal goes unpunished."

The audience clapped, ready for a show.

"It gives me great pleasure to present you the leader of the *Calav-*

*eras*," my dad said. "But more importantly, to accept back into our lives a man who was once like a son to me and my wife."

"Calavera?" Diego asked. "He can't be serious."

"Who are they?" I asked.

"One of the new order cartels that has come to power over the past few years," Tepic explained quickly.

An "old friend" Diego knew nothing about—and an unknown cartel that had to do with my family? I struggled to connect the pieces. "Why would he . . . who is more like a son to him than you, Diego?"

Papá half-turned and beckoned the suited man in face paint I'd danced with. He stepped forward, surveying the room with black eyes that landed on Diego and me. My heart slammed against my chest as the pieces clicked and the puzzle finally revealed itself.

Father raised his champagne glass. "Welcome home, Cristiano de la Rosa."

"*Puta madre*," came Diego's slow curse.

Fear flooded my limbs with the same force and speed it had in the closet eleven years earlier. My mind stripped away the face paint and I saw Cristiano clear as day. He was harder, angrier, an indisputable man who'd seen things. With a rippling red curtain at his back, he appeared like a devil looking down on us from hell.

*No betrayal goes unpunished.* My eyes fell to the tarp. Would he make an example of my mother's murderer here in front of everyone?

Instead of putting a bullet in Cristiano—who'd had a considerable bounty on his head for more than half my life—my father shook his hand.

My stomach turned over.

Flashbulbs popped as reporters captured the moment.

My father drew his shoulders back. "The Calaveras have risen to success faster than any cartel in México's history under the guidance of Cristiano."

The crowd remained silent at first, as if unsure of how to react. Cristiano's role was widely known in Bianca King Cruz's death; Diego had led the charge to hunt Cristiano with the help of most people in this room for years.

"Friends, *por favor*," Papá said in a less jovial tone. "Show my *compadre* some respect so we can get on with it."

People applauded as Diego and I stood frozen. He squeezed my hand until it hurt, but I couldn't speak, even if I wanted to. I would not show dirt respect.

"If my wife were here, I know she would feel the same," my father continued.

*What?* My gut smarted as if I'd been sucker punched.

"This cannot be," Diego said, staring up at his brother. Cristiano watched us back, still as polished as a mannequin.

I had danced with him. Let him touch me, hold me, whisper in my ear. A crook, a ruthless monster, and a cold-blooded killer.

*Did I know somewhere deep down it was him?*

I silenced the thought. I wouldn't have danced with him knowingly.

By the way he set unforgiving eyes on me, Cristiano knew exactly who I was—and he hadn't forgotten anything about that day eleven years ago.

Diego followed Cristiano's heated gaze to me, then pulled me possessively into the crook of his arm.

"Cristiano has come to me with new evidence in the death of my beloved wife," Father said, passing his drink to a member of the staff. "*Que su alma descanse eternamente en paz*," he added, making the sign of the cross as he wished eternal peace on her soul. "Cristiano de la Rosa did not kill my wife."

I covered my mouth to silence my gasp, but it didn't matter—everyone around me was just as shocked. What was my father saying? Why was he dishonoring my mother this way?

Cristiano looked out over the crowd. "It's good to be welcomed back to a home I have missed," he said. "But there's a more pressing matter to address." He held up a gun. The warm light of the chandeliers flashed off burnished gold, sleek silver, and milky pearl.

*White Monarch.*

I grabbed onto Diego's arm. "What's he doing?"

Cristiano handed it to my father, then disappeared behind the curtain. He returned dragging a bloodied-and-bruised older man whose hands were bound in front of him. He released the man's bicep with a push, and he stumbled to the railing, next to my father. Blood soaked his light t-shirt.

Diego stepped backward. "Fuck."

"Who is that?" I asked.

"I don't know," Diego said without removing his eyes from the balcony. "Look away, Natalia."

"This *sicario,* who doesn't even deserve to be named, defiled and killed Bianca Cruz," Cristiano said, "and he is my gift to her family."

I covered my stomach. It wasn't possible. I'd never seen that man—

My father put the gun to the hitman's temple. To the thrilled screams and cheers of the crowd, he pulled the trigger and blew up his head like a firework.

CHAPTER 5

# NATALIA

My bare feet sank into the soil of my mother's garden as I emptied the contents of my stomach onto one of her rosebushes. Diego held my heels in one hand, dodging my wings as he tried to keep my hair off my face. Everything was a blur. I didn't remember screaming with the crowd, running out, or ripping off my mask and shoes.

"Careful for the thorns," Diego said about the bushes.

My eyes watered, blurring the roses' blood-red color. A man's head had exploded. His brains had splattered across the tarp. His body had crumpled at my father's feet. I held onto Diego's arm until I could stand without wobbling.

Loitering by the fountain, Tepic pushed his aviators to the top of his head and chuckled through the cigarette in his mouth. "You okay, Talia?" he asked. "What a show, eh?"

At least Diego still possessed enough compassion to look as ill as I felt, his face colorless and drawn. He smoothed my hair off my forehead gently but said to Tepic, "Shut the fuck up. Can't you see she's sick?"

"What's the matter, Diego?" Tepic asked, getting another cigarette and his lighter from his fanny pack. "You look like you've never seen a man's head blown off. Or blown it off yourself."

Diego rubbed the inside corners of his eyes. "Not in front of Natalia."

*In front of me*, my father had once dragged a drunk out of a restaurant by his hair for waving a gun near my family. My mom had told me to stop crying; that was how Papá handled his business. Dad had returned ten minutes later and ordered a towel and ice for his bloody knuckles followed by a slice of *tres leches* cake. Over the years here and there, I'd witnessed him knock his men around or order to have people "taken care of" and "made an example of." I was no stranger to the stories about him, either—like the one where Papá had supposedly addressed a package with an army general's fingers in it to the mayor and dropped it in a public mailbox.

I had always known my father to be feared, but to me, he was just Papi. Now, because of him, I'd seen a man's brains. I breathed through another urge to vomit.

Careful to avoid where I'd gotten sick, Diego stooped to pick up some of the butterflies that'd fallen out of my hair. "I'm sorry you saw that," he said to me.

"Sorry?" Tepic asked. "She just watched her father take the sweetest kind of revenge. Anyone who's lost a mother should be so lucky to witness what Talia just did."

"It should've been Cristiano," I heard myself say. It had been a long time since I'd wished death on him.

"Not if he didn't do it," Tepic pointed out.

I quelled my shaking and tried to piece together my thoughts. "There's no way he didn't," I said to Diego as he stood. "You were there. You saw. There has to be an explanation."

"I know. Come on out of the dirt," he said, extending a hand to me.

I took it, wiping my bare feet in the grass before I stepped over a row of tiny lanterns. Diego led me to the glowing fountain, set my delicate hair clips on the ledge with my mask, and helped me out of my wings.

"How is Cristiano back?" I asked. "And why does Father believe he didn't do this?"

"I don't know." Diego crouched to strap my shoes back on. "But I'm going to find out."

I stood. "I want to hear it from my father."

Diego pulled me into a hug, shushing me. "Just take a minute to calm down," he said, rubbing my back. "Breathe."

I buried my face in his chest, where it was familiar, where his shirt smelled like soap, suede, and cigars—where it was safe. Warm. I wanted to stay in his arms and pretend I hadn't just watched my own father brutally murder a person. That Cristiano hadn't just reentered our world. That everything I knew about my mother's death hadn't just been called into question.

How had Cristiano pulled this off?

How could my father shame my mother's memory this way?

"I need to see my dad," I said, disconnecting from Diego.

He held my elbow. "Not tonight, my love. You're not even supposed to be here."

"I don't care." I frowned up at him. "I want answers. I demand them."

"Cool off. Let Costa do the same. Can you even look him in the eye right now?"

That hadn't occurred to me, but Diego was right—even though I wanted answers, the thought of facing my dad made my stomach roil again. It would be too hard. Diego knew my mind better than I did in that moment, so I surrendered to the safety of his arms, deciding to wait until the morning to approach my father.

But I wouldn't let him off the hook. Not for this.

I shifted my focus to the other side of the equation—Cristiano. Why was he back? Where had he gone? What had given him the confidence to return with a million-dollar bounty on his head?

"I didn't even know Cristiano was still in the country," I said.

Tepic tapped ash from his cigarette. "Me neither."

"Who are the Calaveras?" I asked.

Diego and Tepic exchanged looks. "You mind if I smoke?" Diego asked me. "I could use one."

"I don't care," I said, drawing back. "Are they a cartel?"

"Stay," Diego murmured, one arm around my shoulders while Tepic passed him a cigarette. As he stuck it in his mouth and lit it, he nodded. "Calavera is a cartel that came to power while you were away," he said, exhaling smoke, "and has been growing at an exponential rate. They move narcotics too, but they're mainly in arms trafficking, like my father was, and extremely private—"

"As they are violent," Tepic added.

"They're like a gang of misfits from all over," Diego said. "Tightly knit. Supposedly make big decisions as a whole. But also a little cultish over their leader."

"Cristiano?" I asked. "And you didn't know it was him?"

"I didn't even know he was back." Diego shook his head. "Their leader was anonymous until now. Most likely hiding behind a front to keep his identity secret."

"Because of my family?" I guessed. "If we'd known where to find him, it would've been Cristiano up there on his knees just now."

"I assume so." Diego took a drag, squinting ahead. "The question is why Cristiano's back, what he wants, and how he pulled this off. I have no doubt he's filled Costa's head with lies."

"Even with that display, you still think Cristiano's guilty?" Tepic asked.

"I don't think it." Diego pressed his lips into a thin line. "I know it."

"You would too if you'd seen what we did," I told Tepic. Cristiano had killed my mother. If I'd walked in a couple minutes earlier, I probably would've witnessed it. Why was Father denying it, and in front of such important people? "It must be blackmail."

"Wow, Tali. Good thinking." Tepic stopped pacing, looking from me to Diego. "That's got to be it, hasn't it?"

"I wouldn't put it past my brother." Diego nuzzled my hair. "He was always dangerous, but if the rumors are true, Cristiano became something else entirely after he fled here."

I kissed Diego's cheek. Sometimes I forgot that the day I'd lost my mom, he'd essentially lost a brother. "What rumors?" I asked. "The ones I heard were mostly in regard to his whereabouts."

"It's, ah,"—Diego grimaced—"not really suitable for your ears."

"If you don't tell me, I'll find out another way," I said. It brought me no joy to hear graphic details about the man who continued to haunt me, but if he was back in our lives, then I had to know what I was dealing with.

"The Calaveras aren't like us," Diego said. "We grew up here. Our home is our identity. These transients from all over the world are here to take advantage of our market." He waved smoke from around my head. "They have no loyalty and no home—literally. Since they didn't have a location to operate out of, they took a town about an hour north of here."

"What do you mean they *took* it?" I asked.

"Like a hostile takeover. The Calaveras seized it to run their operations. Raped the local women, pillaged and stole businesses, enslaved their people." Diego checked my expression. "Now, the whole town is walled off on three sides, and the back abuts a mountainside. Some sadistic shit goes on in the Badlands, I'll bet."

"Badlands?" I asked.

"That's what some people call it. Rough terrain." Tepic wiggled his fingers like a witch. *"Las puertas del infierno."*

*The gates of hell.* That sounded familiar. Suddenly, the designation *Badlands* rang a bell. I'd heard it before but couldn't remember where. "He made his own town?"

"More or less. There are homes and businesses within its walls, but who knows what's true or legitimate. As far I know, nobody has ever escaped, nor has anyone infiltrated and lived to tell the tale."

"They're like a cult," Tepic said, waving his cigarette toward the house with a grimace. "Satanic rituals and shit. They eat snails, speak in tongues, sacrifice virgins, throw rotten fish at whores, that kind of stuff."

I widened my eyes. I'd heard a lot of cartel-related fact that better resembled fiction, but nothing involving any of that. "How do you know all that if nobody's ever escaped?"

"Who knows how rumors start?" Tepic said. "But I don't doubt what I've heard. I just feel bad for the women trapped there who—"

"Tepic," Diego warned. "Stop. You're scaring her."

I would've had to believe all that to be afraid, and I wasn't sure I did. Rotten fish? Speaking in tongues? It sounded pretty far-fetched. Although, I started to vaguely recall a news story from years earlier about a foreign cartel that operated differently than others. Its boss had a long, international reach and an even longer rap sheet. It'd claimed he'd never been photographed or named and had taken more bullets than he had drugs in his lifetime—and survived.

I stared at the fountain, comforted by the sound of running water. Why were women trapped, and how come nobody had freed them? Did Cristiano really have something to do with that? Until the dark day in question, he'd always been respectful of my mother, and she had cared for him. As a girl, I'd caught Cristiano watching me many times with something that'd felt akin to affection. Nothing that'd made me fearful. Maybe I'd just been too young to know better, though.

"What about the women trapped there?" I asked to stop my mind from filling in the blanks.

"It's terrible, Tali, really," Diego said. "You don't want to know. It's my father all over again, which is why I don't understand how Costa could go into business with Cristiano. He represents the same things my parents did."

"Human trafficking?" I asked quietly.

"It's fucked up." He knocked ash from his cigarette, looking somewhere over my head. "But not all that surprising, I guess. Cristiano and my dad are a lot alike, which is why they never got along."

"The women are mostly foreigners if that makes you feel any safer, Tals," Tepic said.

Who could feel anything but disgusted hearing that? My stomach churned. Had there ever been anything redeemable about Cristiano? Why had my mother not only taken him in, but, as I remembered it, treated him with tenderness?

"It makes *me* feel like shit," Diego said, glancing down at me. "I don't want you anywhere near him. If he ever gets you alone, you scream, hear me?"

I had screamed—and screamed and screamed. And nobody had been able to stop him. Not in my parents' bedroom, nor their closet, nor the tunnel beneath it.

I removed my arms from around Diego, suddenly warm. "He can't get away with this," I said. "If any women, from my country or another, are being held by Cristiano, my father wouldn't accept him back."

"And yet it seems he has," Diego said. "It's just another business to Cristiano. He traffics some, and other women are there for him and his gang's use."

I couldn't keep my disgust at bay any longer. Bile rose in my throat, even as I tried not to let my imagination wander down that path. This was the side of my father's world he tried to shield me from, but I was in it nonetheless. Did that make me complicit? What about Diego? Could either of them even stop someone like Cristiano?

"Are you sure?" I asked.

Diego glanced at me and flicked his cigarette butt away. "Jesus," he said, taking my shoulders to hold me at arm's length. "You're pale again. I told you not to ask."

"It's okay," I said. These were things I had decided long ago I didn't want to know about. But now that I *did* know, I was less frightened than I thought I'd be and more quietly enraged. What about the millions of women in my country who didn't have access to the defenses I did? Who was on their side?

Cristiano had always been a calculating killer, that was no shock—but apparently, he'd grown into a disloyal degenerate, a callous crook, a master of mind games. Hades of the Badlands.

Diego massaged my shoulders. "Relax. This is not something you need to worry about. I will always protect my sun—without you, I'd live in the dark. I won't let anything happen to you."

"Cristiano can't get away with all the things he has," I said. What did he have over Papá? It had to be big for him to ignore the horrors

I'd just heard. After all, he'd taken down Cristiano and Diego's father for similar offenses. "He must have a reason."

"Who, Costa? He has none. He's lost his mind," Diego said and gestured at Tepic. *"¿Tienes otro?"*

Tepic passed him another cigarette, then dropped his and used his heel to stamp out the butt. "I'll see what I can find out from Barto and the guys."

Diego nodded him on. "Go."

I tried to wrap my head around why Papá would do this to us. To *himself*. Just seeing Cristiano brought back scores of memories better left to rest.

Had he manipulated my father? Or could there be any truth to his claims?

Was there even a sliver of possibility that Cristiano was innocent?

It was a thought I knew I should ignore, because if he was or wasn't, either answer would only incite more questions. And if my curiosity was an affliction, then my curiosity about a man like Cristiano could be of the fatal sort indeed.

CHAPTER 6

# NATALIA

Some details from the Day of the Dead eleven years earlier were hazy, and some crystal clear, but I'd never doubted that Cristiano had left my mother for dead and had been about to take off with our valuables.

As Tepic returned to the ballroom on a quest for information, and Diego removed his arm from me to light a fresh cigarette, I paced by the fountain and tried to figure out the riddle before me.

Cristiano had forgotten the duffel on the bed, but enough cash and jewelry had gone missing from the safe to set him up for a long time.

Then there was the fact that nobody else could've come or gone from my mother's bedroom that day without being seen. And that the mansion's security system, including the cameras, had been magically disabled, which Barto claimed could only be done quickly and by someone familiar with it. Cristiano, who'd been one of the only guards with the highest security clearance at the time, had known it intimately. Then, getting access to my parents' safe was nearly impossible—it would've taken someone close enough to the inside to find out the combination.

That was as far as I let my mind go. Whatever struggle had caused the tear in Mamá's dress and the bruises on her face—whatever had happened between the intruder entering the bedroom and me skipping in—I couldn't think of without getting sick, so I never did. I knew it tortured Papá enough for the both of us.

And the final detail that didn't add up was the small fact that a *sicario* didn't kill of his own volition. He would've been hired. So if Papá believed Cristiano hadn't done this, then who did? Who had the hitman worked for?

Some of the more conspiracy-minded newspapers back then had speculated rival federations had done it instead of Cristiano, but growing up, I'd dismissed those theories without a second thought.

I stopped pacing. "Could any of this have to do with the Maldonado cartel?"

Diego frowned from a couple meters away. "Cristiano's return?"

"No. My mother's death."

"The Maldonados didn't exist back then." Diego sat on the edge of the fountain, placed his cowboy hat next to him, and scrubbed a hand through his disheveled hair. "They're newer. What do you know about them anyway?"

"Mostly what I've read in the news or what I overheard in the study the other day," I said.

"I thought you wanted to stay out of all this." He sucked on his cigarette, squinting at me as silky strands of his dark-cocoa hair fell around his cheekbones. "Yet as soon as you got here, you were already hiding in hallways like you did as a kid."

"I want to live a respectable and honest life away from all this, but that doesn't mean I want to be ignorant." I couldn't blame his quizzical look. When I was away at school and we spoke on the phone, I *was* ignorant. I'd ask about business because it was his life, but then I'd let him get away with cursory answers.

After my mother's death, I'd no longer wanted to hear about the things I'd sought to know growing up—the handshake deals made over caramel flan with men visiting from exotic-sounding countries. The foreign sports cars, endless vices, and other spoils that came from feeding the world's various drug addictions. The lost boys of the town that the cartel took under its wing, protecting and feeding them while training them like wards.

Back then, I'd do more than hide. I would seek information, curious about the dangers I was always kept from. I'd sneak away from the house and ride my bike a few kilometers to the sprawling, private ranch house on our property that housed boys and men like Diego and Cristiano. There, they'd learned everything about the business—including how to protect and kill for it. From a distance, I'd been introduced to the different kinds of arms and how to carry them. Other things happened in those training camps too, but those I didn't stick around for. I hadn't wanted to learn what could be worse than death.

As far as I knew, the ranch house had been empty since Papá had traded all that for less violence, going from rival cartels' competition to their solution. They now paid him top dollar to move contraband across borders, and since he'd nearly monopolized the shipping market, he could be more discerning than most.

"My father can pick and choose who he associates with," I said. "If he worked so hard to minimize risk and violence, why are we suddenly involved with two of the most dangerous cartels?"

"Calavera and Maldonado have nothing to do with each other," Diego said, raising his eyes to mine.

"Are you sure?" I resumed pacing in hopes that moving would help the uneasiness building in me. "Maybe there's some connection between them."

"I don't see how there could be. Maldonado is my thing. I brought them in."

From what I'd heard in the office, it hadn't sounded as if Papá had been completely on board. "It wasn't my father's call?"

"I brought the contract to him once it had all been arranged." The orange tip of his cigarette flared with a drag. "He would've said no otherwise. Your dad wants to keep doing things as he's always done, but that's dangerous."

"Dangerous or wise?" I stopped in front of Diego and crossed my arms. "If it works, why tempt fate?"

"What do you think happens when a wild animal slows down to rest or to tend to his wounds, or if he gets sentimental about his prey—the way Costa has about Cristiano? Nothing good." He put out the smoke on the ledge, picked up his hat, and leaned his elbows on his knees. "If you're not moving forward, you're going backward," he said. "Adaptation is the key to survival."

I could see Diego's point. We'd done case studies in business school about insolvent companies—those that'd changed too fast, or in the wrong ways. Those that had been left behind.

"Why does adapting have to mean taking on more risk?" I asked.

"Working with the Maldonados isn't any more dangerous than what we normally do—it just sounds that way because they're . . ." He scratched his temple. "Let's just say they're less forgiving than most."

"What does that mean?"

"Can you come here, please?" He reached for me. "We don't get much time together as it is. Why waste it on talking about stuff we can't control?"

It was all I had wanted in the last year—to have Diego's hands on me again. To be ignorant of the dark side of this business. This was exactly why I tried to stay out of these things. Now, I knew too much and had too many questions to overlook what was happening.

Not only that, but I couldn't ignore how invested Diego was in the future of a cartel he was planning to leave behind soon.

I stayed where I was. "What does 'less forgiving' mean, Diego?"

He looked down at the hat as he turned it over in his hands. "They don't do business the way your dad and his friends did. If they don't like something, they get rid of it. They kill unnecessarily and without regard for the rules."

"There *are* no rules," I pointed out.

"Not true. As you know, up until the past decade or so, there was a code. There were *agreements*—like the one my family broke. But older cartel leaders are being replaced with ones who think they're above the law of the land. With the Maldonados, there's no justice—only the word of those in charge."

*Justice*. In a strange way, it did exist in this world. I thought back to what Cristiano had said to me about justice and loyalty before he'd forced me down the tunnel. My father or his men would've killed him without trial based on the damning evidence they'd had. I could almost see Cristiano's reasoning. If the Maldonados murdered who they wanted when they wanted, then that bred more distrust, disloyalty, and violence within their own cartel and amongst others.

"And you made a *deal* with them?" I asked, spinning the diamond on my ring finger. "What happens if you don't deliver?"

"I will, Talia. I've done my homework. I'm talking over fifty percent more profit for maybe nine or ten percent more risk. How can I refuse those odds?"

"Because if there are no rules, how do you know when you've broken one? Or what they're capable of?" I paused. "What *are* they capable of?"

"Things you've asked me not to tell you before."

This was the kind of information I could never forget once I knew. And yet, if it involved Diego's life, remaining in the dark didn't feel like an option. I stilled my fidgeting hands. "I'm asking now. You're caught up in this. So is my father. I want to know what happens if something goes wrong."

"You're overreacting, Tali. I've got everything under—"

He stopped when he picked up on my glare. "Life or death is overreacting?" I asked tersely.

Sighing, he looked away from me. "What happens if something goes wrong with the Maldonados? Death if they're merciful. If not, it's because they can do worse. Enslave a man to do their bidding, hold his family hostage, torture him by killing off his brothers, sell his women and kids."

My heart rate kicked up a notch. It wasn't as if I had no clue of the reach these criminals around me had. But it scared me that although Diego was most likely smarter than the people he did business with, he'd never be as ruthless. "You have to cancel the deal."

He whipped his gaze to me, brows drawn. "I can't do that, Tali. What's done is done, and we need their business anyway. If this goes well, then an ongoing arrangement with the Maldonados would set all of us up for *life*."

"What kind of life is it if you're looking over your shoulder every day? If you're never allowed to make mistakes?" I ran my hands over my face. "No amount of money is worth that."

"You can't even comprehend the kind of money I'm talking about."

"I don't *care*," I said, throwing up my arms in exasperation. "This is exactly the life I don't want—one I'm trying to help *you* escape. Why are you even worrying about an ongoing deal if you're trying to get out?"

"I have to make as much money as I can before I leave," he said adamantly, imploring me with his eyes. "When I get to the States, I'll be back at square one. What will I do for work? I need a bank account with enough zeros to take care of you."

"Diego." I squatted in front of him, set his hat on the lip of the fountain, and took his hands. "That's not how I need to be taken care of. I could have that life if I wanted it, but I don't. I chose to leave, and I thought you wanted the same." I swallowed, searching his eyes. "Do you not want to come to California?"

"I do. I want that so much, but I have to know I can provide for you first. Whether you ask me to or not, it's my responsibility as a man, and I won't be happy anywhere if I can't do it." He moved some of my hair behind my ear and tilted up my chin. "It's not just about the money. This first run will net me enough to come with you, and then you and I will be set until I get on my feet. But if it goes well, it'll also secure the most profitable deal your dad has ever made. It'll prove to your father that he can bring his business into the present, and . . ."

"And?" I asked.

He looked at me with cinched eyebrows, as if in pain. Diego felt everything. I hated arguing with him, but it was important that he see that money and status meant less to me than being with him. I was tired of living a country apart.

He glanced toward the house, avoiding my eyes. "It'll show your dad what I'm capable of. That I'm more than some lackey on his payroll. That I'm good enough for you and can care for you—not just financially, but in every way."

"Oh, Diego." I cupped his jaw, and he leaned into my hand. "He doesn't doubt what a strong, smart, skillful man you are. He just doesn't want me near any of this. It wouldn't matter who you were."

He put his hand over mine, turning his face into my palm to kiss it. "I'm sorry."

"For what?"

"All of this. Worrying you about Maldonado and Calavera. I'm sorry you had to see my fucking *pinche* brother." He brushed his lips up my wrist and forearm, smiling against my skin when I shivered. "I know how those memories of Cristiano affect you," he said softly, "but I'm not going to let him anywhere near you."

Diego *didn't* know. Not entirely. My nightmares were not limited to the horror of finding Mamá in a pool of her own blood. Cristiano had taught me that the gilded fortress I'd grown up in wasn't as secure as I'd thought. He'd robbed me of my carefree childhood. I'd sat in the dark, my nine-year-old mind growing more and more paranoid I might never be found, trying to think of how I could reach the last rung of the ladder without the height or vision I needed. Even if Cristiano hadn't killed my mom, I didn't know if I could ever disassociate him with the fear he'd inspired or the lessons I'd learned too early in life.

Trust no one.

Never draw a weapon unless you meant to kill.

Loyalty didn't guarantee loyalty, even to your own blood.

Anyone, even the most loyal disciple, could turn.

And I had danced with him tonight, aroused by a possessive touch and menacing words that should've sent me running into Diego's arms. I could've screamed like I'd threatened—but I hadn't. What was wrong with me?

I stood, pulled Diego up from the fountain's ledge, and wrapped my arms around his neck. "Thank you for protecting me," I whispered as I brushed my cheek against his. "For wanting more for us. For taking a bullet for me all those years ago. I love you."

"I only wish I could do more." He slid his hands down my back, lowering his mouth but pausing before our lips touched. "I would erase that day for you."

I hugged him more tightly, breathing him in as he pecked me once. Twice. His tongue slid between my lips, tasting me. "My sweet Natalia," he said on a moan.

I loved how he said my name. Even as Diego and I had changed, as our relationship had grown and our devotion to each other had solidified, he continued to say my name the same way—as if he owned it. As if nobody else knew it like he did.

I deepened the kiss. The world fell away, and we were just two people in love who hadn't had enough chances to show it.

His hands moved everywhere—searching, finding, claiming. He cupped my ass and pulled my hips against his, and I groaned.

"God, I want you," he said, his voice hoarse. "I don't know how much longer I can wait."

In that moment, I felt the same. I'd preserved my virginity for him —that part was easy. But keeping it *from* him? I struggled to be good. I wanted to do right by my faith, act with grace as my mother had, and be a woman she would've been proud of. But sometimes I wondered if it even mattered since I would marry Diego no matter what.

His hand dropped lower than it ever had, and the wrongness of being groped outside where anyone could happen upon us made something pull deep in my tummy. From behind, Diego cupped me between the legs and held me in place as he ground against me, rubbing a sensitive spot that made me moan up at the sky. "Oh, *god*. That . . ."

"Hmm?" he asked, running his tongue along the shell of my ear.

"That feels so good," I breathed.

"For me too. I'm getting hard, Tals."

Desire washed over me. This was still new territory for us. It wasn't easy to talk dirty to my best friend over the phone when we'd only ever stolen a few kisses here, a few intimate touches there.

"Tell me something too," he said in my ear. "Are you wet?"

I curled my fingers in his hair, taking two handfuls of honeyed downy strands. I hadn't known a question like that would excite me so much. "I think I am now," I said.

He smiled against my cheek. "You're pulling my hair."

"Oh—sorry." I released my fists.

"I don't mind it. How about you?" Keeping one hand under my ass, he tugged on my curls with the other, causing a butterfly clip to fall out. "Or is it too much?"

He'd been gentle, but I bit my lip as a passion we rarely got to explore warmed the space between us. "It's not too much."

His eyes darkened. "Tell me you love me, Talia."

"You know I do."

"But *say* it, *princesa*." He growled a little, in a way I'd never heard from him. "When I ask, that means I want to hear it."

I was taken aback by the tremor of frustration in his voice, especially because I couldn't think of a time I'd ever denied him anything. That was one thing he and I had never experienced—a chase. We played the games that had been forced upon us by keeping our romance a secret, but maybe the hungry look in his eyes now meant Diego also wanted to hunt a little.

What would happen if I didn't give him what he wanted every time he asked for it?

"No," I said softly.

"No?" He pulled me against him once more, bringing me to the tips of my toes. "Don't keep your love from me, Talia. Ever."

He sounded angry, but his excitement was growing more and more obvious against my stomach. And something about refusing him was equally as exhilarating for me.

I shook my head.

"You don't love me?" He nipped my earlobe. "All I want is to take care of you. Protect you. Love you. And you'll deny me?" He took my face with one large hand, his grip rough but his dancing eyes boring into mine, challenging me in a way that sent a thrill down my spine. His hand under my buttocks crept lower and locked between my legs. He had me trapped, my face secure, while his fingers were centimeters from my most intimate spot. "Tell me how much you love me," he demanded. "I won't ask again."

With footsteps at Diego's back, I jumped back as my heart launched into my throat. We'd let down our guards, which might've made our fondling more thrilling, but that was never smart around here. I hid behind Diego, adjusting my neckline, even though we hadn't been doing anything.

Diego turned just his head to the side. "Move along," he called over his shoulder. "Pervert."

No response. I looked around him and swallowed at the skull in the shadows. One that both arrested my gaze and inspired my instinct to flee. Cristiano had found us vulnerable, away from the team that protected us. I wasn't even sure if Diego had his gun. Cristiano could shoot me. Take me. Hurt me.

But would he? Who was he now? How was he different from the protector I'd grown up with? I couldn't even be sure that version of him was the same man who'd murdered my mother.

If he had at all.

Was I really questioning what I'd seen?

*God*. Cristiano hadn't even spoken yet, and he was playing mind games with me. His composure and coded words from earlier put a match to the embers of curiosity I continually tried to extinguish.

Diego turned, standing protectively in front of me.

The figure stepped into the moonlight. "You were going to take her out here for everyone to see," Cristiano said with an inviting gesture. "Don't let us interrupt."

I shivered at the thought, wondering how long he'd been watching.

Diego put a hand back to stop me from reacting. "What the hell are you doing here?" he asked Cristiano.

Even Cristiano's shrug was threatening. "I came outside to say hello to the brother I haven't seen in years."

"You know what I mean," Diego said. "Why are you in town?"

Cristiano turned his glare on me. "It's time for you to go home."

And leave Diego alone? "No."

"You haven't changed." Cristiano's eyes scanned my body, lingering on my breasts and hips. "And in some ways, you're entirely different."

"Fuck off," Diego said, moving to block me from Cristiano. "She has nothing to do with this."

"So send her away, as she doesn't seem to listen to me. Never did." A whistle sounded over our heads, and I jumped with its visceral *bang*. A burst of shimmering gold lit up the sky. Cristiano shook his head at me, as if disappointed. "I can see your fear from our last encounter has worn off, Natalia. What a shame."

I bit my tongue to stop from retorting *what a shame* it was that he'd lived to see anything at all. It was enough that Diego and I had his attention; it wouldn't help to anger him.

"Tell me," Cristiano said, moving to see me better. "Have you learned how to shoot a gun yet?"

*When you aim, kill.* "Hand me yours," I said, "and let's find out."

"*Cuidado,* Talia," Diego said through his teeth. "Careful. You don't know what he's capable of. Go back to the party. I'll find you."

I kept my eyes on Cristiano as his stayed on me. "What if he tries to hurt you?" I asked.

"Not unless the traitor strikes first," Cristiano said. "Go back to the house, and I promise you my brother's safety."

A second firework sailed through the night sky and exploded blood red. "He's not a traitor, and he's not your brother. I don't know what my father wants with you, but you're not family."

I immediately wished I'd kept my mouth shut. Cristiano came closer, tilting his head as his black eyes took me in. "Natalia Lourdes," he said, drawing out my full name in a way that made it sound sinful, like wisps of breath against a neck that didn't belong to him, and dangerous, like sharpening a knife.

With a sudden movement from Diego, Cristiano turned his head, focusing on his brother. "If you're going to draw your gun on me like you did back then," he said, "aim well. You'll only have one shot, and this time, you'd better be willing to die for it."

Behind him, the shadows stirred. Two shapes with two sharp pairs of eyes took form. Were these the misfits Diego and Tepic had spoken of?

Before anyone could make a move, voices from the lawn made me turn.

Barto approached with two members of our security team. He looked between Cristiano and Diego. "Costa wants to see you both in the ballroom. Now." Barto turned to me. "And you, Natalia. What are you doing here?"

"I was just taking her back to the house," Diego said.

Barto frowned at him, shaking his head. "You'd do better with the truth, Diego."

"Meaning?"

"Costa's likely to be less angry that she snuck into the party on her own than that she came to spend time with you."

Diego licked his lips. "Had I been *informed* we were hosting a known murderer and rapist, I would've obviously sent Tali straight back."

Cristiano barely noticed the insult. Instead, he was watching me. Listening. He'd always been that way, taking in everything around him, processing it like a computer, keeping his observations to himself—to what end, God only knew. Was he plotting ways to terrorize me more? Reminiscing about the life he'd had here?

Fantasizing about dancing in dark corners?

Or worse?

A small part of me couldn't reconcile the human trafficker to the Cristiano I'd known before he'd fled. He'd been next to impossible to get to know back then, even putting aside our fourteen-year age difference. But having only ever been under his protection growing up, I'd never seen him as the vicious killer everyone else had.

Until that day.

Barto nodded at the brothers. "Costa is waiting. Tonight, he's not feeling patient."

Cristiano and Barto exchanged an unfriendly look, which reminded me that before all this, they'd been close. They had come into the cartel around the same age and had risen in the ranks together. Barto, an important member of our security team even then, had been away on business with my father during Cristiano's attack on my mom. Like Cristiano, Barto never said much, but I knew he constantly beat himself up over it.

Barto had lost not only my mother—a member of the family he'd been hired to protect—but Cristiano too, his closest friend and comrade.

"Send someone back to the house with Talia," Diego told Barto.

"It's okay," I said, even though Cristiano still hadn't removed his eyes from me. "I don't need an escort."

As Cristiano passed me on his way toward the house, he stalled. "I'll see you to your bedroom if you like," he said so only I could hear.

The suggestive offer, not made out of graciousness, made me think of our tango. Or perhaps it was more appropriate to call it a mind game than a dance. It was becoming clear Cristiano liked to play. With Father demanding his presence and Barto watching on, I was safe. Instead of cowering at his suggestion, I called his bluff and offered my elbow as I would to an escort. "Let's go."

"Let's go indeed," he said with a hint of a smirk before he walked off with Diego and Barto.

Apparently, my discomfort amused him—but so did my fight.

That didn't surprise me.

Cristiano would pinch a butterfly's wings together just to watch her struggle.

## CHAPTER 7

# NATALIA

Aromas of coffee and cinnamon-raisin toast preceded the *pop* of a toaster as I entered the open, airy kitchen. Papá sat at the breakfast counter with a newspaper as Paz filled a mug with spicy *café de olla* from an orange enamel pot.

"*Buenos días,* Natalia," Paz said as she served him.

"*¿Cómo está?*" I greeted, pulling my damp hair into a ponytail so it wouldn't get my t-shirt wet. Despite my shower, I still had flecks of glitter embedded into my hairline and arms from the night before.

Paz responded, nodded at my father's half-eaten plate of eggs and *pico de gallo,* and asked if I was hungry. When I told her my stomach was still uneasy from the night before, she got me a warm can of Coke Light.

"Good morning, *mi amor.*" My father held up the front page to show me a picture of himself with the governor and his wife. Lower down the page, Papá shook hands with the head Calavera himself. I couldn't even bring myself to think the devil's name. "You wouldn't believe the morning's headlines," he said. "Everyone says it was a great party."

No mention of the murder within its walls? Whatever "journalists" had been in attendance should be stripped of the designation.

"*¿Hace mucho calor, no?*" he asked as Paz set down his toast.

With his complaint about the heat, she set to work opening the windows.

Papá sipped his coffee as I stared at his scabbed knuckles and slightly swollen right hand, remembering how he'd gripped the gun. I knew he'd killed before as sure as I knew my own name. That was no surprise. But to see it with my own eyes, and so carelessly, like plucking an orange off a tree or tossing aside a piece of junk mail. No warning or word of acknowledgment.

A breeze passed through the room, alleviating the heat. "I saw what you did," I said.

"Hmm?" He looked up at me. "What?"

"Last night, at the party. I was there."

He stared at me a moment, then stood and carried his silverware and plate of eggs across the kitchen. He threw them in the sink with a clatter. "Goddamn it, Natalia."

"Why?" I asked.

He turned to the maid as she tried to salvage the cracked dish. "*Gracias*, Paz."

She hurried from the room.

When it came to me, my father's bark was much worse than his bite. I stood my ground. "How could you let that monster back into our lives?" I asked.

"I was going to talk to you today. I didn't want you to find out that way," he said. I knew his scolding frown all too well. "I told you not to go to the party. You defied me."

"If I hadn't, I'd be reading lies for headlines." I picked up his picture with Cristiano and thrust it toward him. "My father, shaking hands with my mother's murderer? How were you going to explain this?"

"With the truth." He came back for his coffee, took the paper from me, and looked at the photo. "Cristiano is innocent."

"It's impossible." My voice broke, but I did my best to swallow down my grief. If I got emotional, his instinct to protect me would prevent him from sharing anything beyond the fundamentals. "Cristiano killed her, stole from us, and left me in a tunnel to rot."

"I should belt you for doubting me. My father would've," he said without any conviction. From my grandfather, that threat would've scared me. He'd had a temper. My dad wasn't like that, though.

"Is he blackmailing you?" I asked.

He put down the newspaper and slid his toast toward him. "No—"

"Papá." I pleaded with him. "Tell me the truth. What does Cristiano have on you?"

"Nothing." Leaning one hand on the counter, he took a bite, then tossed the remaining bread back on the plate as if he couldn't stomach it. "And spreading a rumor like that makes me vulnerable, so watch your mouth."

"What is it then?" I asked, undeterred.

He sighed into his coffee. "If you'd let me get a word in, I'd tell you. You're like your mother, storming in here yelling at me for things I didn't do."

"You shot a man in the head," I cried. "I saw it."

Even as his color drained, he straightened up. "Cristiano has proven his loyalty, Talia. For the last decade, he's done more than built himself a strong, successful cartel—"

"How can you say that?" I fell onto a breakfast stool. "I've heard the kind of 'business' he runs, and it's vile."

"His business isn't anything you should worry about. All you need to know is what Cristiano has done for your mother. For *us*." Birds chirped outside, and a sparrow landed on the sill. Papá shooed it away. "When Cristiano left here," he continued, "he ruthlessly and relentlessly hunted your mother's murderer. He made it his mission to find the motherfucker who entered my house—my *bedroom*—and took almost everything from me. I've had dark moments since learning this. I question Our Lady of Guadalupe for letting this stranger into my home, but I thank her you didn't come into the room any earlier."

With my elbows on the counter, I put my head in my hands. I didn't know what to think. "Who—"

"Let me finish. Cristiano delivered the *sicario*, forced him to his knees, and made him beg me for his life. It took a lot of time and resources to find that man you saw up there. Shooting him in the head in front of everyone was probably the kindest way to kill him."

If Father believed that, I didn't doubt a lack of mercy had been shown behind the curtains. It explained his battered hand this morning—and the man's swollen face and blood-soaked clothing. "And you believe it?" I asked.

"I heard it from the rat's mouth."

"Of course the hitman would say anything Cristiano told him to if he thought it might save his life." I nervously *pinged* the tab of my soda can. "Cristiano wants to clear his name and stop running."

"He doesn't need to be protected from me. He's built himself a cartel that surpasses my own. He has his own success, money, and status now. His network spans the world, and he could've built his business in Colombia, Russia, Bolivia—anywhere. But he returned."

He could've been anywhere, but he was here, turning my world upside down. I gritted my teeth, wishing he'd stayed lost. "Why?"

"Because this is his home. There's greater risk for Cristiano to return than to stay hidden. *Dios mío, me duele la cabeza.*" As he grumbled of a headache, he went to the fridge and removed leftover tostadas and a small *talavera* bowl of salsa. "If I hadn't believed Cristiano about the *sicario*, I wouldn't have hesitated to execute him on the spot. I almost did."

"Why even stop to let him explain?" I asked. "And what lies could he have possibly given to change your mind?"

"Cristiano managed to track down some of your mother's stolen jewelry. Each piece told its own story, and each ending eventually led him one place—to this *sicario*."

"It was jewelry *Cristiano* took," I said, not bothering to keep my cynicism from my voice. "He didn't need to look further than himself."

"If he'd taken the jewels, he would've sold them to survive, wouldn't he?"

"Yes," I agreed. "No question he did."

"And then tracked all of it down again?" Papá shook his head as he stuffed his face with chicken and refried beans. "They were one-of-a-kind pieces," he said as he chewed and swallowed. "The diamonds, rubies, and other precious gems Cristiano returned to me have unique settings I designed for your mother myself. He wouldn't have kept them when he had nothing and could sell them." He wiped his mouth with a paper towel. "The hitman was hired, Natalia. Someone wanted my wife dead."

Hearing it in such certain terms, I touched the base of my neck. At the time, Costa Cruz had been a feared drug lord. It would've been no small thing to hire a hit on a family like ours. I only knew of one other cartel who'd tried that, and the de la Rosas no longer existed, considering the leaders were dead. There was something as sinister about that as there was Cristiano killing the woman who'd acted as a second mother to him. "Hired by who?"

He massaged his temples with one hand. "A rival cartel, apparently."

"But why? Who? And how did the man get in? How would he have disabled the—"

"Slow down, Tali." He shut his eyes and took a breath. "Your old man can't drink like he used to. I have a hell of a hangover."

I went to a junk drawer, found painkillers, and tossed him the bottle. "Which cartel?"

"They're no longer in existence." He fiddled with the childproof cap until it popped open. "I'd deal with them if I could, but they've disbanded already."

"How convenient you can't confirm Cristiano's story." I got him a water bottle from the fridge. "It could be an elaborate scheme."

"To what end?" He shook some pills into his palm and tossed them back. I placed the water in front of him, but he washed down the drugs with a gulp of coffee. "I know you were young and may have forgotten," he said, "but your mother trusted Cristiano above anyone except me, and he cared for her. You too."

I hadn't forgotten. Cristiano had been her protector, but that didn't mean her instincts couldn't have been wrong about him. "He knew how much you loved her, and he wanted revenge for what you did to his parents."

"It wasn't revenge. Take my word for it." He replaced the cap on the pill bottle and looked at it pensively, as if lost in a thought. "It was a confusing time. I fell prey to my rage," he said finally. "I needed someone to blame, and Cristiano had fled, so it was easy to convince myself he'd run out of guilt. There was no other possibility, no evidence but what I had in front of me, and what you and Diego saw. But looking back, deep down, I questioned how it was possible he'd done what he'd been accused of. To assault Bianca and steal from us—it was out of character for him."

"But he did that for a living—he was a *hitman*."

"For us. Not against us. Never did he so much as raise his voice toward either me or her."

My throat thickened. Why couldn't he recognize that his devotion to Cristiano might be misguided? I could admit there was a *sliver* of possibility another explanation existed for that day—but to blindly trust him after all this time? "I know what I saw. I know what felt. I see it in my nightmares, Papá—*please*."

"I'm sorry, *mija*." He reached out for my hand and squeezed it. "It must be hard to see him again, and maybe I should've warned you, but I was trying to—"

"Protect me, I know." I took back my hand and covered my face. "He put a *gun* under my chin. He *shot* Diego. He left me in a *tunnel*."

"He knew I would find you," Dad said. "He was desperate. He understood I would've had no choice but to kill him with the evidence I had at the time."

"I don't know if I can believe any of it," I said, my throat thick as I tried to control my emotions. "I don't trust him."

"You don't have to. You just have to trust me." He returned to the sink for the clay pot and refilled his drink. "I'm sorry for what you saw last night," he said with his back to me. "If I'd known you were watching . . ."

"You wouldn't have done it?"

He turned his head over his shoulder, giving me his profile. "I would've had you removed from the party."

I swallowed. He didn't regret it.

A question I'd been fighting since the night before struggled to surface. If *I'd* believed that was the man who'd brutally attacked and killed my mother, would I have been as horrified?

If it'd been Cristiano up there with his hands tied and face beaten, would I have tried to stop it?

Or would I have reveled in his murder?

"You were there with Diego last night?" he asked.

Papá had heard my questions—now I'd have to answer some of his. I'd implicated both Diego and myself. "Yes."

He dumped sugar into his coffee. "I'll have to have a little chat with him then," he muttered.

"Have the chat with me," I said. "I want to talk to you about Diego anyway."

"Don't bother." His spoon *clinked* the sides of the mug as he stirred. "My answer is no."

"*Papi, por favor—escúchame*. You can't tell me what to do anymore. You have to listen."

"*Bueno*. Go ahead," he said, with an inviting gesture. "But it will fall on deaf ears."

"I love him." He froze, his mug halfway to his mouth. "Don't look so surprised," I said. "You know I do."

He lowered his drink, staring at me. "I know you *think* you do."

"Why do you doubt it?" I asked. "Diego has been there for me practically since I was born. He takes care of me. He treats this family and me with respect. He *loves* me."

"He is dangerous, Tali. Everyone here is. I wouldn't let you date the fucking chief of police."

I looked out the window. Two sparrows played in the terra-cotta birdbath Mom had hand-painted brown and green to look like a tree. Though the landscapers maintained it along with her garden, much of the paint had chipped off. "He's not like the others," I said, turning back. "Diego is sensitive. Sweet. Creative."

My dad seemed to think a moment before he burst into laughter. "My sweet girl. You're smart like your mother. She could teach me about everything from Shakespeare to how to have patience. She'd philosophize on the nuances of morality and ethics, then help me devise the best plan of attack against those who'd wronged me. She'd explain expressionism versus impressionism in a way that made me care."

I had not fully gotten to know that side of my mother. By age nine, I was only beginning to learn the many facets of her personality. But I still understood her innate warmth and intelligence exceeded that of most people. "Do you still think of her every day?"

"What a question, Tali. Of course I do. The day I don't is the day I never think again. But her heart was too pure," he continued. "She could never pull one over on me. When it comes to character, that's where *I'm* smart."

"What are you saying?" I asked, nesting my hands together in my lap. "You doubt Diego's character?"

"No—he has been a good addition to the cartel, and faithful to me. But I wouldn't call him 'sensitive' or unlike the rest of us. He is very much an active part of this world."

"Then why would he want to leave it?" I asked.

My father drew back, looking amused as he dipped crust from his toast into the salsa. "Does he?"

"That's what I want to talk to you about." I wrung my fingers. "Diego's and my plans."

"Your plans." He sighed, reclining a hip against one counter. "Which are . . . ?"

I stilled my hands. This was why I was here. Asking my father to accept us might not be an easy conversation, but it was a necessary one. The thought of leaving here knowing Diego would follow gave me strength. I steeled myself with a breath. "I want you to let Diego leave the cartel so he can come to California and be with me," I said. "I —*we*—want to start a new life there. Together."

He took the sip of coffee I'd kept him from and said simply, "It can't be, Natalia."

Expecting he'd say that, frustration rose in me quickly. I set my jaw. "You're not even listening. He's only dangerous *here*. With *you*.

Once he's away from all of this, he'll be free to start over. To reach his full potential."

"As what?" He set down his mug and rapped his knuckles on the counter as he intoned, "This is in his *blood*, Tali—it will follow him wherever he goes. He can run away from México, but not from this life."

"Then maybe it's better to have him by my side," I argued. "Diego is a natural protector. He confronted Cristiano when he could've run away. He knows how a criminal thinks and won't let anything happen to me."

He chuckled. "I'm impressed with your efforts. That debate class has paid off. But my answer is no."

My head began to throb. I slid out my ponytail holder and scrubbed my hand through my hair. "I know Diego is an important part of your business, but he isn't happy—"

"Maybe that's what he tells you, but it isn't so," Dad said, crossing his arms. "There's no escaping this life for me or him. What would he do in California? Bag groceries? That's all he's qualified for."

I frowned, stung and perplexed that he was around Diego nearly daily and somehow didn't see what I did. "He's smart and resourceful," I reasoned. "He can do anything."

"That means nothing to a man like him. We're cut from the same cloth. Here, he's respected—a businessman, a top advisor. In the U.S., he'll be powerless. He will be nothing."

"He'll be with *me*," I said, rising from the stool. "That's all we care about."

"Diego will never have a normal life. And I know him better than you—he doesn't *want* one."

"He does," I shot back. It earned me a look that made me lower my voice. "You're wrong. He's not made for this world. You're the only thing keeping him here."

Again, he laughed, and it echoed flatly off the tile floors. "You couldn't be more wrong," my father said. "Diego's in too deep. People's fortunes, futures, and *lives* are in his hands. Once a man gets a taste of that kind of power, he can never walk away from it. Not even for a woman."

"But—"

"Enough." He pressed his mouth into a firm line. "Your safety is my number one priority, and Diego can't offer you that. A peaceful, simple life would be death for him." He turned to dump the rest of his toast into the sink. "Go back to school," he grumbled. "Meet someone who can offer you more. Someone worthy."

"He is."

He turned abruptly. "Diego has been an asset to me in many ways," he said evenly. "He's shrewd, and a better businessman than most—even without an education. He's good, but for you, good isn't enough. I want someone great." He paused as he balled and flexed both hands. "These things are not to be taken lightly, Natalia. I loved your mother very much. There is no higher honor in my life than to be called her husband and your father."

"Then you're taking that honor from Diego."

He finished off his coffee and placed it in the sink too. "You will thank me one day."

My face heated. Did he think he was *God*? That he could control love? That he had any right to decide who was great and who wasn't? "I'm sorry you don't see the truth about us," I said, "but you can't stop me from loving him. I'm going to marry him someday, with or without your blessing."

He leveled me with a glare. "No."

"*No?*"

"Marriage is sacred. You will do it once, and only once," he said, raising his voice. "You're too young to know how you feel about him."

"You were twenty when you married Mami," I accused. "She was even younger."

"What your mother and I had was one-of-a-kind. Special. By comparing it to you and Diego, you make a mockery of my marriage."

As he spoke, frustrated tears heated the backs of my eyes. I lowered my gaze to hide them from him. What else could I say to convince him Diego and I had something real? Papá was leaving me no option but to find a way to *show* him.

"When you talk about building a life with someone," he said, "it should only be with the person you're going to die next to."

Shiny black and orange specks blurred on my arm. I fruitlessly tried to pick off the glitter. "Diego *is* that person."

"I don't want you around him anymore. He's already let things get too far with you. You're on the verge of getting your heart broken, and if that happens, I'll have to kill him. Do you want me to kill him?"

I choked back a sob. It was an empty threat, I knew. But for him to react so vehemently was like a slap in the face. I had no misconceptions that he'd disapprove, but he didn't *actually* think he could forbid me from Diego—did he? "He's my best friend," I said. "I don't want to stay away."

Papá sighed, then came around the counter and pulled me into his arms. I fought him at first, but his comfort was exactly what I needed just then—even if he was the cause of my distress. "I'm sorry." He kissed the top of my head. "But nobody risks their life for puppy love."

"Mami did. She cut off her family knowing the danger it would put them in to be associated with the cartel, and she traded small town security for—for *you*."

"And look what it got her, eh? Is that the fate you want?" He took my shoulders and peeled me off. "You have much to learn yet about manipulation, Talia. It won't work on me. I'm your father."

"Please," I begged as he stomped away in the direction of his study.

He turned back. "Diego is this life no matter where he lays his head at night. You might think it's romantic what your mother did for me, but let me tell you—the pain of losing her plagues me every day. You might think you'd die for him, but I won't permit it."

"It doesn't matter what you want," I said. "At the end of the day, we're adults. And you can't keep us apart."

On his way out of the kitchen, he snorted. "Watch me."

My father's blessing meant as much to me as his opinion. He was *the* rock in my life. The one who'd done everything in his power to protect me, and not just physically. After Mamá's death, I could sense how badly he'd wanted to shut down, but he'd pushed through as a newly single parent—for me.

But Diego had been there too. He'd proven his love through a lifetime of standing by me. I had to believe with all of my heart our love was enough for him—even if my father didn't.

CHAPTER 8

# NATALIA

It was a good thing Diego had described his home to me in such detail—it made it easier to find and show up uninvited. A large concrete wall enclosed the property, but the custom look of the wood-and-steel gate and the natural stone driveway gave away Diego's eye for detail.

I rang the buzzer at the end of the drive. Diego had told me not to come, but if I didn't take things into my own hands, I'd never get time alone with him. On top of his work obligations, now I couldn't even spend time with him at home, where Papá might see.

After a few moments, movement in the top right corner of the wall caught my attention. I waved into a security camera. With some yelling inside the house, I heard a door open on the other side of the gate.

"*Por Dios,* Natalia Lourdes," Diego called to me. The gate rumbled as it slid open. He stepped out with a scowl—slightly disheveled and totally sexy in a cream-colored Henley and camouflage cargos. He glanced both ways, pulled me inside, and typed a code on the keypad inside the wall. The gate stalled, then creaked as it reversed closed. "What the hell are you doing here?" he asked.

His exasperation was nothing after what I'd endured from my father the day before. I crossed my arms. "We have to talk, Diego."

Where our compound was a more traditional Spanish-style hacienda, Diego's was sleek and modern. The single-story house was a third the size of Papá's—not even counting our hundreds of hectares of land—but still a mansion for these parts with stacked stone columns, a flawlessly smooth, white exterior, and manicured bushes around the yard. He led me up the walkway to the front door. Floor-to-ceiling glass windows showcased a cloud-like, puffy leather couch, flat-screen TV, and brass-and-mirrored coffee table atop a neutral geometric-patterned rug—plus the armed men who guarded all of it.

"You can't just show up, *mi amor*," Diego said, opening the door. "That's one way to get a bullet in your head."

"I tried texting, calling, e-mailing—everything," I said. "I miss you, and I'm tired of sitting around watching the clock tick down."

"I know. I had to get rid of my last burner." He shut the door behind us and dismissed a guard from the entryway. "I've been trying to make it to the house to see you. Because *obviously*, I miss you too—but it's no excuse for putting yourself in danger."

He was right. I was being stupid for love like my mother. Knowing I'd anger my father wasn't enough to keep me away, though. He wanted to separate us, but that didn't mean he got to. Nobody was immune to love or resistant to the blindness it could cause. I shrugged helplessly. "I'm in love's grip."

Finally, he opened his arms, and I walked into his embrace. "I'm in *your* grip," he said, smoothing his hands down my backside. "I like this summery dress. Where are you supposed to be?"

"Shopping with Pilar."

"And how did you get here?"

"A cab. Security will be looking for me."

"*Ay*, Tali. If you don't get me killed, you'll give me a heart attack. I know Pilar is your best friend, but she's weak. She will give you up."

"She won't," I said. "She's easily spooked, but loyal as they come."

I needed to let her know I'd made it safely. We'd spent the morning in town, browsing the shops before an early lunch. We'd attended a service at the church—a gothic-style structure modeled after Spanish cathedrals with Oaxacan *cantera verde* stone and a domed bell tower. Saints looked over the altar from panels of floor-to-ceiling stained-glass windows, centered by a Virgin Mary. It was one of the only places that reminded me of my mother without inflicting pain.

There were *some* things I missed about Mexico. Grand parades and festivals that shut down the town. Unbreakable loyalty that put family above all else. Goods made by hand with love and attention to detail I could never seem to find in the States.

And Diego, of course.

I craned my neck to look around the place where Diego both lived and conducted business. I hadn't been anywhere the cartel operated aside from home and had only seen photographs and heard descriptions of safe houses, warehouses, and labs. "Can I have a tour?"

"You shouldn't be here," he said. "Someone could tell Costa."

"So send them away. You're the boss, aren't you?"

He shook his head slowly. "I can't. There's too much work to be done."

I played with the placket of buttons at his collar. The ribbed style of shirt only seemed to highlight his tanned neck and muscular pecs. "I've been worried."

"I know, but this is different than sneaking around your own property in a flimsy costume."

My mouth dropped open. "It wasn't *flimsy*. Tepic didn't even recognize me."

He reproached me with a frown not unlike the one Papá had worn at breakfast the day before. "Ditching your security detail leaves you defenseless against anyone who might be looking for vulnerabilities in the Cruz family."

I blinked up at him. "*You* said we no longer have enemies. Most of our rivals were incarcerated, overthrown, or died, and we never made new ones because we're no longer competitors."

"Don't question that the Maldonados—or other cartels we do business with—know who you are. Our enemies won't come looking for weak spots or collateral *after* a fuck-up—they already know who and where to strike to deliver the most pain." He glanced through the entryway windows. "We especially have to be careful now that my brother's back in town."

"What happened when you and Cristiano met with my father during the party?"

Diego inhaled deeply. "How about that tour?" he teased.

I smiled. Because I was also curious about the house, I let him change the subject—for now. He walked me through the living area to a state-of-the-art kitchen with glossy, handleless cabinets and a black-quartz island square under a rack of hanging copper pots and pans.

He pulsed his eyebrows at me. "Want to see the bedroom?"

"I thought you'd never ask."

We linked hands, and he led me down a long hall to the master, a large but mostly bare room with a dresser under a TV, a walk-in closet, and two bedside tables. Dove-gray sheets rumpled his king bed. "Well, now I know—you sleep on the left side," I said and grinned. "I sleep on the right."

"Match made in heaven," he said. "If I'd known you were coming, I would've made the bed. Nobody ever comes in here but the maid, and I gave her two weeks off for Easter."

"I don't care," I said, looking over my shoulder at him as I walked farther into the room. "I like tidying. I'll make the bed when we live together."

"When we live together, there'll be no point in ever making the bed."

My cheeks heated at the fantasy of waking up next to Diego each morning, lounging, laughing, and making love until we were forced to get up. "I can't wait," I murmured, stopping at the nightstand on the left side. It had only a phone charger, two business textbooks, and a picture frame. I picked up a photo of Diego and me smiling at my parents' pool. "I remember this day," I said. "It was the first time I'd ever worn a bikini."

"I remember it too, believe me. The bikini best of all."

I half-gaped at my white bathing suit, grateful it at least wasn't sheer. Diego hadn't yet grown into his broad shoulders, and his chest was smooth, not muscular like now. "How old were we here?"

"You were fourteen," he said.

"Which would've made you . . . a cradle robber."

He laughed. "You know it wasn't like that. You were like a younger sister to me. I remember that bikini because I almost punched my friend in the face for staring at you in it."

I glanced back. "You never told me that."

He stuck his hands in his pockets and shrugged. "And I never told you that when you came home from school two years later, every *puto* within a kilometer radius was talking about the beauty you'd become."

I wrinkled my nose. "You're exaggerating."

"I wish I were. I'd hear them talking about you. '*Qué linda, Natalia Cruz,*'" he mimicked. "That was when I knew."

I bit my bottom lip. "Knew what?"

"I felt more than just protective," he said. "I was jealous."

At times it felt as if Diego and I had talked about everything under the sun. That didn't mean I didn't love hearing all of his thoughts when it came to him and me. "But no other boys ever even *looked* at me," I said.

"I made sure of it."

A pleasant warmth crept over me. With his golden-brown hair in disarray and amusement dancing in his gemstone-green eyes, it was sometimes hard to reconcile the boy he'd been with the man he was now. He'd always been older to me—I'd turned sixteen only four years ago, when he was twenty-three. But he seemed much more comfortable in his skin now at twenty-seven.

"I remember being sixteen and already *crazy* over you, but I thought you'd always see me as a little girl."

"I did," he said. "Until I didn't."

"I'll never forget when you finally began to notice me," I said. "I used to sit on the sidelines and watch you and the guys play outdoor basketball. Then one day, I showed up, and you walked off the court to come talk to me. You'd never done that before."

"The guys teased me for it," he said. "I didn't care. It meant they knew you were mine."

"I never noticed anyone else," I said, glancing back at the picture. "But you know that. When we took this, you were both a best friend and like a brother to me—I didn't really know what was happening, but I was falling in love."

"Then why'd you leave me?"

I set down the photo and perched on the bed to face him. "The same reasons I always get back on the plane. I don't want to end up like my mother. And I don't want to lose anyone else. Papá never gave me a choice anyway. He *still* isn't giving me one."

He furrowed his brows. "Did you talk to him about us?"

"Yes. He doesn't understand that we're serious, no matter how I explain it."

Diego pursed his lips. "I warned you he wouldn't."

"But he wouldn't hear *anything*. He doesn't even want me seeing you anymore, like at all. Not even while I'm home."

He ran his hands over his face and looked to the ceiling. "Let me guess—I'm not good enough for you."

"According to him, nobody is—you know that. It's not personal." I stood and crossed the room to him, wrapping my arms around his middle. "It doesn't matter what he thinks, though."

Diego lowered just his eyes to look down his nose at me. "You know it does. He's your dad."

I shook my head hard. "Not enough to keep me away from you. I'm more worried about other things he said."

He nodded once to prompt me. "Like what?"

I rolled my lips together, trying to think of how to put it in a way that Diego wouldn't get defensive. "Papá thinks men who've only known this life can never leave it behind. Even if they want to."

"Of course he'll say that," Diego said. "It's to plant a seed of doubt in your mind about me." He used both hands to smooth my hair back from my face. "Is it working, Tali?"

I hadn't thought of much since yesterday except the new information involving my mother's death, and what Dad had warned about Diego's entrenchment in this world. I'd fought my father on each point, but with some distance, I worried his arguments might hold some validity. "Could you be happy in Santa Clara with me?" I asked. "It's nothing like here."

"My love . . ." He held my cheeks and pressed his lips to my forehead. "Are you *seriously* asking if I can endure a life where I'm not in danger of being killed—or killing—each day . . . *and* I get to sleep by your side each night?"

I smiled a little. "It does sound ridiculous when you put it that way, but still. What would you do for work?"

"That's why this Maldonado deal means so much to me," he said. "The money I'll make off it will set us up for a long time, Tali. And if your father makes an ongoing arrangement with them, even if I get a small percent for brokering the contract—it will be enough that neither of us will even have to work again."

"But I don't want that," I said. "I want an honest job and clean money. I'm not working this hard for a business degree I'm not going to use."

"It's not about the money, Natalia. It's important to me as a man that I provide for you. That means gifting you the freedom to follow your dreams, whatever they are, free of any financial burden."

"And what about your dreams?"

"I'm afraid to have any until I know I can." He smiled sadly and hugged me to him. "Once I pull this off, I can do anything. Including marry you. I want your father's approval, believe me—it would mean everything to have him see me as a suitable son-in-law. But at the end of the day, once I can support us no matter what, Costa doesn't *have* to agree."

I shook my head. "I could never abandon him," I said.

"Then we'll stay in California or wherever you want, but we're old enough to decide for ourselves. He'll have to learn to accept our plans if he wants you in his life." He smiled. "Because I'm not going anywhere. You will be my wife."

Excitement tickled my tummy the way a sip of champagne fizzed in my mouth. The idea of walking down the aisle to him made me giddy.

"Let's finish this talk over food. I'm starving." He pulled me by my hand. "Did you eat?"

"I had lunch with Pilar," I said as we walked back through the house. When I noticed Diego humming Led Zeppelin, I gave him a quizzical look.

"I've had it stuck in my head since this morning," he said. "There's this new drug in development, and it's called *Escalera al Cielo*."

"Stairway to Heaven," I translated.

"*Sí*." In the kitchen, he disappeared into the pantry. "You remember that guy Juan Pablo Perez?"

"The really good chemist from Nogales?" I asked as I sat at the dining table.

"He's more than really good. He's one of the top scientists in the country now. Probably the world." He returned and handed me a Coke Light. "Tepic told me yesterday he invented a sedative with tetro-something. It's a neurotoxin that comes from . . . *¿cómo se dice? Botete?* What's the word in English?"

"Puffer fish," I said and tabbed open my soda.

"*Sí*. Anyway, it's poisonous to ingest, but Tepic says in the right dosage, it's not fatal."

I sipped my cola. "Why would anyone want to take that?"

"Because, as Tepic put it," Diego said, gesticulating with flourish to imitate Tepic, "it's supposed to be a high more *addicting* than coke. More *life-altering* than ayahuasca. More *euphoric* than ecstasy."

I giggled, raising my soda can. "But is it more satisfying than Coca-Cola?"

"Apparently."

"But why the name?"

"Juan Pablo says it's a round-trip ticket to heaven." Diego came and hugged my neck from behind. "It's peaceful. Euphoric. It starts with tingling in the lips . . ." He kissed the corner of my mouth, then brushed his lips over my neck. "Then moves down to your fingers and arms. It puts you in a trance, and . . ." He tapped me once between the breasts with his fingertip. "Slows your heart . . ." He waited several seconds, then tapped again. "Like that."

I put my hands on his forearms, keeping him close. "That sounds dangerous."

"That's the price for a high like no other." He kissed my cheek and returned to looking in the fridge.

"And with the wrong dose?" I asked.

"What?"

"You said with the *right* dose, it's not fatal. What happens if Juan Pablo gets it wrong?"

Diego leaned out from behind the refrigerator door and cut his finger across his neck. "*Te mueres.*"

"Death. It's literal then—a stairway to heaven."

"He wouldn't put it on the market until it was safe, but I'll be honest. *I'm* not about to risk it." He shut the fridge door and grabbed a mango from a fruit basket. "We don't have shit to eat."

I toed off my flats and pulled my foot onto the chair to hug my knee. I fixed the skirt of my dress even though I wore boy shorts underneath. "Are you going to tell me about the meeting you and Cristiano had with my dad? I talked to him the next morning."

Diego picked up a small knife from a drying rack on the counter. "How much did he reveal?"

"Everything, I hope." If there was more to the story my father had shared, then Papá probably didn't know it. I picked invisible lint off my dress. "He said Cristiano found and returned jewelry that the hitman had sold. And that the *sicario* admitted to being hired by another cartel."

Diego rested his hip against the counter. "That's what he told me too."

"Do you believe it?"

"I . . . I'm skeptical. I'm not sure how—" He blinked at me and shook his head. "I don't know why I'm making excuses. No—I don't buy the story. I don't trust Cristiano, but I've never known Costa to be gullible."

"Exactly," I said. "My father *isn't* gullible. He's trusting his instinct with the evidence he has."

"Something he's known for," Diego pointed out. "Strong intuition. But I'm afraid he's too close to this."

Like my mother had been? She'd trusted her life in Cristiano's hands and had lost it.

"You heard what Costa said at the party—the prodigal son returns." Diego balanced the mango on a plate and sliced a clean curve along the skin. "I think it's obvious he has never been a good judge of Cristiano's character."

"What if Cristiano's telling the truth, though?" I asked. "Why would he come back knowing my father's been hunting him?"

"It's been years. Maybe he thought the old man had softened."

"Papá made it sound as if it took Cristiano that long to track down the jewelry and the hitman." If that was true, I could see why my father had said Cristiano had proven his loyalty. But I'd spent so long hating him, acknowledging anything positive about him felt foreign. And disloyal to my mom.

Diego's knife slipped, and I jumped as it slammed the plate. He glanced at the table, barely noticing, as if lost in a thought. "Whatever Cristiano's reason for returning," he said, "it must be worth risking his life."

"But if the Calaveras are as successful as you say, what could he want from us?"

Diego resumed skinning the fruit. After a few moments, he responded quietly. "Once a man gets a taste of power, his need for it surpasses hunger. It's a sickness that demands more."

Papá had said something similar about Diego. Because he was *somebody* in this life, he couldn't ever be *nobody*. "What's the *more* that he wants?"

He twisted his lips. "He was Costa's star quarterback, as the *gringos* say. Cristiano never failed at any task. Other cartels tried to lure him away, but he stayed true. He was the only one who could talk back to your father and not get punished for it." Diego gently separated the mango's skin, but his knuckles whitened around the knife handle.

"Maybe Cristiano thought he'd one day partner with Costa—or even take over the cartel."

Picturing Cristiano at the helm wasn't that hard to do. He'd worked side by side often with my father and had sat with us at the family dinner table far more than anyone else in Papá's business. "If that's true," I said, "then Cristiano probably felt he lost all that when he had to flee."

Diego nodded. "And now he wants it back."

Even if Cristiano hadn't killed my mother, he'd been blamed for it. What did an accusation like that do to a person? He'd had eleven years to nurse his grudge. I'd never forgotten what he'd said to me before we'd descended into the tunnel: *"Look what loyalty got me."* Those weren't the words of someone who wanted to be accepted home. They were those of a man who felt he'd been wronged.

Certainly Cristiano's definition of loyalty had changed that day.

And that made him dangerous.

Diego raised his voice as he ran the garbage disposal. "Do you know the real reason for the nickname *El Polvo*?"

*The Dust*. That was what some had called Cristiano when he'd worked for my father. "Because he arrives on a cloud of dust, delivering death before the dirt clears."

"That's what people say, but no." He flipped off the disposal and washed his hands. "It's actually because of how he executed his first kill."

"How?" I asked.

"It's gruesome." He dried his hands on a dishtowel. "On second thought, maybe I shouldn't say."

At this point, I was in too deep not to ask. My curiosity was being stoked at every turn and fighting it just made my imagination run wild. "Tell me," I said.

"He got a bucket of sand from the desert," Diego said, rubbing his palms together. "Then tied up a man twice his age and poured it down his throat until he choked to death."

I gripped my neck, suddenly unable to breathe. "No."

Diego nodded. "I've seen him do it. No screaming that way. No blood. No marks. And the bonus of a slow death . . ."

My nostrils flared as I inhaled. I felt that sand in my throat, strangling me. Death by torture—that was worse than death itself.

"After the party, I started looking into the Calaveras more. I've heard all kinds of inhumane things." Diego brought the plate of fruit to the table, removed his shoes, and sat across from me. "Apparently they have a soundproof dungeon where they keep one body part from each person who has betrayed them."

I stopped the question on my tongue—why. *Why* was a dangerous word. I didn't want to know. Dungeons and soundproof rooms and body parts could only mean bad things. Despicable, torturous things. But what was worse—to know the truth, or let ignorance leave me vulnerable? Where Cristiano was concerned, I never wanted to be in the dark again.

"What else have you learned?" I asked. "And don't tell me not to ask. I can handle it."

He shifted in his seat. "The worst, I guess, is abducting children to do his bidding."

As horrifying as that was, my father had taken in Diego and Cristiano for similar reasons. They had food and a place to sleep at night, but also an obligation to the cartel that they could never escape. "Is that different than what you guys do?" I asked.

"The kids in our cartel are like family. Your father never treated us like slaves. I'm talking bigger stuff. The Calaveras have gone as far as to purchase an entire shipment of children for labor."

I recoiled, clamping a hand over my mouth. What even *was* a shipment of children? And how did someone *purchase* one? Bile rose up my throat, and I pushed the mango slices away. "What . . . but how? How can he get away with that?"

Diego ran his sock along my inner calf. It was a small gesture, but still comforting. He lowered his voice, leaning in although we were alone. "Cristiano is powerful. He has even the most pious of government officials in his pocket and within Badlands' walls are all kinds of businesses, big and small. From *supermercados* and hardware stores to drone security centers and freight shipping offices."

"But shipping is your business," I said. "Isn't that stepping on your toes?"

"We own ports and plazas and have arrangements all the way from individual fishermen to fleet management companies, which reduces our risk." He ate a piece of fruit. "Cristiano invests but also has solutions in-house—"

"*Con permiso, señor.*" A boy who couldn't have been more than sixteen stood in the doorway. "*Hay un problema.*"

Diego nodded as he wiped his fingers on his pants. "Speak."

"Tepic is trying to reach you. It's, ah . . ." He glanced at me with anxious eyes. "*Es importante.*"

Diego stood and kissed the top of my head. "I'll be right back," he said, taking out his phone. "Feel free to snoop around the kitchen—unless it's not as much fun when you have permission?"

I stuck my tongue out at him as he left, then texted with Pilar to update her.

By the time Diego returned, I'd finished all the mango. "Sorry," I said as he stayed in the doorway, typing something into his phone. "I guess I was hungry after all. Want me to cut another?"

He glanced up but looked past me, staring off as if he hadn't quite registered that I was there.

"Diego?" I asked, sitting up straighter.

He blinked, and recognition crossed his face. "What?" he asked. "Did you say something?"

"What's the matter?" I got up and went to him. "What was the problem?"

He ran a hand through his hair, then looked at his cell. "Ah, it's nothing, but . . . I have to get back to work." As soon as he stuck the phone in his pocket, it started to ring, and he took it back out. "I'll have someone take you home."

"I can get a cab."

"Hmm?" He checked the screen and ran a hand over his mouth with a curse.

"You're getting pale," I said. "What'd Tepic say?"

"I have to take this, Tali. Don't get a cab." He kissed me quickly on the lips, then retreated. "Sit tight, and I'll send someone in to drive you."

"But—" He was already halfway out the door. "When will I see you next?" I called.

"Soon, *mi amor*. I'll be in touch." As he exited the room, he answered the phone with, "Jojo? There's been a theft."

Despite his unusual behavior, my shoulders relaxed with a small degree of relief. Stolen goods didn't sound like much to be concerned about when a phone call could mean anything from a kidnapping to a RICO charge to the death of a family member.

I put my shoes back on and sat to wait for a ride, feeling slightly comforted.

As far as bad news went, I would take a theft over the alternative any day.

# CHAPTER 9

# DIEGO

Our waitress looked between my brother and me in the low light of a steak restaurant, trying to decide which one she liked better. It'd been a while since we'd been sized up that way. Women had started comparing Cristiano and me once I was old enough to get female attention.

"Brothers?" she asked, placing Cristiano's mezcal on the table.

Don Costa sat back in his dining chair, reveling in the show. "What gave it away?" he asked her.

She twisted her red lips at Cristiano, her eyes glimmering. Apparently, she'd chosen him, not that I cared. With a long nose and features that didn't quite register as feminine, she was no Natalia. "The height," she answered. "Dark hair. Same smile. You look a lot alike, but there's also something very different about you."

"What do you suppose that is?" Costa asked Cristiano.

Who gave a shit? I checked my phone for news from Tepic. We'd been in constant contact with the increasingly dire events of the past couple days, but it'd been a few hours since I'd heard anything.

I prayed that was a good sign.

"One of you is lighter." The waitress returned her eyes to me as she served my tequila. "Must be the eyes."

"Or Diego's soul isn't as charred as mine," Cristiano said with a half-smirk. "Yet."

She laughed. "Enjoy. I'll be back soon to take your orders."

When she was gone, Costa looked me over. "You like her?" he asked me. "We can send a chopper back for you tomorrow if you want to stay the night in the city."

I bit my tongue to keep my temper in check. Anything to keep me from Natalia. I unfolded my napkin onto my lap. "No, thank you."

"All right then." Costa leaned his elbows on the table. All mirth drained from his features as he lowered his voice. "You have fucked us, Diego."

We'd taken a helicopter all the way here, to an exclusive restaurant that topped the city's tallest building, for him to say that. Two tables away, Mexico's attorney general dined with his wife. At the bar sat a rep for one of Bolivia's most pervasive cartels. *Comandante* Trujillo laughed with cronies across the room.

It was no accident that Costa, Cristiano, and I were showing our faces here tonight.

"Two stash houses were hit in two days," Costa said. "Millions worth of product stolen. What do you have to say, Diego?"

No excuse would do. I hadn't slept much and needed to return home to help prepare the next few deliveries, but instead, I was here, putting on a show. "It can only be explained as bad luck," I said.

My brother picked up his drink. "Two direct hits less than forty-eight hours apart? Nothing to do with luck. You have a leak."

"Unlikely." A rat inside the walls would fall on my shoulders, and having a solid team I could trust was one of the things I prided myself on. "My men wouldn't do that."

"Until they would," Cristiano said.

I looked to my brother. Over the last decade, I'd worked side by side with Costa to strategize and build a more advanced tunnel system, to secure long-term relationships with border agents, to arrange reliable shipping via land, air, and water in all corners of the Americas, and more. Cristiano hadn't been there for any of it, so why was he here now?

"How much is gone?" Cristiano asked.

"We're still within reach of what I promised the Maldonados," I said, "but that means we have to be especially careful going forward. No hiccups at the border."

"There are always hiccups at the border," Costa said. "You know that better than anyone, Diego. When have you ever gotten every last kilo across? It can't be done."

Costa spoke with a smile for anyone who might be watching. Rumors were likely starting to circulate, and the first sign of trouble would only breed more of it. Our current clients would pull their cargo until they heard more. A broken link in our system would expose us to weakness. And most importantly—the Maldonados would start asking questions.

Questions they wouldn't like the answers to.

We were here tonight to reassure those around us that we weren't worried, and to crush any rumors that might start circulating about our business or our relationship with Cristiano.

"We have some leeway still," I said, massaging my eyes as they burned from lack of sleep. "I just have to take extra precautions with the transport."

"That's not acceptable." Costa struggled to keep his voice level, but anyone paying close attention would see the tension in his posture. "Failure to deliver means more than retaliation. It's complete obliteration."

That wouldn't happen. If I'd thought there was a possibility of it, I never would've made the deal. I'd even accounted for bad luck. With the odds I'd calculated, doing business with the Maldonados had been a no-brainer. A little risk was good, but there was a point where it became reckless, and we hadn't reached that. I knew my business in and out.

Still, I paired a long sip of tequila with a quick prayer. "I'll handle it."

"Did you see yesterday's news?" Costa asked. "A potential witness in the latest case against Ángel Maldonado was found at the top of a pyramid."

I frowned. "A pyramid?"

"*Of human bodies*," he said. "Every member of his family from Chihuahua to Oaxaca."

There was a time when that mental image would've made my stomach churn. Now, gruesome death was sadly routine.

"This happened while the witness was under twenty-four-seven government protection," Cristiano added. "That's not the Maldonados handling a problem—it's a clear message to anyone thinking of flipping."

I wasn't flipping. I was costing the Maldonados money—equally bad if not worse.

With a vibration in my pocket, I put down my drink and read Tepic's text: *Emergencia*.

*Shit*. What now? Forcing my shoulders down, I excused myself and dialed Tepic as I wound through the tables toward the windowed perimeter of the dining room.

"Diego," Tepic answered breathlessly. "Have you talked to Jojo?"

"I'm still in the city with Costa." I stopped at a floor-to-ceiling glass wall overlooking the city. "What is it?"

"An explosion at the Juárez-El Paso tunnel."

I closed my eyes and clenched a fist. *What the fuck?* That tunnel had been a million-dollar construction in itself, not to mention a crucial channel into the States. "Tell me that's the only news."

"No." He hesitated. "Mike and Felipe were inside. And they didn't make it."

I looked down, massaging my temples with one hand. I was no stranger to losing people on my crew, but it never got any easier. It was personal. Mike and Felipe were more than workers—they were friends. I refrained from making the sign of the cross only so I wouldn't draw attention. "This wasn't an accident," I said.

"No, *patrón*."

"What happened? How much did they have with them?"

After some static on the line, Tepic said, "I'm finding out the exact amount—"

"How much?" I repeated.

"Jojo says they were mid-delivery. Some made it but not all. Five, maybe six containers gone."

"*Puta madre*," I said under my breath. "Make sure every border agent on our payroll knows we have no margins. Pay them more if you have to. And get *every* man we have guarding *every* stash house."

"Some are en route to Guadalajara to meet with Nuñez's guys."

"Bring them back. We need all hands on deck." I glanced at the table to find Cristiano watching me as Costa picked a cigar from a box the waitress offered. "Keep me updated," I told Tepic and hung up.

The cityscape glowed against a starless night sky. I tried to figure out how to break this to Costa. This wasn't human-pyramid bad, but now we'd hit our absolute limit. That was a serious problem in itself made worse by the fact that whatever was happening, it was calculated. And it was in front of Cristiano. Or because of him?

He'd been back less than a week, and things we're starting to fall apart on the most important deal I'd ever made. Natalia had drawn the right conclusion—Cristiano had lost the only life he'd known when he'd been forced from the compound. A life he'd felt he'd deserved, even if it'd been built on betrayal. And now he was back—but *I* was the one who had Costa's trust.

Was my brother here to earn it back?

And how would he regain it?

I didn't doubt he had come home with a plan. Did the Maldonados somehow play into it?

I pocketed my phone and returned to the table. There was no use in drawing out bad news, so I resumed my seat at the table and dismissed the waitress.

"What is it?" Costa asked, puffing on his Montecristo. "I was about to order."

I placed my elbows on the table, leaning in. "A tunnel has been compromised at the border," I said.

Costa nearly choked. As he coughed, smoke billowed around him, shrouding his reddening face. As I sensed his temper mounting, I glanced around to remind him we had onlookers.

When he'd calmed, at least in appearance, he spoke. "We're under attack."

I nodded. "Yes."

Costa looked to Cristiano. "It has to be one of the Maldonado cartel's many enemies who don't like the idea of us working together. Don't they know fucking with us means severing ties to our network?"

"I can find out." Cristiano spun his glass on the table. "But right now, you need a plan."

"Damn right we do." Costa scrubbed a hand over his face and pulled at his long chin. "What are you thinking?"

Why was he looking to Cristiano for guidance? How easily they fell into old patterns. After our parents' murder, Costa Cruz had set us up at the ranch house on his compound, far enough away that gunfire wouldn't draw attention, but close enough that the main house was only a short drive. At the ranch, Cristiano had been fed choice food, armed with the finest "toys," and boarded in a private room while I'd shared everything with the others adopted by the cartel.

Costa and Bianca Cruz had favored Cristiano up until her *untimely* death. But now, I was the one who ate at Costa's dinner table many nights. I had over a decade on my brother of unwavering loyalty to Costa. Of standing by his side to build a business with limitless potential—and profits. And of being there for Natalia whenever she needed me.

Failing the Maldonados could take all of that from me. And if my instinct was right—Cristiano knew it.

"I can still salvage the shipment," I interjected. I couldn't dwell on what was gone. I needed to protect what remained. "We won't exceed the Maldonados' expectations as I'd hoped, but we'll still be within the percentage we promised."

Costa raised his cigar to a comrade across the restaurant. A signal that we had things under control.

But over the past two days, we'd lost more than just control.

"How close?" Costa asked.

"Some of the drop was made." I looked to the ceiling to subtract what we'd potentially lost and the containers that had made it. "If we move everything left, we're likely still within a percent or two of what we guaranteed the Maldonados would make it across the border."

"So you need a ninety-nine percent success rate for what's left." Costa set his jaw. "Not *one* seizure at the border. It can't be done."

"It can if I move slowly, carefully, and strategically," I said.

"You've run out of time for that," my brother said. "You're being targeted, and you need everything in the States immediately."

Cristiano had to comprehend the scope of that operation, even for a company in supply chain management. To mitigate risk, product was stored all over town, then moved in small batches across the border, mostly by individual vehicles. "I can't just send it across all at once," I said.

"And what if another stash house falls tonight? Tomorrow?" Cristiano asked. "You'd be a dead man walking. You, and everyone associated with you. Including Costa."

I pulled at my collar feeling suddenly parched. The situation was dire, yes, but Cristiano was just trying to rattle me. "That won't happen," I said after gulping some water. "I've called in all our security and alerted them to the gravity of the problem. It's all under guard."

"By men who have inside information about where everything is kept," Cristiano pointed out.

"*You* have inside information," I shot back at my brother. "And you were the last to show up around here. So how the hell do I know you're not behind this?"

"*Tranquilo*, Diego," Costa warned. "Calm down."

Cristiano took a slow sip of his mezcal, watching me over the rim. The Cristiano I'd known had never touched alcohol and wouldn't have cared enough to distinguish top-shelf tequila from sludge. Then again, I'd never seen him in a suit until his return, either, and definitely nothing near the fine, custom-made ensemble he currently wore. What was the point of a gangster like him in a bespoke suit that'd surely be ruined by the blood of his enemies? He could show off all he wanted, but while some of us did what was necessary to get by, Cristiano thrived on being a natural killer.

"I've spent the past decade trying to get back in Costa's good graces," Cristiano reasoned. "Why would I immediately turn around and jeopardize that?"

"That's what I intend to find out," I said.

The corner of Cristiano's mouth ticked. "There's no ruse. I can tell you the truth of it. It's that I've missed this—strategizing under fire. Enjoying a meal with the great minds at this table. Spending time with *mi familia.*" He said *family* with an edge that Costa seemed to miss. That, or he didn't want to see it. Cristiano looked between both of us. "It has been too long."

"It has," Costa agreed.

I bit my tongue. What Cristiano missed wasn't family—he'd given that up long ago. It was the prestige and power he could gain by partnering with Costa.

Prestige and power I would earn by pulling off this deal.

"Your brother is right," Costa said. "You need to get every last kilo over the border as quickly as possible."

That was easy for Costa to say. He had nothing but constraints to contribute to the process. He was asking for complete accuracy on an impossible schedule. It wasn't as if he'd be down in the trenches with us. "Even with a full crew, I don't have the manpower," I said.

Cristiano drank some mezcal and studied his glass. "I do."

Of course he did, but I wouldn't allow him to insert himself in my deal. "I'll make it work."

"Then at least let me try to reason with the Maldonados," Cristiano said. With his elbow resting on the back of his seat and a passive expression, he could've been discussing anything from wine varietals to horse racing.

"Why would that make any difference?" I asked.

"We have history," he explained, "and they need my guns more than I need their money."

As Cristiano and I locked eyes, his plan began to take form before me. His timing *wasn't* a coincidence. Cristiano wanted in on this deal. But if I knew him, it wasn't about the money. He wanted the credit. By saving *my* Maldonado deal, *he'd* be the hero. He'd win back Costa's favor. And he'd undercut me in the process. Everything he wanted with one fell swoop.

"I can't guarantee anything," Cristiano continued, "but perhaps it'll help ease the sting if I tell them they might not get the results they were promised."

The results *I* had promised was what he meant. Results that were challenging but should've been attainable. Unless someone with a motive to bring me down had interfered.

Costa nodded along as if Cristiano spoke the word of a patron saint. "That's a generous offer, but a last resort," Costa said. "I'd rather not get the Maldonados involved until we have to. We'll take you up on help consolidating what's left, though."

"I'll make some calls," Cristiano said. "Get your most trusted men together, and I'll get mine. We can store the product in one of my warehouses. Nobody will know the location, and if they do, they wouldn't dare cross me."

Cristiano was hijacking my deal in front of my eyes. How would it look to Costa that I needed to be rescued? How would it look to *Natalia*? With a deep ache in my jaw, I unclenched my teeth. "You expect me to trust my livelihood to you and your unhinged *cabrónes*?" I asked.

"Cristiano is offering to help," Costa said. "Where is this warehouse?"

"At the border of town where the desert starts," Cristiano said and glanced at me. "Nothing to do with the Badlands if that's what you're referring to."

"Sounds like a plan," Costa said. "With both cartels working together, we can pull this off."

"With our two cartels working together," Cristiano said, returning his gaze to Costa, "we can pull *anything* off."

I narrowed my eyes on him. *Aha*. There was more to it than I'd thought. The Calaveras had their own solutions for trafficking, but if they joined forces with us, they could move double the volume *and* restrict their competitors from our services.

But that would mean a merger—one I'd be excluded from.

And not just any merger, but one between the de la Rosas and the Cruzes.

Anyone at the helm of both the Calavera and Cruz organizations would be afforded a power few others could match. Did Cristiano feel he was owed that after the decade he'd lost? Was it not enough that he'd taken our parents from me? Now he was back to take the rest? If so, his endgame was bigger than I'd guessed.

He had reason to push me out . . . but no—it was impossible for him to know that. I was nothing if not careful and always had been. Cristiano would've gone to Costa by now, and this conversation would be happening atop a fresh grave.

"*Perdón*." Cristiano rose from the table with his cell phone in hand. He started to turn but paused. "You may want to consider putting Natalia on a plane, don Costa. In case things get any worse."

I wondered, not for the first time, why Cristiano was concerned with Natalia at all. I hadn't missed the way he'd looked at her at the costume party, first predatorily from the balcony, then later, the way a man regards a woman who has something he likes.

I recognized his interest in Natalia because I shared it as well.

She was more than an interest to me, though. I loved her. She was my weakness.

Did we share that as well?

Did Cristiano have a tender spot for her that he might not even be aware of . . . until someone stepped on it?

As Cristiano left the table, Costa turned to me. "*Are* things going to get worse for my daughter, Diego?"

He said everything he needed to in that one question. It had nothing to do with how the Maldonados could hurt her, but how *I* could. "Natalia is my best friend," I said carefully. "I'd do anything to protect her."

"That won't be necessary. The best thing you can do is put her safety above all else and release her."

I didn't have to be explicitly told to stay away from her—that had always been implied. But it was the closest Costa had come to acknowledging my relationship with her. I wasn't going to get his blessing. Which turned the question from how to get his approval . . . to whether I needed it.

"So I ask you again," Costa said. "Are things going to get worse for Natalia?"

I shook my head, looking into my glass. "No, *señor*."

"Good. As for your brother," he said. "He wants to help."

"And you don't wonder why?" I asked.

Costa sucked his teeth, charting Cristiano from across the restaurant as he made a call on the patio. "No. Because he is grateful I have welcomed him back to his home," he said. "Finish your drink. Then go and express your gratitude for your brother's offer to help."

Cristiano wasn't here to help. He was here to hurt. Or worse . . .

No doubt he thought I'd turned my back on him eleven years ago and blamed me for everything he'd lost. It occurred to me that I hadn't even considered the worst Cristiano could do.

It was true that by saving my Maldonado deal, he'd get credit for it, win back Costa's favor, and potentially replace me. I'd assumed that was the fastest way for him to get everything he wanted.

But perhaps I'd been looking at the wrong side of the coin.

He could sabotage the deal instead.

If it failed . . . the Maldonados would see to my demise quickly and swiftly. Cristiano wouldn't even have to get his hands dirty.

And I'd be removed from the picture entirely.

CHAPTER 10

# NATALIA

Art belonged to my mother. Trying to read brushstrokes or create my own wasn't something I understood. I learned about the world from books or travel, found nature by cantering a horse, and studied history by passing on legends through *corridos*—Mexican ballads.

Art, to me, was living in the world, not observing it. Floating on my back in the ocean on a hot day, finding shapes in the clouds. My aunt's laugh when my nephew took a bite straight out of his birthday cake and came up with a face full of icing. Art lived in people.

It was the way one look from Diego could warm me to my core.

My mom's studio spanned the top floor of the house. With a glass dome in the center and large corner windows facing southwest, it had the best light.

When I was younger, I'd hide in here to see how long it would take Diego to find me. We'd dip our hands in paint and make colorful prints on the tarp Mamá had put down. But most commonly, we'd look at the constellations with a telescope, our own private planetarium.

All the paint and easels had been removed, but the telescope sat on the deck. Tonight, I opened the doors and windows and watched the sun set while I waited for Diego.

When tires crunched dirt, I jumped up and leaned over the rail. A convoy of three cars kicked up dust as they wound up the driveway and parked out front. Cristiano and Diego got out, moving almost lethargically up the walk until my father stepped out of the house to meet them. It was strange, after all this time, to see Cristiano and Diego casually standing next to each other. I leaned out farther to try to piece together their conversation.

". . . forty-eight hours."

"No word . . . Maldonado."

*"Antes de que salgas . . ."*

*Before you* leave? My heart dropped at the thought of Diego disappearing again when I hadn't seen him in three days. As if sensing my anguish, he looked up, met my eyes, and winked discreetly. I watched until they moved inside. As tempted as I was to run downstairs, I waited where I was, knowing Diego would come to me.

*Paciencia* should've been my second name—it was all I seemed to do. Wait. Bide my time. Bite my tongue. A sitting duck, as Americans said.

I killed time by peering through the telescope, but it wasn't dark enough to see much yet. Eventually, the door to the studio opened. I sprang to my feet, hurrying across the wood floors to meet Diego. He caught me in his arms and lifted me for a kiss.

"Why have you stayed away so long?" I rushed out in a whisper, even though we were alone. "I'm set to fly home in a week."

"I'm sorry, Talia. I haven't had such a bad week in recent history. I shouldn't be up here, but I texted because I needed to see you, even for a moment, to get me through." He set me on my feet and gripped my waist. "But if your father catches me here, he'll put you on the next flight out of México."

"He wouldn't. Easter is Sunday."

"Believe me, he would."

Papá wouldn't ruin our holiday for that reason. I touched the brown, coarse stubble on Diego's face. He stank of alcohol, sweat, and cigars, but I was comforted just to be in his presence. "Where have you been? Have you even slept?"

"No." He loosened his already sagging tie. "We went to the city for dinner last night, then flew back. Cristiano and I worked through to just now."

To hear about cartel life over the phone was one thing, but the evidence of its non-stop demands stood in front of me. I hated to think of Diego overworking himself. "You need rest. Come. Sit and tell me everything."

"I can't stay, Tali. If Costa finds me here after dark—"

"He won't." I pulled him to the deck by his hand. Even his palm seemed rougher. "He never comes up here."

"Your father's serious about keeping us apart." Diego sat in an Adirondack chair, following me with his eyes as I went to the linen closet. "It wasn't an idle threat," he said. "At dinner, Costa said he's thinking of sending you back early."

I stopped short, clutching a blanket. "But I've barely spent any time with you! I see you for a few hours, and then you disappear for a few *days*."

He stood to take the wool throw from me. "Sit down," he said.

I fell into the chair next to his. "He didn't mention anything today, and we had lunch."

"Does he ever? He keeps you in the dark to protect you. If he wants you gone, he'll put you on a plane. He wouldn't ask your permission first." He unfurled the blanket over me. "I'm starting to think Costa will never come around to the idea of us. And then what?" He swallowed as he focused on tucking me in. "Would you still want me?"

I reached up to grab his cheeks. "*Yes*," I said, forcing him to hold my gaze. "I'll never give up on us. We'll find a way."

He searched my eyes. Though his were alight, the dark circles under them betrayed his lack of sleep. What had brought on his sudden doubts, and why did my father want me gone so soon?

"I have to ask, Tali . . ." Diego went as still and quiet as the sprawling night around us. "Could you be happy without your father in your life?"

To choose between my dad and Diego? It would be impossible. "He's already lost too much," I said. "If it came down to it, he'd be forced to accept us. I don't think he'd ever make me choose."

"But if he did?" Diego pressed his lips to my forehead before pulling his chair closer to mine to sit. "I just want you to start considering that possibility."

I couldn't imagine not calling Papá whenever I had a question, missed my mom, or simply had the urge. He always spent Christmas with me at school. And just because I only visited once a year didn't mean I wanted to give up the possibility of coming home one day. Having one parent taken from me, I would never willingly give up the other. At the same time, I'd chosen to leave this life as much as I had been sent away.

But not once did I ever *choose* to be separated from Diego.

"And his approval is only half of the issue," Diego added.

Diego didn't want to be separated from me, either. It just wasn't necessarily up to him. I opened the blanket, and he pulled part of it over himself, checking to make sure I was still covered. "You mean leaving the cartel," I said.

"It's not as if I can just put in my two weeks' notice. If Costa thought I was abandoning the cartel without permission or trying to steal you away . . ."

*My father raised the White Monarch, put it to the* sicario's *head, and* bang!

It was an image I doubted I'd ever be able to scrub from my mind.

What would it take for him to "handle" Diego? He'd leveled a threat in the kitchen days earlier, but I hadn't taken it seriously. Diego was practically family to him.

"He wouldn't hurt you," I said. "He has to know what that would do to me." I believed that, but there was another truth I couldn't ignore. Papá hadn't gotten to where he was by letting offenses slide, no matter how sentimental he might feel.

"As long as he doesn't take us seriously, he'll go out of his way to put up a wall between us," Diego said. "He has to realize this isn't a game to us, *princesa*. That we're in this for life."

Diego spoke with such conviction that *for life* inspired a thrill in me. I was his princess, but I was also that to my father—and in his eyes, Diego was just a ward of the cartel, forbidden from entering the proverbial castle walls he guarded.

"Then we'll have to make sure my father understands that if he doesn't let you go so we can start a life together, he will lose me."

"You've told him how you feel. *I've* tried to broach the subject, but he won't hear me. What else can we do to get him to see?"

It would have to be something that couldn't be ignored, dismissed, or stopped. I thought back to my conversation with Papá in the kitchen about loving one person and being willing to risk everything for them. About the ties my mother had cut for my father. About how marriage was sacred and should only happen once. With the person you were willing to die for.

"If we can't tell him, then we'll have to show him," I said. "Even if it means something drastic."

"Such as?"

My heart began to race. I looked out toward bruise-colored mountains as dusk swallowed the day. I was too shy to say it directly to Diego's face in case it wasn't anything close to what he was thinking. "We could always elope."

When he didn't respond, I finally chanced a look at him.

He stared at me with a tenderness that melted my insides and left me a puddle of need and longing. This was the art of life—the art of Diego—and what I would risk my father's wrath for. Diego possessed a potential he would never reach here. He'd supported my decision to go away knowing he'd be left behind. And he wanted the best for me, even if it meant the worst for him. *He* would never make me choose between the two of them.

"Marriage, Tali?" he asked softly, almost reverently.

"It's a lot, I know—"

"It's everything." He took my hand under the blanket. "You're the only one who believes in me enough to trust me with your love. With the *world*. I have tried and tried to show your father the man I can be. I have no one else—my parents gone and a brother I no longer recognize. You and Costa are my family, but he continues to deny me. And you have never once failed to accept me."

Moved by his openness, my throat thickened. "He won't be able to deny you once he sees how devoted we are."

Diego slid his hand up my arm and massaged my shoulder. "I don't understand how Costa freely respects Cristiano but continues to hold me at arm's length. Last night, we were three grown men drinking and talking business, and yet, it's like I was a teenager at the ranch again."

I hated that Diego had grown up feeling second best to Cristiano, who'd been treated like a prodigy just because of his size and capacity for brutality. "There's no way my father can just switch his trust for Cristiano back on."

"It feels that way—like I'm being replaced."

"Never, *mi amor*." I stretched over the arm of the chair to kiss him for all the times we'd had this conversation and I hadn't been able to physically comfort him. "I'll show you so much love and respect that you won't need it from anyone else."

He held the back of my head for another peck. "We will be married," he said, "but I can already declare that I intend to love you until death do us part."

*And death* would *do us part*.

The soothsayer's unwelcome warnings shivered through me. Damn her and her bullshit fortune. I forced her voice from my head and replaced it with a glowing vision of myself in all white, facing a suited Diego. We stood before an altar, hands intertwined as we committed our lives and love to each other. I'd dreamed of it many times at school, but for the first time, calling him my husband felt within grasp. "I wish the day were tomorrow," I said.

"Don't tempt me." He released me to recline back. "I may steal you away and officially make you mine."

"*Stealing* implies I wouldn't go willingly." Under the blanket, I folded my hands in my lap and squinted up, hoping for a shooting star. We needed all the help we could get. "I'll be on a plane soon, Diego."

He nodded slowly. "What're you suggesting?"

"I don't know. Just pointing out that we don't know when we'll be together next, so if we were going to do something drastic . . ." It would have to be now. I absentmindedly picked at my fingernails as I thought. "If the Maldonados gave you twenty-one days, then you only have less than two weeks left until you're out of that. Then it's over, right? But I'll be gone."

He fell quiet as he stared at the night sky, but he didn't seem to be marveling over its wonders. He was working through something in his head, and the longer it took him to figure out his response, the more concerned I became. "What is it?" I asked.

"You know what this reminds me of?" he asked.

I studied his profile. "Catching insects in the rose garden?"

"I don't know why I'm still surprised when you read my mind," he said with a sad smile.

"Up here and out there were the two places you could sneak to for a little bit to keep me company."

"Your mom would always find us and send me immediately back to the ranch."

"She had to. My dad would've been upset. You were supposed to be working, and I wasn't supposed to be around you guys."

"I got to have a childhood through you, hearing about your adventures while I was off doing unimaginable shit to my own people. I never told you this because you were so young, but once, Cristiano used me as bait to kidnap a friend we grew up with."

"What?" I asked, lifting my head. "How come? What happened to him?"

"What do you think?" Diego asked. "He ended up at the bottom of a wash."

"But why?"

"Cristiano found out the kid was paying for his drugs by pimping out his underage sister. To Cristiano, that was enough reason to make our friend disappear."

*Good*, I thought, and immediately covered my mouth. Who was I to say who lived or died? Who was Cristiano to play God? But who was anyone to pimp out a young girl? Around here, justice wasn't always served through the channels it was supposed to be. Most of the police were corrupt, and the ones who weren't were overwhelmed by either trying to prevent or clean up near daily murders.

"I'm sorry," Diego said, removing his hand from under the blanket to take mine from my face. He intertwined our fingers. "That was too much."

"No," I said. "I just didn't realize . . . I didn't think the cartel would handle something like that. Did your friend work in the cartel?"

"No, just a customer. I mean, your dad would never stand for underage prostitution," Diego said. "He might've ordered it done or cut off his dick or something. But Cristiano didn't even go to him. He just popped the kid on his own time."

I rested my head back against the chair with a mental image I could've done without. Had Diego's friend automatically broken some imaginary law my dad held that Cristiano had enforced? Or had Cristiano done it out of compassion toward the girl? Considering the kind of cartel Cristiano ran now, I wondered if any of that benevolence remained. "Do you think the kid deserved it?" I asked.

Diego ran a hand over his stubble and scratched his chin. "Yeah, it had to be done. But I was a kid too, like thirteen or fourteen. I'd known him my whole life."

"That's messed up," I agreed, grateful my dad had moved on from that kind of business.

"You were my break from all of it." Diego kept my hand in his but put his other arm behind his head. "You'd tell me about your adventures of the day. Your mom would take you to the outdoor *mercado* and you'd sneak fruit right from the stands. You'd come home with an orange-stained tongue or dirty fingers from picking wildflowers on the way back. Bianca loved to be outdoors."

"My mom grew up helping my grandparents on their farm." It was strange to call two people I didn't know *grandparents*. They'd wanted no affiliation with anything illegal, and my mom had respected their decision in order to keep them out of danger.

Diego and I had nice memories, but the past couldn't distract me from the fact that he was clearly avoiding the subject of his very dangerous arrangement. "Is something wrong with the Maldonados?" I asked, taking my hand back. "Don't lie to me."

"I wouldn't lie. I just don't want to worry you." He removed his arm from behind his head and shifted to face me. "It's just that—I . . . it looks like someone's sabotaging the deal."

My heart dropped. After what Diego had told me about the Maldonados, even the *threat* of a problem would worry me. "Why didn't you tell me?" I asked. "And what does 'sabotaging' mean?"

"Just how it sounds. There's no reason we shouldn't have been able to deliver what I promised the Maldonados, but *a lot* of their product has been compromised. And it's no accident." He rubbed his eyebrow. "The majority hasn't even crossed the border yet, which is usually where it gets confiscated or stolen. Someone has to be messing with us, but not many would on our own turf."

"How exactly did they target you?" I asked, trying to ignore the sudden tightness in my chest.

"There were thefts at two secret locations and an explosion in one of our tunnels the *exact* time my men were passing through."

*Thefts*. The phone call Diego had gotten when I'd been at his house came rushing back to me. In this case, a theft wasn't better than the alternative. It could mean death.

"Your dad and I have a plan in place to make sure nothing else happens to the rest of it. That's why I was up all night. But until everything has crossed, I'm going to be on edge."

"How could you not be?" I asked. "What happens if anything else goes missing?"

"This is the most we've ever undertaken," he said. "Millions of dollars' worth of drugs. It's not like we can afford to cover it. So that means it's gone."

*Gone*.

I had the same shortness of breath I got whenever I thought too long about Cristiano forcing me to the brink of the tunnel. It had taken no effort on his part. Despite every ounce of fight I'd had, no matter what argument I'd put up, he'd still gotten me to the edge. And then down, down, down.

"What's the plan?" I asked. "Please tell me it involves taking out whoever's behind this."

"It would if we knew who it was. Costa and Cristiano think it's one of the Maldonados' rivals . . ."

I frowned. "But you don't agree."

He flicked his thumb and middle finger a few times, then flexed his hand. "There are pieces of the puzzle that don't make sense."

The only new variables in Papá's business were the Maldonados and Cristiano. But Cristiano was more than a puzzle piece. He *was* the puzzle. Nothing about him was clear—not his involvement in my mother's death, his unusual business practices, his patched together past, nor the men he surrounded himself with. "Cristiano is the wild card," I said.

"Exactly." Diego sat forward and looked back at me. "Jesus, Talia—I swear, you're the only person who gets it. You should be in charge around here."

I blushed. "It's not that big of a leap to make."

"You'd think."

Cristiano had once been the best man to protect us. He'd known our weaknesses. Then, possibly, he'd exploited them. Had he returned to right the wrongs he felt had been dealt him as Diego had suggested? Did Cristiano actually hope to reposition himself in our family?

A pit formed in my stomach at the thought that he had a greater plan. I didn't trust Cristiano, but I *did* trust he could accomplish anything he set his mind to. "So how does your Maldonado deal fit into his plan?"

"That's what I'm trying to figure out. My gut tells me it's some kind of power grab. Like we talked about the other day, an alliance between the Calaveras and the Cruzes would be formidable." Diego leaned his elbows on his knees and ran both hands over his hair. "My father plotted to steal your family's territory. He would've done it if Costa hadn't put a bullet in him." He glanced back at me. "History repeats itself."

"But your father's plan was to kill mine," I said. "Not unite."

Diego shrugged, but not casually. "What's to stop Cristiano from *anything* once he's gained your father's trust?" He gestured toward the darkness concealing the compound before us. "If they merge, Cristiano will replace me. And once I'm out of the picture, there's nobody in his path."

"His path to what?"

"It's a tale as old as time, Natalia. It's only a matter of time before a prince fantasizes about being king."

"He's king of his own cartel," I said.

"Cristiano's anger has been simmering for many years. Maybe he still feels like a prince who never got what he was owed. The taste of power lingers eternal on a man's tongue. Now that Cristiano has his own kingdom, I have no doubt he hungers for a second."

"Are you saying . . ." My throat went dry, and the first image that popped into my head was Cristiano and his bucket of sand. I grimaced. "Are you saying Cristiano wants to usurp my father?"

Diego balled his fists, still leaning forward in the chair. "He'd have to earn Costa's complete faith first. Then, Costa wouldn't worry about turning his back to him. And that's when Cristiano slips the knife in."

With a sharp pain in my jaw, I unclenched my teeth. Cristiano had already taken one parent from me. History would *not* repeat itself. I wouldn't let it. "We have to tell my dad," I said.

"Costa won't hear it. I've tried. Cristiano's reach is too far and too deep. He has to be cut off at the root."

"You have no time left." I knew how stubborn my dad could be, but if I caught him at the right time, maybe he'd listen. "I could talk to Papá."

"And say what? The minute you start asking questions, he'll assume I sent you, put you on a plane, and come looking for me."

I massaged my palm with my thumb as I thought. "What happens if I return to school and one day, I get a call that Cristiano succeeded in taking out everyone who means anything to me? And I'd done nothing?"

"What you did was keep yourself safe. That was the whole purpose of you going to school in the first place." Diego bit his bottom lip, looking over his shoulder at me. Anxious as I was about what he was telling me, his concern for me was kind of *sexy*. "You're out of this life, Natalia. Why dip a toe back in?"

"To help you," I said quietly.

Diego blinked at me, then reached over and tucked my hair behind my ear. "That's not your responsibility. I shouldn't even be worrying you over this—it's just that nobody else sees the truth."

"If I'd defy my own father to marry you, why wouldn't I do everything I could to save your life? Even if it meant going to Cristiano myself?"

"Going to *Cristiano*? No. I'll figure this out, Natalia," he said with conviction. "Believe me. Just the thought of building a life with you fuels me. I'd marry you tomorrow if only I could predict how this deal will end."

Cristiano had taken my fate into his hands once. He'd changed my life in moments. I wouldn't afford him that kind of power again. If he stood between Diego and me, if he deigned to think he could lay a hand on my father, then I had to do something.

I wouldn't lose anyone else I loved to him.

Ever since I'd fallen in a puddle of blood at his feet, our every interaction had been a mind game. Somehow, he'd known who I was at the costume ball and instead of keeping his distance, he'd danced with me. Toyed with me. Touched me. I couldn't deny the rush that had accompanied his hands on me. Maybe I could use that to my advantage.

He wanted to play. I could play too.

The deep distrust Diego had for his brother was most likely reciprocated. That day eleven years ago, Cristiano had denied any part in my mother's death, yet Diego had chosen truth and honor over his own blood. To many men in this world, that was an unforgiveable sin.

And if Cristiano had considered my parents family, then I'd committed the same offense against him with my own accusations that day. But could there be any trace left of the man my mother and father had trusted? Was there more to Cristiano than a ruthless killer?

If so, then there was a chance I could scratch his cold exterior and find the warmth beneath. "I'll talk to Cristiano."

"*Jamás*. Never." Diego frowned. "I couldn't ask you to do that."

"You didn't." I took a breath, hugging myself as the night began to cool. "I need to know for myself why he's here, and what he's planning."

"How? He's not easily cracked, Talia." Diego bit his thumbnail. "And yet . . . I sometimes wonder if he holds a soft spot where you're concerned. Like maybe he cares about you."

That was a stretch. If there was anything between Cristiano and me, it was more carnal. More savage. A thirst for power and a knowledge that the most effective way to hurt my father would be through me. I was a tool for him. After so many years, it likely ran deeper still—an obsession with my family, and maybe even my mother, that had been fostered and stoked to the point that not even an eye for an eye would be enough. Perhaps he longed to defile me while my father stood helpless. I didn't doubt Cristiano possessed a craving for me, even if it was just as simple as a man desiring a woman. But a fondness? No. The only soft spot between us was whichever part of my body he held in his grip. My girlish bicep years ago. My defiant gaze. My arched back as a woman, my hair tickling his forearm during our tango.

My breath sped thinking of the possibilities. Instinct alone had told me as a nine-year-old girl that being the subject of Cristiano's attention was as thrilling as it was dangerous.

I didn't know what exactly tied me to Cristiano, but I understood I could tighten the knot between us if I wanted. If I had the courage. "I think I can get in his head."

"You probably could, but I won't let you." Diego flipped the blanket off himself and stood to pace. "It's too risky."

"I *want* to," I said, following him with my eyes.

He glanced over at me. "But you've always feared him, and with good reason."

What I knew about Cristiano scared me as much as what I *didn't* know. Somehow, the more I learned, the more mysterious he grew. A perverse side of me wanted to test that fear to see if I could glimpse what he never seemed to show anyone.

Nobody ran toward a man like Cristiano de la Rosa. How would he react if I did?

"I have as much reason as anyone to want to bring him down," I said.

Diego raised his eyebrows at me. "I know, but—"

"What other choice do we have?" I asked. "You were right. My father wants my head in the sand. He won't respond well to me asking questions. And Cristiano doesn't trust you."

"You think he trusts you?"

He'd handled me like I was a child once but had spoken to me the opposite. He'd warned me of loyalty and justice and hadn't shielded me from the reality that he could kill me if I didn't help him. "He has no reason to trust me," I answered, "but I think he did once."

Diego ran his hands over his face and looked up at the sky. "I'm corrupting you."

I wrapped myself in the warmth of the wool and got up to stand in front of him. "It's a means to an end. Let me see if I can figure out why he's back, and what he knows about the Maldonados."

Diego rubbed my arms through the blanket as his eyes drifted over my face. Resignation crossed his features as he nodded. "Okay. But you couldn't just go to Cristiano or he'd suspect something. He has to come to you."

"How?"

He blew out a breath. "Well . . . since I've been looking into him, I've discovered that he goes to this nightclub a couple towns over on Thursday nights. If you show up, he'll want to know why you're there. Then, you get him talking."

My heart pounded at just the thought of being alone in the dark with Cristiano again.

"I'd be there of course," Diego said, lowering his voice as he put his forehead to mine. "Watching from afar. Keeping you safe. Believe me when I say—he doesn't lay a *finger* on you."

I nodded slowly. I was walking into the fire. Was it naïve to think I wouldn't get burned? That I could possibly use the unidentifiable, twisted bond that had solidified Cristiano and me years ago to control a conversation with him now?

"Won't he be suspicious if I show up at a place out of town?" I asked.

He twisted his lips. "No. Your father has a lot of eyeballs here who will report your whereabouts back to him, and Cristiano knows that. He'll think you snuck out, because that's what he *wants* to see."

"What does that mean?"

"My brother is a born hunter. He'll assume he caught you out in the wild. Let him hunt. Let him chase. If you make it easy, he'll see right through you." He squeezed my shoulders. "And be careful, Natalia. He's a master manipulator. He'll try to twist your memories or your perspective of him, but never forget what he's capable of or what he did."

*If he did it.* I pushed the unbidden thought from my head. How could I doubt what I'd seen with my own eyes? What I knew in my gut? Cristiano had spoken of justice all those years ago, but nobody had ever imposed it on him.

"I won't forget," I said.

"He's hurt too many people, and he will continue if we don't stop him. Let your fury burn." Diego clasped my hands and brought them to his mouth. Pressing a kiss to my knuckles, and with fervor in his words, he added, "Let it drive you toward the answers we need to stop him."

"I will," I said.

It was a promise. It had to be. Because even if I harbored the slightest doubt about what Cristiano had done, there was no question of what he *could* do.

I feared I hadn't even begun to imagine what he was capable of.

And that if he caught me trying to cross him, I would learn.

# CHAPTER 11

# NATALIA

In the States, there wasn't much of a rush in trying to get past a bouncer who studied my tits harder than my fake ID. But here, at *La Madrina,* while the doorman inspected my license, I could only think about how I was putting my life on the line to get information from one kingpin to save another. And I hated that each time my heart palpitated with trepidation, a tremor of excitement followed.

The bouncer gave Pilar and me a once-over before he unhooked the velvet rope to let us pass. I entered the nightclub with nothing on me but a credit card stuck into the neckline of my black, strapless mini dress and oversized gold hoops that swung each time my platforms hit the ground.

The windowless club had three levels with VIP railed off and overlooking the dancefloor from three sides. A large, rotating disco ball had been hung for the 70s theme, and it reflected white light from a DJ booth against the wall opposite the entrance. The club was dark enough to hide in corners, but a girl could still be seen if she wanted. Somewhere up there, Diego waited in the wings, hidden from everyone, including me—watching, anticipating, guarding.

Pilar and I hit the bar first and the dancefloor next. Diego was convinced I didn't need to do anything to capture Cristiano's attention except show up and dance, so that's what I did, dangling myself out in the open like a fresh piece of meat.

When a gut feeling spurred me to look up, I met a dark and burning gaze from the floor above. In a white dress shirt with rolled sleeves and an open collar, Cristiano leaned his elbows on the rail with a drink in hand. A cigarette dangled from his lips. He'd clearly been staring but didn't flinch or pull away.

I sipped from my straw. *Will you come?*

He shifted against the rail, narrowing his eyes on me.

I turned slightly, holding his gaze as I moved my hair off my neck.

*Oh, yes.* He stubbed out his cigarette and turned away.

He didn't come at first, but I felt eyes on my every move. Was it only Diego? Or both men? To have Cristiano's interest was to put myself in the line of fire, and I was in his crosshairs now, wearing nothing more than a bandage for a dress.

Pilar had picked up a dance partner, and the man's friend slid up behind me.

Before I could react, Pilar grabbed my arm and yanked me to her. "I-I think Cristiano de la Rosa is here."

"He is," I said. "I saw him."

"Then that's him coming over here? Why?" The cubes in her Long Island Iced Tea rattled against the glass. "What does he want?"

"Nothing with you," I assured her.

"This is *Cristiano* we're talking about, he—" She jumped when her dance partner touched her waist. Her drink fell and shattered at our feet. "*Perdón,*" she said, bending to pick up the glass. "I'm sorry. It slipped."

"Don't touch that." I stopped her, urging her back up. "What's wrong?"

"He's a bastard, Talia." Her eyes widened into saucers. "He nearly beat *mi primo* to death, remember? In my mom's shop."

"Your cousin was skimming off the top," I told her. "*And* bragging about it."

"I was there," she whispered. "I ran into the stockroom to hide, but that was where Cristiano took him to do it. I saw the whole thing from behind some pineapple crates."

"I know." I rubbed my eyebrow. "But that was years ago—"

"And your mother?" she asked, raising her voice over the music. "Do you tell yourself it doesn't matter because it was so long ago?"

The man Pilar had been dancing with closed in again as his friend slipped an arm around my waist. I swatted at him, and he backed off. "I didn't mean it like that," I said to Pilar.

"That *monster* is ten times worse now—*why* did your father bring him here?" She took my arm, trying in vain to pull me away. "Please, we have to leave."

"He won't do anything, Pila. We're in public."

"Do you think that matters?"

I didn't have to answer. Cristiano probably got off on taking a life in front of an audience. "Go get someone to clean this mess. I can handle Cristiano," I said, even as a wave of doubt coursed through me.

"He has to be two meters tall. He could pick you up with one hand, Tali." She shook her head. "You can't be alone with him."

"I'm not alone. Look at all these people." My dance partner tried to slip between Pilar and me. "*Déjame en paz,*" I said, pushing him off, hoping Diego wouldn't get jealous and blow his cover. "Go away."

The man showed me his palms but continued dancing near us.

"But—" Pilar began.

I pulled her to me and whispered, "I'm *fine*. Diego's here—no, don't look for him. Is Cristiano still coming?"

"He's walking onto the dancefloor—"

"Go to the bar," I pleaded. "Now."

She was trembling. "I shouldn't leave you."

Within moments, Cristiano's unmistakable presence warmed my back. I inhaled slowly to calm myself, even as my palms sweat. I hadn't knowingly been alone with him since the tunnel.

I wasn't alone, though. Diego was here.

"*Vete,*" Cristiano ordered from behind me.

With the command to leave, the man circling me looked over my head and left the dancefloor.

"Go," Cristiano said to Pilar next.

She nearly tripped over herself as she scurried to the bar.

After a moment, he spoke near my ear. "You're more courageous than your friend."

It went against my every instinct to keep my back to him. The hairs on my nape rose. The mix of my pounding heart and the drink I'd had formed little stars in my vision. I tried to pass off my swaying as dancing rather than nerves. It would serve me right to fall on my face for toying with the devil. Could Diego even stop Cristiano from doing what he wanted? I'd never been scared of the dark while surrounded by this many people.

"More courageous?" I asked. "Or more foolish?"

He grunted. "Where are your guards?" When I didn't answer, he added, "Can you turn around and look at me, Natalia?"

A wild animal like him would sense my fear. I wasn't sure if vulnerability would help or hurt me. I turned just my head over my shoulder but didn't look at him. "*Por favor*. Go. I'm just here to have a girls' night."

"You're a little far from home."

"We didn't want to run into anyone we might know. We're not supposed to be out."

"Ah. You're unsupervised then." He lowered his mouth to my ear. "I won't ask twice. Turn . . . around. Look—at—me."

It was no longer a request. I obeyed, facing broad, pulled back shoulders, somehow both severe and elegant. They squared off to the lean, muscular arms that had pinned me to his body as a girl, that had held me tight as we'd danced a week ago. His skull face paint had enhanced his bone structure then—or so I'd thought. Even without the mask, his angular jaw sharpened with high cheekbones and caved cheeks. A darker, more demanding beauty than his brother's left me breathless. They had similar faces arranged like Greek gods, but where Diego's features yielded to sun-kissed, smooth skin, Cristiano was harsher, weather-beaten with crow's feet around his eyes. His neatly parted hair and clean-shaven face contrasted his stern expression.

I sipped my drink, hoping to calm my nerves. "Why bother asking for anything if you're just going to demand it?"

He licked his lips as his eyes drifted over the short, tight dress Diego had picked out for me. Though Cristiano's eyes were as black as a starless sky, they still glimmered behind his hooded gaze. "It's the polite thing to do."

Had I been brave enough, I would've snorted in his face. He'd just shooed off Pilar with no regard for her obvious anxiety. "Is it *polite* to make a woman tremble with just a word?"

"Very." One hollowed dimple appeared as the corner of his mouth rose. "Sometime I'll demonstrate on you."

My face flushed. He wanted to make me scream and tremble. Despite what I'd heard about his brutality, my mind descended into a shameful vision of being trapped underneath his wide shoulders, begging for a different kind of mercy.

He took my Long Island Iced Tea from me and handed it to a random woman. She started to protest but then looked up and disappeared like the others. "Let me get you a real drink," he said to me.

Diego was right about playing hard to get. It was working. "I have to check on my friend," I said. I took a step, but he wrapped his hand all the way around my upper arm and pulled me back against his wall of a body. "Watch your step, *mamacita,*" he rumbled before he picked me up by my waist, turned, and set me down.

I lost my breath, disoriented by being repositioned like a doll. "What are you doing?"

"There's glass all over." Cristiano signaled across the bar, alerting them to the mess.

He kept one hand lightly at my hip. I shifted to see if he'd let me go. He flexed his long fingers against me, pressing the pad of his thumb into my hipbone. A few degrees south, and he would've found a pistol strapped to my upper thigh—if only Diego hadn't made me leave it behind, rendering me defenseless.

Cristiano started to pull me closer, but I moved away. He dropped just his eyes to mine. If he wasn't six-foot-five as Pilar had guessed, he was within centimeters of it. "What's the matter?" he asked. "You only dance with men in costume?"

"You looked friendlier then."

He pursed his lips as if suppressing a smile. "I wasn't."

"Did you know it was me at the party?" I asked, even though I could guess his answer.

"It's too loud down here. Come with me." He nodded behind him. "Arms up."

Reflexively, I raised them when he cupped the sides of my breasts and slid the deadly weapons he called hands down my waist and hips. "What? Where?"

"Upstairs." He squatted to clasp one of my ankles.

"What are you doing?" I asked, trying to free my leg.

"Security check."

"My legs are bare."

"Nevertheless." One dark eyebrow quirked. "People are creative about where they hide their weapons." He grazed both palms along my outer and inner calf, higher and higher, until his hands were under my skirt. Finally, something else overtook my nervousness—a pulse of heat between my legs as his fingers lingered there.

"Hold onto me if you feel weak," he said, a hint of teasing in his voice.

Nobody around us even flinched, either unsurprised or keeping their heads down. I tried to push his hands out from under my skirt. "I don't have anything on me, not even my phone."

"Is that wise?" he asked.

"I had nowhere to put it."

He paused but didn't remove his hands.

"And I'm not going anywhere alone with you," I added.

"We won't be alone." His lifted his eyes to look directly into mine. "My men are everywhere."

A threat. Perhaps Diego had my back, but he was one man against who knew how many savages. I couldn't go anywhere with Cristiano. Either I'd be leaving myself vulnerable or Diego would try to stop it and put himself in Calavera crosshairs.

Cristiano's gentle touch didn't distract me from the fact that it was still callused, or that his hands, as they moved to my other thigh, had taken many lives. His fingertips started high and then slid down to my ankle, which he squeezed almost tenderly before standing again.

Kicking some glass aside, he gestured toward an elevator I hadn't noticed before. "After you."

"I'm expected to trust that *you* aren't armed?"

He opened his arms. "Frisk me."

My heart skipped at the thought of touching him. The sprawling shoulders and flat pecs under a crisp white shirt. His wide, powerful torso. *He* was the weapon, big everywhere that I could see. What about where I couldn't? My gaze started to drift down, but I stopped it and turned my reddening cheek to him.

"I'll save you the trouble," he said, lowering his arms back to his sides. "Not only am I armed, but one signal from me could light this place up with fireworks."

I flashed back to the barrel of his gun under my chin. Diego couldn't stop his brother then—how could he take on the devil now? I crossed my arms. "I'm not leaving the dancefloor."

White light reflected off the disco ball and flashed over the hard angles of his face. "Then you'll have to come closer so I don't miss a word you say."

That was better than the alternative, so I closed the gap between us with a step. We were nearly toe to toe, but he still had to lean down to speak in a normal tone. "Of course I knew who you were at the party. I wouldn't whisper my wishes to just any butterfly."

I tried to force my muscles to relax. We were out in the open, and he was willing to talk. "Why me?" I asked.

"Perhaps to see if you'd cower. To test whether I'd scared that little girl well enough. The fact that you're standing here tells me I didn't."

"I do cower. You can't expect me not to in front of my mother's murderer."

He started to jut his chin but stopped. "I'm only dangerous to those who cross me or have a right to be afraid," he said. "Do you?"

My instinct was to look up for Diego, but I schooled it. "Did my mother?"

His jaw ticked. "No."

I dropped my eyes. I couldn't think of her now. Even as I questioned what I knew, it felt like a betrayal to even be in the same room as Cristiano without attempting to burn it down. This was for a greater cause, though. The sooner I had what I needed, the sooner I could be free of this place and of him.

I looked up again. "Why are you here?" I asked.

"It's my nightclub."

Words escaped me. If Diego had known that, he'd neglected to clue me in. "That's not what I meant. Why are you *back*?"

"To dance." Cristiano took my hips and pulled me flush against him. With a slow roll of his body, I felt every bump and ridge of what *had* to be a gun. If it wasn't . . .

"I warned you I was armed," he said.

A flush crept its way up my neck. He held me still and moved his hips to the smooth, sultry beat of Donna Summer's "Love to Love You Baby." My body undulated on its own as my hands slid up his chest. He squeezed my backside, moving me against him faster, harder, until we were so synced, he could've picked up my leg and slipped right inside me.

I gasped at the thought and shoved his chest. "Stop."

He didn't budge, but loosened his grip on me, giving me space. "No need for violence, Lourdes. All you had to do was ask."

I inhaled a sharp breath. My second name had been my mother's first choice, but she'd deferred to Papá's love of *Natalia*. "Nobody calls me that."

"I call you what I want—Lourdes. Or maybe Natasha. How do you like that?"

"Years away, and you've forgotten me completely. It's Nat*alia*."

"Forgotten you? No. Not after the way you helped me escape." His eyes drifted to my mouth, then along my neck and chest. "Natasha is what you'd be called in Russia." He moved his hand to my upper back and pushed gently. "Let's go. Our drinks are ready."

"What? Where?"

"Come with me." He guided me through the dancefloor, which was emptier than it'd been before his arrival.

It was slightly quieter at the bar, where he handed me a tall, chilled shot glass of clear liquid. I put my nose to the rim, but it was odorless. "Vodka?"

"Straight from the heart of Siberia. I brought it myself. Have you eaten?"

"I had dinner. Why?"

"Good." He took a second shot from the bar, raised it, and said something in what sounded like Russian, followed by, "*Salud*."

I followed his lead and tasted the cool liquid, holding it on my tongue a moment before swallowing. It was definitely smoother than the drugstore vodka my friends and I drank at school. "You've been to Russia?" I asked, hoping for a clue as to what he'd been doing during the years he'd disappeared.

"*Da*. That means *yes*. I've been many places, but like you, I've returned where I belong. I've come home."

I tucked the information away for later. "This isn't my home."

"Why not?"

"I don't want this life."

"Ah." He clicked his tongue like a wink. "But it lives in you, Natalia, and its roots never stop growing."

It was one of my greatest fears—that I'd seen and learned too much to ever lead a normal life. That no matter what, I'd always be the nine-year-old girl who could trip over the dead body of a loved one at any moment—and then be forced to get right back up and defend my life. "Like a cancer," I said into my shot glass.

"No." He tilted up my chin with his knuckle. "Like a heart. Like blood in your veins. Like bones."

"You're wrong." I tried to focus on anything but his skin on mine, but it only made me more aware of his touch. "Every day I cut more and more of this cancer from my body, and I'm still standing."

"You can't remove it completely. Pretend it's gone if it helps you sleep, but the poison's already in you. You grew up feeding on it, and any predator who comes after you will get a bitter taste. Because you're a survivor. Like the monarch. Like me."

Taken aback, I blurted, "I'm not like you."

He finished his shot and signaled for another. "Let's hope you're never forced to find out."

"With a bounty on your head, you strolled back into our lives. That sounds more like a death wish than a will to survive."

"I'm here, aren't I?" he asked. "I was driven from the only life I knew with nothing but what was on my body. Now, I'm back with the world at my fingertips."

"But it's not enough."

He tilted his head at me almost imperceptibly. "Meaning?"

"You want more than you have. I know that's why you're here." I rested my elbow on the bar. "Give me another reason that makes sense. There is none."

"What about history? A sense of home?" He raised his glass to someone across the room and drank. "I've found myself a family who'd die for me and I for them, but I've discovered a man can travel the world and never find home, Natalia. And *you* will never escape it."

Cristiano was more machine than man, always calculating, always locked and loaded to kill. Perhaps he couldn't help what he'd been taught, but it didn't make it any less true. "Maybe my father trusts you," I said, "but I don't. I know what I saw that day. I believe what I've heard, both when you worked for us and after. You're not here out of nostalgia."

"Why am I here then?" he asked. "Tell me, Lourdes."

"Power. Revenge. If you take out my father and steal his business, you get both." I hadn't meant to say so much, but with Cristiano, candor was best. It was becoming clear he and I could talk each other in circles—I needed answers, though. "And don't call me Lourdes."

"Why not? Because your mother did?"

My heart palpitated once. That was exactly why. It surprised me he remembered. "Yes," I said. "It reminds me of her, and for you to use it is a slap in the face."

"It suits you, though," he mused after another sip. "Natalia is a girl's name."

He thought he had me pegged, but he'd been gone a long time. I wouldn't try to change his perception of me. Any misconceptions could only hurt him—and help me.

"What if you're right about my plans?" he asked, setting his glass on the bar. "Will you stop me?"

I couldn't. He had an army and the means to fund it. All *I* had was a sliver of hope that somewhere in his body, a heart still beat. That maybe he'd cared for my parents and me once. "Don't hurt my family any more than you already have," I said. "That includes Diego."

A smirk ghosted over his hard, chiseled features. "No, I never forgot little Talia, fiercely loyal to someone who doesn't deserve it. Where is my snake of a brother anyway?"

Cristiano calling Diego a snake was like my nine-year-old self stumbling across my mother's body and taunting her murderer for being scared. "You have that one backward."

"Do you still believe after all this time that Diego would stick out his own neck to save yours?" Cristiano asked.

"He already did," I said. "He took a bullet for me. You'll remember —you were the one who shot him."

Cristiano scanned my face a moment, then laughed. It was a foreign sound that caught me off guard, a rumble both dark and delighted. As he reached up, I flinched, but it didn't deter him from pinching my chin between his thumb and forefinger. "You have no idea what it means to be willing to die for someone. Diego took a bullet, I'll give you that. But *for you*? No, *mamacita*. When someone does that, you'll know."

That was bullshit. Diego had been brave. There was nothing else he could've done. And if there was, I didn't blame him. We'd both been in shock—scared and worried for each other. Once he'd been shot, he'd passed out. What did Cristiano expect, that Diego would magically heal his leg, regain consciousness, and throw himself down the tunnel after us?

Why was I even questioning it? Diego had warned me Cristiano would try to manipulate the truth. "You're wrong," I said. "He'll always have my back."

"And yet, the evidence of his cowardice stands in front of me. Diego has sent a woman to do a man's job." He swept his thumb over my bottom lip and released my face. "Where is he?"

I refrained from touching my tingling mouth to erase his uninvited, overly intimate caress. "I don't know," I answered.

"I believe you don't know his exact location, but he sent you."

My heart began to hammer against my breastbone. Cristiano didn't believe I was alone, and I suspected he never had. "You're the one who came to me," I pointed out.

"Diego knew I would." Cristiano turned his head slightly over one shoulder. "Perhaps he's right at my back. Or above us. Or in the shadows of the dancefloor. He's not far, is he?"

If I thought I could fool Cristiano one moment longer, I might've tried, but he was too shrewd for that. I couldn't risk him catching me in a lie and walking away before I got any information. Honesty was likely the best way to get the same in return. "He's here."

Cristiano drew back a little, his eyebrows rising. "Maybe your loyalty isn't as strong as I thought."

"I'm loyal to Diego, but I'm not stupid. Neither are you."

"You may be if you thought you could deceive me." He cocked his head. "I should be mad, shouldn't I?" He cleared some of my hair away, lighting goose bumps over my neck and shoulders. "But I'm more intrigued to know that my brother is watching us now."

I stilled so I wouldn't betray how he was affecting me. "If you touch me, you'll be dead," I warned him.

"Ah, but I already have. Not once, not twice, not even three times," he said, grazing my hip with one hand as he brushed his knuckle under my chin once more. "And now, I'm touching you again." He placed his hands on my jaw, cupping my face as carefully as he might cradle a baby bird. He tilted my head up until I could look nowhere but into his eyes. "I put my hands up your skirt earlier. And where was your Diego?"

Chills made an icy trail down my spine as I tensed, waiting for some kind of consequence to befall Cristiano. And yet, he didn't even look back. His eyes remained unwary.

He turned my head to one side and whispered in my ear, "Understand me. The next time my hands are that close to heaven, they will enter whether Diego is watching or not."

Blood rushed to my head as the tender warmth of his breath warred with such an offensive suggestion. I couldn't respond, my throat suddenly dry, my tongue numb. *Gracias a Dios* I hadn't gone anywhere alone with him—I didn't question his hands would do as they pleased. And to make Diego *watch*? I shivered. How indecent. How obscene and filthy.

And yet, heaven throbbed between my legs. That was the devil's manipulation, making me think I *liked* the idea.

"You're here to do Diego's bidding," Cristiano said. "To get answers for questions you don't even know to ask. But how far would you go to get them?"

He let me jerk my head away. "I have morals."

"You don't even know the game he plays with you—you never did."

"For some of us," I said, "life is more than a game to play, a prize to hold tight, a lesson to be taught. There's more to it than money and power."

"Such as?"

"Love. Ethics." I raised my chin. "*Justice*. You understood that once."

He narrowed his eyes. "You remember that?"

"What you said to me about justice? *Sí*. That there is none."

"There is in my world. I live by my own code, and you may not see it, but it's both fair and ethical." He inclined his head. "For those who are deserving, I ask before I take. I feed those who feed me. I can't control how others interpret things, but I give honesty where I get it. You'll find me dead before you find me a liar."

My chest rose and fell faster as I held his gaze despite the fact that I was stupidly pushing his buttons. "A liar would be an improvement for a murderer like you."

One corner of his mouth twitched. "I'm only deadly to those who've taken risks knowing the consequences. They traded a life of safety for money and power. They deserved it, as do I." He crossed himself in a gross display of blasphemy. What right did a depraved criminal like him have to ask anything of the Holy Trinity? A hint of a smile touched his lips. "If I died tomorrow, I would not say the assassin had no right to do it. Though I'd commend him for accomplishing a nearly impossible task."

"You say you're honest as you lie. You're not fair or ethical; you've executed people who didn't deserve it."

"Deep down, you know I didn't kill your mother, Natalia." Any suggestion of humor left his tone, replaced by graveness. "And that there's more to her death than you're willing to admit."

His acknowledgement of her murder made me step back. I'd heard the denial from my father, but not yet directly from Cristiano since his return. The conviction in his voice angered me. He had no right to dismiss her death. To question what I knew in the depths of my soul. "I saw you," I said. "The gun, the blood, the duffel bag—I . . ." I didn't want to believe there could be anything else to it. A hired hitman made her death even more confusing. More senseless. "You were a *sicario for a living*," I said. I slammed the rest of my shot, and my throat burned with its spicy aftertaste. "You took as many lives as my father and grandfather commanded you to. Maybe one of their rivals paid you handsomely for this order, or maybe it was retribution for what my dad did to yours, but either way, I caught you red-handed."

"You were naïve back then, but you're old enough to know better now. Nothing is black and white." He slid my glass toward a bartender, who refilled the vodka and replaced it in front of me.

I resisted my temptation to drink more. The liquor was dangerously good, and I needed my wits about me. "No, thank you," I said.

Cristiano leaned in. "This *is* a game, Natalia, and you *have* to play—or you'll lose. Learn your lesson should someone care enough to teach you. And never doubt that you *are* a prize to hold tight." He slipped an arm around my waist like we were going to tango again, and advanced until I was backed up against the lip of the bar. When our bodies were flush, he spoke firmly. "Believe me when I say, if Diego's and my roles were reversed, I would hold you so tight, you would forget what it was to breathe. And I would not, for neither money nor power, ever send you into the fire just to see my enemy burn as he has done."

My breathing sped. He was close, his spicy scent as smooth and dangerous as Russian vodka. And he was talking shit about the man I loved. Diego would never put me at risk. He'd fought me on coming here in the first place. There was no way Cristiano could know I'd walked into the blaze on my own, but let him distract himself into thinking Diego had orchestrated this. "Why do you care *how* Diego holds me?" I asked.

"Because *I* held you as a baby," he said intently. "I was responsible for your *life* once." Cristiano's hand tensed over my lower back. "My brother's using you to light the fire, but don't forget—a match also burns."

I resisted the mental image of Cristiano cradling me as an infant. That was what I'd hoped to tap into, but he also knew exactly how to soften me. I wanted to believe he'd cared for my family at some point during the eight years he'd been with us.

"Now, it's *my* turn for questions," he said, easing back. He fixed the roll of one shirtsleeve so it exposed a little more of his dark, brawny forearm. "That night at the costume party when I found you with my brother in the garden—was he forceful with you?"

Unprepared for the topic change, I didn't answer right away. What did Cristiano think he'd seen that night by the fountain? Diego'd had one hand nearly between my legs with his other holding my jaw. From behind, it could've looked as if he'd been covering my mouth as he'd made demands.

*"Tell me how much you love me. I won't ask again."*

"No," I said. "Diego's not like you."

"And how am I?"

"I've heard things. I've seen things. I know what you do to women."

He pressed his lips together, assessing me coolly. "And yet you still tested me by coming here. Some part of you must not believe the rumors."

"I believe them," I said without hesitation so he wouldn't guess the truth—where Cristiano was concerned, I was beginning to question anything I knew.

"You didn't answer my question." He took his cell from his shirt pocket as it vibrated but kept his eyes on me. "Has he ever so much as laid a finger on you without your permission?"

"*No*," I said. "We were playing a game." It was the most plausible excuse—and yet it also held truth.

One of Cristiano's dark, thick brows lifted. Without removing his eyes from me, he answered his phone. "*Sí*." His eyes roamed over the alcohol bottles lining the back wall of the bar. After a pause, he said, "*Adelante*" and ended the call. While typing out a message, he said to me, "Tell Diego to take you straight home. It's not safe after dark right now."

After dark, when the creatures of the night played. "I suppose you would know."

"You're looking for a monster, and you found one in me." He tucked his phone back in his pocket. "But I'm not the one you should fear. Just remember—no monster thinks of himself that way. He's just living by a different code than yours." He nodded once at me and turned to leave. "Goodnight, Natalia."

*Goodnight*? I hadn't gotten nearly what I'd wanted from him. If anything, I only had more questions. This was my last shot. I had to demand his attention. "What's your involvement with the Maldonados?"

He froze. His large frame expanded with a breath, his muscles pulling gracefully under his white dress shirt. Even from behind, he was beautiful—and menacing.

Had I gone too far? I slid a couple steps back along the edge of the bar.

Getting him to talk in hopes that something useful might slip was one thing. But legitimate information was dangerous. If he thought I actually knew anything, that could make me a liability. Or worse—a threat.

After a moment, he turned back. "I have no deal with them. You should be asking Diego this."

"I have, and I know everything he does." I was in too deep to turn back, and I realized I didn't want to, even if I was scared. Finally, I was getting what I came for. "Now I want to know what *you* know."

He returned to standing in front of me. "What I know? My brother's in serious trouble, and if he minimized the danger he's in at all, then he lied to you. He's putting everyone at risk, including you."

"*He* isn't, but someone is. *Someone* doesn't want this deal to happen. Is it you? Are you the one stealing from him?"

His jaw sharpened as it ticked. "Be careful, Natalia. You're out of your depth."

It was the first crack in his composure I'd gotten tonight, and it sent a thrill through me. I wanted more. "I'll come upstairs with you," I said.

He glanced at the glass wall behind the DJ booth. It wasn't a wall at all, I realized, but a one-way window that most likely looked from his office onto the dancefloor. I wondered if he'd been watching me before I'd even noticed him.

"*Nyet,* Natasha."

I turned back to him. "*No,* in Russian," I guessed.

"Correct. I have business now. Maybe another time."

I tilted my head. "Is it easier to think of me differently as a Natasha?"

"Why would I want to think of you differently?"

"So you don't have to see me as the little girl you once promised to protect."

He tilted his head. The pulse at the base of his neck jumped as he let his eyes wander down my dress. "Believe me, I see you just fine as you are. I happen to like the name. I knew a Natasha once." His eyes leapt back to mine. "She sucked my dick like it would end with a mouthful of gold."

My throat constricted. Nobody had ever said anything like that to me. "That's not why I wanted to come up. I won't do that willingly. Not ever. But maybe Natasha said the same thing."

He stilled completely. The lights and music seemed to dim along with his demeanor. "You're accusing me of rape?"

*My mom's dress was ripped*. It was perhaps the one thing I couldn't bring myself to ask about. The answer might be too painful. "You expect me to believe your men do it, but you don't?"

"You insult me. If I want a woman, I can get her without force," he said sharply. "That includes *you*."

I drew back with an audible swallow. He didn't treat me the way others did, yet despite his steely expression and cool gaze, my gut told me he didn't mean it. He only wanted a reaction. Could I trust that instinct, though? In my experience, cartel bosses didn't tease.

And they didn't invite women in skimpy dresses anywhere private to talk.

The dark cloud that'd just fallen over him seemed to lift. "With me, you always have a choice. You're not beholden to my wishes, but I hope you'll still carry them on your wings and deliver them for me." He brushed hair from my cheek, trailing a fingertip over my skin in a way that I had to fight to keep my eyes from falling shut. "Just know that I don't rely on anyone, not even the heavens, to grant my wishes. I make them come true on my own."

He retreated a few steps, holding my gaze, before he turned and walked away.

I hung on his words. What *were* his wishes? What did they have to do with me? I stayed where I was despite my urge to call him back and ask the questions forming in my head.

Because nothing good could come from chasing after *el anticristo*.

Especially if he was saying what I thought he was.

*If you're what I want, then I'll find a way to have you.*

# CHAPTER 12

# NATALIA

Diego's hand slipped higher up my dress as the glowing red hand of his speedometer rose. He sped away from the club through deserted roads as if he also knew of the after-dark danger Cristiano had warned me of.

Only the warm lights of the dashboard glowed against its all-black interior. Silence stretched over the smooth hum of his Mercedes once I'd finished relaying most of my conversation with Cristiano. All in all, there wasn't much to tell.

"Are you okay?" Diego asked for the second time.

"I'm fine." *Because you're a survivor. Like the monarch. Like me.* Cristiano's words echoed in my mind.

"He kept touching you because he knew I was there." He released my leg to grip the steering wheel. "I assumed he'd frisk you, but that's all."

I wouldn't even call what he'd done *frisking*. Cristiano had tested my boundaries as he'd taunted Diego. He'd had his hands everywhere from my ankles to my thighs, my neck and face. He'd touched me in ways only Diego should.

And Diego had let him—or had he not seen well enough the liberties Cristiano had taken with my body? "Cristiano said next time he frisks me, he won't stop his hands at the gates of heaven, even if you're watching."

"Heaven?" Diego's nostrils flared as he hit the steering wheel. "Let him try. I'll cut off his devil hands." He snorted not unlike a Pamplona bull. "Not that you'll ever be in that position again."

I wasn't sure what aroused me more—Diego's possessiveness or the idea of Cristiano boldly taking what didn't belong to him. I only knew that what aroused me, also horrified me. What was wrong with me for getting excited Cristiano might want me when his brother already had me? The same Cristiano who, the last decade, I'd vehemently hated? I shifted in the leather seat. "He only said it to scare me," I said. "It didn't mean anything."

"I know. Still . . . I should knock his teeth out." Diego massaged around his nose. "It wasn't easy to watch. He knows you're mine and that you're the quickest way to get under my skin."

"He only thinks of me as a weapon against you." And if anyone knew how to wield a weapon, it was Cristiano. "I'm sorry I didn't get more information."

"You were perfect." He glanced over at me, running a hand through his hair to get it out of his eyes. "Cristiano *didn't* scare you, did he?"

He'd tried. But had he succeeded? With his comments about Natasha and about how he could have me if he wanted, what unnerved me most was that I *wasn't* scared. "No."

A dog darted into the street. Diego hit the brakes, and I outstretched my arms to catch myself against the glove compartment.

"Shit. Sorry," he said as he decelerated for a yellow light. "You all right?"

I glanced behind us for the dog, but it was gone. "Yes."

Diego stopped the car at an intersection and slid his hand in mine. "You look so beautiful tonight. I can't say I blame him for being so forward. As angry as it makes me, I feel lucky to be the one who gets to take you home."

"Always," I said.

"It's good you didn't go anywhere with him." Diego's phone rang. He released my hand to get it from his pocket as he reiterated, "I would've beaten him half to death if he'd tried to get you alone." He swiped his thumb across the screen and held it to his ear. "*Bueno.*"

As Diego listened to the line, I turned my head toward the faint strains of buoyant violin and guitarrón coming from a corner market. Mariachi music didn't always remind me of the moments before I'd skipped down the hall to hurry my mother for the parade, but in that moment, I saw Cristiano standing in the bedroom, dressed in all black, rising from the ashes. Out front of the *mercado*, a few men smoked, drank, and blared a boombox. Despite opaque, bulletproof windows, I got a chill when one of the men opened his jacket and flashed a gun in our direction. I'd never liked riding around in showy cars when poverty permeated our state.

"I'm not far, but I have Natalia," Diego said into the phone. "I'll drop her off and come." The stoplight changed to green, but he didn't move. "No. I want everyone on site."

"What's wrong?" I asked.

"Some issue at the *fucking* warehouse," he whispered to me. He paused, listening. "No, don't send one of them. I don't trust them around Natalia. Can you break into it?" He snorted. "*Claro que no*. I'll be there in an hour. Just move on to something else until I'm back." He hung up, dropped the phone into a cup holder, and stepped on the gas.

"Is that the warehouse with all the Maldonados' stock?" I asked.

"*Sí*. We moved it all to one spot since none of our regular houses are safe right now. Then it's all going *al otro lado*—into the U.S.—at once." He rested an elbow on the door panel and bit his thumbnail, steering with one hand. "Every call I get, I worry something else has gone wrong."

"Who was on the phone?"

"Jojo. We transported everything to the new location in armored vehicles," he said. "I have the only set of keys to the truck they need to get into right now—and of course, it's impenetrable, so they can't break in, *puta madre*."

I glanced through the windshield. "You said we're close?"

"We just passed the turnoff."

"When does everything need to go?"

"Tomorrow afternoon." He shook his head out the window. "They're loading everything tonight."

I reached over to knead the back of his neck with one hand. "Go to the warehouse. Drop off the keys."

He shook his head. "It's too dangerous."

"Isn't *everyone* in the cartel there guarding it?" I argued.

"Not everyone. In case the hits were due to a leak—which I don't believe—I only have my most trustworthy men there."

"Then what's the danger?"

"No matter how many precautions we have in place," he said, slowing for another red light, "with all the product consolidated in one location, all the risk is there too."

"We're still twenty minutes from the house, which means it would take you forty round trip to get back. This is a priority."

The stoplight changed to green, but he just scratched his chin. "Which won't matter if Costa kills me for taking you to the warehouse."

"He thinks I'm still at the movie theater for a *Star Wars* triple-feature." I checked the clock on the dash—half past nine. "Right about now, Pilar and I are finishing *Attack of the Clones*. The next episode is almost two-and-a-half hours."

"*Dios mío*. You know the runtime and everything?" He reached over to squeeze my knee in the exact spot I was ticklish. I laughed as I squirmed. "Are you this devious in the States?" he asked.

I leaned over the console, batting my lashes up at him. "You'll soon find out."

Someone honked behind us for sitting at a green light before swerving past. Diego barely noticed.

"Mmm." He nuzzled my nose with his, then kissed me softly, sweetly. "You make a good argument, my little C-3PO, but I don't want to risk it." He brushed my hair from my face and tucked it behind my ear. "Even if nothing happens, I don't want anyone to see you there. If it gets back to Costa, or if the wrong person sees you unguarded—"

"I just faced off with Cristiano by myself," I pointed out. "I'll be *fine*. I'll wait in the car. Just go. It'll take five minutes."

"Not even. I'll have Jojo come out and get the keys." Diego sighed, resigned. "You're tough."

"This is good practice for when we're married and I win all our arguments."

He scoffed, seizing my leg again. I squealed, grabbing his wrist as I backed against the door. "Tickling is off-limits."

"I don't think so, *princesa*," he said but smiled and released me. He checked his rearview mirror and swerved into the next lane. Ignoring the red arrow, he flipped the car around to zoom back the way we'd come. The men loitering outside the *tienda* were gone, but as we whizzed by, I could've sworn I heard the echo of mariachi music.

In under ten minutes, we were at the edge of town and approaching a sprawling concrete block. Surrounded by desert, it seemed to have risen from the ground.

"I'm going to park in back so nobody sees you," Diego said, slowing to turn down a dark road. "Do you see a black fob in the center console?"

I opened it and sorted through several sets of keys until I found the one he needed. He rolled down his window and stuck it out as we pulled up to an industrial looking metal gate. As it slid open, Diego killed the headlights and parked in an unlit backlot. He quickly sent off a text, then reclined the driver's seat a little and rubbed the bridge of his nose.

It was the second time I'd noticed him do it since we'd gotten in the car. "Do you have a headache?"

"Yeah. I'm just tired and feeling queasy." He squinted through the windshield. "I've barely slept in days. Every time I close my eyes, I think of what'll happen if tomorrow doesn't go well."

"Come here." I unfastened my seatbelt to give him the best sideways hug I could and kissed his cheek. "You're almost there. By this time tomorrow, the shipment will be on its way and you'll be *that* much closer to pulling off the most impressive deal the Cruz cartel has ever seen."

He turned his head to graze the tips of our noses. "And then?" he asked.

"And then it's you and me with nothing ahead of us but our future."

He tilted his head and kissed me gently. "I love the sound of that. I love *you*."

"I love you too," I said. *Enough to die for you*, a voice in my head said. The fortune teller. Why did she still haunt me when I knew her words held no truth?

A knock at the driver's side made me jump back with a gasp. I clutched my throat, my heart pounding.

"It's just Jojo," Diego said, patting my thigh. I could barely make out a figure until Diego rolled the window down.

Jojo, one of Diego's foremen, nodded at me. "*¿Qué tal*, Talia?"

Even though my heart pounded from the scare, I nodded. "*Todo bien*. All good."

"How's it going in there?" Diego asked, passing Jojo the keys.

Jojo wiped his hairline, leaving a grease mark on his forehead. "One of the semi engines is fucked. We're working on it."

"Where's the mechanic?" Diego asked.

"Not picking up his phone, but don't worry, *jefe*. We'll get him here."

"You checked the fuel and oil levels? The battery?" Diego asked, his brows cinched.

"Yeah, *I* didn't, but Tomás knows all that shit and I think he—"

"Did he disengage the lock?"

Jojo showed us his grimy palms. "I dunno."

"Tell him to try that," Diego said. "If it doesn't work, check the ECM ground wire."

"What the fuck is that?" Jojo asked, wetting his finger to rub grease off his wrist.

"Come on, *cabrón*. Like I don't have enough on my plate?" Diego blew out a sigh. "I'll text Tomás."

Seeing the veins pop in Diego's hands and neck as he gripped the steering wheel, I caressed his right forearm. "Go look at it," I said. "I'll be fine here for a few minutes."

"Maybe if I didn't hire such dumb motherfuckers," Diego muttered.

Diego didn't mean it—he cared a great deal for his men—and Jojo knew it. Jojo smiled with a shrug. "Sorry I couldn't afford to go to college for engines."

Diego rolled his eyes. "Wait there," he said and raised the window before turning to me. "Are you sure? It's dark out here, and you can't turn on the lights or someone might see you. I know that scares you."

Nothing happened in the dark. That was part of why it frightened me—not knowing whose footsteps were coming or going, or who might be at my back, or whether the right or wrong person had found me until it was too late to do anything about it. When Barto had come rushing down the tunnel ladder for me, I hadn't known who he was until he'd held the flashlight under his chin. The shadows had created a ghoulish, haunting mask that hadn't looked at all like the Barto I'd grown up around. I'd gone with him willingly, relieved to have been found, but part of me had questioned him—and everything—until we'd emerged from the tunnel into the closet. Doors had been broken down, my mother's body had been covered, and Papá had crushed me to him for a breathless hug.

I wished there were at least lamps in the lot, but if I said that, Diego would stay when he was clearly needed inside. "I'm not nine anymore," I told him. "I'll be fine."

"I'll just go talk to Tomás and come right back." He leaned over to peck me once more. "Okay?"

"Go."

The dome light came on as he switched off the engine and handed me the keys. "If you see anything—anything *at all*—get the fuck out of here."

"Without you?" I asked.

"Yes." He shut off the light and the car went pitch dark. Not even a sliver of moonlight touched the area. He passed me the keys with the fob. "These are for the gate and the warehouse. Nothing will happen, but I don't care if a jackrabbit hops by and looks at you funny. Just go."

I nodded, gripping the keys. "Got it."

"Lock the door after me and keep the lights off." When he ducked out, I hit a button on the roof to plunge the car back into darkness. I barely made out his shadow as he met Jojo at the back door and disappeared inside the warehouse.

With desert all around me, it might've *felt* as if I was in the middle of nowhere, but I had to remember there were many people here. Specifically, men with guns who'd been hired by my father. They wouldn't let anything bad happen. They were on our side.

Then again, Cristiano had been too when he'd left me in the dark.

Even though it was hard to see, nothing would ever be as pitch-black as the underground tunnel. At least now, I wasn't covered in blood and on the precipice of a future that'd been dimmed significantly. I'd hugged my knees to my chest and tried to stop picturing all the vibrant colors of my mom's dress darkened with blood. What if I'd been ten minutes earlier? Or had heard the shot? Would it have changed anything?

The only thing I'd actually seen in that tunnel had been Barto's shadowed face. All I'd heard was his voice, oddly as cajoling as Cristiano's hours earlier, my own sobs, and the pests scampering around me.

As my chest tightened with panic, I coaxed myself to breathe through it. But no matter how many times I told myself I was too old to be afraid of the dark, fears as deeply rooted as mine knew no age.

With a piercing screech of metal scraping metal, I spun in my seat to look out the back window but saw nothing. My heartbeat echoed in my ears. I turned forward again. The time on the dash changed. In an alternate universe, Pilar and I were starting *Revenge of the Sith*. I closed my eyes and hummed the opening bars to *Star Wars*.

Like a clap of thunder, rumbling motorcycle engines jarred me back to reality. As two bikes pulled up to the driver's side, I ducked into a ball on the floorboard. It went silent again. A large shadow passed Diego's window. My heart pounded as the other biker approached. Keys jingled from somewhere. A silhouette peered into the car. On what looked like a beanie or hat, I made out the small but distinct glowing outline of a white sugar skull. A *calavera*.

They were Cristiano's men.

At Diego's warehouse.

Which held every last gram of the Maldonado product.

Diego had been right—Cristiano *did* have something to do with the robberies. And it looked like he was back for more.

Diego had told me to go if I saw anything suspicious, but he had to know I'd never leave him stranded. I had an opportunity to warn him, and I needed to take it.

## CHAPTER 13

# NATALIA

The Maldonados wouldn't hesitate to kill Diego if he lost any more of their shipment. That was why this deal had been haunting Diego's nights since the first theft. I had no idea how the Calaveras had found the top-secret warehouse, but I knew why they were here—for the drugs.

As soon as the skull-adorned bikers stepped away from Diego's car, I opened the glovebox to get my cell. I sent Diego a hurried text that some Calaveras were out back. The keys to the Mercedes dug into my palm, but I wouldn't leave him here.

I stared at my screen, praying for a response. I couldn't take the chance that these men would ambush Diego and turn the situation with the Maldonados critical. Or worse—hurt him. When a minute had passed without a response, I stuck my phone in the neckline of my dress and sat up. I didn't see the men anywhere, but I couldn't see much to begin with.

I could help. I had to. I knew what it was to feel helpless during and after a tragedy, and it was a form of torture, especially paired with grief. Tonight, I could move soundlessly and use the element of surprise to my advantage to hopefully reach Diego before they did.

I fumbled for the fob to make sure I had the right set of keys, then quietly opened the car door. I ducked behind the side panel, listening as my eyes adjusted. The area seemed clear, so I tiptoed toward the back door, where I deftly tried each key until the lock finally gave.

The door opened to a wide, dark hallway with a light at the end of it. I tugged down the hem of my dress and felt my way along one wall, stepping carefully over boxes. I almost rolled my heel on some screws but managed to steady myself against a crate. As I got closer, men's voices and the *clink* of what sounded like metal tools carried through the doorway. I listened for yelling, threats, or arguing but heard nothing of the sort.

When I'd reached the end of the hall, I inhaled a deep breath and peeked in. It was a garage with two eighteen-wheeler trucks parked side by side. The one closest to me had its hood popped. Diego worked underneath it, standing on a stepladder with a tool belt around his waist and his sleeves rolled.

I scanned the room for the men I'd seen. I recognized my father's soldiers as they unloaded cartons from an armored vehicle, but others didn't look familiar at all. Hadn't Diego said only their most trusted men were here?

When I returned my eyes to the semi, Diego had his phone out. After reading the screen, he looked toward the doorway, and his eyes widened when he saw me. Wiping his hands on a rag, he nodded for me to get back in the hall. I hid as he said something about the engine to the other men. Moments later, he came around the corner and nearly knocked me over.

He grasped my shoulders. "You okay?" he whispered.

"I saw men in Calavera clothing outside," I rushed out. "I think they were sneaking in the back door."

"Yeah, I know. They're with us."

I blinked twice as my mouth fell open. "*What?*"

"This is Cristiano's warehouse." Diego took his suit jacket from over his elbow, put it around my shoulders, and moved me farther from the doorway. "We decided to store everything here after our locations were compromised."

I leaned in and spoke softly. "But what if Cristiano is behind the attacks?"

"It wasn't my decision, believe me, but we're in a crunch." Diego frowned. "I had no other option. I just hope Cristiano has enough of a reason not to sabotage us."

I eased back. "You mean because he might be planning to take it all over."

"Right." Diego glanced over his shoulder. "Jojo says everything's been quiet. They're even getting along with Cristiano's guys. But you still shouldn't be in here."

"I don't want to go back to the car," I said. "The dark . . . it just takes me back to being down there."

"I get it." He pulled the jacket closed and kissed my forehead. "I actually feel safer with you inside. The engine isn't fixed yet, but I see the problem. Tomás can probably take it from here."

"I have two hours before I have to be home. I'd feel better if you guys just fixed the problem," I said. "Because if you can't get the truck to start . . . then what?"

"Then I can't make half the delivery tomorrow," he said. "And all our plans go to shit."

"Then you should handle it. I'll just stay hidden."

"Not here. People are coming and going." He glanced toward the ceiling. "We take breaks on the roof. You could go up there, because I assure you, no one's taking a fucking break tonight. There are lights too. You still have those keys?"

I held up the set. He picked through them until he found the one he was looking for, then walked by me to open the door to the expansive warehouse. He flipped some switches and fluorescent lights flickered on as I entered.

My heels echoed through the building that stored stacks of massive wooden crates and heavy-duty machinery. Attached to one wall was an office with storage lockers. "What is all this?" I asked.

"Calavera contraband. Artillery. Semi-automatics, grenades, drones, IEDs—that kind of thing."

I turned in a circle. No wonder this place was so dangerous. "Where's it all going?"

"Most of it is coming. Smuggled from up north so criminals like us can organize and protect our product. From each other and from law enforcement." He pointed across the warehouse to a staircase. "Just take that up to the access door on the roof. Up there, you'll see lounge chairs and stuff."

"What if someone comes up?"

"Nobody else has keys to this side of the warehouse except me and Cristiano's right-hand man, who's not here tonight. But the door locks automatically behind you, so just in case, take the keys." He kissed me quickly. "I'll be up shortly."

I held Diego's jacket closed as I crossed the room, climbed the stairs to the second level, and continued up a short access hall. At the end stood a single door with a long glass window big enough for me to glimpse the sky.

I stepped out onto the roof. Outdoor LED lights guided me through rows of solar panels and across a helipad.

I found an area of loungers and camping chairs where the men must've taken their breaks, picked up a *sarape* blanket, and sat underneath it near a portable grill. Clusters of stars were the only light in the black, horizonless desert. Behind me, the town twinkled. In that direction, light and life thrived in the dark while the desert had killed the most resilient of men. Why had I chosen to face the direction that was nothing but desert? Why confront Cristiano when being on his radar could only lead to trouble?

Darkness called to me.

That didn't mean I had to answer.

It'd been too easy to enmesh myself in Cristiano's game. Too natural to succumb to the shadows that swarmed my nightmares. Cristiano had said this life lived in me like a heart. Maybe that was true, but hearts could be replaced. A brain couldn't. I wasn't going to walk toward darkness like my mother had.

I leaned my head back. As adrenaline from my emotional and mental warfare with Cristiano wore off, I drifted in and out of consciousness until my phone dinged with a text from Diego that he was on his way up.

I went to meet him at the door. He slipped his arms inside my jacket and scooped me up by my waist, walking us backward. "Nice up here, isn't it? You wouldn't expect it to be."

"I can count every star."

"Funny, I'm seeing stars too . . ." He captured my mouth for a kiss. "Put your legs around me."

He lifted me by my ass, and I locked my ankles at his lower back. "Did you fix the engine?" I asked.

"It's all good." He pecked me. "Everything's on schedule to leave late-morning." His lips brushed the underside of my jaw. "Border patrol is expecting us. Law enforcement is standing by to escort us." He moved his mouth down my neck, warming me with his breath. "We're closer and closer to freedom."

That explained his sudden good mood. I raised my eyes to the sky as he sucked and nibbled the tender skin along my throat. "We're so close," I said, nearly moaning.

"We are."

"And we've been *so* good."

I felt his smile against my skin. "We have."

"Almost saintly."

He laughed hotly into the curve of my neck. "I didn't know saints kissed this way."

My dress inched up the backs of my thighs. He helped it along until my thong was almost exposed. I lifted up to readjust, and the length of him pressed solid between my legs, eliciting my gasp and his pained groan. He wanted me. He was ready for me.

Maybe it was being out in the open, but I was hit with the uneasy question of what my mother would think if she was looking down now. Would she understand Diego and I were meant to be as she and my father had been? They were younger than me when they married. And Diego's optimism was contagious. Finally, I felt as if he wanted to start over in California more than he needed the constant threat of danger that made cartel life both treacherous and exhilarating.

He lowered me onto the cushion of a chaise lounge and kneeled at my feet to remove my shoes. He kissed the inside of my ankle, and I shivered as he grazed his five o'clock shadow up the inside of my leg. He climbed over me, and fixed his mouth on mine, his kiss becoming hungry as our tongues met fast and slippery. "I want you so bad, Tali," he said, panting. "I can't wait any longer to bury myself inside you."

His bold words thrilled me, and as he kissed his way down my collarbone and chest, I doubted my decision to wait. Diego and I were destined. Tomorrow would go well, and he'd come to California.

If it didn't, then I'd have bigger worries than my virginity.

If anything went wrong, wouldn't I wish I'd had this night with him?

We were as good as committed to each other. Why wait for a ceremony?

Diego paused, lifting his head. "Where'd you go, *princesa*?"

"I'm here. I was just trying to remember why we're waiting."

"How much of that vodka did you drink?" he asked with a haphazard smile.

"It's not that. I feel fine. I'm just . . ."

"Horny?"

I laughed. "That goes without saying."

"You have no idea how much it turns me on to know that *you're* turned on." He sat back on his calves. "But if you have to think about whether you're ready, then we shouldn't go any further."

I sat up on my elbows, awed by his restraint. By his *gallantry*. "Really?" I asked.

"Our first time isn't going to be on top of a warehouse. Or any piece of property that belongs to my fucking brother." He stretched out next to me, and I lifted my head to settle into the crook of his arm. "Damn," he said. "It feels good to lie down."

"Do you have to come back here after you drop me off?"

"Yeah I will, even though Jojo told me to go home and sleep since I need to be alert during the delivery."

I glanced up at him. "You're going with them tomorrow?"

"I have to." With his eyes on the sky, his jaw squared as he swallowed. "It's too important for me not to be there."

My heart sank. The last shipment to attempt to cross the border had been blown up, killing two men. "Aren't you more valuable here?" I asked. "Like those people in the movies who stay in the control center during a shuttle launch?"

Diego kissed my temple when I shuddered. "I'll be all right. Don't worry. I'm more resilient than you think, and I'm not planning to meet God any time soon."

I let his resolve soothe me. Because it was that same determination in his voice that told me I wouldn't be able to talk him out of going. A sense of duty ran almost as deeply as loyalty within the cartel. Diego would see this through to the end.

I wanted to be content to sit in peace with Diego and take in these rare moments we had alone, but because the past had crept up on me in the car, my mind kept flashing there. The nebulous shape of my mother's blood on the cold tile. The black, cold-as-steel Glock engulfed by Cristiano's hand. I smelled gunpowder and expensive perfume and heard my father's sobs, as subdued as thunder, the night he'd returned home from his trip. My mother had struggled to warn me about Cristiano. If he hadn't shot her, why had she looked so scared as she'd pleaded with him for my life?

I'd locked these memories away, but Cristiano's presence dredged up more each day. His cryptic words earlier had wormed their way into my consciousness. I'd gotten good at pushing the darkness away, but tonight, it pushed back.

Were there other things about that day I hadn't noticed? Could someone else have gotten into the house somehow? I'd spent almost half of my life seeing Cristiano as a protector—but I'd spent more of it thinking of him as my mother's murderer. Diego, too, had believed the worst in his brother for a long time.

Diego squeezed me closer. "You got quiet. You all right?"

"Are *you*?" I asked.

His eyebrows drew together. "Why?"

"We've talked a lot about how I'm dealing with everything, but I haven't really asked what it's like for you to have Cristiano back—and to consider he might not have done this."

He scratched the bridge of his nose. "I . . . I'm not sure it matters.

Whether Cristiano murdered Bianca or not, too much damage has been done." His chest expanded with a deep inhale. "There's no chance Cristiano and I could repair our relationship."

"Even if he's proven innocent?" I asked. "I've spent a long time blaming him for this too, but as much as I don't trust him, I *do* trust my father."

"Cristiano's not innocent," Diego said without an ounce of doubt. "But neither am I."

I cocked my head into the nook of his shoulder. "What?"

"It's beginning to hit me that Cristiano and I . . ." He shifted in the chair. "We're more similar than I'd like to admit."

Diego and Cristiano—*similar*? Aside from sharing some physical attributes, they were night and day to me. "You're not like him," I said, tracing my index finger over the stubble shading his chin. "Not in a million years."

I lifted my head when Diego repositioned his arm under me, as if he couldn't get comfortable. "He betrayed our family," Diego said, "and I betrayed him."

"You mean Cristiano betrayed my father . . .?"

"No. Mine." He paused, lowering his eyes from the sky to the desert. "When Costa killed my parents, I didn't fully grasp the business they were in. I do now. I understand why they couldn't continue down that path." His face screwed up as if he'd bitten into something sour. "But they didn't need to die for it."

Diego didn't talk about his parents much, but when he did, he got pensive. Still, I'd never questioned that he understood why their death had to happen.

"Our families had a pact not to get into human trafficking. Your parents broke it," I reminded him, flattening my hand over his chest. His heart beat strong against my palm. "But the real reason Papá did what he did was because they plotted against him."

"I know. I get it. But they're my blood, Natalia."

"That doesn't excuse everything under the sun. It *can't*."

"I thought it did. Cristiano went against my parents because he didn't agree with how they ran their business. At the time, I thought him a traitor—and I still do." He wiped his forehead with his shirtsleeve and blew out a breath. "I didn't think anything should ever break the bonds of family. But then I did that exact thing to Cristiano."

"It takes courage to resist blind loyalty," I said soothingly, trying to comfort him.

"Or does it take courage to stick by family no matter what?" he asked. I heard the struggle in his voice and wondered how long he'd been thinking all this. "As Cristiano couldn't excuse my parents for getting involved in things like forced labor or sex slavery, I couldn't excuse him for taking your mother's life—and I turned on him. My own blood."

"You had no other choice, Diego." When he didn't respond, I added, "There has to be a line somewhere, even for family."

"I'm not sure I agree. Sometimes, I get overwhelmed by helplessness wondering if I betrayed my family by joining yours. I hate Cristiano for what he did to Bianca, but perhaps doing nothing was just as bad."

Doing *something* would've meant retaliation. "Did you ever think of taking vengeance for their death?"

He didn't answer right away. As seconds ticked by, I grew uneasy. There was only one person Diego would take revenge on. My father.

"In my darkest moments, yes," he admitted.

My heart thumped once. I'd never heard Diego mention a desire for retribution, but I supposed that was human nature. It wasn't as if *I'd* never wondered how things might've turned out differently if I'd actually known how to operate the gun I'd pulled on Cristiano all those years ago.

"But that's how you and Cristiano are different," I said, balling his shirt in my fist. "*You* are good. You never would've acted on those feelings."

"At the core of it, though, Tali—we've each committed the highest sin in this world. We turned against family, and that's how we're alike." His body depressed into the chair with a long exhale. "It's why we can never repair what's left between us. Even if we're forced to do business together as Costa wants, even if we find a way to make things right again—the distrust between us will never go away."

"You keep saying Cristiano turned against family," I said, trying to decipher what exactly he meant. Did he mean because Cristiano had joined our cartel? "When he hurt my mom, he was close enough to my parents to be *like* family, but they weren't blood as you continue to point out."

"I'm not talking about what he did to your family. I'm talking about what he did to *mine*."

*What*? I furrowed my eyebrows. I didn't understand what he meant, but as Cristiano had warned me hours earlier—I was starting to believe there *was* more to my mother's murder than I knew.

I sat up on one elbow to look down at him. "What are you saying?" I asked.

"You asked if I ever think of vengeance," he said slowly. "I do. But not against your father. He may have pulled the trigger, but Cristiano is the one who told Costa what my parents were doing, and what they were planning."

It took a moment for his words to sink in. I'd never questioned how my father had learned that the de la Rosas were conspiring against him. I wouldn't have guessed the information that would get them killed would come from within their own family. "Cristiano had your parents killed?"

"Yes. That's the betrayal I mean." Diego glanced away. "My brother has no loyalty. He never has. It's what I've been trying to tell Costa. I can't trust him . . . but I *can* trust a man's motivations."

"What are his motivations?" I asked. My mind raced as this new door opened. Could this help reconcile any holes in my past? "Why is he back? I thought it was to avenge his parents' death, but if he caused it, then Papá was right. He's not here for revenge. So what does he want?"

Diego searched the night sky as if it might hold the answers we needed. "By this time tomorrow, the Maldonado deal will either be done or it won't," he said. "I don't know why Cristiano is here. But I suspect we'll find out soon enough."

## CHAPTER 14

# NATALIA

My mother would sometimes braid her hair into a thick, black arrow she wore over one shoulder. It was that way now, but tonight was the first time it twinkled with stars. They winked at me as she held my hand and led me to my bed.

"It's time to sleep, Natasha," she said.

"*Natalia*," I corrected as I got under the covers.

She kneeled next to me. Heavy bracelets *clinked* on her wrists as she touched my forehead, chest, and each shoulder. "You're old enough to know better now," she said.

"I'm only nine."

"The truth is in you like a heart. Like blood in your veins. Like bones." She smiled. "Kiss me goodnight."

I sat up and hugged her neck, resting my head on her shoulder. Somewhere on the compound a shot rang out.

"*Mami?*"

"It's okay, *mariposita*." She laid me back on the bed. When she drew back, blood covered my nightgown. With another shot, she fell over me.

I couldn't breathe. From somewhere in the house, my father screamed at me to get down, but I was stuck under her body. I curled up under the bedspread and hid from the next round of shots. This time, they kept coming, an endless *rat-a-tat-tat.*

"Natalia!"

Jolted out of my dream, I launched forward, gasping for breath, as if someone had been sitting on my chest.

The sky was lightening from black to indigo. Sweat trickled down my temple. I was still in Diego's jacket . . . on the roof. We'd fallen asleep. My father would be looking for us, and—

"Get *down.*" Diego shoved me over the side of the chaise, and I landed on my shoulder on the concrete.

I hadn't dreamed the shots. With another round, I covered my ears and moved my head under the chair. Most everyone I'd known had heard the echoes of a turf war at some point, but this wasn't happening *somewhere.* These shots were being fired right underneath us.

"Stay here." Diego crawled to the side of the roof, rose to his knees, and looked over. "Fuck." He ran both hands through his hair and made two fists. "*Fuck.*"

"What?" I cried just as the shots stopped.

"Shh." He motioned for me to be quiet before slinking back. "The warehouse is under attack. Stay up here."

"*What?*" My heart beat hard enough to shake my whole body. I reached under the chair to grab his elbow. "Don't leave me."

"They're trying to steal what's left, Tali. You know I can't let them. I can't, or else—" He inhaled a breath. "That product down there is the difference between life or death for me."

"They could *shoot* you."

"I won't let that happen." He dragged himself close enough to kiss me. "It'll be okay."

"Diego," I said shakily. "Let me come with you."

"Talia, you *must* hide under here. Give me the keys. Listen. Are you listening?" He took the keys from my shaky hands. "Do you have your phone?"

I nodded quickly. "Yes."

"If I don't make it back, stay hidden." His words were soothing, but

I heard the crack in his voice. When more shots sounded, he flinched. "Don't come looking for me. Text Barto—he'll find you. I'll be back for you in no time."

I clung to his arm, tears blurring my vision. Was this what I'd been warned of? *I see pain. I see betrayal and violence. And much death.* What were the chances Diego would go downstairs and never return? They weren't odds I wanted to take. I choked back a sob. "Don't go."

"I have to, *princesa*."

My hair fell over my right eye, but I refused to release him. "I'll come with you."

"It's too dangerous. It's for your own protection, and those are my men down there. I can't leave them stranded."

"But I need you." My heart had already been irreparably damaged losing one person—I couldn't say good-bye to another. I wouldn't abandon Diego. "You can't die. You can't."

"I'm not dying today, Talia. No way in hell." He lifted the black veil of my hair and settled it over my shoulder. "When I go, you'll be by my side, okay? I'm with you, life or death."

With a thick throat, I nodded. "Life or death," I rasped.

"Good girl." He kissed my forehead. "I love you."

He angled to get his 9mm from its holster, maneuvered out from under the chair, and sprinted across the roof.

"I love you," I whispered back.

Night's cloak lifted as the sun peeked over the distant mountains. With the whir of a helicopter, I curled all the way under the chaise and clutched Diego's jacket closed around myself. A spotlight flashed over the roof. With a whistle from above, an explosion on the ground shook the building. The helicopter circled one more time, dropping grenades that rattled every bone in my body. I covered my mouth. Tires screeched, and the helicopter flew off.

With unsteady fingers, I shot Barto a quick text. After what could've been thirty seconds or five minutes of silence, I crawled out. The helicopter was nowhere in sight, so I peeked above the concrete ledge. The rising sun cast rich purple shadows over a vast desert. Behind me, the town woke up, cars honking and people screaming.

Men yelled below me. The blasts had stopped, so I risked getting to my feet to look all the way over the side of the roof.

Flames raged below, licking the side of the building, jumping from one wood container to the next as black smoke billowed from the windows. I had to get off the roof now, or I'd be trapped. I needed to get to Diego. I snatched my shoes off the ground, ran for the door, and grabbed the handle, but it was locked.

I slammed my fists against the industrial metal door, then my stiletto against the sliver of glass. I traded it for a discarded lead pipe and smashed the window. It shattered, leaving a space just big enough for me to get an arm through. Smoke wafted out, curling around me before it disintegrated in the wind. My eyes watered, and my nostrils burned. I whipped off Diego's jacket to cover my mouth, knotting the sleeves at the back of my head.

I rose onto the tips of my toes, feeling around. My skin heated fast while glass sliced into my forearm, but finally, I managed to grab the handle. I cranked it, opened the door, and ran down the stairs holding the jacket in place. I tried to blink away the burn blurring my vision as plumes of smoke surrounded me. I leaned over the railing and jumped back as heat scorched my hand. Movement below caught my eye. It looked as if men were running in and out. I waved the jacket and screamed for help. Flames engulfed almost everything on the ground floor, consuming the base of the stairs. If I didn't get through, I'd have to jump over the side of the roof.

I started down the steps when someone caught my waist from behind, picked me up, and carried me back up the stairwell. "Diego?" I cried.

Strong, sinewy forearms pinned me to a hard body, easily wrapping around my torso. A voice rumbled against my back, deep and full of grit. "Try again."

*Cristiano.*

I struggled to turn, and when we were back on the roof, I kicked his shin. He released me, and I stumbled back, spinning to face him.

"What are you doing here?" I choked out.

"Ladder," he said, coming toward me. "*Now.*"

"What ladder?" I backed away. With my eyes watering, he almost seemed like an apparition from the night before, still in his open-collar white dress shirt and wrinkled suit pants. It didn't take long for me to connect the pieces. "You did this."

"We have to get out of here."

"I'm not going *anywhere* with you." I snarled. "Your brother's inside."

"You have no other choice." He grabbed me by the arm. I wrestled with him, my chest tightening in panic as he easily yanked me toward the ladder. Suddenly, I was nine years old again and his puppet, pulled along like I weighed nothing, forced to the edge of nothingness.

I coughed as smoke suffocated my lungs. "Let *go*."

He took my shoulders and shook me. "*Wake up,* Natalia. This warehouse could blow any second."

It hit me then what was inside—gunpowder. Artillery. Explosives. Fear gripped me as easily now as it had the last time Cristiano had torn me away from my loved ones when they needed me most. But this time, I wasn't afraid of what Cristiano would do to me. I feared for Diego. I didn't think I could survive the crumbling of my future if he was taken from me. I tried to wriggle free. "I have to tell him."

"He knows. Diego can take care of himself, and if he can't, it's already too late."

I pushed him away. "Fuck you. I'm not leaving him."

"What are you going to do? If you run back in there, you'll burn alive. Down is the only way out." He didn't give me a chance to answer. In one mighty swoop, he had me off my feet and over his shoulder.

"What are you doing?" I screeched.

He strode toward the edge with no signs of stopping. For a split second, I believed he was going to launch me over the side until we reached an access ladder I hadn't noticed before. "What the fuck were you doing up here?" he growled, descending down the side of the building swiftly, as if he didn't have an adult female hanging over his back. "I told you to go straight home."

"He's your *brother*."

Upside down, I spotted Diego's Mercedes. We were at the back gate. The fire roared on all sides but hadn't reached the lot yet. On the ground, Cristiano set me on my feet and scanned my legs and dress. In the cold light of breaking dawn, he seared me with a different kind of heat than he had the night before. He didn't seem to like what he saw anymore. "Get on the horse," he said.

Near the open gate, a man on a horse held the reins of a rearing black stallion. I wasn't going anywhere without Diego. I turned to run around front where the semis were parked, but Cristiano snatched my elbow, pulled me back, and hoisted me up. I struggled, trying to kick him as he carried me toward the exit. He put a hand to the horse's nose, and when it'd calmed, Cristiano dropped me on its back.

"You can't do this," I said, my throat thick. "We can't leave Diego here."

He grabbed the horn and butt of the saddle, trapping me. "Your misguided loyalty is going to get you killed, but not today." He pulled himself up, took the reins in one hand, and wrapped an arm around my waist to secure my back to his front. "Hold on," he said and spurred the horse with a "*Hyah!*"

The stallion jerked into motion, and we exited into the desert. I squirmed against Cristiano, fighting to look back. The other rider took off in the opposite direction to catch up with a group of men on horses. I braced myself for a bone-rattling explosion, and another irrevocable shift in my life. "He's going to *die*," I said.

"Cockroaches survive fire. Butterflies, on the other hand . . ." He tightened his hold on me. "They go up in smoke. You'll see your Romeo again, I guarantee it."

"Let me go." My imagination jumped ahead to Diego's funeral. The only black dress I had was the one on my body. The last one I'd seen him in. A scrap of fabric. I'd have to buy one. Or dye something black. Another dress for another funeral . . .

"Please." My voice cracked, but I clawed at the solid bar of his forearm, trying to free myself, prepared to fall off if I had to. I didn't expect him to release me, so when he did, I braced to hit the ground.

He grabbed me again, capturing my upper arms and pinning them to my sides. "I can't leave Diego there."

"You're not," he said. "I'm forcing you away."

"Take me back."

"Have you learned nothing from your mother's death?" Cristiano held me in a grip so tight, his fingertips dug into my bicep. "If you're drawn to this life, fine—but you can't be so fucking reckless."

My vocal cords protested, but I continued to fight. "I'm not drawn to it. I want no part of this."

"You're lying to yourself, but if you want me to make that true, say the word. I'll put the fear of God into you and send you sprinting back to California for good." He put his mouth to my ear. "I thought I'd scared you straight years ago, but I'm happy to try again."

In that moment, any thoughts of Diego vanished. I remembered who I was with—the devil himself. "Where are you taking me?" I asked, twisting my torso against him.

Riding one-handed, he slid his coarse palm higher up my bare shoulder. "I suppose I could take you anywhere, couldn't I? Imagine if I showed up at the gates of hell with an angel like you."

Where young women were trapped and used, bought and sold. Dread spread through my body to my toes and fingers. There were worse things than death in this world, and Cristiano wanted to teach me a lesson. My heart hammered as his suit pants scraped my bare outer thighs. "But—why w-would you . . . you can't—"

"Mmm, there it is, the fear," he said as I struggled to beat back my panic. "Don't worry. You get used to the underworld's fire." He put his scratchy cheek to mine. "And I suppose, in exchange, *I* could be persuaded to give heaven a try."

We'd left the warehouse behind and were galloping along the edge of town, toward the thick of trees that surrounded the compound. Even when I recognized we were on our way home, my shivering didn't subside. The power in Cristiano's every touch, in his words, reminded me that despite the time that had passed, and despite the fact that I was no longer a child—I still held no chance against him. His grip on me never relented. He was in control of my fate.

I couldn't fight Cristiano. I was in both God's and the devil's hands now. Wherever he chose to take me, I had to go.

"That's it," Cristiano said when I sank against him, his voice suddenly hoarse. "I suspect you'll even like the feeling of surrender."

For possibly the first time since it'd happened, I recalled crying into Cristiano's neck as he'd taken me down the ladder into the tunnel. I'd had a strange albeit fleeting sense of safety. Despite all the things he'd done and the rumors I'd heard, I'd been programmed as a girl to see him as a protector no matter what he was, and somehow, a piece of that trust in him still remained.

The sun rose between two mountains as we steered away from endless desert. Wind whipped my hair the way it hadn't in years—not since the last time my mother and I had ridden the Cruz property, cataloguing different types of vegetation, a project for my science class that'd turned into a regular weekend activity for us. The fresh morning air felt good—reinvigorating even. The thought came with a wave of guilt. How could I think that when there was a possibility Diego had taken his last breath?

Cristiano rode up the long drive toward the house. A team of men in black scurried around trucks and tanks like ants on a hill. They stopped to look as we approached, some of them raising their rifles, only lowering them once they saw me.

Cristiano halted the stallion, hopped down, and reached for me. I slid off the other side and gasped as I landed on my bare feet. Pain shot through my soles, but I ran into Barto's open arms.

"We were looking for you all night," he hissed.

"There was an attack," I rushed out. "And a fire at the w—"

"I got your text." Barto frowned as he rubbed between my eyebrows and showed me his soot-darkened thumb. "Diego took you there?"

"Is he alive?"

"I just spoke to him."

Barto clutched me to him as my knees gave out in relief. With gritted teeth, I turned my glare on Cristiano, who stared daggers right back at us, his eyes narrowing on Barto. "He did this," I told Barto.

"Who, Cristiano?" he asked. "Did he hurt you?"

"No, but—"

I jumped with a *bang* behind me. My father stormed down the front steps, the door swinging in his wake. "Natalia Lourdes King Cruz. Where the fuck have you been?" He stopped abruptly when he saw Cristiano. "You brought her back?"

"I called him about the warehouse fire," Barto said.

"I was already on my way, so I said I'd look for her," Cristiano said.

"*And*?" Papá demanded. In a rumpled button-down and jeans, he looked as if he'd gotten dressed in the dark. "You have as much in that warehouse as we do."

"More," Cristiano said.

"Yet you bring my daughter back to me yourself? The warehouse could explode. You should be there putting out the fire."

Cristiano pushed back some of his jet-black hair that had fallen over his forehead. "She was stuck on the roof," he said. "Everything else can be replaced. Protecting your family has always been my priority."

My father's ashen face stilled. He charged forward and shook Cristiano's hand with vigor. "Your courage will be rewarded. What the devil was she doing there?"

Cristiano glanced over. "Ask her."

Papá turned on me. Shadows marked his face like bruises. "What happened? Why were you there?"

As my immediate fears of losing Diego and being kidnapped by Cristiano subsided, I was left with my father's fury. "*Lo siento, Papá*."

"You're *sorry*?" His voice rose as he stepped toward me. "Answer me when I question you. *¿Qué la chingada* were you doing there?"

I tried to stand tall in nothing more than a skimpy dress as my father, all his men, and Cristiano stared at me. "I—I . . ."

"She spent the night there," Cristiano supplied. "With Diego."

Father took one look at my outfit, hair, and makeup, and he grabbed me by the arm. "He better pray he burns alive. I will kill him for this."

"No," I cried. I'd managed to keep my emotions in check since I'd been torn from my dream earlier, but now, they overcame me. "It's not what you think," I said as my voice broke. "We were talking and we fell asleep—"

"Get inside." He shoved me up the stairs to the house. "Indecent *brat*."

"Papi—"

"Do you think this is a game?" he bellowed, throwing me into the foyer so I landed on my behind. Standing over me, he seethed, "It wasn't enough I lost my wife and the love of my life? I should lose you too? You want me to spend the rest of my days mourning my entire family?"

While anger reddened his face, pain was clear in his eyes. My chest stuttered as I tried to hold in my breaking sobs. "No. I'm s-sorry."

"I have *enemies*, Natalia. Do you know what they do to daughters like you? Kidnap, rape, and beat you half to death as—"

"Enough," Cristiano said.

"As they videotape it all for me. Then they cut your neck. Is that the memory you want to leave me with?"

My throat closed hearing him talk more candidly than he ever had around me. "But I was with Diego—"

"You will never—*ever*—see him again. You're forbidden."

I closed my fist against the tile. "You can't do that," I said.

"Do not talk back to me." He raised his hand, and I ducked to cover my head. "My father would've belted me a hundred times by your age for all the ways you've defied me."

"Enough," Cristiano repeated. It was the calmest, most controlled threat I'd ever heard. I peeked out from under my arms. Cristiano filled the doorway but said no more.

Papá started as if broken from a trance. He began to shake and lowered his arm before limping forward to steady himself on the foyer table. "I can't lose you too," he said shakily as tears filled his eyes. "Nothing scares me more than that possibility, *Lourdesita*."

He hadn't called me "Little Lourdes" since before I'd left for school. And he'd never even come close to laying a finger on me. He was in pain. I scrambled to my feet and hugged his waist. "I love you. I never want to hurt you."

His heart pounded against my cheek. "I'm—I'm sorry, *mija*. You're not the one I'm angry with, and you know I would never . . ."

"*Yo sé,* Papi. I know." I buried my face in his chest and cried until he kissed the top of my head.

"All right, Talia. I have to deal with this fire. Go upstairs and get cleaned up." He pulled away and said over my head, "Ride with me."

"I have transportation," Cristiano answered.

I'd almost forgotten he was there.

"I'll see you at the warehouse then," my father said on his way out the front door. He disappeared into a black car. Trucks rumbled and shuddered with power. The first in a line of cars tore down the winding road, and the rest followed, kicking up clouds of dust.

The house became eerily and unusually quiet. For everyone except a couple guards out front to leave, it had to be serious. For them to leave me alone with a killer, it had to be life or death.

And it was. Reality dawned. The warehouse . . . the goods inside. The damage done was enough to seal Diego's fate. There was no escaping a loss of this magnitude.

"You're responsible for this," I said. Had Cristiano's talk of games the night before been a warning? If so, he'd made a move that would put us all in the crosshairs of the Maldonados. "My father trusted you. *Diego* trusted you, and you tried to kill him."

"If I had, he'd be dead."

"Like your parents?"

He took a step toward me. "Meaning?"

"Diego told me everything. If you'd have your own parents killed, you wouldn't hesitate to do the same to anyone else."

As he advanced, I retreated until I was up against a wall. "And you think I'd destroy my own livelihood to do it?" he asked.

If it meant getting what he wanted, I wouldn't put it past him. Which suggested he'd go to great lengths to grant his own wishes. To position himself at my father's side and strike when Papá least expected it. To see Diego gone.

To take back what he thought he was owed.

What did loyalty mean to a man who'd betrayed and been betrayed by those he'd trusted? Even if he hadn't committed the murder, what loyalty remained after eleven years on the run? A feral cat could be domesticated, but it would never stop looking over its shoulder.

If Diego's suspicions were right, then Cristiano wouldn't stop until he got what he'd come for.

The question was—did I fit into this somehow?

The answer, I feared, I was about to learn.

"My father's expecting you at the warehouse," I reminded him.

"I'm not going to the warehouse." Cristiano wore no expression. He spoke with the ease and confidence of a predator who'd cornered its prey and had the time and proclivity to savor picking it apart. "I'm staying right where I am. Now, come here."

## CHAPTER 15

# NATALIA

Was this how my mother had felt? Cornered by Cristiano with nobody in the house to protect her? *No*. It was worse for her. Cristiano wasn't breaking my trust like he had hers. And he couldn't destroy my sense of safety in my own home. He'd already done that years ago. It wasn't the first time Cristiano and I had squared off under this roof.

His eyes lingered over my dress. "Did my brother do that?"

I followed his gaze to the blood and dirt smeared on my legs. As soon as I noticed the bruises on my forearm and wrists, and the cuts on my ankles and feet, they began to throb. "I already told you, he isn't like that."

Cristiano came toward me, and I backed away, suddenly aware of the glass wedged in my feet. When he was close enough that I could inhale his smoky mix of sweat and burnt wood, he said, "You can limp to your bedroom, or I can carry you there."

My breath caught in my throat. "My bedroom? Why?"

"Use your imagination."

I could think of no reason Cristiano would want to take me upstairs except for the obvious one. What chance did I stand against him? He might as well have been made of marble for all his muscle.

Resisting him would be like fighting a statue. He knew that. Maybe he wanted my struggle. If it was he who'd tried this with my mother, her fight had cost her her life.

But if he touched me, he'd lose any shot at uniting our families. I had to believe that was reason enough to stop him from hurting me.

"My father would murder you in cold blood," I warned.

"Understood." He moved aside to let me pass.

With Cristiano at my back, I crossed the foyer to the dining room and made my way to the stairs. On the second floor, I stopped at my closed door, remembering how I'd skipped down the hall to my mother's room. He reached past me, turned the handle, and pushed it open. "Inside," he said.

I took a breath and stepped over the threshold. With the curtains drawn, my room was dark. He shut the door behind himself, stood at my back, and moved my hair over my shoulder before lowering the zipper of my dress.

"Strip," he said.

Fear and curiosity warred inside me. Was Cristiano so weak that he'd risk his chance at an empire just to have me? If he raped me, killed me, or both, there'd be no question as to his guilt for doing the same to my mother. He'd be back on the run.

My trust in him was buried somewhere deep, and I drew from it now. I was hit hard with a memory I hadn't thought of in over a decade—my mother and I encountering a young Cristiano while gathering flowers in the garden for one of Mamá's parties. I had to have been five or six, which would've made him almost twenty. He'd never picked flowers, he'd told us, and we'd giggled as Mamá had made him carry our baskets of bouquets around for the afternoon. It was one of the only instances I could remember him without a scowl. Even when he'd promised me he was a monster far worse than any that dared hide under my bed, he'd spoken gravely.

"My mother is watching," I said into the dark. If any part of him regretted what'd happened to her, maybe he'd soften.

"I'm not going to hurt you," he said.

I supposed that was the best I could ask for. To come out of this no more wounded than I already was. I pulled down my dress and stood in my thong and strapless bra.

He placed his palm on my upper back. "Walk," he said.

I raised my eyes to the bed in front of me. He could have me any way he wanted, and nobody would stop him. Everything I'd saved for Diego would be taken in a flash. Was there anything left of that man who'd been so devoted to our family that he'd carried baskets of flowers for us? There had to be. I wasn't sure how I knew, but like the way he'd nonchalantly referred to Natasha, my gut told me Cristiano only wanted to see how far he could push me.

I straightened my shoulders and stepped toward the bed. When I neared the footboard, he applied pressure to my back, guiding me away from it and toward the en suite bathroom instead.

Inside, he flipped on a dim overhead light. I watched in the reflection of the mirror over the sink as he circled me, his eyes roaming over my back. He set his jaw, inspecting my body almost clinically. Just another Natasha.

He stopped at the counter to empty his pockets. With his attention diverted, I studied him back. His stark white dress shirt had been marred by smoke, ash, and what looked like blood. My blood, I realized, from when he'd carried me down the access ladder. Without thinking, I dropped my gaze and sucked in a breath at the bulge in his pants.

He glanced up at me, his watch *clinking* as he set it on the Italian marble countertop. He tightened the roll of one sleeve, securing it at his elbow, then the other. The mere sight of his powerful, sinewy forearms made me light-headed. They were weapons in their own right. Every part of him was, it seemed, down to the beast straining against his zipper. Most of the men I knew couldn't match his strength. What chance did *I* stand against him if he tried to overpower me?

He stepped forward, towering over me, soot smudged on his admittedly handsome face—he looked the way I imagined the Grim Reaper might if he shopped in the finest apparel stores and possessed the chiseled features of a god. "Wash the cuts," he said.

I tensed. "What?"

He moved around me and turned on the faucet to the bathtub. "The cuts on your arms and legs. I told you to watch out for glass, did I not?" He grunted. "I can't help but think you ran through it just to spite me."

"I did it for Diego," I said, although it was only half-true. "And I'd do it again."

He looked over his shoulder at me, his gaze shadowed. "So you continue to remind me, even though I was there. I watched you run into the fire for him."

I limped to the tub. "You were wrong earlier. Butterflies aren't delicate."

We switched places. He pulled open my top drawer and started pushing products around. "No?"

"During a wildfire, they don't go up in smoke. They bury themselves in soil."

He moved to the next drawer, shoving aside my hair dryer. "Another way they're survivors."

I perched on the inside edge of the tub so I wouldn't have my back to him. He kept his to me as he rifled in my drawers, his muscled back rippling under his dress shirt. He dumped my makeup bag into the sink, picking through items while I gently soaped my right arm and hand.

He went through every basket, drawer and cabinet, including the medicine one over the sink, gathering things and placing them by the side of the toilet.

I moved on to cleaning my feet. Eventually, Cristiano sat on the outside lip of the tub and held out his hand for the soap. I gave it to him, and he reached in to clean my other foot. He alternated between lathering the soap over my cuts and massaging my ankles. "What happened to your shoulder?" he asked.

I hadn't realized I was holding it. Or the throb of pain when I raised my arm. "I fell."

When he seemed satisfied with my feet, he stood and lowered the lid of the toilet. "Sit," he said to me before disappearing into my bedroom.

I moved from the bath, dried myself off, and slipped on my purple satin robe. Seated on the toilet, I swayed a little, recalling the sensation of riding for the first time in over a decade. For some time, I'd craved that feeling of driving a horse again the way I had with my mother on one side, but the longer I put it off, the harder it was to get back on.

Cristiano returned with my desk chair. He sat in front of me and handed me a towel of ice. "For your shoulder."

I inspected it as if it might be hiding mini daggers before deciding to take my chances. I held it to my arm. "Thank you."

He took tweezers from the counter and grasped my wrist. "This is a deep one, but it'll be the worst one."

I'd sooner faint than show him my pain. I made a fist with my opposite hand as he squeezed my skin.

"Why were you at the warehouse?" he asked quietly as he inspected the cut. Somehow, he was more menacing when he was calm and collected than when yelling.

"Diego stopped to check on a problem."

"And he decided *that* was the right place to fuck you? You're a foolish girl."

"*Foolish*?" I bit out, my temper flaring. "For your information, we barely touched."

"I don't believe you."

I set my jaw. "You don't know a single *thing* about him, me, or our relationship—"

One corner of his mouth crooked. "There it is."

"What?"

Belatedly, dull pain radiated from a spot on my palm. He held up the tweezers to show me a thin but substantial shard of glass. "If you can take that, the rest should be easy."

I shut my mouth. I hadn't even felt it. He'd tricked me to distract me.

His expression defaulted to a scowl as he turned over my hand to inspect my knuckles. "You should never have gone anywhere without your guards," he scolded. "Not the club, and especially not the warehouse."

"I don't need to be looked after," I said firmly, but my heart skipped. Perhaps what scared me most wasn't Cristiano's reputation, but the fact that he was unreadable. Unpredictable. That he had not only the strength to shove me down a dark tunnel but that he might do it for no other reason than to amuse himself. *How* could Father trust him?

"You'd feel differently if there wasn't anybody to look after you." He tweezed a few small pieces from my forearm. "You've never had to survive in the wild. You're just the kind of prey some predators are looking for—one with a false sense of bravery."

He had no right to accuse me of that. We'd faced off when I'd been weaponless and small enough that I'd only come up to his waist. I'd held my own for a kid. "I *have* survived," I said. "Not all danger is physical. I've navigated through a different kind of wild, one you know nothing about."

He worked silently a few moments. "You forget I've lost parents too—and a brother as far as I'm concerned. I was thrown out of the only life I knew and forced to fend for myself."

"You have only yourself to blame for the consequences of your actions."

He glanced up at me. "You still think I'm guilty?"

"Yes," I said. No matter what questions I had, he'd latch onto any weakness I showed, so I kept my mounting doubts to myself.

"Nah," he said. "I'm innocent. You know I am. Yet my brother chose not to believe me, even though it would end my life. So what do you suggest I do about that?"

I tried not to let his twisted truths worm their way into my consciousness. He was only trying to manipulate me against Diego, that was all. "*Nothing*."

Like Diego, Cristiano had long, full lashes. But behind them, his dark, calculating eyes betrayed the differences between them. "You know I can't let something like that slide."

Goose bumps spread over my skin, prickling my hair under my silky robe. "So you are here for revenge."

He returned to the task in front of him. "I reached out to him once, about four years after Bianca's death. Did he tell you? I wanted to come home. To tell Costa the truth and pledge my loyalty to him."

I shifted on the seat. I'd only been thirteen and already away at school. I hadn't heard anything about Cristiano reaching out then or since. "What happened?"

"He said he'd broker a meeting between your father and me, but it was a setup. He tried to have me killed." Holding my wrist in one hand, he ripped open a bandage with his teeth and stuck it on one of my cuts. "There's no trust amongst us, and there never will be."

It wasn't as if my father or Diego told me much to begin with, but that seemed like an important detail to keep from me. And if they'd hide that, what else didn't I know? Could I even believe Cristiano?

"What about me?" I asked quietly. "I said you were guilty too. You must think I also betrayed you."

I swallowed when he didn't respond. If Cristiano had anything to do with the fall of the Maldonado deal, he must've known they'd come after Diego—and the people he cared about. "I guess that was your plan all along. We didn't give you a chance to prove your innocence. My father and Diego hunted you for years. Now, the Maldonados can take us all out in one fell swoop and you command both cartels."

"If you believe that, why aren't you running for your life?"

"I wouldn't leave my father or Diego behind."

"You don't know what you're toying with, *mamacita*," he said, shaking his head. "Where was Diego when you were on the roof alone? *He* left *you* behind."

"He had to salvage what he could of the product. When he ran downstairs, the fire hadn't started yet. He couldn't have known that would happen." I adjusted the ice pack. "He was coming back for me."

"It only matters that you believe he would've."

He released my arm, and I pulled it back, cradling it to my body. "That's not fair. Diego has been there for me my whole life."

"It must be coincidence that staying by your side also serves his best interests."

I wanted to ask Cristiano what he meant, but giving him the chance to spin more lies felt like a betrayal to Diego.

I bent my knee as Cristiano picked up my foot and placed it in his lap. He held my ankle in one hand and ran his fingers along my arch. I jerked but tried to hide that I was ticklish. His touch firmed and my reflex to squirm disappeared. A sharp, pleasant thrill traveled up the inside of my thigh. My instinct should've been to pull away, but warmth coursed through me instead. Satisfaction bloomed like surrendering to a protective embrace as arousal tightened my insides.

Cristiano had a face made to lure prey, a voice as powerful as the sensation of skin on skin, a presence that demanded my attention. But I knew the danger he presented—how could I possibly harbor any attraction to him? What had given me the confidence that he hadn't brought me up here to hurt me? My body and mind betrayed me.

As he dug the tweezers into a particularly sensitive spot, I clenched my fist around the towel of ice and sucked in a breath. He raised his eyes to mine. "Mmm," he said. "*Qué interesante.*"

"What's interesting?" I breathed.

"You're excited by a little pinch."

"I am not. I'm in pain."

"And a part of you likes it." He blinked lazily at me. "A part of *me* likes it."

I inhaled. *Please tell the heavens it is my dying wish to hear you scream.* The warmth he'd awakened in me simmered to a tingle between my legs. Why did things that should intimidate me arouse me instead? So far, his threats had been hollow, but just because Cristiano was handling me gently now didn't mean I was in the clear.

"I'll bet you wish your guards were here now," he said with an almost imperceptible smile.

"I want my gun back," I said.

He paused, then glanced up at me. "Will you learn how to use her?"

"Yes."

He extracted more shards and wiped them on a towel before

setting aside the tweezers to spread antibiotic ointment onto the wounds. "Better?" he asked when I put down the ice pack and rolled my numb shoulder.

I mumbled my agreement as he applied bandages to the deepest cuts. He smoothed his thumb back and forth over the final one to make it stick but didn't stop there. The pad of his finger slid to my ankle, and he turned my foot over to inspect it. It tickled slightly, but resisting the urge to squirm only made me more aware of his palm as it grazed upward. His breath shallowed as he looked over my leg, then glanced at me. His pupils dilated, and his eyes grew darker.

My heart pounded, not just because his hand kept going but also with surprise for the effect I had on someone as taciturn as Cristiano. He wanted me and wasn't hiding it. My traitorous body came alive under his firm but deliberate examination. I shouldn't notice how good his touch felt. I *should* have cared that we were alone and nobody could hear me scream.

As Cristiano moved the hem of my robe aside, I slapped my hand over his, stopping him in his tracks. "I'm waiting until marriage," I blurted. I wasn't sure why I said it, or why I thought that might deter him.

His lip curled in a way I could only interpret as angry. "A virgin?"

I swallowed as an electric current passed between us.

His fingertips dug into my thigh. "You've saved yourself," he said slowly, half statement, half question. "And you think using that as an argument won't have the opposite effect you want it to?"

My brain scrambled to keep up. It sounded as if he meant my virginity was something he'd want, but I couldn't fathom why. I wouldn't know what to do with a man as experienced as he was.

*But I could learn.*

I forced the thought away. "I've saved myself for Diego," I said. "You'd be taking that away from him. From *me*."

His nostrils flared. "You think I'd go as far as to rape you in your father's home?"

My thigh pulsated with warmth where his hand had stopped, my skin sensitive under his rough palm. "I think back then, whatever plans you had were interrupted by my mother or by me. And I think you're too smart to make that same mistake twice."

His gaze drifted down between my legs, where only a silky piece of fabric hid what he so clearly wanted. "Plans? Regretfully, I have none for *you*, Natalia."

He stood and returned to the sink to replace his watch and the contents of his pockets. I waited, tense as a bowstring, until he left the room. And I didn't breathe again until I heard the front door close.

Once the immediate fear of what Cristiano might do subsided, a violent tremble overtook me. I waited for relief to come, but adrenaline coursed through me. Now that I was alone, I felt as if I should do something. I was safe, but would it last? How long until he returned? Until he struck again?

I hugged my shoulders, dropped to my knees on the bathroom floor, and crossed myself. I thanked *La Virgen de Guadalupe* for sparing myself and Diego.

Then I prayed I'd never see Cristiano again.

CHAPTER 16

# CRISTIANO

In my office overlooking *La Madrina,* I fixed a drink. Mid-afternoon, the nightclub was quiet as the cleaning crew scrubbed the downstairs floors and walls. In a few hours, the bar staff would prepare for all the sinners who'd spend their Good Friday night celebrating tonight's theme—*la iglesia roja.* Red church. Sturdy construction would mute the thump of bass, and the dancefloor's crimson glow would make my office look like an opium den.

I'd been up most of the night, but I felt invigorated. Serving justice could do that to a man. With a third direct attack on his deal, Diego would've worked everything out by now—but he'd be missing the final piece. "You can expect my brother any minute," I said to Maksim, who stood straight-backed by the door to my office.

"I figured."

I held up a bottle of *Rey Sol Añejo.* "Drink?" I asked.

"Nah." Max chewed on a toothpick. "Guess I should have my wits about me. His claws will be out."

"He'll fight, but not physically. He can't win. Instead, he'll try to manipulate the game board."

Diego had run out of moves, though. After over a decade of being hunted by my brother, our day of reckoning had come. Only, I wasn't the one caught in a trap. For a third of my life, I'd been mislabeled a traitor, had been forced from friends, family, and a life I'd valued, and I'd done whatever I'd had to in order to survive. And in mere moments, Diego would pay the price for it.

I swirled my drink, breathing in caramel and tobacco. "Try not to kill him if you can help it."

Max's two-way radio beeped and Alejo's voice came through. "We've got a visitor."

"Bring him in," I said.

Max removed his assault rifle from across his body and held it with one hand. "You got it, *jefe*."

"*Oye. Muy bien*. Your Spanish is coming along."

With barely a chuckle, Max went downstairs to meet Diego and his other escorts. I shrugged into my suit jacket and stood at the one-sided glass wall. I wasn't in the habit of spending so much time at the club, but it'd been easier to conduct business here than drive back and forth from the Badlands. The evening before, I'd been on a call to Turkey when my men had alerted me of Natalia's presence. I could still see her now, all bronze legs and arms, the ends of her black hair brushing her waist as she'd moved her hips to disco. Her wide, nervous eyes as she'd turned to face me on the dancefloor.

I shouldn't have been surprised to return home and find Natalia so enchanting—she'd always fascinated me, but not just with her beauty. She tested boundaries, even when fearful. *Especially* when fearful. She'd manipulated her parents in childish but effective ways. She held unwavering devotion to my brother. Her sheltered childhood had given her a false sense of safety as an adult, but I'd hoped her mother's death, and our encounter that day, would scare her into obedience. I didn't know if it was more frustrating or charming that it hadn't.

She'd still dangled herself as bait in front of me, a man she knew to be dangerous. A man she believed was her mother's murderer. Every time I tried to scare her, she returned for more. Even hours earlier, when I'd stood at her back in her bedroom and had practically watched her imagination run wild with all the possible things I could to do to her while we were alone, she hadn't cowered long.

She should cower, though. Testing boundaries got her into trouble. Case in point—she'd stupidly spent last night in the most dangerous place possible.

With Diego. *For* Diego.

It hadn't occurred to me they might be there. None of my men had seen her. I gripped my glass at the thought of Diego alone with her all night. It was like the unnerving feeling I'd gotten when I'd come across them in the courtyard at the costume party. Jealousy had warred with my fury. Any other time, I would've been delighted to catch Diego in a vulnerable moment, but Bianca Cruz's dying words had been for me. A plea. And no matter how far I'd run, or how hard I'd worked, I'd never forgotten them. And that tied me to Natalia in ways she didn't understand.

Maybe Natalia Lourdes was no longer my responsibility, but that instinct to protect her remained. Seeing her again had reawakened an unwelcome fondness for her, but my fascination wasn't nearly as innocent as it'd once been. But who could blame me?

She had mesmerizing violet eyes that could charm a man to walk into a burning building.

Long legs that could wrap around him for days.

And I hadn't stopped thinking about that virgin pussy since this morning.

Diego wouldn't know what the fuck to do with a *panocha* like that. I knew exactly what I'd do with it, though. And it would start with my tongue buried so deep inside her, I'd be tasting her for weeks.

With a knock at the door, I took a moment to collect myself. This was why I didn't fuck with sirens like Natalia King Cruz. I was thinking about *her* when I'd spent years anticipating this final standoff with my brother. Costa had cleared my name, and I was back where I belonged—but I still had one more loose end to tie up. I couldn't let Diego's faithlessness in me go unpunished.

And I was going to revel in every moment of what was to come.

I turned from the window. "*Pasen*."

Maksim entered first, followed by two of my men as they

restrained Diego. Max tossed a semi-automatic pistol next to the bottle of tequila on my desk. "He's clean."

"My brother shouldn't cause you any trouble," I said, picking up a second glass from the drink tray to pour a fresh one. "He's smart enough to know he's cornered."

"Your head of security has a glass eye and your bouncer a severe limp," Diego said. "They'd be lucky to get a shot anywhere near a target."

"I'd think twice about insulting anyone in this room." I gestured at a club chair. "Have a seat."

"I'm not staying," Diego said. Covered in ash and soot, with cuts along his face and hands, my brother looked as if he'd been up all night fighting for his life. Which, I supposed he had.

"*Siéntate*," Eduardo ordered.

"You were expecting me." Diego sat on the edge of the chair. "Why not show up at the warehouse like a man to face those you ruined?"

"I had something to attend to at Costa's." I held out the tequila to him. "Here."

He waved off the drink. "Costa was with me."

"*¿Seguro?* Are you sure?" I asked, offering it again. "It's top-shelf. A special edition sent especially from a tequila bar in Guadalajara."

"I'm sure what's 'special' about it is a dram of poison," Diego said.

I gave Eduardo the glass. "Enjoy, *compadre*," I said.

Ed nodded as he accepted it. "*Gracias, señor.*"

I returned in front of Diego, picked up my drink, and sat back against the edge of my desk. "Costa left his poor, trembling daughter alone in that big house this morning. And during such a dangerous time." I frowned into my drink. "I took it upon myself to offer her my protection. And my comfort."

Diego narrowed his eyes on me. "What'd you do to Natalia?"

"Nothing she didn't enjoy—don't worry."

"*Vete a la chingada*," he said, jumping out of his chair. "Fuck you, *pinche puto pendejo.*"

As Diego released a string of curses, I held up a hand to stop my men from drawing their weapons. Had I hit a nerve? When it came to

Costa and his family, Diego put on an admirable performance, but today, we had no audience. Could it be that his feelings for Natalia were *genuine*? I smiled. That would make this even more interesting. Diego was about to lose more than I could've even planned for.

"You almost *killed* her this morning," Diego said.

She wasn't supposed to have been at the warehouse, nor was he. It was a fuck-up on my part, but I wouldn't let him see that. "*Tranquilo*," I said, keeping my tone light to calm him. "I simply bandaged her up." Bandaged her up and resisted my every urge to fuck her until she forgot my brother's name. If waiting years for this moment with Diego wasn't evidence of my unrivaled self-control, removing my hands from Natalia's smooth, firm thigh was.

A round with me and she'd question everything she knew—including her devotion to Diego. It hadn't occurred to me until now that she might actually mean something to him.

"She was trapped on the roof of the warehouse with no way out," I said. "Luckily, I was there, or she'd have been burned alive."

"You say that like it was a coincidence," he said. "You planned it that way."

"Planned it? No. I was supposed to watch from a distance as your hopes, dreams, and livelihood went up in smoke." I took a sip. "I hadn't intended to risk my own life for your Natalia." Despite the silky vanilla-almond flavor the tequila had left, '*your Natalia*' tasted bitter on my tongue. *My Natalia* sounded better, but I couldn't entertain that thought.

After this, she'd never forgive me.

"You did this, Cristiano," Diego said evenly, taking a step toward me. "The hits on the safe houses. The tunnel explosion. The warehouse fire. You're responsible for all of it. And now, I have nothing to offer the Maldonados but ashes."

I stood to meet him. "I warned you one shot was all you'd get," I said. "You missed. That was your mistake."

"I've never taken a shot at family. That was you."

"You put me in front of the firing squad, which is worse," I said, holding his stare. "First, by accusing me of Bianca's murder, then years later when I reached out to you for help. You sent men to kill me as soon as you knew where I was, and they came home empty-handed. Never take aim if you can't hit the bullseye. You missed both times."

"You went to Costa, our family's enemy, with information that you knew would get our parents killed," he said, balling his fists. "I tried turning you over to Costa, yes, but that's no different than what you did to our mother and father."

"It's completely different. The victims of my crimes are never victims—they know exactly the risks of the life they lead." I picked up the tequila bottle in the likeness of a smiling golden sun and pulled off the top. "Our parents were getting deeper and deeper into trafficking innocent children and women," I said. "I went to Costa for help because you and I were too young to do anything, and they had to be stopped."

"Nothing breaks the bond of family," Diego said. "Costa might've pulled the trigger, but you murdered them. Their blood is on your hands."

I made a show of checking my knuckles. They were callused and scarred from years of defense, offense, and survival. But there wasn't a spot of blood on them. "You're one to talk about breaking family bonds." I refilled my drink. "Do you know what tomorrow is, Diego?"

Diego took my drink off the desk and gulped from it. "Holy Saturday."

"The burning of Judas." I filled another glass on the tray for myself. "We'll be celebrating here at the club in case you know any traitors. There's still time to make an effigy."

"Then make it in your likeness." His nostrils flared. He thrust the glass in my direction, and tequila sloshed over the side as he pointed. "You killed *our parents*."

"Costa did."

"And he has paid half the price," Diego bit out. "His debt will be settled once his daughter chooses me over him. Once he realizes I can take her away from him if I choose. But *you* haven't been made to pay at all."

"I've paid, believe me. The Cruzes were my family, and they turned on me for a crime I didn't commit."

"They are not your family!" He shoved a hand in his hair and turned around, pacing to the glass. "They never were. You don't deserve one after what you did to ours."

The Cruzes *had* been family to me once, especially Bianca. Costa's wife could've easily cast me off or ignored me as she had Diego—who, I was certain, she'd seen through from the start.

But she hadn't. She'd cared for me the way a mother should when she had no reason to. But she'd never get to speak her truth—so I would do it for her.

"Bianca *was* family," I said. "You didn't know her like I did."

"No, I never got the privilege," Diego said, turning back to level me with a glare. "We all know how *well* you knew her. Despite Costa's pardon, the state they found her in speaks for itself."

I dropped my glass and charged at him, seizing him by his shirt. "I never touched her, and you know it. You talk of loyalty but reek of betrayal, and that's why she kept you at arm's length. It's why Costa will *never* let you near his daughter. They only trust you so far."

Diego grabbed my lapels to try to push me off, but Max drew his gun in a split second. Glass eye or not, my right-hand man had as unshakeable an allegiance to me as I did to him, and that made him a killer of the deadliest sort. Diego clenched his teeth but let go of my jacket.

"You've planted some bullshit ideas in Natalia's head," I said, "but don't think I don't know where they came from. You're the one with plans to take over, not me."

Diego laughed grimly. "I'll do it the noble way. I don't have to force a woman like you. My plans are to marry Natalia, who loves me, and stand by Costa's side until he's ready to hand over the reins."

I released him with a shove. It was uncanny, my ability to sniff out when my brother was lying. Why other certain people couldn't see it, I had no idea. "You fused yourself to Natalia when she was most vulnerable. Bianca would never have allowed you to get so close to her. You saw an opportunity and you took it. And if Costa wasn't going to give you what you wanted, you were going to use Natalia's love for you against him."

"You'd have done the same," Diego said. "The difference is, Natalia fell for me, not you."

I had traveled the world in search of the kind of loyalty she gave Diego. I'd lost any family bonds I'd had or formed. My parents were dead. Bianca was dead. The only man I'd ever looked up to had thought I'd violated and murdered his wife. I'd gone through great pains to surround myself with men and women I trusted my life to every day—ones I'd give mine for in return.

Yet I remained haunted by the day Natalia had risked her life for my *brother*. A man who didn't deserve her. To have what I'd built was one thing. To have the unflinching devotion of a woman like her, to be loved the way Bianca had loved Costa, was surely nirvana.

But devotion to the wrong man could get you killed; my mother was evidence of that.

Diego made Natalia weak—I was doing her a favor.

Because Natalia had proved a woman who couldn't be moved with words or reason. It had to be with action and force.

"Natalia didn't fall for you. She was manipulated." I stalked closer to him, enjoying the way he pulled back his shoulders, as if he thought he stood a chance against me. "You slowly secured her loyalty to you over anyone else, so when you were ready to make demands of Costa, he'd have no choice but to give in or lose her."

"That doesn't mean I don't love her or see him as a father," Diego said. "I know what's best for all of us."

A monster didn't always perceive himself that way. But I saw right through my brother. "It was an admirable grab at power, not unlike something our father would've done, but it didn't work. And in the end, it doesn't matter, because it won't change your fate."

"Once the Maldonados hear about the fire, they'll come looking for me." A vein in his forehead appeared as he tensed his jaw. "I can't recover from this."

"No, you can't."

He swallowed, his hands twitching as if he had to resist throwing a punch. "So, here I am. You have me where you want me. What do you want, Cristiano?"

"Nobody gives me what I want. I take it."

He ran a hand through his hair and made a fist. "I've cost them over a hundred million dollars. They'll crucify me. And Costa. And everyone who ever spoke a word to me."

I undid my jacket as I rounded my desk to make a fresh drink. "You knew the risk of writing a check you might not be able to cash."

"I would've been able to—if not for you."

"There is no use in *if*, Diego." I sat in my leather chair and leaned back. Diego continued to stand tall, though I read the agitation in his eyes and hands. "What's done is done."

"So that's it. You'll ruin the Cruzes too? Stand back and watch as the cartel takes revenge on everyone involved—me, my men . . . Natalia?"

I didn't respond at first, letting that sink in for Diego. He had fucked with me, and now I had the power to destroy him and everyone he loved. His precious Natalia too, who'd be especially devastated since she'd been lying to herself for years that she wanted nothing to do with this life. Now his sins would be hers.

When recognition of my reach began to cross his features, I spoke again.

"Ángel Maldonado and I happen to have an amicable relationship," I said, crossing an ankle over one knee. "For his mercy, I will pay a hefty price, but it can be arranged—for those I find deserving, at least."

His shoulders loosened just a little. "I figured as much. So what do you want in exchange for that 'hefty price'?"

"From you? Nothing. I'll pay the toll to spare Costa and his family —who have acted as *my* family."

"And me?" he asked, drawing back. "Your own brother?"

"You've been in my shoes." I opened the top drawer of my desk and took out a box of Cubans. "You had the chance to save my life by speaking to my innocence, but you didn't."

"I was trying to protect the family you claim to love. I had no reason to believe you weren't guilty."

I cut the tip of one cigar and glanced up at Diego to scrutinize his reaction to what I said next. "I'm not sure I believe that."

His jaw set as the pulse at the base of his neck quickened. He flattened his hands on my desk. "Whatever lies you've convinced yourself of, you can't hide from the truth. You'd murder your own brother."

"No. The Maldonados will do it for me." I flicked my lighter and held the flame to the end of the cigar. "You left me at the mercy of another—now I'll do the same for you."

"Why not just shoot me here?" he asked. "Don't you have the guts?"

"I hope for a long, prosperous relationship with Costa if he wants one."

"And killing me might jeopardize that."

"I'm not killing you. You got yourself into this mess. I'm simply not going to help you." I puffed on the cigar, feeling gratified, then offered it to him. "Eye for an eye, Diego. It's more than you deserve after everything you've done."

He ignored my gift and straightened up, regaining composure as if he'd grasped an answer that could earn his freedom. There was none, but I'd play along until I got bored. I'd waited for this moment too long to rush it.

"You want to see me stripped of everything? My family, my money, my woman?" he asked. "You hold the cards, Cristiano. *Tienes todo el control*. I'm at your mercy—but you cannot let the Maldonados go through with this. They won't just kill me... they will make an example of me—"

"As they should." I traded the cigar for my drink. With a celebratory sip of tequila, I ran my tongue over my teeth, pleased to find revenge had hints of peach and sweet agave. "There has been a snake in the grass far too long, and it's only fair somebody separate its deceitful mind from its body."

He began to pace in front of my desk. "Name your price, then."

"There's none."

"There's always a price. Whatever it is, however high, tell me now."

I watched him quietly, reveling in the way his eyebrows knitted together when the truth dawned on him. *This* was the final puzzle piece he'd come looking for today, the one thing he couldn't figure out. What did I want in exchange for taking mercy on him?

Nothing.

I hadn't manipulated him into this position to extract anything. Because of him, I'd suffered. For years, I'd been on the run, looking over my shoulder for a *sicario* in the dark. I'd lived with the knowledge that the people I'd cared for most had thought me a traitor. I had pulled myself from nothing and built an empire. I was wealthier than God and surrounded by a steadfast army. I'd made peace with Costa. All that remained was to see my brother pay for his sins, which I suspected ran deeper than he was willing to admit.

And now I would.

And now he knew the truth.

Betrayal had a price, and even family had to pay.

"Confess your sins and pray for mercy," I said. "But you'll get none from me."

Diego had plans to take over Costa's cartel and drag down Natalia as he followed in my father's footsteps, but I wouldn't allow it. The world would be a better place devoid of any de la Rosa men, but especially without the two of them.

Diego shut his eyes, his chest expanding with each deep breath. When he looked at me again, his gaze burned with hatred. "You can't do this," he said.

"It is done." I looked to Maksim, Eduardo, and Alejo—my friends and my *compadres*—as I spoke to Diego. "You can run. I did for years. But I expect you won't make it months." I returned my eyes to my brother. "Then again, perhaps you'll surprise me."

"Or *perhaps* I'll spend my final days in California. Natalia is headed back soon. She'd like to have me with her."

I flattened a hand on my desk. I could order the Maldonados not to kill Natalia, but there was no guarantee they wouldn't if she purposely got in the way. I hadn't been able to stop my mother from supporting and defending my father's decision to get into the sex trade industry.

"You'd be putting Natalia at risk. You know what they'd do to her. It would be selfish. Are you a selfish man, Diego?"

He glanced away.

I didn't need an answer. I'd convince Costa to keep Natalia close in the coming days. With his help, no harm would befall her. I took a final pull from my cigar and stood, cracking my knuckles. "Do as you please with your final days. We're finished here." From my pocket, I took a silver coin and flipped it at him.

He caught it and turned it over in his palm. "What's this?"

"The ferryman demands a toll to take passengers to the underworld," I said. "This one's on me. Safe travels to hell, *hermano*."

Diego stood his ground, raising cold, bitter eyes to mine. "I'll beg if that's what it takes. Whatever you want, it's yours."

"You have nothing to offer me. What've you got that I can't buy for myself?"

"Besides my loyalty—information," he said. "I know everything there is to know about Costa's business. I can give you inside access. Together, we can take over his cartel and you can rule them both with me as an advisor."

"I have no need for Costa's business, but if I did, I'd manage to secure it fine without you." I signaled for my men to remove Diego.

"Help me leave town," Diego said, growing louder as he rushed out his final pleas. "This will be the last you ever see or hear of me. You can tell everyone, including the Maldonados, I attacked you and died as a traitor. Tell them anything."

I rose from my chair, buttoning my jacket as I strolled around the side of my desk to face him. "You've plotted against Costa; why should I believe you wouldn't do the same to me? I can already see the wheels turning in your mind as a plan forms. I won't spend my life looking over my shoulder anymore."

"I will, you have my word," he rushed out. "I'll disappear completely."

"Your word means nothing. A parasite doesn't change its ways." I nodded to Maksim. "Remove him."

Eduardo and Alejo rushed forward like a stampede and took Diego's arms, forcing him toward the door.

"*Suéltame*," Diego said, struggling against them. "Get off!"

As they dragged him backward, I turned back for my cigar.

"You're wrong, Cristiano," Diego said. "About one thing, you're wrong."

Despite the desperation that remained in his voice, something about it had turned chilling, almost satisfied. He wasn't entirely defeated as he should be. Nor was he filtering himself anymore or hiding behind a persona he'd crafted.

It was enough to get me to look back and raise a hand to stop my men. I smiled. "Tell me what I'm wrong about."

His breathing evened out as smug certainty tainted his words. "You say you have everything you want—but that isn't true. Some things can't be taken. Some things must be *given*."

I narrowed my eyes on him as red light flickered and faded downstairs. "There's nothing in this world you have that I can't take for myself."

"Then you're no different from our father."

I drew back. He was right—because my father had taken *people*. If Diego was saying what I thought he was, then even *I* had underestimated the lengths he would go to to save himself. Something stirred deep inside me, a desire I tried not to acknowledge for fear of where it could lead.

"Don't think I don't know your weak spot, brother," Diego said. "Because it is mine too."

I raised my chin. I couldn't protest. I should've stopped him by now, but I hadn't—because in this area, I wasn't sure I wanted to be strong. "That's not yours to give."

"It is. Call off the Maldonados." He bowed his head and spoke ardently. "Spare my life, and I will deliver it to you."

I should've had Max finish him off there for trying to tempt me. I had a plan. More importantly, I had a code, especially when it came to human lives. I hadn't encountered many reasons in my life to break it.

But this possession wasn't only something I wanted. It was something *Diego* wanted.

And that made it all the more precious.

## CHAPTER 17

# NATALIA

I sat at my dresser in a daze, unsure of how long I'd been brushing my hair and willing my phone to ring. I hadn't heard from Diego since the warehouse had burned, and my father was making arrangements to get me out of Mexico. Diego had to know how worried I was. And how that anxiety ruled my imagination. If the Maldonados knew about the warehouse, Diego could very well be dead by now.

Until I spoke to him, there was nothing I could do but pray for his safe return. I traded my brush for a match. When I struck it, fire flamed. I held it to the wick of my Virgin Mary candle, lit a few others on my dresser, and closed my eyes.

But I didn't think of Our Lady or God or even Diego.

Instead, the devil came to mind.

Cristiano had fooled everyone around him—except me. I still hadn't completely processed Cristiano's involvement in the death of his own parents. At only fifteen, he'd come to my father, the head of their rival cartel, with information that he knew would seal their fate. How could my father have trusted someone who'd committed that kind of betrayal against his blood?

And now, Diego would pay the price.

No, I couldn't think like that. Diego would pull himself out of this, and I had to hold on to that hope for both of us. Whatever it took, I wasn't going to let him go. I couldn't. Having Mamá ripped from my arms was enough heartbreak for one lifetime. Diego wasn't just the love of my life—he was my past and future. He anchored me. We had a long life ahead of us—a cliffside California wedding, children that would resemble each of us, safety and security that had been earned over a lifetime.

Saying good-bye to all of that would be too difficult to bear.

I'd protect it however I needed to.

Diego had already shaken hands with one devil. Whether it was the Maldonados or Cristiano who held his fate, we'd take it back—even if it meant making a new deal.

No matter what my father said, I wasn't leaving Mexico until I knew Diego was safe.

I paid no attention to the first couple taps at my window, but when the third came, I jumped up. Barely noticing how my feet smarted, I ran onto the balcony, tying my robe closed, and leaned over the side. On the dark lawn, a shadowed figure looked up at me from under a black hoodie.

My heart leapt. "*Diego*," I said. "I've been trying to reach you."

He held a finger to his lips. After glancing left and right, he scaled the trellis along one wall he'd used before to sneak into my room.

I scanned the yard as he climbed, making sure nobody saw. As he reached the top, the wood lattice under his foot snapped. He jerked, cursing as he almost lost his footing. I reached for him, and a vision flashed—his fingertips centimeters from mine before he lost his grip and fell to his death.

I shook the harrowing thought from my mind. "Careful," I whispered.

He grasped my hand and heaved himself up the rest of the way. I grabbed his cheeks and pulled his mouth to mine. He thrust one hand in my hair, holding me as he devoured me for a kiss that tasted of soot, smoke, and death. My fingers traveled his face, brushing over cuts and bumps. I drew back to take in the bloodied bruises on his cheekbones, nose, and forehead.

Seeing the evidence of his fight against that morning's attack made my chin wobble.

"Oh, no, *princesa*. Don't cry," Diego said softly. "Let me in. After the last twenty-four hours, it'd be a waste for me to get shot here."

I moved so he could climb over the concrete balustrade. Once inside, I hugged his neck. "I'm so scared."

"Shh." He rubbed my back. "Come. I need you to be strong for me."

I swallowed down the urge to cry and reluctantly released him. "What's happening?"

Diego sat on the edge of the bed, put his elbows on his knees, and ran both hands through his hair. "Please forgive me for last night. Please. I need you to know that I came back for you, but you were gone."

"Against my will," I said. "I would never have left you, either."

"Cristiano." As he cupped a hand over his other fist and squeezed it, the tendons of his forearms went taut. "Did he hurt you?"

The fear and concern in his eyes made me go to him. He pulled me onto his lap and wrapped his arms around me. "No," I said. "He forced me to leave and brought me home."

His fingertips dug into my hip. "I want to curse him and thank him all at once. He may have saved your life, but it was only so he could flaunt that in my face."

"You've spoken to him?"

"Yes." Diego looked up at me, his expression pained as he caressed my back. "First, just promise me he didn't lay a finger on you."

I nearly shivered remembering Cristiano's threatening presence behind me in my bedroom. My thoughts as they'd strayed to the possibility that he'd unapologetically take what I'd saved for Diego. The way he'd held my wrist and provoked me with words to distract me from the pinch of the tweezers. His fingertips trailing up my leg, his grip on my upper thigh, his unusual reaction to hearing about my virginity.

I smoothed Diego's brown hair from his forehead. It was no less silky for whatever trauma he'd been through. "He dropped me off," I said. "That's all."

"Really?" Diego's expression eased. "He never touched you?"

"Really." I was surprised at the lie, but relief crossed Diego's face for the first time since he'd arrived.

"I never should've taken you to the warehouse," he said. "Being around me puts you in danger."

Because my father had said the same to me many times, hearing that from Diego almost felt like a betrayal. I drew back. "That's *my* choice to make," I said. "Papá wants to send me home early, but I'm not leaving you."

"When?"

"Sunday. He says we'll go to Easter Mass, but the helicopter leaves before nightfall."

"I'm doing everything in my power to get us out of this," Diego said. "I need you now more than ever—you are my strength." He glanced out my window, setting his jaw as if he were fighting himself. "But Costa is right. You shouldn't be here. I'd never be able to live with myself if anything happened to you."

"But you just said you need me." I gritted my teeth to stem a fresh wave of tears, but not because I was sad. I hated that Diego and my father wanted me gone when this was the only place I should be. "I won't abandon either of you."

"This isn't a game, Tali," he said, looking back. "When the Maldonados come for me, they'll come for us all." He lowered his voice. "We owe them a lot of money."

I would've had to have been a fool not to know that, but hearing it sent chills down my spine. "How much?"

"Millions and millions," he said quietly. "More than we can ever repay."

I covered my mouth. "There has to be a way out. Can you borrow it from somewhere? Ask for more time?"

"Years wouldn't be enough. Retribution is taken with a long arm and a firm grip. Not even Costa can protect us."

"Then we have to leave," I said, standing, ready to run the second he agreed. "Fuck this life! Just come with me."

"I can't." He reached for me. "You know there's nowhere I can run they won't follow."

I went to my closet. "Well, we can't stay here," I said, wrestling my suitcase from the top shelf. "Since when are we sitting ducks? Why not at least try to disappear? We can get passports and start over—"

"Please, Talia," he said, rising from the bed. "Don't pull away from me."

He caught my elbow and drew me into his embrace. Cupping my face, he kissed the tears that'd escaped down my cheeks. "Forgive me," he whispered, sliding his hands everywhere on my body. "I'm desperate."

His hungry lips found mine, and I grasped his hair as he took my mouth. I arched into him, letting him walk me backward toward the bed. He untied my robe and slipped his hands inside to grab my ass. His kiss grew more feverish. This time, he didn't stop it, as if sensing this might be the last time.

As that reality hit me, I choked back a sob but tried to hide my despair with a moan.

Diego wrenched himself away and strode to the other side of the room. "We can't do this." His hair fell forward, and he tucked it behind both ears. "My God, Natalia. You are so beautiful . . . but we can't. I'm weak."

"Then let us be weak together."

He paced the room. "It was a mistake to let myself fall in love with you, but I could no more help it than I could growing older each day."

My gut smarted as if his words had delivered a punch to my stomach. "You don't mean that."

"How can I not?" His anguished eyes met mine. "I'm a dead man. I'll never have you. Not now."

"Don't talk like that." My throat thickened again. "You'll find a way out of this, and then my father will understand—"

"Your father? He's the least of our worries." Diego unzipped his hoodie, balled it up, and tossed it on my reading chair. It slipped over the arm onto the floor. "It's *over*, Tali—don't you see?" He strode back and forth, his muscles straining his black t-shirt each time he thrust his hands in his hair. "Even if I found a way out of this, Costa would never forgive a failure of this magnitude."

"Then there's nothing keeping us here," I said, reaching for him. "We have to go."

He avoided my eyes as if it was easier to pretend I wasn't here. "They'll find us, and when they do, they'll kill us both. I can't put you in that position." Finally, he stopped moving and pinched the inside corners of his eyes. "I'm as good as dead. The only peace I can have now is knowing you're safe."

My chest stuttered with a panicked breath. Fear crept into every part of my body. I had known it was bad, but seeing Diego come apart in front of me made everything even more real. He'd never expressed anything close to this level of anguish. "We'll elope," I said. "Papá will understand how much I love you, and he'll find a way to stop the Maldonados. He has that power."

"He doesn't," Diego said. "If he did, he would've stopped them already because he . . ." His jaw squared as if he were checking his emotions. "He's in just as much danger as I am."

*No*. My heart fell to my feet. I'd lose the two people who meant the most to me in the world. I put my hands over my face. "They'll kill him too."

"I'm sorry." His voice came out strangled. "I'm so sorry, Tali."

I wanted to sink into a ball on the floor, but that wouldn't help. As despair weighed on me, I forced myself to hold it together. I picked up his hoodie to fold it over the arm of my chair. "There has to be another way. There must be."

"There . . ." He hesitated. "There is."

I glanced up at him, unsure I'd heard him correctly. "What is it?"

"It's not on the table," he said. "I won't involve you in any way."

*Me*? I could do something? I didn't care what it was. I hurried over to take his hands. "If I can help, let me. *Please*."

He brought the backs of my hands to his lips. "I don't deserve you. You should walk away now."

"You must know I'd die for you if it came to that," I said firmly.

He swallowed, his eyebrows cinching. "Tali."

"I would," I said. "Now tell me what can be done."

With obvious trepidation, he paused for a breath, seeming to struggle to get the words out. "The Maldonados are too powerful. Nobody who would help us can match them. They don't fear us—but they could."

Hope surged in me. There was a way—that was all that mattered. Not all was lost. I would take a sliver of hope over nothing. "How?"

"Neither your family nor mine is strong enough to stand against them alone. But together . . ."

*Together*. Two families standing as one. Unified.

"You've been part of our cartel longer than you haven't," I said. "We *already* stand together."

"Not officially."

To bind our families in a legal sense meant . . .

*Marriage*.

My heart soared. Relief and joy—and a sense of rebellion—spread through me. They thought they could destroy us, but we'd fight back. My father thought he knew better, but he'd see that keeping us apart wasn't the answer. Taking Diego's name was not only a privilege, but now it was my destiny. I could save us—and I'd be getting exactly what I'd always wanted.

"We'd stay in the shipping business but bring on a weapons and narcotics division," Diego explained. "Each cartel would benefit from the others' infrastructure. Pooling our resources, network, and cash, we'd become a formidable front."

"Father would forbid it," I cautioned. "He'd never let us go through with it."

"Once it was done, he'd be forced to see it was the only way. Our houses, united, expands his empire. He'd control the movement of his own drugs and guns—we'd be untouchable."

"But where do the drugs and guns come from?" I asked.

"Cristiano."

My stomach dropped. So it had come to that—making a deal with

Hades to get another devil off our back. "But he set all of this in motion. Why would he help us?"

"Because it gives him power. Even more than our parents had. More than your father has. More than the Maldonados." He closed his hands over mine, pressing my palms together as if we were both in prayer. "That was his goal all along, and this is the fastest way to get it. He gains more than he did as Costa's partner—the protection of family. He knows what it means to bear the Cruz-de la Rosa name."

I got a silent thrill hearing our names together that way, even if it meant tying us to Cristiano. For once, I didn't feel so helpless. I could act. Wanting to marry Diego—to take his name and give myself to him in every sense—no longer felt small, selfish, or disobedient. With our promise to each other before God, I'd be saving us all. There was no holier union than that.

"But *would* Cristiano help us?" I said. "Have you asked?"

"It came up when we spoke earlier, but I'd decided not to ask this of you."

"I'm glad you did," I said.

"If you go, Tali, you at least have a chance of survival. Your safety can be arranged, and you can continue your schooling. Agreeing to this means—"

"I stay. I know." None of that mattered now. I could figure out my school situation later. "Did Cristiano agree when you spoke to him?"

"He's greedy and calculating. For once, it works in our favor. But a warning—I'd have to be willing to promise him anything to get him on our side. Even if I don't mean to keep those promises. Once we're safe and can regroup, we'll strategize a way to separate from him." Diego gently took my face, thumbing the corners of my mouth. "I wish it had never come to this, Tali, but it's where we are. Would you do this for me?"

My heart skipped. I didn't need a proposal or pretty words or a grand gesture. I just needed Diego. "Life or death. I belong to you in either."

He swooped down to wrap his arms around my waist and lift me off my feet. "What have I done to deserve your love and loyalty?"

"*Everything.*"

He brushed kisses along my neck and jaw, eliciting a shiver from my body. I had no idea how it was possible that moments ago, everything had felt hopeless, and now I couldn't stop smiling. "How do we do it?" I asked.

He caressed my cheek with his stubble, a scrape that soothed me with its familiarity. "On Sunday, pack your bags before Mass. Bring them. Don't breathe a word to your father, or he'll try to stop us." Finally, his eyes danced as his posture straightened once again. It felt good to be able to take away his worries. "When we were kids, you wanted to go to Antarctica."

I laughed. "Are we going on a trip?"

"No, but is the coldest place on Earth still on your bucket list?"

"I thought it sounded exotic—it was always so hot here. The grass was greener and all that."

He smiled. "I'm not even sure they have grass there. So where do you want to go?"

Fleetingly, I thought of my life in California, and all the dreams I'd had for us there. Was that over? Or on hold? I couldn't think of that now. Nothing mattered more than the man standing in front of me. "Why?" I asked. "Will we have to leave for a while?"

"No, *mi amor*." He lowered me onto my feet. "Just indulge me."

*Ah*. A honeymoon? He kept me in his arms as I kept mine around his neck. I lifted one shoulder, trying not to seem too giddy. "I've been many places with Papá. New York, Buenos Aires, São Paulo . . . and I've seen even more with my school friends." I ran my palm down his wide, muscular chest. "But I've not yet been to Southern Europe. I'd like to see Tuscany."

"Make me a promise," he said, absentmindedly twirling the ends of my hair around his finger. "If things get hard, if you miss me and we can't connect, promise me you'll dream of us under the warmth of the Italian sun. When it's dark, and you're worried the light won't come again, dream up ideas for us to do once we can get there."

As tempting as it was to fall into that fantasy, all I heard was what he wasn't saying. Was there a chance we'd be separated? "Diego . . ."

He kissed the tip of my nose. "Just know that it may not be right away, but we'll make it to Europe one day. When the time is right."

I balled his t-shirt in my fist. "You're making me nervous."

"*I'm* the one who's nervous." He raised his eyebrows. "See the sweat on my temple?"

I blew gently on his hairline to cool him. "What is it?"

He took my hands, kissed each of my palms, and held them between us as if we were standing at the altar. "I can't ask what I want to ask. It wouldn't be right. But . . ."

I blinked up at him. What could possibly make him nervous when his life had just been on the line—and still was?

*Oh.* With the realization, I involuntarily rose onto my toes with excitement. We were promising our lives to each other. I didn't need a proposal—but now that I was getting one, I couldn't keep my grin at bay. "Yes?"

"Natalia." He smiled down on me, gently squeezing my hands. "Make an unworthy man happy. Meet me at the church this Sunday."

# CHAPTER 18

# NATALIA

It was a question that had only one answer.

There wasn't a sliver of doubt in my mind that I'd marry Diego. He'd been my best friend and my love for a long time, but now, he'd finally be my husband. "Yes," I whispered. "I will meet you at the church on Sunday."

He lifted my hand to kiss my ring finger. His lips lingered there until he pressed his forehead against the back of my hand. "*Por favor,*" he whispered. "Holy Virgin Mary."

"What's wrong?" I asked at the overwhelming sadness in his appeal. "Why don't you look happy?"

"I am, but I fear what lies ahead."

The gauzy curtains of my balcony fluttered, causing the candles on my dresser to flicker. I pulled him by his hand toward the bed. "Then lie with me and forget."

"Tali . . ."

"It's not a request." Diego and I had waited long enough. I had no more doubts about making this union. My heart hammered as I slipped my robe over my shoulders. "I almost lost you today," I said, tugging on the sash to open the bow. My robe fell to my feet, revealing my negligee. "And I'll be damned if either of us leaves this world without having spent a night together."

"You *may* be damned, Tali."

"I won't, because I know what's true in my heart." Sunday, we'd commit ourselves to each other before God, but tonight, we'd make love as husband and wife in our souls.

"And what's true?" he asked.

I put my hand to his cheek. "That I love you."

"And I you." His eyes roamed over my short, strappy nightgown. "You are so lovely in indigo silk that matches your eyes."

"*Mi madre* said a lady never wore anything less than the best to bed."

He smiled crookedly at his basic black tee and chinos. "I'm underdressed."

"You're *over*dressed. If you want to see more, you have to show more."

He arched an eyebrow. "A motto I can stand by." Bathed in candlelight, he grimaced as he slowly pulled his shirt over his head.

"Are you hurt?" I asked.

"A couple bruised ribs, nothing more."

I gently pressed my lips to a purple mark blooming on his chest and then a small gash on his right bicep. "I'm sorry."

"I'm not. I'm still standing. And here with you, no less."

I touched the button of his pants, pausing to ask for permission. It came in the form of his low-lidded stare as he wet his lips. I undid his pants and pushed them down.

He cast them aside, took my chin, and tilted my eyes up to meet his. After a tender kiss to my forehead, then the bridge of my nose, he gathered up the hem of my negligee. I raised my arms so he could slip it over my head.

He stepped back, gripping the purple silk as his eyes drifted down my bare breasts and stomach to my lacy underwear. I kept my shoulders back even as nerves tickled my tummy. He'd never seen me this way. I knew he'd been with other girls—and that I actually meant something to him. But as he stared, doubt took over. Had he been expecting more? Was he worried about my inexperience? Or was it simply too strange to see his best friend naked?

He wore only boxer briefs, but it wasn't much different than seeing him in a bathing suit.

"Well?" I asked finally.

"My life is on the line," he said, swallowing, "and yet, I don't believe I've ever experienced such happiness."

My heart fluttered, pumping relief throughout me. "I've heard it only gets better from here."

He grinned, then swooped down to hug my waist and litter kisses on my neck until I laughed.

"You were never *this* ticklish when we were younger," he said, lifting me so my legs wrapped around him.

"Well, you never tickled my neck, did you?" I arched into him as he lowered me to the mattress and climbed over me. I bent and opened my knees to make a home for his hips.

"Would you like to hear my ode to you now?" he asked when we were mouth to mouth.

I nodded breathlessly.

He cupped my cheek, thumbing the apple of it. "She is a heavenly creature cut from the finest cloth with which God had to work. A fabric *so* fine, that to be dressed in it is to be a king, and to forget anything that came before it." He paused as candlelight flickered over his face. I ran a fingertip along a cut near his hairline. "Her love is all-consuming and more addictive than any high. It can twist fantasy to truth and make honest men lie—without blame. Those hopeless to receive it turn mad."

I didn't know any other man who felt so deeply, much less possessed the gift of expressing it so beautifully. A tear of love and joy slid down my cheek. "Diego."

"There is no greater pleasure than to be in the presence of your love," he finished.

I put my arms around his neck and pulled him down to me. He kissed me, running a hand along my waist and under my backside, then drew me against him.

I gasped softly as the length of him slid over my thigh. I was both eager and tentative to finally touch him. I wanted to do it right, to know that I could make him feel good.

He brushed his lips along my neck, and I quivered as he kissed my collarbone, then down my chest. "I can't believe we've held off this long," he said.

"Our patience has been admirable."

"Our patience has been *foreplay*," he said, running his tongue along the skin under my nipple, "and it will be rewarded."

In that moment, the sensation of his breath cooling my tender skin was the best thing I'd ever felt—until he pulled my nipple into his mouth and sucked, sending ripple after ripple of pleasure down my stomach.

"*Oh*." I moaned, inadvertently drawing my shoulder blades together to give him more access.

"I'm trying not to rush, my love—but I can't wait much longer to be inside you," he said before lavishing the same diligent attention on my other breast.

My heart skipped at the thought of unleashing a fire between us that had been simmering for years. I wanted to tear through our patience, but I was grateful for Diego's slow, careful movements that forced me to savor this.

He took the elastic band of my underwear between his teeth and tugged it down, murmuring, "*Jesucristo*."

Calling for Jesus between my legs inspired thoughts of heaven and hell. As Diego discarded my panties, parted my thighs, and slid his tongue over my core, I was reminded of his brother's hands threatening to trespass. No, I didn't think of Jesus, or my Diego and his tender promises, but of the antichrist's violent passion.

I thought of Diego's brother.

I jerked my head to the other side as if it would rid him from my mind, and my eyes landed on the framed Virgin Mary over my dresser.

"Diego," I said, shoving away thoughts that could only be blamed on the stressful events of the past few days.

"Hmm?" His response vibrated before he plunged his tongue inside me.

I gripped his hair with the unnerving sensation. It felt neither good nor bad, just new. A friend of mine in California liked to brag that her boyfriend ate pussy like he was trying to get all the meat off a chicken bone, and ever since, I'd been scared just at the thought of it—but Diego's gentle tonguing wasn't anything like that.

"Talia?" he asked.

"Hmm?"

"You shouldn't be this . . . quiet."

"I'm not—I think I hear something," I said.

He stilled, glancing up at me. "Really?"

I shook my head, putting a finger over my mouth to quiet him. Footsteps echoed in the hallway. Papá was unlikely to be anywhere but his bedroom or study this late, and since my mother, he'd never had overnight visitors. Nobody wandered the halls of the second floor except the housekeepers, Barto, or the security team.

"I don't hear anything," he whispered.

Neither did I.

Perhaps they'd been phantom footsteps, sleek dress shoes that'd followed me to the foot of my bed earlier that day. Cristiano had cleaned me, bandaged me—tended to me without my explicit permission. He hadn't violated me, but if he had, he wouldn't take care like Diego did. Cristiano would eat pussy like a wild animal feasting on its kill, fending off any other predator foolish enough to approach. *I'm scarier than any monster.* Twin threads of revulsion and desire pulled sharply in my tummy, and I sucked in a breath at a visual that should've appalled me.

"There she is," Diego said. He slipped his arms under my hips and gripped them as he pulled me hard onto his mouth.

"*Ay*," I breathed on a moan.

"*¿Te gusta?*" he asked and then dove back in. He went from licking and sucking my most intimate spot to making love to it with his mouth. His tongue plunged deep and flicked over my clit. When he added one finger, and then another, my back bowed as I cried out.

"This is just the warm-up," he said, smiling at me from between my legs. "But no matter how wet I get you, or how careful I am, you might bleed."

"I know. The maids will think it's my period."

He climbed up my body and kissed my breasts again, sending spasms of pleasure through me with each pull of my nipple into his mouth. He took one between his teeth and pinched, and I bucked my hips into him.

"I think you might be ready for me, Tali."

"I'm ready," I said, nearly panting. A flush had worked its way up my chest; I was burning up for him.

I threaded my fingers through his hair, focusing on the way he dragged the tip of his tongue up my breastbone to the base of my neck. His fingers trailed down my side and over the curve of my hip. Just his presence made my head swim and my toes curl—what could lay ahead except more bliss as we fed a hunger we'd been forced to conceal for so long?

I lowered my hand between us, cupping my palm over his hardness. With just that simple touch, he was already pleading me with his eyes. "Don't stop there," he whispered. "Give me more."

He pushed his underwear down and kicked it off the bed. Finally, I held him, skin on skin, the full remarkable length of him in my hand. He was bigger than I'd imagined—not that I'd known what to expect or had anything to compare it with.

He would be my one and only. My forever.

The perfect first time with my perfect man.

Diego smiled down at me as if we shared the thought. "You're glowing."

His hair fell in a dark curtain around his face. I pushed some strands of it behind his ear. "I'm happy. I'm ready."

He nudged my legs apart. "You'll tell me if it's too much?" he asked.

I nodded and glanced between us, taking him in for the first time. Pink, long, hard—and all mine. Perfect. And naked. There would be nothing between us, and as much as I wanted to feel every inch of him, seeing him prepare to enter me also forced me from my fantasy into reality.

"Wait," I said.

He lifted up on one arm. "What is it?"

"We should get a condom," I said.

He took himself in his hand, sliding the head over me in a way that made me bite my lip. "You have no idea how fucking good it feels without one."

I moved onto my elbows. "I'm not ready for . . . you know. I'm not taking the chance that I could—get pregnant . . ."

"I want our first time to be pure." He grazed his fingertips over my cheek and lowered his mouth to my ear. "Let me empty myself in you, just this time. Mark you as mine, first and always."

A primal desire for the same rose inside me. I wanted that too, but with such uncertain days ahead of us, we couldn't take the risk. "Then we'll have to wait," I said, and started to close my legs. "Once our future is more—"

"Wait." He grabbed one of my thighs, staying it.

*Was he forceful with you?*

I hated that Cristiano's unfounded accusation popped into my head. Maybe violence ran in their bloodline, but Diego wasn't his brother or his father. He'd never pressure me as Cristiano had implied.

"I'm sorry," he said after a second, releasing my leg to get up from the bed. "You're right."

Though he tried to hide it, I sensed his frustration. I was disappointed as well. I drew a throw from the end of my bed over myself as he picked up his pants from the floor. "You're leaving?"

"*Leaving?*" He gaped at me. "Not unless you toss me over the balcony, and even then, I can't promise I won't climb back in." He took something from his pocket, made claws, and crawled with exaggerated movements over the bed to me. "I won't be deterred," he said, snatching the blanket and tossing it away. He tickled my sides until I squirmed. "I'll keep coming back for more."

I laughed, relieved that he wasn't angry. "I'm sorry, Diego," I said. "I don't want to stop, but—"

"Stop? Are you mad?" He flicked up two fingers. Between them, he held a foil packet. "*Nothing* will ruin our first time."

I flopped back onto my pillow as my anticipation returned. "Thank God."

"Thank *me* for being prepared. *El Señor* has *nada* to do with it." With a sexy grin, he used his teeth to tear open the packaging. "Still ready for me?"

I sighed happily up at the ceiling. "I've been ready."

"Get under the covers," he said, drawing back the comforter.

I slipped between the sheets. He rolled on the condom and climbed in after me. "Kiss me," he said from above.

I lifted my head to meet his lips. We each took a breath, and then he opened my mouth with his, running his tongue over mine, nipping my bottom lip. He grasped the side of my neck, his thumb caressing my throat as he deepened the kiss.

"Are you still wet?" he murmured, lowering a hand to touch me. I spread my legs for him, and he found his answer there. "Good, my love. Very good. I love you, Natalia."

I nodded, struggling to speak as I prepared my mind and body for what was to come. "I love you too."

I held my breath as he lined himself up between my hips, then fisted the sheets as he began to press inside me. "Good?" he asked.

My body resisted at first, but with a push, he slid in partway, and I exhaled with relief. Any pain I might've experienced was non-existent under Diego's care. "Yes, weird."

His eyebrows rose. "Weird?"

I covered my mouth. I'd meant to agree with him. It *was* good, of course. I was exactly where I wanted to be. But in a way, it was also strange. I had dreamed of this moment, worried it might never come. Diego had always been around, watching over me, protecting and shielding me. I remembered looking up to him as a girl, too young to recognize I was falling in love with my best friend.

And then realizing he was more than a best friend.

He was a man, and I was head over heels for him. I hadn't come down to Earth since; I was still floating on cloud nine.

In his green eyes, I saw everything—a *past* that consisted of pain and support and unconditional love. A *present* that added to the framework of our promising *future*. He'd looked upon me this same way many times, with hope and tenderness.

"We've known each other so long. We've talked about this and now we're doing it—what I'm trying to say is . . ." I glanced away. *Weird*? I felt silly I'd picked the wrong word to describe this.

He turned my face back to his and pecked me. "Keep going. Tell me every thought you have in that beautiful brain."

I smiled a little as my muscles loosened, and I relaxed deeper into the mattress. "The weird part is that being with you now *isn't* as strange as my friends said the first time would be. I'm . . . I'm happy."

"I know you are," he said. "I recognize my own feelings in your eyes."

He slipped his arms under me to cradle my shoulders as he nuzzled my cheek. He pressed his lips there, then to the corner of my mouth.

I wrapped my legs around him and urged him deeper.

"You've been one of the only constants in my life," he said. "There were times even Costa overlooked me. But you, well . . . your love continues to anchor me."

"And me," I said.

He relaxed on top of me, giving me more of his body weight—he finally let go. I wrapped my arms around his neck as he entered me completely. He stayed rooted there a moment as our breath synced, then drew back and drove inside me. I bit my bottom lip, expecting some kind of pain, but it only felt right. And his first plunge only made me crave the next.

As I picked up the rhythm of his lovemaking, I met his thrusts with my hips. Each move he made came with a tender caress or a look of askance, making sure I was comfortable. He was every inch the gentleman, but I sensed there was also a hunger for me he kept bridled so as not to hurt me. I looked forward to unleashing that passion in him.

His drives became hungrier, faster, harder. His hand slipped between us and he knew just the right place to touch me to bring me to the edge. He looked down on me, arresting my gaze. Any time I got shy or my lids started to fall shut with pleasure, he called me back. The electricity between us crackled, pulling me out of this world and into a deeper state of love with him. It was just us, nothing else existed, and suddenly my body was spasming, drawing him deeper, contracting around him as he shuddered and came along with me.

Neither of us moved for a while, and I didn't want it any other way. My only desire was to stay in Diego's embrace and receive the love he showered on me.

To be with him for as long as time would allow.

And to bask in the glow of knowing that in only two nights, I'd officially be a de la Rosa.

## CHAPTER 19

# NATALIA

Bells pealed overhead as Pilar and I navigated our way to the church. We opened the gate, passed the garden, and found an unlocked door in back.

How Diego had secured the church so quickly, and on Easter, I had no idea, but he'd sent word that someone would come for me when it was time.

Inside, I found us an empty room with some chairs and a full-length mirror. I set down a garment bag and tote, disturbing a cloud of dust motes that sparkled in the light coming from gothic-style windows.

"Can you get out my dress?" I asked Pilar, unpinning my hair since I'd put it up to set.

"Why are we here?" She unzipped the bag.

My hair fell to my waist in large shiny black curls. I looked at Pilar in the mirror. "Because I'm getting married today."

She froze, her hand in the bag. Slowly, she withdrew a cream lace dress. "*What?*"

I turned and unzipped my Easter dress to shimmy out of it. "It's a long story, but Diego's in danger."

"And?"

"And a wedding will get him out of it." I reached for the bridal gown. "Hand me that."

"Get *him* out?" she asked, handing me the slinky lace. "Or bring *you* in?"

I waved a hand. "We have a plan."

"Natalia . . ." She made a noise akin to a whimper. "It's just, I know how important marriage is to you, and that you've dreamed of having a beautiful ceremony with all of your family there. You can't do it as part of a *plan*."

I stepped into the long dress and slipped my arms into its full sleeves. "I *want* to marry him," I said, walking over to take her hands. "It's not just a plan. If it works, I'll save Diego. If it doesn't . . ."

Pilar paled. "What?"

Then at least Diego and I would have this day together.

Heaviness weighed on my chest. I didn't want today to be anything other than perfect, though. I took a cleansing breath and forced the thought away with a smile. "I'll be Diego's wife, Pila, and our two families combined will be too powerful to challenge."

She frowned. "Exactly what kind of danger is he in?"

My body tightened, but I focused on survival. I needed to keep positive thoughts and prayers for all of us. I drew my hair over one shoulder and turned, then frowned at the black strappy heels on my feet. "Damn. I forgot to bring my silver shoes. Will you do me up?"

"Where'd you even find a gown this late?" she asked, moving behind me to start with the bottom button.

"It was my mother's." I admired the dress in the mirror. The high-necked ivory bodice was fitted but not tight, and the lace around my neck was intricately crafted. The dress had buttons all the way from my lower back to my nape.

"Costa doesn't mind that you're wearing this?"

"He doesn't know. I had to sneak the dress out."

Pilar touched her forehead. "*Dios mío*, if Costa finds out I helped, he'll put me in the grave."

"Don't worry. You'll be the last thing on his mind. He'll be either too relieved to care, or he'll kill Diego—which I hope he doesn't, because we're going through a lot of trouble to keep him safe from the Maldonados."

"The *Maldonados?*" She muttered something and made the sign of the cross. "*That's* who he's in trouble with?"

"*Sí.* It's scary, I know. That's why we have to go to extreme lengths."

"Hopefully they involve *una bruja*. He'll need black magic to immortalize himself if he has upset them. Or to resurrect him from the grave."

When she'd done the last button, I turned in the mirror. The dress just grazed the tops of my heels. I frowned. "It's too short."

Pilar squatted to inspect the hem. "I can let it out quickly. It won't be perfect, but because of the lace, you won't be able to tell much."

Pilar got a sewing kit from my bag, squatted at my feet with a seam ripper, and did her best to lengthen it. "You won't miss having Costa walk you down the aisle?" she asked.

I didn't have to consider my answer. I would, of course. The thought of it had been plaguing me for days. "Yes," I admitted. "But once Diego and I are safe and everything is as it should be, we'll have a real wedding and a huge celebration, hopefully in California." I could envision it perfectly, a cliffside resort where we could have an outdoor ceremony in late summer as the sun set on the water, then a reception on a dancefloor strung with lights. "You can be my maid of honor. I'll throw you the bouquet so I can set you up with a handsome American."

"A *gringo?*" she asked, incredulous.

"*Bueno, un chicano.*"

She smiled a little. "What about Manu?"

"You're too good for him," I said, but I knew there was slim chance of getting Pilar out of the marriage her parents were hell-bent on arranging.

She waggled her dark eyebrows as she tugged on the lace. "Are you ready for your wedding night?"

I failed to suppress my smile. I shouldn't tell Pilar what Diego and I had done, but I was too giddy. "We already had it."

Her mouth fell open. "*¿En serio*? Really?"

I nodded hard. "Friday night, he stayed with me."

Her eyes widened. She lowered her voice. "At your dad's house? How was it?"

"Magical. He was such a gentleman, and made sure I enjoyed every second." I searched her face for judgment. When she didn't respond, I continued, "People say your first time is bad, but it didn't hurt at all."

"Well, that's the most you can ask for."

I agreed. There was a great deal of passion between Diego and me that we hadn't even explored because he'd been holding back so as not to hurt me. I could only imagine that next time, we'd be tearing off each other's clothes like animals. "It was perfect."

Pilar sat back on her heels. "How's that?"

The dress swung at the bottoms of my heels. "Better. What am I missing?"

"A bouquet."

I gasped, covering my mouth. "I completely forgot."

"Just take something from the garden," she said.

I glanced out the window. "Do you think Father Rios will mind?"

"Without the money your family has donated, there'd be no garden at all."

"There's a flowerbed out there in my mother's name."

Pilar came up behind me and rubbed my back. "She's here now. I'm sure of it. Anyway, without a bouquet, you'd be offending the Virgin of Guadalupe."

"Ah, *verdad*. I need an offering in exchange for her blessing." I removed my shoes, gathered up my dress, and walked across the lawn behind the church. Sparrows chirped in the trees as I entered the garden that bore roses, lilies, marigolds, dahlias . . .

I closed my eyes and breathed in their fragrance, curling my toes in the springy, freshly cut grass before I picked red roses and white lilies and arranged them into a small bouquet.

I glanced up at a hovering monarch butterfly. I'd never seen a rare, elusive white one, and likely never would, but nonetheless, I stopped to appreciate this one in all its colorful beauty. It passed over the roses and landed in a ray of sunshine atop a lone group of marigolds.

I smiled to myself until it hit me—marigolds were the flower of the dead. "Mami?" I whispered.

It wasn't the season for monarchs, not like autumn. They'd been everywhere during my mother's funeral, so close to *Día de los Muertos*. As a girl, I remembered each year when they'd migrate south from the States and Canada in awe-inspiring kaleidoscopes through town—especially dazzling in our yard where Mamá had planted milkweed. I regretted how she and I had captured them just to feel their wings flutter against our palms. How must it have felt to be trapped?

The same as my mother had in her final moments?

"*Lo siento mucho,* Mamá," I said, my throat thick. "I'm sorry."

I hated to admit that I understood what Diego had meant when he'd spoken of a deeply buried desire to avenge his parents' deaths. It was the kind of thing I never poked at for fear of awakening a thirst for revenge only the life of my mother's murderer could quench. And that was why I'd tried to leave this life behind. Family bonds, wealth, vengeance, and violence—it was a vicious cycle of sins and pain. I was still leaving, I told myself. Not now, not yet, but when things had settled, Diego and I would have our fresh start anywhere but here.

The butterfly fluttered her wings. "What is it?" I asked.

What wish was she trying to deliver? Or was it a message? A breeze passed through the garden, ruffling leaves. I realized I was gripping the stems of my bouquet, and a thorn had pricked me. I sucked my fingertip and tasted metallic just as I got the sudden sensation I was being watched. I glanced around, but nobody was there.

Thoughts of my mother, and hope that she was looking down on me, should've brought happiness, but suddenly, a sense of dread permeated the fragrant air.

The wind picked up, blowing my hair into my face as the monarch flew off through the trees. I watched until she was out of sight. In the distance, the sky had darkened to a deep blue-gray, the way it only did in the desert when a storm approached.

I wished my mother was here to see me exchange vows today, but since she wasn't, I would carry her with me into the church. I squatted down to add the marigold the butterfly had landed on, the most brilliant of the bunch, to my bouquet.

I didn't doubt she'd bless my union with Diego or that she'd be at the church today in whichever form she took. She would have understood my urgency, my passion. She had loved deeply too and had given up a family to gain one.

She had known Diego was worth saving as a child and had taken him in. She would approve, I knew it.

The bird above my head stopped chirping and flew away the same instant a shadow moved over me. Two dirt-sodden boots stopped beside me, inciting a memory from eleven years earlier I often tried to forget. Blood-splattered boots and a Glock in the devil's grip. I raised my eyes, hoping to finally meet Diego, but half-expecting Cristiano. I dropped my bouquet with a gasp.

A man with pockmarked skin, scraggly, graying hair, and an angry, diagonal scar across his face looked back at me. "They're ready for you in the church, Miss Natalia."

He was hard to look at, ugly as sin, scowling even as he smiled—the stuff of nightmares. I swallowed dryly. "Who are you?"

In one hand, he held a gun at his hip. With the other, he ran a fingernail between two of his teeth and then inspected it. "I'm just s'posed to take you in."

He leaned down, and I flinched, shooting out my hand to catch myself before I fell back in the dirt. He picked up my bouquet, dusted soil from the lilies, and held it out to me. "Don't wanna forget this."

I brushed off my hands, clutched the bouquet to my breast, and hurried back to the church. Pilar waited out front with my shoes and a lace *mantilla* veil, looking uneasy.

"Who is that?" she asked, helping me back into my heels. "He came looking for you."

"I don't know," I answered.

She held up the veil and draped the ivory Spanish lace over just my hair and shoulders. "I've never seen him before," she whispered.

I glanced over my shoulder to where he waited by the door. "Diego sent you?" I asked.

"*Da*."

*Da*. Yes.

Did my father have any Russians on his payroll? It could've been, though I didn't recall one.

The man stepped forward and held out a small black box with a white satin bow. "From your intended."

I exchanged a look with Pilar, and the pit in my stomach dissolved. What was Diego up to? With renewed excitement, I took the present, slid off the ribbon, removed the top—and inhaled a sharp breath at the familiar rosary inside.

"What is it?" Pilar asked.

My eyes watered as I handed her the box and held up the gold chain of rubies and pearls. I ran my fingers over the Sacred Heart center and intricate gilt crucifix. "It's an exact replica of my mother's." I shook my head as a tear threatened to fall. "How did he remember it so well?"

"And when did he have time to make it?" Pilar pointed out.

That was an equally impressive feat. Perhaps he'd known for some time he would give it to me on our wedding day. I held it to my heart. "Thank you," I said to the man, who just shrugged his wide shoulders.

I looked over myself once more in the mirror. The beads spilled from my hand, and for the first time, I glimpsed the grace Barto had said I'd inherited from my mother. I could think of no better way to meet my groom.

We hurried to the front of the church, me with my head bowed, Pilar on one side and the Russian on the other. When we climbed the steps and reached the carved wooden doors, he pulled one open for us.

Bells began to chime. I had only an hour before Barto was supposed to pick me up to meet the helicopter. One hour to meet my fiancé, return with my husband, and break the news to my father.

"Are you coming in?" the man asked Pilar behind me.

"*Sí.*"

"If you insist." He grinned. There was something funny about the eye with a scar over it. He closed the door behind us as we entered a small antechamber that opened to the grand, high-ceilinged church.

Light spilled through the stained-glass windows, and candles lit the aisle to the altar, which was surrounded by fresh flowers, including the red roses and white lilies of my bouquet. I passed into the nave slowly, taking it all in. I would've never thought Diego could pull this together so quickly.

My heels echoed off the empty pews as I walked deeper into the church. Father Rios stood at the altar, his head bent as he murmured to himself, reading from the book in front of him. I would have to remember to thank him later for ending his services early to perform this without notice.

Three men in suits stood around the priest with their backs to me. My stomach dropped. I flattened my hand against it to quell my nerves, welcoming the coarse lace under my palm as I picked up my pace. I looked for Diego but stopped after only a few steps. My betrothed wasn't amongst them. Two of the men had rifles strapped across their suit jackets. And the third, even from behind, was unmistakable. A constant presence in my nightmares, a monster even to monsters—the devil himself.

What was *he* doing here? I took a step back.

Cristiano turned his head over his shoulder, giving me his profile. His jaw sharpened as he paused there. I didn't realize I was holding my breath until I began to feel faint. Finally, he turned and faced me. "What a beautiful bride you make, Natalia," he said, meeting my eyes. "Not that I expected anything less."

He had no reason to expect me *at all*. How dare he show his face on my wedding day? The beads of my mother's rosary dug into my palm. He looked wrong next to the elderly, homely priest—and at the altar, where Diego should've been.

The heavy door to the nave closed behind me with a *click*, causing candle flames to flicker and sigh. The distinct, pungent smell of marigolds invaded my nostrils.

Perhaps the monarch hadn't come to deliver a wish or a message—but a warning.

*Run.*

## CHAPTER 20

# NATALIA

Sunshine streamed through the archways on both sides of the church, but it didn't touch me in the center. The aisle that would lead a bride to her groom remained dim and candlelit.

The aisle that ended with Cristiano de la Rosa.

He stood in Diego's spot wearing a perfectly cut suit and a satin tie as sleek and jet-black as his styled hair. His eyes trailed from my lace-adorned neck, to the rosary and bouquet in my hands, to my ankles. Even in such a modest dress, his perusal stripped me bare. Heat warmed my cheeks. He acted as if he had every right to linger his gaze on the curves of my breasts and hips. As if he was deciding where to start. As if he owned me.

The room had gone still, not even a breath exhaled.

A pit formed in my stomach. There was a chance Cristiano had come to stand for his brother, but with the way he looked at me—possessively, but with more satisfaction than longing—I knew he wasn't here just to show support for the joining of our families.

"What have you done with Diego?" The panic in my voice reverberated off the pews around us.

Cristiano's eyes shifted over my shoulder. I turned. Diego stood at the door, sagging under the weight of something I couldn't name. It didn't matter. He was here. I ran to him and threw my arms around his neck, breathing in the heady fragrance of my bouquet and Diego's soapy scent.

He hugged me back until Cristiano barked a single warning that echoed off the high ceilings. "Diego."

Diego moved his hands to my shoulders and peeled me off, separating us. He seemed to have aged years since I'd last seen him. "My dearest Talia," he whispered, his green eyes searching mine. "My love. You know you are, don't you? My only love?"

It felt like a good-bye. Since I'd stepped into the garden, dread had been slowly gathering in me like the dark clouds on the horizon—and a storm was about to hit. I moved back and stepped on the bouquet I hadn't even realized I'd dropped. I held the rosary with both hands, as if in prayer. "Please tell me Cristiano is only here to see this merger through."

Diego scrubbed both hands over his face, then smoothed back his hair. "Everything is gone, Talia. I can't replace it, and I can't pay for it. If the Maldonados aren't already on their way, they will be soon, and they'll come after *all* of us."

"I know," I said. "I *know*, but you said you had a plan—you said . . ."

"Cristiano has admitted to the attacks. He sabotaged my deal with them."

*I knew it*. It should've come as no great shock, but heat rose up my neck and cheeks as anger brewed inside me. I gritted my teeth. "Then let *him* pay for it."

"I can't prove it. I have no credibility or influence with them. But *he* does." Diego nodded over my shoulder. "There's only one way out, and it's through him."

The only way out was to form an alliance and stand against the Maldonados. We'd already figured that out, so what did Cristiano have to do with it? "What do you mean?" I asked.

"Cristiano will settle our debts and smooth things over with the Maldonados, but only if . . ." He trailed off as if he couldn't bear to say more.

"Only if *what?*" I asked. "What about our plan? By marrying and uniting our families, we'll—"

I froze.

*Make an unworthy man happy.*

*Meet me at the church this Sunday.*

Diego had never actually proposed.

He went to touch my face but stopped himself at the last second. "I swear to you, Natalia," he said so softly, I almost didn't hear him, "I will fix this. Trust me. *Please.*"

I reached out for something to steady myself as I became lightheaded, but there was nothing. "This . . . you . . ."

Cristiano cleared his throat. "My patience grows thin, *hermano.*"

Diego glanced over my shoulder and wiped sweat from his forehead with the butt of his palm. "I told you there'd be a union of families today—"

"No." I was shaking my head—slowly at first and then harder. I ripped off my veil as it loosened. "*No.*"

Diego gripped my shoulders. "It's the only option. Cristiano will throw us at the mercy of the Maldonados unless you agree."

I breathed out a shuddering gasp, and a laugh of disbelief escaped. The space around us sharpened into a distortion of reality, as if I'd been hit with *déjà vu*. "Unless I agree to . . . to what?"

Diego nodded once. "To marry Cristiano today."

My heart thudded painfully. I dropped the veil and my rosary clattered on the wood floor. Marry *Cristiano*? I couldn't. I *wouldn't*. I shifted my gaze over Diego's shoulder to Pilar, whose eyes flitted from the men at the altar to us to the armed Russian next to her—guarding the door. Had this been planned? When? How long had Diego known?

My limbs weakened. The church's grim atmosphere said it all. I wasn't here for my wedding but for something much graver. "I can't," I whispered. "You can't ask this of me."

"That's his condition to help us." Diego glanced at the ground, and his brown hair eased around his cheeks. "I can't save us. But you can."

"*Why?*" I asked.

He squatted to pick up my rosary, clutching the beads in a fist as he spoke through his teeth. "He covets you, but he knows he cannot command you, or it would make him like my father." He lifted his eyes. "He has refused my money, servitude, power—everything." Diego stood and pressed the rosary back into my hand. "I offered to leave town so he'd never see me again, but he's determined to see me dead."

"He has refused power?" I asked, raising my voice. I couldn't look at Cristiano, but I'd make sure he heard me. "This *is* a power play. He unites two families, consolidating power for himself while stripping you of yours."

"The only thing he wants is you—and for you to willingly go to him."

I gaped at Diego, who wore a special-occasion gray suit as if he'd tried to look *nice*.

"This has *nothing* to do with me," I said evenly. "There has to be another way."

His jaw firmed as he swallowed. He pinched the inside corners of his eyes, and a tear escaped. "There *isn't*, Talia," he cried. "I'd never ask this of you if it wasn't my last resort."

"The Maldonados will come for us once they have their money," I said, trying to get him to see. "*You* said they don't forgive failure. That they'll make an example of you."

"They respect Cristiano. He can keep them at bay, and even if he couldn't, they cannot come against him and your father." His brows cinched. "Even they aren't that powerful."

I didn't want to believe it, but I knew I hadn't even begun to fathom the kind of havoc the Maldonados would wreak—not just on us, but those around us. I could almost sense them closing in now. I touched my throat as if *El Polvo* poured sand down it. *That's* who I was to marry? I had to choose between the lesser of two evils—to be married to a vicious murderer or face a mob of them.

I looked down and released my fist. The rosary beads had made indents in my palm. "The Maldonados . . ." I said. "They'll listen to Cristiano? You're sure?"

"Yes. But not until he's gotten what he wants."

*Me.*

No. I couldn't do it.

I took Diego's hands. "You and I can get married. Cristiano will still be united with my father. We'll leave. Let them have it all."

I started to turn, but Diego pulled me back. "I tried. It won't work. Walk down the aisle to him—or walk out. I'm desperate enough to beg you to do this for me"—his voice broke as his nose reddened—"but I will respect whatever you decide, Tali. I've always been willing to die for you. That hasn't changed."

"*Please,*" I said, looking at our intertwined hands. I held one up, showing him my initials on his ring finger, knowing it would say more than I could. "Please. There *has* to be another way."

Diego didn't speak, but another tear slid down his cheek. "We wouldn't be standing here if there was an alternative," he said finally, pulling his hands away. "This is it. The last option. To deny him what he wants is to put a bullet in all our heads."

"Then let them kill us!" Frustration overwhelmed me, and a sob rose up my throat. If I left here with Cristiano, I'd be stripped of a future anyway. "What kind of life would I lead with him?"

Diego inclined toward me, speaking near my ear. "It's only until I can get to you," he whispered. "I'll do anything to free you. I'll build an army against him. He won't hurt you, Tali. If he wanted that, he would've done it by now."

"No. He wants to hurt *you,* and he'll use me to do it. What do you think he'll do with me once we leave here? We'll be *married,* Diego."

He turned his face away, swallowing. "I can't think of it. If I suspected he had any intention of hurting you, I'd die first. He won't. I'm asking you to do this and hang on for me, Talia. Can you?"

Pressure built in my chest. I'd declared not days ago that I'd save him any way possible. This was what I'd been called to do to prevent us from meeting a gruesome death. "I . . ."

"You must understand—you'll be safe with him while we settle things with the Maldonados. More than you'll be anywhere else."

My jaw tingled. I was safest in the grip of a devil. Nobody was willing to budge, negotiate, or listen to reason. I pressed my hand to my chest as my anger gave way to fear for what Diego and Cristiano truly believed was about to happen. I wasn't sure Diego understood that once I belonged to Cristiano, he wasn't going to share. I would be his to do with as he pleased.

"Once he marries me," I said quietly, "he'll have only one use for me, if even that. I won't be able to escape him."

"That's enough," Cristiano said from the altar. I refused to turn and look at him. "Come to me now, Natalia, or I'm taking the deal off the table."

"Life or death, Diego," I begged. "I'm yours in either. Where you go, I will follow."

"And they will hunt us like dogs."

I swallowed through a painful lump in my throat. They would find us, but at least we'd be together. At least *I* wouldn't be left at the mercy of Cristiano. He'd restrained himself around me so far, and hadn't given me much reason to believe he'd hurt me—but I had no idea how he'd act once he thought he owned me like one of the women he kept behind Badlands' gates. Except *I* would belong to the master himself. "Then we'll face the Maldonados together," I said.

"And Costa?" Diego asked.

My heart stopped. *Papá*. They would come for all of us. Me, Diego, my father. Tepic, Jojo, Pilar. My father's family. Maybe even my mother's, who were the only ones wise enough to stay far away from this life. And it would touch them anyway. Unless I did this.

I would do this for Diego, but I *had* to do it for the man who'd given me life, who'd loved and protected me always. If I didn't, maybe I would find my father dead on the cold tile floor before they killed me too. Or took me. Was I better off enslaved to them or Cristiano? I hated that the answer was obvious.

My nose tingled, and I shut my eyes as resignation set in.

"The Cruz cartel will cease to exist," Diego said. "They'll execute those at the top to warn others, keep the ones they have use for, and discard the rest."

My core seemed to have frozen. I wrapped my arms around myself as the cold hit, inciting a shiver deep inside me. "You can't put their lives on me," I said. "Maybe I can save them, but *you* did this. Father did this. Cristiano did this. I'm innocent."

"Be that as it may," Cristiano said from behind me, "I've named my price. Turn around, Natalia."

*No. No.* I wouldn't. I grabbed the lapels of Diego's suit and pulled him close. "Please," I implored one final time. "Find a better way. Don't ask this of me."

*Defeat.* That was what I'd seen in the slump of his shoulders earlier. I could name it now because he drew up, lengthening his spine. His resignation morphed into resolution. "Okay," he said. He hesitated, then slowly enveloped me in a strong hug. He looked over my head to Cristiano. "I'm sorry. She won't do it."

I waited for relief, but it didn't come. In the following silence, my insides tangled. Cristiano's menacing presence pervaded the church. With the reality of how I'd just changed the course of things, my head filled with visions of what came next. A massacre. Bloodshed. News stories that would never be reported. Deaths that would stand for nothing and happen in vain.

"I never truly thought she'd go through with it," Cristiano said finally. "You've asked too much of her love."

*Bastard.* My teeth mashed together. My love wasn't weak as he implied. Perhaps he didn't know true love because he wasn't capable of it. He was wrong. *Life or death.* I repeated it to myself, trying to bring my courage up to meet my indignation. *Life or death.*

"Put Natalia on her plane out of the country," Cristiano continued. "Once Ángel Maldonado finds out, it's out of my hands. I can't protect even her, though I will try."

Diego's heart pounded against my cheek. "It's all right," he murmured in my ear. "I understand."

"My offer is off the table," Cristiano announced. "Max, pull the car around."

I pressed my face into Diego's chest as he smoothed my hair away and shushed my cries. I didn't want to leave this spot, but I heard the resolve in Cristiano's voice. In his footsteps down the aisle. These could be my last moments with Diego, and if I survived, I'd have to live with knowing I hadn't saved him. I would rather die by Diego's side than marry my enemy, but even death did not seem to be an option for me. Only for Diego.

Clutching the rosary, I lifted my head and asked in a watery whisper, "You'll come for me?"

He spoke into my hair, only for me. "As soon as I can. I just need time, and this is the only way to buy it."

What awaited me when I turned and faced Cristiano? What unspeakable things did he have planned once I left with him? At least with the Maldonados, there was a chance they'd kill me quickly. Cristiano and his bucket of sand wouldn't rush his torture.

Cristiano's footsteps neared.

"Wait," I said into Diego's neck. "*Espera*. Wait."

Diego tensed, then loosened, and he breathed a loud exhale near my ear. "My girl," he said, ghosting his lips over my temple. "My savior. Thank you." He rubbed my back briefly, then slid his hands to my upper arms. "Turn and go to him."

"I can't." I hiccupped. "I can't do it."

"Strength, *princesa*." Diego squeezed my shoulders affectionately, then spun me around.

Cristiano stood halfway down the aisle, tall and imposing, not a hair out of place—and utterly lacking in any softness, understanding, or empathy for what he demanded of me.

I stared at him from under wet lashes heavy with mascara. What a farce, getting made up. And in my *mother's* dress. It was profane, a sin against her sacred day with my father. "Why?" I asked Cristiano.

"I believe the words you're looking for are 'thank you.'" Cristiano walked closer to us. "Diego would be halfway to the grave if not for me."

"His life is in danger *because of you*. And you don't need me to pardon him. Look inside yourself for forgiveness, Cristiano. You were human once—he is your *brother*."

"He ceased to be anything to me long ago—and now, he is nothing to you. He deserves to die. All I did was push fate along."

"You can stop it."

"My price is very, very steep, Natalia. I can't be expected to let him go unpunished, can I? So he can make an attempt on my life?"

By Diego's words pleading me to hold on just now, he did have plans. And Cristiano likely knew it.

Cristiano stuck his hands in his pockets, looking down on me. "Didn't I warn you about him? You should've listened. At least with me, you'll be safe."

"Safe? With you? You're forcing me into marriage."

Even as I straightened up, Cristiano seemed to grow bigger. He filled the room, demanding everything of the space around him. "There's always a choice, Natalia. If there wasn't, I'd throw him to the wolves and take you anyway. Who'd stop me? Diego? He's giving you up. Your father? He isn't here. I can easily take you, but I'm offering a choice. Come with me willingly, or go and say your good-byes."

Without moving from his post, Max said, "The car is here, boss."

Cristiano checked his phone. "*Vámonos.*"

I shut my eyes and tears spilled down my cheeks. There was no more time, and no more I could say except my decision. "I'll do it," I said in darkness, then opened my eyes.

With slow, deliberate movements, Cristiano slid his phone in his jacket pocket and closed the space between us. "A lesser man would make you beg for another chance—I already took the deal off the table. But a simple 'please' would go a long way."

I dug my fingernails into my palms until they throbbed. "I won't beg."

"Oh, you will, *mariposita*. But I can be fair. I'll go first." Our gazes met, and for a moment, it was just the two of us. "Marry me, Natalia. Please."

"You're mocking me."

"I'm not." He stared into my eyes, seeming almost unsettled, as if battling something inside himself. "I've not made this arrangement lightly. I would like very much to call you my wife."

"Then you will. But I want to hear, from *your* mouth, what will happen if I don't. Diego has said it. You should have to as well."

He arched an eyebrow. "Now you're being smart. It's only good business to hear the terms of an agreement."

"This is my term—promise me you won't hurt my father."

"I have no quarrel with him."

"Swear it on my mother, who placed all of her faith in you."

He pressed his lips into a line. "You have my word."

Perhaps it was foolish to believe him, not that I had much choice, but I took him for his word.

One corner of his mouth rose into a crooked, sinister smile as he looked to Diego. "Now for the other terms you failed to mention to her."

I glanced back. Diego's shrewd green eyes were fixed on his brother. I could read the hatred in them. Cristiano wanted to torture him, and it was working.

Diego loosened his tie and turned his head out the window.

"At a loss for words? I'm happy to fill her in." Cristiano rubbed his jaw and took a few paces to one side, stopping at the end of one pew. He turned to me. "Diego has confirmed what you shared with me the other night—that you're waiting for marriage."

Diego put a hand to my back, spreading his fingers between my shoulder blades, a warning to keep my silence. Cristiano thought I was a virgin. "Why does that matter?" I asked.

"Because I want to be your first. Your last. Your only. And because denying him brings me pleasure," Cristiano said. "So there's no question—the deal is contingent on the consummation of our marriage."

My head filled with images of Cristiano's massive arms trapping me to the mattress. An ache formed between my legs as his beautiful but cruel face hovered above mine, his broken soul taking what he wanted. His broad shoulders blocking out everything else. Everyone else. *Your first. Your last. Your only.*

Had Diego come to my balcony knowing any of this? He said he'd spoken to Cristiano but had decided against bringing me into their deal. My heart said Diego wouldn't lie, but doubt formed in my mind, mingling with a tinge of humiliation over my complete faith in him. I hadn't breathed in so long that I gasped with an inhale. Had Diego taken my virginity after promising me to his brother?

Cristiano tilted his head at me, smoothing a hand over his jacket. "You *are* a virgin, aren't you, Natalia?"

To admit the truth would mean Diego's death. To lie, I feared, could mean my own—I would have to take the secret of my night with Diego to the grave. "Yes," I said. "I am."

He narrowed his eyes and took a step toward me that echoed around us. "You're sure?"

I dipped my head in a firm nod. "Yes."

"Then you, Natalia Lourdes King Cruz, and your virginity—are mine."

Surrounded by people who stood by and did nothing as Cristiano imposed his will on me, my face burned. As he declared me *his* and promised to defile and abuse me, his men stood back. And Diego—he had *arranged* this.

*You will die for him, your love.*

"What's your decision, Natalia?" Cristiano asked.

I inhaled a deep breath and exhaled the things I could not control. I had to trust that Diego wouldn't accept a life without me in it. He had to have a greater plan that would put Cristiano in the ground—this couldn't end any other way. Because I knew without being told that when Cristiano said till death do us part, he would mean that literally. Even when my use to him had run out, I wasn't naïve enough to believe he would release me.

To save Diego, I could hold on until he and my father came for me. I had known strength and poise in my mother. She'd fought back and lost, but her determination would live on—in me.

"*Que será, será,*" I said. "My answer is yes."

Cristiano stilled, his eyes dark, bottomless pits that stewed with plans—the games he would play, and the violent delights he would take. "Then it is done," he said with a rumble. "I will make you a very good husband, Natalia. Come to me."

I glanced back at Diego.

"I'm not leaving," he said. "I'll be right outside, waiting."

"You'll watch every moment," Cristiano said to him, then turned to me. "And you will not look to him again. You're finished with him. Now, come."

# CHAPTER 21

# NATALIA

Candles flickered along the aisle, burning a fiery path to the man watching me from the altar.

Cristiano de la Rosa—my future husband.

I picked up my bouquet and twined the rosary around the stems. As everyone around us looked on, I took one step toward him, then another, wobbling in my heels as the room tilted around me. I steadied myself on a pew. Cristiano tightened his shiny tie but didn't rush me.

Father Rios avoided my eyes, but when I reached him, I saw the tears in his. The suited men with guns flanked him—a bridal party from hell, hired to enforce Cristiano's will. To force fate's hand—and mine, in marriage.

I kneeled on the pillow before the priest. Organ music I hadn't noticed stopped.

"Pilar." Cristiano faced the back as his voice echoed around the room and vibrated in my chest. "*Trajiste un lazo?*"

"I-I . . ."

I didn't have to look back at my friend to know she was scared—I heard the fear in her voice. "Yes," I answered for her. "There's a lasso in my bag."

"Bring it to me," Cristiano said.

Pilar's rapid but light footsteps sounded toward us. She handed him the shoulder bag.

"You can sit," he told her, pointing to a pew behind me and said to no one in particular, "I like this tradition, this unification of man and wife." He took out a black rope and inspected it, tossing the bag aside. "Where'd you get this?"

"It's the tie from my curtains," I murmured. "That was the best I could find on short notice."

"It will do fine. Someone else lassoes us, no?" he asked the priest. "I haven't been to many weddings."

"The priest or a family member," one of his men answered. "I can, *padrino*. I did it for my sister."

Cristiano hummed. "I'd like to do it myself, if it's acceptable to the reverend."

As if anyone would stop him. Cristiano came to stand in front of me, waiting until I looked up. Even when I wasn't on my knees, he towered. Now, he reached the sky. He ran the silken cord through his hands as if deciding the best use for it. He tied the ends of the lasso together to form a circle, then tugged to tighten the knot.

Cristiano squatted in front of me and looped the rope around my neck, letting his fingers brush my throat and collarbone.

My back ached from holding it so straight, but I couldn't loosen if I wanted to. I avoided his gaze by looking at his suit. I'd never seen such fine tailoring in all my life, even though my father had benefited from my mother's good taste.

Cristiano pulled the lasso taut enough that I could feel it when I swallowed. He lifted my face by my chin. With a rough touch, he used his whole hand to palm away my tears. "I wish my bride not to cry on our wedding day." He kneeled beside me and handed me the remaining cord. "Now you."

Finally, something I could happily agree to. I twisted toward him and coiled the *lazo* around his neck to form an infinity between us. To leash me to him. I gave the rope a tug, and he arched a dark, scolding eyebrow at me.

If I'd had the guts, I would've asked why he'd bothered with this charade at all. As "willing" as Cristiano demanded I be, summoning tradition didn't make this anything more than an extravagant kidnapping.

As fresh flowers perfumed the space around us, and tall candles warmed it, the priest recited a prayer with a shaky voice and obvious trepidation. I had to keep myself from looking back at Diego.

Cristiano's shoulder touched mine, and only then did I realize I'd been shivering. Despite the way he bullied and intimidated, he had that kind of soothing touch, one that would still you, if not with serenity, then out of dread. It confused me now the way it had when he'd frisked me at the club, or when he'd bandaged me up after the warehouse fire.

The way he'd slid his hands up under my dress and then robe . . . and I hadn't run away either time.

And his touch wouldn't end there. As Father Rios married us, my wifely duties were placed upon me. Cristiano hadn't hesitated to put his hands on me before, even knowing I was spoken for. That I was opposed to it. There was no question he would demand everything from me.

My trembling started anew, and he turned his head. I kept my gaze forward, even as the priest's speech slurred, or perhaps it was my mind that blended and muffled words to protect me from what I was hearing.

Father Rios went quiet, breaking me from my stupor.

After a moment, Cristiano said, "I do."

"Natalia," the priest said, "do you take Cristiano to be your wedded husband, to have and to hold from this day forward, for better, for worse, for richer, for poorer, in sickness and in health, to love, cherish, and obey till death do part you . . ."

*Obey*. I hadn't heard a word of Cristiano's vows, but somehow, I doubted he was under any obligation to obey *me*.

They both stared.

My chest was tight from holding my breath. I couldn't bring myself to say the words. I looked to the guards on each side of the priest. One had a face tattoo, a wrinkled dress shirt, and stood unevenly, but was dressed in the finest artillery. He gave me a close-lipped smile that made wrinkles around his eyes. The other wore a matching gun and restrained grin, with deep dimples and scars that peeked out from his collar.

I returned my eyes to Father Rios, who seemed to be whispering his own prayer while waiting for my answer.

Cristiano turned to me, laced our fingers together, and raised my hand between us. "He has asked if you'll take me as your husband, Natalia."

*I can't. I can't say it.*

After a moment, one of Cristiano's men said, "She does."

"I heard it too," the ugly guard said.

"*Por favor,*" the priest pleaded. "I can't proceed without her consent."

"Nor can I," said Cristiano. My palm perspired in his rough one. He squeezed it gently. "Tell him, Natalia Lourdes."

Father Rios' fallen expression took my heart down with it. He was as trapped as I was. I straightened my shoulders and looked at Cristiano. His dark eyes danced. The sharp lines of his angular face almost softened with something like happiness. "I do," I said to him.

Cristiano stood and helped me up. He reached for my left hand. "I don't have your ring yet." From his pocket, he produced a considerable but simple diamond in a gold setting and slipped it on me. "For the sake of the ceremony, until we find one that suits you."

"I don't need one," I said.

He glanced at the priest, who nodded for him to continue.

"With this ring, I thee wed. With my body, I thee worship." Cristiano commanded my attention, and again, the others fell away. As his dark eyes drank me in, I only wondered how, if he'd not been to many weddings, he knew what to say. Or why he seemed to say it with such vehemence, as if he meant it.

It wasn't like he needed anyone in this church, not even the reverend, to believe it.

"With all my worldly goods," he continued, "I thee endow—*en el nombre del Padre, y del Hijo, y del Espíritu Santo. Prometo amarte y respetarte todos los días de mi vida. Amén."*

He hesitated, as if he half-expected me to repeat the words back to him.

*I promise to love and respect you for all the days of my life.*

My new husband was turning out to be a riddle.

But I wouldn't mock the church and say what he asked of me.

We were mercifully interrupted. Out of nowhere, a man in cowboy boots and a matching hat appeared and clomped down the aisle to us. "*¡Felicidades!*" he said. "Congratulations to the happy couple."

"Remove your hat in the church," Cristiano said.

"Of course." The man did as he was told and held out a folder.

Cristiano opened it, looked over some paperwork, and rearranged the pages. Satisfied, he turned the file around for me. "Sign."

I glanced at the sheet on top. "What is it?"

"To legalize the marriage with a civil ceremony."

"Why all this trouble?" I asked, shaking my head. "You could take me to the Badlands and imprison me there whether we're legally married or not."

"I have my reasons." He nodded at the cowboy, who patted his pockets before producing a pen. "Sign."

I started to protest, but what could I say? And what did it matter? Signing on the devil's dotted line was no more permanent than the verbal agreement I'd already given. I had lost, and I feared I'd need my strength to fight bigger battles later.

The man started to put his hat back on, then seemed to remember Cristiano's order and held it to his chest. "I'll need those medical records, *compañero*. They're supposed to be done weeks in advance."

"I'm grateful for all the concessions you've made for my wife," Cristiano said, returning the folder to the man once I'd signed. "You have a friend in Calavera."

"*Gracias*, de la Rosa," the cowboy said, slipping the paperwork under his arm. He bowed to me, replaced his hat, and returned from wherever he'd come.

I found myself staring at Cristiano like everyone else in the church. He thought himself a god and expected the same of others.

He'd called me his *wife*. My fingers and toes curled. I was what my mother had been to my father. In some ways, it was a stretch—the devotion between them had run deep, the love profound, and here I was marrying a man I knew little better than a stranger. Yet that wasn't true. Cristiano had been a constant presence in my life, even after he'd left. There were similarities to our marriages too. My mother and father had trusted Cristiano with their lives and now, I was putting that same faith in him.

Trusting him with my eternal life as we descended into hell.

Promising him my love everlasting while my heart belonged to another.

Cristiano turned to the priest. "Finish it."

Father Rios nodded. "You may kiss the bride."

Cristiano gestured for my bouquet. For strength, I called upon a moment in which I hadn't feared Cristiano. A sunlit afternoon many years ago when he'd carried baskets of daisies and morning glory. I'd held Mamá's hand on our way back to the house, turned, and caught him smelling the flowers. He'd winked at me. I'd laughed, thinking it funny back then that it was more unusual to see him toting flowers than it would've been a gun.

I prayed, for my sake, that man still lived in him.

He took the bouquet from my nerveless fingers, unwrapping the rosary from its stems. "What do you think of it?" he asked.

"What?" I looked between us. "The rosary is from you? But how did you know?"

"It's not a replica. It was your mother's."

I could clearly remember her turning these beads through her slender fingers in this very church. The memory brought tears to my eyes. Now, I truly had a piece of her, but under such dire circumstances.

He pocketed it, then passed my bridal bouquet to a guard, who handled it with surprising care.

Cristiano cupped his hands around my jaw. He had to stoop a

good deal to meet me, even as he lifted my face the rest of the way. He waited there, his unforgiving eyes boring into mine as if trying to read my mind. I had only one mounting thought, though.

*Please, let this be another nightmare, for the darkness I've resisted welcomes me too easily.*

*Let Cristiano dematerialize into the black shadow that haunts my sleep.*

*Let him have mercy.*

*Let him release me.*

He pressed his lips to mine, their yielding fullness a stark contrast to the firm hands that held me in place. He inhaled sharply, as if he'd surprised himself as well. My heart pounded. His mouth parted, and mine did the same, granting him access that he seized, plunging his tongue inside to find mine just as eager. I gripped his elbows as his fingertips dug into my cheeks, my knees threatening to give out. A kiss that promised lovemaking in one breath and fucking in the next.

He drew away, leaving me gasping. I kept my eyes closed as the silence grew weighty between us. Why did giving into his kiss feel like walking into darkness—a temptation I knew I *should* resist? I half-expected a soothing whisper from him, maybe even something sweet.

I eased my eyes open. He kept my face in his hands but had his head turned toward the back of the church. "Envision me taking her with the same fervor on this, our wedding night, brother," he said, then kissed me again.

I jerked away and slapped him. The sound of it echoed through the church—skin on skin, and Pilar's loud gasp—whereas my regret was immediate.

Cristiano glared at me, working his jaw side to side, anger clearly building within him.

Even with the realization of what I'd done, rage burned in me. For the way he'd flaunted the kiss, something that should've been sacred no matter the circumstances. For how he'd used me to become even more powerful. For how he'd stolen my senses and tricked me into enjoying the kiss.

"You've ruined me," I said to him, and turned to look down the aisle at Diego. "And you let him."

I picked up my dress and strode down the aisle. If Cristiano didn't like it, let him shoot me in the back.

"Talia," Diego said, pressing his palms together in supplication. "Wait."

I pushed by him. "Go to hell."

Max blocked the door, stopping me with a curt shake of his head. There was nobody to help. Nobody but me.

I spun back and stood in front of Diego as my vision blurred with tears. "You were careless with my father's business and careless with me. Now I'll pay the price."

"You saved my life," he said. "I will forever be grateful to you."

I grabbed the lapels of his suit to push him away, but I couldn't. I didn't want him to go to hell. I wanted him to stay with me. Diego took my wrists. I fisted the fabric and buried my face in his chest. "You *know* what he has planned for me."

Without turning, I sensed Cristiano at my back before he spoke. "Take your hands off my wife, or I will add them to my collection."

I squeezed my eyes shut. I would soon see Cristiano's rumored museum of body parts with my own eyes.

"I'm sorry," Diego said, and we released each other.

"She is mine," Cristiano said. "Say it."

The tie of Diego's knot hung loose, defeated. I hated that he had put me in this position, but I hated how Cristiano rubbed it in our faces even more.

"She is yours in the eyes of God," Diego said, "but in every other way, she is mine. Saying otherwise won't change the fact."

I turned to Cristiano to plead with him not to react to Diego's baiting words, but he stood calm.

"As I told you before, brother," he said, each word slow and clipped, "once this was done, there'd be no turning back. She is mine. If you, or anyone, touches her again, I will rain down a fury the likes of which not even the Maldonados have seen."

Chills spread over every inch of my skin. He only said it to goad Diego, but his possessiveness gripped and thrilled me in ways that scared me.

Cristiano lowered his eyes and locked them on me. "Get out."

Instinctively, I knew he wasn't talking to me.

"Out!" Cristiano bellowed. He looked around, meeting eyes with each of his men and then Diego. "Everyone leave. You too, Max, and take the priest. I have business with my wife."

The church emptied quickly—too quickly. I couldn't even get a handle on my trepidation over being alone with him.

When it was just us, Cristiano walked forward until we were face to face. "Next time you slap me," he said, "save it for the bedroom."

I let out a shaky breath. My only comfort was being in the church. I had to believe he wouldn't punish me for my insolence in God's house.

He looked me up and down. "Hit me, rage against me, call me names. But I have two rules you won't break twice. First, Diego will *never* touch you again. And second, you will not *ever* lie to me, even one more time."

I racked my brain for what he might be referring to. "I didn't lie," I said quickly.

"No?" he asked. "What did you think would happen when you came to my bed and didn't bleed?"

I swallowed my gasp and did my best to school my shock. He knew I wasn't a virgin—yet he'd gone through with the wedding anyway. "Not every woman bleeds," I said, careful to speak honestly.

"Not with Diego, I'm sure. He treats you like you're breakable. I won't. With me, you'd have bled, and perhaps you still will in other ways." He raised his chin. "Remove your dress."

*What*? My jaw went slack. He couldn't mean for me to strip down *here*? I ceased to breathe or function in any way but to stare at him—and shake all over with the force and speed of my hammering heart.

"Y-you can't," I said, my mouth completely dry. Even Hades would wait until he was back in the underground for this next part. "We're in a church."

"White doesn't suit you, my lovely wife." He circled me until he was at my back. I didn't even have the wherewithal to try to keep him in my sight. He wouldn't do this here. He *couldn't*.

He trailed a finger up my spine until he'd reached the top button of my dress, just under my hairline. He gripped the back of the collar with both hands, slipping his knuckles between the fabric and my skin. It was a warm caress that spurred panic in me as I realized what he was doing.

"Stop—"

He yanked the dress open, ripping my mother's lace.

I opened my mouth, and my chin trembled. I thought I'd already known the worst of him, but he would prove me wrong. When his footsteps sounded again, I did my best to inhale back the urge to cry. My weakness would only spur him on.

Cristiano finished his circle and stood in front of me again with darkened eyes and lowered lids. "Now, take off your dress, Natalia—and let me see what my brother's freedom bought me."

# VIOLENT ENDS

## BOOK TWO

The devil has a name, and it's Cristiano de la Rosa. On my wedding day, he was the last man I expected to see standing at the altar. He wants to make me his queen. His brother wants to rescue his princess.

Getting Cristiano to lose control becomes the name of the game, and the stakes are life and death. But as truth and lies blur, loyalty is tested, and our chemistry threatens to reach the melting point, the prize grows less clear. Either freedom no longer means what I think it does, or Cristiano is as devious as everyone says, and he's mastered the art of playing my mind.

All I know for certain is that nothing is certain.
And all you need to know? This is a love story.
But even love stories have to end.

## CHAPTER 1

# NATALIA

The devil had a name—Cristiano de la Rosa—but from this day forward, I would call him *husband*.

The cozy church where I'd spent Sunday mornings over a prayer book with my parents stood still and quiet except for the echo of broken promises and ripped lace. Mid-day, sunlight flooded the pews around us, but only candlelight touched the darkened aisle.

In a sharp, tailored suit, my new husband stood before me, waiting for me to finish stripping off my wedding gown so he could thoroughly claim ownership before we'd even left the church.

Cristiano had forced my hand in marriage, and the man I'd envisioned spending my life with had agreed to it. Had *tricked* me into it.

"My new *bride* is shy." Cristiano smiled tightly, finding pleasure in the designation, likely just because he'd imposed it on me. "But I only required my brother meet two terms to validate this arrangement, and you've already broken one."

Cristiano had expected me to come to him a virgin, but Diego hadn't delivered me that way. The implication was clear—would I break the second term, too? I couldn't. Cristiano had already invited me to walk away from all of this, but there would be a price for that, and the people I loved would pay it.

Consummate the marriage, or the Maldonado cartel would obliterate all of us.

"I'd hoped our first time might be different," I said, grasping for a way to change an inevitable outcome. He'd asked me to marry him when he could've dragged me down the aisle. He'd respected the ceremony, lassoing us in a show for our few onlookers. If there was a shred of humanity within him, I had to try to tap into it.

"As had I." He tilted his head, his eyes scanning my front, as if I was a puzzle to be solved. "But you chose to give your virginity to another. I was prepared to take you to bed and handle you gently, but it seems I no longer have a need for that." He stepped toward me, six-foot-five inches of suited muscle and dark beauty with a clean, masculine scent. "You *have* been thoroughly broken in . . . haven't you?"

I shivered as I slipped one arm through the wedding dress, mourning the beautiful, ruined lace my mother had worn to wed my father. "No," I whispered.

One thick eyebrow arched. "I'm sorry?"

"I haven't," I insisted. "Diego and I did it *once*. He was gentle. I'm not . . ."

"Broken?" he suggested. "Like a wild horse."

I turned away from his penetrating gaze as his black eyes danced. To sully the wedding altar, to slap God in the face, to force Diego to endure my ruination from the other side of the door—it was what I'd sold Cristiano in exchange for our lives. Not just mine, but my father's, Diego's, and anyone else close to the Cruz cartel. Men who'd protected my family, who'd *raised* families under my father, and who'd helped raise *me* after my mother's death.

I drew my other arm through its sleeve and pushed my dress down until it pooled at my feet.

Cristiano wet his lips, his eyes drifting to the ivory lingerie I'd worn for a wedding night I'd planned to share with Diego. Diego and I had made love, but tonight, I'd been ready to give in to the passion we'd been forced to bridle for years. *How naïve.*

Cristiano dipped his head. If I hadn't known better, I'd have thought it was in reverence. "Beautiful."

I shifted from one heel to the other. "You've seen me in my underwear before."

"In your bathroom, after the warehouse fire." He nodded, his angular jaw firming. "But I didn't let myself look at you this way. All I'd have seen was what I couldn't have." His broad chest expanded with an inhale as he raised his chin. "Now, all I see is everything I *own*. Every last inch of you, my darling."

My heart skipped. We'd been married mere minutes, yet he acted as if I was his possession. "Just because we're married doesn't make this consensual."

"As I've said before, you always have a choice. You can walk out of this church now and into my brother's arms. I'd ask you to stay, but I wouldn't force you."

As irritation flickered in me for his word play, I retorted, "But you *would* allow a rival cartel to exact revenge for the money Diego lost them."

"It cost me a great deal to call them off. More than Diego can ever repay." Cristiano shook out his wrist and adjusted his steel watch without breaking eye contact. "But as long as I have you, his debt is forgiven, and they won't lay a finger on you or anyone you love."

His solid footsteps resounded through the pews as he circled me and stopped at my back. Perhaps he'd rip off my underwear the way he had my dress. I didn't care—unlike my mother's gown, they were worth nothing.

He parted my hair, drew it forward over my shoulders, and spread a hand against my bare upper back. "Not until this moment have I allowed myself to want you."

I swallowed dryly. Something new had entered his voice. Longing. Desperation. As if he'd been in need of something I was now offering. I waited for him to push me down, bend me over a pew, and conquer.

"How was he with you?" Cristiano asked quietly. "Did my brother destroy you, or did he leave me the pleasure of that task?"

"Diego was . . ." Words to describe the man I loved, once at the tip of my tongue, didn't come as easily now. He had betrayed me, but how thoroughly? If he'd been willing to trade me, was there a chance he'd also taken my virginity knowing what was in store for me? He wouldn't. He *couldn't*. Only a monster would do that, and the de la Rosa family already had enough of those. I'd known Diego practically my whole life, and I'd know if he was that evil. "He was sweet and caring," I continued. Even if doubt entered my memory of that night, I couldn't let Cristiano see that. Weakness was one thing I could no longer afford to show around him. "At least I'll know that kindness once in my lifetime, and I will cling to that memory every time I'm with you."

Cristiano chuckled deeply and lowered his mouth to my ear. "I look forward to watching you try. Your lips will know one word when I'm inside you—my name—and you'll feel only one thing—the pleasure I'm giving you."

I shut my eyes as the inevitable closed in. "Please make this quick."

"Never." Starting at my shoulder blade, he slid a finger up under my bra strap. "*Quick* is not the way to fuck a woman like you, at least not until after I've thoroughly explored you."

I drew a small breath at his bluntness. What kind of torture would it be to have such a controlled, dangerous man explore me with his full attention? Sweet or cruel? A mix of both, I guessed. That wasn't the terrifying part, though. By the tone of his voice, he intended for me to enjoy my undoing.

He pressed his hands to my shoulders. "Stay here," he said before walking away.

I stared down the aisle toward the discarded pillows where we'd kneeled, which were backdropped by paneled, stained-glass saints. Our Lady of Guadalupe silently stared at me. I'd never given her my bouquet in exchange for her blessing of our union, but then, we didn't deserve it.

Some of the candles had gone out, likely with the way everyone had rushed out of the building with Cristiano's command to leave. Was Diego envisioning Cristiano shredding my clothing at this moment? The merciless way he'd use me? The fervor with which Cristiano had promised to take me after our first kiss as man and wife?

I hoped he was, and that each and every one of Diego's thoughts tortured him.

Any suffering he endured would never match my own.

This was *his* fault.

Cristiano's footsteps returned, and with barely a touch at my back, my bra popped open. He slid it off, dropping it on the ground. We were starting. My heart beat in my stomach as I anticipated his callused palms on my skin.

"Is quick really what you want? For me to tear through you hard and fast?" His voice deepened with unmistakable lust. "Or would you prefer I draw it out? Make you enjoy it? *Crave* it? What would be worse?"

I shuddered despite the warmth of the church. To enjoy it would be a betrayal to myself—a crime I had a feeling I'd commit. Already, my nipples stuck straight out, tingling in anticipation of his hands. Every time he touched me, my body responded—from our dance at the costume ball to his wandering fingers as he'd bandaged up my feet after the warehouse fire. But no matter the draw that existed between us, I would never admit to craving it. I'd sure as hell never ask for it.

What would be worse? I could comprehend pain, resistance, and hatred in a moment like this.

But to be pleasured by the devil and enjoy it? That felt like the highest sin.

"Get it over with," I said.

"I only ask out of curiosity," he said, pressing his hand to my back and guiding me forward. "It won't change the course of things. Now, my little butterfly, brace yourself on the pew."

I inhaled deeply, bent forward, and gripped the lip with both hands, offering my backside to him.

"What a sight," he said. "My imagination is getting the better of me. Maybe if you ask nicely, I'll sodomize you this way sometime."

Reflexively, I clenched my cheeks. I'd be naïve to think he had any limits, but my mind hadn't yet wandered to the sordid details. He made it sound as filthy as possible, so different than I'd ever heard.

Considering how he might use me, might violate me in such a

forbidden place—my breath came short. It was what he wanted, to inspire fear. Being at his mercy in the most vulnerable ways possible, surrendering to him, was like falling at the feet of a hungry beast.

My body answered the thought with a sharp but pleasurable pang somewhere in my depths. *Oh, God*. What was wrong with me?

*"I suspect you'll even like the feeling of surrender,"* he'd said to me on the horse days earlier.

Could he have been right? Maybe I had the same dark nature inside me that he did, a craving to be bent to a man's will. But I wasn't an animal. I wouldn't allow myself to enjoy it just because it satisfied some carnal desire.

His first touch came as a grip around my ankle. "Lift your foot," he said.

I looked down between us and did as he said. Kneeling behind me, he held a black lace garment in his hands. "What is that?" I asked.

"Step into it," he instructed, waiting until I did. "Now the other foot."

He stood, sliding a long, floor-length dress up my body. The skirt fell to the ground with a small chapel train, almost like a wedding gown itself. "You're dressing me?" I asked.

"Regretfully."

"But . . .?"

He waited. I couldn't bring myself to finish the sentence. He'd sworn to defile me. Why wasn't he?

"We'll get to that," he said, reading my mind. "I quite like the idea of your thoughts running wild with all the things I'll do to you tonight—mine will be doing the same. By the time I put my hands on you, I'll have violated your sweet body every which way in my fantasies."

Another throb between my legs, harder this time. To cancel out my body's traitorous reaction, I challenged him. "You told me once you have no need to force a woman," I said.

"I don't." He zipped up the dress. "But, when I'm through with you, any shred of innocence, any scrap of the girl you were, will be gone—and that's a pretty thorough violation if you ask me."

"Why would you want that?"

"Because you're no longer someone's sweet, pure, naïve *princesa*. You don't live in the ivory tower anymore. You own it. You're going to learn to rule from it, because that's what it means to be Calavera royalty. And this dress is far more suitable for a queen."

Chills spread over my body with the threat and promise that I was one of them now. A Calavera. Like a crown, black lace turned me from eager bride to the cartel's first lady. The intricate bodice molded to my chest and waist, and the wide neckline stopped at the top of each shoulder, nearly baring them.

From behind, Cristiano skimmed his hands down the fabric clinging to my breasts and settled them at my waist. "The thought of nothing but lace between us all night is enough to drive me mad." Grit hardened his words, and the rawness in his voice vibrated in places that shamed me. "But I don't want any other men lusting after you. Perhaps I should warn them before we arrive that should their gazes linger, I will carve out their eyeballs."

"What men?" My breath came faster with his suggestive touch and graphic threats. "Arrive where?"

"I suspect they already know." Cristiano continued his thought, pressing his hips against my lower back and announcing his need. "After the trouble I've gone through to get you, and the sacrifices I've made, they won't question that what's mine is *mine*."

I was helpless in his grip, his large hands tightening around my waist, his erection strong against my back. Could there exist a certain kind of contentment in giving myself over to the inevitable? In submitting to a man who was so strong and sure of himself and his plans for me? By the way his command made my heart race, I suspected there was some beauty to be found in resignation.

But I wouldn't give him the satisfaction.

I couldn't afford to remember that there was a time when I'd felt safe with him. Even eleven years earlier, as a scared little girl who'd walked in on Cristiano standing over my mother's dead body, I'd found an odd and unexpected sense of comfort in his arms later, as he'd carried me down into a pitch-black tunnel.

"You say what's yours is yours," I echoed back to him. "But I've heard the rumors about your men. Will you let them touch me? Use me? Tell me now so I know what to expect—do I belong to you or to the Calavera cartel?"

He ran one palm up my chest, his skin warm on mine, and loosely wrapped it around my throat. "Whatever happens, mark my words—you will love it."

*No*. The idea of serving multiple men made me want to run more than anything had up until now. And the suggestion that I'd enjoy it? Equally obscene and horrifying.

"I'm going to let go of you now. If I don't, I'll take you in God's house, and I may not be able to stop until dawn breaks."

He released me, leaving me breathless and confused. My legs shook as I stooped to gather my pile of things.

"Leave it all," he said. "My men will discard it."

I picked up the precious ivory lace of my abandoned wedding dress, running my bare fingernail over the long rip. "I want to bring it."

"You won't need it where we're going. Max already put your bags in the car."

"It was my mother's," I said quietly.

I looked up at him as I had eleven years earlier when he'd stood over her as she'd bled out. Over me. With blood on his pants and a gun in his hand. I remembered him as the most vicious yet protective man in my world.

His power and strength had only multiplied since then.

Pressing his lips into a line, he crouched and took the fabric from my hands. After gathering it and my bra into his arms, he stood. "Come."

"Where are we going?" I asked.

"Home."

## CHAPTER 2

# NATALIA

Despite gray skies, there was no shortage of people in the plaza on Easter day. The scent of fried plantain filled the air as locals danced and filled their bellies with horchata and empanadas, and kids begged for candies, balloons, and toys from vendors.

It seemed as if the only person missing from the festivities was Diego.

A pair of black Land Rovers with tinted windows idled at the curb in front of the church. Cristiano led me to the second one, handed off my things to the driver, and opened the door to the backseat.

Getting in meant surrendering myself to Cristiano. Once inside, I was as good as lost to the world. My cell phone was in the bag I'd brought to the church and had been taken somewhere. I wasn't naïve enough to think I'd be getting it back any time soon, if at all. I squinted around the square. "Barto's supposed to pick me up any moment. He thinks he's taking me to the airport for my father."

"Then you'd better get in so he and I don't have a confrontation," Cristiano said. "Quit stalling."

I crouched to unbuckle the strap of one shoe. "My feet ache," I explained, furtively scanning the steps of the church and then the crowds for Diego. Laying eyes on him one last time wouldn't change my situation, but it didn't feel right to just leave.

"He's gone if he knows what's good for him," Cristiano said, calling my eyes up as he looked down on me.

Just like that, my entire life had been flipped on its side. Diego was nowhere to be seen, and his brother filled my vision and called me *wife*.

"Forget the shoes," Cristiano said, "and get in the car—and don't mention his name again, or so help me God, I'll—"

"You'll what?" I asked, standing. "Separate me from my loved ones and condemn me to a life I never wanted?"

He narrowed his eyes. What could he say? It was true. My fate was sealed.

I ducked inside before Cristiano could respond. He removed his jacket as he went to the first SUV and spoke to the driver. I fixed my gaze out my window, memorizing the town square. Until I saw Diego again, my last memory would be the defeat in his stance as Cristiano had ordered everyone but me from the church.

My heart sank. Diego had given me away. He'd had no choice—Cristiano had decided he'd wanted to unite our families, and his cartel with my father's, so he'd made it happen. Nothing could've stopped him.

But still. The person I loved, the man I'd been willing to defy my father to marry, had let me walk down the aisle to someone else. And not just anyone. His cruel, notoriously violent brother.

Was Diego sorry? How long had he known about this?

My chin wobbled, but I stilled it in an attempt to pull myself together. Fuck Diego for putting me in this position—and fuck *me* for still trying to catch once last glimpse of him.

Cristiano tossed his suit jacket onto the seat next to me and slid behind the driver. "Why do you care where my brother is?" he asked, raising a partition between the front and back seats.

I turned from the window to Cristiano. "He was going to be my *husband*."

"Diego gave you up to save his own ass. He's not worth your time." Cristiano studied me as we pulled away from the curb. "You should be thanking me for stepping in."

*Thank* him? My blood simmered. Between our union and Cristiano's human trafficking business, I doubted there wasn't anything he couldn't justify to himself. "You left him no other choice."

"There's always a choice." Cristiano tugged at his shirtsleeve, then held out his arm. "Do you mind?"

I looked at his hand. "What?"

"My cufflinks."

We slowly made our way through the square decorated with papier-mâché figures, multi-colored flags, and flower bunches. Men in sombreros and women costumed in traditional ancient dresses with woven baskets on their heads moved aside, peering through the tinted windows, some of them tossing out angry words at our intrusion. We weren't supposed to be driving through here.

"You can remove them yourself," I said.

"But I'm asking you to."

Was an ask ever truly that with Cristiano? I heard the demand in his words. Hesitantly, I pulled his wrist to me and slipped the sterling silver bar of a grooved cufflink through its hole. "What would you have done in Diego's shoes? Or mine, for that matter?" I asked. "Although, I suppose you'd have to know love to truly understand the lengths you'd go to for it."

"I should warn you, each time you say my brother's name, a vision comes to mind. One I don't like. So unless you wish to provoke me, you won't speak his name again."

His cuff hung loose. He nodded at it, so I rolled it up, my fingers grazing a vein of his thick, dark-haired forearm. "What vision?" I hedged.

Once I'd secured his sleeve at his elbow, he shifted to give me his other hand. "If I vocalize it, it's likely to anger me. Not wise when you're trapped back here with me."

Diego's name could've called up a memory for Cristiano that haunted me as well. Eleven years earlier, Diego had accused his brother of murdering my mother knowing it would cost Cristiano his life. Diego had chosen justice over family, and in the cartel, betraying family was the ultimate sin. I could still see Diego clear as day, aiming his gun at Cristiano and me, and I wasn't even the one he'd wanted to shoot.

I removed the other cufflink, clutching both silver pieces in my palm. "I don't think I've ever seen a more composed man than you were in that church," I said to see if I could gain some insight into what made him tick. "Now you're angry. What changed?"

It was his turn to look out the window. Cristiano didn't have to acknowledge any of my questions, and that made answers precious. No matter the topic, anything could be considered a clue to the man behind the calavera mask. Who was Cristiano? What did a man as cold and callous as him fear? Desire? Love?

And why did I care?

*Information.* Once the only vice of a girl whose family told her nothing under the guise of protection, and later a burden when I'd wanted to forget everything to do with this life, could now be the thing that saved me. It would be easier to survive my enemy if I knew what he wanted. What he expected. What drove him.

Not just survive him, but maybe even escape him.

I was metaphorically chained to Cristiano by the power he held over the lives of the people I loved. I couldn't run. But that didn't mean there weren't ways to free myself of him.

I grazed a fingertip over the smooth skin of Cristiano's wrist, lightly enough to make it seem like an accident. "What made you angry?" I pressed.

He continued to stare out the window for a beat, then turned to me. "Jealousy is new to me, but I no longer allow emotions to overtake me, so I was able to conceal it in the church."

*Jealousy?* I schooled my expression to hide my surprise, both at his answer, and that he'd answered at all. Perhaps his response shouldn't have caught me off guard, though. Cristiano had expected me pure. Was he upset that he'd gotten his brother's hand-me-down? Or was it simply the primitive urge of a husband who'd wanted to have his wife first?

He'd threatened to remove Diego's hands just for touching me—but what had Cristiano thought would happen? He'd walked into the middle of my relationship with Diego. He'd disrupted our wedding.

He'd *won*.

When he reached for my ankle, I sprang back.

"Is the ache from the shoes?" he asked, pulling my foot into his lap. "Or the cuts?"

My heart pounded as the hair on my arms rose. I could never forget that Cristiano could—and would—touch me at any moment. I shifted my back against the door so I was facing him. "The cuts have nearly healed."

"You had a good doctor." The corner of his mouth lifted as his big fingers struggled with the stiletto's delicate buckle. Days earlier, my fear of Cristiano had been overridden by how gently he'd tweezed glass from my feet. Instead of taking advantage of a situation, he'd helped me.

We cleared the town and accelerated down a two-lane highway, surrounded by desert on both sides as we barreled toward the storm clouds gathered ahead. I crossed my arms. "You're a doctor, captor, and husband all rolled into one," I said. "Lucky me."

"Say that again." He tossed my shoe aside and met my eyes. "I like the way that word sounds on your tongue."

"Captor," I said. "I'm your captive, and I have no doubt it brings you pleasure to hear that."

"Not that one. *Husband*." He moved my foot a few inches over until my arch aligned with a bulge at his zipper. "You are my wife, and it brings me perverse pleasure to both say it *and* hear it."

My throat dried as he lengthened and grew against my foot. He was aroused, and I was at his mercy.

Rain pattered the roof as the sky darkened. "How long until we reach the Badlands?"

Cristiano wet his lips. "Another half hour or so."

I weighed my options. I had no idea what awaited me inside the gates. At least twice, he'd warned of taking me later. Better it lasted thirty minutes than through the night. If luck was on my side, maybe once would be enough for him to tire of me and move on.

"Just enough time to consummate our union," I said.

He stilled, blinking at me. "I'm sorry?"

I pushed through the instinct to shut my mouth. I could endure him for thirty minutes. And even if I couldn't, I'd have to find a way. "You said the marriage wasn't valid until we consummated it."

"Correct."

"Then the people I love aren't safe until the ink is dry."

He cocked his head, squeezing my foot as he ran a firm thumb along my sole the way he had after he'd removed all the glass from it. A sharp, delicious twinge pulled inside me, and I shuddered to hide that his touch tickled. "You're so eager that you want me to take you here the first time?" he asked, sounding genuinely curious.

"I want it done," I said.

"You cowered from me in the church."

"To be violated as Our Lady of Guadalupe looks on is heinous." I should've been more afraid of what I was asking. I was tempting the beast to defile me. But I tried to appeal to logic. The devil I knew was here, now, and the clock was ticking. "To be had in the backseat of a car,"—I swallowed—"feels truer than anything yet."

"Not in the least," he said immediately, curving a hand against the smooth black leather seat. "This isn't suitable for my bride."

"I'm not your bride—I'm your prisoner. You want to be my husband? It's too late for that. You will take me as your captive, not your wife."

He set his jaw and reached for my other leg. Instinctively, I pulled away at the thought of him taking hold of both my ankles, but the backseat didn't give me much room. He captured my foot and set to work freeing it from its satin confines. "You're speaking from anger," he said. "I understand. You feel betrayed—as you should. He traded you, but take comfort in the fact that *I* never will."

"Where's the comfort in that?"

"You'll learn to find it."

Though I faced him now with both feet in his lap, I turned my head away. "For my sanity, I hope I do."

My jaw tingled. *Trapped*. At least he acknowledged it. But how literal would my captivity be? Momentarily, I'd forgotten to fear not just Cristiano but the place he called home. The Badlands had been described as dangerous, cultish, lawless—a wasteland for women and children. To add insult to injury, it was set against—but walled off from—the Pacific Ocean that sprawled from Mexico's west coast. And I would be in the center of it all.

"What are you thinking about that makes your toes curl?" he asked.

I flexed my feet, forcing myself to relax. I had to remember Cristiano was nothing if not observant. Even as a girl, I'd been the subject of his attention, which unfortunately meant he might know me better than I was comfortable with.

Having liberated my feet, he inspected the soles.

"Have you taken more bullets than drugs in your lifetime?" I asked.

He raised just his eyes. And a single brow. "Pardon?"

"That's the rumor about Calavera's leader."

"I have never taken drugs," he said.

"And bullets?"

"What do you think?"

"I think . . . yes. You have."

He squeezed my heel. "Good guess."

He seemed simultaneously amused and grave. I ran my tongue along the edge of my teeth. "Do you have a foot fetish?" I asked, just to see what he'd say.

"So many questions." He seemed to consciously flex his grip, as if he'd forgotten he was holding onto me. "Why do you ask?"

"First you cleaned my feet in my bathroom the morning of the warehouse attack, and now you're fondling them."

"I cleaned *you* in the bathroom," he said. "Now I'm touching *you*. Maybe I have a Natalia fetish." He sat back in his seat but kept my feet where they were. "So, *la narcoprincesa* is curious about my habits and fetishes. She must be wondering what awaits her in the Badlands."

How did a broken society function? If they were as devout to Cristiano as reported, what would they make of me? I didn't know much about his business, either, except he moved weapons and women. Virgins, everyone in this world knew, were valuable. If he hadn't married me, I'd be agonizing over the possibility of being sold. Maybe I *did* need to be worried about that.

I shivered and caught him staring at me. In an afternoon, Cristiano had already gotten what he'd wanted from me—the power two families and cartels afforded him. But at the end of a kingpin's long day of destruction, he was still a man, and he looked at me with a man's eyes. His gaze wouldn't release me, nor his large hands.

He would have me tonight.

It was all there in the way his eyes devoured me. I had to face the truth. I'd given myself to Diego on the promise that he'd be the only man to ever have me. Now, I was facing a lifetime of servitude to his ruthless brother.

I could not cower or run. Cristiano would get what he wanted. And one day, he'd tire of me.

A man like him was not made for one woman.

Having a wife would be more of an inconvenience to him than anything. I hoped, out of respect for our history, he'd keep me somewhere tolerable. That I'd be housed and fed decently as my father had done for him. That I'd be called to his bed when needed, and otherwise left alone. But I didn't dare expect anything.

Not after the things I'd heard.

What was it Diego and Tepic had told me? Rumors about Calavera's mistreatment of whores, and satanic practices that involved eating snails, sacrificing virgins, and chanting in tongues. Nobody could confirm nor deny what went down on the devil's playground, because apparently, no trespasser had ever lived to tell the tale.

Diego had promised to come for me. My father would try, too. But I couldn't depend on them against the all-powerful Cristiano. If I wanted out, I'd have to find a way from within—and until then, I just needed to hold on.

In the literal sense, too, it seemed. I latched onto the door as the SUV jostled when we pulled off the main highway. Lush, green mountains rose from the barren desert, vibrant against the clouds. I knew the Pacific spread behind the mountain range. It was a trifecta of natural beauty, and it didn't surprise me he'd taken this particular town so he could erect his man-made hell.

He liked beautiful things, so he made them his.

"Do you get carsick?" he asked.

"Not usually."

"Good. It gets rough here. The roads leading up to the gates aren't paved."

"We're here already?" I asked.

"The distance from your father's house isn't great. It's the terrain that slows people down."

I gripped the side panel as we made our way down a rocky dirt road. "Why don't you fix the roads?"

"That would make it too easy to get in."

*Or out.*

My stomach dropped. Up ahead, stone walls rose from the desert like a fortress, sectioning off hectares of land that abutted the mountainside.

*The Badlands.* The designation made sense now. It was hard to get to, and anyone who made it in wouldn't be able to make a hasty escape.

A smirk ghosted over his features. "By the look on your face, you've heard the rumors. I ruined this town—defiled, disgraced, and ran out its people. That I rule it with an iron fist." He slid his hand under the hem of my long dress, up my calf. "Maybe you can open that fist, Natalia. Turn it from iron to liquid mercury and sculpt it to your liking. As your mother once did with your father."

I ground my teeth together. "If I'm forbidden from mentioning Diego, then you should be forbidden from speaking about my mother."

I tried to pull my leg back, but he seized it. After a brief hesitation, he let go. "I knew Bianca well," he said. "She had influence—and a spine of steel to stand by Costa's side. You're not there yet, but you have it in you."

"She'd be horrified by what you've become. Of how you treat women. And by whatever you have planned for me."

Color crept up his neck until he looked away. I slid my legs from his lap and bent my knees to my chest, hugging them as we bounced toward iron gates several times taller than the men guarding them.

Silence settled between us as tires crunched dirt and rocks hit the bottom of the car. That was as much as he was willing to acknowledge my mother, it seemed. Or the brutal conditions that lay ahead. I'd find out soon enough what was true and what wasn't, but where there was smoke, there was fire. I could see the walls and gates for myself. They hid secrets, and people, and in this world, that could mean nothing good.

He was confused if he thought I'd ever develop a tolerance to treating humans like commodities. If he thought my mother would *want* that for me.

We stopped in front of a gate. The walls were thick enough that their stone housed checkpoints, as if we were crossing a border. Men with guns and clipboards stepped out as the gates opened inward.

Blocking my view was a grumbling semi. I craned my neck as we passed it. Men hopped out of the back and pulled down the door, and I glimpsed people in the trailer.

Who were they? Were they arriving or being taken somewhere? I *needed* to ask. But what would I do with the answer? I was as stuck as they were. I squeezed my legs more tightly to my chest and inhaled a breath to calm my racing heart as we entered *"las puertas del infierno,"* as Tepic had called them.

*The gates of hell.*

To mentally prepare myself, I closed my eyes and envisioned the worst—a scorched-earth ghost town, patrols with AR-15s nudging beggars and prostitutes along, heavy chains weighing down exits and people. Brothels and abandoned storefronts, warehouses of guns and drug labs, failed absconders hanging like examples from trees.

Medieval but effective.

When my curiosity became too much, I opened my eyes and looked out the windshield.

Envisioning the worst had proved futile.

Nothing could've prepared me for *this*.

# CHAPTER 3

# NATALIA

It could've been Main Street in any affluent town. Clean and maintained buildings spread before us, tucked under the verdant, towering mountainside that would've shadowed the Badlands had the sun been out. This wasn't a ghost town—whatever the Calavera cartel had done to the people who'd lived here, the structures and homes had not only remained intact, but seemed to have been improved. Their red brick facades were bright, stucco white walls clean, and not a crack could be seen in the pavement or concrete.

It was in even better shape than where I came from.

No longer bumping and jostling, we started a slow tread as the road into the Badlands smoothed from potholes and rocks to paved roads and cobblestone. We drove down the wide, main road bordered by shops that went directly from the gates to the foot of the mountain.

I took my chin off my knees and released my legs to scoot closer to the window. Though the walls were high, the town was big enough that I couldn't see where it began or ended. Just beyond was the ocean, taunting the prisoners with salty air and the promise of an endless horizon they couldn't see. I wondered if anyone ever tried to escape that way, and how far they got.

Two young girls in t-shirts and shorts stood under a deli awning, watching us pass. They had plastic bags of groceries in their hands and umbrellas tucked under their arms. *Their freedom was stripped, but at least they're dry,* I thought wryly. Men on horses steered to one side, nodding at us. A group of women traveled as a pack and carried baskets of fruit on their shoulders; one smacked another on the shoulder as we drove by.

The rain started and stopped, and hardly a passerby didn't stop to stare as we drew closer and closer to green foothills dense with trees. I didn't know what to make of what I saw. Disoriented and slightly dizzy, I sat back in my seat.

"More than meets the eye?" Cristiano lowered the partition. Clouds darkened the sky, but the driver switched off his wipers as the rain became a drizzle. "You can see the house ahead," Cristiano said.

I didn't try to hide my curiosity. I ducked to peer through the windshield and spotted it instantly—a multi-story house built into the mountainside with white walls, a red terracotta roof, and crisp lines that offset curved archways.

"I can keep an eye on things from up there," he said.

I didn't doubt Cristiano had eyes everywhere.

It turned out the main road didn't go straight through to the base of the mountain. We made our way around the perimeter of a large plaza, not unlike the one we'd just come from, also anchored by a church. I wasn't fooled. Diego and Tepic had suggested the Badlands used storefronts and mundane businesses for money laundering. The church could've been a decoy for something else or just a cruel joke for false hope in a godless land.

People had set up stands in the same manner they had back home, though most were packing up their goods, and some stalls had been abandoned in the rain. A pair of children ran barefoot from booth to booth, jumping up and down with their hands cupped, tugging on the dresses of women who were boxing up everything from painted, wooden knick-knacks to talavera tiles to vibrant clothing.

"Begging for chocolate," Cristiano said.

"So sad," I murmured.

"Sad?" he asked. "They just want Easter candy."

Oddly, women wore colorful dresses and had decorated their stands with flowers, red, white, and green crepe streamers, and matching flags. With trash bins full of paper plates and plastic Solo Cups, it almost looked as if we were arriving at the end of an event.

"Pull over," Cristiano said, and the driver parked at a curb close to the square. Cristiano opened his door and strode toward a woman who was removing dresses from hangers and folding them into a crate.

When she noticed him coming, she stepped back, waving him away. He held something out to her, grabbed her hand and pressed it into her palm, then squatted before a yellow blanket displaying leather *huarache* sandals.

I had no idea what he was doing, but the woman clearly objected to it.

Cristiano headed back, his dress shirt dotted with raindrops. He slid in next to me and passed over a pair of brown leather sandals. "These will be more comfortable," he said.

I took them because I didn't know what else to do. Turning them over in my hands, I admired the detailed craftsmanship and high-quality leather. He stared ahead as we continued on and didn't look as if he expected a "thank you."

"These are well-made," I said. "They look expensive."

"Maricela is highly skilled. I've told her to charge more, but she refuses, so I gave her double."

"You paid her?"

"Of course." He glanced over as I ran a fingertip along the thin soles. "They remind me of the ones you were wearing . . . the ones you had as a girl."

*Ah. Yes.* I pinched the smooth leather strap. These were an understated, adult version of the woven *huaraches* I'd worn until the leather had been darkened by dirt and sun, and the frayed straps had started to come loose. "My mom hated them. She said—" I stopped myself. I'd been wearing those sandals the day I'd found Cristiano in her bedroom as she'd lain dying on the floor.

"What did she say?" he asked.

"Nothing." Cristiano didn't deserve to share in my past, however trivial. I bent over to pull on sandals like the ones I'd worn so ragged, my mom had teased that they were only a step up from bare feet. "It was nothing."

The car wound up the mountainside and turned onto the circular driveway of Cristiano's house. Upon closer inspection, the white, Spanish Colonial-style home had wrought-iron window grilles, and a stone walkway that led to a massive, arched, dark wood door. "You don't have a gate?" I asked as we parked. Anyone from town could hike up to his front door.

"Wait here," he said, taking his jacket from the seat and exiting the car.

I turned away from the house to peer beyond the cliff it sat on. Clay rooftops, stone buildings, greenery, and desert comprised the town. Businesses and activity gathered in the middle, around the main street we'd driven down, and from there spiraled off pockets of neighborhoods.

A slim woman with delicate, elfin features and long, reddish-brown hair descended the front steps to meet Cristiano. He handed her his jacket, touched her shoulder, and gestured to the car. She twirled her considerable hair into a bun on top of her head as she nodded before walking to the trunk.

Cristiano opened the door to the backseat and offered a hand to help me out. "This is Jazmín," he said as I unfolded from the Land Rover. "She'll see that your things are handled."

The woman and I met eyes. She was indisputably pretty and close to my age. How had she gotten here? I studied her for any signs of mistreatment. In clean, pressed black pants and a white button-down, and with no outward signs of trauma, she almost seemed normal.

Jazmín bent her head toward me. "*Bienvenida, señora.*"

"I can get my own bags," I told Cristiano. "She doesn't need to do that."

"Jaz has been preparing for you the last couple days," he said.

I tucked some of my hair behind my ear and straightened my

dress. Even with the low-heeled sandals, the hem just barely grazed the ground. "Why am I wearing this?" I asked.

Cristiano glanced from me to Jazmín. "I apologize. Natalia seems to have forgotten her manners."

My cheeks warmed. I hadn't responded when she'd welcomed me, and she wasn't the enemy. "*Mucho gusto,*" I said to her as she removed my bag from the trunk and slung my mother's dress over her elbow.

Cristiano led me up the steps to the sturdy wood-and-iron door. The tiled entryway had high ceilings with dark beams and round-top windows that would've lit the space if the sun had been out. Instead, a chandelier made of wrought iron glowed above us and matched the railing of a staircase with blue and orange painted risers.

Jaz entered behind us. "We had to move everyone into the dining hall because of the rain." She gave him a small smile. "It's a little cramped, but they don't notice."

"Drunk?" he asked.

"Very. And extremely curious."

"I have no doubt," Cristiano said. "I'll give Natalia a quick tour on our way to the party."

I couldn't hide my surprise. "*Party*?" My life was falling apart, and Cristiano wanted to celebrate? "You can't be serious."

"Do you have any laundry?" Jaz asked me, readjusting the strap of my bag on her shoulder.

"I—what? I can unpack myself," I said, stepping toward her. "I'll just go to my room if you'll show me—"

Cristiano took my elbow and drew me back to him. "Jaz has it under control. I want you by my side right now. They've put a lot of time and effort into tonight. You'll make the rounds with me."

My lips thinned into a line. "You can't force me to enjoy a party."

He turned to block Jaz from my view and put his mouth to my ear. "Enjoy it or don't," he said quietly. "But you'll do as I say, and you won't question me in front of anyone again. Jaz asked you something. Answer her."

He straightened up again, and I was faced with Jaz's unreadable expression. The last thing I wanted was to be rude to someone who might be in an even worse situation than I was, but being thrust into a party an hour after my life had been ruined seemed cruel.

"My things are clean," I said to Jaz. I'd done all my laundry at home before I'd packed. "Except . . ." I glanced at the ruined wedding dress hanging over her shoulder. Even if the delicate lace could be repaired, was there any point?

"Except?" she asked.

"Never mind. It's all clean." I cleared my throat. "Thank you."

"*De nada*." Jaz started up a staircase, gripping the iron railing as she climbed the stairs over the front door. She cast me a narrow-eyed glance before disappearing through a rounded doorway.

"It will make my staff happy to know you're happy to be here," Cristiano said. "And when my staff is happy, so am I."

"But *I'm* not."

His posture eased with an exhale. He tipped up my chin until our mouths were aligned and he could bend and kiss me if he wanted. "Then fake it for their benefit."

I dropped my eyes to his lips when he wet them, then quickly turned my face away. "Why should I?"

"I already told you why. It makes *me* happy. And you want that." He guided my head forward and waited until our eyes met again. "But if that's not a good enough reason, then do it because I command it."

I had a feeling I'd get used to hearing that response. But if I had to endure his will, then he was also stuck with me. I didn't have to play nice when we were alone. "Fine," I agreed. "It'll be good practice anyway."

"For?"

"Faking what I don't enjoy."

He pursed his lips into what could've been a smirk. Before he could decide if he was amused or annoyed, footsteps sounded behind me, and Cristiano dropped his hand and stepped back.

The two guards that had stood by Cristiano's side in the church entered, and we proceeded down a hallway, past a long, wooden bench with muted cushions, to an airy living space that opened to a dining room—but as there were no people in it, it must not have been the one Jaz had just referred to. Though lines and curves anchored the tidied, Old World Spanish-style room, it was warmed by clay pottery over a stone fireplace, a gold-and-maroon tapestry covering one wall of the dining area, and trees in ceramic pots. Flimsy, sheer white curtains were drawn halfway, and windowed doors showcased a covered concrete patio with dining tables and couches, and a sizeable pool that rippled with occasional drops of rain.

The kitchen appeared more lived in—and less suited to Cristiano—with deep-orange walls, cornflower-blue shutters, and a green tea-colored wood table. A stout woman reached for a tray of hors d'oeuvres on the counter, and it was impossible not to notice the burn scars up and down her arms. She spared me a quick glance before she side-stepped a man in a chef's hat.

Cristiano gestured around the room rattling off names that went in one ear and out the other. My mind was at capacity for the day. "*Fisker* is the main chef," he added.

A blond, skin-and-bones man standing over a large pot nodded at me. "Fish stew?" he asked.

I looked to Cristiano, who asked, "Are you hungry?"

"N-no," I told Fisker. He didn't look healthy. Nobody in here did. Where had they come from? "But thank you."

Cristiano turned to exit but bent to whisper, "Don't let his gaunt appearance fool you. He was a fisherman in Denmark and knows food as well as any world-renowned chef I've met."

Cristiano nodded for me to follow, and we were moving again. Down another hall, past closed doors and small windows. I thought I detected the din of voices and music, but it wasn't until Cristiano opened one of the doors that a cacophony of singing, hollering, and mariachi overwhelmed me.

"Soundproof rooms," Cristiano explained the disparity in volume. "One of the best investments I've made in the house. The party can rage on while I—we—sleep. Or *we* can rage on while they dine."

His tone was teasing, but I doubted he'd meant it as a joke. He dipped his hand to my lower back and guided me down a small, dark passageway. We stepped through the doorway to the top of a staircase, as if entering a basement, and stopped at a half wall overlooking a subterranean dining hall. Distressed wood beams formed an X on the high ceiling, and candlelight sconces made shadows on white walls. Three long, sturdy picnic tables centered the room, where people ate from a restaurant-style buffet.

At one end of a community-style table, a group of women sat interspersed between children with plates of frosted cake. Their long skirts and dresses resembled what the women of my town had worn to church that morning. They sneaked bites of dessert from the children and laughed across the table from each other.

Cristiano urged me forward by my lower back, and though my hands were only figuratively tied, it still felt like walking the plank. "This is your home now," he said, removing his hand. "These are your people."

*How did they get into this situation?*

"They're just celebrating Easter."

I glanced back at him, not realizing I'd spoken aloud. "Easter?" I asked. "*Here?*"

"It's not as if we've left the country. We still have holidays here."

But anything beyond basic survival would be a luxury for people being held and worked against their will. And they were, weren't they? The alternative was that they lived in the Badlands willingly. As one of Cristiano's victims, I just didn't see how that could be.

"Do you think people in distress eat cake?" he asked as if reading my mind.

Maybe, if it was the best they could make of a bad situation.

My heart fell. I should've been with my father, sitting down for an Easter feast now, or on a plane back to my friends and my life in California. Instead, I was surrounded by the lost and forgotten.

My gaze caught on an older man who glanced up and made eye contact. He lowered his beer mug to the table with a frown, and people fell silent in sections as they noticed us. The music stopped. Wide eyes stared. The number of women and children both surprised and saddened me. Mothers drew their children to their sides. Men stood straighter. They feared Cristiano, but their eyes were trained on me. Did they fear me too? Or was their fear *for* me?

"I can't be a part of this," I whispered.

"But you are."

"Why?" The intensity of their glares made me want to move behind Cristiano, which was ridiculous. *He* was who I wanted to hide *from*. "Why parade me around like this?" I asked under my breath. "You don't need me."

"You will learn all the things I need, and soon, I hope. But as of today, you don't know enough to say what I need." He kept his distance but spoke only for me. "Tonight, you'll meet your people, and they'll see they have nothing to fear."

"Fear?" I asked. "*Me*?"

A portly man raised a frothy ale and shouted, "Are the rumors true, *patrón*?"

Despite looking as if he'd just come from the fields, the man must've been one of Cristiano's inner circle to address him with such an informal term of respect.

"*Sí*," Cristiano said, moving away from me. "I've formed an alliance that will benefit both parties."

An excited murmur moved through the crowd. The man banged the bottom of his mug on the table so loudly, I stepped back and hit Cristiano's body. He grabbed my shoulders and released them as if the lace had burned him.

Other men slammed their mugs and beer foamed over, dripping onto the tables as they offered celebratory shouts. "*¡Epa!*"

"It should be a prosperous year—" Cristiano started.

"Who cares about business," another said. "Who's the girl?"

Cristiano chuckled as if sharing an inside joke. "In order to make the deal, I've taken a wife."

I glanced over my shoulder at him, but he kept his distant eyes on the crowd as if I weren't there at all.

Though a few men and women smiled, and the children were mostly awed, some of the enthusiasm left the room.

"My bride will stay here with us out of convenience," he said, adding under his breath, "unwilling though she may be."

Cristiano started down the stairs, leaving me standing there alone. Up until then, he hadn't been so dismissive. He hadn't been dismissive *at all*. Not once since he'd turned up at my father's costume party. Even as I'd been forced down the aisle to him, he'd watched me with curious, hungry eyes. In the car, he'd shown interest and a modicum of warmth as he'd asked after the state of my feet.

And he'd claimed to be jealous. So he wasn't completely indifferent to me. Was he? Earlier, he'd claimed he'd wanted me by his side. Now, he didn't even seem to care if I descended into the party with him.

I hadn't realized the warmth of his attention until he took it away —especially in a room full of strangers.

Perhaps now that I was caught, I was little more to him than a product of the merger. And that was what I'd wanted, wasn't it? To be nothing to him? To be left alone?

The security guards were suddenly at my back, and my only paths were back through them or down the stairs. They looked even unfriendlier than him.

I followed Cristiano.

As I hit the basement level, a young boy ran up to Cristiano without any hesitation. I braced myself, though for what, I wasn't sure. Perhaps anger from Cristiano at being approached that way.

"*Mira*," he said, opening his mouth and pointing at his missing front teeth.

Cristiano stopped. "What am I looking at, Felix?"

The boy grinned wider. "I lost the second one."

"That's too bad," Cristiano answered. "You won't be able to eat any cake."

"Yes, I will," he declared. "I already had a piece."

A woman—Felix's mother, I assumed—took his hand to pull her son away. "*Perdón, señor*," she said to Cristiano as she eyed me. "He's just excited for the *el Ratoncito Pérez* to leave a gift under his pillow."

"Who wouldn't be? There will be one there tonight, Teresa," Cristiano said and looked to a member of his security team.

The guard nodded in acknowledgement, then limped away to speak into his two-way radio.

"*Gracias, señor,*" Teresa said and thanked him again before turning her eyes on me. "She's beautiful."

"You need anything else from me for the project we discussed?" Cristiano asked.

"No." Teresa shook her head. "But it helps to see her for myself."

In any other situation, I would've demanded they not speak about me as if I weren't standing there. But I couldn't be sure who was friend or foe—or who worked for Cristiano and who was in my position.

Teresa guided her son away, and I found a sea of unreadable faces looking back at me.

"Eat, drink," Cristiano bellowed to them, gesturing at their tables. "Don't let us interrupt the fun."

The music resumed, and people turned back to their food, beverages, and conversation. It felt wrong to drink and sing. People almost seemed . . . *comfortable.* I could see that they were well-fed, and they acted as if they were safe. In some way or another, the people here must've been employees of the cartel and their families. Which made this the office Easter party.

Cristiano nodded at the buffet. "You should be able to find something to your liking."

"I'm not hungry." I crossed my arms over my stomach and hoped it wouldn't growl. To me, it just wasn't the time for tamales and cake. "What was that with the boy's mom? Some kind of code?"

"Code for what?" he asked.

"You expect me to believe that exchange was really about what the Tooth Rat would put under a kid's pillow? Did you just order someone decapitated or something?"

The corner of his mouth twitched as he led me to the spread of food. "No, *mi amor.* Just handled. I'll do the same to you if you don't eat something."

My stomach was in knots. "Food is the last thing on my mind."

"What *is* on your mind?" he asked.

"I'm tired," I lied. "I don't see the purpose of being paraded around for people who don't seem to want me here. Is there somewhere I could lie down?"

"*Sí*," he answered. "My bed." Amusement flashed across his features. He was testing my limits. Trying to scare me.

"Fine," I said. "I'll eat."

"Good to know that threatening my bed works on you." He handed me a paper plate printed with party balloons. "While Felix and his mother are here, Eduardo will put a hundred pesos under the boy's pillow. I've also hired her for something personal, but it's nothing deceitful. Not as exciting as a beheading, just a small favor."

I eyed Cristiano for signs of sarcasm but was only met with a casual shrug.

A young man walked over, his arm extended in greeting. "*Felicitaciones*," he congratulated Cristiano, shaking his hand before turning to me. "*Y usted también, señora*. You make a lovely bride."

I couldn't tell if the man was mocking me by extending his congratulations to me as well—Cristiano had made it clear to all that this was nothing more than an arranged marriage.

"Doesn't she?" Cristiano remarked as if I were a prized pig, and barely glanced at me as he said, "Go make yourself a plate."

I understood his order for what it was—they needed privacy. Diego and my father had dismissed me the same way many times. In a way, Cristiano's true colors were a relief. This was the ice I'd expected to find in my new husband. It was a wonder he didn't melt in hell.

As I turned, Cristiano touched my arm, leaning in so only I could hear. "But stay close. I should be able to reach out and touch you whenever I please."

He returned forward, leaving me with his clean scent, promised heat, and a chill that raced down my spine.

Dusk encroached, and true darkness would fall soon. And when it did, Cristiano would touch me *whenever he pleased*.

## CHAPTER 4

# NATALIA

Standing over a hand-painted sink, with cobalt blue and white shiny tiles at my back, I stared at myself in a bathroom mirror, my wide, nervous eyes and pale face bathed with warm, honeyed light. Over an hour into the Easter party, and it was the first moment I'd had alone. Cristiano carried on conversations and shook hands as if I didn't exist, yet if I ever left his side, he'd reprimand me with a look or a clipped command under his breath to return.

I touched the dark circles under my eyes, and my new wedding ring caught the light. I inspected the small, meaningless diamond Cristiano had probably found in a pawn shop. Or, more likely, one of his men had been ordered to pick it up.

*"In order to make the deal, I've taken a wife."*

Literally.

How far back had Cristiano planned this? For Diego and me, the union had been sudden, but had Cristiano known my fate since the night of the costume party? If so, then he'd played with us—and I feared the game wasn't over.

Cristiano had admitted as much at his nightclub. This was all a game, and I had to play, or I'd lose.

But how did someone like me, with nothing except the clothes on my back, beat a man who had every resource available to him?

I had only one thing to offer—one bargaining chip.

I hadn't forgotten Cristiano's threat to Diego earlier.

*"Envision me taking her with the same fervor on this, our wedding night."*

I pressed my hand to my stomach as my insides wrenched. How long until Cristiano ended the party and took what he felt he was owed? I needed to prepare for tonight, mentally and physically. For me, sex was no longer about love. It was an exchange, and perhaps a tool I could use to make my time here bearable.

With a knock on the bathroom door, I opened it and met Alejandro, the guard who'd shown me to the bathroom and who'd also stood for Cristiano at our wedding. "*Don* Cristiano is asking for you," he said.

"Can't I use the restroom in peace?"

"It's been twenty minutes."

"Don't have the shrimp," I snapped at him.

I thought I detected a smile in his eyes, but he remained passive. "Noted."

He led me back through the house. In the kitchen, people continued to buzz, coming in and out with trays, though it seemed to me everyone had eaten plenty. Jaz stood at the sink washing dishes with her head down. Her bun sagged, and pieces of her red hair had come loose around her face. I'd thought she was young and pretty before, but as I studied her profile, I realized she was beautiful.

I stopped where I was, and without consulting Alejandro, I seized an opportunity to gather more information while Cristiano wasn't around.

I walked over to her. "Do you need any help?"

She looked at me with brown, startled eyes. "No. This is my job."

I rolled my lips together, glancing at Alejandro. "How long have you worked here?" I asked.

"Years."

My mouth fell open. She looked my age. "Is it . . . did you live here before? Are you being paid?"

"*¿Qué?*" Her gaze shifted over my shoulder to Alejandro. "I don't know what you're talking about."

"Where are you from?" I asked, touching her forearm.

She flinched back. "I'm from *here*. This is my home."

"Is there a problem, Natalia?" Alejandro asked behind me.

Everyone in the kitchen went quiet. The chef leaned against a counter and slurped stew from a bowl like a server on his dinner break. The scarred, elderly woman glanced at Jaz and me, and then quickly away.

I faced Alejandro. "I was asking for . . . aspirin."

Jaz turned off the faucet, yanked off her rubber gloves, and slapped them against the counter with a *thwack*. "I'll bring you some, *doña* Natalia," she said with obvious sarcasm and a glare before walking away.

"Come on," Alejandro said. "Jaz will find us."

I'd clearly upset her, and I hoped I hadn't gotten her into trouble. "How old is she?" I asked.

"Not sure. Early twenties?"

"But she's worked here years?" I asked. "Doing what?"

He frowned at me. "What do you mean? She's part of the household staff. Cooks, cleans—that kind of thing."

"But is there more that's . . . required of her?"

"Well, it's a big house," he said, his eyebrows drawn. "She helps keep the rooms in order, manages the landscapers—"

"Never mind," I said with a sigh. I just didn't understand how such a young girl had come to work here, and whether she was in any kind of trouble. She didn't seem to be. So what was the truth about the Badlands?

Alejandro veered us away from the party and toward the living space we'd walked through earlier.

"Where are we going?" I asked.

He gestured in front of us. Some of the main room's French doors had been opened, and the scent of rain and wet soil drifted in from the patio I'd seen earlier, the pool just beyond. Cristiano sat at a round table with a group of men, his back to Alejandro and me, an ankle over one knee and a cigar in his hand. Alejandro continued outside and went to take the last open patio chair, leaving me in the doorway.

Cristiano drummed his fingers on the arm of his chair looking anything but bored. He almost seemed relaxed as he acknowledged Alejandro but didn't notice me behind him.

"It's all right," he said after a few moments of silence. "Continue."

"As I was saying, Cortez is demanding more from us than the buyer paid," the glass-eyed man said after a sip of his drink. *Max*. He'd brought me from the church garden to the wedding earlier that day.

"The shipment is invaluable, but he doesn't need to know that," Cristiano said. "Pay him a fair sum, nothing more."

Max nodded through a cloud of white smoke. "If he doesn't like it, he'll like the alternative even less."

I stepped lightly onto the patio so as not to draw attention. Though both Alejandro and Max knew I was there, it still felt like I was doing something wrong. But picking up even a few words of Cristiano's conversation could help me puzzle together what exactly was happening inside the Badlands' walls.

Cristiano placed both feet on the ground, leaned his elbows on his knees, and pointed his cigar at Max. "But make *sure* he understands that our payment is a courtesy I won't extend twice."

I held my breath, certain Cristiano would turn around and tell me to leave any moment.

"Next time we catch him transporting for BR," Cristiano said, "I'll *take* the shipment. Nobody gets paid shit. And I can't guarantee he'll walk out alive."

"Agreed," Max said.

Cristiano sat back in his seat. "Gentlemen, there's one thing you should know about my new wife: you should be even more alert than usual. She has been taught since childhood that eavesdropping is the only way to get information."

A few of the men chuckled as my cheeks warmed. He hadn't even looked in my direction—how had he known I was standing there?

"So you'll handle that then, Max?" Cristiano asked.

"*Sí, jefe*."

Waiting to be dismissed, I folded my hands, and my knuckle caught on the diamond on my finger. It would take getting used to. It seemed blasphemous to wear it, a mockery of the marriage I could've had.

"What else?" Cristiano asked. "As much as I like you all, there's only one person I want to spend my wedding night with."

"There's the matter with Sandra," Alejandro said.

"Right. You think she's ready?" Cristiano puffed his cigar, but he still didn't send me away. He knew better than to assume I'd leave on my own, which meant he was allowing me to listen in.

Sweet, woodsy cigar smoke wafted toward me. Only Alejandro refrained from partaking. "She won't look this young forever," Alejandro said. "She can easily pass for fourteen."

"She's been going to Solomon about a year," Cristiano said. "She's ready. Put her on the corner."

I gasped, only mildly more shocked by Cristiano's suggestion than I was that they were talking business in front of me.

"If Sandra says she's too scared, send her to me," Cristiano added.

"You can't put a fourteen-year-old on the streets," I blurted.

Everyone except Cristiano turned to me. "She's not fourteen. She's eighteen."

"But you're trying to pass her off as underage?" I asked. "It's sick."

Cristiano finally looked at me. "Perhaps it was a mistake to let you stay. You're asking the wrong questions, and you don't have the stomach for this yet."

I pressed my lips together. He was giving me a choice, which was more than anyone in a position of authority had ever done before. I could stay and continue to gather information that might help me understand what was happening under this roof, or I could run and hide in my room.

As if responding to some silent signal, the men ashed their cigars, stood from their chairs, and nodded at Cristiano on their way inside. The one with the face tattoo and limp—Eduardo, I thought Cristiano had called him—was last to get up, hesitating before he shut the door behind himself.

Once we were alone, Cristiano turned to me. "Sit."

I obeyed, hoping it would earn me a chance to say my piece. Because despite being in a similar situation, or maybe because of it, I couldn't stay quiet when a young girl was being taken advantage of.

"I do have the stomach for this," I said as calmly as I could so he wouldn't get defensive. "But that could've been *me* on the corner. You protected me as a child once. Do you still have it in you?"

Cristiano eyed me passively. "What do you mean it could've been you?"

"If your father had struck against mine as he'd planned, he'd have left me an orphan. What do you think he would've done with me? Despite their pact with the other cartels in the area, including Papá's, your parents were secretly trafficking humans."

"I'm aware." A vein in Cristiano's temple pulsed as he glanced over his shoulder and into the house. "My father wouldn't have been as kind to you as I have been today. As I have been your whole life."

I swallowed. I couldn't deny that was true, but it wasn't a strong enough argument to justify what he was doing. "You're no different from him now, but you can still change."

He smashed his cigar into an ashtray. "You don't know what you're talking about," he said with a sudden sharp edge to his tone. "I'm nothing like him. I wouldn't exploit a woman, no matter her age."

"If that was true, I wouldn't be here."

He shot up from his chair, nearly knocking it over. "I didn't buy, sell, or trade you," he said, going rigid. "You're here willingly."

*Willingly*. Diego had used the same word. Was it a clue as to what justifications brewed in Cristiano's mind? He seemed set on believing I'd come here by choice. That he hadn't forced me into anything. Diego had told me all about how Cristiano had been so opposed to his parents' budding business in human trafficking that he'd gone as far as to enlist Papá's help to put a stop to it—even knowing there was only way to stop it.

My father had killed Cristiano and Diego's parents for sins similar to Cristiano's. Trafficking people. Exploiting young girls. Plotting against our family.

So what had changed for Cristiano? Why had he stood up to it back then, only to turn around and build an even greater empire on the backs of others? He'd obviously seen and done enough to turn him into a different man. One worse than his father if the rumors were true, and if he justified his actions by convincing himself that anyone came to him willingly.

The door opened behind us. "*Señor?*" came a small female voice.

We both glanced over at Jazmín as she stepped out with a decanter of amber liquid.

Cristiano smoothed out his dress shirt, rolled his neck, and sat back down, once again cool and unruffled. "Come," he said to Jazmín.

She brought him the bottle, and he refilled his drink, nodding at her other hand. "What's that?"

She passed him a pill bottle and set an Evian on the table. "For Miss Natalia," she said.

He furrowed his brows as he studied the painkillers. "What's wrong?" he asked me. "Headache?"

"Yes," I said, which wasn't a complete lie. By the end of the night, I wasn't sure what kind of pain I'd be in. The thought made me queasy and opened a door in my mind I'd been trying to hold shut. How was I going to make it through this? I'd only had sex once, and it had been the complete opposite of what I was about to endure.

My chest started to cave, and I dug my fingernails into my palms, barely managing to keep from breaking down. That was probably what Cristiano wanted, to know the kind of power he had over not just my body but my mind.

"You barely touched your dinner," he said with a frown. "In fact, you look a little pale. You need to eat more."

"I can bring something," Jaz said.

I shook my head. "I'm not hungry."

"Bring us a little bit of everything," Cristiano said with a nod.

Jaz didn't move but bit her bottom lip and laced her fingers behind her back. "*¿Señor?*"

"What is it?"

"She was asking questions," Jaz said quickly, her eyes flitting toward me under her lashes. "About me and where I came from."

Cristiano scolded me with a look. "Why are you questioning our staff, Natalia?"

"They're not *my* staff." I set my jaw as frustration simmered underneath my skin. "I was curious, that's all."

"So ask *me*. What did you tell her?" he asked Jaz.

"*Nada*. Nothing at all." She shook her head hard. "I don't know her. I don't know who sent her. And I don't trust her."

"*Me*?" I asked.

"You trust *me*, don't you?" Cristiano asked her. "Do you think I'd bring someone here who was a threat to you?"

After a moment, Jaz slowly shook her head. "No."

"Natalia's only curious. Like you, she's also suspicious of those around her." He popped off the top of the bottle and shook two pills into his palm. "Can she take these or do I need to be worried you might poison her?"

My heart thudded in the ensuing silence until Jaz laughed. "If I were going to poison her, I wouldn't be so obvious about it."

He winked. "That's what I thought."

There was an easiness between them I didn't understand. She wasn't fearsome so much as . . . flirtatious?

"Jaz, please draw the curtains for us," he said.

"*Claro*. Of course," she said with a nod and returned back inside. A pit formed in my stomach as she shut us off from the rest of the house.

Cristiano opened the water bottle and handed it to me with the pills. I tossed them back quickly.

"Come here," he said.

"I am here," I said. We weren't a half meter apart.

"Closer." He took my hand and brushed his mouth against the back of it. "It has taken all my effort to keep my hands off you tonight."

Memories flashed across my mind—him cradling my face at the nightclub, running his roughened palms up my leg in my bathroom, encircling my ankle in the car. His touch so far had been callused but never cruel.

A thread of unwelcome desire tugged inside me at the idea that he'd been anxious to touch me again. What had stopped him earlier? Why did I care when I should just be thankful and let it lie? I didn't want to respond to his touch. I *couldn't.*

"Any closer and I'll be on your lap," I said.

"You've read my mind."

"You've ignored me tonight."

"I'm not ignoring you now." He stared at me expectantly. Now that we were alone, his full attention was back on me. I could see why so many people sought it. First, the boy who'd lost his tooth. Then, throughout the night, many people had approached Cristiano, vying for his time. He hadn't looked at any of them the way he looked at me now.

He tugged on my hand until I was standing, then pulled me across his lap. "This is where I like you," he murmured, hugging me against him. "Never question my attraction to you."

"What am I?" I asked, my heart rate kicking up as hardness pressed against my hip. "Something you stole from Diego? A way to hurt both him and my father?"

"*You,*" he said, nuzzling my neck, "are my *wife.*"

"You mocked me in the church, and you're mocking me now."

"I'm not." He slid a hand under my hair and ran his thumb up to my scalp. "You're mine. I wouldn't give you away, Natalia. I'm not my brother."

My heart missed a beat. The sting was fresh. Diego was both the person I would've called for comfort and the reason I was here. Perhaps Cristiano was right—Diego had given me away, along with my trust. But did a betrayal that deep slice right through my love for him? I didn't think it was that simple—I wanted to strangle him and then fall into his arms, anger and grief warring in me.

But I couldn't think of it now. When I had Cristiano's attention, mine needed to be on him. I had to play my cards close to my chest until I knew what Cristiano planned for me. He required all my energy and left me little to worry about Diego.

"At least Diego never held me against my will."

"You're not my prisoner." He massaged my neck. "You can leave when you like, but then the deal is off."

"You gave us your word that if I married you, we'd all be safe."

"Not only have we *not* consummated the marriage, but our arrangement was made in bad faith on Diego's part. I proceeded anyway, but my protection only extends to your family so long as it is mine. As long as *you* are mine. Leave me, and my obligations go with you. One phone call to the Maldonados is all it would take."

He wanted me. Even a dead person would be able to feel his need pressing against me. But it was there in his words, too. *Mine. His.* Diego had made a risky deal with one of the most powerful cartels in the country to transport their narcotics across the Mexico-US border, and he'd failed, costing them millions of dollars. Now, the only thing keeping them from retaliating against my father, his family, and his cartel, was my new husband. Cristiano. A man who had the means, the connections, and now, a reason, to keep the Maldonados at bay.

I tried not to give in to the feeling of Cristiano's strong fingers working my tendons. "Why?" I asked. "What do you want with me?"

"I want details." He put his mouth in my hair. "Tell me, Natalia. How was it with him? Where did you do it?"

I tensed. Surely, he didn't mean my night with Diego? "That's sacred," I hissed.

"Nothing you've done before me is sacred. As your husband, your secrets are mine."

"And let me guess—yours *aren't* mine," I said. "How is that fair?"

"I never said that. Ask what you like. I'll do my best to answer. But not until I've gotten my answers. Where did my brother dishonor you? Your bedroom?"

"Dishonor?" I snapped. "That's the height of hypocrisy coming from you."

"*Dishonor* is a gentle word for what he did." Cristiano curled a hand on top of my thigh. "He lied to both of us. He broke my terms and stole from you in the most malicious way."

I took a breath, containing a shudder as I tried to keep up. "What do you mean?" I asked. "He lied to you, yes, but—"

"But nothing," Cristiano said. "You know the truth. When we made the deal, I'll bet my life you were still a virgin."

"He wouldn't . . ." My mind raced. I had trusted Diego all my life—I never would've opened up to him that way otherwise. Only two nights ago, he'd climbed up my balcony and into my bed. And this morning's wedding had not been spontaneous. "When did you make the deal?" I asked.

And I prayed. *Any time before Friday night.*

"After the warehouse burned," Cristiano said, "and Diego had no more options."

I turned my face away as my throat closed. *Friday morning.* I didn't want to believe it. Cristiano had more reason to play with my mind than Diego did to hurt me that way. To have traded me for his freedom was hurtful and cowardly, but to have come to my bedroom after having made this deal? Ruthless. Unforgivable.

When I looked back, Cristiano studied me. He'd given me this look in the past, one a student might give a complex math problem. He resembled his brother in that moment. Diego had worn the same frustrated expression trying to solve the Maldonado equation once it'd started to go wrong.

What had gone wrong, we'd find out, was Cristiano. He'd sabotaged Diego's deal by stealthily stealing, attacking, and burning the Maldonado's shipments before they'd ever made it near the border. If Diego had manipulated my virginity from me, then he'd broken my trust beyond repair. But that didn't mean I could believe a word from Cristiano's mouth, the man who'd orchestrated this entire plot.

"I've answered your question," Cristiano said. "Now answer mine. Where did he take from you? Your bedroom?"

Lights blurred together along with Cristiano's words. I barely heard what he'd asked. "Yes," I said absentmindedly.

"*Mmm.* That lucky piece of shit. I wouldn't have minded having you there, where you thought you were safest, where you slept and dreamed . . ." His hand slid up the lace covering my outer thigh. "Where you've touched yourself."

Everything sharpened back into focus. "How do you know that?"

"A guess, but I'm not wrong, am I?" I felt his smile against my cheek. "Did he warm you up at least?"

"Stop," I whispered.

"I will, once you tell me what I want to know. He betrayed you—don't protect him."

Protect him? It was my natural instinct. But did I owe Diego that anymore? "I'm protecting myself," I said. "Why does it matter how it was with him?"

"It humors me to know how he botched your first time, and what I'll have to do to redeem it."

"He didn't *botch* it. Far from it." Cristiano's arrogance fueled my anger. Both men had knocked me back and forth like a tennis ball. Despite my fury with Diego, he was turning out to be the easiest way to get under Cristiano's skin, and in that moment, I wanted that. I needed to hurt him. "He did warm me up," I said. "With his mouth. And it felt *amazing*."

"Amazing?" Cristiano repeated, sounding amused. "A trip anywhere is amazing until you've been to the moon. Then what?"

"We had sex," I said, and amended, "*amazing* sex."

"And you didn't bleed," he said.

"No, but I had an orgasm, which I much prefer."

His grip on my thigh tightened, and he shifted under me. "Did you?" he asked. "Or are you making that up?"

"You told me not to lie to you—that's the truth. I didn't even know I could get so wet, and it took practically nothing for—"

"Enough," he snapped, his lip curled. "Did he use a condom?"

"Yes," I said. "Or no. I guess we'll find out in a few weeks. Will you want me then, baby and all?"

He took my chin, turning my face to his. "Watch your step. You're entering dangerous territory, my love. Condom or no condom?"

I'd never seen Cristiano unravel, and it hadn't taken as much as one might think. His breath came fast, his eyes dark. I knew without knowing—few saw this side of him and lived. It should've scared me. It did. But it was equally electrifying to drive such a powerful man to the edge so quickly and keep him there.

"Tell me honestly," he said, "and in exchange, I'll invite your father for dinner tomorrow night."

Tears instantly filled my eyes. *Papá*. I would've done anything to see him in that moment. "My father?" I asked. "You'll let me see him?"

"No doubt he has questions."

"*Questions*? He'll be worried sick!"

"Then I'll bring him here and show him he has nothing to be concerned about." He flexed his fingers against my thigh. "That you're in good hands. Unyielding hands. That is, if you tell me what I want to know."

I swallowed. "We used a condom."

Cristiano's expression eased slightly. "Smart girl."

I hadn't realized I'd sunken deeper into his lap until the door opened again, and I vaulted forward.

"*Ay*," Jazmín said. "*Perdón*."

"It's okay," Cristiano said, beckoning her while keeping his eyes on me. "But discretion, please, Jaz."

"Yes, yes," she said, hurrying to the chair. "The curtains are still closed."

"Good." Cristiano took a plate from her, and she disappeared as quickly as she'd arrived.

"What're you hungry for?" he asked. It sounded like a threat.

I surveyed the serving plate with fried chicken, rice, beans, plantains, and more. None of it sounded appetizing when my stomach was nothing but nerves for what was ahead.

"Dessert?" He slowly forked off a pale-blue frosted bite of Easter cake and held it up to me.

"You already announced our marriage," I said. "Why are we hiding behind curtains?"

"Eat," he said.

Tit for tat. Indulge his questions, and I'd get to see my father. Eat his food, and I'd get my own answers. It was enough to get me to open my mouth and let him feed me a bite.

"It won't be possible to keep much from Jaz," he explained. "She's everywhere. But while you and I get to know each other, I prefer privacy. People are curious about you." He nuzzled under my ear. "As am I."

His breath tickled my neck, and I cursed my body as it warmed, threatening to arch into him, my nipples pebbling. It came as no surprise a man so adept at manipulating people's minds could also do the same to a woman's body.

He offered another bite, and I leaned in to take it.

"You're pretty when you eat." He thumbed frosting from the corner of my mouth and licked his finger. "Not like me. I went through a period where food was hard to come by, and if I didn't fight to eat, I might not eat at all."

My heart panged at the thought of anyone going hungry until I realized the cause of his struggles. He'd fled the home he'd known for eight years, ours, because of his involvement in my mother's death. I didn't care how many *sicarios* he brought me—unless we could go back in time, I'd always believe his guilt before his innocence.

"You have plenty to eat now," I said, pursing my lips. He didn't deserve all that he had.

"I do." His voice rumbled as he added, "And I'm voracious, *mariposa*. I take big bites. I eat like I won't get another meal. I gulp down the finest wines and unwrap my candy fast, lick and suck until I get to the sweet core,"—he nipped the shell of my ear—"because I'm greedy for the juicy center."

I shivered, reading his words perfectly. I'd once envisioned Cristiano like an animal fending predators off his spoils. I had no idea what was to come, but I knew I'd be his feast, his candy, the frosting he licked clean. Tremors of dread mingled with a craving to be devoured as Diego had promised but not delivered.

Shame washed over me. What prey harbored even the smallest hope of being caught?

*Stupid* prey. *Senseless* prey.

Cristiano would have his way with me and discard the carcass.

"If my brother warmed you up with his mouth," he said, "I will make it my new life's mission to set you on fire. Are you ready for our wedding night?"

"Why do you think I wanted the aspirin?" I asked.

He drew back as if I'd slapped him. A second time. "Meaning?"

"You can make me sit on your lap and feed me sweets, but it doesn't change the fact that you'll push me down on a mattress later and take what you want."

After a moment, he released his hold on me. "I'm not making you do anything," he said. "Sit where you like."

It almost felt like a trick, and perhaps it *was* a mind game. As long as we didn't consummate the marriage, I'd be on edge knowing he could call things off at any moment. That was, assuming Cristiano was even true to his word. I stayed where I was, deliberating as my weight rested on his large wall of a chest.

Neither of us moved until he said with an edge to his voice, "Go now, *mariposa*. If I'm not forcing you, then you're pressed against my cock *willingly*, and my control slips fast."

I stood quickly. I wasn't sure what I wanted, but slipping control was enough to scare me off for now.

He pulled a chair so close that it wasn't a far cry from sitting on his lap. I took the seat, and he passed my plate over. "I'm not the one who forced you into this marriage," he said, all the rumble, grit, and sex in his voice gone. "I tried to warn you about Diego."

I paused with a bite halfway to my mouth. "You manipulated him into a position where he'd have to give me up or lose his life."

"Is that what he whispered in your ear at the church—that I stole you from him?" Cristiano asked.

What other explanation was there? There was no question that's what had happened. Diego had given me away, but Cristiano had stolen me as well.

I put the fork down and pushed the cake away. "He didn't have to whisper anything. I know what I know—neither of you are innocent."

"And you decide what's true, do you?" he asked. "You don't have even a shadow of a doubt that I killed your mother, so it must be true."

I choked a little, barely managing not to cough. If that *wasn't* true, then it would turn Cristiano from a murderer on the run to an innocent man fleeing persecution. I refused to believe that. Cristiano was the last person who deserved my sympathy. "Yes," I said. "I still think you murdered her."

"You want to believe it, because you want to believe the worst in me. You'll excuse Diego anything. Imagine how you'll feel if none of it is true."

"I have eyes and ears. You were standing over her with a gun and blood on your clothes, ready to make off with the contents of her safe." I could admit to myself that I had shreds of doubt as to whether he'd done it. But how would being falsely accused have shaped the man he was today? It still made him a wild card—but one with an axe to grind. And it still didn't excuse the business he ran now. Emotion bloomed in my chest, and I channeled it into anger. "You'll put a young girl on the street," I accused, my voice rising. "That's the lowest of the low, and it can never be forgiven."

"I agree," he said coolly. "But you refuse to listen to my side or to see reason." His jaw firmed as he nodded at my plate. "Eat your cake, Natalia. Live in that world where Diego is a prince. When you want answers, and you've got the guts to face them, let me know." He stood, took out his phone, and said with finality, "When you're ready for the truth, I'll be here."

I jerked my head up. "That's it?"

"What's it?" he asked as he typed.

"I can go to bed?"

"You sound disappointed."

Ending the night now meant I'd wake up and go through all of this again tomorrow. He would devour me—it was inevitable. The sooner we got it over with, the sooner I'd know my family was safe. "I told you—I want this done."

"Don't worry. It will be done. I don't need you to believe me to fuck me." Narrowing his gaze on me, he slid his phone back into his shirt pocket. "But I intend to take my dessert in the bedroom."

## CHAPTER 5

# NATALIA

Night had fallen, covering the town like a blanket. Out front, freedom spread in every direction from the precipice on which Cristiano's home sat. But even in the dark, I could feel how abruptly it stopped at the Badlands' gates. A light flickered here and there to the soundtrack of a hooting owl but it was otherwise silent and the horizon black.

"Put a smile on your face," Cristiano said as we stood in his driveway, waiting to see off the next wave of guests.

On the patio, he'd been unable to keep his hands off me, but now, distance was all he seemed capable of. I was once again invisible until I was a nuisance or had done something wrong, like frown.

I forced my mouth into what I hoped looked like a smile when an elderly couple exited the house, the old man walking on a tilt. His wife took both my hands and rushed out a goodwill prayer as Cristiano helped her husband down the steps. Nobody seemed to have cars except Cristiano himself—once they left, they descended into the night on foot.

After the final guest, Cristiano held open the front door for me. This was it. We were alone, and there was no more time. I entered the house to the *clink* of dishes from the kitchen. Lingering smells of fish stew and baked goods lent me no comfort. As I trailed behind him, Cristiano glanced over his shoulder, as if ensuring I hadn't made a break for it.

In the kitchen, cleanup had begun. Staff members in rubber gloves and aprons filled the dishwasher, topped plastic containers, and scrubbed the ovens.

"We'll continue to eat like kings for a few days," Cristiano said, and some people laughed. "Everyone raved about tonight's fare, Fisker. Well done."

Applause filled the room as I hovered in the doorway, trying desperately to piece the scene together. Nobody seemed distraught. Either the staff members were resigned to their situations, or like tonight's guests, they supported, benefitted from, and profited off Cristiano's business.

Even beautiful Jaz had something quietly ugly and fearful about her, like an elegant cat that purred to lure you in, then used its claws on you. She sat on a countertop, feet dangling, watching me as she dried dishes and slid them onto the top shelf of a cabinet.

As Cristiano spoke to a man who looked like a butler, I inched toward Jaz. "Can I have something to drink?"

She gestured around the kitchen. "It's all yours. There's filtered water from the fridge or bottles inside, along with soda, beer, and anything else you want."

It wasn't mine. Just because I'd married Cristiano didn't mean I had a right to anything in his home. I opened the fridge and found a sparkling water I hoped would settle my nervous stomach.

I took a few long sips. Fizz bubbled up my chest, and I pressed my hand to my chest, trying and failing to conceal a burp. Everyone but Jaz laughed—even Cristiano.

An embarrassed smile crossed my face. "Excuse me."

"Jaz," Cristiano called across the kitchen. "Please show my bride to her bedroom."

She cocked her head at him. "Her . . . bedroom?"

He nodded once, and Jaz sighed, conveying her disappointment. Perhaps she, too, had thought he'd toss me in a locked cell and forget about me. Or maybe she knew what was to come, and it was jealousy that plagued her. It didn't seem like a stretch that there could be more to their relationship than employer and staff. That didn't sit right with me—that Cristiano would abuse his power that way, then flaunt it in front of the household and me. And if he was an unfaithful husband—did I care? Was there any chance he *wouldn't* be?

Cristiano took the dish in Jaz's hands and popped it on the top shelf. "I'll finish this," he said. "Go."

Jaz shrugged as she hopped off the counter and gestured for me to follow. "Come on."

"I'm sorry if I made you uncomfortable earlier," I said as we climbed the staircase. "I was just trying to help."

"We don't need your help," she said.

So I was coming to find out. The question was why? I glanced at my interlaced hands. "And if I need yours?"

As we hit the second floor, she dove into an exaggerated curtsy-bow. "I'm at your service, *doña* Natalia. We all are. It's our jobs."

"I hope we can be friends." We continued up to the top floor. "Coming from university, where I knew lots of people and had rarely a dull moment, I'm afraid I'll get lonely."

Jaz didn't respond. I'd been willing to give up all that so I could have Diego, but now I had neither him nor that life. And how would I fill that hole in my chest? As night closed in on me, all that I'd lost did too. But I couldn't let it weigh on me tonight. I had to be strong when Cristiano called for me later.

At the end of a hallway, Jaz used her shoulder to shove open a heavy plank door with iron hinges and hardware that made me feel like I was boarding a pirate ship. A breeze passed through the dark room, fluttering the white gauzy curtains of an elevated, four-poster bed. Only the moon shone through arched doorways that opened to a balcony. Jaz flipped a switch and warm light bathed the thick white walls and red-clay Saltillo tile. A weathered, leather chest sat at the foot of the bed across from a sitting area with a red velvet couch, russet-colored coffee table, and stone fireplace.

I turned in a circle. The room paralleled the rest of the house with dark wooden support beams that cut across a white vaulted ceiling with an antler chandelier as a centerpiece. "*This* is my room?"

"*Sí*," Jaz answered.

As far as jail cells went, it was undoubtedly the most luxurious one in existence. I removed my sandals, picked up the hem of my dress, and made my way to the balcony. I hadn't even scratched the surface of the bedroom's magnificence. As I neared, the world spread out before me.

Stars shimmered like a city in a black sky that bled into the horizon and became the ocean. Waves crashed below. A refreshing sea breeze misted my face, almost delightful enough to make up for my circumstances.

The house had been built through the mountain, desert and town behind us, jungle around us, and nothing but ocean and sky before me.

"But it's so wonderful," I said to myself. I lived on a *bluff*, directly over the water, and had never seen anything like it. "And so big."

From my balcony, it was nothing but ocean and sky. And a long drop to the small strip of beach below. I stared down into the darkness as I once had into a tunnel.

There's always a choice, Cristiano had told me more than once.

There was always a way out.

"It's the master," Cristiano's deep, contented voice answered behind me, rumbling like thunder through the beauty of this new world. "If you're thinking of jumping, don't. You're forbidden."

I turned and braced myself against the short, stucco wall. A cream and brown woven hammock big enough for two swayed in one corner with the breeze. "I'm *forbidden*?"

"Rule number one in my home," he said, his hands in his pockets as a sinister smile tugged one corner of his mouth. "Don't die."

Jaz was nowhere in sight—it was just the two of us. "Why do I have the master?" A knot formed in my stomach as the truth hit me. "Where do you sleep?"

"In the master." His smile broke free and slid over his face. "Where else but by my wife's side?"

But I wasn't his wife. I was, at best, the product of a merger and a convenient mistress, and at worst, a slave to his every whim. Someone to call to his bed when he wanted and to send away when he was finished. What exactly did it make me if I wasn't that? What would compel him to sleep by my side each night when he didn't have to?

With a gust of wind, I hugged myself and walked by him, back into a flickering room. The nights were cooler by the water, and Jaz had lit the fireplace and iron candlesticks on the mantel. "I assumed . . ."

"What?" he asked. "That our marriage was for show?"

"Yes. I mean, no," I said carefully, trying to slow my racing heart. "I know you have certain expectations of me. But there's no need to encumber yourself with a true wife. I don't expect us to sleep in the same bed after we . . ."

"After we what?" he asked, not bothering to hide his amusement.

He wanted to make me uncomfortable by forcing me to say it, but I wouldn't let him. I turned around, lengthening my spine. "I figured I'd go back to my room after you fuck me."

He inhaled deeply, fisting his hands in his pockets. "There is no *after* I fuck you, Natalia," he said. "I'm always fucking you. I should like to be able to roll over and be inside you. To slide down between your legs at your request. To unwrap your pussy and suck on candy at all hours of the night."

My skin pebbled with the alarming conviction in his voice. His filthy mouth was fit for a devil, and I had no doubt it would be just as bold between my legs. Ashamed by the way I quivered at the thought, I kept my back stick-straight. "Most men would be happy to take what they want and send their whore away. I'm fine with that arrangement."

"I'm not." His dress shoes clapped the terracotta as he stepped into the candlelight. Gone was any inkling I might've had that his bullishness was for show, or that he acted so profanely just to frighten me. His desire for me showed in his face and in his ragged words. "In case you haven't figured it out, I'm not most men. You're my wife, not my whore, and don't ever call yourself that in or out of my presence again. Every night, you will eat at my dinner table. And every night, you will sleep in my bed."

"Every night?" I asked, my voice breathy even to my own ears.

"*Every* night," he replied on a growl.

"Until you grow bored of me."

"You may wish for that," he said with furrowed brows that made it hard to tell if he was teasing. "But don't count on it."

I swallowed. Just like my confusion over his interest in my virginity, I didn't understand what would possess him to shackle himself to me when he had the luxury of freedom. The sex, I understood, even if the heat between us continued to bewilder me. We were matched enemies, and that ensured a modicum of respect between us, however small. Walking that fine line between hate and admiration only seemed to kindle our sexual attraction. But I could be both curious to explore that explosive spark and also *not* want to sleep with him.

I'd only planned to give that gift to one man.

My plans didn't matter anymore, though.

There was no denying Cristiano when he'd been stoking the embers between us since he'd returned into my life as a haunting calavera. Except then, our chemistry had been harmless.

But a true marriage? It couldn't be. I'd play a dutiful wife for others as I'd been forced to tonight. I'd placate Cristiano while I listened and watched for opportunities to get myself out of this situation. But what was the purpose of pretending in private that I was anything more than his plaything?

"Forever is a long time to sleep next to someone," I said.

He prowled closer until we were toe to toe. "As you'll grow used to the heat behind the gates of Hell, so will you come to enjoy sleeping by my side—and the safety it affords you."

"Safety from whom?" So far, I'd only lamented what had been stripped of my old life, and feared the dangers that came with being in

Cristiano's grip—but I'd not yet considered any outside threats that came with this new one. "Who do I have to fear more than you?"

"I don't want to find out. Where you sleep is non-negotiable." He raised my chin with his knuckle. Candlelight danced over his face, creating shadows around his eyes much like the dark circles he'd painted on as a sugar skull mask. "In my bed, you'll be safe, Natalia—and in my bed, you'll be *mine*."

The crackling fire was no match for what sizzled between us. Alarmed, I took a step back, and he came with me. A dance with a complex man who had many faces. Earlier, he'd been cold and distant. Now, he was no less hard, but somehow equally warm. I couldn't fathom him so attentive and serene outside this room. For a man as controlled as Cristiano, there was something alarmingly thrilling about getting a side to him others didn't—and to unpeeling his layers. "Are you so insatiable that you need me to be within reach all the time?" I asked, embarrassed by the rasp in my voice.

"Oh, *yes*," he said as if it were a threat.

"You can have any other woman," I said. "Those you can't charm, you can take. Why me?"

He circled me as he had in the church, and my breathing sped. But *unlike* then, when I'd been too stunned to keep up, I turned my head and watched him until he disappeared behind me.

The hairs on the back of my neck stood up as I felt his eyes on me. He would touch me any moment. My body would respond. It already was, my legs unsteady, my heart racing as my mind wandered to a thought I'd had before—what it might feel like to be trapped beneath such a strong body with broad shoulders that shielded us from the world as I took all he had to give.

And he had much to give, I was sure—even before it suddenly pressed into my backside.

He wrapped his arms around my middle, enclosing me in a strong, warm embrace. We faced a floor-length mirror framed by hand-painted talavera tiles that I hadn't noticed before. Cristiano towered behind me in the reflection, hugging my back to his front. His massive hands slid up my stomach and cupped my breasts through the black lace.

"Why you? See how perfectly they fit in my hands?" he asked, watching my face. "They were made for me."

Cristiano was hot and cold, ignoring me one second—and the next, so hopped up and hungry that I felt like a drug he needed in order to stay upright. The only other thing that seemed to take him from zero to sixty was a certain trigger word from my mouth. Cristiano held all the control in our relationship, but I had to grasp it where I could. "They fit that way in Diego's hands, too."

He snarled near my ear, squeezing my breasts until the place between my legs shamelessly throbbed. "I know you only say that to anger me, and it works. It makes me jealous as a dog. Before you were mine, I hated the thought that you were his. Now that you belong to me, it's enough to drive me insane that he had your heart and your pussy first."

The room threatened to spin as my emotions ping-ponged between anticipation and trepidation at being at the mercy of such a powerful and hungry man. To know I'd soon submit, and to have him grow harder against my backside. This was it—what it had all been leading up to. He moved one hand up my neck, jerking my face to the side and my mouth up to his.

"Kiss me," he said.

With our mouths centimeters apart, I fought the infuriating urge to close that small space between us. "No," I said.

"No?"

"You'll have to take it from me."

"There are many women who'd like to be standing where you are."

"I know," I said.

He flinched as surprise crossed his features. "Do you?"

"You're handsome, rich, and powerful. I'm sure many have spread their legs for you. And I'll spread mine, too. But I'll be wishing someone else was between them."

He tightened his grip on my face, holding me still as he lowered his mouth to mine. "I've endured many years of disappointment and suffering, Natalia. I can take a lot. But if you're going to provoke me in this way, you should know—I'm not sure I can control my response."

His warm breath caressed my lips as I swallowed his harsh words. As soon as he'd spoken them, I understood that was what I'd been trying to do—test his control. And if *he'd* meant to scare me, it was working.

Or maybe it was something other than fear that made my heart pound.

He grazed the bridge of my nose with the tip of his. "The thought that he has had you before me means I will work twice as hard to erase him. To claim *you*. Now, don't keep me from that another moment." He nearly bared his teeth. "*Kiss . . . me*."

"No."

He took my mouth, plunging his tongue deep as mine lashed back at him. He slid a hand between my legs and cupped me through my dress, sending bolts of pleasure crashing through me as he rubbed me in the exact spot to make my knees buckle.

I didn't realize I'd shoved my hand in his hair until he groaned and growled. He held me in place and thrust his hips into my backside like a bull ramming a fence that detained him. Cristiano was going to fuck me. I'd known it for hours, but now it was happening. And my body was already giving into him, grabbing at him, yielding for his bruising kiss, growing wet under his firm grasp.

He turned me around, cradled my face, and devoured my mouth again. I fisted his shirt, pulling him closer as he walked me backward.

I gasped for more. For him.

And then in shock.

What was I doing? Minutes in Cristiano's arms, and I was surrendering? It couldn't be. The bastard didn't get to take and take with no consequences. He didn't get to win in every way. He'd succeeded in tearing Diego and me apart, but he would never *have* me.

I released his shirt and dropped my hands to my sides. The pulsing heat between my legs remained, but I ignored its demands and slackened my jaw. Cristiano curled his fingers into my hair, kissing me harder.

There was no point in fighting—our terms had been agreed upon. But if he was going to consummate this marriage, it would be with the understanding that I didn't want it.

That was our reality. If I let myself escape into a fantasy and enjoy this, I'd be playing his game—and losing.

And if he thought I wanted this, he'd never see himself for the monster he was.

He drew back, his breathing labored. "What is it?"

My dry throat made my response hoarse. "Nothing."

"What did I tell you about lying to me?" He squeezed my arms, bringing me to the tips of my toes until our mouths nearly touched. "Don't deny me, Natalia. You want this. I need it."

*Need*. To be needed by a man as dominant and typically dispassionate as him was a heady feeling. It inspired my unsettling—and dangerous—impulse to obey his orders. He made it too easy to fall under his spell. I had to douse any embers of passion between us and detach in order to come out physically and emotionally unscathed.

Sex couldn't always equal intimacy. I'd thought I'd had that with Diego, only to find he'd broken that trust. Sometimes sex was an exchange of the world's most valuable currency—power—and it was the only playing field where I rivaled Cristiano.

I tilted up my mouth and put my tongue in his with the same enthusiasm I'd show a brick wall.

He didn't kiss me back. "What are you doing?" he asked.

"I vowed to obey you." When his grip loosened, I wriggled free and backed away toward the bed. "That's what I'm doing," I said, removing my wedding ring to set it on the nightstand.

"Put that back on."

"As you wish." I replaced it, sat on the edge of the mattress, and lay back.

"I asked you what you think you're doing," he said slowly. "Answer me."

"Do you want me a different way?" I spread my knees and stared up at the ceiling as I gathered my dress. "This is the only position I've known."

"Never mind what I want. What do *you* want?"

"We have a contract. You brought me here, so take what you've bought."

"Did you sign anything?" he asked.

"I took vows before God. Before you. It's my duty—"

"Stop."

I parted my lips and took a breath. A breeze passed through the room and the fire roared in response. Cristiano was known for taking what he wanted. He'd declared he would many times. He'd made it clear sex was non-negotiable.

And yet he kept his distance. It was my unwillingness that stopped him. That puzzle piece snapped nicely into place. If he needed me to want this before proceeding, that gave me something I could use against him.

"Close your legs." It took me a moment to register his order. With his face turned toward the fire, he fixed his collar. "I said close them."

I dropped the hem of my dress and sat forward, bringing my knees together. "Why?"

He smoothed out his shirt. "Go to bed."

I almost couldn't believe it had worked. He could be stopped. Victory rushed to my head like alcohol, and for a moment, I was high. I'd won.

Except, I hadn't.

Reality came crashing through. Until the people I loved were safe, I hadn't won.

*"My protection only extends to your family so long as it is mine. As long as you are mine. Leave me, and my obligations go with you. One phone call to the Maldonados is all it would take."*

"Wait," I whispered as he turned and walked to the door. "Wait!"

He didn't.

He reached for the handle, and I jumped to my feet. Cristiano wouldn't guarantee anyone's safety until he'd had me in the most carnal way. We would consummate the marriage regardless of what he or I wanted—I'd make sure of it.

Now, I knew how to stop him—but I'd always known how to start him up.

I ran across the room, my bare feet slapping the tiles until I stopped short. "Please."

He froze.

"You can't go," I said, grabbing his bicep with both hands to pull him away from the door. "We had a deal."

He arched an eyebrow. "I changed my mind."

I tugged him toward the bed with me as I repeated, "Please."

With a lazy blink, the same desire he'd worn earlier returned to his face. He'd told me once I would beg. He *wanted* me to beg. My dignity had been stripped away in the last twenty-four hours. My virginity had been stolen, my love rejected, and I'd been forced to my knees before God to pledge my obedience to the devil. What more did I have? I was the only person who could keep Cristiano's wrath at bay.

And I knew what he needed to give himself permission.

Only one word—*please*—had warmed his demeanor just now.

I dropped to my knees. I wasn't begging for sex but for the lives of my father, everyone who worked for him, and any innocent person who'd pay the price of Diego's deal. I had no idea how far the Maldonados would go, and I wasn't going to find out.

"Please what?" he asked.

"Consummate this marriage as you promised you would."

His chest heaved. "I don't like the word *consummate*. Choose another."

"I . . ." My throat thickened. I doubted he meant *make love*, and whatever shred of dignity I retained wouldn't allow me to call it that anyway. "Fuck," I said. "Fuck me, Cristiano."

He seized my bicep, urging me to my feet and spinning me around. "You're willing to take whatever I give to save Diego?" he asked, hauling my hips back and making his erection known as he walked us toward the bed. "This is what you want?"

What I *didn't* want was to admit that my quaking was just as much born of desire as it was fear. But I had to if I was going to break his control. "I want this."

He fisted my hair and bent me over the lip of the bed. Despite the fire's warmth, I shivered. Cristiano's dominance finally matched his threats, and it was as thrilling as it was terrifying. He held me down as metal *clinked*, and his zipper *purred*. He pushed my dress up over my ass and pressure weighed against the crotch of my underwear. I gripped the comforter, fighting warring urges to push him off and gyrate against him. I thought I'd wanted gentle, but gentleness had deceived me.

I wanted the monster.

*Break me so I can break you.* What would it do to him to lose control? To look himself in the mirror tomorrow knowing deep down he'd taken me against my will? I would soon find out.

He closed his body over my back, his mouth in my hair. "This is how you like it?" he asked, pinning my hands to my sides. "Answer me."

"Yes."

He thrust, and my damp underwear pressed against my opening as he begged for entry. "No other woman has ever gotten me this hard. I could break right through your panties. Maybe my brother put his dick in you and moved around, but I'm going to wreck your pussy and show you what it truly means to have your virginity taken. To have it *destroyed*."

*Ohh, God.* I sucked in a breath. In any other moment, his words might've confused me, but now that I was poised to be thoroughly shaken and ravaged, I understood what I'd experienced before him was simply a tremble. "Whatever you command is yours," I said through gritted teeth.

He groaned in my ear. "You thought what he gave you was an orgasm? Child's play. When I'm through with you, you won't even remember my brother's name. You will clench on my cock so hard, you'll suck me dry. I will show you,"—he thrust again—"how a man fucks his wife. How an animal fucks. So tell me. How do you want it the first time? Like an animal or as my wife?"

I needed him to fill me, to rid me of the confusing, *consuming* ache between my legs.

I needed him to break me once and for all so I could hate him for it. So he could hate *himself* for it.

"Animal," I said.

"I see," he said evenly. "The beast scares you in the light, but not only do you crave it after dark . . . you become it. I'm not surprised—I knew it all along." He released me and stood, taking his heat with him. "That's why you've soaked the tip of my cock right through your underwear."

I began to shake, trying to connect his words to his actions. With a *zip*, the moment disappeared into thin air. I glanced over my shoulder to find him doing up his pants. "Why are you stopping?"

"I told you once," he said, buckling his belt, "I have no need to force myself on a woman."

My body flushed as I became acutely aware I was still baring my ass to him while he was fully dressed. "But I told you I want this."

"You lied."

"I won't fight you," I said.

"You should. You should fight *anyone* who touches you against your will. Diego tricked you into sleeping with him—I won't do the same, no matter how hard you pretend to beg for it."

I scrambled into a sitting position, pulling my knees to my chest. "But what about our deal?"

"Indeed," he said, his eyes wandering over me as he walked backward. "What about it?"

He turned and left the room. The silence following such chaos was deafening, and I covered my mouth as a sob ripped through me. I'd stooped to a level I never thought possible, and Cristiano had still managed to make me feel even lower. He was right. In the dark, my desires were shameful. I'd wanted him to follow through with his threats.

But he was also wrong. My begging for the beast hadn't been pretend. What kind of animal did that make *me*?

And in the end, I'd failed. Cristiano claimed he wouldn't force himself on a woman, but he would. It was only a matter of time before he did, and until then, we were all still in danger. If he thought walking me down an aisle, filling my stomach with world-renowned cooking, and lying with me on the finest sheets made him anything different than a captor, then there was no question he was a master at justifying any sin to himself.

And I might be in the best position to show him who—and what—he truly was.

## CHAPTER 6

# NATALIA

Bright light flooded my dreams. I'd been on an airplane soaring through cotton-ball clouds, headed somewhere that wasn't here.

In Cristiano's bed.

I cracked my lids as Jaz yanked apart the white curtains and opened the door to the balcony. Sunshine, warmth, and ocean air filled the room as waves crashed through the silence.

Cristiano hadn't come back to bed until well after I'd cried myself to sleep. I barely remembered the mattress dipping with his large body. With as riled up as he'd been, was there any question what had kept him out so late?

I sensed the bed was empty now, but I still held my breath as I checked over my shoulder. He was gone.

I sat up against the headboard, rubbing sleep from my eyes. "*Buenos días, Jazmín.*"

"Oh, *perdón*," she replied without inflection. "I forgot you were here."

"What time is it?"

"Late. *Don* Cristiano is waiting for you downstairs." She disappeared into the closet and called, "He sent me to get you dressed."

"I thought you forgot I was here," I said.

She didn't respond. It didn't matter. I was going to see my father today, and together, we'd find a way to fix this. We had to. If Cristiano respected my father as he claimed, then this was his chance to prove it.

"What do you want to wear?" Jaz asked. Hangers scraped in the closet. "You don't have much."

"I was only planning on staying in México for two weeks," I grumbled.

"The rain has stopped." Jaz returned from the closet with my jean shorts. "It's pretty warm today—" She stopped short and screamed.

I whipped my head around, following her gaze to the patio. Under the grand arched doorway, backlit by sunlight, stood the tall, muscular silhouette of a man with a gun in each hand.

My heart jumped into my throat as I scrambled to Cristiano's side of the bed and Jaz lunged for the top drawer of his nightstand as the man stepped into the room.

Broad chested with dark, spiky hair, a wide jawline, and impeccable posture, I recognized him instantly. Relief filtered through me. I laid eyes on a friend, not an enemy.

Jaz yanked a semi-automatic from Cristiano's drawer, racked the slide, and leveled it on him.

"It's okay, Jaz," I rushed out.

Footsteps barreled down the hall. Cristiano burst through the bedroom door in a suit and tie, his gun raised. "Barto," he said, cinching his eyebrows a millisecond before his jaw clenched. "What the fuck—"

"Don't take another step." The head of my father's security team, a man who'd been blindly loyal to my parents since I could remember, aimed both pistols at Cristiano. "I've been hearing for *years* about Calavera's impenetrable walls and top-notch security." An uncharacteristic grin crossed Barto's face. "Yet here I am on my first try."

Cristiano's knuckles whitened around the grip. "How?"

"You forget, I grew up with the same training you did," Barto said, walking forward when Cristiano did. They stopped before their extended guns touched, eyeing each other—Cristiano, in his tailored suit, aimed his pistol at Barto's chest, and Barto, in head-to-toe black, kept both of his on my new husband's head.

Though the two men were similar in stature, Cristiano had both height and muscle on his former comrade. Apparently, they were matched in other ways, though—Barto had pulled off the impossible feat of breaching my gilded cage's security system, and I was secretly cheering him on. He'd been Cristiano's closest friend at the ranch, and my father's number one since my mother's death, after Cristiano had vacated the position.

"What'd he tell you, Natalia?" Barto asked, keeping his eyes on Cristiano. "That you'd be safe here with a whole town to protect you? I've disproven that completely, and I'm sure I don't need to tell you—it's the people within its walls you need to fear."

"Get in the closet, both of you," Cristiano ordered Jaz and me over his shoulder.

"Barto won't hurt us," I started. "He—"

"*Now*."

"Not until you put your guns away," I snapped at Cristiano. Leveling my voice, I tried my luck with Barto. "There's no need for them. *Please*, Barto."

With obvious reluctance, he made a show of lowering one gun. "Now you," he said to Cristiano.

Cristiano followed suit but didn't completely holster his gun until Barto had put away both of his.

Jazmín kept hers raised until Cristiano said, without turning around, "*Está bien*, Jaz. I'm good."

Once we'd crossed the room and entered the walk-in closet, she hugged the gun to her chest while I stayed at the doorframe where I could see and hear everything.

"Is it true?" Barto asked.

"It is," Cristiano said instantly. "We're married."

"You'll pay for it, you know."

"I'm sure you hope that's true, but you're in for disappointment." Cristiano crossed his arms over his chest. "You're threatening what's mine, Barto. And just because it has been mine less than twenty-four hours, don't think that means I won't protect it fiercely."

Barto shrugged. "A man who calls his wife 'it' has no regard for her."

I stopped just short of shouting my agreement. Finally, I had a true ally on my side.

"We'll handle this as Costa sees fit," Barto said. "But I see his only daughter in the bed of a man she has hated for over a decade, and I can only assume you forced yourself on her. For that alone, I hope Costa locks *you* in a room with someone who'll repay the favor."

"Are you offering?"

"Fuck you."

"Fuck *you*," Cristiano said. "You know me better than to think I'd hurt Natalia."

Barto snorted, his posture easing marginally from his militant stance. "You're not the person I knew. You're a stranger, and I don't trust you. Costa wants to give you a chance to explain. Me? I'd have already put a bullet in your head."

"You would rather she belonged to Diego?" Cristiano asked, arching an eyebrow.

Barto narrowed his eyes, shaking his head. "We're not talking about Diego. You've interfered with Costa's family. For some reason, he wants you alive, but he'd believe that you attacked me and I had to defend myself. Especially with Natalia as my witness."

"Good luck getting her to lie for anyone but Diego," Cristiano muttered.

I pursed my lips. It wasn't exactly the time to passive-aggressively raise grievances. "I think I'd make a concession in this case," I offered.

Cristiano clenched his jaw. "Get back in the closet."

"Change, Natalia," Barto said. "You're coming home."

"She's my wife. Where she goes, I go. Costa is invited here." Cristiano turned his head over his shoulder while keeping Barto in his sight. "Tell this brute of a bodyguard, Natalia."

"It's . . . true," I conceded. "Cristiano was planning to invite my father over today."

"Forgive Costa if he's lost any reason at all to trust the man who might have murdered his wife," Barto said.

Barto still believed Cristiano was guilty. Or was it that he was beginning to waver in that conviction? Barto generally didn't use words like *might* or *maybe*.

"He wants to see you both at the house," Barto said. "Now."

"Where he, or Diego, or anyone can try to ambush us?" Cristiano straightened his tie. "Costa can come to me."

"Diego isn't there," Barto said.

Where was he? I refrained from asking, knowing any mention of Diego from me would change the entire tone of the conversation, and not in my favor.

They stared at each other, distrust radiating from each of them, an interloper and a kidnapper in a standoff. We were going to be here all day.

I exited the closet, approaching them slowly, like I might a pack of wild dogs, and touched Cristiano's back. He stiffened, his tensed muscles only reinforcing the obvious power beneath my hand. "Please, can we go?" I whispered. I hoped Papá wouldn't need any convincing to get me out of this marriage, but on my turf, I'd have a better chance of making my argument. "Your problem is not with my father."

"Nobody will try anything," Barto said. "You have my word."

Cristiano kept his eyes on him and sniffed. "It holds no weight."

I spread my hand on Cristiano's back to see if I could get him to relax. "It does to me," I said gently.

After a pause, Cristiano's shoulders eased. "Given he's family, I'll extend Costa the courtesy of going to him." He raised his chin. "You going to tell me how you got in here?"

"It could've been an inside job." Barto's mouth twitched, as if resisting a smile. "Do you trust your team?"

"With my life. I know you didn't have help from in here."

"Maybe I did." I'd never known stoic, dependable Barto for an antagonist, yet he clearly enjoyed having caught Cristiano off guard.

"Or maybe I bypassed all your security measures, your walls, your guards, your team, all on my own."

"Then I'd suggest you come work for me," Cristiano said. "If I trusted you wouldn't knife me in the back."

"Then you have more sense than I thought," Barto said, and to me, "Go on and change, Natalia."

"You don't tell my wife what to do. You're lucky to be standing here after you broke into my bedroom. Any man who steals a look at my wife in her nightgown should enjoy the view. It'll be the only thing to comfort him on his way to hell."

Barto's lip curled, but he didn't move. "I've seen her in her pajamas more times than you ever will."

Cristiano stepped forward. I grabbed the back of his shirt as he looked Barto in the eye. "There will be no second warnings. Next time you enter my home, you're dead."

Barto's eyes shifted to mine. The determination in them both comforted and concerned me. Was it that he believed Papá would get me out of this? Or that he couldn't? Was Barto just reassuring me he'd never give up?

Cristiano and my father were each bullheaded—neither would back down until he got what he wanted. The question was whether Cristiano wanted me in this life as much as my father wanted to keep me out of it.

And whether what *I* wanted mattered to either of them at all—or if it ever had.

Cristiano let me tug him back. "Get dressed," he said under his breath. "Be quick."

I ducked back into the closet, where Jaz already had an outfit ready. "He should've killed him on first sight," she muttered, holding out a pair of lightweight jeans. "I don't know why he didn't."

"They trust each other, despite how it looks," I said as I drew my nightgown over my head. Neither man would've lowered his weapons and left himself vulnerable in the presence of a true threat. Jazmín, for instance, didn't know Barto at all, and if the way she kept a gun in one hand was any indication, she was prepared to send him to the grave before she ever gave him a chance to officially meet her.

"Who is he?" she asked.

"He works for my father. He and Cristiano used to run security together. Barto has never forgiven himself for my mother's death," I explained quietly, "even though he wasn't even in town at the time." I hooked myself into my bra. "He won't let anything happen to me."

"*Cristiano*, you mean," she said, frowning. "*He* won't let anything happen to you."

*Right*. Jaz was living in denial if she thought he was the hero here.

As I stepped into the jeans, she took a few steps toward me. "If this is some kind of trap . . . you won't get away with it. I promise you that."

I froze, staring at her. "If what's a trap?"

"You. Here. The marriage. All of this."

"*I'm* the one who's trapped." I balked at her. "Why can't you see that? I'm the victim, just like you."

"I'm no victim." She tilted her head at me. "You expect me to believe you're innocent? He's been acting different ever since we heard about the abrupt wedding. You think you can sit on his lap or touch his back, and he'll do whatever you say? I see what you're doing —using sex to get your way."

I blinked at her, racking my brain. "What are you talking about?"

"You can control a man with your mouth, but not by telling him what to do. Cristiano caves because he wants to believe he's found what he's looking for in you. I know better. I know all the tricks, *puta*. I had to learn them to survive."

My eyes widened. Tricks? *Me*? The accusation caught me off guard until the truth hit me—she was right. Cristiano showed me a different side when we were alone. And he *had* heeled just now when he'd agreed to go to my father's. More than once the night before, too, he'd been reduced to basic needs and desires I knew I could fill.

The pieces I'd been collecting fell into place. I hadn't purposely tricked Cristiano into anything. But I was more powerful than I'd realized.

None of that made me a whore, though. I was a survivor, just like Jaz.

"You and I are on the same side," I told her. "But if you can't see that, then we're opponents of your own making." I snatched my t-shirt from her, suddenly regretting I'd trusted her enough to undress in front of her. "And it's *señora de la Rosa* to you," I leveled at her as I pulled on my shirt. "Call me a whore again, and I'll have Cristiano throw you out."

"He would never," she said without an ounce of doubt.

I had far less confidence, but that didn't mean I couldn't fake it. I tipped my chin down. "Who do you think he'd choose?"

"Me, if he's smart. And he is. Smarter than you. We may be forced to wait on you," she said, "but we don't trust you. He lets you in his bed and drops his guard, but rest assured, if ever I come in here and find you've betrayed the man we consider our savior, you won't make it off the property."

She left before I could tell her to get out.

## CHAPTER 7

# CRISTIANO

As we drove up the tree-lined road to the Cruz house, Natalia's father came into sight, his wrinkled face set in a scowl and his arms crossed over his chest. Waiting at the top of the front steps under the porch, he was tall enough to reach up and touch the metal sconce over his head.

Or rip it out and beat me with it.

If I hadn't known him almost twenty years, I might've been intimidated.

We parked on the rustic, Tuscan pavers Bianca Cruz had not only picked out but helped install herself—the way she'd painstakingly overseen every remodel or addition to this house.

As I exited the SUV, Costa raised his chin. "You'd better have one hell of an explanation, de la Rosa." Natalia jumped out of the car before I could get her door. Costa kept his eyes on me as he extended one arm to her. "Come here, *mija*."

Natalia went to her father, looking up at him with big, hopeful eyes. "Papá."

"Did he hurt you?"

"No, but—"

He nodded shortly at me. "Talk. Fast, before I draw my own conclusions."

I stuck my hands in my pockets and sauntered up the front steps with Max at my back. Barto took his position by Natalia. She should be by my side now. I'd grant her and Costa this time to adjust, but I'd never been known for my patience. "Our houses are one now," I told him.

"If this is an effort to take over the Cruz cartel—"

"Not a takeover. A partnership." I glanced at Natalia. Once, it'd been part of my job to keep an eye on her. Now, I was finding it hard to look at much else. And as time went on, it seemed, she looked back with a little more defiance. And a little more familiarity. "If not for me," I said, "Diego would be dead."

"A sacrifice I'd be willing to make in exchange for my daughter's safety," Costa said.

"Then talk to him," I said. "But Diego didn't only jeopardize his own life. He put you, your cartel, and your daughter at risk. Until I stepped in. So you can thank me."

"He *has* thanked you," Natalia said, her cheeks beautifully flushed, her hair slightly undone, "by not wringing your neck for kidnapping his daughter."

Boldness agreed with Natalia. It always had, even when she'd demurred from it. But that didn't mean I'd step back and let her accuse me of *more* crimes I didn't commit. "Kidnapping? I didn't drag you down the aisle." And I wasn't the one who'd dragged *her* away from the door when *I'd* been trying to leave the room the night before.

*God reward me for my restraint when my dick was painfully hard against her underwear and begging for relief . . .*

I cleared my throat and returned my eyes to Costa. "I've kept her alive. I've kept her safe."

Costa's eyebrows lowered along with his register. "And she wears a ring."

I nodded once. "A condition of our arrangement."

"Look at your daughter, *don* Costa," Barto said. "She's terrified."

Natalia cowered against her father. It was for show. Not since we'd left the church had she shown true fear. Even when she'd trembled against my body the night before, there'd been determination in her voice. One could even detect a hint of submission in the way she'd fallen against me during our kiss if one was looking for it.

And I was *always* looking for it.

Even if Natalia had been experienced enough to fake her arousal, she had no reason to. The kiss in the church, and then later in our bedroom, had swept her off her feet. She was right to be afraid of that, but she'd be wrong to deny it.

"I found her in his bed," Barto continued, "and seeing as she's hated Cristiano since the day she discovered him standing over Bianca's body, I can only conclude the worst. Will you let him get away with that?"

"Never. Cristiano will explain himself, believe me," Costa said, still staring at me. "I want her out of this life. What gives you the right to keep her in it?"

"I make my own rights." Now wasn't the time to assure Costa his daughter was safe from me—well, for as long as she resisted. Once she allowed herself to ask for what she wanted, I couldn't guarantee there wouldn't be some carnage, all of which she'd enjoy. "I'm not the one who put her in danger. I pulled her out of it. The Maldonados are no longer a threat, but that can be undone."

Natalia glanced briefly to the top floor of the house—Bianca's old art studio—and I followed her gaze. She and Diego had spent time there as children, hiding from Bianca, playing when Diego should've been working.

Costa turned, steering Natalia into the house. "Go wait in your room. I'll talk to Cristiano and work this out."

"What? *No.*" She pulled away, looking up at him. "I'm not going to sit around while others decide my fate. That's how I got into this in the first place."

If she hadn't been trying to escape me, I might've applauded her. Natalia had been bent to the will of others since before Bianca's death, but it had only grown worse in the years after. Diego, her father, Barto and his security team—and even myself. We were all guilty of it.

But as a kid, she'd stood up to me, a man with a reputation that would terrify most girls, with nothing but grit and determination on her side. And her White Monarch.

She had it in her to rise to the job of cartel queen, but the steel spine that ran in her blood needed space to grow. And encouragement.

"She should be present for this conversation," I told Costa as I followed them into the foyer.

"Of course. But let's you and me speak first." Costa kissed the top of Natalia's head when we reached the door to his study. "Go on upstairs."

"Let me rephrase," I said. "She *will* be present for this conversation."

Natalia turned to me, her light, purple-blue eyes wide like saucers. It was all the thank you I'd get from her, but I wasn't expecting anything more. Natalia had been a precocious and smart child who'd found a way around the rules and limitations put upon her. She wasn't anyone's pawn, but she'd let herself fall into that role for my brother.

Diego, who'd put his hands on her, knowing she was my future wife.

I tried not to think of it, because that was exactly what Diego had hoped to achieve by fucking her—to get under my skin.

Not to ease Natalia into her first time, and not to claim her for any romantic purpose before he released her. But to have something over me I could never get back.

Costa turned to face me, his chest out. "You're telling me what's best for my daughter?"

"No. I'm telling you what's best for my wife. She's no longer to be kept in the dark about this world, her life, or our cartels. She's in it now, as Bianca was."

Costa's expression pinched, and his eyes narrowed on mine as he seemed to read me like a book. He ushered Natalia into the study, but turned and lowered his voice so only I could hear. "You don't know what you're getting yourself into, son."

"I don't follow."

"Bianca never should've married me. Don't you think I knew that from the moment I set eyes on her? But I did. Marry her. And I don't have to tell you how much I loved her." He glanced into the study, and I followed his troubled gaze to Natalia. "I did all that knowing what the outcome could be—so some would say I got what I deserved. I worry for Natalia's fate as I did her mother. But I also wouldn't wish my pain or guilt on any man."

Costa was worried I'd get my heart broken, was he? Coming from anyone else, I would've laughed in his face. But the old man had gone through the worst of it, and he was protective of those he loved. Given our history, and mine with Natalia, it hadn't taken him five minutes to see that something flickered in me for his daughter. But he didn't need to warn me of the danger of attachments.

"Would you go back and change it if you could?" I asked.

His eyebrows sank. He took a step closer to me, each of us rising to our full heights, then nodded into his study. "Inside. Now."

Costa stood before Natalia and me like an emperor looking to make a head roll. With Max and Barto competing to guard the door, I stayed by Natalia's side, forming a united front with her, even if she didn't want that.

"Let me see if I have this right," Costa said. "You kidnapped and married my daughter without my permission, and in exchange, you're keeping the Maldonados from eliminating every last one of us."

"That's Diego's version of the story, so it's not entirely accurate. But the outcome is nevertheless the same—Natalia and I are married."

"Give me one reason I shouldn't have it annulled and put Natalia on a plane back to California."

I glanced sidelong at my bride. "I think that reason will mean more coming from Natalia herself."

Her eyes flitted up to mine, as if I'd called on her to recite the North American Free Trade Agreement. In Costa's bright, sunny office, her irises appeared violet. "Cristiano has agreed to cover

Diego's—the Cruz cartel's—debt," she said, and turned back to her father. "Without Cristiano, the Maldonados are still a threat to all of us."

"Natalia understands this is greater than me and her. With this union, you and I are family. Our loyalty is to each other. You have my protection, not just against the Maldonados, but against anyone who dares cross us." I smiled tightly. "That would've always been true if I hadn't been forced from this home. We're stronger together."

"There were other ways of merging," Costa said.

"This way, we're respected as one family. With the exception of Diego, of course." I put my hands in my pockets and shrugged. "Thanks to me, the Maldonados have pardoned Diego. But he has not been pardoned by me—or you."

Natalia swallowed. "What do you mean?"

"We're partners now." I glanced from her to Costa. "Together, our families will accomplish great things. But Diego's no longer my family or yours. He has nothing left—you will cut him loose or the alliance dissolves."

"Diego has nothing left but this cartel," Natalia said flatly, as if she were concealing any emotion she might have about that.

Smart, but frustrating for me.

"A prison of his own making," I said, eyeing her. "I promised to let him live, nothing more."

"Despite his flaws, he's been loyal to us," Costa said. "Why would I cut free a good man?"

Anger simmered below the surface. I'd been treated like a criminal for eleven years, and Diego was *loyal*? He was *'a good man'*? "If Diego is a man, then I am a god," I said, "and which would you rather have protecting your family?"

Costa grunted, leaning his hands on his desk and looking over my shoulder at Barto. "Against Diego's advice, I welcomed you back into my life," he said, shifting his eyes back to me. "I trusted a man I wanted dead for over a decade. Since then, you have taken my daughter, stripped your brother of everything, and attacked my cartel as I sat across the dinner table from you."

I took a pack of cigarettes from my pocket and offered it to Costa, but he shook his head. "Regarding the attacks on your houses and tunnel, I wish it could've been different," I said. "It was necessary, and I'll repay you."

"You killed my men."

"A cost of doing business." If I were in Costa's shoes, I'd have security marching up here now to take me away, but he'd never been as sentimental about his army as I was mine. He treated his men better than most, but taking Diego and me in was the closest he'd come to forming attachments—and that had been at Bianca's urging. "I owe you a great debt—"

"You could let me go—"

"Not *that* great." I cut Natalia off and resisted from smirking, simply because Costa wouldn't see the humor in it. "But I will do what I can to mitigate the loss of good men. As far as the rest, you can place the blame where it belongs—on Diego."

"He said you'd say that," Barto spoke from behind us.

"He took a risk working with the Maldonados." I picked a cigarette and the lighter from the pack. I generally only indulged in smoking at the club, but I was feeling accomplished these days. "If Diego's deal had gone well, he would've made another and another until he'd eventually failed and put you all at risk. I just . . . sped things along."

"You don't know that he would've failed," Natalia said heatedly.

"I do. He wants more. He feels he's owed. That blinds him, and that's how mistakes are made." I winked at her. "If you can't see how I've protected you, consider my interference a preventative measure."

"Owed?" Costa asked. "What for?"

At one of the study's long, wide windows overlooking Bianca's garden, I lit my cigarette. She'd put a lot of work into the backyard, the roses especially. I pushed the window open wider, sat at the sill, and faced my new wife. My budding rose. "Diego's grievances against this family run deep, but I don't blame you for not recognizing that. He's a master of disguise and manipulation."

She glared at me. "Some would say that was you."

"He was never the loyal charge you thought him to be," I said, tearing my eyes from her to look at Costa. "I don't relish being the one to break that to you."

Costa came around his desk. "What're you saying?"

"I came to you as a boy when I was lost and in need of help," I said. "You brought me to this very room. We formed a plan. You trusted me then, and I'm telling you to trust me now. Diego never forgave us for what we did."

Costa drew back. "For your parents?" he asked. "That was years ago. He was—what—eight at the time?"

"He has seen it as a betrayal ever since. I set it in motion, but you aimed the gun, and you pulled the trigger. We each watched our mother and father die by your hand."

"Against Bianca's advice," Costa mused, walking to one of the other windows and looking out. "I did that to ensure you boys understood that even though I was taking mercy on you, I was the boss, and I was not to be fucked with."

I took a drag. "He has fucked with you. And me."

"Bianca warned me that could happen. She never worried about you," Costa continued, glancing at me, "but your brother . . . she wondered if seeing that had irreparably scarred him. I called her paranoid."

Natalia's eyebrows met in the middle of her forehead. "You never told me that."

"As I said. I thought it was bullshit, so after her death, I didn't give it much thought."

Out the window, I tapped ashes from my cigarette. "He sees us as responsible for the loss of his parents, his family's business, and perhaps most importantly—his legacy."

Costa returned to his desk, but sat against the front of it this time, crossing his arms over his chest. "He blames you too?"

I nodded once. "He never forgave me for it."

"How would you know?" Natalia asked. "You weren't here. He was. He stayed by my father's side for almost twenty years."

"Diego is loyal," I agreed. "To himself, and his needs. Staying here suited him." I raised my eyes to Costa. "He's always been good with strategy, hasn't he? He knows when short-term sacrifice equals long-term gains."

I knew Costa was thinking of how Diego had convinced him to work with the Maldonados, despite the risk involved. The business they would've gained from such a prolific cartel would've set them up for years to come—if not for me, of course.

Natalia's defense of my brother was weak at best. She was listening to what I had to say, but until she could grasp the full meaning of it, her default was to act defensive.

But the doubt was in her. She was beginning to see the truth about Diego. As I tended to and nurtured her distrust, it would grow, and her devotion to him would shift easily. I just needed to cultivate a weak trait of my own to get us there—patience.

I studied my cigarette, considering the best way to word what came next. I raised my eyes to Costa. "Diego's plan was always to earn Natalia's love so he could use that against you to take your business."

Costa's response rumbled through the room. "That's a bold accusation."

He could call it what he wanted. It was also the truth. I'd waited longer than I would've liked to tell him that, and yet, it was Natalia's reaction I watched for. A flush worked its way up from the collar of her tight little t-shirt. Her nipples hardened when she was angry—interesting. Where would she direct her wrath?

"He said he didn't care about the business—he just wanted to save enough money so we could live comfortably," Natalia said, her jaw working back and forth. "He said we were going to California."

"I'm sure he also said he'd marry you." I inclined my head toward her left hand. The small ring was missing a diamond fit for a queen, but that was on its way. "And that he'd love you. Protect you. Yet here we are."

Her sexy lips twitched in frustration. "How can I believe a word you say?"

"Don't, then," I said, and looked to Costa. "Believe your gut. Logic and reason. Believe a man's motivations when he shows them to you."

Costa massaged his jaw, lost in thought. "How?" was his only response.

I brushed ash from my pant leg. "Diego lied to Natalia as part of a greater plan to make her love and trust him," I explained. "Then, when it came time, he'd ask her to choose. You or him." Natalia's face reddened. I did so enjoy when she flushed and blushed, such a desert rose . . . and I looked forward to watching her bloom under more intimate circumstances. "She would've chosen Diego."

"You don't know that," she said immediately.

"You chose Diego the moment you agreed to marry him against Costa's wishes."

She shut her eyes briefly. "*Papá*" wouldn't take kindly to this new information.

"What's he talking about, Natalia?" Costa asked. "Is that true? I'm sure it's not." His thick, graying eyebrows fell nearly to his chin as he leveled a glare on her. "Diego knows better than to propose marriage to my daughter. And she knows better, too. Don't you, Natalia?"

She turned fully to him. It didn't surprise me that she took a small step back in my direction. Suddenly my protection didn't sound so bad. "We had no choice," she said. "It was all we could think of to save the family. The Maldonados were closing in—"

"Get to the point," Costa barked. "When Cristiano says you agreed to marry Diego, what does he mean?"

A beat passed, and I resisted from jumping in. This was a battle Natalia had to fight, even though she wouldn't win. "Just as it sounds," she said quietly but without wavering. "It's the reason we were at the church on Sunday."

"How? Diego said Cristiano ambushed you after Mass."

"He did." She touched her ring, then stilled her hands, drawing up straighter. "But everything was already in place, because Diego and I had planned to do the ceremony right after. Quickly. Because the Maldonados—"

"Fuck the Maldonados. Are you telling me you were going to go behind my back when I *specifically* told you to stay away from Diego?"

He took heavy, deliberate steps toward her. "When I forbade you from even *seeing* him again?"

"That's why we had to do it," she cried. "I knew you'd say no, and Diego told me it was the only way to save the family. If I'd come to you first, we might not even *be* here right now."

Costa and I met eyes over her head. "See what I mean?" I asked. "As soon as Diego realized he was in too deep and that I could make it all go away, his first thought was what—or whom—he could trade for his life."

"I just assumed that he . . ." She spoke to herself, her eyes on the floor. "He never actually proposed. I just assumed."

"Because he never intended to make you his wife," I said as gently as I was capable of. "Only to make you *mine*."

As the level of his deceit settled onto her slender shoulders, I had warring urges to gather her in my arms and hunt down my snake of a brother so I could bring her his head. It bothered me to acknowledge that in this moment, especially with Costa looking on, distance was probably what she needed most.

She bent her head briefly, but picked it back up to meet her father's blistering gaze. "If you had listened from the start, I wouldn't have had to go behind your back."

"Then I suppose it's a good thing Cristiano was there!" he bellowed.

Even Max flinched, and I couldn't help a small laugh—the man had faced down far scarier men than Costa, but never an irate father.

Natalia whirled to me, fire blazing in her eyes. "Do you think this is funny?" She jerked a hand back at Costa. "Tell him, Cristiano. We were all in danger."

I looked to the back of the room—not to Max, but to the second ever invader to make it inside my home. The first, an overeager and overqualified *Federal*, was now on my team. Even though Barto and I had been tight-knit comrades once, I'd be a fool to trust him with sensitive information. "Privacy, please," I said to both men.

Max stepped to the door instantly, but Barto waited for Costa's signal before leaving the room.

Once the three of us were truly alone, I spoke to Natalia. "The threat was against Diego for the millions and millions he'd cost the Maldonados. Of course, that threat extended to the Cruz cartel. Costa knows that. It's why he was sending you away."

She glanced at her father. "I was doing what I thought—"

"But." I cut her off, and silence fell over the room as my audience waited. "Diego lied about the danger you both were in. I told him I'd make a deal with the Maldonados to protect you. To protect everyone but him. He was the only one who'd pay the price."

Natalia's face paled as she shook her head. "No. I don't believe you."

"In a final, desperate attempt for his life, he offered you up as my bride," I said.

Costa walked up behind Natalia as she began to shake, her fingers curling into balls. He placed his hands on her shoulders. "Why would you accept, Cristiano?"

"Our families would unite," I said. "We'd both become more powerful. You have a better infrastructure for distribution within México than I do—"

"Your business brings in far more than mine," Costa said evenly. "There's more to it than that. So why?"

My eyes drifted from his down to Natalia, whose gaze burned with anger. But for once, it wasn't directed at me. She had every right to feel enraged. I was, too, for her. In moments like these, stripped down, she was the young girl I'd silently protected from the wings. I saw the headstrong, smart woman she had become but which had been blunted by Costa, Diego, and a sheltered life in the cartel. I saw Bianca in her, as well as a woman I didn't deserve, but one I hadn't hesitated to take. And now that she was my wife, and I had decided I could—and would—keep her, I saw our future.

Costa leaned back on his heels, looking between us. "I see," he said, even though I hadn't responded.

"Diego promised he'd get her to marry me of her own free will, and she did, Costa. I didn't kidnap her. I gave her a choice—she made it."

Natalia's shoulders fell. Either she was still processing the depth of Diego's betrayal or she was realizing that this deal was done, and Costa wouldn't save her.

I was torn. As I willed her to get back up and fight for what she wanted—always, no matter what—I also hoped this was one battle where she'd stand down. I would make her a good husband. And in order to get Costa on my side, I was willing to use all the tools I had to convince him of it. Without his blessing, I'd be forced to choose between the wants of a man I deeply respected and my own.

Costa had always known me to be a good man, even when I'd stood accused of murdering Bianca. If he'd ever truly believed I'd done it, I'd be rotting six feet under right now.

"Natalia knows she's free to walk away at any time," I said. "But if she does, I'll have no more stake in this fight. I'll be forced to walk away, too. I won't send anyone after you, but I can't promise they'll stay away." I glanced at Natalia, shifting on the windowsill. "As I've told your daughter, my protection extends to your family as long as it's mine. And that will remain true when threats like the Maldonados or Diego are nothing but an afterthought."

"And if we refuse?" Costa asked.

I flicked my lighter open and closed, darting my eyes between the two of them. "If I hadn't stepped in, Diego would've pulled off his deal with the Maldonados and made another, building his fortune. Knowing your objections, he would've convinced Natalia to marry him in secret by promising her the world—or in this case, promising to get her *out* of this world."

She took her bottom lip between her teeth, and I had to look away so I wouldn't be tempted to take her sexy, plump lip between *my* teeth.

"Once he'd secured her hand," I continued, trying to gauge Costa's reaction, "and her undying love and loyalty, he would've gone to you with an ultimatum." I paused, then returned my gaze to my wife. "If you didn't hand over the cartel, he would turn Natalia against you."

"I wouldn't have betrayed my father like that," she said. "And I wouldn't stay here and run the cartel with Diego."

"You would've protested . . . at first," I said, nodding. "But he works a long game, Natalia. And the proof stands before me." I tilted my head. "You agreed to give up your life in California. To marry Diego behind Costa's back. In time, there's nothing you wouldn't have done for my brother."

She shook her head. "That's not true."

I squinted at her with one final drag. "Once you were willing to do anything Diego asked of you, then *Costa* would have to do anything Diego asked of *him*."

"You make it sound like I'm just a pawn," she said. "I have a mind of my own."

"Just imagine if he'd gotten you pregnant."

She snapped her mouth shut.

"The leverage he would've had over you . . ." I inhaled a deep breath through my nostrils, more agitated at the idea than I would've thought possible.

And that motherfucker had come close.

Thank fuck for condoms and Natalia's good sense enough to use one—but she'd better believe I'd be inquiring after her period starting now.

Costa squeezed her shoulders with a dark chuckle. "Fortunately, that's not possible for a virgin."

"She's not a virgin," I said.

Natalia's mouth dropped open. "You *asshole*."

Costa flexed a fist as a much greater tide of anger rose in him than in her. I'd known Costa a long time and it had once been my job to read his moods, understand the things he didn't say, and anticipate his needs. He had a temper.

He cast her aside and marched at me. "Tell me how the fuck you consummate a marriage with a bride who wants nothing to do with you."

"I haven't," I said, meeting his eyes, waiting for understanding to dawn. "You have my word—the marriage hasn't been . . . made official."

Costa's neck corded, another swell of rage overtaking him. He looked over his shoulder at Natalia. My mind flashed back to days earlier, when he'd found out she'd spent the night with Diego and thrown her to the ground. It would be the last time in my presence.

He paced toward her, seething. "Diego? He did this?"

I flicked my cigarette out the window and got to my feet, ready to intervene if necessary.

"*We* did this," she answered solemnly, her posture stiff. "I was there too."

"Is this a joke to you?" He blew by her and slammed his fists on the surface of his desk. "How could you let him?"

She flattened her palm to her breast as her chest stuttered, her confidence clearly shaken. "Because I *loved* him," she said, her voice breaking.

"Only because he manipulated you," I said.

"And what about *you*?" she accused, whirling to me. "You've gotten everything you wanted while taking my chance at a happy life."

With a deeply buried pang of guilt, my control slipped. "Then go."

Surprise momentarily flashed across her face, followed by resignation. She wanted to keep making me the bad guy. To make me into my father. I wasn't him, and I wouldn't let her reverse all the work I'd done to make sure of that.

"I warned you about this," Costa snapped at her.

Her chin wobbled. "I thought I loved him—maybe I still do. I don't know, Papá. He hurt me."

"*Qué chingado*, that motherfucking *bastard*." Costa swept his hands over the desk so everything in his path went flying. "I told you if he broke your heart, I'd kill him, and I don't make idle threats."

"I'm as responsible as he is." Natalia swiped a tear away, taking a breath. "It was my choice to make—you couldn't have stopped it."

Costa ignored her, turning to me. "I will ask you this once. By marrying her, do you have my daughter's best interests at heart?"

"Yes." I took a few steps so I could look him in the eye. "And no."

He frowned. "Excuse me?"

"I've always sworn to protect your family. If I hadn't been in the wrong place at the wrong time during Bianca's murder, I would've been here by your side every day the past eleven years." I paused. "I'll make it up to you now and deliver on my promise to Bianca that I'd protect her daughter—even against Diego."

Costa shook his head. "Bianca had her concerns about him. Though she accepted Diego into our family, she suspected he was hiding something, or that he resented us, and I knew the feeling—I had that same instinct. But his words and actions were always loyal, for so many years, and he never gave me reason to turn him out."

"He's clever that way. And he has something I don't—great patience," I said. "But that may be the only thing. I've got him beat in most other ways and now that your family is mine, your enemies are mine. Do I think Natalia deserves this life? No. But I do think she's made for it."

She flinched almost imperceptibly. It was a lot to take in; she needed time to process.

Costa's rage ebbed, but I knew it sat close to the surface. "I want Natalia to be with someone who loves her, treats her well, and protects her."

"Did Bianca have the same concerns about me that she did Diego?" I asked, because I had complete confidence how he'd answer.

"You know she didn't," Costa said. "She trusted you and thought you capable of great things."

With the word *great,* Natalia looked crestfallen. "You said you didn't want me with a good man, but a great one," she whispered.

Costa turned his head over his shoulder to her. "I did, yes."

"Then Bianca would support our union, as should you," I said, reluctantly peeling my eyes from her. "As long as Natalia's under my roof, you have my word I'll do my best to see her loved, treated well, and protected, as you've asked of me."

"Then under your roof she will be. But if I hear a whisper of harm against her, you will have a father's rage to deal with, and I don't think I have to tell you what that means."

"Understood."

I could practically hear Natalia's teeth grinding from where she stood, any despair vanishing. "You talk about me—my virginity, my *mother*, my past and future—as if I'm not in the room." She whipped her eyes to me. "Both of you."

She had been knocked down in this fight, but she struggled to get back up. Now that Costa had acknowledged her as my wife, I knew he'd take my lead. I nodded for her to continue, silently encouraging her.

"I have been traded between families, and brothers, even by my own father." She paused for a few deep breaths, struggling not to cry as she addressed us both. Her forearms tautened as she made fists and pressed on. "You can't tell me who to love, and you don't get to shame me for sleeping with Diego when it was *my* choice. It was my mistake to make."

Tension I hadn't even realized I'd been holding drained from my muscles. I exhaled through my nose as her words etched themselves into my mind. She knew she'd made a mistake. This early on, that realization was the best I could hope for. She may have been holding strong to the shreds of what she thought was love for him—I couldn't fault her that. It would dissolve and fizzle, because it was never real. But for her to acknowledge that Diego had betrayed her meant she'd soon be strong enough to push him out of the way for good.

And I'd be standing in his place.

"I am not your pawn," she said. "You can move me around, buy me, sell me, berate me, but you won't break me. I've known the greatest pain a woman can—first losing my mother, and then having my heart pulverized and my love violated so ruthlessly. But I haven't broken yet, and I won't."

She stormed out of the room and slammed the door behind her.

She was hurting, but I wouldn't pity her. She'd been bent but not broken, as she'd said. It was necessary in order for her to come back stronger and one day take her place as my queen.

Because now, there was no question she would be. Costa had been my biggest obstacle in the way of this marriage.

Natalia was mine now, and nothing could change that.

For every door she slammed, I would open another. I'd pursue her. I'd break down that defiance until I found myself in her sweet core.

She would cross over into the darkness. And I'd be waiting with open arms.

Costa pulled a box of cigars from his desk. "You say my enemies are yours," he said, picking one out. "But yours are also mine. And I've heard rumblings."

*Belmonte-Ruiz*. They were coming for me, and they had every right to. I'd been fucking with their business for a while now, but I'd gotten more aggressive lately. Before I'd ever known it would put Natalia and Costa at risk. It was a train I couldn't stop, and one I didn't want to.

"What you've heard is most likely true," I said, approaching the desk. "I have it under control, but I'm happy to bring you up to speed."

"Do." Costa slid the box of cigars toward me before cutting his own. "Tell me everything."

"There's only one thing to tell." I held up a cigar to the light and ran it under my nose with a long inhale, indulging in the ripe cherry and tobacco aromas. "I'm going to bring Belmonte-Ruiz down."

# CHAPTER 8

# NATALIA

The doors and windows to my mother's art studio had likely been shut since Diego's and my last visit. I hauled open the heavy curtains and let sunlight into the still and quiet room. Cacti and brush dotted the vast desert surrounding the house—a stark contrast to the mountainous, verdant, sea-misted landscape of my new home.

The familiar, dusty vista of my childhood did little to soothe me. Two men I'd trusted more than anyone, and one I barely trusted not to murder me in the night, had completely and utterly failed me. I'd had to fight simply to be in the room as Papá and Cristiano had discussed the trajectory of *my* life.

If I wanted out of my marriage, I couldn't rely on anyone else. What did getting out even mean? I couldn't run, so I'd have to step into the ring with Cristiano and pull no punches. Escape couldn't be physical, so it had to be mental. Emotional. In order to know what it would take to win against Cristiano, I had to *know* Cristiano.

When the door opened behind me, I closed my eyes. I didn't have to turn to know it wasn't Cristiano—the air in any room shifted entirely when he entered.

I'd chosen the art studio on purpose. If Diego was in the house, he would find me in here, the room my father and his staff rarely entered.

*"Princesa."*

I'd know Diego's voice anywhere. A confusing mix of anger, love, and hurt flooded through me—along with hints of relief. I realized I'd thought there was a chance I'd never see him again.

I turned around. Aside from dark stubble, he looked no better or worse than he had the day before. Our wedding day. His golden-brown hair swayed past his ears as he strode across the room.

Before I could process anything, he'd gathered me in his arms. "I knew you'd come up here, my sweet Natalia," he whispered. "Costa sent me to the ranch, but I couldn't stay away knowing you were here." He kissed my cheeks, nose, and forehead. "Hardly any time has passed since I've drunk from your lips, and yet I feel a painful thirst."

He pressed his mouth to mine. The familiar feel of his kiss comforted me. It would've been so easy to sink into. A day earlier, I would have. A day earlier, I had. But everything had changed.

More than ever, I wanted to ignore reality, but more than ever, I couldn't. And Diego was to blame for that.

I put my hands on his chest and pushed him away. "Drink from somewhere else, you . . . you lying, manipulative *bastard.*"

Diego's eyes widened as my own shock hit. I'd never called him anything close to that before.

He raked a hand through his hair and made a fist. "Natalia. I know you must be angry—"

"You tricked me." My heart pounded as I drew on the strength I'd started to find in my father's study just now. "I showed up at the church like a fool thinking I was walking into eternity with you. I gave you my *virginity.*"

"I know—let's just slow down," he said, taking my hands and bringing them to his mouth. "Please. You have every right to rail at me, but first, I just need to know if you're okay."

His lips warmed my knuckles as they had many times before. Before, when we were shy and new at this. Before, when we'd had to hide our developing love from others. Before—when I had been his.

That mouth had soothed mine, had formed words I'd never forget, and now . . . lies I'd never forgive.

"Don't." I yanked my hands back and turned my face away. "I can't even look at you."

"You know I had no choice—"

"There's always a choice." Cristiano's refrain was bitter on my tongue because I hated to admit it was true. Diego'd had more of a choice than I had. He'd put his life and the lives of the people I loved on my shoulders. "You chose to make a risky deal. You chose to trade my freedom for yours." A vision washed over me—Diego climbing up the wood lattice to my bedroom. I'd been so scared he would fall. Now I wondered if it would've been such a bad thing. "You came to my bedroom and stole *everything* from me."

*"Tali."*

I stepped back from him, resisting the pained way he said my name. "You don't even deny it."

He shrugged helplessly as if lost to some higher power. "I was scared if I told you what was going to happen, you'd make me leave, and we'd never get the night we deserved. I had no idea if it would be our only chance to—"

"So it's true." I'd hoped Cristiano was wrong, though I'd suspected he wasn't. Hearing how Diego had plotted to deceive me made my skin crawl.

He swallowed as tears filled his eyes. "Forgive me."

"How can I? You made one of the most important decisions of my life for me. And I'm not even talking about the wedding." A wave of grief rolled through me. "You hurt me."

"I know."

The man who stood in front of me had never given me any reason not to trust him—until now. He'd wanted to know if I was okay? It was a simple question I'd answered countless times before. Too simple. Physically, I was unharmed. The last twenty-four hours had been a whirlwind of emotions from fear and anger to curiosity and even unwelcome desire. My request to Diego should've been straightforward—help me break free of Cristiano's chains. But as my expectations of the Badlands had been wrong, so was my trust in Diego also weaker than it'd been the day before.

I crossed my arms and moved to look out one of the glass doors. "You don't get to care how I am anymore."

Silence filled the room as Diego's eyes burned into the back of my head. "But you are okay," he said, as if it'd just dawned on him. Relief threaded his voice. "He didn't consummate the marriage. I knew he wouldn't when we made the arrangement."

My first reaction was to doubt him, but curiosity got the better of me. I glanced over my shoulder, and then turned to face him. "How could you have possibly known?"

"I put two and two together. He insisted you come to the church willingly. That extends to his bed as well." Diego massaged his jaw, looking to the side as if thinking over his next words. "Cristiano can't see himself as our father. He has twisted and manipulative ways of justifying his actions—even to himself." He paused and met my eyes. "You have to stay alert at all times, Natalia."

There was no other way to deal with Cristiano. Having a conversation with him was on par with navigating a chessboard. "I know that," I said.

"Do you?" He peered at me. "Because he's already coming between you and me."

"*You* came between you and me," I said.

"That's what he wants you to think. Who benefits most from a divide between you and me? Between Costa and me? I warned you Cristiano would try to do this."

I swallowed audibly. I'd always believed anything Diego had said. That he'd had my best interests at heart. Now, I questioned all of it.

But Cristiano had fed these doubts in my head. I'd be a fool to think he wouldn't play with my mind just like Diego would. Neither brother was innocent.

"He'll tell you I took your virginity to get back at him instead of the truth—I wanted one night with the woman I love. He'll say I plotted against your family." Diego was most handsome when he was pained—or acting like he was. His eyebrows met, wrinkling his bronzed forehead as he scrubbed his hands through his hair. "Fuck. If Cristiano can kill your mom and convince Costa he *didn't*—I wouldn't even be surprised if he tried to pin that on me, too. Just like he blames me for all the hardships he endured after he had to flee from here."

I had to look back out the window to keep from giving into him. With his serious, pouty frown and disheveled hair, still in the rumpled clothing he'd worn the day before, he was made to look tormented.

Cristiano *had* said, or insinuated, some of the things Diego accused him of. I doubted Diego's words now more than ever, but that didn't mean I trusted Cristiano, either. Who could I believe? At this point, I couldn't even put my fate in my father's hands.

"Cristiano said Papá and I were never in true danger—that he was willing to make a deal with the Maldonados so only *you* would pay the price."

"Of course he did. A convenient lie." Diego didn't even seem ruffled, as if he'd expected such a brash accusation by his brother. He approached my back, gathered my hair in a hand, and moved it over my shoulder before running a knuckle down my spine. "Please turn around. We don't have much time together, and I don't want to waste a moment not looking at you."

I closed my eyes. "Don't touch me."

"I have a plan."

I hadn't known I'd been expecting those words until he voiced them. I glanced at the ground, inhaling and exhaling through my nose. Diego had a plan—sure. But for how long had it already been in play?

I suspected Cristiano would tell me it was time to join the game if I had any chance at winning. Diego's deception stung worse because I'd loved and had planned a future with him, but I had to recognize that things had changed. I could mourn the loss of him another time. Now, I needed to get my emotions in check, or else they'd consume me, and I'd never get my freedom back—from any of them.

I turned to meet Diego's soulful green eyes. "There's my girl," he said, smiling as if the past few minutes hadn't happened. He took my hands, slouching as he studied them.

This time, I didn't pull away. If Diego was as smart, cunning, and patient as Cristiano made him out to be, then he likely had either knowledge or a plan that could help me dissolve this marriage. Whether that meant finding a way to get Cristiano to lose interest in me or bringing him down from the inside, there had to be a way out.

Diego ran a thumb over my wedding ring. "It was my mother's."

I drew back. I'd assumed it was meaningless. "Are you sure?"

"Yes. I'm surprised he kept it." He frowned. "It means nothing to him, and it has no real value to a man of his wealth."

"Maybe it's sentimental," I said.

Diego squeezed his hands around mine. "He had her *killed.* I prayed to her, to Bianca, to my dead ancestors to keep you safe from him." He clenched his jaw. "My prayers have been answered. You remain mine. Your heart, soul, and body."

I wasn't his. Not anymore. It hurt for me to admit that, but his betrayal had been too thorough. It was also liberating in a way. I had only myself to look out for now. "Belonging to Cristiano leaves no room for anyone else," I said. "You must know your brother has a possessive side."

"But you *are* mine, first and always. It's written right here on my body." Diego shifted our grip to expose his small tattoo, our initials along the inside of his ring finger. "You're what I want, Tali. Try to hold my brother off. Make sure he knows you don't want to sleep with him, and he'll keep his distance."

"What do you *think* I've done?" I asked, slipping my hands from his. "Begged him for it?"

Except, I had. And I might've rubbed it in Diego's face if I wasn't so ashamed of it. That not only had I begged for *my* life, but also for the life of a man who'd traded me, who'd used me.

But worst of all, I had fallen into Cristiano's kiss. Nearly melted at his touch. And then begged for his destruction. His desire had incited my own.

I'd felt Cristiano's carnal need against me more than once, and it was undeniable. Diego might think Cristiano would wait, but there was a line, and Cristiano would cross it. The question was who would be in control when he did—him or me?

"I'm sorry. You're right." Diego wet his lips, glancing at mine as if there was a chance in hell I'd give in to a kiss. "I'm soothed by the fact that I'm still the only one to have you. And if all goes according to plan, I will be the only one."

I lifted my chin. I wanted to know the plan. Not because I thought he'd be successful, but because any information was power—and if I was going to save myself, I'd need all the power I could get, wherever I could grab it. "How are you going to get me out?"

His mouth slid into a smile. "All those snooping skills you've been honing will finally be put to good use."

My scalp prickled. "I can't snoop in Cristiano's house. If he catches me . . ." I didn't need to finish my sentence. A leak in any cartel would be plugged and sealed as fast—and as ruthlessly—as possible.

"You're as stealthy as anyone I know. I need you to look for information on a cartel."

"The Maldonados?"

"No, not those hotheaded idiots—although, continue to ask Cristiano about them. It will distract him." He inclined his head, growing more serious. "The Belmonte-Ruiz cartel is more organized. They know what they're doing."

*Belmonte-Ruiz*. Was that the "BR" Cristiano had mentioned on the patio the night before?

"Tali?" Diego ducked his head to catch my gaze. "Do you know something about them?"

I hesitated. Cristiano had trusted me with information our first night together—a privilege I'd rarely been afforded with Papá, and one it had taken me years to earn with Diego. Even though Diego had finally confided in me about the Maldonados, it was clear now, given my current situation, there was just as much he *hadn't* told me.

For the first time, I didn't know where my loyalty lay. It wasn't with Cristiano, but that didn't mean it was with Diego.

And I didn't need to be told that anybody outside of a cartel was an enemy to that cartel—and anybody who fed enemies information might as well be dead.

"I've never heard of them," I said, and it wasn't a complete lie. "Who are they?"

"I've told you Cristiano and the Calaveras are deeply entrenched in the sex trade," Diego said. "His cartel has been ambushing and stealing Belmonte-Ruiz shipments."

"Shipments?"

"People."

Blood drained from my face. That aligned with what Cristiano had said the night before—that payment was a courtesy and next time, he'd take the shipment. I was disgusted but not surprised he'd referred to *people* so callously.

"Why would he do that?" I asked. "And how is he getting away with it?"

"He's hard to get to. Hard to bring down. That's where you come in. If you confront him, he'll just spin it somehow." Diego got a cigarette from his shirt pocket, then seemed to think better of lighting it. "Play dumb, but act smart. Listen. See. Hear. And report back to me what you find so Belmonte-Ruiz can do the dirty work."

I shook my head. "I'm not doing anything until you tell me exactly who they are."

"Belmonte-Ruiz?" He stuck the cigarette behind his ear. "The most successful traffickers of forced laborers and sex slaves in the country."

The contents of my stomach turned over. "Why would I want to help them?"

"You don't. But they have more reason than anyone to bring Cristiano down. He's costing them money and resources and making them look like fools." Diego glanced over his shoulder and lowered his voice. "Nobody on Cristiano's team can be bought. Trust me. They're loyal dogs. But you're in a better position than any of them. Be my eyes and ears on the inside, and I'll handle getting Belmonte-Ruiz the information they need to take out Cristiano and his business—and to free you."

Diego wanted me to snitch. I didn't need Cristiano to tell me not to go through his things and not to repeat anything I'd heard. Anyone who'd grown up around here, no matter how sheltered, knew that narcs were one of two things—undiscovered or dead.

If Diego was willing to risk me getting caught going through Cristiano's things, that told me two things.

Whatever he felt for me, it wasn't selfless, and that meant it wasn't love.

And that this wasn't a plan to save me, but to save himself.

"And then what?" I asked, to see what he'd say.

"And then we go to California like we planned."

I would've laughed if it didn't hurt so much. I'd wanted California and that life with Diego more than I'd wanted anything except my mother back. California seemed like a distant dream now, though. And if I was honest, it felt *wrong*. The perfect life I'd had there suddenly and starkly contrasted with the dire fates of the women whose lives were being played with by warring cartels.

Diego checked the door again and reached into his back pocket. "Come here, Tali."

Curious, I inched closer to him. He hooked a finger into my waistband and tugged until we were face to face. "Diego," I warned. If Cristiano caught us like this, we'd both be dead. "I told you not to touch me. I don't want you to."

"I know you're scared of how my brother will react, but don't lie and tell me you don't dream about our night together."

Even before all this had come to light, I hadn't thought about the sex we'd had much at all—I was too busy trying to survive. And now, thinking of it only made my mouth sour. "I don't think about it. I can't."

"Then maybe I need to refresh your memory," he said quietly, lowering his mouth to my cheek. "We could steal away into the closet for a kiss."

His hot breath on my cheek made my heart pound. It wasn't exciting. It felt calculating, as if he were trying to get something from me. And even if I'd wanted to have a few final moments in fantasyland, the thought of Cristiano bursting in kept me firmly rooted in reality.

"He will cut off your hands," I said to Diego, trying to take a step back.

"Wait." He kept his finger hooked in my belt loop. Reaching between us, he slipped his hand into my pocket, where he deposited something rectangular. "You'll need this so we can stay in touch. A burner phone."

"Diego, I can't," I said, swallowing as my nerves flared. "Cristiano will find it."

"Then make sure he doesn't. I've disabled the ringer. Delete any text conversations we have immediately. And if he does find it, it won't reveal anything. It has only one number in it—mine. It's saved under your dad's name, though."

"He'll never buy that."

"You're smart and resourceful. Convince him, Tali. I've seen how he looks at you, and you don't even realize the power you have over him. Over both of us." He cupped my cheek, thumbing the corner of my mouth. "If he's about to find the phone, if his hands wander somewhere you don't want them—redirect them. Use his desire for you against him."

Diego was woefully naïve when it came to his brother's prowess. Cristiano could not be misdirected or distracted when he set his mind to something. And if I were going to use my sexuality against anyone, it would be on *my* terms. Not Diego's.

"I believe in you," he said. "I'll do everything I can on my end to make Cristiano pay for putting you in this position."

With one hand on my cheek, he slipped the other around my waist and leaned in.

I pulled back, trying to wriggle free. "Stop," I insisted. It felt strange to deny him when only days ago, I'd have done anything for a few minutes alone with him. "I told you not to touch me."

"That's Cristiano talking, not you." He tilted my chin up, waiting until I met his eyes. "You're only giving them what they want. First your father, now my brother. They're determined to keep us apart."

"Determined?" I heard behind me. My heart leapt into my throat as Diego's eyes shot over my head. Slow, controlled footsteps echoed through the room. I closed my eyes, knowing what I'd find when I turned around. Knowing how bad this looked, and that *I* would pay the price, not Diego.

"*Determined* is not the right word," Cristiano said. "Try resolved. Hell-bent. Try this—I'll stop at *nothing* to keep you two apart."

With deliberate movements, I pushed the phone as deeply into my pocket as it would go. I didn't even want it, but I couldn't let Cristiano see it.

I turned around. Everything about Cristiano was buttoned up—not just his suit jacket and perfectly knotted tie, but his tense frame and locked jaw betrayed his discontent.

"We were just talking," Diego said.

"That's not the way it looks to me." He kept his eyes on Diego. "Come here, Natalia. Behind me."

Leaving Diego's side would expose him to his brother's wrath. *Good.* It was becoming apparent that Diego would use my body as his shield as long as I let him, but Cristiano used himself as mine now—just as he had that morning with Barto.

I went to Cristiano, whose dark, endless eyes bored into mine a moment before he shifted them back to Diego. "And what did you talk about?" Cristiano asked him, dark, sinister amusement lacing his words as he moved in front of me. "The weather?"

Diego smirked. "We spoke of the impossible."

Cristiano didn't stop until they were face to face. "I'm not in the mood for riddles."

"I said there was no way you'd pleased her more than me," Diego said, lengthening his spine. "And she said you had. That she'd never been so satisfied as she was on her wedding night because her groom never touched her."

"*Diego*," I said, covering my mouth. I had shared that in confidence. I was already going to be in trouble—why make it worse for me?

Cristiano grabbed Diego by the shirt. "I hope those ten minutes alone with her were worth it. Now tell me which hand you'd prefer to lose."

"Enough," came a bark from the doorway. I turned as my father took a few measured paces, his expensive loafers silent on the wood floors.

Cristiano released Diego with a shove.

"Cristiano has *attacked* me." Diego fixed his collar, looking to me for backup. I wouldn't offer it—not to either man. "He has attacked your family," he continued, "and proven what I've known all along—he isn't the man we once knew."

"None of us are," Papá said, pausing at my side.

In that moment, they were two wards of the cartel, standing before their fed-up *jefe*.

Papá sighed as if he carried the weight of the world on his shoulders. "When night falls, I'm alone in the dark with only my character. The choices I've made, if I've kept my word—and whether I've stayed true to myself and my instincts."

I looked up at my father as lines crinkled around his eyes. He wouldn't end this. The deal was done. He was the man in my life, but today, my trust in him had eroded just a little.

Cristiano gave a satisfied rumble from his chest. "What do your instincts tell you, *don* Costa?"

Papá looked between the both of them. "Leave my home. And don't return."

I didn't have to see which brother his eyes had landed on, but my nerves flared nonetheless. A day ago, I would've fallen to my knees and begged my father to pardon and forgive the boy I loved, but Diego's sins were too great—and his betrayal had cut this family too deep.

"I am not the enemy here, Costa," Diego said, a tremor of panic in his voice. "You're alone at night because you lost your wife. We may never have hard evidence Cristiano was behind it, but you know in your heart he was."

"I know in my heart that he wasn't," my father said.

He'd said it before, and his mind was made up. I hoped, for my sake, he was right.

Diego narrowed his eyes. "You seem to forget Cristiano blew up one of our tunnels and killed a number of our men at the warehouse last week—an attack which almost took Natalia, too."

"A nearly inexcusable offense," my father agreed. "But one you're guilty of as well, since you made the deal in the first place. Cristiano has promised to make it up to me."

"I'm not the enemy," Diego repeated with conviction.

"No?" Papá asked, fisting his hands. "You never planned to fuck me over? Never thought about it?" His body seemed to grow bigger beside me. "Never wondered what it might be like to back me into a corner—and use my daughter to do it,"—his voice boomed so loudly, the windows nearly shook—"and break her heart and *fuck her* when I explicitly told you to stay away?" He thrust his finger at the door. "Get out!"

Diego's jaw looked painfully tight as he stared at us. Hearing my father talk about me that way, my cheeks burned with the heat of a thousand suns, and I wished for a trapdoor to open up and swallow me.

"You nearly got us all killed," Papá said evenly, but no less threatening. "You went behind my back and tried to take Natalia from me."

"And I failed." Diego seethed more quietly than my father. "But Cristiano succeeded. He's the one who's fucking her now—in more ways than one."

Cristiano turned his head, looking cool and collected, but his neck corded. For a moment, I thought he might make good on his promise to remove one of Diego's body parts.

"And that's no longer your concern," my father said. "My instincts—and those of my beloved wife, God rest her soul—tell me this is where you and I part ways, Diego."

And that was it—Papá's word was the final one. Barto waited by the door, and Diego was forced to walk through his past—by his brother, his benefactor, and his lost love—and toward as uncertain a future as mine.

"May God protect you when I can't, my love," Diego said softly to me as he passed. He glanced over his shoulder at Cristiano. "And may He protect you from the devil—as He has me."

I was beginning to learn it wasn't God's job to protect me, and it certainly wasn't Diego's. Even Papá hadn't been able to reverse this. The job was mine. I wanted to go back to the way things were—to fall into Diego's embrace and believe that he'd fix this. To let my trust in my father overflow as it always had. But they had both failed me, and the sting was fresh. Neither had given me any reason today to believe he wouldn't fail me again.

I was on my own.

## CHAPTER 9

# NATALIA

Taking the terrain at a higher speed than we had yet, I jostled in the cab of Max's pickup truck on our way back from my father's house. We sailed over rocks and potholes right up until we entered the gates of the Badlands and Max slowed down.

Cristiano had taken two calls during the ride home, neither of which had offered anything of value with his monosyllabic responses.

When Max parked out front of the house, Cristiano spoke his first words to me since we'd left my father's. "Wait there."

As he came around to my side of the car, he removed his jacket and undid his cuffs. He opened my door, rolling up his shirtsleeves and looking expectantly at me.

"What?" I asked.

"You will always sit in the car until I come to the door for you. It's a show of respect."

"You can't command respect," I said. "It has to be earned."

He took my waist and spoke low in my ear as he lifted me from the truck. "Put your claws away. I'm the one showing *you* respect."

"I'm not a dog." My feet landed in the dirt. "You don't have to train me to stay until you tell me to come."

"Only time will tell," he said.

I wasn't on my feet two seconds before Cristiano spun me around by my shoulders and yanked my back against his body. He wrapped an arm around my front and something cool and flat pressed against my neck.

I lost my breath entirely, my body registering a millisecond before my mind that he was holding a knife. He knew. He'd seen Diego press his lips to mine. He'd seen him slip the cell phone into my pocket.

"Wh-what are you doing?" I managed.

"I'll tell you what I'm *not* doing," he said, his voice pure grit and gravel in my ear. "I'm not standing here shaking like a leaf, letting panic overtake me. That's what *you're* doing."

"Why?" I choked out. "Why are you doing this?"

"Does anyone need a reason to hurt you? Scare you? Touch you against your will?" He marched me forward to the lawn in front of the house. My heart pounded painfully as I felt the phone against my hip with each of our long strides.

"I'm sorry," I pleaded.

"For what?"

"For betraying you."

He paused, and I could've sworn I felt *his* heart beat against my back. "When did you betray me?"

"Diego touched me, but I told him not to. I tried to stop him."

"And you think I'd punish *you* for *his* gutless actions?"

When I swallowed, my throat moved against the blade. I was afraid to even speak. I sure as hell wasn't going to nod.

"*Do something,* Natalia." When I didn't respond, he growled. "I said fucking *do* something."

Tears filled my eyes. I didn't know what he was asking. Did he mean something sexual? But I was firmly in his grip. I'd made a grave mistake dropping my guard with Cristiano for even a moment. Now, we were going to consummate the marriage as I'd wished—but with a knife to my throat.

I closed my eyes and moved my hips back against him.

He inhaled a sharp breath and threw the knife on the ground. "If that's your move, then I won't say no." He laid a heavy hand on my shoulder. "Get on the ground, facedown, so I can fuck you."

"No," I cried, my throat protesting. "Not like this."

"You're grinding against my dick, Natalia. What did you expect?" He tried pushing me to my knees. "Get down or fight back."

"I c-can't," I said. "I can't fight you."

"Then I'll teach you how," he said, releasing my shoulder and stepping away.

I clutched my throat, whirled around, and backed away as a tear slid down my cheek. "*What*?"

"I wanted to see what you'd do in that situation, and I have to say, Natalia—I'm sorely disappointed. You wilted like a flower. I thought you were a survivor."

"Fuck you." The unbidden words rasped from me as tears built in the back of my throat, but I wouldn't take them back. "What's the matter with you?"

"I could've beaten you. Raped you. Slit your throat. And you didn't even try to stop me." He picked up the knife, wiped the blade along his pants, and sheathed it. "Nobody should ever be able to touch you against your will, Natalia."

"You're the only one who would," I shot back.

"And you stand there and let me, trembling and freezing up the way you did last night."

I gritted my teeth, anger overtaking my fear. "What am I supposed to do?" I accused. "I'm half your size. You're probably five times stronger than me."

"Yet I possess the same weak spots you do, *mamacita*. You just need to know where they are." He looked almost amused as fury burned through me. With a smirk, he said, "Show me the self-defense moves you learned after I stole you away into the tunnel eleven years ago."

"What are you talking about? I don't know any."

"As I suspected." He shook his head at the ground. "Your father threw you on the ground. Diego tried to kiss you earlier when you told him not to. And me? I don't have to tell you I could've done any number of things to you back in that tunnel—as I could right now. What's it going to take to get you to fight back?"

I shuddered as I stared at him, but not just with aftershocks of fear. He made me sound completely helpless while conveniently ignoring the circumstances. "I may never even *see* Diego again," I sniped at him, "so you don't need to worry about him touching me."

"Fuck him. This isn't about Diego. It's on you." Cristiano's chest rose and fell a little faster as he cracked his knuckles. "It never occurred to Costa to teach you how to sever a brachial artery or handle a handgun? It never occurred to *you* to learn to defend yourself?"

I removed my fingers from my throat, but the ghost of the cold metal blade remained. "I *did* defend myself. I left this life. You're the one who brought me back in."

"If your father had ever upset the wrong people . . . don't you think they'd have been able to track you down in California? Did you think that precious, flimsy bubble you created for yourself would keep you hidden? You don't know the simplest self-defense. Can you even operate a bottle of pepper spray?"

"Is there more to it than point and spray?"

"For fuck's sake, Natalia." He ran a hand through his black, normally smooth hair. Now that he'd disheveled it, it stuck up. "Given the malfunction rate, taking a few minutes to learn would behoove you."

"I was doing just fine until you took me." I scowled. "Why are you teaching me this?"

"Do you think I want a wife who'll crumble the moment an attacker puts his hands on her? I need you to fight back." The edge to his voice faltered as he added, "I need you to save yourself and come home to me."

I drew back. Cristiano wanted to arm me . . . but did he not realize I could use what I learned against him? There was almost something *romantic* in his response, and despite the heat, a shiver worked its way through me. "What if I *am* home?" I asked. "Barto got in."

"Believe me, I'm aware. I wasn't planning to work on this with you so soon, but today was enough to open my eyes to the fact that I can't be everywhere you are all the time."

That was why he'd reacted so aggressively, then. And scared the shit out of me just now. Not that I was about to admit that I probably wouldn't have taken this little lesson so seriously otherwise.

He widened his stance and looked down his nose at me. "First, you have to change your mindset. You're in control of your life. You *can* take down an attacker of my size. With a knife to your throat, you might get cut, you'll likely get hurt, but you *can* fight for your life and escape. Come here," he said.

"No."

"Get your ass over here *now*."

I took a moment to catch up and process what was happening. Cristiano was *actually* going to teach me this. How to fight. How to protect myself. That was something nobody else had ever given me. Not even Mamá. Protection had always come from someone else. But as this morning had proved, I couldn't always rely on others. That put me at risk. And Cristiano, apparently, wasn't having it.

I exhaled and stalked toward him until we were toe to toe. "Now what?"

"Turn around."

When I did, he carefully enveloped my shoulders and drew my back against his front. He positioned the sheathed edge of the blade to my neck again. "Show me how you'd fight me off."

I grabbed his forearm and pulled, but he didn't budge.

"You can't compete with my strength," he said, "so don't try."

"Then I'd kick my heels into your shin or aim for your groin."

"Don't tell me," he said. "Show me. It's how you'll learn."

I stomped on his foot, but his shoes must've had steel toes for all the good it did. He just laughed. I couldn't angle to kick him, so I bucked my hips back into his groin.

"You're moving too much," he said. "Either you just slit your own throat or gave your assailant a hard-on."

Without thinking, I pinched the skin of his forearm between my teeth.

"You're a biter," he said. "I sort of suspected you might be . . ."

My tongue flickered over his skin, tasting salt. To my horror, my nipples tingled. I removed my mouth to see I'd left a red mark.

"Usually," he said, "your chin would be locked by my forearm. I'm just not holding you as tightly as I would if this were real."

"Maybe you should," I said and mimicked, "How else will I learn?"

"Relax, Rocky. We'll get there. I'm just walking you through it now." He strengthened his hold. "If you were ever in this position, it'd likely be a planned attack. But not necessarily. Given what we do, your attacker could easily be drunk or high—his pain tolerance will be elevated, and he won't be fazed by a nibble, or, depending on what he's on, something as severe as a stab wound."

"I wouldn't 'nibble' an attacker," I said. "I was demonstrating on you."

"Next time you demonstrate," he said low and gravelly in my ear, "feel free to sink 'em in. I've been looking forward to unleashing your wild side."

"That makes one of us," I muttered.

I felt his silent laugh against my back as he straightened. "If you're going to rely on inflicting pain, you'd better not miss, and you'd better not be half-assed about it. If you go for the eyeballs, gouge them. If you bite, draw blood."

I shuddered. "You're going to teach me to gouge out someone's eyeballs?"

"No. Max is," he said. "He's an expert at it."

"What a weird expertise," I said.

"How do you think he got his glass eye?"

I shuddered. "Yuck."

"Yeah. Anyway, the point is—if you try to hurt the assailant and fail, you'll only anger him." Cristiano repositioned the knife under my jaw. "Listen. You don't want the blade to go sideways or up, or else you're dead. So what does that leave?"

"Down."

"Right. Now, the weakest part of me within your reach is my wrist. Sneak your hands up—slowly," he added as I followed his instructions, "so I don't know it's happening. If you can create some kind of diversion—asking random questions to distract him, for example—that helps, too."

I slid my hands up the front of my body. "Have you ever been to Disneyland?" I asked.

He barked a laugh, and I seized his wrist. "Not yet," he said. "Now pull down, away from your throat."

"I just did that. I'll never be able to budge you."

"That's why you have to know a man's weak spots. My forearm is a bar—you won't move that, but with practice, you *can* move my *wrist*."

I didn't see how that was possible, but I tried. I focused on the weakest part of his wrist until I'd drawn the knife a short distance away. "Like that?"

"Yeah. Now trap my forearm with your right shoulder, and rotate —no, don't twist," he corrected. I resumed my original position and tried again with less *twist*, and more *rotate*. "This is where you leverage your body weight," he said. "Always put your body into it. Rotate toward me."

Since Cristiano wasn't using his full strength, I was able to keep a hold on his wrist and turn into him, contorting his arm at an unnatural angle so the knife was now aimed at his side. "Then you'd stab me," he said. "Keep going."

I glanced up at him. "Stab you?" I asked hopefully.

He raised an eyebrow at me. "No. Keep *rotating*."

I reversed under his arm, bringing his wrist with me until he was forced to bend at the hip, and I was standing over him.

With his face inches from my hip, I suddenly remembered the phone. My heart, already thumping, began to pound as his eyes shifted.

How would I explain it if he found it? Would he even give me a chance to?

My mouth dried as possible punishments ran through my head. Cristiano had earned his nickname, *El Polvo*, for a reason. The Dust. He'd poured sand down the throats of those he'd deemed deserving of a slow, painful death—and no doubt he'd find a certain poetic justice in that particular fate for a snitch with a big mouth.

"Wrestle the knife from me if you can," he said.

I released my breath finally, praying I could get upstairs soon and stash the burner.

"But if not," he added, "at the very least, you can knee me in the face and run away."

I released him. "You'd catch me."

"I would, yes." One corner of his mouth quirked as he straightened. He looked almost comical in a loosened tie, wrinkled dress shirt, and slacks, with sweat dotting his hairline. "But we're going to train you so *nobody* can catch you, *mariposita*."

"Who's we?"

"Solomon, Alejandro, Max, me. We all fight differently, so you'll learn from each of us." He unknotted his tie and slid it off. "Your main goal is to incapacitate the attacker long enough to run away," he said. "You're tall but skinny—we're going to build up your strength so you can fly. Solomon will teach you to assess the situation and make a quick decision—outrun him, stab him, or knock him unconscious. It'll depend."

"Kill him?" I suggested.

"If that's what it takes," he said grimly.

"Who's Solomon?"

"Our resident expert on martial arts. As former Israeli military, he's got experience in street fighting, Krav Maga, Muay Thai, and more." He sniffed, wiping his upper lip on his sleeve. "Let's try again."

"Are you sure you're up for it?" I asked. "I'm not the one breaking a sweat."

He scowled. "I weigh twice what you do, and the sun is fucking strong today."

I shrugged, not bothering to hide my amusement as I turned my back to him.

As his arm surrounded my shoulders, and he pressed the knife to my skin, he said, "Natalia?"

"Yes?"

"If we're going to keep doing this, don't wiggle your hips. It won't do either of us any good if I develop a conditioned response to holding a knife at your neck."

As his meaning registered, I flushed and glanced at the ground. "I *didn't* move my hips."

"Maybe it's a subconscious way of physically preparing yourself, but either way, make it stop." He raised the knife, forcing my eyes up. "Be stealthy," he said, "but don't hesitate. You're not grabbing my wrist —you're yanking it. Use speed, leverage your body weight to bring it down."

"Cristiano?"

He shifted behind me. "Hmm?"

"Did you know, according to Jewish folklore, a pomegranate has exactly six-hundred-and-thirteen seeds?"

"What?" he asked. "I—"

With his wrist firmly in my grip, I rotated, and this time, while we were tangled, I poked the sheathed blade into his ribcage. "Bang, you're dead," I said quietly.

His eyes met mine over his shoulder. A moment in our shared history passed between us. I'd just repeated back to him the words he'd said to my nine-year-old self in my parents' closet before he'd whisked me away down the tunnel.

"Who knew pomegranate trivia could save your life?" he asked, and I was grateful for a reprieve from the gravity of the memory.

"The name Solomon made me think of it." We separated, and I was surprised to find myself out of breath. At least I'd have more than enough free time here to get in shape. "Supposedly King Solomon had his crown modeled after a pomegranate. Thank you, religious studies," I said. "Can I see the knife?"

His eyebrows rose. "Not yet."

"Afraid I'll hurt you?"

He removed the knife from its leather case and showed me the fine, smooth edge that ended in a sharp point. "You'll hurt one of us if you try."

"So that's it?" I asked.

"For today, yes. It's an introduction to get comfortable with panic. If we reenacted this for real, you'd be dead before you even registered what was happening." We briefly met eyes, and he added, "I don't want that, so you'll have to learn how to stay calm and practice these moves until you know them with your eyes shut." He turned the blade, and it caught the light. "When I'm not here to practice with you, Alejo or Solomon or someone else will."

I squinted up at him. In the sun, his coal-black eyes were closer to the color of coffee beans. "You don't want me dead?" I asked, testing out how it felt to tease him.

He put the knife away and wiped his hands on his pants. "Of course not."

"Just trapped." My humor faded. I glanced beyond the cliff, out toward the Badlands' gates.

With a knuckle under my chin, he gently turned my face back to his. "I want to make sure you're prepared," he said. "At some point, you may find yourself in a position where you'll need to defend yourself."

I'd *already* found myself in that position. "What makes you think I wouldn't use what I learn against you?"

Searching my eyes, he lowered his hand back to his side. His demeanor shifted away from its rare lightness—espresso beans darkening to pitch black. "Dinner will be served shortly." He turned toward the house. "Wash up."

## CHAPTER 10

# NATALIA

*Dinner will be served shortly. Wash up.*

Like any other command from Cristiano's mouth, he'd ordered it nonchalantly and with no room for argument.

It wasn't nonchalant to me.

Balanced on the edge of his bed after our impromptu street fight, I waited for him to vacate the shower. Since the day before, I'd been married off, shuttled to a new home, shuttled back to my father's, told this was my new life, and held at knifepoint.

And now, Diego was trying to turn me into an information mule. I'd wrapped the phone in a bra and shoved it to the bottom of my overnight bag until I could decide what to do with it.

*Use his desire for you against him,* Diego had said.

Wiggling my hips against Cristiano had been enough to get his attention. It was becoming obvious it was important to him that I be willing, but I was sure his patience had a limit. A perverse side of me wanted to tempt him just to prove that he was no better than his father or brother. That I was here because I had to be, and that he'd fuck me against my will with no more thought than he'd give to fucking me against a wall.

But did I have the guts?

I tiptoed to the bathroom, careful to stay out of view. In the mirror, I could see the hazy outline of his bronzed, naked form through the steamed-over shower door.

He flipped off the water and stepped out before I could retreat. "Well, well," he said, nude and dripping on the bathmat.

My face burned. I was mortified, but for some reason, I didn't want him to know it. I fought my instinct to run and hide in the closet and held his gaze instead.

I could face him.

Just as long as I didn't look down.

He grabbed a towel from a hook and came around to face me, scrubbing it through his hair. "How long were you standing there?"

"I just walked in," I said.

"Two minutes earlier, and you would've gotten a show."

He wrapped the towel around his waist, and it was then I realized I'd been clenching every body part that could be clenched—teeth, fists, ass cheeks. I urged myself to relax. "I don't know what that means."

"I'm not used to sleeping next to a woman I can't touch," he said. "It makes things a little hard . . . *¿Comprendes?*"

It took me a second, but inexperienced as I was, I understood. It literally made *things* hard. "Because you have no privacy?"

"The physical contact we just had downstairs isn't helping."

My heart thumped. I'd felt it, too, but I wasn't about to admit it. And I'd been right. His patience was too thin for him to wait for me to be willing.

*Not that I ever would be,* I reminded myself.

"Good to know holding a knife to my throat turns you on," I said.

He arched an eyebrow and went to the mirror, inspecting his stubbled jawline. "Shower's all yours. There's a towel on the counter."

I picked it up, went to the closet, and closed the door so I could strip down. I found a deep drawer with a hamper in it, dumped my clothing inside, and secured the towel under my armpits before returning to the bathroom.

Still wrapped in his own towel, Cristiano stood in front of the mirror and shaved up under his chin. His back was not only tan and smooth but very broad. I wondered if he lay down, whether it could fit two of me. I'd never seen anything like it, the way his muscles rippled beneath the surface, the embodiment of his capabilities, his weaponry—his power.

"You . . . you won't look, will you?" I asked, pulling my towel tighter.

With his head tilted back, he lowered just his eyes in the reflection. "If I do, I'll have to jerk off again, and the shower's occupied."

I frowned. "In a house this size, surely you can find somewhere else to . . . do that."

He rinsed the razorblade. "Is that an invitation to look?"

"No."

"Why shouldn't I?" he asked. "You belong to me."

"I don't belong to anyone."

"You're Natalia de la Rosa. You bear my name. You've said vows in front of God."

"That doesn't make me your property," I argued. I didn't know why I bothered when he was clearly *trying* to get under my skin. "Are you *my* property?"

His eyes had moved down to my bare legs. "Sorry, what?" he asked.

"Selective hearing," I mumbled, opening the shower to turn on the water.

"It's cute," he said.

I glanced back. "What is?"

"How you're worried I'll only *look* at you."

He was capable of so much more, as he'd proven out front. I was no match for his strength, and no matter how he trained me, I never would be. As if my feet were made of lead, I suddenly couldn't move. "You said you wouldn't force yourself on me."

"I did say that." The razor scraped his skin. "But I can change my mind, can't I."

It was a statement, not a question.

A reminder.

A threat.

A bluff?

If Cristiano had wanted to take me, there would've been no better opportunity than our wedding night. He could've dominated me if that got him off, or given himself permission if he'd needed it once I'd begged him to get it over with.

But he'd held back.

If he truly thought of me as property, he would've staked his claim on me. I was the one in command, and I suspected he knew I was nobody's property.

I dropped my towel. He froze, keeping his eyes on mine. My heart pounded as I bared myself to him. As I showed him my body on my own terms. As I demonstrated for him that I retained a small measure of control, no matter what he said or did.

It wasn't until I'd turned and stepped into the shower that I released a massive exhale. The last man who'd seen me that way had turned around and passed me off like a baton. I'd shown Diego much more than my body that night—I'd exposed *all* of myself and had held nothing back. At least, the self I'd been days ago. I hadn't been enough. And I was pretty sure that was a good thing.

I shook as I stood under the stream of water, but at least I still stood.

But the problem with testing Cristiano's control was that I didn't know what might break it. Once he crossed the line, then I'd know where I stood. I'd know for sure who he was. I'd know my place here. His restraint put me in a frustrating limbo.

He talked a big game, but so far, he'd only smiled when it came time to bare his teeth. I needed him to break. To show his true colors.

I couldn't beat a monster I didn't know.

AT DUSK, the back patio glowed with strung white lights, and a square, candlelit table set for two. I'd found my way here on my own since Cristiano had disappeared while I was in the shower, and I hadn't seen Jaz since that morning.

A temperate evening with an air of romance suited the long, floral, strapless dress I'd bought in Mexico City a few summers earlier. I'd found it hanging on the back of the closet door after my shower. Cristiano sat at the table, an ankle crossed over one knee as he scrolled on his cell phone. His shoulders were as high as his eyebrows were low. This time, he definitely didn't sense me standing there. I'd snuck up on him—a first.

I recognized the tableware as fine china and silver, impeccably set in the organized manner my mother had tried to teach me as a girl. A bottle of white chilled in a marble wine cooler.

"Are you expecting company?" I asked from the doorway.

The frown he'd been wearing disappeared as he slipped his phone into the pocket of a white, linen dress shirt open at the collar. His eyes drifted over my dress. "*Hermoso*. It's beautiful."

I smoothed my hands down the front of the dress. "The staff does all this for you?"

"For us." He stood and pulled out the chair next to him. "Sit."

I walked by him to the seat across his instead, to the only other place setting. "It seems someone prefers me to sit here."

He reached over and grabbed the corner of the placemat to slide it next to his. "Yet I have the final word."

In all things, I was sure. I took my place beside him.

"Wine?" he asked, drawing out the frosty bottle of Sauvignon Blanc.

My mouth watered for a taste—not of the alcohol but of an escape. A way to dull my senses. But I had to be sharp as a tack to keep up with Cristiano. "No, thank you."

"It's French. Or would you prefer something of the Russian variety?" His eyes twinkled the way they had the night at the club, when he'd pulled two shots of chilled Siberian vodka from nowhere.

"I find myself suddenly on the wagon," I said.

"*¿Qué significa?*" He made a face. "What does it mean?"

"Sober," I explained.

"Ah. Probably wise, but I hope you don't mind if I partake." He poured himself a glass and didn't bother to look, smell, or swish before taking a gulp. "That was quite a show earlier," he said, examining the glass. "I don't know whether to thank you or spank you for it."

My breath caught in my throat. "Why would you spank me?"

"You thought it would rattle me. And it did. I enjoyed it, but that doesn't mean I condone it."

"It was only fair. You showed me yours, I showed you mine." I put my napkin on my lap, averting my eyes. "Now we're even."

He snorted. "Hardly. You didn't even look."

"You don't know that."

"If you'd seen what I've got to offer, you'd either have dropped to your knees to give thanks—or fainted."

I gaped at him. "Your arrogance knows no bounds. Diego was—"

"Nothing compared to me." His mouth slid into a sinister smile.

"Such humility," I mocked.

"I know when to be humble and when it isn't necessary. In this case, I know what I have." His eyes drifted over me. "But I have yet to know my own wife. Though I'm certain she has no reason to be humble, either."

"I'm not a piece of meat," I said.

He picked up his knife and scraped the blade across the tongs of a fork as if sharpening it. "*Bon appétit, ma chérie.*"

Hunger glinted in his eyes, but not for food. It wasn't the first time I'd pictured him devouring me like an animal.

The chef stepped onto the patio and set down a plate in front of each of us. "*Escargot à la Bourguignonne* in garlic-herb butter. Enjoy."

I frowned at the dish, confronted with the first of the many horrible rumors I'd heard about the Badlands. "Are these . . . ?"

"*Escargot,*" Cristiano said blankly. "Have you been to France?"

"No," I said, wondering how a half-dozen snails had made it onto my plate. Tepic had warned of satanic rituals like this—but compared to what my mind had conjured up, this was fairly ordinary. I couldn't help it—I started to laugh.

"What's so funny?" Cristiano asked. "Snails are a delicacy in France."

"I know. It's just . . . I heard these rumors about Calavera."

He used a two-prong fork to remove the meat from its shell and dip it into the sauce. "Well?" he prompted.

I pinched one between my tongs. "I heard your cartel is like a cult."

"What's that got to do with snails?"

"You eat them and other strange foods, then you speak in tongues, sacrifice virgins, and throw rotten fish at whores."

Cristiano chewed, nodded, and didn't deny any of it. "I suppose to people who'd never been outside of México, likely those spreading these rumors, foreign foods like drunken shrimp, bratwurst, bird's nest soup—or snails—would seem strange."

"So that's all there is to it?" I asked. "What about the other rumors? Are they true?"

"I know when to keep my mouth shut." He swallowed and sat back in his seat. "So if I address them for you, you give me your word what I tell you doesn't leave this house."

My laughter faded. Suddenly, I wasn't sure I wanted to know. Surely not all the rumors were as innocuous as French food. That would mean facing the truth about my time here.

"Oh, no," he said, shaking his head as he read my expression. "You don't get to back out now. Tell me you can keep my secrets. I intend to have all your secrets, too, so it's only fair."

I thought of the mission Diego had charged me with. If I accepted, from this point on, I'd be passing along sensitive information I'd been sworn to keep. At least last night, I hadn't yet agreed to anything.

So who had my loyalty?

After today, there could be only one answer. Me. I was loyal to myself. I couldn't trust the reasons why Diego wanted the information, but I wasn't going to kneel for Cristiano, either. Nor would I give up the phone just yet. As of now, it was my only communication with the outside world.

I glanced at the table and back up. "You have my word."

"Fisker—*oye*," he called out. "How many languages do you speak?"

The chef sauntered onto the patio wiping his hands on a dish-towel. "Fluently? *Cinco, señor*."

"So that's Danish, Spanish, English . . .?"

"German and Swedish. And some French." He turned to me. "You look surprised, *madame*. But it's very common where I come from, and in the Badlands too."

"My men are from all over the world. They speak everything from Russian to Chinese to Swahili." Cristiano gestured at Fisker. "In how many languages can you say snails?"

"In more than I speak. *Escargot, snegle, caragols de terra, slakken, caracoles*—"

"This is Natalia's first experience with them."

"Ah, but you requested them?" he asked Cristiano, who nodded. Fisker turned to me and added, "Butter is the key. Dip generously."

Cristiano dismissed him with a "*Merci*." When we were alone again, Cristiano said, "To an uncultured ear, some languages, especially all at once, might sound—"

"Barbaric," I finished.

"But what's *barbaric*," he said, "is the Scottish wedding ritual I partook in last year."

I glanced up, my eyebrows cinched. "What was it?"

"Our Scotsman found himself a lassie, and in his super rural part of the country, they have some outlandish customs. The bride and groom are blackened with soot, feathers, and more, and paraded around the night before the wedding to ward off evil. We then covered the bride in the worst things we could find, like dead fish, sausages, and curdled milk . . . and tied her to a tree."

My jaw tingled as he sat there chewing his food like it was no big deal. "That's disgusting," I accused. "How can you allow that?"

"Should I judge someone else's culture? They have their ideology, and she was a willing participant. Some people might find it strange that you and I were lassoed."

"No one more than me," I muttered.

He chuckled. "The happy Scottish couple was married right here on the property, and they're expecting a son next month."

"So how do people know what happens in here if nobody has lived to tell the tale?"

"Rumors find a way, and that's not true, anyway. People can leave any time they want, but most choose to stay."

I didn't know enough yet to say if that was true, but why *would* they stay?

"And drones," he added. "We capture or shoot them out of the sky on a regular basis, but occasionally I'll allow one to spy on us—if I think it helps."

I was almost afraid to ask. "Helps . . .?"

"Let the people talk," he said, waving a hand. "That's my logic. What the idle mind conceives is far worse than what I can do. If people want to believe we have no internal compass for right or wrong, and that we'll brutalize intruders who would do us harm, I won't correct them."

I blinked. Either he was fucking with me or he was fucking with the world. "You *don't* brutalize intruders?"

"Who'd do us harm?" he asked, sucking his teeth. "Of course we do."

I narrowed my eyes. "What about the virgin rumor?"

"Well." He dipped another snail. "That I'm not sure about, although I have some ideas where it started."

I studied him a moment, then finally gave in to the aroma of garlic and butter and picked up a shell. I followed his lead, extracting the meat and dunking it in the sauce. It looked even slimier drenched in melted butter. I stared at it, steeling myself to put the creepy crawler in my mouth.

"Are you sure you don't want wine?" he asked with a hint of a smile.

I tested the snail with my tongue, but all I tasted was the flavoring. "I'll have a little," I conceded.

Cristiano eyed me as he poured Sauvignon Blanc into my glass. "I chose this meal for a reason."

"To rattle me?" I asked, mimicking his earlier accusation.

The corner of his mouth twitched. "No. It's a tribute to your mother, actually."

I froze with the tiny fork in front of my mouth. Hearing anyone talk about her was enough to catch my attention, but walks down memory lane were few and far between. Diego hadn't known her very well, and Papá could be stingy where emotions were involved. Cristiano was one person with actual memories who I'd never been able to talk to about her. "What?"

"The meal I had prepared for you tonight is one Bianca made for me once, start to finish, after a trip to Paris with your father. I had snails at your house—imagine the reactions of my brother and the others at the ranch when I told them *that*."

I could only imagine. Diego had often shared rice and beans from a community vat. "Was I there?"

"Yes, but you were too young to remember."

Sadness tugged at my heart as I shook my head. "I *don't* remember."

"There's probably a lot you don't."

As much as I wanted to hate Cristiano and anything to do with him, the food before me took on new meaning. I put it in my mouth and chewed, and though the gelatinous consistency was unnerving, it wasn't nearly as gross as I'd thought. With warm butter and garlic, it resembled seafood.

"Imported from California," Cristiano murmured. "Like my young bride. I look forward to teaching you about the world."

I had to stop from warning him his arrogance was showing. Perhaps the women he normally dated weren't very worldly, but he knew my parents had liked to travel. "I've been places," I said smartly. "And I've spent more time than you in North America. I can show you some things, too."

"Of that I have no doubt." His gaze darkened. "But I have fourteen years on you—and believe me, I intend to use them."

Fourteen years, several countries, and likely countless women in his repertoire. How was *I* the one who'd ended up here? "Do you have other wives?"

His eyes nearly fell out of his head before he bellowed a laugh. He seemed more and more relaxed as the night went on—more than I'd ever seen him. Was it the wine, or something more? "That would make me a polygamist," he said.

"It wouldn't surprise me."

His smile faded instantly, and he blinked his gaze toward the pool a few moments. "Fear not. You are my one and only," he said and cocked his head as I glanced at my plate. "You look disappointed to hear that. Do you want me to keep other women?"

"I'm sure it doesn't matter what I want," I said. "You didn't come to bed until, like, three or four this morning I think. When you left the room, you were suitably . . ." And without warning, I lost my breath remembering the ravenous way he'd trapped my body, whispered in my ear, and probed the aching spot between my legs. He *must* have gone to see another woman—and how had he treated her? With the same hot and cold regard? Had he pretended she was me? Had he *wished* she was? "It doesn't take a genius to figure out where you were," I finished.

"And where was I?"

"Is there a brothel in this 'town'?"

"I don't pay for sex."

"Maybe Jazmín then," I said. "She's beautiful, and very loyal to you, it seems."

Cristiano rubbed his jaw, watching me. "I must say . . . if you're wading into the waters of jealousy, I quite like it. I like it very much."

"Jealousy?" I mocked. "That a man who would rape me probably raped someone else instead?"

"Jealousy," he said in a corrective tone, "of a woman who doesn't want her husband with anyone else. Even if *she* doesn't want him."

I picked up my drink and took a sip that half drained it. "A tribute to my mother," I said, shaking my head into the wineglass. "What a crock of shit."

"I beg your pardon?"

"I think you made all that up about my mom to toy with me."

The pocket of his shirt lit up with a call. When he made no move to answer it, I said, "Your phone is ringing."

Fisker stepped onto the patio with our next dish. "Duck confit," he announced, delivering an aromatic, beautifully presented duck leg with caramelized apples in front of me.

Cristiano sat back in his seat, his eyes suddenly glued to me as he reached into his pocket and appeared to send the call to voicemail. "Don't wait for me," he said. "Go on."

I started to say it was impolite to eat until he'd also been served—but who cared about manners at a time like this? Politeness was almost a form of capitulation, of following rules set by someone with more authority than me. I picked up my fork and knife and took a bite.

The rich, tender meat and crispy skin instantly transported me to my past. I'd eaten this before at my mother's dinner table, right before she'd passed. "This is familiar."

"I suspect you haven't had it since childhood," Cristiano said.

I looked up at him and took longer than necessary to chew so I wouldn't have to admit I'd jumped to conclusions. Maybe he *was* taking me for a walk down memory lane—but why? Another mind game?

And to what end? To make me feel safe?

Even if it was a game, memories of my mother were more temptation than I could resist—they'd always been hard to come by. In the years following her death, my father had grieved fiercely but privately. At some point, that had changed, but it had always been rare to find him in a state that he could open up about her. Most other adults who'd known her weren't the sort a young girl would pepper with questions.

How much did Cristiano remember? How much was he willing to share?

And what would each revelation cost me?

"She made this for you?" I asked.

"Everything Fisker will serve tonight, she made." He looked down on me in a way that made me feel like he was imparting wise advice. "Who cooked for you in the years before you went to boarding school?"

"The staff or myself," I said. "But Papá wasn't this adventurous. We mostly stuck to regional dishes. Things he grew up on."

"I figured as much."

It was strange to think Cristiano had figured anything at all. "You wonder about my diet?" I asked with a hint of a smile.

"Mostly how things were after her death. After I left," he said. "What do you remember about her?"

I frowned at him. "What do *I* remember?" I asked. "A lot. More than I can say by dessert."

"Then tell me about dinnertime."

Studying him, I used a napkin to pat sauce from the corner of my mouth. I wasn't sure what he was getting at, but maybe my memories would trigger his. "She hummed when she plated the food. That's how I could tell when it was time to eat." I could still remember the tune, though I never hummed it aloud. It took me to a simple yet blissful point in time I'd never be able to get back to. "She always served herself last. I think she was lactose intolerant because I remember her getting stomachaches if we had cheesy meals, and she never liked ice cream."

"Sometimes she brought *queso fundido* to the ranch," Cristiano said.

"With chorizo." I smiled sadly and took a sip of wine. I wanted these memories, but they were also little knives in my heart. What hurt the most was the time we'd lost. I would never completely know my mother, the kind of woman she was as an adult—the friend she would've been. Seeing her through others' eyes was the best gift I could receive.

I hoped Cristiano understood I was grateful, even if I couldn't bring myself to show it. I suspected he did. "Why did she like you so much?" I asked.

He paused as if caught off guard, and it took him a moment to answer. "I like to think she and your father were both great judges of character."

"I like to think that, too, which is why their regard for you is so confusing."

His mouth parted with surprise before he breathed a laugh. "Bianca took me in. I owed her my loyalty, and she knew she had it."

"What kind of man turns his back on his own family to fight for their enemy?" I asked.

"Listen . . . I don't pretend to be moral in any way. Much of what I've done is inexcusable. But some things are so vile, they can't be forgiven."

"I agree," I said, raising my chin. If he had stopped his parents' descent into human trafficking, how could he excuse himself for the same crimes?

"She trusted me," he continued after a moment.

"But why?"

"It's not hard to gain someone's trust; it's just too easy to lose it. I tried to be there when she needed me. I never lied. I was forthcoming. When she and your father disagreed, I didn't automatically side with him. I told them what I thought was right. I always did with Costa, even if I knew he wouldn't like the answer."

I glanced toward the kitchen as Fisker brought Cristiano a plate. He dug in before the chef had even turned his back. "What did you and Papá disagree on?"

"Not a whole lot, but I remember once," Cristiano said, gulping down a mouthful of fowl with wine, "he wanted us to light up a location. He thought it housed two gang members responsible for a drive-by that took out some of our men. He was trusting his gut, but I was trusting mine, too. Despite his order, I wouldn't move until I had proof."

Though Cristiano was as calculating as Diego, it was in a different way, and I couldn't quite put my finger on why. Most men around here shot first and aimed later. "Why not?"

"Costa was right—the men were in there. But I was right, too. There were also women and children in the house who would've paid the price if we'd attacked."

Maybe that was it. Diego looked out for himself, and Cristiano looked out for others. Which was nice and all, except that nobody seemed to be looking out for me. Diego had acted in his own best interest by offering me up, and Cristiano in his by taking me.

"Weren't you so noble, then?" I asked, sitting back. "And I suppose you feel that Diego and I forced you into a life you'd once looked down on."

"Only as much as I have forced this life on you."

So what did that mean—we were even? Hardly. Even if he'd been wrongly accused and pushed out of the cartel, at least he'd had his freedom. "Do you still think you're the voice of reason?" I asked, my temper rising. "Did you think if you cornered me, you could then convince yourself that you had *saved* me?" I rolled my eyes. "Maybe you hoped I'd see it that way, too."

A server I didn't recognize cleared our plates as we stared each other down.

"Did you roll your eyes at me?" It was a warning more than a question. Cristiano grabbed a toothpick from a tin and stuck it in his mouth. "You're certainly brave for someone who thinks I'm capable of murder on a whim."

That image of him didn't match the man sitting in front of me, who'd restrained himself many times over in the weeks since he'd returned. Who was he? How long until he showed me? I was rolling my eyes and sniping at him because I was *frustrated*. "I think you still need me, so you're playing nice," I said. "I just don't know why, or for how long."

"I never needed you."

The cutting words snipped at my already short wick. "Then why am I here?" I retorted.

"Because I wanted you."

My heart thumped beneath his suddenly darkened gaze. All playfulness evaporated from between us and in its place was whatever inexplicable charge had existed the night of our costumed dance. Of the morning he'd bandaged my feet. Or of any time since I'd arrived when I'd been under his spell.

"I told you that merging our families through marriage wasn't my idea. I have no *need* for you and your family. Only desire." He relaxed into his seat again and chewed on his toothpick. "I took you, yes. The idea of having you as my bride appealed to me for several reasons. But now, I can't imagine things any other way."

# CHAPTER 11

# NATALIA

As Cristiano paced by the pool on a call, I rationed what remained of my wine. I picked up the glass. Backlit by the turquoise pool, it glowed ethereal blue. It was tempting to drown myself in the wide, generous wineglass after the day I'd had, but I had to be smart.

I'd wasted too much time being gullible. I'd hated Cristiano for his elaborate plan to get me to the Badlands, but it was Diego who'd orchestrated the whole thing. Forty-eight hours earlier, I would've sworn on my mother's grave it wasn't possible.

But I knew it was the truth.

As I tilted my glass, watching the translucent liquid pool to one side, I recalled something Diego had told me before we'd slept together.

*I'd have to be willing to promise him anything to get him on our side. Even if I don't mean to keep those promises.*

Now, thanks to Cristiano, I was thinking like Diego. If he were here now, he'd spin the tale in his favor. He'd tell me he'd promised Cristiano the world to get him to agree to help us, but that he'd planned all along to free me once the coast was clear.

I righted the wineglass. Two more sips, I decided, but then I'd stop.

I doubted I'd get tipsy after the snails, duck, mixed salad, and cheese, but I wasn't taking any chances. Reading a man like Cristiano required my full, unadulterated attention.

Especially when *I* had *his*.

I drizzled honeycomb over blue cheese, impressed by the meal we'd just eaten. Recreating world-class fare my mother had made might've been a way for Cristiano to distract me from the truth of my situation—but the walk down memory lane was welcome nonetheless. It was as close to time spent with her as I'd get.

Cristiano made his way back to the table, tucking his phone into his shirt pocket. "I have to leave town for the next couple days, so we're going to go over some things."

And of all people, I had brash, taciturn Cristiano to thank for my night with Mamá. Not that I would.

I swiped my index finger through the remnants of honey on my plate. "Rules?"

"If that's what you want to call them."

"You already told me the first one—don't die."

He slid his chair from the table and sat. "Be kind and courteous to the staff. It's not their fault you're here, and they just want to make you comfortable—that includes Jaz."

"I have no problem with Jaz." I drew a sad face on my plate, then sucked honey off my finger. "She has a problem with me."

"She's, ah . . . protective."

I didn't miss the way he stared at my mouth or momentarily lost his words. This was what Diego had meant by redirecting Cristiano's attention where I wanted it to go. "Protective of . . .?" I asked softly.

He inhaled and looked away—which made it hard to mesmerize him into spilling his secrets. "Of me. And herself. She wants to be here, if that's what you're getting at."

"Why?" I asked.

"Gratitude." He dipped his head, his eyes darkening. "And, of course, reparations."

A sense of unease worked its way through me. Was Jaz indebted to him somehow? Or he to her?

"Courteousness should be obvious," he said, "as should this—you're to stay on the property."

"Are these just the rules while you're gone?" I asked.

"They're the rules until I say they're not."

"So I'm confined to this house for my foreseeable future?"

"Correct. There's plenty to keep you occupied here."

"Such as?" I asked.

"There's a game room, movie theater, indoor pool. Just let one of the staff know what you want to eat. If we don't have it, they'll procure it."

Hanging out with a staff who was paid to be here didn't appeal to me. I missed my friends. It felt strange to wonder about companionship when the day before, I wasn't even sure I'd have a proper bed or a warm meal.

He leaned back in his seat, drumming his fingers on the table. "Anything a girl could ask for, and I suspect it's still not enough. We also grow fruit, vegetables, and flowers out back if that interests you."

"My mother liked to garden," I said, but of course, he'd know that. I'd never tended my own, but I'd helped as a kid, and it'd been a long time since I'd sunk my hands in fresh soil. "That's something, I guess."

"Landscapers maintain it, but you can help as long as you stay between there and the house."

"Who will I talk to?"

He winked. "You can always call me."

"I don't even want to talk to you when you're here."

"No?" He gestured away from the table. "You're free to go up to our room."

*Our room.* He was mocking me. I stood, and he eyed me as if he knew my next move before I did. Perhaps he did. He'd called my bluff. Cristiano's company wasn't ideal, but it was preferable to being alone. The more time we spent together, the more likely he was to open up. Learning as much as I could about him and this place could only be valuable. Somewhere, somehow, I was going to figure out how to pull the pin that would implode this cartel like a grenade—or at least its leader.

Cristiano had spent an entire day with me when he surely had better things to do, and I couldn't fathom that would happen very often, so I had to seize what time I had.

I sat back down. "Arguing with you is more stimulating than staring at a wall," I reasoned. "Barely."

"Every day, you'll continue learning self-defense," he said, resuming our conversation. "That should keep you busy." He ran his tongue along his front teeth and added, "But I suppose I could also arrange to have one of your professors brought here if you'd like."

My jaw dropped. I could never forget for a moment the all-powerful reach of a kingpin in this world. "Oh my God. You can't just keep . . . *taking* people," I said, blinking rapidly. "Especially not an American professor. It's not right—it's unfathomable."

He set his elbow on the table and massaged his jaw. "I—"

"People have lives and families and—and dreams and goals." A fleeting vision crossed through my mind—palm trees in the wind, coolers of beer on the California beach with my friends, even all-nighters at the library before finals. And that all had amounted to what? The same life I'd had as a child. Occupying myself in a big house while keeping one eye over my shoulder. Losing all that was bad enough. Now, I was putting others at risk? "That professor could be a mother or father. Do you have any idea the uproar—"

"For Christ's sake, Natalia." He sighed heavily, dropping his face into his hands. "I didn't mean I'd *kidnap* him. I'd make him an offer to come and teach you." He glanced up. "I'd *pay* him. A far superior salary to what he currently makes. At least double—whatever it took."

I scoffed to hide my laugh at how wistful I'd become over his suggestion. "Oh."

"*Oh*," he echoed. "Not everything has to be done with brute force."

"And I'm sure a professor would feel perfectly comfortable turning away someone like you from his doorstep."

He rested his hands on the leg crossed in front of him as his mouth turned down. "What does that mean, 'someone like me'?"

"You're twice the size of some men. Anyone would be right to feel intimidated by you."

"You don't."

"*Of course* I do."

"Not really, though," he said. "Is it because you grew up around me?"

I gaped at him only a moment, then shut my mouth. I wasn't going to indulge him in a conversation about how scared or not scared of him I was. That was just another way for him to exert power. Since I didn't care for the direction of the conversation, I changed it. "How do you know Barto won't break in again?"

His knuckles whitened around his shin. "Max and I are taking care of it."

"You know how he got in?"

"We have video."

"So you know?"

He narrowed his eyes. "We're still reviewing it."

That was a *no*, and I could see it bothered him. I sipped my wine, using the glass to hide my smile. "Are there cameras outside the house?"

"Of course, and after Barto's little show, we'll be installing more as soon as possible. Inside and out."

"So you and your men can watch me at all times of the day. I'll never have any privacy." My jaw tingled. "Perverts."

"We're not per—it's for your own safety." He inhaled through his nose and flexed his hand a couple times. "No man will ever lay eyes on your naked body again."

"What if I strip down right here in the middle of the patio? You're telling me there aren't cameras here?"

"You wouldn't, but my team knows when to look away anyway. You have my word."

"Your word doesn't exactly mean much," I pointed out.

"Then consider that shielding you from them isn't for your peace of mind. It's for mine. If Max ever looked at you, he knows I'd remove his other eye."

"Why?" Now that my basic needs had been met, I could focus all my attention on the man in front of me. Who he was, what drove him, what held him back. That would only help me navigate whatever was coming my way. "You've told me I'm only yours, and you haven't even touched me. Why do you care what happens to my body?"

"Because I'm selfish and possessive over what's mine."

"This home is yours, and you share it with others. You invited half the town here last night."

"And you think I should invite half the town to your body?"

*He'd never.* I pushed the unbidden thought away, irritated I'd assume there was any horrific thing Cristiano wasn't capable of. Maybe he'd been possessive, and even protective, since he'd returned to town—but that didn't mean I was safe with him. "I thought when I came here, I'd be treated like your other women."

"What women? I don't own anyone else," he said, wetting his lips with a hint of a smile before it vanished. "How are women around here treated?"

"Worked, passed around, sold."

The flash of irritation over his face told me more than words could —I'd poked at something he didn't like. His brows lowered. "We don't treat anyone that way, no matter their age or sex."

"Just me then. How many women have you sold?" I asked. "Is that why you go to Russia?"

His eyes shuttered. "I'll answer your questions in time, I promise. But not when you're on a mission to malign me."

"I'm not," I said, relaxing into my chair as I ran a fingertip along the rim of my wineglass. I still had a sip left before I'd cut myself off. "I'm genuinely curious."

"This isn't a two-sided conversation." He tracked my hand with his eyes. "You won't listen to reason now."

I sighed and told the truth, hoping sincerity would gain me *something*. "If you're hurting women, or anyone, I won't be a part of it. Not even as a bystander. And children?" I asked. "Do you take them, too?"

He slid his drink away by its stem, wine sloshing against the glass. "I don't take anyone."

"You took me," I challenged.

"That's not true."

"I wasn't willing, and we both know it." I picked up on the irritation in his voice, but I had a feeling getting to the bottom of it would teach me something important about Cristiano, especially if he didn't want me to know. "If you'd take one person, you'd take others, and how is that different from smuggling people like weapons or narcotics?"

He inhaled audibly. "Marrying you is *not* equivalent to human trafficking."

"Why not?" The cracks in his composure sent a thrill through me, spurring me on. "It's playing with a human life."

"That's enough," he ground out through clenched teeth. "What right do you have to question me when—"

"True, prisoners don't generally have many rights."

He rose to his feet and his palm slapped the table. "You don't know the *first* thing about my business, and you haven't made any honest effort to learn. You see what you want to see and believe rumors without substantiating them. I won't indulge that behavior."

Despite the menacing way he towered over me, triumph surged through me. Finally, an honest reaction. One that gave me more insight into this man. The fact that this was a sore spot for him confirmed what Diego had said.

Cristiano was just twisted enough to believe he was different from his father. He considered himself the hero of his story.

"Another rule that may need reiterating," he started.

"I already know what you're going to say." *Don't question me. Don't snoop. Mind your own business.*

I'd heard it in one form or another as long as I could remember, but this situation was different. My life and my future might depend on my ability to learn my surroundings—and the man standing in front of me—inside out.

He arched an eyebrow, regaining his composure. "Please—enlighten me."

"All the regular cartel stuff. Don't touch anything of yours, don't explore the house or eavesdrop or talk to the staff."

"You can do all of that," he said.

"Really?" Let's see if he felt that way when I tried each of them while he was away.

"You're free to roam and to talk to whomever you want," he said, "as long as the person is comfortable with it—which Jaz was not the night you got here."

I continued my list, ticking off items on my fingers. "Don't challenge you—"

"I invite you to."

"—or drink your two-thousand-dollar-a-bottle liquor—"

His eyebrow quirked. "Costa's rule no doubt."

"—and don't share sensitive information or repeat anything I hear or see—"

"Well." The air shifted as something cold passed over his face, and he inclined his head, leaning over me. "Sensitive or otherwise, *no* information leaves these walls. None. That's not a rule, it's a way of life, and I'd assumed it would go without saying. You can eavesdrop all you like because I know you understand—opening your mouth would be a death sentence."

I hadn't told Diego anything, but my throat still constricted thinking about the phone upstairs. I laced my fingers in my lap, squeezing them together as I held his gaze. "I wouldn't."

"And none of those are what I was going to say anyway," he said, smoothing his hand down the front of his shirt. "You will be at my dinner table and in my bed every night. Even when I'm not here. If ever the day comes when you're missing from either, I'll assume you're gone."

I blinked up at him a few times, recalling his same words from the night before. "That's a rule?"

"It's *the* rule, sweet butterfly," he said. "If you're not at my table or in my bed, I'll have no choice but to assume you left."

"I can't even step off the property," I pointed out.

"Can't and shouldn't are two different things. I haven't chained you to a post. If you want to leave, you'll find a way—as those who are whip smart and resourceful tend to do. You've been honing those traits since childhood."

To my dismay, I blushed. Whip smart? Resourceful? Papá hadn't thought so. More like disobedient and sneaky. Or stealthy, as Diego had called me.

Cristiano set one hand on the table next to me and the other on the arm of my chair. No, he hadn't chained me up, but his body trapped me now. A powerful frame that acted as a reminder that my *husband* could flip at any moment and take what he wanted from his wife.

"I don't think I need to repeat myself," he said, "but I will so there's no confusion. If you fly away, so does my protection. I said I wouldn't set the Maldonados, or whoever else holds a grudge against your family, on the people you love—but I've been known to change my mind."

I'd grown too comfortable today. My stomach fluttered with fear but also with a sense of satisfaction. *This* was more like it. Now, he was treating me the way I'd expected, and it made more sense than serving me a four-course dinner garnished with memories of Mamá.

His threats weren't idle. I'd always known of his ruthlessness. But for some reason, he seemed to be holding back with me, and that only confused my time here. Hoping to provoke him to see if he even *knew* how far he'd go, I asked, "What does it mean to change your mind?"

By the way his bloodless knuckles curled on the table, my prodding worked. "Let's work through this, shall we? I could set them loose like a rabid dog in a chicken coop. They'd snap the old rooster's neck—that's *Papá* to you—and tear chicken-shit little Diego limb from limb. They'd definitely knock Barto off his high horse and obliterate all the men who'd ever breathed a word near your father, including townspeople. Maybe even Pilar. Definitely your mother's family at their farm north of here."

I stilled. It made perfect sense that Cristiano knew of them—it'd been his job to once—but it disquieted me nonetheless. I'd never met my mother's parents since she'd chosen cartel life with my father and had severed ties to keep them out of danger. But they'd always been in it, emotional leverage in the shadows, and they likely didn't even realize it.

"But what about you? How would you fare without my protection?" Cristiano continued. "Such a beautiful girl who can't fight . . . they would find you. Easily." He ghosted his knuckle under my chin. "You've accused me of many things. What was it? Worked, passed around, sold? You were worried I'd invite half the town to fuck you." His dark eyes reflected the cool blue of the pool as he passed them over me. "You must understand, Natalia. They would do all of that and worse. And never forget that I could, too, with less than a snap of my fingers."

I'd hunched back into my seat, cowering from him, but when my attention snagged on one word, I straightened. "Could?" I asked. "Or would?"

His eyes drifted down to the strapless neckline of my dress. Instead of answering, he said, "Don't give my staff any trouble while I'm away, and we can take out the horses when I return."

Cristiano would go all the way up to the line, but something kept him from crossing it. He had the power and inclination to treat me however he wanted, or at least scare me so badly that I never stepped out of line. And he had the reputation to back it up. But he wouldn't. Why not? What was that raw place in him I'd touched when I'd equated my being here with human trafficking?

"You have horses?" I asked.

"You already met mine, remember?"

How could I forget being forced onto a saddle and stolen away from a burning warehouse while the love of my life had been inside. Or that confusing mix of relief and safety as I'd submitted to the things I couldn't stop—the wind in my hair, Cristiano's body cocooning mine, the sound of hooves pounding the solid ground as the desert had spread out before us.

My most unbearable memories of my mother were those of laughing and riding free on our horses. Nothing took me back to those days like the smell, sound, and *feel* of riding a horse. I worried if I ever took the reins again, I'd keel over from a broken heart. I looked away. "I don't ride. Not anymore."

"Then you can stay in the house while I go."

I jerked my head up and met his glittering eyes. "You're a dick."

Still bent at the hip, he removed his hand from the table to pinch my chin between his thumb and forefinger. "Not yet, but I can be if you like. Perhaps as payback for slapping me in the church in front of my men, I ought to gather the staff out here and spank you for your attitude. Now, *that* would make me a dick."

"You won't," I said.

"How do you know?"

*Because that would be over the line.* "You just gave me your word you'd never let anyone lay their eyes on me," I challenged, "and I'm pretty sure that includes my bare ass. But maybe I'm wrong. Maybe you'd like to let Alejandro take a swat."

"Go upstairs," he bit out before I'd even finished my sentence. "You'll find a closet full of new things, all in your size. Don't touch a single garment." He paused to let me connect the meaning of his words to his fiery gaze. "Take off your clothes and wait for me in bed."

My heart skipped. He sounded more serious than he had yet—and more menacing, which was welcome. We both knew what he was, but he hadn't fully stepped into the role yet. A captor, rapist, and monster with heroic restraint had kept me on edge more than anything.

Whatever he was, I was ready to face it. I shoved my seat back from the table, took one last healthy gulp of wine, and marched upstairs.

In the closet, I slammed the door. Each hanger had been filled during our meal—floral summer dresses, beaded ball gowns, silk blouses in every color of the rainbow, wool slacks. T-shirts and jeans piled to the tops of each shelf. The stilettos, pumps, sneakers, and sandals lining one wall were so dazzling that I had to force myself to look away so I wouldn't lose focus.

I wasn't here to play dress up. To fall into the role of wife and keep house. I was something much uglier—a captive who'd been bestowed with a closet of beautiful things but had been sent to bed with nothing.

My dresser drawers were filled with satin and silk, lace, rhinestones, and scalloped trim. I stripped down and rifled through *his* drawers instead for the most unattractive thing I could find.

He wanted me naked in his bed? He'd have to look me in the eye as he stripped me of *his* clothing and *my* choice.

I pulled on his sweatpants, knotted the drawstring as tightly as I could, and threw on a matching black sweatshirt.

As I whirled around to march out of the closet, I stopped cold. My wedding dress hung elegantly on the back of the door, clean and pressed on a cream, padded, satin hanger. I approached it slowly, with bated breath, as if it might dissolve beneath a sigh. I ran the ivory lace through my hands and removed the hanger from its hook to turn it, inspecting the back. The lace that had ripped in a clean line along the column of buttons had been repaired, and the damage was barely noticeable. Somebody very talented—and very *fast*—had fixed this. But why?

Was it possible Cristiano had felt a shred of remorse upon discovering this had been my mother's dress?

I saved the thought for another time. Right now, I couldn't think of any decency that might be buried under his cold demeanor.

With a sound in the next room, I replaced the hanger and walked out of the closet.

Cristiano unbuckled his watch by the bed. He glanced briefly at my outfit, then back down. "We'll have to work on your listening skills," he said, his watch clattering on the nightstand.

I continued to my side of the bed and slipped between the sheets before turning my back to him.

But within seconds, he was standing over me.

I stared forward, avoiding him as he took his time unbuttoning and removing his shirt. As he discarded it, I caught the shadowed ridges of his abdominal muscles.

"Look at me."

I was afraid I'd lose my nerve if I did, but when he reached out, I flinched, rolling onto my back as I raised my eyes to him.

"Let me list all the things you think could stop me but wouldn't," he said, peeling the top sheet away from my body. "Sweatpants. Your period. Diego. Your father."

He ghosted the back of his hand down the front of the sweatshirt. I didn't even have to feel it to sense his hand stop at the tie of my pants.

"I know what *will* stop you," I said.

"Tell me."

Cristiano wanted to test me. I could play that game, too. He wasn't the only one who could take us to the edge, but would he push me over . . . or pull me back at the last second?

My heart raced as I let one leg fall open. "Yours."

His gaze darted to my hand as I placed it on the inside of my thigh. "My what?" he asked hoarsely.

Diego had been right about one thing—Cristiano had somehow convinced himself he was different from the other unforgivable people in this world who played with human lives. He'd played with mine, and he didn't get to ignore that. "Your father."

He froze as if a chill had fallen over the room—while *my* body continued to warm. Even though he towered over me, it felt as if I was the one looking down on him. A shadow passed over his face, and his jaw firmed, its angles sharp enough to cut glass. But nothing sliced as deep as words. "What did you tell me once?" I asked. "Nobody thinks they're a monster?"

He swallowed with a quick nod.

He hadn't even touched me, but his magnetic hand continued to hover. I resisted the urge to lift my hips to meet it. "You run the same business your father did on a much larger scale. Somehow, you've justified that to yourself, but if nobody else will tell you, I will. You *are* your father."

He made a fist, veins winding like vines around his dark forearm. I let my eyes travel up to the solid, thick muscles of a powerful bicep. *Tense* muscles that looked as if they were on the verge of exploding like his temper. "You're wrong."

"I don't think I am." And as someone from his past, how did I fit in? Cristiano could've had anyone in his bed, but he'd chosen me. Maybe it was only that I meant something to Diego. But perhaps it was more. He'd watched me grow up. He'd protected me from people like him.

His long lashes lowered. The promise of his father was enough to scare him off, I was sure. He unfurled his hand, flexing it. I left my leg open, expecting him to withdraw but tempting him to give in to the darkness behind his eyes.

He stretched his long fingers and brushed the stiff fabric. Reflexively, I grabbed his wrist. I'd called his bluff, and he'd called mine right back. Realizing he was going to touch me, a thread of desire yanked inside me. Hands the size of my head that had wrapped around men's throats, and had both commanded artillery and cradled me as a baby —they wouldn't relent until they'd made me feel terrifying things, like euphoria. Bliss. Or worse, connection. What if Cristiano made me feel so good that I began to crave—or *need*—a man I was supposed to fear? Already, I had the unsettling impulse to pull his fingers down so he could soothe this new ache when I should've pushed him away.

With lightning speed, he flipped his hand to capture *my* wrist.

I exhaled a soundless gasp. My helplessness was instant, along with a new, deep-seated yearning to submit. Being in his firm grip turned the gentle pulse between my legs into an angry throb. He could overpower me without much effort. And I wanted it. Every heated look, every restrained touch, and each inciting, sizzling word he'd uttered in my ear since he'd come back into my life suddenly culminated inside me, demanding relief.

I lifted my hips just enough to draw his eyes back to them.

He released my wrist, my skin prickling with the loss of his heat. After rounding the bed and unbuttoning and removing his pants, he climbed under the covers next to me.

Warmth spread through me. My nipples tingled as I waited for him to roll over and be inside me like he'd promised he would.

*Promised*? He'd meant that as a threat.

But I wasn't scared. I was turned on, and he wasn't doing anything about it.

*That was it?*

After what felt like minutes of nothing, I moved my head over my shoulder. Silence. Then, for the first time in this bed, I turned to him.

On his back, he had his eyes on the ceiling, but they drifted to meet mine.

All pretense evaporated, and I bit my bottom lip.

He licked his.

The small distance between us nearly crackled with heat.

And yet, Cristiano somehow remained cool. Just like our wedding night, he'd made me admit the worst to myself—that I wanted it. All so he could assert his dominance by leaving me on the ledge alone.

"I knew you wouldn't do it," I said, acid on my tongue, and turned forward again.

Suddenly, he was at my back, his mouth at my ear. "Tell me something, sweet Natalia." He reached over me, took my hand, and pushed it past my waistband, down the front of my pants. "What filth runs through your mind when you touch your pretty pussy? What do you fantasize about?"

Unable to hide my sharp pang of desire, I sucked in an audible breath. "Not you."

Over my underwear, he used my own fingers to apply pressure to my clit. "I already know that," he said, heat gathering beneath his touch. "Because you need permission to go into the darkest corners of your fantasies. I can give you that."

He held my hand there but didn't move. He wanted me to scrape the barrel of my mind, and he knew I wouldn't do it on my own. Just the thought, just hearing *pussy* spill from his lips, my stomach filled with butterflies. I chased the feeling, pushing my hips against my palm, and was rewarded with a rippling ribbon of bliss.

"Getting fucked by me doesn't scare you. You're only afraid you'll enjoy it. And that afterward, you might want it. And that you won't be able to resist *asking for it*." He met my next thrust, pressing my hand against the pulsating knot between my legs. With the thrill it inspired, I bit my lip to contain my whimper. "That's why you won't call yourself my wife. It's easier to play my captive. Follow that path, in the privacy of your mind. I will you to. See how long it takes you to come."

I slipped into that rare and mystifying sense of safety I'd found with him before. I'd been in more precarious situations with him than this one, and he hadn't hurt me. I'd known he wouldn't. I trusted that instinct now, closed my eyes, and let myself fall into pleasure's tightening grip. Nobody would know if I wondered how it would feel for Cristiano to turn me over and press me into the bed. Nobody, not even him, knew that I was grinding against our hands as I fantasized about opening to him. About how completely and brutally he would fill me, even though it was wrong on every level.

"I can sense your disappointment that I haven't broken you in yet —but I will." His hips pressed against my backside, and this time, I couldn't hold in my moan. The size and solidity of his erection was intimidating but not surprising—what caught me off guard was how it answered a primal, unwelcome need inside me to receive him. "You'll take me in each one of your three holes," he continued, urging his hips against my ass so I was stuck gyrating between my hand and his cock. "I like that your holes *could* belong to anyone—but they don't. They belong to you. My wife. That pleases me to no end."

I groaned an ugly and guttural sound I'd never heard from myself as my arousal reached new heights. If Cristiano viewed my body as property, that meant no part of me was off limits. In that raw moment, I was more turned on by what I didn't know than by what I did. I'd only thought of him on top of me, breaking me in—not all the other ways he could ruin me. A blissful feeling spread through me, his seduction as quick and ruthless as it was slow and mounting.

"How does it feel to hear me defile you, Natalia?" he breathed in my ear.

"Call me Natasha," I said, the name he'd used in the nightclub. Natalia was his past, his bride, his future, but Natasha was just his toy. It would be easier for both of us to think of me that way.

But he said, "No, *Natalia*." He gripped my hand more tightly and my fingers stroked my clit as we moved together. "*Your* pussy and *your* ass will stretch to fit me, and it will be *your* sweet, pouty lips that suck me sloppy—until I explode down your throat."

My body shook with an impending explosion, his hot and profane mouth putting my climax within reach.

He removed the sweet, pulsing pressure against my clit and used his index finger to swipe mine against the crotch of my underwear. Missing the weight between my legs and taken aback by how wet I was, I sucked in a breath.

"I suspect I'm the first man to soak your underwear clean through." He withdrew both our hands and brought them to his mouth to suck on my dewy finger. "*Mmm.* My first taste of heaven. I imagine it will inspire a thirst so deep, even drinking from you every day wouldn't satisfy it." His chest rumbled against my back. "I wonder if the same will be true when an angel like you drinks from the devil," he mused, as if perusing a menu and trying to decide on a lunch order. "Will you come to crave it? Or will you do it just to please me?"

Adrenaline pulsed in me with the blood rushing through my veins. "Or will I spit it out?"

He answered with a sinister chuckle. "You think you can only drink from your mouth?" he asked. "I will spill myself into all your holes, and I won't relent until your body has drunk every last drop I have to give. Until you're mine through and through."

I was going to climax just from his words. I *needed* to. The ache firmly rooted in the depths of my tummy cried for more. I tried to put my hand back down my pants, but he lowered it to the bed, pressing it into the mattress in front of my eyes. "Final rule," he said in my ear. "Your orgasms are mine. You will not come until you ask for it. Until I stick my cock in you and tell you to."

He rolled away as shudders of pent-up frustration quaked through me. I opened my mouth to protest, but what could I say? Was I willing to ask for it? That was what he wanted. And I had no doubt—once I asked, he'd make me beg.

His breathing evened out within moments, and he fell asleep as if it were nothing at all, leaving me wide awake and alone with my thoughts.

As need vibrated in me, my longing for release became so agonizing, I almost wished I'd just broken down and asked.

That I'd begged for my own destruction.

CHAPTER 12

# NATALIA

The cicadas' song vibrated the heavy air. Sweat trickled from my temples and under my breasts as I stood on dry grass, trying to mirror Alejandro's stance as he droned on about the importance of stability during a fight.

If my self-defense lessons with Cristiano were equal parts terrifying and exhilarating, the ones with Alejandro were downright yawn-worthy. He was lucky he was so easy on the eyes, because he spoke in a monotone, without inflection. And he never got too close to me.

Cristiano was such a master of diversion that a few nights before, I'd forgotten to feel relieved that he was leaving town and I'd get some measure of freedom from him. For days, I'd mostly just read by the pool, watched TV or movies, and snacked.

The air was thick, as if polluted and dirty, even though I hadn't seen one car within the Badlands' walls aside from those in Cristiano's flock. A need for relief weighed on the sky. Things seemed desolate, as if it hadn't rained in years, even though it just had.

I massaged my side through a cramp. My period had just started, and even though I was bloated and disgusting, everything seemed to turn me on since Cristiano had left me aching.

The more I tried not to think about him turning my own fingers against me or the orgasm he'd denied me, the hotter I got. That uneased throb spurred me on, and as my hormones went haywire, each day I *wished* Cristiano would return and finish the job he'd started. One firm touch between my legs had inspired all kinds of things in me, but when I'd tried to replicate it in the shower the next morning, it'd simply felt like touching two body parts together. No fire, no easy walk to the brink of pleasure.

Cristiano had demanded ownership over my orgasms, and it shamed me how easily my body had complied.

"Natalia?" Alejandro asked, pausing with his hands hovering in the air. "Are you paying attention? Adjust your back foot inward a bit."

"This would go a lot faster if you just arranged my legs the way you wanted them," I said.

Either he blushed or he was getting a sunburn. He looked away and continued his narration on how to protect my liver from a potential strike.

Alejandro wore a long-sleeved shirt despite the heat, and I wondered if it was due to the raised, pink skin peeking out from his collar. I'd first noticed his scars in the church as he'd stood by and watched Cristiano marry me. "You look hot," I told him.

"It's pretty humid," he agreed. "I think we're in for another storm."

Every person in this house had a story that could help piece together the mystery inside these walls. The chef had served me politely enough, and Jaz had reluctantly helped me around the house, but nobody wanted to talk to me.

Alejandro's scars might tell his story best of all. "Why don't you take off your shirt?"

"*Ay*." He widened his eyes. "Have you met your husband?"

"Sometimes I wonder," I said to myself. "But what do you mean?"

"He'd wring my neck. Cristiano's become a jealous bastard."

I coughed a laugh, shocked. Would he call his boss a bastard to his face? For the first time, a thought hit me—maybe he would. Maybe they were actually *friends*. I hated to admit that would explain the easiness between Cristiano and his staff much better than the story I'd concocted—that Alejandro's and the others' loyalty and respect had been forced on them.

"Maybe if it was Eduardo training you with his pot belly and limp." Alejandro snickered. "But I've had my fair share of female admirers, and Cristiano knows it."

I laughed at his unexpected confidence. "You're about as humble as he is."

"I'm not bragging, just relaying the truth."

I bit the inside of one cheek as I glanced at the edges of his scars. "Can I ask what happened?"

"Um." He scratched behind his ear. Maybe it was forward, and none of my business, but he'd actually been acting friendly, unlike others. "I've had them since childhood. I was an orphan, and not a very happy one."

"I'm sorry," I said. "Are they from your foster parents?"

"The keepers of an orphanage. They seemed welcoming enough in the beginning, but looks are deceiving, Natalia."

He said it as if imparting wisdom. I was surprised he'd said it at all. Even though Cristiano had said I could ask the staff questions, I'd assumed Cristiano had put some kind of moratorium on most topics. "How did you end up here?" I asked.

"I grew up near Tijuana." He wiped his sweaty temple with his shoulder. "Once I was old enough to run away, I went wherever I could to make ends meet. I met Cristiano in Bolivia when I was nineteen, and he took me under his wing, so to speak."

"How?" I asked. "Did he live there?"

"No, he was there trying to start a business."

"What business?"

"The Calavera cartel," he said as if it was obvious. "It was a small operation then, but I didn't have much else, so I joined the cause."

*The cause*. Sure, if he thought the fortune they all made off their business dealings was a worthy movement. "You mean you worked for him."

Alejandro shrugged. "When Cristiano learned my story, he asked if I could fight. I'd never been formally trained, but I'd picked up plenty of moves on the street. Within only a week of knowing him, he brought me to meet others like me. Friends that would become family."

*Others like him.* A shiver worked its way down my spine. Was Cristiano's "small operation" in Bolivia to lead the lost and desperate into a life of their choosing, or of servitude? "Do you mean other orphans?" I asked, picturing Cristiano as some kind of savior in disguise, looking for workers the way my father had brought boys to the ranch.

"No—well, not exclusively." He reached his hands toward the sky, exposing a sliver of his washboard abs. "Mind if I stretch? My joints are stiff, which is why I'm pretty sure it'll rain tonight." I gestured for him to proceed. Whatever he needed to keep the conversation going. "I was talking about Max, Eduardo, Jaz, Daniel, Solomon, Fisker—you know. The others."

The misfits Tepic had mentioned. I couldn't very well call Alejandro that to his face, though. I nudged the toe of my new, ultra-fancy performance sneakers in the grass. "I don't understand."

"Those of us who had no one." He linked his hands and turned his palms up before bending to one side. "Society cast us aside and forgot about us. Our families turned us out or sold us." His forehead wrinkled with a frown. "Hasn't Cristiano explained this to you?"

"No . . ." I didn't want Alejandro to stop talking, but a pit formed in my stomach. Would he get in trouble for revealing things he wasn't supposed to? "I'm not even sure he'd like us talking about it."

"Never said not to," Alejandro said, stretching the other way. "Cristiano is discreet given his position, but inside the walls, he's more of an open book than you'd think."

"You're joking," I deadpanned.

"No, *señora*."

"Don't call me that," I said. "It makes me feel old. I'm only twenty."

"That may be, but you're married now, and no longer a *señorita*."

"Just because a book is open doesn't make the story true. I don't know what's fact and what's fiction. Cristiano married his enemy's fiancée," I pointed out.

"I know. I was there."

"So why would he tell me anything or let me into all of this? He doesn't trust me as far as he can throw me."

"I'll bet he can throw you pretty far. Have you tried asking him anything about the cartel?"

"A little. He explained some of the rumors, like the rotten fish and the snails thing."

Alejandro opened his mouth as if to respond but just blinked at me. "Huh?"

"Never mind. It's the other stuff that he hasn't explained, and I'm sure I asked . . ." Hadn't I? Cristiano's fuse had run out quickly when the trafficking had come up. He'd accused me of believing hearsay, of not entertaining both sides of the story, and he *had* denied some of his practices, but not given me an explanation for them.

"Have you asked what we're about, though?" Alejandro asked, cocking his head. "What we're doing?"

"I know enough. You deal in arms, and you traffic women and children."

He stepped back as if I'd shoved him. "Those are the rumors, yes, but . . ."

"What? Am I wrong?" Why wouldn't I assume the worst in Cristiano when he'd forced this life on me? Even if there were shreds of decency in him, that didn't make him decent. "Isn't that what you guys do? Isn't that what you did to me?"

Alejandro's jaw slackened. "Is that . . . is that how you feel?"

Raising my eyebrows, I crossed my arms. "Why wouldn't I? You were at the wedding. You saw."

His eyebrows drew together as sweat dripped down his temple. He swiped it away with his sleeve and turned his face away, shaking his head. "Jesus, Natalia . . . I mean, you should really ask him about all of this. Don't let him off the hook until he explains what we do here."

"You just told me we're allowed to talk."

"We are," he said. "But it doesn't feel like my place to explain. When Cristiano gets back, try putting aside what you've heard and go in with an open mind."

"Will it change the fact that I'm here against my will?" I didn't expect an answer, but I wanted Alejandro to see things from my side. I sighed. "Forgive me if I find it hard to keep an open mind."

Alejandro glanced at the ground, looking uncomfortable. "I get it, I do. But if you could just *try* . . ."

"If you think this is about anything other than Cristiano's need for power and control," I said, "you need your head checked."

"I *do*," he said, squatting to tie his shoelace and then glancing up. "I mean, the first part . . . not the head check. Cristiano is a control freak. He needs to live in that space—he's a provider and a guiding light for more people than I can count. Sometimes, it's destructive. But in some cases, it can save lives."

"Destructive," I repeated, frowning. "Do you know what I gave up to be here? I *loved* someone else. I had a future with him—"

"Diego's a piece of shit."

My mouth fell open. My reflex was to block the insult, to defend the man I thought I'd marry, but even hearing his name lit a fire inside me, and not the kind it used to. Diego *had* done awful, unforgivable things, but that had nothing to do with this. "The point is, now I'm here, spending my days wandering around a house that isn't and never will be, mine. I'm learning how to defend myself in case anyone, including my 'husband,' tries to hurt me."

Alejandro rose slowly, a frown tugging the corners of his mouth. "He wouldn't hurt you, not ever."

"He already has."

"How?" he asked. "You tell me right now if Cristiano has put his hands on you. I would kill him. He may be rough around the edges, but he's making an effort."

Taken aback by the vehemence in his voice, I scoffed. *This* was making an effort? Cristiano had held a knife to my throat in this very spot. He'd pointed a gun at my head as a child and had left me in the dark to fend for myself. A week ago, he'd almost killed me in a warehouse fire.

But then he'd carried me from a burning building and bandaged me up.

And though he and I had been alone two nights, only arousal—and a demanding need—had resulted from his hands on me. So, no. Maybe he hadn't inflicted any physical violence or force on me, but still.

"I meant emotionally," I said.

"I'm sorry for that," Alejandro said. "I've endured physical and emotional abuse, and they're equally painful in different ways."

He spoke evenly, but the pain of his past came through anyway. Suddenly, my plight didn't seem as severe. "I'm sorry."

Shrugging, he nodded toward the house. "Come on. We can pick this back up tomorrow. Cristiano wants me to show you the cellar."

"A wine cellar?" I asked. "Why?"

One side of his mouth curved, and a deep dimple dented his cheek. "It leads to the panic room. If you ever hear the alarm go off, that's where you go."

I blinked at him. "How big *is* this house?"

"It's designed for a kingpin," Alejandro said. "And a kingpin needs a place to go if and when shit goes down."

"Then why doesn't the property have tunnels?" I asked since my father had commissioned them in his house.

Alejandro arched an eyebrow. "Who says it doesn't?"

It was a relief, finally, to have someone treat me normally. Jaz couldn't seem to stand me. Eduardo, the other guard from the wedding, had a face tattoo and seemed largely unapproachable, and the rest of the staff had kept their distance.

Alejandro and I walked back side by side. "Are you married?" I asked.

He laughed. "No. It's not easy to meet women in this life."

"Do you want to?"

He scratched the back of his neck. "Yes. But I prayed to God many times for a family, and he gave me one. *This* one. My devotion lies with Calavera and Cristiano always."

I didn't understand how somebody so cruel could command loyalty from so many people, but Alejandro seemed to be proof it was possible. He had a genuine air to him, and I believed him when he said he wasn't in a bad situation.

I followed Alejandro back into the house and through a multi-car garage I hadn't yet seen. We passed a Jeep with mud-splattered tires, a sleek, black Mercedes-Benz G-Class, and a monstrous Ford F-150—and that was only in the first section of the garage. "How many cars does one man need?" I asked.

"They're for cartel use, and they're how we get in and out. We have another garage off the premises where we keep the good stuff. McLarens, Audis, etcetera."

Well, I supposed there had to be *some* spoils in exchange for the risks they took. Alejandro opened a door to a staircase and flipped on a light. "I'll meet you down there," he said, pulling out his two-way radio. "I'm going to have one of the guys run this like a drill so it feels real. I'll let the staff know so nobody freaks out."

"How will I know which alarm means to go down there?"

"There's only one," he said. "Trust me—you'll know."

I descended the stairs into the cellar. Stacks of wine bottles lined the walls, some behind glass in refrigerators that emitted a warm glow. I walked the perimeter of the room until I reached a steel door that must've led to the panic room. I tried the handle and was surprised to find it open.

I stepped into the dark and tried a switch. Fluorescent lights hummed to life overhead. The large concrete box had clean, gray floors, a windowed office, and multiple doorways. Industrial washing machines and dryers sat against one wall. Boxes and crates were piled next to a row of bicycles. Definitely not the panic room, but still not a place I was sure I was allowed.

I glanced over my shoulder and walked in, peering into a large closet of cleaning supplies and equipment. I was about to move on when I noticed transparent bins of women's sneakers and sandals, separated and marked by size, stacked almost to the ceiling. I flipped on the light to see what was in some smaller tubs piled in another corner.

My jaw tingled as my eyes adjusted to what was in front of me.

Assorted sizes and colors of bras and underwear.

*What the fuck?*

I made my way to another doorway. This one led to a whole other room, as big as Cristiano's bedroom. Metal shelving lined the perimeter, stocked with more folded pants, t-shirts, and sweaters than a person could ever need. Even stranger, I realized as I picked up a pair of jeans, it was only women's and children's clothing.

Countless boxes were labeled in Spanish for toothbrushes, toothpaste, hairbrushes, and other toiletries. Down the center, on a long metal slab of table, travel-size toiletries were grouped like some kind of assembly line. At the end were boxes of plastic zippered bags stocked with everything from shampoo and conditioner to cotton balls to aspirin bottles. Like toiletry bags I'd pack for a trip.

It made no sense. I'd expected to find a museum of body parts—and I still did—but this was more akin to a drugstore.

*Drugs*. It hit me. People smuggled narcotics in all sorts of creative ways. I picked up a tube of toothpaste, cracked the seal, and squeezed some out. I smelled and tasted it, but there was nothing suspicious about it.

I broke open a plastic toothbrush, half-expecting something like cocaine to come spilling out. But as far as I could tell, it was just a regular toothbrush. Frustrated and confused, I threw the evidence of my snooping into a garbage can and left the room, glimpsing more boxes, this time with packaged food like trail mix, nut bars, and dried fruit.

Was this some kind of processing center for the women and children Cristiano trafficked? And if so, where were they? Surely he kept them somewhere else in the Badlands . . . but then why hadn't I seen a single one?

I turned to leave and came face to face with a whiteboard that took up half of one wall. It was divided into four sections—*Missing, Taken, Found,* and *Belmonte-Ruiz.*

I covered my mouth with one hand as my eyes roamed over myriad photos of women and children taped to the board under each section. The images had names scrawled beneath them except each column also had a subsection titled *No photo*.

I ripped off a printout of several stapled pages that had been taped to the board. Thumbnail photos filled each page. Some faces had been crossed out in red.

A door slammed, and I dropped the dossier. Footsteps on the stairs had me hurrying back into the cellar as quickly as my heart raced.

Alejandro jogged down the steps and stopped short at the base of the stairway. His eyes drifted from my head to my toes.

*He knows.*

Surely there were cameras everywhere, and that included down here. Someone had seen me snooping.

Alejandro was a friend, though—wasn't he? As he tilted his head, my mouth went dry as a desert. Maybe the sun peeked through the clouds. Maybe its warmth was inviting. But that didn't mean it couldn't also scorch you.

I took a step back as Alejandro took one forward.

His mouth twitched into a friendly grin. "Ready to panic?"

CHAPTER 13

# CRISTIANO

I leaned in the doorway of my spacious dining room as my delectable wife, completely oblivious to my presence, licked the tongs of her fork between bites of Black Forest cake. Her dark hair curled around her shoulders and arms, encircling her like dying black roots.

It'd been a few days, but my desire for her burned just as hot as it had in our bed. Back in her presence, I could sense my emotion overtaking my reason. How to stop it? And why?

Because attachments were dangerous. They blinded men. They exposed us. They hurt us. I'd learned that lesson early. And now, I'd relearn it. I wanted to trust Natalia, but I couldn't yet. I'd thought to get what I wanted from her, I had to give the same. A safe space to speak the truth. It was the first thing I'd asked of her after we'd said our vows—honesty.

And my honest reaction to my security system picking up the signal of an unauthorized phone in Natalia's things while I was away?

A deep-seated need to remind my wife whom she answered to, and that I'd been a far kinder and more generous husband than I needed to be.

Natalia Cruz—Natalia *de la Rosa*—was a handful. And she was a problem. She'd proven herself untrustworthy just by having the phone, not to mention all the system breaches it could cause.

But the bigger problem was that Natalia put me at odds with the one person I feared most—myself. I'd married her for purely selfish reasons. The things I wanted to do to her were everything I stood against. Everything I hated. They were part of a past I'd overcome.

I prided myself on having a code.

For her, I'd broken it.

Would I go even further than that? I'd resisted her the other night, but just barely. She knew my patience held on by a tenuous thread, and when tugging on it got her no reaction, she yanked on it.

The right thing would be to set her free—but the moment I'd let myself think of her as mine, I knew that wasn't possible.

Did keeping her cancel out anything I'd accomplished the past several years?

Did my urges to defile her undermine those I'd helped?

Her fear both excited and calmed me. Her tears were mine to collect and soothe. Her pussy was mine to devastate and worship. And lick and explore and fuck. All in due time. But what did it make me that I wanted to do it now? That I had taken her in the first place and wouldn't let her go?

She might never come around. I was not a patient man. I never waited for anything anymore. I took. If my self-discipline with her faltered, I worried I'd enjoy it, and that would make me as bad as those I sought to take down.

That made me my father.

But not even that knowledge was enough to make me walk away.

I strolled into the dining room, staying on the rug to mute my steps. When I reached her back, I wrapped my hands around her neck.

She froze in her chair. *Wrong reaction, little girl.*

After a moment, she tilted her head back all the way and met my eyes upside down.

"Haven't you been training with Alejo?" I asked.

"He talks too much."

I nearly laughed at the unexpected response but managed to maintain my composure. Her safety wasn't a game. "Excuse me?"

"He won't let me practice." Her throat constricted against my palms as she swallowed. I refrained from tightening my grip around the slender column and shifted my focus to the chocolate frosting at each corner of her mouth. "I think he's afraid to touch me," she added.

"Then he's smarter than I give him credit for." I lowered my mouth to her forehead for a kiss. I wanted more. Was it so much to ask that a husband could kiss his wife's lips? I moved down her cheek, but the tension in her body remained.

*She'll come around,* I reminded myself. It was no victory to take from someone who didn't want to give.

But then again, I'd been suffering for my lust for some time.

I slid my hands under her chin, tilting her mouth up to mine. She parted her lips for a gasp—or a sigh?—and clearly fought to keep her eyes from fluttering shut. One flicker of my tongue and I'd get that chocolate right off her lips.

I hoped she'd been stewing in her own juices since I'd left her wanting in our bed.

I hoped at that moment, she was questioning the wetness between her legs.

I reached by her and plucked the cherry off the top of her cake. Straightening, I popped it into my mouth, discarding the stem on her plate before I fell into the seat next to her. "You weren't going to eat that, were you?"

She scowled, wiping her mouth with a napkin as she picked up her plate and stood. "I'll just have to get another slice."

I smiled. "Be my guest."

I watched her until she'd disappeared into the kitchen. Who was I kidding? My attachment to her was already forming. It was hard to avoid that when she'd been under my protection as a child. Now that she was a woman, and my wife, the affection I'd once had was something else entirely.

Her vulnerability was also mine, though. She was my responsibility. Was I doing everything I could to ensure her safety? A week ago, I hadn't known I'd be bringing her here. Now that it was more than the staff and me in the house—now that I was more exposed—it was time for a full security check-up.

Max and I had come to the conclusion that the only way Barto could've entered my bedroom that Monday morning was by scaling the cliff beneath my balcony. It seemed impossible. The beach below the house acted as a port and had its own robust defense in place, yet they'd never seen him. We'd inspected every camera and triple-checked each passageway in and out of the house to no avail.

While security had always been the top priority in the Badlands, it was also important to me that townspeople felt welcome and could take shelter in the house if they ever needed to, no questions asked.

But with Natalia under my care, and with a target on her back as my wife and Costa's only daughter, it was becoming clear I'd have to take greater measures to protect the house.

Max had begun meeting with ex-military to get us up to date on biometric technology—fingerprint scans and voice and facial recognition, and new steel-fortified, bullet-resistant doors with automatic locks. I'd been taught hand-to-hand combat and marksmanship as a boy growing up in a cartel, but I'd learned what it meant to fight for my life on the streets. I hated that I needed all the latest gadgets to protect myself and my people. I'd installed a large, open balcony in the first place so I could taste freedom at all hours of the day and night. I didn't want to board myself up in a house. But I couldn't be everywhere all the time.

I'd laughed Max out of the room when he'd tried insisting on installing cameras in my bedroom. If I needed men watching me as I slept, then I deserved whatever attack was coming to me.

But Natalia was in my bed now. I wanted the ability to lay eyes on her at all times if need be.

At the very least, I'd have to go overboard on our wing of the house and in the bedroom.

Natalia returned, not with cake, but with two plates full of food. She set one in front of me, avoiding my eyes as she sat. "You didn't eat dinner yet?" I asked.

"I was going to skip it."

In lieu of another multi-course dinner, I'd asked Fisker to prepare two balanced meals since we weren't staying long. I'd assumed Natalia had already eaten hers.

"I can appreciate cake for dinner," I said carefully, trying for amenable where I could afford it, "but the chef says you had mostly salad, wine, and dessert while I was away."

"You're keeping tabs on what I eat?"

"I want you to build strength." If she noticed the pomegranate that I'd requested on her plate, she kept it to herself. I pointed my fork at her food. "So, eat your chicken. What else did you do while I was away?"

She took a bite. "I'm sure you watched from your ivory tower. I can't imagine it was very entertaining, seeing as I mostly just wandered around the house."

"You're bored. Noted." She needed company, and I'd get her some, though it might be a reminder she should be careful what she wished for.

"Alejandro showed me the panic room." She hesitated, presumably deciding whether to ask about what she'd seen downstairs. "I saw what was in the basement. That . . . that warehouse room."

I chewed, pleased with her honesty, even though it didn't make up for the phone. I'd already known she'd snooped, but I hadn't expected her to bring it up herself. "Great, isn't it?" I asked. "It's like a mini superstore down there."

"How can you joke about something like that?" Her eyebrows cinched. "What was all that? And the whiteboard with the pictures? I want to know what goes on under this roof."

"All you have to do is ask, Natalia. You don't need to sneak around. This is your home. You can go where you please."

"This is *your* home."

"And you are my wife. What's mine is yours. I trust that whatever you see, you'll view with an investigative eye and an open mind." I paused to let that sink in. She'd seen quite a bit down there, and based on the other rumors she'd brought to me, I had no doubt her mind was running wild with potential scenarios. I tilted my head. "I trust you in our home."

At least, I had.

"I haven't done anything to earn that trust," she said.

"You haven't done anything to break it . . . have you?"

She drew a short breath. I'd have to teach her how to perfect—or even begin to hone—her poker face. I knew she was thinking of how she'd stashed a phone Diego had surely given her. *I* was. Diego was the last person I needed knowing about the goings on of my home, because he wouldn't hesitate to use them against me.

"No, I haven't," she said finally. "So how do you explain the food, clothing, and toiletries down there?"

"They're for the women who arrive here. To make the transition smoother. Whether they choose to stay or go, there's always an adjustment period. Most of them have nothing."

She picked up a glass of water and peered at me over it. "But you're why they have nothing. Aren't you?"

I sighed and rubbed the inside corners of my eyes. If she would just ask before insulting me, I would answer honestly. But she continued to dig her heels into her assumptions, and she'd have to dig herself back out once she learned the truth.

It was my own fault she chose to think the worst of me, but that didn't make it any easier to hear.

"If there's any kind of abuse, I won't live here," she warned.

That tone was new, not quite an accusation, perhaps even cracking the door open to a real conversation. But it was too hard to resist watching her get riled up. "Where will you live?" I asked. "In the stable?"

She pursed her lips, reminding me of the petulant child I'd once known. That fiery attitude she'd had before Bianca's death was returning, and I didn't mind the burn. In fact, knowing me, I was pretty sure I'd be sticking my hands into the flame anytime the opportunity presented itself.

After a bite of chicken, I said, "Going downstairs into the panic room must've brought up some old memories, no?"

Her answering silence spoke volumes. I wasn't wrong, but I was probably the last person she wanted to open up to about the day I'd locked her in a closet with me and threatened her life before Bianca's body was even cold. But who understood better than me? We'd both stumbled across the body. We'd both loved and respected Bianca. We'd both descended into the darkness together.

"It was fine," she said, but her body language told a different story. Her shoulders rose nearly to her ears. "Alejandro made me feel safe."

*Safer than I did.* I ignored the jab and continued my thought. "I think about that day a lot. Especially lately. What it must've been like for Bianca. For Costa, when he got home. And for you."

Had she talked through it with her father or a therapist? With Diego? All of it—every last detail? It was a heavy burden to carry, watching a parent die.

"Why were you so cruel that day?" she asked, her posture easing with her tone. "I was covered in my mother's blood. I was in shock. And you had no sympathy." She picked up her water again, and I noticed she'd pushed her wine away. "You made me think you were going to kill me," she said, glancing into the glass. "Or worse, take me with you."

I needed no reminder of the things I'd said. I didn't regret any of them. It'd contributed to getting her out of there and off to California. I only regretted that I hadn't scared her off Diego. "My life was on the line, Natalia. You and Diego were accusing me of murder. I was scared, too. But I was also angry. You ferociously defended Diego, but not me."

"I was *nine,*" she said. "All I knew was what I saw."

"I *wanted* to frighten you," I added quietly.

She took a breath. "You succeeded."

"I don't think I did." But given the night I had planned, I might. "I've been watching you closely ever since my return—as closely as I did when you were young."

"You watched me then?"

"Of course. I was responsible for your life. And in a world as grim as ours, a child like you was a ray of sunshine in the dark." She'd had a laugh that'd made murder and mayhem bearable. And Bianca had trusted me around Natalia. Nobody else would've left me, a hitman with a long rap sheet, alone with their kid back then. Now, I was responsible for rays of sunshine all over the Badlands. "If anything had happened to your parents, I was supposed to get you out of the house and take you somewhere safe."

"She told me once to go to you in an emergency," Natalia said, slackening against her chair. "But you didn't take me. You left me in the dark."

"I couldn't take you where I was going. Not as a fugitive. It would've been kidnapping." My chest tightened. In the seconds before I'd left her down there, she wouldn't let go of my neck. I'd scared her so badly, she'd actually wanted the monster. "At least in the tunnel, you were stowed away until Costa could get to you."

"Like a doll on a shelf."

An action figure maybe, though she had yet to own the role. "I don't see a timid girl who was broken by her mother's death," I said. "I don't see a porcelain doll who needs to be shelved for her own protection."

She took her entire bottom lip into her mouth, seemed to think as she bit down, then released it. "What do you see?"

"A woman trying to break through the restraints placed on her—including the ones of her own making. I understand why you went to California—I'm glad you did. You needed the distance and protection from this world. But you're not a girl anymore. Losing your mother the way you did is no longer an excuse to run away from the life you were destined to lead. I have forced your hand, but in time, if you're the woman I think you are, you'll come to see that you're right where you belong."

She blinked her gaze around the main room, her eyes drifting from the still fireplace to the pottery above it. But she understood I was talking beyond the literal. I could practically see the wheels turning in her head. "And where do I belong?" she asked.

A sense of pride gathered inside me, tinged with a lust for the devotion I'd always wanted from her. "Next to me," I said. "At the head of the Cruz-de la Rosa empire."

"What if . . ." She glanced at her hands fidgeting in her lap. "What happens if I'm not the woman you think I am?"

"The same thing that happens to anyone who's not cut out to rule. You'll fall in line, or you'll perish."

"Then I'll perish," she said without inflection but raised her eyes to look upon me with renewed fire. "If you think for one *moment* I will rule a cartel responsible for bringing horror to human lives, then you *will* learn what I'm capable of."

I couldn't help my smile. That was exactly the woman I thought she was, and I looked forward to bringing out this ferocious, protective side of her. "I hope I do."

"I won't stand by your side if you inflict pain and slavery on others. If you wanted that, you should've chosen a different wife. If I find out the rumors are true, I will stand in your way at every turn. I will not fall in line."

*If, if, if.* Her accusations were yielding as doubts crept in. Pride and lust surged through me again. This time, the lust was more carnal. The impulse to spar with her, to see just how close I could bring her to falling in line. And the pride was that of a husband watching his wife grow. "Spoken like a true queen. This is the Lourdes in you," I said, referring to her regal second name. "But how long would you hold strong to your ideals? You promised to obey me. I don't need to remind you that defying me could bring danger on your family."

"Yet you do remind me quite frequently."

I had to stifle my chuckle.

"What would *you* do?" she asked. "Would you choose the right thing over family? If it meant saving countless lives?"

"I already did." My amusement vanished. "And I'd do it again."

"But that doesn't make any sense. You turned your father in because he was involved in human trafficking. But he never took it as far as you have."

"You don't know that, do you?" I asked, my tone verging on snapping. I wanted to be patient with her, but it got under my skin when she compared me to him so easily without verifying anything that she assumed was fact. At some point, I needed her to realize that she was doubting and maligning me without evidence, while I saw nothing but potential and goodness in her. And even if I was her own personal beast, I was still nudging her toward a better version of herself. "You've made a lot of assumptions and accusations, Natalia, but not once have you asked about the specifics, or even generalities, of my business."

She smacked her water glass on the table. "I'm asking," she said with a frown, as if I hadn't just invited her to.

I stuck a toothpick in my mouth, somewhere between wanting to teach her a lesson and trying to be patient with her. One minute, her curiosity allowed her to listen, the next, she was obstinate for no reason. "Then I will show you."

But not until she ate. I'd already finished my meal, and she'd barely taken three bites.

I shifted to take a velvet box from my back pocket and stuck it squarely on the table in front of her plate.

Her gaze bounced between the box and me. "What is that?"

"Your wedding ring. Teresa made it. Remember Felix, the boy with no front teeth? His mom."

"But I already have one. It's—oh. I see." She glanced at her hand, then slid off the ring I'd put on her finger in the church and placed it in front of me. "It was your mother's. You must want it back."

That wasn't why. My mother's ring had been a stand-in. It wasn't good enough for my wife. I'd found it amongst Bianca's jewels, the ones I'd recovered for Costa over the last several years. It meant nothing to him so I'd pocketed it, meaning to melt it down. It'd come in handy, but now I could get rid of it. I tossed it aside, opened the little box, and slid it closer to her.

Her eyes widened. "Cristiano. This is . . . *enormous*."

Indeed it was. I'd explained to Teresa what I'd wanted, but she'd insisted on meeting Natalia before creating it—to capture her personality, apparently. Who needed personality when you had a big, fat rock to back up your confidence? I'd wanted something bold. A jewel fit for a queen. I'd told Teresa to recall the biggest diamond she'd ever worked with—and then find one double the size.

Natalia would wear my ring, a piece of jewelry so heavy, she'd feel the weight of me at all times.

"Is it real?"

I arched an eyebrow, suppressing a laugh. "Natalia, for fuck's sake. Of course it is."

She gave me a minx-like smile—she was messing with me—then slipped on the emerald-cut diamond set in a diamond band.

I picked up the box. There was more inside—a two-tone, gold-and-silver ring with a fine, almost invisible pearl inlay strip around the center, engraved inside with our wedding date and one word.

*Mine.*

I passed it to her, and she slid the rings together to form one. She spread her fingers, peering at them. Would she recognize why I'd chosen it? She placed her splayed hand on the table, admiring it in silence.

She only raised her eyes to watch me push on my ring. My band matched hers, but without the pearl and with a different word inside.

*Yours.*

I was a married man.

I didn't wait to hear what she thought about it. She wasn't in a place to thank me for anything yet, and if she was going to tell me she hated it, because it didn't come from Diego, I was in no mood to hear that.

"You haven't touched your fruit," I said. "In Greek mythology, pomegranates are the fruit of the dead."

"That was true for Persephone," she said right away.

Ah. I wasn't expecting such a smart comeback. Between us, we seemed to possess a wealth of knowledge on tempting berries. "If you see her time in captivity as a death sentence, then yes. Some would be willing to die in order to become the queen of hell, though." I sliced my pomegranate open to get to the juicy red center. I couldn't wait to sink my teeth into Natalia, too. "*Es un delicia inigualable.*"

*A matchless delight.* Her cheeks pinkened as she watched me scoop out the seeds. "Jaz," I called, and she appeared in the doorway. "Pack Natalia a bag. We're not staying here tonight."

Jaz nodded. "Yes, sir."

Natalia stilled, her palm still pressed to the table. Her fingers curled. "We're not?"

"You said you were bored." My tone dropped, making it sound like a threat—and I was fine with that. "We're going out."

"Out?" She met my gaze. "Where?"

There it was. The slight tremor of fear in her voice that she tried to hide. It did something to me, owning that fear. That was at least one thing Diego had never gotten from her. Perhaps he'd made her quiver, but *I* could inspire the deepest tremble. I would make her shake.

I'd make her beg.

Natalia jumped up before I could answer. "*Wait,*" she called across the room, but Jazmín was long gone. "I can pack my own things."

"Sit and finish—you'll need the energy," I said. "Jaz will do it."

The phone wouldn't last another night.

With an audible swallow, Natalia lowered herself back into the chair. "Where are we going?"

"To *La Madrina*. You remember my nightclub?" I allowed myself a smile at the way her spine lengthened. "But first, I'm going to introduce you to the Belmonte-Ruiz cartel."

# CHAPTER 14

# NATALIA

In Cristiano's closet, I quickly dug through the bag Jaz had just packed while Cristiano showered. During his absence, I'd gotten my hands on a sewing kit and stitched a secret pocket into the lining for the phone. I tore through her precise folding and the tops she'd rolled into neat, tidy torpedoes until I felt the weight of it in my palm and breathed a sigh of relief.

"All there?"

I jumped at Cristiano's voice behind me, then tucked the phone back into place, piling clothing on top of it. "Yep."

I turned around and darted my eyes away. I didn't think I'd ever get used to the way my heart skipped seeing him in just a towel—all the trim, powerful muscles that lay in wait beneath his clothes. The fact that his body had pinned me to the mattress several days ago made me want to sneak another peek when it should've made me desperate enough to throw myself over the balcony just to escape. I'd never felt that kind of firm, promising weight on me, not even with Diego. And it made my insides tighten with desire.

I was a traitor to myself and my gender.

And Cristiano was a smirking jerk who seemed to read my mind.

“We’ll leave in ten minutes,” he said. “Wear the same black dress you had on the night you came to my club.”

But it was so *short*. So revealing. I’d only worn it around Cristiano knowing Diego was nearby. And we were meeting the Belmonte-Ruiz cartel, a thought that immediately dried my throat. I was supposed to meet sex traffickers in a skimpy dress? “I don’t think it’s clean,” I lied.

“Even better. Put on the dirty little dress you wore for me that night.” His pupils dilated as he looked me over. “We can roleplay what would’ve happened if you’d come up to my office like I’d asked you to.”

"What if there are people I know at the club?”

“Doubtful as it’s out of town. But you don’t need to worry about that. You won’t be seeing anyone I haven’t arranged for you in advance.” He turned his back to me. “I don’t like surprises.”

My eyes drifted to the carpet. “And yet a life in the dark is nothing but surprises.”

“At least it’s not boring, eh? Now, where’s that dress?” He discarded his towel on a chair and surveyed his extensive suit collection. “I want to watch you squeeze into it.”

I lost my breath at the sight of his ass. I could’ve flicked a quarter at it and ducked as it ricocheted right back at me. Smooth with bronze, concave cheeks, it had more definition than his top-of-the-line TVs.

I slipped out of my robe and took one of the last clean pairs of underwear from a drawer.

“Leave them,” Cristiano said.

I froze. “But I’m still on my period.”

He grunted his disapproval. “How much longer?”

“A few days probably.” I proceeded to pull on the most unflattering underwear I had. “I found tampons in your bathroom. You must spend a lot of time with women to keep those handy.”

“Jaz put them in there for you,” he said.

I slipped into my dress, feeling his eyes on me. I’d been told on enough California beaches that I had a good ass, but it wasn’t the product of the gym. I never worked out, though that would have to change if I were going to continue with the self-defense classes.

"Is there a fitness center here?" I asked.

"I'll get someone to dust it off."

I looked over my shoulder at him. "You don't use it?" I hadn't meant to sound so surprised. He wasn't beefy by any means, but muscles like his went way beyond genetics.

"Nah. Get my exercise in other ways. You can't design a better glutes workout than squatting outside a drug lab with binoculars for eight hours. Nor can you spar with friends like you can fend off enemies. Sharpens reflexes. Builds muscle." He winked. "And stamina."

I stared at him, trying to decide if he was exaggerating. "I never thought I'd have a killer for a husband," I muttered.

"What do you think Diego is?"

The question caught me off guard, but it was warranted. "He may have killed, but he isn't a murderer at heart."

Cristiano snorted. "You still believe that?"

I supposed I couldn't. If he was willing to lie and deceive so thoroughly, then it was likely he'd also created himself a new persona.

"And how about you, *mariposa*?" he asked. "Are you a killer? If I ask you to knot my tie, will you try to strangle me with it?"

I turned as he tucked his dress shirt into his pants. "If I thought I could get away with it," I responded wryly.

"I'll take my chances." He stepped toward me, took my waist, and lifted me onto the island in the middle of the closet. "Do you know how?"

"I learned when I was nine."

He spread my knees, and my dress rode up as he settled himself between my legs. He smelled of the same soap I did and the cedar shampoo in his shower. "Nine?" he asked.

"My father taught me how to do Diego's tie for my mother's funeral."

His Adam's apple bobbed as he swallowed. "I see."

As I pulled the wide end up, he lifted his chin and kept it there even after I'd looped the tie and tightened the knot.

"Give me your hand," he said. When I did, he brought my fingers up and pressed them gently to the hollow of his neck, under his Adam's apple. "Remember I said we all have the same weak spots?"

"Yes."

"This is one. The trachea—or windpipe. If your attacker ever exposes this to you, hit him here."

"I would think higher." I moved my hand up to his Adam's apple. "Wouldn't this be worse?"

"No." He stretched his thumb away from his other four fingers to show me the webbed curve between them. He held it to the middle of my throat and squeezed. "If *I'm* attacking *you*, there's no chance in hell you're going to be able to strangle me."

"You'd be surprised at the strength that comes with a rush of adrenaline."

"Natalia, I can crush a skull. You're not going to win unless you're strategic." He contracted his hand even tighter. "See how much effort it takes? Do you feel anything?"

"Not really."

He lowered his grip, pressing his palm into the base of my neck, and immediately, I was choking. Alarms fired in me, my hands flying up to grab his forearm just as he released me. "You felt *that*," he said.

I moved my fingers to my throat as my heart pounded, the terrifying sensation lingering. "Right away."

He took my hand, spreading it into an L-shape the way his had been. "It has the same effect on me that it does on you. You can hit someone there—hard—to incapacitate or disorient them, giving yourself time to run or do more damage."

He slid his hand under my jaw and pressed his thumb and index finger into the sides, where I'd been taught to take my pulse. "These are your carotid arteries. You can strike them to do damage, but if you have a knife, even better. Cut both of them at the same time."

My throat constricted, and I struggled for my next breath. Cristiano had an unsettling obsession with throat-related murder. "At the same time?" I asked. "How?"

"Don't just stab your assailant in the neck. Stab through it."

I inhaled sharply with the gruesome mental image, but also—I could barely admit in the depths of my mind—embarrassment that his savagery was a turn-on. His hand was hot and tight around my neck. I wrapped mine around his wrist, not to pull him off this time, but to try to channel the utter strength he held against an opponent. A beat passed between us. "How many men have you strangled?" I asked softly.

"Are you asking if the rumors about *El Polvo* are true?"

"I know they are. Diego saw you pour sand down a man's throat until he choked to death."

"I did." He spoke without inflection or emotion, his hand loose around my neck.

"What did he do to deserve that?"

"I'll tell you what he didn't do. He *didn't* kill me first—and that's what matters." He grazed his thumb under my jaw. "Such a pretty, slender throat," he said, his eyes drifting down. "I'll bet there are many who'd love to get their hands on it."

"You're the only one who has."

He looked pleased by that, even though I hadn't meant to flatter him. He dipped his head but kept his gaze on me. "And I'm the only one who ever will. That's my promise to you."

A threat . . . or a promise. He'd be the only one to keep my fate on a precarious edge.

"You don't have to worry about the sand," he said, moving his mouth closer to my ear. "That would be such a waste. A throat like yours would bruise and tighten and succumb so beautifully under a man's hands."

A shiver prickled down my spine as cords of fear and desire tangled in me. I couldn't stop swallowing. "How many women have you choked?"

"With my hands? None."

"But you've strangled some?" I asked.

"No." His crow's feet deepened as he suppressed a grin. "I was being suggestive, but I'm glad to see it was lost on you. I assume that means mine will be the first cock you gag on."

A gasp sucked the air from my lungs with the delicious, maddening pull I was coming to expect between my legs whenever he spoke about dominating me.

"And before you accuse me of abusing a woman's mouth," he added, bracing his hands on both sides of me until our mouths were close, "I'll let you in on a secret. Some women love it. They shouldn't call me *El Polvo*. They should call me *El Gallo*."

"The rooster?" I asked at the same moment it clicked. The *cock*.

"More women have willingly choked on my rooster than men have been forced to eat my dust."

Of course, Cristiano de la Rosa's attempt at a joke would be both sinister and provocative. I didn't laugh, mostly because I was too focused on trying not to picture the look that would cross his face the first time I took him in my mouth. Would he become even more domineering when I kneeled for him? Or would I steal his control?

"How many men have you killed?" I asked.

"Countless."

"How many women have you been with?"

He searched my eyes. "Tell me why you're asking, and maybe I'll answer."

"I want to know if I'm one in a long line of many, or if you intend to take our vows seriously."

He went uncharacteristically silent, as if racking his brain for a response. "And how would you feel if I promised the rooster belongs to you and only you?"

"I would feel that the rooster was in for a long nap. And that he perhaps should not bother waking at all, as he'll be in for great disappointment."

The corner of Cristiano's mouth twitched into a lopsided smile. I, too, almost smiled. *Almost*. At his sudden playfulness, in part, but also because there was something appealing about Cristiano never taking another woman again.

Not even me.

My hardwired female instinct saw the romanticism of keeping a wild man, but even as my fantasies wandered, the angry, bitter part of my brain wanted to torment him with our vows until death did us part.

"We should go," Cristiano said. "Everyone's waiting."

"Everyone?" I asked.

He took his blazer off a hanger and wrapped it around my shoulders. "Wear this until we're alone again."

I put a hand on his chest before he could help me down. "Wait."

With our faces inches apart, dark, nearly black eyes, looked back at me. Nose to nose, I could see their deep brown color and slight amber flecks.

"Hmm?" he asked, staring at my lips.

His skin warmed my palm, even through his shirt. I imagined all the strength under my hand aimed at anyone who tried to come at him. At me. At *us*.

"Your knot is crooked," I said. As I adjusted his tie, a tiny black spot in a sea of white fabric caught my eye. I ran my fingertip over it. "There's blood on your shirt."

"That's why I chose it," he said gravely. "I don't want to ruin a second one."

A KILOMETER outside the gates of the Badlands, Cristiano parked in the driveway of a large, freestanding garage.

This, it seemed, was the everyone who'd been waiting for us: two SUVs, a Dodge Ram, an Audi, and a couple of shoddy Hondas—all black with tinted windows.

Cristiano stepped out of the car and joined a circle made up of some of the men who'd been at the Easter party. I knew better than to follow or even open my door until Cristiano came for me. Instead, I watched from where I was as a very young blonde girl in a denim skirt and a tank top exited one of the SUVs.

Cristiano gave her a once-over before circling her.

I knew that walk. That stare. That scrutinization. He'd done it to me on our wedding day before he'd ripped off my dress.

As she kept Cristiano in her sights, Max approached her from behind, grabbed her elbows, and yanked her down onto her knees so she crumpled like a ragdoll.

She thrashed, threw her head back, and he released her as he keeled over. Jumping to her feet right from her knees, she turned and kneed him in the face so he fell back onto his back.

She put a foot on his chest in triumph, then backed away.

Cristiano smiled as he helped Max off the ground, then slapped him on the back and nodded at the girl before she got into one of the SUVs. The rest of the men dispersed into other vehicles that left the garage.

Only Cristiano remained, looking in my direction. As he walked over, he signaled for me to lower my window.

"Who was that girl?" I asked when Cristiano neared. "Where are they taking her?"

He stuck an arm on the roof of the car and leaned inside. "If you want answers, come with me." He straightened and called over his shoulder as he walked away, "But you might not be ready. If you're not, Eduardo can take you home."

When Cristiano had mentioned the Belmonte-Ruiz cartel, all sorts of scenarios had run through my head, most ending with me in the trunk of a car. But we'd come this far without Cristiano hurting me—or letting me get hurt. And I was finding that being in the dark was far worse than anything I'd learned yet. I held fast to the instinct that he'd keep me safe as I popped open the door and exited the car.

My spiked heels stuck in the rubber garage floor, but I wobbled along to one of the Hondas, where he opened the trunk and handed me a bulletproof vest. I'd seen plenty in my lifetime, but I'd never worn one.

"What's this for?" I asked, holding it with both hands.

"What do you think?" He shot me a grim glance. "Still want to come?"

I put the vest on under the blazer and pulled back my shoulders to keep from slouching beneath the weight.

Moments later, we were pulling out of the garage in the Honda.

The first in a line of vehicles took off in the opposite direction of the Badlands, and we followed.

"Why are we in this car?" I asked.

"To remain inconspicuous."

It wasn't a long drive, but Cristiano's silence made it seem that way. With permanently furrowed eyebrows, he focused out the windshield, only breaking his concentration to speak into a two-way radio.

As darkness spread around us, I glimpsed a side of him I'd expected to see more of—the determined security team member I'd known as a girl. It was how I knew we were heading somewhere important, and in this world, that was usually synonymous with dangerous. There was an allure to seeing him in his element. I could picture him wearing the same grave expression in the bedroom as he found ways to exert his dominance. Maybe he was this serious, too, each time he'd had to jerk off because he wouldn't let himself touch me.

He could control my body, but he couldn't control his own. The thought made me shiver with a heady mix of lust and control.

Cristiano cursed as we took a pothole too fast. He slowed the car as the pavement became uneven and we entered an unfamiliar neighborhood. Dim, yellow streetlamps barely lit the people sitting along a chain-link fence on upside-down crates, smoking and watching us.

"Where are we?" I asked.

"Get down in your seat," he ordered.

I slipped low enough to appease him but continued watching through the window as we turned a corner onto an unlit street. As we passed an alley, a flame lit a ghoulish-looking face and disappeared.

Cristiano parked, turned off the engine, and lowered his phone between his knees to send a text. "The side panels and windows are all bulletproof. The car looks like shit, but it's secure and runs well," he said absentmindedly. "Nobody should get close enough to try anything, but you may hear gunshots. Try not to scream."

"That's like asking you to look approachable or gentle—it's just not the natural way of things."

He stopped typing to look at me sidelong. "You had gentle. How was it?"

My cheeks warmed as I slouched against the car door. How could he *possibly* know what it'd been like with Diego? But he was right. It was gentle. Satisfying. Pleasant.

Nothing like being told I was going to get my mouth fucked and throat choked.

I bit my lip a little too hard and forced my eyes back out the window, ignoring his question. A woman walked down the street, her blonde hair as impossible to miss as the moon in the sky. "Cristiano, look," I said. "Isn't that the girl Max was just fighting?"

He shut off his phone and stuck it in a cup holder, sinking down with me. "That's Sandra. She's Estonian."

She sat on a bench and took out her phone. I'd never been here, but it didn't take a genius to see this wasn't a good neighborhood. She should be paying attention to her surroundings. I balled my hands in my lap and surveyed the area. "Why is she so far from home?"

He sniffed. "Her aunt sold her to Brazilian traffickers when she was thirteen," he said. "Unfortunately, we only got her out a couple years ago, so she was forced into prostitution for a while."

My stomach dropped. *That* was a betrayal unlike any I'd ever heard. What Diego had done to me paled in comparison. "Her own aunt?" I repeated, my nose tingling.

"People get desperate. The weak ones break." He touched my hand. It took me a moment to realize he was trying to uncurl my fist. I opened it, and his warm palm took mine. "Young, light-skinned, light hair—she's easy bait, but this is the first time we've put her in the field. The important thing is that she wants to be here. To help."

It took me a moment to adjust to the simple act of holding his hand. Was it for comfort? I checked myself before reacting to the word *bait*, remembering what Alejandro had said about trying to keep an open mind. Cristiano had also said *help*. I relaxed my hand into his. "Is she the eighteen-year-old who looks fourteen?"

"Yes."

I closed my eyes. "I'm trying not to think the worst, Cristiano."

"And what's the worst?"

I glanced over at him. "That *you're* prostituting her now."

"I've spent a fortune on girls like her." His eyes grew distant as he looked at her with obvious affection. "It's why I've worked so hard to earn it. They're worth every penny."

Again, I had to work to read his ambiguity so I wouldn't jump to conclusions. He'd told me earlier in the week that when I was young, he'd tried to scare me. I sensed he was doing that now. "What do you mean?"

He squeezed my hand. "Sandra has intimate, inside knowledge of these operations. Sad but true. Just by sharing what she knows, she has helped us free more than twenty girls—and more tonight, we hope."

My heart began to pump, and I felt the rush of blood in my veins. "I don't understand."

His two-way radio went staticky, and a voice came through. "*Hay viene un hombre.*"

Someone was coming. Cristiano stuck a baseball cap on his head. I started to glance over my shoulder, but he grabbed the back of my head and shoved my face into his lap. "What—"

"Suck my dick like your life depends on it," he said. "Or at least pretend to."

"Cristiano—"

"I shouldn't be making jokes—this is serious. Stay down. He's about to walk by." He curled his fist against my scalp then smoothed a hand over my hair. "Do you know this area?"

My irritation with talking to his zipper dissipated as uneasiness settled in. "No."

"It's a forgotten neighborhood. The next one over is a hotbed for trafficking, but law enforcement in both is owned by Belmonte-Ruiz, and they're paid to look the other way. Every person we've seen is either a drug addict, dealer, or prostitute, and they're *all* spies for BR. We have to blend in, or we'll stand out."

"Fortunately, playing your whore isn't too much of a stretch," I said, even though I was near purring by the way he stroked my hair.

His hand stilled. I doubted he even realized he'd been petting me. "In that case, if you have any impulses while you're down there, feel free to indulge them."

*Your curiosity is an affliction.* Papá's words continued to haunt me into adulthood.

With Cristiano, my curiosity was as strong as ever. He was an enigma. My favorite part of business school had been case studies of the inner workings of companies—their mistakes and triumphs. Here was one right in front of me. Nothing about him added up. Nothing about *him and me* added up. Not only could I stomach being this close to him, but I felt safe here, as I had the other times I'd sought solace in him when *he'd* been the one to put my life in danger.

Was it because he hadn't shown me cruelty yet? Or was it that I knew, instinctively, he never would—no matter what evidence I mounted against him?

"How much longer do I have to stay down here?" I asked.

"He's gone. I just like having you there."

I sat up quickly to glare at him. In his black baseball cap, he looked younger, slightly less menacing, and he almost verged on . . . boyish. "I thought you weren't making jokes."

"It wasn't one." His eyes shone, but he didn't keep them on me long, shifting them to the blonde instead. "The Belmonte-Ruiz cartel has been tracking Sandra since we put her on these streets a few days ago. They know she doesn't have a pimp yet, or she'd be working a street in the next neighborhood. Hopefully they'll pick her up tonight."

A small tremor of panic worked its way through me. "But you won't let them take her, will you?"

The man who'd passed our car earlier approached Sandra, and after a quick exchange, she handed him a lighter. With a few drags of a cigarette, he said something, and she smiled.

"He just complimented her looks," Cristiano said. "Sometimes they grab girls. Other times, though, the girls go willingly."

There was that word again. *Willingly*. I was beginning to think

Cristiano thought it meant something different than the rest of the world.

"They're lost and looking for connection," he said in an instructional tone. "Protection. Could be that they come from a shitty, abusive home and this is one way out."

Sandra fidgeted with her hands in her lap.

"Anyway, this guy?" Cristiano continued. "He's feeling her out."

An SUV rounded the corner and crept toward them. The smoker said something, laughed, and nodded discreetly at the car. Sandra turned her head over her shoulder, and her grin vanished as she shot to her feet.

I sat forward as she took off in a sprint, but Cristiano shoved me back into my seat. "Don't call attention, for fuck's sake."

The man flicked his cigarette away and ran after her. "But you have to do something," I hissed.

The SUV reversed, trying to catch up with her, tires jumping what was left of a crumbling curb before the car screeched onto the sidewalk to block her path.

"Cristiano," I said more firmly. "*Do* something."

Cristiano said nothing. Did nothing. The man grabbed her, and she struggled against him. Suddenly, he howled like an animal, jerked, and fell, clutching his leg. The driver bolted out of the car and stopped at his partner's feet, his face scrunched in confusion.

Sandra whipped a knife from under her skirt, raised it over her head, and plunged it into the top of his neck.

I covered my mouth to conceal my gasp, but it filled the car.

"See how she stabbed *into* his spine, not through?" Cristiano asked. "I hope you're taking notes."

My stomach churned violently as I watched blood spurt everywhere. The man who'd approached her on the bench writhed on the ground, trying to yank what looked like an arrow from his leg.

A third man I hadn't seen ducked out of the passenger-side door and crept along the side of the car that was hidden from Sandra.

"Fuck," Cristiano said, grabbing his two-way and barking into it, "Now. Go!"

The blood was excessive and I hadn't seen that much of it since my mother's death. The thought, the sight, made me woozy, my jaw tingling as bile rose up my throat. The third man snuck up behind Sandra until she whirled. He smacked her across the face, and she stumbled back, tripped over the smoker's foot, and landed on her back.

The man jumped on top of her with a pair of handcuffs, wrestling her wrists to the pavement.

Cristiano sat forward. "Come on," he said in a way that sounded as if he was cheering her on.

A Honda screeched around the corner, followed by a convoy of speeding cars. They skidded to a halt in the middle of the street, distracting the man long enough for Sandra to knee him in the balls.

"Yeah," Cristiano said, hitting his palm against the steering wheel triumphantly.

As my attention darted between him, Sandra, and everyone else, my head began to swim, but I narrowed my eyes, focusing on the scene in front of me.

As men from the warehouse swarmed out of the cars, Sandra's attacker released her wrists. She punched him hard enough to send blood and teeth flying.

She shook out her hand, and gold flashed in the headlights. She had a ring on every finger—thick, heavy bands and gems. Not even brass knuckles. Just rings.

I glanced at the massive diamond on my finger. Earlier, I'd regarded is as stunning and elegant—if not over the top. Now I saw it as a potential weapon.

Just the motion of bending my head to look down made me feel queasy, so I raised it again, trying to ward off the sick feeling.

Cristiano unbuckled his seatbelt and tossed the hat aside. "*Stay*," he ordered. "Or so help me God, I'll leave you here tonight."

I shrank down in my seat but kept him in my sights as he marched across the street, rolling up his shirt sleeves. The menace in that one move, in the way he exposed his veiny, hirsute forearms, made sweat trickle down my temple. Who could ever stop Cristiano when he was hell-bent on anything?

One thing I knew—it would take more than physical force.

A man like Cristiano could only be brought down through mental and emotional warfare—carefully chosen words, intimate, deliberate touches, manipulations and schemes so subtle, he would never see them coming.

But as far as what he was walking into now? I wasn't worried for his safety, though I was surprised by how vehemently I wanted it—especially if the alternative was him getting hurt and me having to fend for myself.

By the time he reached them, Max had the smoker and the third attacker on their knees by the curb. The man with the knife in his neck *had* to be dead.

When Cristiano reached them, he squatted to face the first man who'd approached Sandra. They exchanged words until Cristiano seized him by the neck—or was it his *trachea*?

Cristiano released him and circled the two men. He stopped behind the smoker, accepted a machete from Max, and decapitated him in one clean slice. I covered my mouth to hold in my scream as the body slumped over, bleeding and convulsing.

Vomit rose up my throat, and I swallowed over and over to force it back down.

I wanted to look away, but I forced myself not to. I'd wanted answers, and I was getting them. I wasn't sure what they meant yet, and perhaps I'd regret having them. But I was beyond the point where I could turn a blind eye.

Cristiano moved behind the last one and paused. I held my breath as I waited for him to send the last man's head the same way of the smoker's.

But Cristiano passed the machete back to Max and gestured for Sandra to take his place. She didn't hesitate—just sliced her blade across the man's neck, leaving him a bloody heap with the others.

I'd heard the rumors, but I'd not yet seen Cristiano in action. He'd delivered death without hesitation—and faster than it would've taken me to cross the street to him.

That was the vicious killer I'd grown up with. The man who'd stolen me out from underneath his brother. That was also the man whose tie I'd fixed earlier, who'd just made a crude joke, who'd served me duck confit over a bed of precious memories.

That was my husband.

And he'd been right—I wasn't ready.

I put my head between my knees and retched.

# CHAPTER 15

# NATALIA

Black, vomit-splattered pavement blurred with tears as I emptied my stomach again. The car door had been opened, and a hand had gathered my hair into a too-tight ponytail, away from my face.

"You puked *in* the car and somehow managed to avoid *your* shoes," Cristiano said, wrapping my hair around his wrist. "Mine weren't so lucky."

I wasn't sure if I was crying in response to the vomit or for what I'd just seen. I looked past Cristiano's blood-splattered pantlegs. Max had a bound-and-gagged woman over his shoulder as he hurriedly transported her from the back of the attackers' SUV to one of Cristiano's. Eduardo did the same with a different girl. "Where are they taking them?"

"Got it all out? We have to move," Cristiano said. "Get up."

"I can't," I said, the words grating from my raw throat.

"*La policía* will be here soon," he said. "And as I told you before, they're not on my payroll. Either they'll find an abandoned car and a pile of vomit or they'll find an abandoned car, vomit, and you." He took my elbow. "Let's go."

I let him yank me out of the car as Max shut the doors to his SUV and climbed back behind the steering wheel. Blood and guts painted the broken pavement.

"They're taking the girls somewhere safe," he said, dragging me along.

Disoriented, I tried piecing the scene together. "Then why are they still gagged?"

"So they don't scream and fight. If Belmonte-Ruiz sends men after us, or if law enforcement shows up, it'll get ugly. We need to go *now*. You're walking too slow."

He ducked, hauled me over his shoulder, and carried me to the Audi.

After settling me into the passenger's seat and securing my seat-belt, he removed his shoes, went to the trunk, and returned with a fresh pair.

Within seconds, we were speeding away.

I gripped the door handle in an attempt to quell my uneasy stomach. "During the Easter party, you said you weren't going to pay for another shipment," I said. "You were going to take it instead."

"That's what I did."

*He rescued them?*

That would change everything. *Everything*.

It would mean he wasn't a monster at all—at least not to them. Only to me. "I don't understand."

"Belmonte-Ruiz is the leading sex trafficker in the country—one of the top in Central and South America. They're not easy to get to, so I interrupt them where I can."

"Like you did to Diego?" I asked, trying to relate everything together. "You sabotaged him to force him into a position where he'd be vulnerable."

"Pretty much. Nobody who traffics for Belmonte-Ruiz is safe from me. I try to intercept shipments or in this case, hit their own men on a small job." Cristiano steered into the next lane with one hand on top of the wheel. "Basically, the Calavera cartel doesn't traffic people."

"Then what *do* you do?" I pleaded. "Help me understand. After everything I've heard, I don't get why you'd help anyone."

He set his jaw, staring forward. "Because you came in here with your mind made up. You saw what you wanted to see, but it's time to open your eyes."

"You're asking me to believe that all this—this . . . that everything I've seen—the women's clothing in the basement, Sandra as fourteen-year-old bait, and the rumors about the Badlands—it's all . . . it's . . ." Overwhelmed by confusion, I put my face in my hands, shaking my head. "That's not what this world is. If you steal from another cartel, you die."

"We've been hitting Belmonte-Ruiz for months, and I'm still standing," he said. "And they aren't the first cartel we've brought down."

"But all those people in the Badlands," I said. "The gates—"

"Are to keep those who'd hurt us *out*. That's all."

"When we drove in, I saw people in the back of a semi."

He shifted in his seat, frowning. "It was headed south. We were taking people home—Guatemala, Brazil, Chile, wherever. It's not like we can just send them on their merry way once we excavate them from bad situations. They need help to get home and get acclimated. And we have to be stealthy about it because of the circumstances." He ran a hand over his mouth and rubbed his jaw before glancing over at me. "The Badlands are full of slaves and whores, Natalia. And laborers, misfits, and ruthless people."

I looked back at him, meeting his eyes a second before he turned them back out the windshield. "That's what I've been saying all along," I said.

"I never denied it. You were just looking at it from the wrong angle. It's not a prison. It's a sanctuary. They're not abused. They're rehabilitated."

*Holy shit.* A coat of goose bumps sprang over my skin. Why had it been so hard for me to see it? Why was it hard now to admit that it made sense?

Because Cristiano was still my captor. My bad guy. He'd done the opposite of all this to me—so how could I be expected to see him as anything else?

"What about me?" I asked. "You can't get angry that I assumed everything I'd heard was true. *You took me.*"

His nostrils flared as he swerved into the next lane and took a turn too fast. I braced myself against the door. The Audi's smooth hum filled the silence until Cristiano smacked his palm against the steering wheel. After a few moments, he spoke calmly. "It would seem you're the one exception."

Of course I was. *How convenient.* Cristiano got to be a hero to everyone else while keeping me locked up in his house. I crossed my arms and leaned into the corner. "I see. And Sandra? Is she also an exception?"

"No." He stopped for a red light, and I registered my surroundings. We were almost at *La Madrina*. "She's had two years of therapy and rehab, including one of intense physical training—twice as hard as what you've been doing. She wanted to see those men suffer." His grip tightened on the wheel. "She understood that the best way to help was to draw them out. There were about a dozen pairs of eyes on her, ready to spring into action if she needed help." He snickered. "Well, eleven and a half if you count Max."

I didn't laugh. "Where are Max and Eduardo taking the other girls?"

"To the Badlands. There's a team there to receive them. Clean them up, feed them, set them up in a safe house with whatever they need while they adjust. That's the purpose of the toiletry kits you saw." He blew out a sigh. "Then we learn who they are and where they came from."

I fingered the unfamiliar, obtrusive diamond on my hand as I eyed him. "And then?" I asked softly.

When the light changed, Cristiano hit the gas and turned in the direction of the club. "We try to get them home. If they don't have a home or don't want to return—like Sandra—then we have good, fair work and modest housing for them in the Badlands."

My heart sank as the truth of the situation overwhelmed me. These women had been in the worst situations imaginable. Cristiano and his team had saved them. I had not only doubted him, but accused him of unspeakable things. Considering the lengths he went to in order to help, my character assassination must've been shitty to receive.

My throat thickened. "They stay willingly?" I asked, feeling smaller than ever.

"Yes. They have jobs and pay rent like anyone else. Because after what they've been through, many of them want to *be* anyone else."

I wrinkled my nose. "You . . . charge them *rent*?"

"You don't miss anything, do you?" A half-smile slid across his face. "Working gives them a sense of purpose. The Badlands are a safe place for them to do it. I don't need the rent money—I put it back into the community. But none of them came here for a handout. Most like to feel like they're contributing."

I shifted in my seat, grateful for the dark cover of night to hide the range of emotions surely playing out on my face.

How could I have missed all this?

How were girls and boys and *humans* enduring this every day, and why weren't more people helping?

I looked down at my hands. Had I made a terrible mistake treating Cristiano with such disdain, even though he was still guilty of his crimes against me?

"What about the men?" I asked. "Where are they from?"

"All over—and right there. Many of the residents who live within the walls were there when we arrived."

"The town you plundered, raped, and pillaged."

"That's the rumor, yes. And I thank you not to dispel it, since it keeps our reputation intact."

If Cristiano hadn't said something similar at dinner a few nights earlier, I might not have believed him. But it seemed he not only appreciated his bad reputation—he needed it to continue the work he did.

"We needed a town in a strategic location with natural security like the ocean to protect our backs, the mountain over our heads, and the flat desert to see anyone foolish enough to approach. We found that, and we took it." He flexed his hand on the wheel and leaned an elbow on the windowsill. "But we came to the townspeople with respect," he said. "We worked out an amicable deal with those who wanted to stay and compensated those who didn't—all with non-disclosure agreements, of course."

It was like a fairytale, and I wanted to believe it. But regardless of what Cristiano had done for others, there was one person who wouldn't get a happy ending.

As he pulled into the lot behind *La Madrina*, the tires tread over a track to a sliding gate. He parked, exited, and helped me out before taking my bag and his suitcase from the trunk.

"We're sleeping here at the club?" I asked, removing Cristiano's jacket and then the bulletproof vest.

"*Sí*." I tried to take my duffel from him, but he hoisted it over his shoulder. With the cell phone tucked into the bag's bottom, I probably didn't need to worry, but Cristiano seemed to know all. He had yet to punish me for anything like snooping or snarky comebacks and barbed words—but if he thought I'd used the phone at all to get in touch with Diego or *anyone* outside this cartel, his threats would no longer be idle.

*"Opening your mouth would be a death sentence."*

He turned to me. "Leave the vest. Put your jacket back on. I won't have club rats ogling my wife."

It didn't much matter what I wore. We used a private entrance in the back and rode upstairs in an elevator reserved for him and his team.

We walked out of the elevator and across a carpeted hallway that thumped under my feet. He unlocked his office and held the door open for me. It was an extension of his club—sleek and black with shiny surfaces and gold hardware. Computer monitors with surveillance footage made up the wall behind his desk. A bar cart in one corner held decanters, glasses, and spirits in varying sizes. I went to the floor-to-ceiling window overlooking the club. Aqua, turquoise, and seafoam green lights splashed over the patrons and made shimmery, squiggly lines on the dancefloor.

"Tonight's theme—*Bajo el Mar*," he said.

"Under the sea." So many people, and they probably had no idea they were being watched. "How long did you spy on me before you made your presence known?"

"Long enough to know you were looking for me. Long enough to fantasize about stealing you away to my office."

"And here I am." I turned to face him, wondering why he'd brought me here. Was he planning something? Or was a change of scenery supposed to be a gift to me? The spot of blood I'd seen on his shirt earlier was now one of many. "You wore a tie just to murder a man?"

"No. I wore it to murder three." He dipped his head with a sinister smile. "How about a drink, *mi amor*?"

How easily we slipped back into our roles—Cristiano in control, and me trying to make sense of things and even anticipate his next move. "You don't have what I want."

"I own a bar. Try me."

"Coca Light."

He cocked his head. "Of course I have it."

"Warm," I said. "That's the only way I like it."

He paused. "I'll have them put it in the microwave."

Despite my uncertainty over what was happening around me, I almost laughed. "I mean unrefrigerated."

He winked and kept his eyes on me as he picked up his desk phone and placed my order.

I glanced around the dimly-lit office shaded blue by the ocean theme. "Do we sleep on the couch?"

"We can if you like. It'd be cozier."

"What's the alternative?"

"I have a bed on the next floor."

I raised my eyes to the ceiling as if I might be able to see through it.

I could barely feel the vibration of the music below. "It's so quiet in here."

"The walls are soundproof so the noise doesn't disrupt me while I'm working. As are the walls upstairs." He grinned. "So you and I don't bother the patrons."

Another attempt at humor. But also, perhaps, a threat. Maybe outside the Badlands, there were no rules. Maybe willingness was more subjective here, in a dark club, where he'd tried to get me up to his office before. Could everything he'd told me tonight be canceled out by the fact that I was the exception?

Could I appreciate that he was a savior worthy of praise and loyalty, but also hate him for making me his only victim?

I had to keep my eyes and ears open. I admired the things he did, but to me, he was still the same man he'd been before the past couple hours. I couldn't take the chance that if I gave in and saw him as something other than the devil, I might stop fighting for my freedom.

I stared at him, utterly perplexed at the puzzle before me. This was exactly what I'd feared. Not knowing whether to hate him or to feel something else entirely.

"I need to change my tampon," I said.

He blinked at me, opening and closing his mouth. "I—I can send one of my employees out for some. Did Jaz not, uh, pack some for you?"

An ember of delight sparked in me as he stammered. Even the most composed man in the world could be derailed by menstruation. "I have some," I said. "I just meant I need to use the bathroom."

"Ah." He nodded at a closed door to his left. "Through there."

I hesitated. "Are there cameras in there? I don't want an audience."

"For God's sake, Natalia. No. I don't surveil toilets."

My pleasure grew at the offense he took. It wouldn't hurt to remind him that while he called me his wife, I was still his prisoner, and that even when he treated me well, he was only the hero in his own story—not mine.

I picked up my bag and started across the room.

"Leave that," he said.

I paused. "What?"

"The bag," he said evenly, and with no room for argument. "Put it on my desk."

My heart thumped once. I looked back at him. All teasing had left his face, and his dark demeanor had resurfaced. What did he want with the bag? I feared the answer was obvious. “I need it,” I said.

“No, you don’t.” He nodded in front of him. “There.”

Inhaling through my nose, I carried it to his desk, setting the bag down slowly. I wanted to protest more, but that would raise a red flag.

I took a tampon from the inside pocket and glanced up, trying to gauge his shift in mood. There was an indisputable hardness in his eyes that hadn’t been there a moment ago.

Could he possibly know about the phone? And how?

Leaving the bag felt more like surrendering it, but I had no choice. If he knew enough to search the bag, then he knew what he was looking for.

My gut smarted as I made my way to the bathroom.

I had the distinct feeling that the hero had left the building.

# CHAPTER 16

# NATALIA

Compared to the nightclub below, the marble full bathroom off Cristiano's office was eerily quiet. I stood at the door, steeling myself to face the possibility that Cristiano had found the phone Diego had given me. I'd uncovered things about Cristiano tonight I never could've imagined. Good things. But I didn't have him pegged in the least. He could still flip on a dime.

I exited the bathroom and found him towering over his desk—and the contents of my overnight bag.

"Coca Light, warm." He nodded to his bar cart, which held a glass of soda that must've been delivered while I was in the bathroom.

I took a sip hoping the carbonation would soothe my stomach—uneasy from both my earlier nausea and my current nerves—but otherwise kept my eyes on him.

"You know," he said, his eyes shadowed by heavy brows, "Diego was standing right about where you are now when he figured out the truth."

My fingers tingled with alarm. "What truth?"

"I cannot be bought off or dissuaded from getting what I want. Whatever I desire, I find a way to take it." He opened the top drawer to his desk. "But my brother proved me wrong."

I spun the giant rock on my finger and moved closer to the door. "How?"

"He gave me you. And in exchange, I let go of something I'd wanted for a long time. But I don't have you, Natalia. Not yet. Not the way he did."

When he glanced down into the drawer, I quickly scanned the items on his desk for the phone, but it wasn't there. "I could've told you that before I walked down the aisle," I said. "I could've saved you the trouble."

Cristiano took out a gun, and my back went straight as a rod. He'd found the phone—there was no question now. Holding the 9mm up to the light by its pearly white grip, silver and gold flashed.

I stepped forward, my heart pounding as I recognized the White Monarch. I looked down at my rings, and it clicked—the reason they'd felt so familiar. The two-toned metal and pearl inlay wedding band complemented the gun. All it needed was a big, fat diamond in the middle.

The last time I'd seen the White Monarch was in the moments before it'd blown out a *sicario's* brains. "Where'd you get that?" I asked.

"When you pulled this on me eleven years ago, my life didn't flash before my eyes—yours did. The child I'd protected since before she could walk had turned on me. You know what else I saw?"

He didn't wait for my answer.

"Your loyalty to Diego. You offered yourself up in his place. I saw Bianca in you that day. Your mother would've followed your father to the grave. You risked your life for my brother's. I admired that." Still holding the gun, he leaned his hands on his desk. "And I *hated* it."

I pulled his jacket closed around me. "Why?"

"I already told you—because *I* wanted it. I'd pledged my loyalty to your family, and that included you. But in a moment, it all vanished into thin air. Nobody would risk their life for me, though I had for them, over and over." He unknotted his bloody tie and discarded it on the desk. "So I left, built a steadfast cartel around me and made my own family," he said, undoing the buttons at his throat. "Why, then, is it not enough? Why do I still think about that moment you pulled this on me?"

"Is that why I'm here?" It wasn't the answer I wanted as to why he'd married me, but it was an answer nonetheless. "Some elaborate scheme for revenge on a scared nine-year-old girl?"

"No, *mi corazón*. My scheming is done. It didn't go the way I'd planned—Diego's still alive—but only because he knew what I wanted, even when I didn't." He gently slid the gun across the desk. "Just when I was about to throw him to the dogs, he stood where you are now and offered something I couldn't take on my own."

I released a breath I'd been holding. "Me."

He nodded once. "You."

"You could've taken me at any point. You didn't need Diego to do it."

"That's where you're wrong."

Because Cristiano wouldn't *let* himself take me. He'd needed Diego to give me. Maybe he'd thought that my loyalty was part of the bargain, but something like that couldn't be forced.

"Diego is more cunning than you think," he told me. "I didn't even recognize my own want for you until he showed it to me. I'd never let myself think I could have you, so it was never an option in my mind. Diego gets credit for pinpointing a weakness and exploiting it. But he doesn't get to keep any part of you."

"Of *me*?" I asked. "He doesn't have me. He doesn't have *anything* anymore."

"You can't be loyal to both of us, Natalia. It'll get one of the three of us killed, and it won't be me."

"He *doesn't* have me." Cristiano had to know that—didn't he? Feeling short of breath, I walked a few steps toward him and steadied myself on a chair. "But neither do you. Do you honestly think loyalty can be demanded?"

"Yes. So tell me—who are you loyal to, Natalia?"

After this past week, the answer came easily. "Myself, and no one else."

A vein in his forehead ticked, and he nodded at my bag. "Where's the phone?"

My heart stopped, even though I'd known where this was going. "Diego gave it to me," I said, focusing on keeping my voice firm and steady. "I didn't ask for it."

"Where is it?" he demanded.

I swallowed as his patience ran thin. "Sewed into the bottom."

He rifled through his drawer and slammed a pair of scissors on the desk. "Get it out."

As I approached, he jerked his desk phone to his ear and punched a single digit.

I could see that I'd angered him—but did that mean what he'd said it would? Since I'd arrived, he'd been all bark and no bite. He'd warned me leaking information would lead to death—period. But Cristiano wouldn't kill me.

I hadn't shared any information. I was only guilty of accepting and hiding the phone.

*He wouldn't hurt me,* I told myself.

What then? How would he punish me for hiding the phone? Did he have it in him to lock me away, chain me, starve me? The answer was easy—yes, he did. He hadn't gotten where he was without ruthlessness. Torture, destruction, and murder. And you didn't torture, destroy, and murder without having developed some degree of detachment from people.

He'd lavished beautiful clothing upon me, fed me the best food, and surrounded me in comfort. He'd kept his distance, as had his men, warned away from touching Cristiano's "things." He was teaching me how to fight them—and him.

He'd liberated women and children, mostly, I realized in that moment, without credit since he'd been underground until a couple weeks ago.

He wasn't a rapist or an abuser. But he *was* a murderer.

And I?

I was his one exception.

He leveled his eyes on me as he held the phone to his ear and waited. After a moment, he spoke into the receiver. "Send Scratch upstairs with his equipment."

My stomach dropped. *Equipment*?

He shoved the contents of my bag onto the ground and picked up the little black phone. "What did you tell him?"

"Nothing," I rasped through my dry throat.

Cristiano swiped swiftly and expertly before holding up the screen to show me the one saved number. "*Padre*. You expected me to be so fucking dumb that I'd believe this phone was from Costa?"

"No," I said.

"You don't even call him that. You call him *Papá*. Tell me how you still believe Diego cares for you when he put you in this position."

"I don't," I said, "but even if I did, I take responsibility for my own actions."

"Oh, yes," he said. "You will."

The hair on the back of my neck stood up. Cristiano had only been this cold to me in the company of others. His iciness, paired with the mention of *equipment*, sent a chill down my spine. "I didn't share information," I said as panic tightened my chest. "You have my word."

He resumed looking through the phone. "If there were texts, you've deleted them, but one of my tech guys can easily recover them. Tell me honestly, Natalia. What information did you give him?"

"Nothing," I swore again.

He slipped the phone into his shirt pocket and came around the desk. "If you're conspiring with him against me—"

"I'm not—"

"Let . . . him . . . *come for you*," Cristiano intoned, raising his voice. "I am *not* him. I won't let you go so easily."

"Easily?" I exhaled. "What would you have done in his shoes?"

"For the woman I claimed to love? Built an army to protect her or died by her side. But I wouldn't give her to another man, especially one I knew to be dangerous. And I won't let him have you."

The stark confession, which came so easily to him, shocked me. Did a man like Cristiano even *know* love? Did *I*? I'd been the one stupid enough to fall for a phony like Diego. *I'd* been the one begging him to flee with me, to die with me if it came to that. And he'd refused. Words meant nothing anymore—only action did. Now, I stood before his brother, who was turning out to be the complete opposite of what I'd thought.

Cristiano continued around the desk until he was standing over me. "He'll have to kill me if he wants you back."

I tried to hold my shiver at bay, but every inch of me was vibrating with adrenaline, both from Cristiano's frightening threats . . . and his exhilarating promises. "I imagine he wouldn't be the first to try."

He snorted. "Not hardly. *Pero todavía estoy aquí.* I'm still standing before you, so you can guess what happened to those who failed. As I told you once before—betrayal can only be treated as a life or death matter."

He was trying his best to scare me, and though it was working, I wouldn't give him the satisfaction of knowing it. I raised my chin. "Are you going to hurt me?"

"Don't you think I should?" He stood in front of me, blocking me from the exit. "If you were a man in my cartel who'd gone to the enemy, what the *fuck* do you think I would do to him?"

I gripped my neck. *El Polvo.*

"Exactly," he said.

"I *didn't* betray you. I swear it."

"Are you certain?"

"*Yes.*"

"But you're wrong, naïve girl."

I gritted my teeth. "I'm telling the truth."

"I know you are. But the phone synced with the Wi-Fi at the house. And that may mean nothing to you, but it means a hell of a lot to me, my security team that works very hard to secure our town, and to Diego—an enemy. And I assume *all* my enemies enter *every* situation with the worst of motivations. Especially him."

My hairline began to sweat. I'd already known this was bad, but it was much worse than I'd thought.

"He could've gotten access to sensitive information." Cristiano's lips pressed into a bloodless line. "He'd have known your whereabouts anytime the phone was on. He could be standing outside the door right now, ready to ambush us, thanks to his ability to track us here."

None of this had even occurred to me. I shook my head, at a loss for words. "I didn't know."

"It doesn't matter. You knew enough not to bring the phone into my house, and to cut off that line of communication. You did it anyway, knowing what it could cost you. You broke an unspoken rule that I *did* speak." His pupils seemed to eat his irises—completely black eyes with not a single fleck of light to be seen. "You fed information to an enemy."

"Not on purpose," I said, battling against a rising wave of dread. I looked to the gun. I'd thought loyalty couldn't be forced, but maybe I'd been wrong.

"You haven't learned your lesson, even though Diego so brutally taught it to you," he said. "So I ask you again. Who are you loyal to?"

I didn't want to show fear, but I couldn't help it. Cartel law was no joke. I'd been shielded from it, but I was no longer someone's innocent daughter. I was *in* this life now for better or worse. And I wasn't going to cower.

"My answer is the same. Myself," I said, mustering all the conviction I could, even as I wrung my trembling hands in front of me. "Every man in my life who means anything to me has broken my trust—even you."

"I can't break promises I never made," he said coolly. "Deceiving me has consequences, but when the going penalty is a slow, tortured death, I hope you'll find this punishment more than fair."

With a knock, Cristiano looked over my head and called through the door, "*Espérate*."

He'd told someone to *wait*. "What are you going to do?" I asked, glancing back.

"You wanted to be a captive. You wanted me to impose my will. That's what I'm doing."

My heart stopped. "Who's at the door, Cristiano?"

"Scratch. Best tattoo artist in the region. You're a member of the Calavera cartel now—and you're going to own it."

A pit formed in my stomach as I looked between Cristiano and the door. "You're going to—to *brand* me?"

"You're already branded, sweetheart, but this way, there'll be no question."

My heart pounded. Cristiano was going to put his mark on me. Permanently. There would be *no* mistaking who I belonged to with the Calavera name inked on my body. It was barbaric, possessive, and it was making my breath come fast. Part of that was anger that he could be so callous—but *most* of it was something else. Something deeper. Murkier. Cristiano hadn't even officially claimed me yet, but he wanted to tell the world who I belonged to.

And that spoke to an inky darkness in me I'd been trying not to give in to for as long as I could remember. It nudged the basest of my desires awake, just like the ones Cristiano had whispered in my ear on only my second night in his bed.

*"I won't relent until your body has drunk every last drop I have to give. Until you're mine through and through."*

The tender place between my legs responded to the claim of ownership now just as it had that night. Why did I want to be dominated like this? Why had I never known it until Cristiano?

I'd struggled for control since I'd stepped foot into the church. I was terrified but also tempted to let go, just for a little, just to see how Cristiano would respond.

"There *is* another option," he said, tilting his head.

I released a breath, but disappointment tinged my exhale. Why? My body wasn't his property. But if ever there were a man who could own a person in every way, it would be Cristiano. And he'd picked me to be his. He'd married me, brought me into this cartel, and he was going to fuck me, no question. He'd decided I was his, so I was. What would a tattoo mean or even change?

But I wasn't as easily fooled as I used to be. "Another option" would only cost me in some other way. "What is it?"

"One last chance to pledge your loyalty to your husband. But now, I want you to do it on your knees." He walked around to my back and cleared my hair from my neck. After a soothing squeeze of my shoulder, he grazed his hand down and very gently molded his hand to the curve of my ass. "You will beg my forgiveness, you will promise *never* to betray me again—and then, I'm going to let you off with a warning. But not before I put you over my knee and punish you with a spanking."

I inhaled a sharp breath, my ass cheek already stinging with his promise. His enormous hand heated my skin while barely touching it—with only the *thought* of him exerting his dominance.

My legs threatened to buckle. Which was exactly what he wanted—to prove he could get me to my knees, and then that he could get my body to betray me by making me enjoy my punishment.

I was wet already—but he'd known I would be. I hated that he did, especially before I did. Getting spanked and enjoying it was a form of capitulation all on its own, but that he also wanted me to beg? And to mean it?

They should've been easy demands to meet. Swear to keep his secrets, plead him for mercy, and receive a punishment that terrified me not because of the pain it might inspire, but because of the pleasure it definitely would.

I *had* betrayed his trust. I'd put him, Jaz, Alejandro—the entire household, the entire town—at risk. I understood. He couldn't let that slide.

And any fool could say and do what was necessary to save her own life. If my mother was watching, God rest her soul, she would understand. Any idiot could see that being taken over one knee like a petulant child was a thousand times preferable to a permanent tattoo.

But my spine lengthened instead of bowed. It occurred to me that was what Cristiano had been teaching me to do. To show strength and fight back. And I'd warned him I'd use it against him.

"No," I said.

"I beg your pardon?" he asked against my hair.

Submit on my knees or learn what it meant to have my loyalty forced. I'd wear the tattoo like a badge of honor. I clung to the deep-seated knowledge that even though Cristiano'd had plenty of opportunities to hurt me already, he hadn't. "You can shove me down, but I won't beg."

"You put my men at risk, along with every single person in my household."

I bowed my head. "Then do what you have to do."

His hand disappeared from my backside. "If you're trying to provoke me, you won't like the result."

Except, I *wasn't* just denying his loyalty to prove he couldn't demand it. And my trust in him would never be absolute just because he'd kidnapped me. I was hit with the realization that there was a deeper, more powerful reason holding me back.

I could never willingly let Cristiano have me in the ways he demanded . . . and it had nothing to do with his actions over the past few weeks, or with Diego.

"You want my devotion and my loyalty, but they're based on trust and respect," I said calmly over my shoulder. "I have neither for my mother's murderer."

"I already *brought* him to you," he said through his teeth. "I hunted your mother's murderer. I put him on his knees and handed Costa the gun. For closure. For Bianca. For *you*."

Maybe he was right. Maybe with everything I'd learned about him tonight, I should've known with complete certainty that he wouldn't have hurt my mom on purpose. And perhaps it'd been an accident, or perhaps he'd given the *sicario* access, or perhaps a million other possibilities. But as long as I had even a *shred* of doubt, I could never fully trust Cristiano.

I turned to face him. "I can't know for sure."

"*I* can. I *do*. I'm not her murderer. She didn't die because she was shot in the stomach—she bled out. Do you know how long that takes?"

I blinked at the ground, unprepared for this argument. "Several minutes," I said, having looked up as many details as I could remember over the years.

"At the very least. Could be ten, fifteen minutes—or more." He took my arms and drew me close. "What fool would stay at the crime scene that long? I walked in moments before you did."

"You were cleaning out the safe—"

"All the money in the world is useless if I'm dead."

"It doesn't matter. Don't you see that?" I wriggled free of him, backing up until I hit his desk. "Even if the *sicario* wielded the gun, someone else gave the order—but who?" I asked. "As long as I have questions about your involvement, I will doubt you. A wife cares for her husband in sickness and health, she lies with him willingly—she loves him. I will never do any of that for a man who could have killed my mother."

The skin at his collar reddened as his chest expanded with an inhale. He turned his head over his shoulder. "*¡Adelante!*"

As the door opened and heavy boots pounded the floor, closing in on us, my nerves flared—but they were anchored by a shameful thrill of excitement. Cristiano knew how to make me enjoy a spanking, I had no doubt. But he would never suspect being marked this way spoke to a terrifying—and utterly confusing—desire in me.

I tried to see around him, but his shoulders were too wide.

A bald, lumbering man with a chest-length red beard and a black bag over one shoulder stepped into my peripheral vision. He pulled on a glove. "Where do you want it?" he asked in a low, rumbling voice as rubber snapped against skin.

I could feel that same sting, Cristiano's big hand landing squarely on my ass, spanking me into the submissive role he knew would leave me wet.

But I wasn't going to beg for anything.

"Turn and face the back of the room," Cristiano said to me.

As I did, my eyes landed on the White Monarch he'd left on the desk.

He noticed it, too. We exchanged a look before he slid it outside my reach.

My trust in him would never be absolute—and it seemed the reverse was true, too.

From behind, he slid the lapels of his jacket to my elbows, trapping me and exposing my upper back. "Last chance to say mercy, *mariposa*." He spoke quietly so Scratch wouldn't hear. "Tell me you've learned your lesson. I warned you once. No lie, no betrayal will go unpunished. Say mercy, and I'll turn that sweet ass red in return."

He wanted an out, but not for me. He'd walked right up to the line, and now he expected *me* to pull him back so he wouldn't cross it. So he could sleep easy at night knowing he wasn't his father.

He was. And I'd be the one to prove it to him.

I met his burning gaze over my shoulder, and I could see that no part of him doubted I'd concede my loyalty and my dignity. "I won't beg for anything, even your forgiveness, and I won't be willingly bent over your knee as punishment."

He drew back. It gave me a secret thrill to surprise him. Now, the tables were turned, and *he* had to decide what to do. "Careful, sweet girl. The thought of spanking you until you're dripping wet turns my dick to stone. But my cartel's name on your skin? I'll truly own you then, and I don't think I need to tell you what that means."

Heat pulsed in me. I didn't need to be told because I felt it, too. His hand would only dominate my ass for tonight, but the act of permanently marking me said ownership in a soul-deep way.

"Give me a reason to do it, and I *will* take it," he warned.

"Take it."

He searched my eyes, perhaps looking for any doubt or reservation. After all, I had to be willing, or I suspected he wouldn't go through with it. His expression eased as he tilted his head and seemed to find the answer in my gaze—one that pleasantly surprised him.

Cristiano wanted my loyalty, and as with anything else he desired, he would take it.

But that wasn't enough. He would make sure the world knew it.

He'd make sure I never forgot.

I belonged to Cristiano now, and I'd have it permanently stamped on my body for all to see.

# CHAPTER 17

# NATALIA

The butterfly stung. I peeled back the bandage on my shoulder. Orange wings shimmered iridescent within black windowpanes. Slightly whimsical and a touch artistic, I was grateful to see it was a tattoo I would've chosen for myself, although until tonight, I would've balked at the script, sugar skull, and red roses inked around it.

In the mirror of Cristiano's bedroom on the top floor of his nightclub, I read the tattoo reflected back at me over my shoulder.

*Calavera Cartel.*

Yes, I'd agreed to it, but that didn't change the fact that the asshole had branded me like I was cattle and sent me upstairs to bed like I was a petulant child. I'd tried to sleep, but I was drunk on a cocktail of emotions. A bitter aperitif of adrenaline, anger fizzing like soda water, an infuriating sweet-and-sour clash of irritation, and worst of all—secret excitement from Cristiano's absolutely arrogant and unapologetic claim over me. I was sure he couldn't wait to pluck off the cherry garnish and slice clean through it with his teeth. And it would be irreversible when he did.

Cristiano liked permanence—no room for question. An entire town nobody could take from him, a Catholic marriage to bind our souls, a tattoo to remind me of my place. Or was it a warning to others? Nobody else would get too close to me when they saw who I belonged to.

When we'd danced at the costume party, my fury was aimed as much at myself as at him for my unsettling attraction to a man who'd so flippantly come on to me while knowing I was spoken for. Not many men would take another man's woman, then threaten to *remove his hands* if he touched her again.

I was angry at myself again, this time for the secret thrill that came with being staked by a man as wild and hard to pin down as Cristiano. Could the thought of it both make my pussy flutter with excitement and *also* piss me off? Could I have both allowed it to happen *and* use it to prove he was a bastard to decorate my body like a wall in his home? He had no right to assert his dominance in such a permanent, irrevocable way, even if it aroused the hell out of me.

And like splashing alcohol over a wound he'd created, he'd done it an hour after I'd learned he was an *advocate* for women.

I was the *exception*. The one captive. Keeping his dick in his pants allowed him to convince himself he was different. That he was a protector. That he'd made up for his father's sins.

*No monster thinks of himself that way. He's just living by a different code than yours.*

Frustration over my traitorous reaction, and with Cristiano himself, simmered close to the surface. I needed somewhere to direct it. I knew just the man to receive it. If Cristiano's definition of evil was a man who liked his women helpless, then I'd hold up a mirror and show him the reflection of a soulless beast.

I turned away from my naked body. The black and gold bedroom on the top floor of *La Madrina* looked like the kind of bachelor pad you'd find in a nightclub. It shared the same soundproof walls and one-sided window as Cristiano's office so he could look out over the dancefloor in complete silence. I imagined him standing here, choosing a woman, and having her sent up to him. And the thought of him touching someone else, putting his *mark* on someone else, made me even more eager to rail at him.

Surely the playboy mini-mansion was woman-friendly for the many guests it saw. I found pink disposable razors, a blow-dryer, lavender-scented deodorant, and a black satin robe in my size on the back of the bathroom door.

The bedside clock read one in the morning, and once again, I was alone. He was a hypocrite to demand I sleep in his bed while he came and went as he pleased. Every day he asserted more dominance over me, and tonight, he'd taken control over my own body. But I suspected neither of us completely grasped the power I possessed.

I slipped into the robe, leaving my shoulder uncovered as I cinched the sash around my waist. Descending the staircase to return to his office, I was unsurprised to find Eduardo out front, his back straight and hands crossed in front of him. Even as I approached, he kept his eyes trained forward, as if I were Medusa, and one look would turn him to stone.

*If only.*

I reached for the door handle, but Eduardo blocked me from it.

He held his two-way radio to his mouth. "Your wife is here."

"*Un momento*," Cristiano responded and cleared his throat.

Another power play, making me wait to see my own husband. I folded my arms over my chest and muttered, "Asshole."

"He's not," Eduardo said, his voice quiet but sharp.

I balked at him. "Excuse me?"

He rubbed his face over the tattoo darkening his cheek. "You're lucky to have his protection and affection."

"*Lucky*? You were in the church when we married. You know the truth of the situation."

"The truth is, he's our leader. He puts all of us before himself. He puts *you* before himself. And *we* reciprocate—but do you?"

It was, in much subtler words, the same threat Jazmín had leveled at me my first morning in the Badlands.

*"If ever I come in here and find you've betrayed the man we consider our savior, you won't make it off the property."*

The office door opened and a petite, slender blonde in skinny jeans stepped out. Her damp hair made wet spots on a white t-shirt.

She waited for me to move so she could pass, but I was too stunned. My already sizzling anger boiled over. I didn't *want* to move. He was seeing another woman in the middle of the night *while I was upstairs*? Regardless of our arrangement, he was my *husband*. Her eyes sparkled as she ducked her head and went around me with a small smile.

Eduardo grunted what sounded like a laugh.

"Come in, Natalia." Cristiano called my attention to where he stood at his desk in a white, ribbed undershirt. His gaze drifted down my body as he picked up a tumbler of alcohol. "I thought I told you to go to bed."

"I'm not a child," I said.

"Then don't make me spank you like one, or that tattoo would've been for nothing."

My insides tightened with a rush of desire, but equally potent mortification ripped through me as Eduardo listened on. On some level, I must've believed Cristiano when he'd said there was nobody but me, because now, the blow of seeing a woman exit his office had turned my feet—and possibly my throat—to concrete.

"Eduardo's standing *right there*."

Cristiano sighed. "I can see to it that to him, you're only one of my prized possessions. Like a car or watch. That my men hear nothing, see nothing, touch nothing, and wouldn't think of you as a female."

I gaped at Cristiano. "He thinks of me as a *car*?"

"He might, if he knows what's good for him—but would you like me to enforce that on him?"

I slammed the door to the office and walked in. A white terrycloth robe, far too small for Cristiano, had been discarded on the couch. "So every other man should see me as nothing, but you can enjoy your whores whenever you feel like it?"

Cristiano's eyebrows dropped, disturbing his normally unreadable expression. Confusion played over his face like film slides. "I see. Earlier she was a victim, now she's a whore? What changed?"

"What are you talking about?"

"That was Sandra," he said, shuffling some papers to one side of his desk. "The bait from earlier."

I glanced from the robe to his bare, muscled arms. "You're *sleeping* with her?"

He scoffed. "God, no. She showered, and I changed shirts because we were both wearing another man's blood. Well, several men's."

"What was she doing in here then?"

"What are *you* doing in here?"

I didn't answer, because I wasn't even sure I knew. He had tattooed me and sent me away—and didn't seem to hold any remorse over the extreme punishment. I wondered if he'd every truly thought I'd beg. And then, let him spank me—even if he suspected I wanted it.

I'd thought, maybe foolishly, I could turn Cristiano against himself. That I could gain a measure of control and freedom—not by escaping, running, or petulance, but by luring out his demons so he could no longer hide from them.

If I was enticing enough, could I undermine his work, his willpower, and his self-control, and *finally* get him to cross the line?

He ran a fingertip along the rim of his glass. "Sandra was here to discuss a top-secret project," he conceded when I didn't answer.

A large ice cube melted in another glass on his desk. "Have you cheated on me?"

"Is it cheating if you don't care?" he asked. "Although it seems you might at the moment."

"It makes me look stupid."

"To whom? As I said, my men see nothing, say nothing, think nothing about you." He set down his tumbler. "You shouldn't be down here. I sent you upstairs for your own good."

"Why? What will you do? Call Scratch back?" As if given life by my acknowledgment, my exposed *mariposa* tingled. "Go ahead. Mark me once and you might as well mark me everywhere."

"I intend to, just not with ink."

"Another baseless threat."

"Baseless?" He whipped his undershirt over his head, every muscle in his arms and torso flexing as he pulled it off. "Careful, Natalia, sweetheart. You tempt me."

I bit down on my lip at the embodiment of his power, surprised that my first thought was how elegant and sensual such profound and brute strength could be. *My* strength didn't lie in my muscles, but I wanted to prove that it didn't make me any less powerful. I stepped toward the desk. "But you're a master of resistance."

"Not tonight." He balled up his shirt and tossed it on the couch with the robe. "I haven't had so many sleepless nights in a row since I was on the street. My willpower isn't as strong as it has been."

"That explains the girl."

"All it explains is why I sent you away." He heaved a sigh and his eyes drifted to the paperwork and laptop in front of him. "Believe me, I wish your accusation were true," he said, rubbing the bridge of his nose. "To care so little that I could be buried in someone else's pussy right now."

I clenched my teeth, stemming jealousy at the thought—and then satisfaction that he'd resisted something he clearly wanted . . . for *me*.

"Especially when you stand there looking like you came here to fuck." His expression turned pained. "I need it, Natalia."

An answering ache between my legs caught me off guard. It was becoming clear that each time he voiced a need, my body's primal response was to question how I could fill it.

I couldn't imagine him asking *anyone* for what he needed. As he'd said before—he *took* what he wanted. He didn't ask. So what stopped him now?

I took another step forward, and he moved back.

*This* was where my power lay. Tonight, his weakness was on display. Perhaps because he'd thought I'd gone to bed and had naïvely let down his guard. I forced words from my mouth before I could chicken out. "What do you need?"

"You're the one who came to me," he said. "So I ask you *again—why* are you here?"

"It's hard to change the tattoo bandage when I can't see it that well." A small fib. I raised my chin as I delivered a jab just to irritate him. "Although, if it gets infected, maybe they'll remove it for me."

"Anyone else in my position would have killed you in a *heartbeat* for putting his livelihood and team in jeopardy—I shouldn't need to remind you of that."

"I shouldn't need to remind *you* that kidnapping me didn't make my loyalty automatic."

"It's your duty as my wife." He pressed his knuckles to the surface of the desk. "We're family now, and family comes above almost anything else."

"I'm not your family just because you put words on my skin. I'm not your property, either."

His eyebrow rose in challenge. "You're both."

I breathed through my urge to rage at him. That was why I'd come down here, but I needed to be smarter . . . to keep my cool the way he did . . . and to find and employ the *right* weapons, not the obvious ones.

He'd told me once I'd have to play the game, or I'd lose, and sex was the only defense I had.

He'd made it very clear he didn't want to be his father. I'd made it very clear I didn't want to be his wife. But he'd proceeded anyway. So would I.

"But none of that means I'll fuck you against your will," he said with finality. "So leave. I have a lot of work to do. I'll fix your bandage in the morning."

Cristiano wanted me. It had been written on his face since before I'd even known it was his eyes I was looking into. Under Calavera face paint as he'd asked for a dance, his want had shown. It showed now, and it'd grown into *need*.

He had the strength and prowess of a lion. He could tear me apart. Perhaps he would.

He'd promised in the church that I'd bleed in other ways.

But at some point, I'd shifted from trepidation over that—to trepidation over what would happen if I *loved* it.

Even when I hadn't known what to call it, that fear had weighed on me from the moment he'd put his hands on me on the dancefloor and threatened to take me from my fiancé and make me his.

I untied my robe and let it drop. "I'm neither your property nor your wife until you claim me."

Dark, ravenous eyes raked over me, and I felt them like hands. "Claim you?" He nearly growled. "What happened to consummating the marriage?"

Exposing myself this way, I had to contain a shiver of fear while my nipples hardened with the hungry way he looked at me. "This isn't about that. I'm not doing this for Diego."

He walked forward until he towered over me. "Let me see my tattoo."

It took me a moment to register his meaning. *His* tattoo. He owned it, even when it was on my body. I wanted to tell him to go to hell, but I needed to control my reaction. Slapping him in the church had been satisfying, but it hadn't accomplished anything. Getting him to break down and fuck me against my will? *That* would be much more effective.

I turned, and he hovered his fingers over the ink. "I hope it serves as a strong enough reminder of who you are and where your loyalty belongs."

"I expect it will," I said, facing him again.

He raised my chin with his knuckles. "You're more exquisite, more finely drawn, than any piece of art I've collected over the years."

"I'm glad my body pleases you."

"As am I," he said, his voice deep enough to register in my mind as desire. My own craving for him reared its ugly head. "But it's more than that, my Natalia. *Mmm*. I do like the sound of that. My Natalia. What once was his is now *mine*."

"I'm not thinking of Diego now," I said. "But you are."

"No. No more. He's an echo—and you, darling, are a symphony." He bent his head as if he might kiss me. "I sent you to your room out of anger, but also because seeing my name branded on your body gives me the most raging hard-on I've ever had. It's a dangerous combination. I haven't been in a situation where I didn't trust myself in years. I can't say how I'll react."

My heart pounded with his thinly veiled warning. I could already feel his hands on me, consuming every inch of my skin, charting new lands, conquering curves and valleys. I was the one in dangerous territory, though. I had to hold strong. He could have my body, but he would never possess my heart. That wasn't on the table. Diego had broken it, and Cristiano was the last man who could put it back together.

I turned my cheek as he leaned in to kiss me.

He stayed there a few moments, his breath warm on my cheek. "You're turning away from me?"

"No. My body is yours, Cristiano. But I won't kiss you."

"You've kissed me before."

And each time, I'd lost any sense of my surroundings, and that was why I couldn't let it happen again. Not until I'd grown stronger and held more control. "I can lie back on the couch for you. What more do you want?"

"I want to know what it will take for you kiss me the way you did on our wedding day."

"I'll keep your secrets as I've promised. I will obey you as I swore before God. But I *won't* kiss you."

He pinched my chin and turned my face to his. "You are my wife. You will kiss me when I say."

A thrill ran through me. As I suspected, he only possessed so much willpower.

The same thought must've dawned on him because he released my face and picked up my robe. "Go to bed."

I put my hands over my breasts. "You're rejecting me?"

He held the robe open, and I reluctantly slipped into it. "You're on your period anyway," he said.

"You said that wouldn't stop you."

"And it won't." A wolfish grin spread across his face as he adjusted the shoulder of the robe so it didn't touch the tattoo. "With the life I've led, do you think a little blood scares me?"

"Then why are you sending me away?"

He tied my sash into a firm knot. "Do you have any idea what you're asking for?"

Disappointment seeped through me. My only weapon against him had failed me. "I'm not asking for anything," I said sharply. "I'm giving you what you need."

"And *I'm* not asking you to submit to the inevitable," he said. "Only that you come to me because you want to."

"That will never happen."

"Then I will never fuck you, because I am not a rapist." He walked around to my back, gathering my hair into a loose ponytail and freeing it from the collar of the robe. With his mouth at my ear, he said, "Don't get me wrong. I could bend your naked body over every flat surface of this office. I could chain your ankles to my bedpost and fuck you raw for days on end. I could push your tits up against the window and make you look down on everyone as I finger you with such restraint that you'd beg me to finish you off while your juices drip over my hand and run down the glass."

I couldn't breathe. My thighs shook, and it wasn't from fear. An entire *world* of possibility opened up to me—a frightening world in which I actually wanted to experience all the things Cristiano had just said. In which I craved to be humiliated, dominated, and *ruined* by the king himself.

"Nobody's stopping you, Cristiano," I said breathlessly.

"You know what's stopping me."

"You're not interested," I said to provoke him.

"Back up and feel how interested I am."

I did, closing the distance between us. My heart pounded as I pressed my ass against his hardness. I reached back to touch him, but he caught my wrist. "I could do all those things to you and more, Natalia. But it would mean nothing to me if you didn't want it. Go back upstairs and don't come to me again until your sweet pussy is so wet with need for me, that if you sat on my lap, I'd slide right in."

I opened my mouth, silently gasping from his words, from the tidal wave of arousal that washed over me. I wanted all of that. But his determination not to break spoke volumes.

Nothing scared a man as powerful as Cristiano. But *this* did. The fear of becoming his father ran deep in him. As deep as his cock was hard.

"Fly away, *mariposa*," he said heatedly in my ear. "I can picture exactly what I want to do with you first, and I'm dangerously close to giving in."

I drew back my shoulders triumphantly. "What do you want?"

"To see how far down your throat I can fit my cock."

I inhaled sharply, shocked, and yet the words were nothing to him. He tossed them between us like a bag of groceries, amused at how I stood there gaping.

"I have work to do." He turned his back. "Go."

He didn't have to tell me twice. The idea of a penis in my *throat* was enough to send me upstairs—but slowly. I could barely walk as desire mounted in me. Why? It was beyond wrong to be aroused at the idea of taking Cristiano so brutally in my mouth. If Diego had ever said such a thing to me, I might never have spoken to him again. But to hear Cristiano tell me what he wanted to do to me so resolutely, without apology, my instinct to kneel and let him push the boundaries of my comfort—and my body—was alarming. I was tempted to throw myself at his mercy and have him exert his ceaseless dominance over my mouth. And equal was my craving to get *him* to pass his limits and give in to his desires—so he could hate himself for it.

Something was changing, but it wasn't in him. It was in me.

Yet, perhaps *changing* was the wrong word. What if all along, I'd wanted those filthy things he'd said, but I'd been denying myself?

I'd known when he'd taken me in his arms at the costume party despite my refusal that my power came from his weakness for me.

I had failed tonight, yet it didn't feel like it. I'd tested the waters, and they were warm and inviting. Having something he wanted—to fuck me—and something he could never have—my devotion—emboldened me.

Just as much as my building desire for him terrified me.

## CHAPTER 18

# NATALIA

I woke in the dead of night to a warm, soothing touch. I didn't remember falling asleep, only lying on my stomach, replaying Cristiano's filthy, arousing words over and over again. I'd had to resist from touching myself so he wouldn't walk in and catch me in the act. So he wouldn't see firsthand the effect he was having on me.

Cristiano cleaned my tattoo with a damp towel so gently that I closed my eyes and let him finish without protest.

Afterward, he cleared my hair from my neck and smoothed his hand over my back as my mother had done when I was small. "Marked but still flawless," he murmured.

I drifted. Maybe. I wasn't sure. He'd stopped touching me but still weighed down my side of the bed. I opened my eyes, blinking over my shoulder until he came into view, sitting with his head in his hands.

"What's wrong?" I whispered.

He shook his head. I didn't actually expect him to confide in me, but he said, "A problem I can't solve. Every time I get close, I seem to end up further from the answer."

I sat up, pulling the sheet with me and tucking it under my arms to cover the cream negligee Jaz had packed for me. The raw emotion in his face made my heart do something funny. Something unwelcome. I didn't need to have spent much time with Cristiano to understand he wouldn't show this side of himself to many people. For any cartel leader, vulnerability could mean death. But for Cristiano, control was everything, and in this moment, I sensed he didn't have it.

"I'm sorry."

"Don't be sorry. Be useful."

*Of course.*

There was only one way he saw me as useful, and that was on my back. I was an idiot for offering my condolences. I started to lie back down to sleep when he spoke again. "Advise me."

"What?"

"Be useful and advise me on this issue," he said.

"You have men for that."

"They tell me to drop it." He shrugged one shoulder. "That I've been pursuing it too long. They don't see the payoff, only that I'm emotionally attached."

Having had the most emotional attachment possible severed—that between a mother and daughter—I understood. "There's no room for emotional attachments when you choose this life."

He stared at me as if he'd seen a ghost and his voice dropped so low I had to lean in to hear him. "Do you really believe that?"

"I don't know," I admitted. "They're dangerous. But I wouldn't want to know anyone who didn't have them—those attachments remind us that we're human."

Elbows on his knees, he bent his head and scrubbed his hands through his hair. "Despite what you may think, I *am* human. I do feel the loss of things I once had and crave those I never can, no matter how badly I want them."

"What things?" I asked.

"My needs aren't different just because I'm . . ." He gestured at himself. "This."

My heart tugged. Of course I'd known I didn't have to show Cristiano the monster inside himself. He knew his demons, as we all did.

"Never get attached," he said. "*Never.*"

I sensed he was speaking from experience—intimate experience. He'd learned that lesson the hard way. "Who taught you that?"

He hesitated, then looked over at me, both drinking me in and fighting himself. "My father. But I am attached. So, tell me, Natalia. What would you do in my position? I have a gut instinct I can't ignore. A theory I can't prove. A need that only this missing piece can meet."

He'd shown me carnal need earlier, but this one ran deeper. Why come to *me* for help? He was the one man in my life who shouldn't care about anything more than my body. And what he was asking here was no small thing—my opinion, my advice. On cartel business.

For that grave reason alone, I attempted to put aside my situation and walk in his shoes. He had more than a cartel in his care. He had an entire town, and most people in it had suffered in some form or another. They depended on him. He'd been described to me as a leader, provider, savior—even a guiding light. I hadn't believed any of it until I'd seen it with my own eyes. Most men would either buckle under the pressure or let that kind of authority go to their heads. Maybe he had done both, but he was still standing.

Or sitting, rather—at my bedside, so he could talk this through with *me*.

I shifted against the headboard. "What do you stand to lose?"

"There may *never* be payoff, but there will *always* be risk." He blew out a sigh, thinking. "My resources are better spent other places—commanding a business that allows me to keep the Badlands running. I'd be taking up resources that save lives."

Helping others was more than important to him. It was his way of life. I still wasn't sure why, or if he had ulterior motives, but if people were better off in the end, wasn't that for the best? "And what do you have to gain?"

He dropped his hands between his knees. "Peace of mind. And something I want very much. Suddenly, it's within reach—if I'm right and can prove my suspicions."

I inched a little closer. "Is it dangerous?"

His eyebrows cinched. "How so?"

"You traffic weapons. Is it something that will give you inexorable power over other cartels?"

"What if it was? Would you tell me to grab it before someone else could?"

I pulled my knees against my chest under the sheet. The right weapon in the wrong hands could be devastating. But to use it as an offense wasn't any better. Obliterating others to save myself was something I didn't think I could live with. "No."

"Smart girl. A weapon of mass destruction was a good guess," he said. "But wrong answer. We'll have to work on that."

I frowned, a sliver of dread twisting through me.

"This mission isn't just for me, but my reasons for pursuing it are selfish—"

"How?"

He blinked at me, moonlight bathing him. Even when I'd hated him fiercely, I hadn't been able to ignore how devastatingly handsome he was. But in this moment, with his pain showing, his beauty was a thing of wonder. "It's selfish because as someone who's had nothing, I recognize how much I have now," he said. "And I'm grateful for it. But I want more, Natalia."

"More?" I asked under a coat of goose bumps. "Power? Money?"

"It's not about money. I've already spent enough money and time pursuing it, only to come up empty-handed."

"Then why continue?"

He cupped one hand over the other, forming a fist nearly as big as a child's head. His knuckles whitened, and a familiar tremor moved through me. I'd seen this kind of contained fury before, and I'd missed it—in Diego.

"Revenge?" I asked.

He stared straight ahead. "When is it ever not about that?" he asked.

"But it's never only that." Cristiano, like his brother, had also witnessed his parents' death. It was a scene I'd envisioned many times, but for the first time, I saw him in the room, too—not just Diego. "Revenge stems from other things, like pain. Are you in pain?"

Slowly, to my surprise, he nodded, but to my even greater surprise, it broke my heart a little. They'd only been boys. *This* boy, in front of me, had experienced something from which he hadn't healed. And he was here now, asking for permission to find what he needed. Maybe even looking to me for more. That was a new kind of power, not sexual or physical, and not the kind of emotional we'd been dealing with up until this point. These wounds lived deep, amongst distrust and lost hope.

"I've been through this with Diego," I said. "If it's revenge you seek, leave it. If it's against me or my father, I beg you to see how we've already suffered."

"It's not against you, my lovely wife. I promised you earlier tonight, and I meant it—where you're concerned, I'm done scheming. But for you, I still want many things. Not just revenge, but closure, happiness, even love."

My throat threatened to close with the conviction in his voice. Revenge and closure. Those two things could tempt the devil. They fit easily into my life, but into many areas—revenge and closure for my mother. My father. Or against Diego. Cristiano, too. Happiness and love were murkier—and much scarier coming from Cristiano's mouth. "You're a formidable man. I don't need to tell you that."

"I am."

"So why can't you take this like you do everything else?"

"It can only be given."

An eerie feeling fell over me with the familiar words. *I* had been given to him. So was it a person? Was he trying to command the same loyalty, devotion, and fidelity from someone else that he'd tried to from me?

"I *have* tried taking it regardless," he said with resignation. "Now, what I wonder, is just how much I'd give up." He paused, running both hands over his face. "I have unmet needs. And a fierce desire for answers. I want to regain a sense of what I lost. I want . . ."

My heart pounded with the yearning to understand how *I* could give such a powerful man and equally broken boy what he wanted. Maybe even what he needed. "What?" I asked softly.

"If I go on, I may confront things I'm not sure I want to know. And in the end, there's no guarantee I'll get what I want." His jaw firmed as if it was difficult to admit. "No guarantee I'll even meet those needs."

It was clear to me he had to do this. There was nothing Cristiano couldn't have if he set his mind to it. But I also knew Cristiano had to figure that out on his own—and I could help him get there.

"Not knowing the truth will drive me mad." Frustration seeped into his voice. "But if I keep looking for it, I may go mad before I get there."

"Then leave it," I said.

He pulled back, his eyes finding mine. "Just like that?"

"Could you get hurt?"

"Tell me you don't want me to, and I'll promise you I won't."

I bit my lip to hide a smile, thankful for darkness to conceal my pinkening cheeks. "Will it hurt others?" I asked.

"Only those who deserve it."

"Did those men tonight deserve it?"

"You tell me." The silhouette of his Adam's apple bobbed as he swallowed. "I don't need to explain where they meant to take Sandra and those girls—or what they meant to do."

I'd seen the bound-and-gagged with my own eyes. I'd seen more these past couple weeks than I had in a lifetime, beginning with the inside of a *sicario's* head. Papá had tried to keep me from witnessing the dark side of this world, and pretty much everything else—while Cristiano had made me watch him deliver death by machete.

Was he steeling me for things that may come my way? *Our* way? Protecting me by arming me? He'd put his body in front of mine more than once, and deep down, I knew he would again if I needed him to. But if ever the day came that he wasn't there, then what?

"My father and Diego never would've brought me along tonight," I said.

"It was risky," he admitted. "But such is life. The more you see, the less it will shock you if you ever encounter it. I can't have you puking every time you see blood and guts, or this marriage will never work."

My stomach protested, despite the fact that it was another attempt at a sinister joke.

"I wouldn't have brought you if I wasn't ninety-nine percent confident in my team," he said.

"And the one percent?"

"One-hundred percent confidence is a death wish. And if you weren't confident in *me*, you wouldn't have come. Were you scared?"

I stared back at him. "Yes. But I won't be as scared next time."

"And even less the time after that," he said with a nod of approval. "Do you see me differently now?"

I tilted my head. Contoured by shadows, his bicep flexed. I *did* see him differently. He had always been a man who could hurt me and innocent people. But now, he was *also* a man who could hurt others. Those who *weren't* innocent. The ones immune to the law. Sinners to which God had seemingly turned a blind eye. There were plenty of those around who were never made to pay for their crimes.

I had a very powerful husband, not just in physique, but in dominion. His reach was long, far, and unforgiving.

If I'd learned anything from my mother, it was that behind every powerful man stood a stronger woman.

And if I'd learned one thing from *Jazmín*, it was that I could *control* a powerful man with my mouth—and not by telling him what to do.

Indecision warred on his face. The dark, hauntingly beautiful face that hid fears, grief, and heartbreak. I could tell with eyes like his that he'd seen things. He already knew the answer he was looking for, but he needed me to confirm it.

Would I let him suffer, or would I free him to pursue and conquer what ailed him?

I glanced at my hands and considered the best way to urge him forward. What came to mind was the universal currency around here —one we'd both been dealing in. Power, and it came in endless forms. "How much money do you have?" I asked.

His eyebrow rose at the brusque change in topic. "Enough," he said. "And more coming in every day. You'll never have to worry."

I peeled back the sheet, put one foot on the ground, and then the other. After rising from the bed, I stepped softly until I stood before him. He followed my every move with bottomless eyes, willing me closer so he could suck me into his universe.

He'd come to me for help, vulnerable and fighting himself.

The real domination would be harnessing the kind of power he wielded. Using his own weakness to turn him against himself, against everything he stood for. I'd wanted that for a while.

But I wanted other things, too, and not all of it made sense.

Now that his walls had begun to crumble, I wondered if I could achieve the impossible feat of filling such a man's voids and needs.

My more carnal desires surfaced, too, but what it all came down to was . . .

I wanted to get on my knees to see if I could bring the great Cristiano de la Rosa to *his*.

I kneeled between his legs with butterflies in my stomach and nothing but him in my vision.

"If I'd known money would be the thing to bring you to your knees," he said, "I would've bragged about my fortune relentlessly."

"I already know you have money. More than my father, and he's a multi-millionaire." I willed my hands steady as I reached up and opened his belt. "That's not why I asked."

"Why then?"

I slid the fine leather band through his pant loops and set it on the bed. "If money is no object," I said, "there's nothing you cannot buy."

"Nothing."

"This thing you want to find. Tell me, truly, why you want it. Maybe it becomes revenge or money or sex—but at your core, what is your unmet need?"

The lust in his eyes burned so hot, I suspected he wouldn't even be able to form a coherent answer. "I'm looking for the key that unlocks something I've wanted for a long time." He jutted out his chin. "Not something. *Everything*."

Though my throat dried with the prospect of what I was about to do, my mouth watered. He'd said this was what he wanted tonight, but it was more of a need. And he seemed to think that I of all people could fill it. Had anyone ever reciprocated that kind of trust in me?

I had no keys to give—whatever he ultimately needed, it wasn't here tonight. But I was.

I sat back on my calves and lowered the zipper of his pants. "Why should a man like you ever have a need that isn't met?"

"I tend to agree."

Dark hair gathered like a storm cloud at the root of his hidden cock. There'd be no turning back once I freed him from his underwear. There was no need to be scared. I was in control here, and that was saying something. I'd heard about giving head plenty of times, just as I'd heard about receiving it—and that had been a more pleasant experience than I'd expected.

"Have you done this before?" Cristiano asked.

I stared at the bulge twitching to be liberated. "No."

"I'm glad. But tonight, I'm in no state to be your first." It was a warning, but not a refusal.

When I shifted my hand and brushed against him, he sucked in a breath. "Why not?" I asked.

"It took everything in me—and I mean everything—not to fuck you in your wedding dress in the church. I want to own you so badly, it scares even me. Now, seeing my cartel on your body for eternity . . . I've been tortured with need since the first ink touched your skin."

*He* was telling *me* he didn't want this? Or he was giving me an out. An opportunity to retreat. I didn't want to, and I didn't want to ask myself why that was. I'd been prepared to take all of him on my wedding night, and then again earlier when I'd gone to his office in my robe.

"What state *are* you in?" I asked.

"The one where I find your limits and push them. I'm fine to sit back and let you kiss on my dick for hours while you figure it out—one day. Not tonight. Tonight, I want to fuck something."

"There are lots of somethings downstairs."

"You're right. I don't want to fuck any of them. I want to fuck you."

I needed to get up. He was warning me. This had been my goal and my fear—to unleash his inner demons.

*"I'm scarier than any monster,"* he'd told me as a child to chase away my nightmares.

But it was also my desire—to see his worst. I was prepared to let him use me, because I was prepared to hate him.

I *wasn't* prepared for the alternative. To accept him, to crave him. To . . .

I pushed the thought away.

His own inner battle played out on his face. He was just as tortured as I was bewildered by my own desire to do this.

"This is my last attempt to scare you off." He took my jaw in his big hand and lifted my face to meet his gaze. "I will fuck this mouth. I will fill this throat, first with cock, then with cum. And you know what I'll do after that?"

I shook my head. I couldn't even conceive what more he *could* do.

"I will protect this mouth and this throat from any motherfucker who even looks at you wrong. Every part of your body will submit to me, and every inch of you will know the protection of a man who would lay down his life to keep each hair in place." He stood to his full height, doubling in size and menace. "No man will touch what's mine to suck and lick and fuck. No man will take what you give only to me."

Sitting on my heels, I had to tip my head back all the way to see him. Raw, throbbing desire replaced any fear his words should've inspired. "And does that work both ways?"

"You have my devotion in and out of my bed."

"*Diego* got a tattoo for me."

"You want me to reciprocate? I can. What would you like?" He cuffed my wrists in one hand and tugged me up onto my knees until I was face to face with his groin. With his free hand, he pulled out his cock. "Shall I get 'Property of Natalia' scrawled across it?"

I swallowed my gasp as the source of his confidence revealed itself. Had I never seen another penis, I still would've known it was larger than average, and equally intimidating in its girth.

It begged to be sucked. The engorged purple head asked for entry.

Had I lost control of the situation? Or was I getting exactly what I wanted? Shackled by his hand, I was his prisoner. I was at his mercy. I was his. And I could've exploded for all my pent-up desire. We'd spoken of unmet needs? I had one. *Relief.* I could soothe and be soothed if I would let myself.

"Open," he said, "or go back to bed and stay away until you're ready."

I inhaled through my nose, wet my lips, and parted them. "I'm ready."

"Good girl," he rumbled. "Don't close until I say." He slid past my teeth without pretense, feeding himself into my mouth. "You have a lovely, wide mouth, Natalia. I noticed it instantly at the costume ball."

Unable to respond, I moved my tongue under the silky skin of a rigid, veiny shaft. He had promised to fill me, and he was a man of his word. He left no room for anything else. No thoughts in my head, nothing but his dark pubic hair and taut, godlike belt of muscles in my sight. Only my own saliva slickened the way.

"When I saw you," he continued, "I thought to myself—what a fucking woman Natalia has become. I wasn't ready for that." He kept pushing, approaching the back of my mouth. "But don't think that just because I was and am your protector that I'll treat you like you're breakable while you're in my bed." He stared down at me, his gaze menacing one moment and adoring the next as he tightened his one large hand around both of my wrists. "Even trapped and filled by me, you already know you're in charge here, don't you?"

As he thrust deeper, I swallowed to keep from choking. In that moment, I knew nothing but the weight of a man's cock on my tongue and his tip begging entry to my throat. It stripped me of anything but pure satisfaction that I could pleasure him.

"That's it," he said, caressing his thumb on the inside of one of my wrists. "Open your throat, *mamacita*. Show me what you can do."

I had no idea what to do. All the talk in the world couldn't have prepared me for being dominated by a man of his size and prowess. My mind rejected this, told me to fight back, but my body, my instincts, my throat, yielded for him, welcomed him, and I found my pussy pulsing for how he demanded my submission.

"Breathe through your nose," he instructed. "Open. Take me deeper."

To feel him in my mouth was strange but natural, as if I were a creature made to receive him. But when he breached my throat, it took all of me not to push him out. I gagged and tears flooded my eyes. "There's no sight in the world like watching you try to take as much of my cock as possible."

I wanted it between my legs. I'd sworn to myself I wouldn't beg for it, but my body betrayed me, nearly shaking with longing to take him the one place I knew he'd truly possess me.

"*Qué bellísima*," he murmured. "Such a good girl has no reason to fear me."

He withdrew. Once the tip of his cock reached the tip of my tongue, he glided back in, but only partway. "Suck," he said, releasing me.

I hollowed my cheeks and did as he said, using my hands to cover what I couldn't reach with my mouth.

"*Sí, Natalia*," he said with a groan. "Now grip my hips and see how deep you can go on your own."

I dug my hands into his skin and tried but didn't make it nearly as far as he'd been able to push himself.

"Look at me, *mi amor*," he said. "It's one of the many things I'll demand of you, but perhaps the most important. Keep your eyes on me when my cock is in any of your holes—even when I take your ass."

Butterflies erupted in my stomach. He was so crass, and now that I was on my knees for him, ruled by arousal and desire, I could admit that I fucking loved it. I had been treated so carefully my entire life, with kid gloves and placating words. Cristiano was the opposite of all that—and unlike any man I'd ever met. I pulled back, panting for breath. "I will never let you do . . . *that*."

"You will. And I'll find a way to watch your face as I press every last inch of myself into the tightest hole on your body, until you think you're going to break in half."

I wiped saliva from my mouth, so turned on that I was nearly ready to agree to what sounded like the ultimate ruination.

"I didn't say you could stop." He cupped the back of my head, pulling me to him. "Flatten your tongue."

I didn't have to; he flattened it for me. When I forced it to relax, he took advantage, pushing even deeper down my throat. Once he was anchored there, he held my head in place and moved his hips, slowly at first and then faster. And now, I understood what it meant to have my face fucked.

When I gagged, he stopped. "Your virgin mouth can't take it, can it? You still need breaking in."

I blinked away the tears that had gathered as I'd choked on him. He was letting me put a stop to this, but I didn't want that. Not even close. I'd gotten on my knees willingly, and I was at his mercy, stripped emotionally bare.

Only honesty remained.

And the truth was, I needed this.

I loved the primal way he used me. The look of admiration that came with each "good girl." The sense that he'd do almost anything in his power to have me continue.

I drew his hips closer, pulling him marginally deeper into my mouth.

"Use your nails," he said.

When I dug them into his skin, he inhaled sharply. "Do exactly that if it's too much. I'm not going to ask again if you need a break. Use your nails and I'll stop. *¿Entiendes?*"

I nodded—as best I could with a mouthful of cock—that I understood.

He resumed his pillage and plunder. "Take it deep for me just a little longer, *mi amor*. You'll know it's the last time when I spill down your throat."

He pushed back as far as he could before I clawed his hips and came up coughing.

My heart pounded as I regained composure. I opened my mouth and he was back inside in a second, impaling me. As he fucked the opening of my throat into yielding for him, he looped his fingers into my hair, massaging the back of my head until I jerked away to catch my breath.

He pumped his fist over the monstrous length of him, my saliva glistening and dripping in the moonlight. "Enough?" he asked as the corner of his mouth lifted. "I can paint your face a pretty, pearly white instead and coat your throat another time. Just say the word."

I would not. This only scratched the surface of all the ways he was going to ruin me, but the same was true for him. He was at my mercy just as much as I was at his.

I leaned in. The tip of him was swollen and purple. I could practically read his need for release. He slowed his furious stroking as I put just the tip in my mouth, sucking on it like a lollipop then licking under the ridge.

His fingers curled against my scalp. *"Fuck."*

At the intensity of his curse, I darted my eyes to his face, wondering if I'd done something wrong. Instead, I met a half-lidded gaze that said I was doing everything right. This time, I slid my mouth along his shaft on my own, keeping my eyes up.

His lips parted for what would surely be another command, but then he clenched his jaw shut, glancing up at the ceiling. "God, that's so fucking good. *You're* so goddamn good."

*This* was control, and I understood why Cristiano wanted it so badly. It was heady to watch the face of such a powerful man screw up with need and desperation—all for *me*.

He took both sides of my face in a firm but gentle hold and used my mouth to finish himself off. He left my throat alone as he thrust hard and fast into my mouth, his fingers gripping tightly. "I'm coming." His massive body shook with his impending explosion. "Your mouth is too hot and sweet to resist. And now, it's finally mine."

He shoved to the back of my throat and shuddered as he came warm and sticky down my throat. The moment he pulled out, he towered over me, placing his hand under my jaw and angling it up. "Swallow me, Natalia." I started to cough, but he held me there. "Swallow."

I gulped him down, but it was more than I thought possible and some spilled over my chin. He stroked his cock slowly as it settled between his legs, as spent as I was.

As he walked away, I fell forward onto my palms, reorienting myself. It was oddly satisfying to work and be worked and to feel the result dripping down my throat and over my chin. Not once in my life had I ever been handled so ruthlessly, with such fervor, or been broken down and so relentlessly exposed.

"You're sufficiently ruined for one night," he said from somewhere in the dark, my thoughts apparently running through his mind as well.

I looked up. He was wholly naked now, his cock hanging between his legs, his thigh muscles working as he approached me barefoot and with a damp towel in his hand.

"That's what you wanted, wasn't it?" I asked hoarsely.

"For longer than I care to admit," he said. "I suspect you won't admit you wanted it, too."

I couldn't, not in that moment, but I wouldn't deny it, either. I reached for the towel, but he took my elbow and helped me up. He put his knuckle under my jaw to raise my head and look me in the eye as he smoothed the warm, damp towel over my chin. "You will learn to swallow every last drop," he said gently. "But I must say. You were *incredible*."

I smiled, then turned red, embarrassed by how good his praise felt. "You're only saying that so I'll do it again."

"Perhaps. Or perhaps it's the truth." His eyes scanned my face and landed on my lips. When he bent his head, I was tempted to lean in and meet him.

But that was enough to make me angle away.

A kiss was a different kind of submission. It was one thing to let myself enjoy how he handled my body, but my heart couldn't take the same beating.

Cristiano didn't move, hovering near my cheek. "Still no kiss?"

"I can't really stop you."

"As I've said, there's no joy in that for me. You were incredible just now because you wanted this as much as I did." His hot breath warmed my cheek, and he spoke with a thread of desperation. "Tell me why you won't kiss me."

"It should be obvious. Sex is sex, but a kiss is more."

"We haven't had sex."

"But we will. And you'll know exactly how to make me enjoy it. But that's my body, nothing more."

He turned my face back to his as he wet his full lips. He was a good kisser. He'd managed to draw me in for a few seconds amidst the horrors of our wedding day. He'd nearly convinced me on our wedding night that I wanted him. He cast a spell with his kiss, and I couldn't afford to stray from reality.

"You're wrong," he said, sounding almost amused. "This goes far beyond your body. You need things, and I can give them to you. I want to give them to you."

"Why?" I whispered.

He pressed his lips to the corner of my mouth. "Someday soon, maybe when you least expect it, I will repay what you did for me tonight."

"How?" I asked. "I have nothing down there to jam down your throat."

He smirked. "And *gracias a Dios* for that."

"Speak for yourself. I should like to see *you* suffer for *my* orgasm."

The corner of his mouth quirked. "I imagine I will." He touched his lips to the other corner of mine. "You took my cock like a champ. In return, I'll eat you like my life depends on it, and believe me, I value my life."

*Oh my God*. I was frustratingly aware of the throb between my legs. It had started in his office and hadn't subsided since.

"Unless you'd like to collect on my debt now?" he asked. "Just ask."

To be relieved of that ache was almost too good to pass up. Accepting his advances, or even submitting to them, was one thing. Asking for something felt wrong, though. I shook my head and forced myself to turn away before I changed my mind.

He took my elbow and pulled me back. "Kiss me once," he said. "In exchange, I won't lay so much as a finger on you for a while, not even if the kiss tempts you to more."

Disappointment at the loss of him struck me first followed quickly by horror. I didn't want to miss his touch or wander down that path. To cover up that confusing feeling, I quickly agreed. "Deal."

"I'll pretend you said that with a little less vigor." He frowned. "Would you like to think on it a moment?"

"No. How long is a while?"

"Days. Maybe even weeks, if I'm unlucky."

*Weeks*? He seemed to both keep his hands to himself and touch me non-stop. "And you won't touch me at all?"

"Not even to help you from the car."

"All right." I closed my eyes and waited, but nothing came. When I looked again, he was pulling back the sheets of his bed.

"*Ven aquí*," he said, lying down.

"We had a deal."

"Come here," he repeated.

I trudged back to my side of the bed, climbed in next to him, and curled into a ball with my back to him as I had every night.

After a moment, he tugged me close with a loose grip on my bicep. I glanced over my shoulder at him and met his eyes, dark with demands once again.

He ghosted a finger over the tattoo. "Mine," he said. "*Mi mariposita*. My rare and unusual, beautiful white monarch."

"You're wrong," I whispered. "He made the wings orange, not white."

He barely traced the outline of it. "The butterfly's orange color warns of its poison," he explained. "It's dangerous to be colorless. And you, my wife, are toxic to predators."

"This isn't just a reminder to me." I had suspected as much. "It's a warning to others."

"She is mine." He moved some of my hair behind my ear and pressed closed lips to my mouth. His hand tightened around my arm, but he stayed still, not yet pushing for more.

He angled his shoulder over me, cocooning me. His butterfly. It shouldn't have surprised me to feel him harden against the cushion of my ass. *I should like to be able to roll over and be inside you.* I tried to think of anything to keep from wanting that. To keep from falling into him as he slid his hand down my forearm, squeezed my wrist, caressed my hip and the curve of my ass.

I wanted him to keep going. To slip between my thighs and relieve me of the arousal he'd inspired, to chase my shame away without permission so I didn't have to face that I wanted it.

I had to think of anything else or I wouldn't just ask him for more —I would *beg* for it.

Out of habit, Diego came to mind. Had it felt like this to kiss him? Like I was standing at the edge of a black hole, and he was both pushing me over the edge and pulling me down into the dark? I'd always known that darkness was too easy to walk into, and now, Cristiano knew it, too. He'd drag me down, ruin and defile me, while Diego had wanted to keep me pristine.

No, the kiss with Diego hadn't been a magic spell like Cristiano's, because it wasn't just about sex. I believed Diego had loved me on some level, as much as he was capable. And that on some level, *I'd* known that what I'd had with Diego wasn't real.

Cristiano was real. Raw. His honesty could be brutal, but it left no room for pretense, and my body responded.

I moaned greedily and thrust my tongue into his mouth first, then gasped at my forwardness.

Cristiano smiled against my lips. "Goodnight. Sleep tight knowing you're safe from me for a time. And should you realize that isn't what you want, take comfort in the fact that this is far from our last kiss."

When I awoke next, it was to a dark and empty room, yet I sensed dawn had broken. I rose from the bed and opened blackout shades to find the sun rising in the distant desert.

Below, Cristiano carried his suitcase to a town car.

No wonder he'd promised not to touch me. The sneaky bastard was going somewhere.

Cristiano was a master of words and manipulation, and that wasn't news to me. But in place of the fear I'd been clinging to, I suddenly wondered if I could keep up with him. If I could learn to decipher the true meaning behind his words, thoughts, and actions—and play on his level. Something told me he wanted that, too.

And just like that, already, that small shift in mindset was working.

I knew without asking why he was leaving.

He was going in search of answers that would fill whatever void existed in him. Of the key that could unlock the something—the *everything*—he wanted.

Or he'd drive himself mad trying.

And where would that leave me?

## CHAPTER 19

# NATALIA

A dark-haired, petite mirage of a girl wrung her hands in front of a dusty black SUV. I shielded my eyes from the sun as Alejandro took a beat-up suitcase from the trunk.

As I ran down the front steps, my flip-flops slapped against the stone. "*Pilar*?"

My best friend threw her arms around my neck. "*¡Dios mío, Natalia!*"

I took her by her shoulders so hard that she winced. Loosening my grip, I looked her over. "What are you doing here?"

Her crystal green eyes widened. "I have no idea."

I whirled around. "What the hell, Alejo?"

He shrugged. "Cristiano said you might be lonely while he was away."

"So he *took* my friend?"

"No." Alejandro winked at Pilar. "*I* did."

Her cheeks flushed as she glanced away, but *I* didn't. I scowled at Alejo and grasped Pilar's elbow to pull her up to the house. "What happened?"

"I was at the market getting milk," she said. "I was making *arroz con leche* for Manu, and—"

"For *Manu*?" I asked, leading her through the foyer. "You bake for your family's *panadería* for a living. Why are you making anyone anything when you aren't working?" I waved my hand. "Never mind. What happened next?"

"He,"—she nodded behind us at Alejandro—"told me to get in the car. I recognized him from . . ." She lowered her voice as if someone might be listening. "The wedding."

"And you got in?" I balked. "That's one of the first things we learn as kids. *Never* get in the car or you're as good as dead. He didn't hurt you, did he?"

She chewed her bottom lip. "You know me. I don't have to be ordered to do anything twice."

It was true. My sweet Pilar had no backbone, and she never had. I hated that Cristiano had dragged her into this, first by burdening her with being a witness to our wedding ceremony, and now by bringing her here. But I was glad Alejandro hadn't been forceful, and truthfully, I wouldn't actually think he'd be. "He brought you straight here?"

"My bag was already in the car when I got in. He packed it for me. I don't know when or how." Her eyebrows met in the middle of her forehead. "Now all the ingredients are just sitting on my kitchen counter."

"*Puta madre*, fucking domineering asshole—" When Pilar shuddered, I forced myself to calm down. I would deal with Cristiano later. "Don't worry." I attempted to soothe her as we approached the house's main room. "Alejandro is a good guy. I mean, as good as it gets around here."

"I've been worried sick for you," she said under her breath, then stopped at the grand dining table with brass candelabras. She took in the fireplace, wooden coffee table with wild dahlias, and the regal tapestry on the wall. Turning in a circle, she surveyed the majestic room. "I didn't know what to expect. I thought it . . . I thought *you* would look . . . different."

She'd probably been expecting wreckage and devastation. I wrapped the slinky, colorful cover-up I'd found in one of my drawers over my bathing suit and pursed my lips. "Looks can be deceiving."

"*Vengan.*" In the doorway, Alejandro ordered us to follow and turned back for the staircase. "You'll be staying upstairs, Pilar."

"For how long?" I demanded.

I didn't expect an answer, and I didn't get one.

At the second floor, I left Pilar with Alejandro and promised her I'd be back in a moment. I continued up to Cristiano's bedroom and went to my nightstand. When I'd returned from *La Madrina* last weekend, I'd found a cell phone in the top drawer with only one number programmed in it. *His*.

I'd considered it some kind of annoying joke after our last encounter with a phone, but now, I prayed it actually made outgoing calls.

And that appeal was answered. He picked up on the first ring. "How are you, my beautiful bride?"

"You asshole."

"*Ah*. I assume Alejandro delivered Pilar." His shit-eating grin was unmistakable, even over the phone. "I thought you'd be pleased—you said you were bored."

"I didn't mean you should kidnap my friend."

"Relax. It's only for the weekend . . . unless she wants to stay longer, that is."

"She has a life. A fiancé and a family business. You can't just rip her out of it for no reason."

"Not for no reason," he said. "For you. I thought seeing your friend would make you happy."

Pilar was like a light in the dark, but I wasn't going to force this life on her for my own amusement. "She's scared half to death."

"So show her she has no reason to be," he said over some static on the line. "You have free rein of the house. All I ask is that you continue your lessons with Alejo—and bring Pilar with you. I get the feeling she couldn't tiptoe over an ant without shedding a few tears."

Pilar might be prone to trembling, but that didn't mean she wasn't tough in her own way. My nostrils flared. "You—"

"I know, I know. I'm horrible." He cleared his throat. "I'm also heading into a bad area, so I have to go."

"Bad?" I asked, straightening as alarm jolted me. I'd be surprised if whatever mission he'd left on was legal or safe—after all, if this thing he wanted so badly was easy to get, he'd have made it his a long time ago. But for someone in this life to consider an area *bad*, it had to be dangerous. "What do you mean bad?"

"Er—bad for reception," he clarified.

Surprisingly, relief passed over me—and with that, my irritation was free to return. Especially with myself over finding out that my gut reaction to Cristiano in danger wasn't joy, but . . . *concern*.

"Is there anything else, Natalia?"

"Yes," I said. "About a million things."

I thought I heard his breathy chuckle through the phone. "Will you call me tonight?"

"No."

"I like seeing your name light up my phone, *mi amor*. Call me when you're in bed, and tell me how it went with Pilar."

He hung up before I could protest.

I hurried down a floor and followed voices to one of the bedrooms. Pilar stood at the foot of a bed, gaping at the ornate, four-poster frame, large window overlooking the water, and beamed ceiling. "Do you have a room like this?" she asked me as I entered. "There's a fireplace."

"Yes, I do," I muttered. "Cristiano's room."

"Oh . . ." Concern creased her forehead as understanding dawned. "Oh, no. I mean, of course. It makes sense, but—I'm sorry."

Alejandro, standing in the doorway of the walk-in closet, stared at us with one eyebrow arched as if we were speaking another language. "Jaz will unpack your things," he said.

"I spoke to Cristiano," I said, pursing my lips at Alejo before turning to my friend. "You're not stuck here forever—just for the weekend. Did you have plans?"

Pilar sat on the edge of the bed. "Well, Manu's *arroz con leche*—"

"Never mind the *arroz con leche*," I said, exasperated.

"He really likes it," she said slowly. "He expects it. When I don't bring it over, he won't be happy."

Alejandro typed something into his cell phone. "Manu's the fiancé?" he asked without looking up.

"If Manu has a problem, he can take it up with Cristiano," I said, ignoring Alejandro. What did *he* care?

"I don't know," Pilar hedged, sticking a fingernail between her front teeth. "Are you sure?"

"Don't worry. Any man in his right mind wouldn't challenge the Calavera cartel," I reassured Pilar and sighed. There was nothing really left to say. "Did you bring a bathing suit?"

"*No sé*." She glanced at Alejandro. "Did I?"

"There's one in the closet," he said. "Cristiano gave me a list of things to pick up."

"And I was at the top of it," Pilar said.

Alejandro laughed heartily, while I just stared at her. She wasn't generally one to make jokes, especially in a tense situation. "Go change," I told her, tearing my glare from Alejandro. "We'll get in the pool. It's supposed to be especially warm today."

Alejandro tucked his phone back into his pocket, dipped his head, and left the room, closing the door after himself.

In the walk-in closet, Pilar's little suitcase sat in one corner, but I wasn't sure why Alejandro had bothered with it. We found ourselves staring at enough outfits to last her a month. "*Jesus*," I muttered to myself. "What, does Cristiano own a woman's clothing brand?"

"Is this stuff yours?" she asked me.

"I think it's for you." I shook my head. "Cristiano's doing."

She fingered a light, floral dress. "This is from that boutique you and I go to in the plaza at home. Do you think Alejandro went shopping for me?"

Alejandro was no Cristiano, but he was certainly a big, burly, scarred—and armed—guy who had no business shopping for women's apparel.

Pilar and I exchanged a look and despite myself, I laughed. Taking my cue, she also giggled.

At the dresser, I opened drawers until I found a couple bathing suits. "Imagine what the salesgirl thought when a man like him bought all this," I said, handing her the only one-piece. "There's even a sun hat."

"I think maybe she didn't notice," Pilar said, pretending to inspect the suit's fabric as she blushed.

"What does *that* mean?"

"Oh, come on. You didn't notice?" she asked. "His face is a *bit* distracting."

I lowered my voice. "He is handsome," I agreed. "And he may be nice. But he's also dangerous, Pilar. All these guys are."

Her emerald eyes turned into big, sparkly gems. "I didn't mean—I was just saying . . . I don't mean that anything makes up for what Cristiano did. I'm sorry I laughed earlier."

"Don't be sorry," I said gently and pulled her into a hug. "Laughter is good. That's why Cristiano brought you here—he knew it would make me happy."

She drew back, her eyebrows cinched. "Really?"

"Yes." I needed to try to stay positive about him and my situation. It would be a lot easier on Pilar if she felt safe and realized I wasn't in any immediate danger.

I went to leave the closet—Pilar was as modest as it came and wouldn't even change in front of me—but she stopped me. "Are . . . are there cameras in the house?"

"Not in the bedrooms."

She mouthed, "Microphones?"

"No, at least I don't think so," I said, frowning. "The house isn't surveilled to spy on us. It's to protect us." I rolled my eyes inwardly. That was something Cristiano would say.

"But will you show me where the cameras are?" she asked, twisting the bathing suit through her hands. "I mean, if you even know. If you want. It makes me anxious to think I'm being watched."

I went back and kissed her cheek. "Of course," I said soothingly. "Don't be anxious. I'm the one he wants, not you."

"I still can't believe you're here," she said.

"Neither can I most days," I said as I left to give her privacy.

I had to admit, though—I was getting used to things. Cristiano had been gone almost a week, and I'd even been bored enough to miss him in a way—or at least his stimulating conversation. With him gone, what I looked forward to the most were the self-defense lessons I did once or twice a day. Solomon wasn't as afraid to get physical with me as Alejandro was, and he was more patient than my brutish husband. I could already feel my body getting stronger in small ways.

When Pilar came out of the closet, she took modesty to a whole new level. To go down to the pool, she'd pulled on drawstring pants and a navy cotton shirt with sleeves long enough to hide her hands. Since I could make out the shape of a swimsuit underneath, I didn't question her.

Downstairs, I walked her to the patio and down to the sparkling infinity pool set amongst the jungle and overlooking the ocean. I'd been spending my days there, too, since Cristiano had left. Even during intermittent showers, I'd sit under an umbrella with a book.

I almost felt a sense of pride as Pilar lifted her sleeved hands to her mouth and gasped, "Wow."

Navy-and-white striped lounge chairs and matching cabanas surrounded the pool with a swim-up bar. It sat at the edge of the world, facing the ocean. The thing that got me was that I couldn't imagine a *single* person in this house using the pool, least of all its master.

As I stripped down and tossed my cover-up on a chair, one of the staff who helped Jaz on occasion approached us with large, sweating glasses of water. "Would you and your friend like lunch, *señora*?" she asked.

"Are you hungry?" I asked Pilar.

Her face seemed set in a permanent expression of shock. "I guess?"

"Tell the chef to surprise us," I said.

"There's a *chef*?" Pilar whispered as the woman walked away.

"More than one." I set my water on a side table. "We have a lot to talk about."

Pilar removed her pants and perched on the edge of a chair cushion.

"Don't sit," I said. "Let's cool off in the pool."

"I can't swim," she said.

I furrowed my brows. "You've been in the pool at my house."

"I stayed in the shallow part, and there were always people around. I knew I'd be safe."

"There are people around now," I said, taking her hand and pulling her up. "Come on. We'll just go in to our waists. I shouldn't get my tattoo wet anyway."

"You have a *tattoo*?"

"Like I said, I've got a lot to share. Let's—"

She stopped, leaning back with all of her body weight. "Wait. Natalia—"

"What?" She wasn't afraid of water. We'd swum at my house and had been to the coast lots of times. I shielded my eyes and located Alejandro, standing—and most likely sweating—between the pool and patio. "As you can see, Alejandro is our shadow today." I called to him. "Can you swim, Alejo?"

"*Sí.*"

"There. See?" I told Pilar. "I promise, he won't let you drown."

"I've gained weight, and I'm self-conscious."

"You haven't gained a kilo since I've known you." I crossed my arms. "What's the matter?"

She hesitated, her posture wilting. "Nothing," she said and turned her back to peel off her shirt, revealing bruises up and down her arms and sides.

I gasped. "*Pila*. What . . .?"

"Please," she said softly, taking my hands. "Don't make a thing of this. They don't really hurt."

Anger burned through me, turning my vision spotted. No wonder she'd been trembling when she'd arrived. I whirled around, charging toward Alejandro. "You fucking *asshole*," I said.

Alejandro drew back, his eyebrows cinched. *"¿Qué?"*

"When I tell Cristiano about this, he'll skin you alive. And if he doesn't, my father will."

"What are you talking—"

"Natalia," Pilar called, her footsteps shuffling after me.

Alejandro's gaze shifted over my shoulder, and his brows dropped. "Are those bruises? *Hijo de la chingada,*" he cursed. "I didn't do that, Natalia. I would never—I told you about my history."

As soon as he said it, I stopped short, knowing it was true. I started to apologize when the actual truth hit me. My scalp prickled, and I turned back to Pilar. "Manu did this?"

"The fiancé," Alejandro said through gritted teeth, staring daggers at the marks on her arm.

"Has this happened before?" I asked Pilar.

Absentmindedly, she scratched her shoulder. "It looks worse than it is."

She was uncomfortable with Alejandro here. He raised his eyes to meet mine, and a current of anger passed between us. I was so furious, I didn't even know what to say. Pilar had been promised to Manu for months by her parents, and they wouldn't hear her protests.

*Well, fuck him.* Manu had no idea who he was dealing with.

Alejandro seemed to follow my line of thinking. Slowly, he dipped his head in a nod. As he turned and walked away, he took his cell phone from his pocket, and I didn't need to ask who he was calling.

"I'm sorry," Pilar said. "I didn't want to say in front of Alejandro in case it got me in trouble . . ."

"Say what?" I linked my elbow in hers and guided her toward the shallow end of the pool. "Why would you get in trouble?"

"After your . . . ah, wedding . . . I was so scared for you, I ran straight to your house."

"Wow. You *must've* been scared," I said. "You're terrified of my father."

"I didn't go to him." We waded into the pool, and she sat on one of the steps, submerged to her chest. "I found Barto and told him about the wedding. He's always been nice to me."

*Ah.* I didn't need to imagine how Barto would react hearing the story from a terrified Pilar. No wonder he'd shown up here the next morning with such a chip on his shoulder. "What does that have to do with Manu?"

"Nothing yet. Barto helped calm me down. He wanted all the

details, and I was having trouble getting them out, so he made me a drink."

"A *drink*?" I asked, as amused as I was shocked. "I've never seen him take a sip of alcohol."

"He didn't have one," she said quickly. "We started talking about life and other things until I was finally composed enough to relay what had happened in the church."

"Hmm." I leaned my back against the lip of the pool. "Barto's always been good in a crisis."

"He spoke really softly and tried to soothe me, but I could see him fuming on the inside. He really cares about you, Natalia."

"I know," I said. "I think he sees me as a kid sister."

"Anyway, afterward, Barto drove me home. My family and Manu's were at the house and had been looking for me since I hadn't come back from Mass."

I grimaced. "And you'd been drinking."

"Manu smelled the alcohol. Once Barto left, Manu exploded. He's still angry about it, which is why I was making him *arroz con leche*. He wants me to do more considerate things like that."

"Oh, God, what a fucking manipulative asshole," I said, rolling my eyes.

But my words hung in the air, taunting me. How come I could see Manu's manipulation so easily, but I'd missed every warning sign with Diego? And my own father? And now, I was in the grips of another controlling man. One I'd gotten on my knees for willingly—and had controlled right back, if only for a few minutes.

And yet, I couldn't imagine Cristiano guilting me into baking him treats like Manu.

In fact, I had a feeling if Cristiano thought, in any way, he was remotely responsible for Pilar's bruises since the wedding had started this—he'd harness that guilt into making it up to her.

"I'm so sorry," I said. "What about your parents?"

She shook her head. "They turn a blind eye, as you'd suspect. They just want this marriage to go through."

My heart sank, and suddenly, swimming in the sunshine in my expensive bikini while being waited on seemed like *the life*. Overindulgent, even. "Was this the first time he hurt you?"

"No."

Here, I'd been anticipating the worst from Cristiano while Pilar had been enduring it from Manu. "Why didn't you tell me?"

"What could you have done?"

"My father is one of the most powerful men in the country," I said. "We would've figured something out."

She tucked some hair behind her ear. "Barto said the same thing."

I watched her smile to herself as I stretched my arms along the pool's edge. "He knows about this?"

"Not the bruises, but he came by the house to check on me a few days later. I asked him not to do that again because Manu could get jealous. And we started talking about the whole arranged marriage thing . . ."

Barto wasn't much of a talker. At all. Thinking of him sitting and conversing with my friend not once but twice made me smile. "I take it he wasn't a fan?"

"No. He said if I ever needed help getting out of it, to come to him. He'd talk to your father."

Considering how Cristiano was going after Belmonte-Ruiz, I could only imagine how he'd receive this news . . . and what he and I would do to rectify it. "Well, now *we're* going to get you out," I promised.

She swallowed. "It's not possible, Natalia. Manu has been pursuing me for a year, and he comes from a good background. My parents want him as a son-in-law."

"But that doesn't mean it has to be."

"I can't exactly go home and tell them I won't do it. They'll throw me out, and then where will I go?"

Cristiano's invitation rang through my mind. It had frustrated me then, but now, it was a godsend. "You can stay here as long as you want," I said.

"Here?" she asked. "But Cristiano—"

"Would love to have you. Believe me, he'll be more supportive than you know. We have so much room."

*We?* I didn't blame her for looking confused. I was as well. This life had been forced upon me. I'd come into it kicking and screaming. And now, not even two weeks later, I was inviting her into it? Referring to Cristiano and myself as *we*?

There may have been a world full of people with more freedom than me, but that didn't mean they were safer. Whether or not I wanted to be here, it hit me just how much worse off I could be.

"It's not . . ."

She waited for me to continue. "What?"

"It's not as bad as I thought it would be," I admitted and teased, "but if you tell Cristiano that, I will toss you in the deep end of the pool."

"I'm too scared to tell him *anything*." She fidgeted with the strap of her suit. "Are you just saying that so I won't worry about you?"

Ever since my arrival, I'd made the worst of my situation. Had I even *tried* to consider it as anything else? There had been more surprises than anything. I'd never imagined such a beautiful cage, eating the finest foods and sleeping in Egyptian cotton next to a man who made my body feel things I hadn't thought possible—and we hadn't even slept together. *That* was a surprise—the heady feeling of getting to my knees to comfort a man as stoic as Cristiano and actually enjoying it.

"You don't have to tell me what he's done to you," she continued, "but I'm here if you want to talk about it. Nessa went through something like this."

"Nessa?" I asked. "Your half-sister? I didn't know that."

"A guy she trusted, he . . . anyway, I've talked to her about it." Her posture lifted. "I mean, obviously it's not even *close* to what Cristiano has put you through—"

"He hasn't," I said, looking away. My gaze caught on the rings weighing down my hand. They were collars. Glittering splendors in the sunlight . . . and possibly even weapons.

"Hasn't what?" she prompted.

I sighed, turning back to her. "We haven't had sex."

Her jaw dropped nearly into the water. "How is that possible? Is he gay?"

I couldn't help laughing. I'd have given anything to see Cristiano's face if he'd heard that. "He's definitely not."

"How do you know?"

"He's . . . vocal about the things he wants to do. And we've, you know. . . done a little." God, I wasn't *that* shy about these things—I'd talked a lot with my friends in California. But it was Cristiano who made my cheeks heat. The wrongness of fooling around with him. Curiosity over what he'd do when he saw me next. The unsettling urge to call him tonight from our bed.

With my thumb, I spun the diamond on my ring finger. "The way he talks, it's just . . . it's filthy, and scary, and . . ."

Pilar waited. "Do you like it, Natalia?" she asked quietly. "Do you like *him*?"

"No," I said, stopping the horrifying thought in its tracks. "God, no."

"What if you did?" she asked. "It would make life here a lot easier."

"That's not a good reason to fall in love."

"I don't mean love. No, not at all. I mean, what if you find a way to . . ." She pulled her hair off her neck and fanned herself. "Never mind. It's dumb. I'm not the one in this situation."

"No, what?" I prompted. I hated when Pilar doubted herself, but if I was honest, I was more curious about what she had to say. I fought every day—against Cristiano, my situation, and sometimes even myself. To hear someone tell me I didn't have to could alleviate some of my guilt. "What if I find a way to accept this?" I asked. "Is that what you mean?"

"Or at least not hate it. Only until you get out of here. Maybe you can compartmentalize his past and the horrible things he does to others. For self-preservation."

"But he doesn't force me, Pilar. And I don't hate what he does to me. So I don't know what to think. To see him as anything other than the man who stormed my wedding and ruined my life . . ."

It would change everything. But I didn't *want* things to change. Cristiano had forced my hand in marriage—how could I ever forgive that? Especially while the reason behind my mother's death remained uncertain. To form any kind of attachment to Cristiano would mean I'd only have to sever it later.

"You said you haven't had sex, but you also say he's done things to you." Pilar crossed her arms over her stomach. "From what I know, Cristiano is really convincing, Natalia. You have to be careful. Go somewhere in your mind if you need to until you get out. But you can't ever *want* to stay."

"Of course not," I said. With a sinking feeling in my stomach, I knew that wasn't what I'd hoped she'd say. I waded away from the wall. "It's just that he's complex. It makes it hard to know how I feel about him. One minute, I think he's going to lock me away and strip me of everything, and the next, I learn that he's not *totally* the villain I thought he was."

"Has he done that?" she asked, her tone completely serious. "Locked you up?"

"No. Not unless you count staying in the house. I'm not allowed to leave the property."

"*You*? But you never let that stop you before. How many times has Barto wanted to ring your neck for slipping by him?"

I laughed. "When I was a kid? More than I can count."

She looked kindly at me. "You're laughing. I'm relieved, Natalia. I was so scared of what I'd find when I got here. I know it doesn't mean you're happy, but I'm just glad you're okay. For now."

*For now.*

She squinted ahead, seeming to process everything. "But he's always been the villain around our parts. Do you still think he killed your mom?"

"I can never let myself believe otherwise. What if months from now, I find out he *was* somehow involved? As long as I have doubt, I can't fall for him."

Pilar stayed seated but glided her arms through the water. "Wow. I didn't know love was on the table."

*Fuck.* I hadn't even realized what I'd said. "The heat must be getting to me. Falling for him was the wrong way of putting it, obviously. More like tolerating him."

"And Diego?" she asked. "What about him?"

I blanched. Once a prayer to me, his name sounded foreign now—I thought about Diego less and less each day. I blew out a breath. "Diego . . . is not who we thought he was. He can go to hell, actually."

"*What?*" Her eyebrows shot up. "You've been head over heels for him since I can remember."

"Things change fast around here," I said, pacing through the water. "This is going to sound crazy, but try to stay with me. First of all, Diego was the one who orchestrated all of this. The wedding to Cristiano was his idea, and he *tricked* me into showing up."

She chewed on her thumbnail. "How do you know that?"

"Cristiano told me."

"And you believe him? I don't understand," she said. "Two weeks ago, you *hated* Cristiano, and you were smiling ear to ear thinking you were going to marry Diego."

It would be nearly impossible to explain what the last couple weeks had been like. "It still hurts," I admitted. "Diego lied to me. I saw a future with him. I gave him my *virginity,* Pilar. I was smiling because I was on cloud nine."

"I remember."

"And then I find out he made the deal with Cristiano before we even had sex. Diego knew he and I weren't going to be together."

She looked at her hands under the water. "That doesn't sound like Diego."

"He *admitted* it."

"But what if he had to?" She raised her eyes again, concern clear in them. "Maybe Cristiano has something over him. Obviously you don't trust Cristiano, so why would you believe anything he says?"

I turned to pace the other way, glancing toward the house, maybe because of what I was about to admit. "I trust him more than Diego."

She gasped. "Your shoulder! That's the tattoo?"

I turned my head as she stood to get a better look. My butterfly was brighter out in the sun. I liked her more and more each day, but that stayed between me, myself, and I. Not only did I not want Cristiano to know, but I was also a little embarrassed to admit I didn't hate it when the circumstances around it had been so ugly.

Pilar frowned. "Does it say *Calavera Cartel*? With a skull?"

"Yes," I said, adding wryly, "A gift from Cristiano . . ."

She balled her fist at her mouth. "A *gift*? You didn't want that, did you?"

How did I explain that I could've stopped it? That I could've begged his forgiveness and let him spank me instead, but I'd chosen not to? How did I say, without sounding as if I were justifying it, that I *knew*, deep down—if I'd truly not wanted it, Cristiano wouldn't have gone through with it?

It all sounded like defending an abuser to Pilar, someone who was actually living the life I'd feared I would. "I could've said no," I promised.

"Then why didn't you? That doesn't make any sense." Pilar's face contorted with concern. "Talia. If he'd force a tattoo on you, he'd do much worse. Believe me. Can't Diego get you out of here somehow?"

"Diego's all talk, Pilar. That's what I've been trying to tell you. I'm done with him." I went to the pool's infinity edge. On the horizon, the ocean seemed to touch the clouds. "He used to promise he'd come to California with me, but he was never going to."

Ever.

It was hard to believe he could've been so convincing. That I'd hardly questioned him.

Looking back with fresh perspective, though, there'd only been excuses, delays, and Diego entangling himself more and more in cartel life while promising me he was getting out.

Cristiano, on the other hand, had wanted what I had to offer so much that he hadn't let anything stand in his way. It was a twisted way of looking at things, but there was some comfort in it, I supposed.

Diego and Cristiano had faced off. Cristiano had fought for me, and Diego . . . hadn't. So, if fate and fortune demanded I be with one of the brothers, maybe I'd somehow ended up with the right one.

I looked up at white-cotton clouds, wondering what the future had in store for me. "Cristiano says he never would've done what Diego did . . . and he never will. That he'd never let me go, let alone give me to another. Apparently, *my* prison sentence is *his* wedding vow."

"*Dios mío*," Pilar said.

At the small tremor in her voice, I swam back, hoping I hadn't frightened her. "Cristiano takes all this very seriously."

"I can see that." When I caught her looking at my ring, she lifted a slender shoulder. "It's blinding me, Natalia. But it's just jewelry. Don't let diamonds blind *you* from the truth. That's probably what he wants."

I spread my fingers, frowning at the rings. "I could care less about Cristiano's wealth." If anything distracted me about them, it was that he'd put actual thought into the design. It was such a kingpin move, matching my rings to a gun, but in its own way, it was sweet.

*Sweet?*

Cristiano?

Never before had the word been used to describe him, I was sure. He was rough around the edges, weather-beaten, a man who'd seen and done too much to have any sweetness remain intact. And yet with me, and only me, there was something there. He yielded. He showed vulnerability. He considered me where others hadn't . . .

I pushed the thoughts away.

That was dangerous thinking about a man who I could never care for.

"I'm getting out of this marriage," I said resolutely, as much to Pilar as to myself. "Without Diego, and without my father."

"What about Barto?" she asked.

"Nope. He's under Papá's control. I've got to do it on my own."

She leaned in, speaking softly. "How can you? You might be crafty enough to get by the guards, but it's not as simple as that."

"No, it isn't. Running away isn't an option." I chewed the inside of my cheek. "Cristiano can hurt me the most without touching me."

"So how do you escape a man who has the means to find you wherever you go? You need help."

"Nobody can help me," I said. "I'm on my own, and I have a plan. The more I know about Cristiano and the Calavera cartel, the more power I have."

Admittedly, the plan didn't sound like much of one. Getting to know Cristiano had proved to be a wild ride. It seemed like every time he opened his mouth, something I didn't expect came out. And his actions were even more unpredictable.

But it all formed a bigger picture, and I had to believe once that revealed itself, I would understand what was best for me. That was my goal now—taking charge of *my* life as much as I could.

"I've learned so much already," I murmured. Not just about him, but about this world. And maybe even myself.

"Like what?" she asked.

"The Calaveras are nothing like they seem." I scratched my chin on my shoulder and glanced at my *mariposa*. "To be honest, this isn't the worst tattoo I could have. Calavera represents the opposite of what you'd think. The wings are almost symbolic."

Pilar's forehead creased—she looked like she was going to blow a gasket—and I realized how backward all of this sounded. I opened my mouth to clarify, but that would mean I was defending Cristiano. Explaining his actions. And the way Pilar looked at me, I felt like a sucker.

"Cristiano, unlike anyone I've known around here, evens the score," I said carefully. "He does good things as well as bad."

"The arms trafficking?" she asked.

"No, that's legit, but the profits he earns from that—and they're considerable—he puts toward other . . . endeavors."

"The sex trade," she almost whispered. "I've been hearing that for years about this place."

I nodded. "Did you see anything when you drove in?"

She shook her head. "I had to wear a blindfold, but Alejandro was nice about it. He sort of gave me the option without really giving me an option, you know?"

I smiled a little. "I do, all too well." I paused, trying to think of how to word what I wanted to say. Since Cristiano had left the morning after we'd slept at *La Madrina*, I'd been asking myself what I believed and what I didn't. His story added up. But my feelings about it didn't. "I can't really say too much. But whatever you've heard about the Calavera cartel, there's another side of the story. A good side."

"Good?" She looked over her shoulder. "Not a single thing I've heard could be described that way."

I shielded my eyes against the sun reflecting on the water. "Just trust me."

"I do, Tali, but . . . that's the complete opposite of what everyone says." She blinked a few times. "I mean, how could some of it not be true?"

"I'm not saying they're angels, believe me." I rubbed the inside corners of my eyes, knowing how it sounded—like I was excusing Cristiano's behavior. "Cristiano is still . . . he's . . ." I couldn't find the words, because I didn't know myself. I knew what I *wanted* to believe about him, but what I actually believed? Not the best but not the worst, either.

"He's scarier than any monster," I said quietly.

I'd let that soothe me as a child, but it wasn't until my mother's death that the words had taken on a negative meaning. On some level, as a young girl, I must've known something good in Cristiano.

And now . . . I wanted Cristiano on my side. He was the law in a lawless land, a dark hero for those who needed one. A protector.

Things I might've called him to his face, if only he'd been that for *me*.

And now, thanks to my guidance, he was out there searching for something that would only make him more powerful. That was all a man like Cristiano wanted. No matter what he'd divulged about his mission, it was the only thing he would pursue to the point of madness.

*Power.*

That was the *everything* he'd claimed was within grasp.

The everything he'd confront danger to get.

And that could either hurt or benefit me, depending on which Cristiano I was dealing with.

When he returned, it would most likely be as an even more powerful husband . . . or a more formidable captor.

# CHAPTER 20

# NATALIA

Cristiano's bed was irritatingly comfortable and welcoming—nothing like what I'd expected riding to the Badlands with him.

I stared up at the ceiling, thankful Pilar was under the same roof as me and away from Manu. We'd actually managed to have a good time lunching by the pool, followed by popcorn and a movie, but I could tell she was anxious over Cristiano's return.

I was the one who should be anxious—yet my mind was occupied by my earlier conversation with Pilar. She was skeptical of his business, but I'd tried to defend it. Could I believe and respect him while despising what he'd done to me?

I reached over to the nightstand and took the cell phone he'd left me from the drawer. He'd told me to call, and there *were* things I wanted to discuss with him.

"I have to talk to you about Pilar," I said when the line clicked.

"Good evening to you, too," came Cristiano's familiar, rumbling voice over a din of background chatter that sounded like a restaurant.

I flopped back onto my pillow and twirled my hair around my finger. "Good evening."

"I've already spoken with Alejandro," he said tersely.

"And?" I asked.

His voice went distant as he excused himself from wherever her was; he didn't speak again until the background quieted. "Tell me what you'd like me to do with him, Natalia. The fiancé."

Chills covered my skin. I'd never been asked to determine anyone's fate before, and if I knew Cristiano, he wasn't asking if I thought we should write Manu a threatening e-mail. "I don't know," I said.

"Yes, you do. Don't get shy on me. Don't you want justice for your friend?"

"Yes . . ." I counted the number of antlers in the chandelier to avoid asking myself what kind of justice seemed fair for a pig like Manu. Someone who'd beat on a woman half his size should feel that same wrath turned on him. And with my husband hanging on the line, I had the means to make that happen. "She's afraid of you. You beat up her cousin," I said. "She saw the whole thing."

"I remember. He was a thief. I should've killed him."

"For stealing?" I asked.

"No. For sexually abusing Pilar's half-sister."

My mouth fell open as the chandelier's faint, warm glow blurred. Pilar had mentioned supporting Nessa through that. "*That's* why you did it?"

"Costa didn't give me permission to kill him, even though I disagreed and told him so," Cristiano said. "Instead, I left him lacking in the one place that matters."

I shuddered. "You mean you . . ."

"No, but I'd be surprised if the thing between his legs could even twitch on its own."

"Oh my God."

"So about the ex-fiancé," he said almost cheerfully, ignoring the fact that he'd probably just scarred me with that mental image.

"Ex?" I asked, wrinkling my nose. "She won't leave him."

"Then he'll have to leave her."

I fell silent. I had some idea of what that meant, but I was afraid to ask for clarification. I wasn't sure it mattered what Cristiano intended to do to Manu, only that it would be bad enough to keep him away.

"It seems we don't even have to be in the same room for me to scare you," Cristiano said.

Manu deserved whatever was coming to him. All I had to do was order the punishment, and my husband would enforce it. Cristiano could deliver justice when everyone else Pilar cared about had failed her—but to feel pride over that posed a question I wasn't sure how to answer.

*Did* I belong in this world as Cristiano kept suggesting? Had I ever really left? Just because I'd been deaf, dumb, and blind to my father's business while in California didn't mean I could erase the years I'd been raised in the middle of it. It didn't mean I wasn't my father—or my mother's—daughter. Papá served justice, as Mamá had.

"I'm not afraid. But why would you do all that for Pilar?"

"She needs someone stronger than him in her corner. Now she has an army of us. But that's not what you're asking." With shuffling on the line, it got even quieter. "You're wondering why I should help her when you feel I've done the opposite for you."

My stomach rose with a deep inhale. Who was in my corner? Who was stronger than Cristiano? Perhaps *I* could be. I was learning the ropes from the master himself, after all. "You can see why I'd think that."

He didn't respond right away, and when he did, I had to listen hard to catch his words. "I've asked myself the same." He cleared his throat. "All I can tell you is that I'd help Pilar regardless of your association with her, but the fact that she's your friend makes it all the more personal. I will handle this, Natalia. And I will take her under my protection if that's what she wants."

I shook my head, gratitude for his help and contempt for my situation warring inside me. "I don't know what to say."

"Say nothing. In any case, Alejo will be happy to handle this while I'm away. He seems overly concerned for a girl he hardly knows. Perhaps he's got a thing for her."

"It might be mutual," I said, allowing a small smile. "*Although* . . . she did speak about him the same way she did Barto."

"Barto?" Cristiano sounded annoyed. "What's he got to do with anything?"

"He helped her, too, after the wedding." I reached up and played with one of the bed's gauzy, white curtains. "I can't really blame her. They're both handsome men, Barto and Alejandro."

Cristiano growled. "You'd call them handsome, but your own husband, you treat like Quasimodo."

I laughed. Cristiano was the last man on Earth I'd think of as insecure, and perhaps the last man who had reason to be. He was beautiful in a way normal men could never touch. His own brother was strikingly handsome with clear green eyes, high cheekbones, and hair that begged to be touched. But there was still no comparison. Paired with a face and body right from Mount Olympus, Cristiano's darkness devastated.

*And I'd die before I admitted that to him,* I thought willfully.

"Speaking of Alejandro, you need to let him spar with me," I said.

"No."

"Why not?" I asked.

"He could hurt you."

"So let me get hurt, Cristiano. You let me fight with Solomon. Is it because Alejandro's good-looking?"

"You're not helping your case."

I sighed. "If I don't practice what I'm learning, I'll be useless in a real fight."

"You're my wife, and I don't want him putting his hands on you." His anger fizzled with his words. Cristiano didn't truly believe Alejo would try anything. "Fine," he conceded. "I'll talk to him before tomorrow's lesson—but when I get back, you'd better be advanced enough to take me on."

"Thank you," I said, biting my lip as I tried not to entertain all the ways I could take him on. Silence settled over the line. "You should get back to your thing."

"What thing?" he asked. "I'm talking to my wife. That's my thing."

I stretched my legs under the covers, pointing my toes. "Have you found what you're looking for?"

"Eager for me to come home, eh? Or perhaps the opposite, in which case you'll be glad to learn I've had a setback."

"How?" I asked.

"The trail has turned cold. I wasted two days."

"Are you still in the country?"

"Yes."

"Have you asked my father for help?" I asked. "You have a stronger worldwide network, but within México, Papá is well-connected."

"This is a matter I have to handle on my own," he said. "I don't want to tell Costa until I have every confidence that it's true."

"That what's true?" I asked, sitting up straighter. "Does it involve him?"

"Yes."

With a flurry of jitters, I spread my hand over my stomach. "How?"

"I would tell you, Natalia—I promised to answer your questions. But like with your father, I don't want to until I know more. Because it involves you, too."

I curled my hand into the sheets, intrigue rising in me and clashing with wariness. In this new world of mine, anything could happen. Nothing was off-limits. I'd been lucky in my situation so far, but that could change. "I don't know how many more surprises I can handle, Cristiano."

"You can handle a lot. I wouldn't have married you if I didn't think so. You prove it to yourself more every day."

I wasn't sure where his confidence in me came from, but he had a point. Almost two weeks at Cristiano's, and I was physically, emotionally, and mentally stronger than I'd been when I'd arrived.

"What if you don't find what you're after?"

"Then I suppose it will be some time before I return. I'll be tempted to come home for the same reason I have to press on, but I won't return empty-handed unless I have to."

A reason that involved me. Something that tempted him to come home—and also drove him. I tapped my chin, trying to piece it together but coming up short. "You are the most cryptic man I've ever met."

"I choose to find the compliment in that. I'm grateful to have graduated from asshole, monster, and devil to 'cryptic.'"

I bit my cheek to hide my smile. "Wishful thinking. But if you do this for Pilar, then I promise to cross one of those off the list."

"Then I will do this for Pilar. And I will do it for you."

He still hadn't said *why* in any way I could fully comprehend. Why he'd handle everyone from Manu to the Belmonte-Ruiz cartel, and all the dangers in between, if it meant helping women. There was only one explanation for that.

It had to be personal.

And personal was exactly what I needed if I had any chance at even beginning to understand him. And to understand if escaping him was still the best thing for me.

"Have there been women you couldn't help?" I asked.

He went silent for so long, I wondered if he was still on the line. Maybe I shouldn't have pressed.

With a firm, sudden knock, I vaulted upright in the bed. "Someone's at the bedroom door."

"It'll be Jaz with my dry cleaning," he said.

"*Dry cleaning?*" I wondered aloud, picturing Cristiano in one of his pressed suits. Despite the nature of his business, he was almost always clean-shaven or neatly trimmed, sporting fine Italian loafers and Swiss watches, and his black, inky hair was never too short or too long. "What's the point?"

"Not every interaction I have ends with bloodshed," he said. "Are you decent?"

I glanced down at the silky red camisole and shorts that had one day appeared in my dresser drawer. "My mother instilled in me the importance of dressing as well for bed as I would for church," I told him. "Even when I'm alone."

"Mmm." I heard his contentment over the line. "Send Jaz away and tell me every last thing you're not wearing."

"*Cristiano.*"

"I promised I wouldn't touch you for a while—I never promised you wouldn't touch yourself."

While he *listened*? God, how obscene. And tempting. It was turning out that I loved the utter filth that spilled out of him when he got excited. With that thought, I shifted the phone from my mouth and called, "Come in, Jaz."

"Use my imagination, I guess," Cristiano grumbled to himself.

The door flew open and Jazmín breezed in with armfuls of suits and shirts sheathed in plastic. "Excuse me. I'll be quick."

"No rush," I said as she passed into the closet without even a glance in my direction. I moved back against the headboard and lowered my voice. "She hates me."

"Give her time."

Hangers scraped in the closet as Cristiano's line remained quiet. I checked the clock. It was almost nine. I wanted to ask where he was, and not just because it could be a clue as to why he was gone. I was curious about what he did outside these walls. About his life. About whether he was with anyone. Where he was, what he was doing.

About him.

Every layer I'd unpeeled had revealed something I hadn't expected. And with his promise to help Pilar, I felt myself opening to the idea that he could possibly be not just a hero to others, but to me—even if he wasn't one *for* me.

Did that mean I cared? Whether I wanted to admit it or not, my trepidation and hatred of him had been waning. Would other feelings rise in their absence? They had to. The only thing more improbable than falling in love with Cristiano would be indifference toward him.

"I'm sure you're needed at your party or whatever," I said, hoping he'd offer up something without me asking.

"Yes," he agreed, but made no move to get off the line. After a brief silence, he said, "Don't worry about Jaz. She hasn't known much kindness."

I was lucky that most of my life, I'd had an abundance of that, despite the betrayals and death I'd seen. There was still a wall between Jaz and me—more like every brick was still in place. But that didn't mean I hoped we wouldn't break it down. I could afford to show compassion.

I swung my legs over the side of the bed and prepared to say goodnight. Plastic wrap crinkled in the closet, then it went quiet. Nine o'clock wasn't late at all. Maybe Jaz and I could talk—even over a drink. It seemed as if Cristiano would welcome that more than he would mind.

Anticipating Cristiano would end the call, I stuck my head in the closet to address Jaz and nearly knocked my forehead into hers. She jumped back and the wood hangers in her hands fell, banging against each other.

Had she been *listening* to our conversation?

"Everything okay over there?" Cristiano asked.

"Um," I said, stalling as Jaz's eyes widened. I'd never caught her spying on me, but that didn't mean it was the first time. I wouldn't forget anytime soon how she'd ratted me out to Cristiano the night I'd arrived at the Badlands. When I'd been scared and alone. *She* looked scared now. I opened my mouth to respond, but nothing came.

I'd just decided to show her kindness, and I myself had sure as hell been caught eavesdropping on more than one occasion. Plus, whatever Jaz had against me, she was loyal to a fault to Cristiano, and I didn't want to give him reason to question that.

"Everything's fine," I told him, raising my brows at Jaz. "I dropped my hairbrush in the bathroom."

"I see."

"So, goodnight then," I said.

"Goodnight. I—uh . . ." He paused.

My heart missed a beat. Cristiano didn't stammer over his words, and that sent up a red flag in me. "What is it?" I asked, backing away from the closet, keeping Jaz in sight until I turned and walked onto the balcony for privacy.

"I'm only one man, Natalia," Cristiano said. "And there's a world full of evil to contend with."

My nerves calmed at the absence of alarm in Cristiano's voice. But the melancholy in it touched something deep inside me. It was hard to imagine a man as strong and tightly coiled as Cristiano feeling sad, so I never really wondered if he was.

I rested my elbows on the stucco wall, squinting out over the inky black ocean. "What's wrong, Cristiano?"

"When you say my name that way, nothing."

I had also sensed the shift in how I addressed him—I was starting to feel at ease, but I didn't necessarily want to admit that to him.

"You asked if there are ever women I can't help," he said. "I wish I had a different answer."

I remembered how I'd once peered over this wall and wondered if it could be a way out. My *only* way out.

*Don't die*. It was Cristiano's first rule.

I'd cheated death already, though, if that soothsayer from my father's party weeks ago was to be believed. I hadn't forgotten her prophecy about Diego and me. *You will die for him, your love.*

If she'd been so prescient, why hadn't she warned me about the kind of person Diego would turn out to be?

"You'd have to be a superhero to save them all," I told Cristiano as a breeze sent a shiver down my bare shoulders. "And superheroes don't exist."

*But you come close.*

The unbidden thought scared me. It was true—for others. Not for me. Cristiano held the key to this tower. He could unlock the door and free me, but as long he'd put me here, he couldn't save me.

"I cannot describe to you, nor would I ever try, the things I have seen," he said slowly. "Things no man should ever witness. The sex trade runs so deep, and touches parts of the world, of the internet, and of men, that even the strongest army can't beat. But we can still fight." He paused as a gripping sorrow passed through the phone from him into me. Cristiano had taken on a beast that could never be killed. How did that feel for someone as mighty as him? "I'm sorry it's this way," he continued. "I do what I can. The people I care about, I will protect, and those I didn't, I will avenge."

My heart stopped a moment, and his grave words hung heavy over the line. I'd never doubted Cristiano had demons, only that he'd ever show them to me. Or anyone.

"Those you didn't?" I repeated softly. "Who?"

A beat passed, and then another. I thought he might actually answer until he said, "A story for another time, my love. Now, it's really time to say goodnight. Sleep well. I will, knowing you're one of the protected."

The line went dead, but I made no move except to raise my head to the stars twinkling above us. I was one of the protected, which meant he cared, and though that should've come as a surprise, it didn't. The tenderness in his voice didn't match the man I'd thought I'd married. This man had a past that I'd lived alongside him and which I still knew very little about. How could I, when I'd been so consumed with hating him?

Cristiano had lost people he'd cared about, but hadn't been able to protect, and he was trying to make that right by doing everything he could for strangers.

Unless it wasn't about strangers at all. Cristiano had lost my mother when it'd been his job to protect her. And perhaps he was trying to make *that* right . . . but how?

The answer sat on the tip of my tongue but also eluded me.

Silence fell over the night as the waves lulled. With a noise at my back, I spun around.

Framed by the clean, white arched doorway, Jazmín looked almost devilish with her dainty, sharp features and red hair. "What are you doing here?" she asked.

"*Me?*" My heart rate kicked up a notch. "This is my bedroom."

"I mean in the Badlands." She took a step toward me, narrowing her eyes. "You may think he's blind. That he's too wrapped up in you to see anything else, but *I* see everything."

"He's hardly wrapped up in me," I said, also stepping forward. "If you saw *anything*, you'd know that. Maybe you're the one who's blind."

Jaz made two tiny fists, her mouth sliding into a frown. "I meant what I said. If anything happens to him, you'll pay the price. If he doesn't come home, you'll have all of us to face."

"Why wouldn't he come h-home?" I asked, stumbling over the strange word. It wasn't the first time I'd referred to the Badlands that way, but it was the first time it felt . . . true. And the first time fear had *ever* entered my heart that Cristiano might not return.

"Every time he leaves these walls, he's in danger. But this time especially, and you don't even *appreciate* it." She shook her head up at the night sky. "He's wasting time and resources that could go to people who actually need it."

I wrinkled my nose, trying to make sense of her words. Cristiano was in search of something he desperately wanted. Something he needed. And he'd said it involved my father and me.

I'd thought power was the only thing that drove a man like Cristiano, but power was a fickle bitch that wore many masks.

Sex. Money. Revenge.

Cristiano had only hinted that it wasn't any of those, but he'd never confirmed anything. He *had* told me he was done scheming, though. What, then, could possibly drive him to put himself in harm's way? And why, when I'd spent the last few weeks wishing to be free of him, did the thought of him in danger inspire concern?

"I don't know what you're talking about, Jazmín," I said. "He didn't tell me where he was going. He barely said good-bye when he left."

"He went because of you. Because you told him to. Because even though he gives you *everything*,"—she gestured emphatically around the palatial room where I rested my head each night—"it's still not enough."

"I never asked for any of this," I said, my voice wavering until I reminded myself it was true. My cheeks warmed, my temper rising as I repeated, "I never asked for *any* of this."

"But you're lucky to have it, and have you ever *thanked* him? Ever returned any of the kindness he shows you?" As she took another step, I straightened. I was taller than her, but she possessed a scrappiness I never would, no matter how much I trained. "Out there, he's exposed. The deeper he gets into this, the more dangerous it is."

"What is *this*?" He'd said he'd look until he found what he needed—

or until it drove him mad. I'd told him to go, but I'd had no idea I was the force behind his search. "What's he looking for?"

"It's not my place to say—"

"You inserted yourself in this, now tell me what puts *my* husband in danger," I demanded.

Slowly, she crossed her thin arms, glaring back at me. After a moment, she gritted her teeth and looked out over the water. "He knows you'll never trust him, and never believe him, without proof." She turned back to me. "And even if he doesn't know it yet, he loves you too much to live with that."

Waves crashed against the shore as silence fell over each of us. Cristiano was controlling, dominant, aggressive, even cheeky at times, but was he loving? My heart answered with a skipped beat. I'd known from the beginning that Cristiano hadn't done any of this out of hatred or indifference—how did I not ever *once* consider it might be love? I wouldn't believe that unless I heard it from his mouth, but I realized there was a chance it was true.

As tempted as I was to explore that possibility, the first half of Jaz's thought demanded my attention. "Proof of what?" I asked.

"I've said too much." She shook her head as she retreated. "Tell him to come home. If he doesn't make it back, *you* won't make it out. We need him. This town needs him. We can never repay him for what he's done for us . . . but we'd all jump at the chance to."

Her threat was clear. Nobody would bat an eye if I paid the price for their hero's fall. But Jaz didn't intimidate me. Her concern only demonstrated how truly worried she and the others were. *That* scared me—the idea of losing Cristiano. For now, it was as much as I could admit in the privacy of my own thoughts.

There were people out there who wanted Cristiano dead. I'd known that when I'd told him to go. In my mind, he was invincible, but in my heart, I knew that wasn't true.

Cristiano was on a mission I'd sent him on. I didn't even care what he'd gone to find. There wasn't anything I could think of that was worth risking his life.

I could call him back.

But why did I care? Why would I tell him to retreat when I'd done nothing but try to think of ways to get away from him?

*The people I care about, I will protect.*

He had sworn me his protection, but he was out there now, unprotected.

And *my* care could bring him home—if I could allow myself to want that.

CHAPTER 21

# CRISTIANO

I'd traveled across the country, brought along two of my most trusted men, and worst of all, left behind my new bride—only to come up empty-handed. Now, I navigated a small crowd in a warmly lit hotel ballroom with chandeliers overhead, hit songs on the speakers, and a fresh mezcal in my hand.

Max, Daniel, and I had kicked up mud on our way through dirt-road towns, hitting up local bars and banging on doors to ask questions that put targets on our backs—all in an effort to excavate information from those who were willing to sell at the risk of their lives.

But the remaining members of the long-disbanded Valverde family were nowhere to be found since they'd changed their identities and gone into deep hiding. Either that or they were dead.

So I was hitting somewhere even more dangerous—the elite. Those who had more, demanded more, but also possessed an even greater weakness for money than the poverty-stricken towns we'd just come from. The right offer to the right person could produce information. But the wrong inquiry to the wrong one? These people had enough money and power to wipe anyone from existence.

Some—myself included—would call me a fool for trying to raise one rival from the dead when I already had another to contend with.

Belmonte-Ruiz wanted my neck after the attack Sandra had helped us pull off, the most recent in a line of several. But the information the Valverde family possessed could be invaluable—proven by the fact that I was still trying to track them down.

Natalia had been right, though. What was all of this for if I couldn't have everything I wanted?

Tonight was my first politician's event. Everything I'd done up until now had been under the radar and cloak of anonymity. Every government and law enforcement official, judge, or ally of mine had been secured via a complicated but nearly impenetrable network that spanned the world.

Now that my identity had been revealed, I was coming to collect on years of staying clear of polite society.

I hadn't been invited, but that didn't matter. Senator Raúl Sanchez wouldn't dare turn me away knowing the influence—and capital—I had to offer.

The crowd was a thing to see, particularly the confused and anxious expressions of the state's elite when they recognized me. And, of course, as they took in disheveled, Russian Max and his glass eye, and my completely hairless associate Daniel.

"I hear congratulations are in order." Sanchez shook my hand, but I didn't miss his furtive glances. I was both a liability and an asset, the latter being the kind better kept in the wings.

"Thank you, Senator."

Coming up to my neck, he had a habit of looking at my chin rather than into my eyes. "How are you finding your new bride?" he asked.

"Expensive." I adjusted the knot of my tie. "She has a credit card with her new name on it and nothing but time to kill."

"Welcome to married life." He clinked his drink with mine. "I hope she at least pays off the card both timely and *abundantly*."

"Do you think there's any woman who denies me?" I asked with a dismissive wave. "I have access to the best pussy in the world. The girl doesn't even come close. I needed the connection to her family—that's all."

"I've heard Costa's daughter is quite the beauty, though."

An ember of fire lit at the base of my chest. I breathed through my nose, calming my instinct to put him in his place. He should be so lucky to ever lay eyes on Natalia Cruz *de la Rosa*. I forced out the only acceptable response. "Exaggeration. She's a plain and boring brat."

"Nonetheless, she has brought you even greater fortune and power," he said with a sip. "I'm happy you could make it tonight."

"How happy?" I asked, ready to move on from the subject of Natalia. "I'm looking for the Valverde family."

"Now's not really the time, de la Rosa." With a tissue from inside his jacket, he patted his hairline. "Have you gotten a chance to visit the silent auction?"

"Now is exactly the time." I had a low tolerance for political smoke and shadows and would sooner be back at the hotel working than shoveling this bullshit, but I'd exhausted all other options. "The sooner I get what I need, the sooner I'll leave."

"I never had any association with Valverde," he said out of the side of his mouth, "and that's the God's honest truth."

"Then give me the name of someone here who can help me."

"I haven't even heard the name *Valverde* in years. How would I know what you need?"

"Wrong answer. Try again, *compa*. Give me a name."

He forced a smile that couldn't even pass as an *attempt* at genuine and raised his cocktail across the room. To me, he spoke under his breath. "See the gentleman in the wheelchair to the left?"

I followed his gaze to a man in a bespoke suit with wrinkled skin and thinning gray hair. Despite his sunglasses, I knew the face underneath was hard as nails. It'd been years since I'd seen him, but I recognized him instantly. "*El Búho*," I said.

"Once wise and all-seeing."

"Now blind and senile," I said, frustrated by yet another useless lead.

I'd gone to The Owl as a twenty-something in need of help, and he and his family had done everything they could, but it hadn't been enough. I appreciated the man he'd been, but at almost a hundred years old, I'd heard through the grapevine that his mind was worthless now.

Sanchez clucked his tongue, shaking his head. "Not so fast. Those secrets are still in there, and he just might be out of it enough to share some." The senator shrugged. "But what's true and what's lies? You'll have to decide for yourself. He's your best bet at information here, though."

I started toward the old man, but Sanchez called me back. "He's on a tight leash. Family doesn't let him talk to anyone anymore."

*Sure*. But I wasn't anyone.

My phone buzzed in my shirt pocket. I slipped it out and kept the screen close to my chest as Natalia's name flashed. *Well, well*. It wasn't the ideal place to talk, but the fact that she'd called at all was reason enough to pick up. I did love when she obeyed—almost as much as when she didn't.

I got Max's attention and nodded toward the man in the wheelchair. "Bring me *El Búho*. I need a few minutes alone with him."

I'd barely put the phone to my ear when Natalia blurted, "I have to talk to you about Pilar."

My free hand curled into a fist as lust rooted itself in me. Being called upon by Natalia for help was one of the sweetest things I'd experienced to date. It would be my perverse pleasure to hear Natalia ask me to deliver a certain fate to the woman-beating molester.

I smiled to myself then schooled my expression for anyone who might care enough to take note. "Good evening to you too," I responded.

I thought I detected a sigh as she said, "Good evening."

Recalling Alejandro's account of her best friend's bruises and the cowardly fiancé was enough to turn me from doting husband into Manu's personal nightmare. I tugged at my collar as my chest burned. "I've already spoken with Alejandro."

"And?"

I excused myself from the senator and made my way through the crowd with Daniel at my back. He opened the patio door for me, and I stepped out onto a balcony.

Two women in gowns smoked between sips of martinis. My presence was enough to get them to stub out their cigarettes and clear the area. I gave Daniel a nod, and he returned inside. I could speak freely to my wife knowing he was guarding the door.

Natalia had called for help, and I was more than happy to answer. My mind was already running through the ways I could make Manu pay. I tried my best to keep the growl out of my voice so as not to scare Natalia. Although, I'd quite enjoyed watching the evolution of her responses to my attempts to instill fear.

"Tell me what you'd like me to do with him, Natalia. The fiancé."

As she spoke, I listened with all the attention I had. It wasn't always easy, pretending she was nothing to me, but it was necessary. Even amongst my own townspeople. Natalia had taken it in stride the day we'd arrived at the Badlands, or perhaps she'd just been relieved I'd kept my distance. She was in enough danger as my wife—even the slightest suspicion that she meant anything to me put her even more in the line of fire.

Although, there was a flip side to that. Perhaps the best way to go about this marriage would be to show everyone just exactly how prized my new wife was. And let them even *think* about coming for her.

I preferred to stay on the line with Natalia, but once the conversation turned to the past, talking over the phone wasn't the way to go. I ended our call and glanced out over the balcony as I sipped my liquor, welcoming the burn down my throat. With Natalia around, I'd been thinking more and more of the life I'd had before all of this. Of my time at Costa's, of my parents and brother . . . of others I'd been unable to help. Of things I would go back and change if I could.

Things I should've prevented at all costs.

At a noise, I spun around. A small, white-haired woman looked over the balcony with her back to me. I glanced at the door, where Daniel still stood.

"*Oye*. How'd you get out here?"

She turned slowly, her black, beaded dress trickling like a waterfall. She had more pink lipstick on her teeth and on the mouthpiece of a long cigarette holder than she did on her lips. "What a handsome man," she said, her watchful eyes resting on me, "a beauty rivaled only by her."

*Her*? Who did she mean? It didn't matter. She'd listened to a private conversation between my wife and me. "Didn't anyone ever teach you not to sneak up on a man that way?"

"So toss me over. Isn't that what the cartels do?" She shrugged a thin shoulder and leaned against the balcony wall. "Nobody will see, and if they do, they won't challenge you over an old, faceless woman."

Whatever she'd meant by bringing up cartels, I didn't care for it. With an uneasy feeling, I said, "Leave."

"I'm not finished with my cigarette, my friend."

"Friend? You don't even know who I am—if you did, you'd do as I say."

"Ah, yes. You are well-known for your treatment of women." She sucked on the cigarette holder and set a frail elbow on the edge of the wall. "Despite the rumors and your cold demeanor, I can't help but think I'd be safer with you than anyone else at this party."

I took a step toward her, completely aware of how menacing it would seem. "Who are you?"

"You were wrong just now, my friend—I *do* know who you are," she said. "And what you want, who you love, and who you seek."

My jaw tingled, and not from the drink. I set the glass on a wall. "Then tell me how to find it."

"You're closer than you think."

"That's vague." I went to take a cigarette from my jacket, but I'd left the pack in the car. When I glanced up, the woman held one out to me. Cautiously, I stepped closer to accept it.

"Don't give up." She flicked a lighter open. The stacked, mixed metal rings on her fingers clinked as she cupped her hand around the flame for me. I had to bend considerably to reach her. Wrinkles deepened her leathery skin as she peered at me. "And when death strikes, don't fall down."

"I don't intend to."

"And know when to *back* down. You don't always need to fight—"

"I will *always* fight."

"Brains beat brawn, *señor*. You have both. But there's a time to throw a punch and a time to be patient. And calculating."

I tipped my head back and blew smoke at the sky. This cigarette was not an indulgence, but an attempt to ease my frustration, all the dead ends and false starts—and this cryptic old woman wasn't helping. "Give me something I can use," I said. "Is there someone here tonight who can help me?"

"You've spent a long time leading others. Someone here can lead *you*—if you let them."

"You," I deduced.

She grinned. "I'm just an old lady with a bad back."

"Tell me then. Without details, nothing you've said means anything to me."

"I can tell you the senile man is indeed wise, but that you'd be wiser than him if you left right now. Before your chat."

*Senile man* . . . The Owl. She might've been nearby when I'd been speaking to Sanchez. I wasn't going anywhere until I spoke to *El Búho*.

"I can say that you were on the right path, but it's about to split." She rubbed her teeth with her index finger, but the lipstick didn't budge. "And you'll have to decide how badly you want the prize."

*My* prize. Natalia got this look sometimes when she was suppressing a smile or laugh. She did it enough around me to signal that she thought feeling happiness in her situation was wrong. That would change, though. "Badly."

She sighed as if she'd done all she could to convince me otherwise. "Then you should value it more than life itself, because that will be the cost."

"Whose life?"

She shrugged. She didn't know. *Because she doesn't know* anything, I reminded myself. I almost *wanted* to listen to her, which showed how desperate I was. "Then at least tell me if I'll succeed in obtaining what I want."

"No." She put out her cigarette.

"No I won't, or no you won't tell me?"

She nodded at my mezcal on the wall. "I'd dump that out if I were you."

Alarmed, I inspected the glass. "Poisoned?"

"Drugged. But it's not doing your heartburn any favors, either."

I frowned at her, then burst into laughter—even as I asked myself how the fuck she'd known about my heartburn. I must've been rubbing my chest.

She winked at me and knocked on the glass door.

Daniel turned to open it, and his non-existent eyebrows rose as the woman pushed by him. "What the—"

"Don't ask," I said, shaking my head after her. She had balls of steel to corner me that way, then spout a bunch of bull. How had she even gotten out here? I looked to the balcony several floors up as if she'd been airdropped in like a package of canned goods.

I didn't have time to wonder, since Max wheeled the blind man in sunglasses through the doorway.

"*¿Quién está ahí?*" the ancient man asked before he was even all the way on the balcony.

"You're safe," I assured him. "I just have some questions I need answered."

"*Vete a la chingada*. Fuck off." He turned his head in every direction, looking remarkably like an owl. I half-expected him to *hoot*. "Where's my wife?"

"Dead," I said, tapping ash from my cigarette. I nodded at Daniel and Max, who closed the door and resumed guarding the balcony.

"You may not remember me, but I'm a friend to your family," I said.

"Cristiano," he said.

I paused with my smoke halfway to my mouth. Pleased by his coherence, I nodded. "*Sí, señor*. You remember?"

"No. I can't remember. That's what they tell me. Can't see, either."

"I'm sorry. I thought the dementia was more advanced or I would've visited."

"Visited where?" he asked, a thread of panic in his voice. "Where am I?"

I scratched my eyebrow as he started to squirm. "It's me. Cristiano de la Rosa," I said. "I'm looking for the remaining members of the Valverde family from the northwest."

"Cristiano." He grumbled, shaking his head. "Your father's playing with fire."

"Not anymore," I said. "The fucker's dead. I'm with the Cruz cartel now, and we need to get in touch with the Valverdes."

"The Valverdes and the Cruzes are enemies," he informed me. "Vicente and Costa are fighting over the old de la Rosa turf like vultures."

Once my parents had died, Vicente Valverde had pounced on their cartel's carcass, resulting in years of battling with the Cruzes over their narcotics territories.

The Owl was stuck in the past, but that might not be a bad thing. "Do you know who wins?" I asked.

Costa would, eventually. Largely because the Valverdes had vanished one day, practically into thin air. The Cruzes had absorbed all that remained of the fallen cartels. And when Costa had decided to trade risk for stability, he'd used some of those territories as currency to build out and focus on the shipping side of his business.

*El Búho* gripped the arms of his wheelchair with knotty, spotted fingers. "I have to get home. My wife is waiting."

With a tap on the glass, I looked up and met familiar dark, sparkling eyes. *Tasha*. She arched a manicured, scolding eyebrow at me—*busted*. She'd caught me pumping her grandfather for intel.

Then again . . . could she and her smirking red lips get the old man to hoot?

I nodded at Daniel and Max to let her onto the patio.

Natasha Sokolov-Flores stepped out in strappy, cherry-colored heels and a matching dress that stopped just below the curve of her ass. Her curled auburn hair brushed her cleavage as she came toward me. "Cristiano. It's been a while."

# CHAPTER 22

# CRISTIANO

All my hopes were pinned on a blind, senile man in a wheelchair. The closure and proof my wife needed to allow me to smash through the lies she'd been told currently lay with The Owl.

Tasha, his granddaughter and my old friend, leaned in to kiss me on both cheeks. "How've you been?"

I nodded once. "I didn't know you were in town."

Her red lips curled up at the corners. "Then I won't be offended you didn't call."

"Is that you, Tasha?" the old man asked.

"*Sí, abuelito,*" she answered. "I'm right here."

"I recognized your perfume."

As did I. Tasha and I had hooked up enough times to turn me into a dog whose mouth watered at the hint of Chanel No. 5.

"*Tsk, tsk,* Cristiano," she said quietly to me. "What are you doing sneaking my grandfather into dark corners?"

Tasha had a powerful bloodline. Her mother—the daughter of a self-made, well-connected Russian mobster—had been married into a Mexican dynasty. Natasha—Tasha or Tatia—had been born the baby of her family and was more interested in the spoils the arms and narcotics trade afforded her than the business itself. But she knew more than she let on. And she could be of use to me now.

Fleetingly, I wondered what my Natalia at home would think of me standing here with *Natasha,* the woman I'd teased her about in *La Madrina* weeks ago. I'd told my then-unknown future bride that Natasha had sucked my cock like it'd end in a mouthful of gold. And she had, but I'd said it to shock Natalia. What would my bride say about it now that she'd given me the gift of her beautiful mouth? I'd heard repressed tremors of jealousy in Natalia's voice before—over Jaz, Sandra, or just at the prospect of my infidelity. After I'd fought so hard for just the chance to earn Natalia's devotion, I gave in easily to the satisfying feeling that she might one day be possessive over me.

Or that maybe she already was.

Without thinking, I picked up my mezcal, then froze as the old woman's words from earlier filtered through my consciousness.

*I'd dump that out if I were you.*

Strange woman. And seemingly very intuitive. I didn't believe in clairvoyance but perhaps she'd seen something. I glanced into the dregs of the glass, feeling better than ever and tempted to finish it off. But I was too far from the safety of the Badlands' walls to take any chances.

I set it back down. "I'm looking for any remaining members of the Valverde family," I told Tasha.

The Owl answered. "You want the locations of their gravesites?"

Tasha pursed her lips to suppress her smile. "There's your answer. Now, how about we get a drink?"

Not so fast. Clearly, the old man's mind wasn't *completely* gone. "I don't believe they're all dead," I said, though I'd been told they were plenty of times.

"They might as well be." Tasha crossed her bare arms. "They haven't been relevant in years."

I arched an eyebrow at her. "Then giving me information on them shouldn't be a problem."

With a sigh, she squatted at her grandfather's side. "Grandfather? What do you know about the Valverdes?"

"I know nothing about nothing," he said.

She glanced up at me as she spoke to him. "You know so much, though. It's me, Tasha. Are there still any living members of the Valverde family?"

"Who? What?"

"Listen to me, *abuelo*," she said firmly, and then repeated, "Where are the living members of the Valverde family now?"

"They're all dead. All of them . . . but there are men in the south who say otherwise."

Tasha covered his hand with hers. "Where in the south?"

"If you've hit Guatemala, you've gone too far."

I would've laughed if I wasn't desperate for this information, which could not only bring some peace to my world, but also get me where I was meant to be—back home. Running the Badlands. Unearthing things most thought were better left to rest. And teasing, learning about, and sleeping by my Natalia.

"Which town down south?" I pressed.

"Go fuck yourself," he said. "I know nothing about nothing. Where's Elena?"

"She's not with us anymore, *papi*," Tasha said. "You remember."

*Perfect*. I'd been reduced to getting information from, first, an aging mystic-for-hire, and second, a once great man who now didn't know his own wife was six feet under.

Tasha shook her head and stood. "I think that's the best you'll get. 'I know nothing about nothing' is his mantra."

"I just need to know which town," I said.

She took my cigarette from my hand and placed it between her lips, staring at me as she took a drag. "Use that devious brain you're so famous for." She parted her lips, and smoke curled around us. "Where would *you* hide? If it were me, I'd look for either the deepest hole or the highest mountain."

I shifted my gaze behind her and nodded at Max. "Take him back."

When Tasha and I were alone, she set the cigarette on the ledge next to my drink, pressed a hand to my chest, and leaned in for a kiss.

I drew back. "I'm married now. Didn't you know?" I teased, since it was unlikely she'd heard.

One dark eyebrow rose almost imperceptibly. Though she'd grown up in the eye of the tornado that was this world and had perfected her mask, I could tell she wasn't deterred. "When? I didn't know you were looking for a wife."

"It's an arranged marriage," I said, showing her my ring. *Or more accurately,* I thought, *a forced one.*

"Who makes a more powerful alliance than me?"

"I didn't know *you* were looking for a *husband,*" I pointed out.

"I'm not." She smiled a little. "But for the right cock, I might make an exception. And, baby, there's isn't a cock more right than yours."

I snorted. "My wife's is a different kind of alliance."

She played with one of the buttons of my shirt. "You mean because her family offers some other vice we don't? Business is expanding, you know."

"No. Not that. I mean . . . they don't give me as much power as yours would have. But she brings other things to the table."

"Such as?"

"It's not something I can really put into words."

"I see." She licked her lips. "You love her?"

"No." I wanted that very clear to anyone around me, including Tasha, even if I did trust her.

"Who's the family?" she asked.

"The Cruzes."

"Ah. Bianca's daughter." Tasha eased back but kept her hand on my chest. "She's young."

"Twenty."

"I knew you when I was twenty," Tasha said. "I wasn't naïve enough to fall in love, but if I had been, I wouldn't have stood a chance against a man like you. She must be following you around like a lovesick puppy."

I grunted. *I* was the one constantly trailing *her*. Watching her. She was on my mind too much. I normally traveled with more men, but

I'd left everyone except Max and Daniel behind with instructions to keep her safe.

Barto breaking in had shaken me. In my absence, I'd increased security tenfold around the Badlands, even if it meant traveling light. And I wouldn't relax again until I was back in her presence.

"This is an arrangement between her father and me," I explained. "She could care less what I do."

Tasha's button nose crinkled with a smile. "A shame. She doesn't know what she's missing . . . but I do. What does it matter if we spend one night together?"

I'd walked right into that one.

She pursed her plump, red mouth. A mouth that sucked dick like a pro and enjoyed every minute. Her eyelids lowered as if she was also remembering her lipstick smeared all over me. But there was something even better about my wife's nubile, naked mouth tasting a man for the first time. Tasting *me*. And I was going to break in that pussy as a faithful husband.

And if I never gained Natalia's complete trust? If I came home empty-handed? What then? I'd be forced to choose between life as a celibate husband or an adulterous one.

It was a line of thinking I couldn't afford to follow. I'd press forward to the south as The Owl had suggested, and if I didn't find what I needed, I'd go deeper, harder, and more ruthlessly into the dark corners of this country, no matter the risk.

If I wanted Natalia to fall completely into me, without any reservations, then I had to be successful.

And I would be.

"It matters," I said.

"Because she gives you a different kind of power than anyone else could," Tasha concluded. "She's your past. The things you lost. The people you failed. That doesn't mean she can be your future, Cristiano. You should be careful."

A chill passed over me, despite the fact that it was a warm night. Her instincts hit too close to home, and I didn't like it. "You're warning me about my marriage?"

"If you're putting the pressure of the past on her and expecting her to fill those voids, you'll probably be disappointed. There are plenty of other women you could make a family with. Why does it have to be her?"

My heart thumped once. I'd asked myself the same thing over and over since Diego had begged for his life in my office.

Why did it have to be *Natalia*? Why couldn't I have let her go and stayed on course to bring my brother down? Why did I still feel drawn to her, and protective—even after she'd betrayed me and she continued to turn her head when I tried to kiss her?

In weak moments as a young man, I'd confided things in my friend Tasha. I hadn't seen her in at least a couple years and was surprised she could read me so easily. Then again, she'd been there from the start, when each side of her family had tapped their local and Eastern European connections to get me as close as possible to righting past wrongs. Wrongs that continued to plague me.

Was Tasha right? I missed the warmth and acceptance Bianca and Costa had given me after all I'd known was the dismissal of my own parents as they'd busied themselves playing with innocent lives.

I didn't expect that from Natalia now, but I could be a persistent motherfucker when I wanted something. And I wanted the home, the contented life I'd once had before I'd been forced to give it up.

"By seeking out the Valverde ghosts, you're plunging yourself into the past," Tasha warned. "Whatever you want them for, it must be connected to her."

I kept my mouth shut. I appreciated Tasha's help, but I wasn't about to share any more than I already had. "Enjoy the party," I said.

She rose onto the tips of her toes and pressed her lips to my cheek. "Are you sure I can't convince you to come back to my apartment?" She cupped her hand around my dick, and it twitched against her palm. "I'm wearing that invisible underwear you love so much."

It would be so easy to lose myself in her for tonight. I couldn't remember being so riled up in all my life as I was waiting for Natalia to invite me into her bed. Not even when I'd first fled the Cruz's home and had gone an embarrassing amount of time without a woman. I was crazed for Natalia, evidenced by the fact that I'd broken down and fucked her mouth when I'd promised myself I'd wait until I knew for sure it was what she wanted.

But in Natalia, I saw the potential for so much. As Tasha had just said—it was a lot to put on one person's shoulders, but I had faith. A night with another woman might not be much, especially around here, but to me, it was one small way of giving up hope in Natalia and me—and that, I wouldn't do. Not yet.

I removed Tasha's hand from my crotch. "I appreciate the offer, but I'm certain."

She pouted. "I lied earlier. Every other cock I've met is better than yours, simply because they didn't deny me."

I laughed. "If it makes you feel better, it's not my cock that denies you."

"Your heart?" she asked.

"No," I said. "The same thing that rules everything else—my reason."

"Very well," she said, backing away. "You know how to reach me if you change your mind."

I longed to bury myself somewhere warm and wet, but whereas in the past, any woman would have been good enough, now, only one would do.

Natalia was a conquest that would undoubtedly conquer me back.

I had seeds of hope that I might yet earn her devotion. That hope drove me. It was why I stood here now.

I walked back into the party, motioning for Max and Daniel.

"What now, boss?" Daniel asked, plucking a mint from a glass bowl on our way through the lobby.

"We go south," I said as we headed outside, passing under the bright lights of the hotel's awning. "Start gathering satellite images of the terrain and mountain ranges," I continued, stopping at the valet stand, "and putting out feelers for information from existing and potential sources." I glanced around for one of the parking attendants, eager to move. "We have plenty of contacts at the México-Guatemala border, which—*puta madre*," I cursed. "Why the fuck did they make us valet if nobody's working?"

Due to the high-profile nature of the event, we'd been forced to hand over the keys to the Suburban, but for such a high-end hotel in this city, the service was shit.

"I'm on it," Max said, sauntering into the small booth. He swiped our keys and took off running.

My phone buzzed, and I slipped it from my pocket to check the screen.

*Natalia.*

Twice in one night? Maybe one day, that would be the norm . . . but now, it wasn't right. And it set off warning bells.

With a quick glance at Daniel, I said, "Get ahold of Alejo. Check on things at the house, yeah?"

"You already had me do that hours ago," he said, snickering at my overprotectiveness of Natalia.

"Do it the fuck again or I'll leave you in that party," I threatened.

His eyes flew open. It was enough to get him on his phone. He stepped away to call Alejandro as I swiped my finger across the screen. "Natalia," I answered. "What is it?"

"Cristiano. I'm—I'm sorry to call again, and so late."

"It's not late." Surveying the space around me, I stuck a hand in my pocket and paced toward the lawn for privacy. "Call me any hour of the night. I leave my phone on for you."

She took a breath, and with that small inhale, I sensed some hesitation. Was it possible to read her just through respiration—tiny, sexy gasps, light exhales, heavy pants? *Fuck.* Perhaps I was descending into madness already . . .

"What is it?" I repeated. "Is something wrong?"

"No," she said, but it wasn't as resolute as I'd have liked. She almost hedged on fearful. "Everything's fine. I just . . ."

With the ensuing silence, my hand sweat around the phone. Why the fuck was one damned call and a few simple words making my heart pound?

I felt . . . panicked. In a way I hadn't in a long time.

And the only explanation was Natalia. My attachment to her was fully formed now, and that was a problem for me.

It was weakness.

And it was a problem for her, too, if she never came around to the idea of me. Because I had no plans to let her go.

"You don't sound fine," I said.

She sighed. "Where are you?"

"Not far. If you need me, I can get on a helicopter, just . . . ask."

She wouldn't. What reason would she have? Things between us had shifted, but not to the place where she could ask me for something like that.

More silence. The longer it spread over the line, the more uneasy I felt. What was going on? An ache pulsed at my temples, my thoughts jumbling. I felt like I was in a snow globe that'd just been shaken. "Why are you asking?"

"It's just that you didn't tell me you were leaving, not explicitly. And you didn't say how far you were going. So I just feel like, as, you know, your . . . I should know where you are."

*As my wife.* No longer my captive? Finally, the SUV pulled up. I glanced over my shoulder as the valet got out of the driver's side. "Talk to me, *mi amor*," I said, turning forward again. "What's going on?"

"I've just been thinking a lot about our conversation at the nightclub last weekend," she said softly.

"Why didn't you bring it up earlier?"

"I didn't realize . . . well, you said you were looking for something, and it might be dangerous."

I racked my brain for what might cause Natalia to stumble over her words or beat around the bush. If she wasn't in trouble, could she possibly just be . . . shy?

"What are you trying to ask?" I firmed my tone in case she needed to be told. "Tell me now."

"I want to know if *you're* in danger—for real. Like actual, real danger. And if so, are you sure this mission is worth it?"

*Ah.* I leaned back on my heels as a soothing, unfamiliar warmth bloomed in my chest. She was concerned? For me? In these last weeks, she'd been resisting me at every turn. The last eleven *years*, she'd hated me for what she'd thought I'd done. Even the smallest inquiry about my life was a breakthrough—and here, she was actually checking in on my wellbeing. I couldn't help my small smile. "Natalia."

"Cristiano," she answered, and I heard her own smile over the phone. She knew she'd pleased me.

"Are you *worried* about me?" I asked.

"Well, if worrying about what the people here in your household, and in all of the Badlands would do without you . . . and if being concerned over the futures of the mistreated women and children your resources could help . . . if all that means I'm worried about you, then I suppose I am."

I would take it. Every word of it. She couldn't say the things she wanted to—it was too early for that. But the meaning behind her concern came through. And I appreciated it.

"I'm not in too much danger," I said, downplaying the risk. Traveling farther and farther from my home would always expose me to enemies and potential threats.

"I don't believe that," she said, her voice rising to its normal tone.

"Any time I leave the Badlands, there's a chance something could go wrong," I admitted. "Especially since I've only got two men with me."

"Why didn't you take more?" she asked. "Is it because they're here with me?"

Realizing I'd been strolling around the lawn, I stopped and looked for Daniel. Where *was* he anyway? And Max? My eyes landed on the Suburban as it idled by the valet stand, unattended. Had I seen that a valet had pulled it around? Max was the one with the keys.

"Where are you?" Natalia asked.

I frowned, still scanning the area. A wave of uneasiness weirdly similar to nausea hit me. "At a political event, but that's not important. I'm planning to go south from here."

"Why?"

It wasn't that I wanted to keep the details from Natalia, but I needed more information before I shared anything. If I told her what I was looking for and came up short, it could drive an even bigger wedge between us. And if my instincts about this were right, it could potentially break her heart—again. And like Costa, I didn't take that lightly. I'd vowed to protect her, but if my suspicions proved true, it would be a deeply emotional betrayal I couldn't shield her from. I wasn't going to breathe a word until I was one-hundred-goddamn-percent sure.

"Does it have to do with politics?" she asked.

"No."

"What then?" she asked. "Can't you give me any more hints as to what you're looking for?"

I shut my eyes briefly. *Closure.*

"I don't need it," she said immediately.

I blinked my eyes open against the awning's bright lights. I hadn't said the word aloud. Had I? What the fuck was wrong with me? Words never slipped out if I didn't mean them to.

"If you're doing all this to give me closure over something, don't," she practically pleaded.

Of course I was doing it for her—but I was no saint. I had my own selfish reasons, too. I turned back for the hotel and jogged up the steps to check the lobby for Daniel. "You don't even know what I'm trying to find."

"It doesn't *matter*, Cristiano."

"It does to me."

"But why?"

I massaged my jaw, thinking. "Tiny Dancer" played over the hotel speakers, and it was damn loud. When had I last put on a record and listened all the way through? And what kind of a thought was that right now? The song carried outside as I returned through the revolving doors and headed for the car.

If Natalia knew why I was gone and I came home empty-handed, she'd never fully open for me. Without this, there'd always be a part of her heart I'd never touch, no matter what happened. I knew it. *She* knew it. She was the one who'd sworn to me that without closure, she and I could never reach a level of complete trust.

"You don't have to do anything for me," she said. "Not if it, you know—not if you're not safe."

Her measured words spoke volumes. If Natalia didn't want me to put myself in danger, that meant on some level, however deeply buried—she might . . . *care* about me.

And not only was it hard for her to say, but after eleven years of seeing me as the worst man in her life, it was probably impossible.

I was moving from *monster* to the man she'd call *husband.*

But that alone wasn't enough. I wanted it all. I wanted her to *ask* for what she wanted. And I hoped what she *wanted*—was for me to come home. "Natalia. What are you trying to say?"

"I . . . I want you to—to—"

I missed the end of her sentence as my ears began to ring. I stretched my jaw, working it side to side . . . only to realize the sound was coming through the phone.

A piercing wail that drowned out Natalia as my spine went rod-straight.

My heart thudded in my chest as I strode to the car. I'd recognize that alarm anywhere.

"What *is* that?" Natalia yelled over what I knew was an earsplitting noise on her end.

"The house alarm. Where are you?"

"The bedroom—"

"Get down to the panic room, through the cellar—like Alejandro showed you, Natalia. Now!"

The ground under my feet turned to jelly, and I stumbled as I rushed to the Suburban.

*When death strikes, don't fall down.*

I righted myself, ignoring the way my head swam.

"Your car, *señor* de la Rosa." I turned and came face to face with one of the young valet parkers. I looked over his head for Max at the same moment the kid lunged into me full force. My shoulder flew into the Suburban's side panel. Pain radiated from my bicep as I bounced off it, swung at him—and missed.

I never missed.

*What the fuck?*

Bright lights burned my vision. Whether the house alarm echoed in my ears or blared from my cell phone, I wasn't sure. *Natalia.*

My back slammed up against the car door as I was pummeled again. The valet did his best to get in my face while I towered over him. I could easily pick up two of him and crack both skulls together—but my reflexes had slowed to the point that I could barely even push him off.

My mezcal. It'd been fucking *drugged*. I gritted my teeth and tried to propel myself forward. I had many lives depending on me—including Natalia's.

With the bolstering thought, I managed to knee the valet in the balls, and a sharp pain burnt up my stomach to my chest.

He disappeared, but I couldn't move my head fast enough to get him in my sight.

My muscles fatigued, and I had to steady myself against the car or I'd fall. My phone, still in my hand, vibrated and lit up with Natalia's name for the third time in one night.

I stared at it, willing my hand to move so I could answer it. I swiped my finger across, but couldn't get the phone to my ear. "Natalia," I managed to grate out.

And her piercing screams answered.

*No.* Fuck! No. *The alarms. The cellar.* Was she in there? I tried forcing the question from my mouth.

With a flash of motion at my side, the valet threw himself at me again. "A gift from Belmonte-Ruiz, *cabrón*," he said. "You've fucked with us for the last time."

Time slowed. I blinked against the blinding lights above the awning as they brightened and sharpened. Elton John's crooning slowed to a deep, lethargic warble. My head fell forward, and I caught sight of a bloodied knife in the valet's hand. Where was the blood coming from? And why was it dripping at my feet?

With a brutal thrust, he plunged it into my side, and searing pain followed.

As he withdrew it, I gasped for air and tried shooting out my hand to grab his neck, but exhaustion weighted my movements.

The world undulated around me. My ears tuned back into the screams.

*Natalia's* screams, as they mixed with the house alarm.

My vision blurred. I focused everything on getting the phone up to my ear.

I heard my name. I grasped for it. "Cristiano—" Her voice—small, terrified. "Cristiano!"

*Get to the cellar.* My knees buckled, and I fell onto them, but only one thing mattered—the shrieking of the woman I'd protected as a baby, a child, and now as my wife. They could not, *would not,* be the thing I heard as hell pulled me under. I couldn't go down in fear that she was being hurt. That another man had entered my bedroom. Cornered her when she needed me most. That he'd do all the unspeakable things I'd been fighting against. Put his *fucking* hands around the delicate throat I'd promised her only *I* would ever touch. My entire body burned at the thought that anyone would even broach the gates of Heaven—*my* goddamn Heaven—which I'd barely tasted and had never even breached.

Anger surged in me as the worst possibility of all hit me. I forced myself to my feet with everything I had and managed to wrap my hands around the fucker's neck. Belmonte-Ruiz would not take my wife from the Badlands and into a worse hell than the one where I was headed.

I squeezed with the strength of a body that had faced death countless times and was still standing. A body that had taken down men three times the size of this scum. A body that had triumphed.

And then I reached into the depths of my reserves for even more—the reserves that had kept me alive in the past, the ones that I'd always fallen back on to save my own life. Now, I called on them for Natalia.

But the body I'd always depended on, which had stumbled but never fallen, that had racked up kill after kill—it failed me now. My vision darkened as I dropped him and fell back onto my knees, wheezing for breath.

I couldn't slip into the darkness. I fought against it. To lay my eyes on her and know she was okay, to kiss lips I'd barely begun to learn. To speak the things I couldn't imagine never saying . . .

I mouthed her name. I needed to return to her, to my . . . my . . . "*Natalia—*"

"Don't worry about Natalia." It took every effort to lift my head and meet the Belmonte-Ruiz member's eyes as he stood over me with his bloody dagger. His mouth slid into a menacing smile. "Your wife is next."

# VIOLENT TRIUMPHS

## BOOK THREE

I've become a queen to the forsaken, a leader to thieves, and the wife of a man who instills fear in all who cross his path. He was the husband I didn't want. Now, I can't fathom life without my king.

I should've been ready for anything. Like the caterpillar that feeds on poison during metamorphosis, I was raised in the dangerous world of cartel crime. But nothing could've prepared me for Cristiano de la Rosa, his brother's poison, or the Calavera cartel.

This is still a story about a love strong enough to topple households, unite enemies, and divide brothers. Resilient enough to bring down those who would try to destroy it . . . and selfless enough to make the ultimate sacrifice.

But I was warned, and so were you. Death's day always comes.

This time, it will find what was once a caterpillar is now a butterfly—and hell hath no fury like the White Monarch.

# CHAPTER 1

# NATALIA

*I suspect you might even like the feeling of surrender.*

Cristiano's distant words echoed through the darkness falling over my mind. He hadn't meant submitting to death, but the hands around my neck demanded that.

The back of my skull throbbed where it'd been slammed against the tile floor. One moment, I'd been trying to tell Cristiano something important over the phone. The next, dragged through our bedroom and pinned on my back by an immovable weight.

Now, pinpricks of white light pierced the black. Stars in the night sky, promising peace. It wouldn't be difficult to walk toward them. The dark had always been a fierce presence within me. Unknown. Ever-inviting.

Surrender would be simple. My body and my training had failed me—I hadn't even fought back. Or maybe nothing up to this point had been real. Maybe this had all been a dream, and I was being torn from sleep.

As my windpipe closed under the grip around it, my screams relented. The shrill house alarm faded into a peaceful buzz. My fear ebbed, an ocean of tranquility rising in its place.

*Heaven.*

Mamá waited with open arms.

*Go to her. Be with her again. Submit.*

I wasn't waking up; I was dying. Cristiano was the last person I expected to see at the gates of Heaven, but there he was, waiting in his suit and tie. Thank God. Wherever I was going, Cristiano was there, and he wouldn't let anything hurt me.

He and my mother would be the light, the serenity, the prize for giving in to death.

All I had to do now was succumb. Go to him . . .

*Cristiano.*

"Cristiano is dead." A scratchy male voice took hold of me the way strong hands locked around my throat. "You have nothing to fight for," he said. "Go to sleep."

The word scraped through the dregs of my consciousness. *Dead.*

That was why Cristiano waited for me at the gates to eternity.

But he could not die. He was *untouchable.*

What was a world without Cristiano de la Rosa? Grief flooded me, but just as quickly, it ebbed. And in its place, fury swelled. Someone had *killed* Cristiano.

The voice above me thought I had nothing to fight for, but it'd just given me a reason.

Nobody—*nobody*—would get away with murdering my husband.

*Fight, Natalia. Surrender is not an option.*

Reality flickered. Carotid arteries. No oxygen. I forced myself out of the encroaching darkness. Clawed at the tightening fingers around my neck. I arched my back until I was looking upside-down in the bedroom mirror propped against one wall. My first night here, we'd stood in front of it—Cristiano wrapping his arms around me from behind, demanding my submission. I hadn't given in then. And over time, I'd grown stronger. Mentally, emotionally—and physically. Under Cristiano's guidance.

I wanted those moments with him back. For him to survive so I could look him in the eye and tell him I'd resisted, and I'd won.

Because he'd taught me how. He'd taught me strength.

With a clicking noise, I struggled to turn my head and see where it was coming from, but my vision blurred. Moonlight glinted off metal. A knife? *Fuck*. I began to thrash under him.

"*Shh*," he said. "This won't hurt."

I had no defenses against a knife. No weapon. Nothing on me but flimsy satin pajamas and plenty of exposed skin. But my breath . . . it was coming back.

*Change your mindset,* Cristiano had told me. *You're in control . . . you* can *take down an attacker . . . you* can *fight for your life and escape.*

That was all I had to do. Escape. Run. I wasn't at the level I needed to be to win, but I had the will to survive on my side—and the fact that he'd removed a hand from my neck to pick up the blade. I only needed to incapacitate him long enough to outrun him and get to the panic room.

My first self-defense lesson on the lawn had taught me more than hand-to-hand combat. There was the art of diversion. The magic of distraction.

*Have you ever been to Disneyland?* I'd asked Cristiano as his bar of a forearm had locked around my neck from behind.

The sound of Cristiano's answering laughter heartened me.

Words scraped from my throat. "Cristiano . . . isn't . . . dead."

The attacker's face bent toward mine, giving me my first close-up glimpse of him in the dark. Crooked nose, foul breath, beady eyes. "What?"

"He's not dead. I can"—I let my voice falter—"take you to h-him."

He leaned closer. "*¿Qué?*"

I rammed my forehead into his mouth, and blood burst from his lip. "*¡Cabrona*!" he cursed.

The butt of my palm slammed into his trachea. Plastic clattered to the ground. I only had enough strength to shock him, but it was all I needed. He loosened his other hand around my neck, and I punched him in the same spot, harder this time.

Alarm crossed his face with his guttural shout. The fact that he could shout at all meant I hadn't crushed his windpipe. I fisted my left hand and made good use of the extravagant diamond Cristiano had saddled me with. I jammed my wedding ring into the man's throat over and over until he'd released me completely to grab his own neck. Blood trickled onto me as he wheezed so hard, my own chest went tight.

With a bare foot, I kicked him in the crotch, crawled out from under him, and jumped up. I'd taken only two steps when his hand grabbed my ankle, and I fell forward. My head cracked the mirror. It teetered, and I rolled away a split second before it toppled to the ground.

The short fight had winded me, but I wasn't done. He hadn't gone down yet. Movement from the corner of my eye spurred me to get back up. I grabbed the biggest shard of broken glass within reach and got myself to stand. The moment I was on my feet, the man seized me from behind. He pinned my elbows to my sides with one arm, grabbing at the glass with his other hand. I held onto it until blood dripped down my fingers, but he wrestled it from me and put it to my throat.

"Nobody . . . told me . . . you'd fight back," he panted, struggling to speak. If his mouth hadn't been in my ear, I wouldn't have heard him over the blaring alarm. "Your husband teach you that?"

"Fuck you."

"It's a nice surprise. Very *exciting*. But I'll cut your throat if I really have to." His front flush against my back, he lifted my chin with the glass as his tone turned from amused to foreboding. "Your husband stole from us. This is the price. For every woman Cristiano took, we'll kill two inside these walls."

I'd been in this position before, at the mercy of a menacing man and his whims. And I'd been just as scared.

But Cristiano had taught me a valuable lesson that day he'd simulated jumping me on the lawn.

I was not to be underestimated. I'd survived my time in the Badlands by doing my best to protect myself from every angle—mentally, physically, emotionally. Cristiano had pushed me as far as he could without injury. But now, I had to be willing to get hurt.

I yanked on my attacker's wrist with all my body weight. The glass sliced the length of my throat as I rotated until the man's arm was twisted at an unnatural angle. I wrenched it as far back as I could and kneed him in the nose. He stumbled backward through the archways to the balcony as blood gushed from his face.

Run? Or stay and fight? I had to decide—

"*Maldita perra*." He charged at me with the shard of glass. "You fucking bitch."

*Too late*. I'd broken the first rule Cristiano had ever taught me.

*Don't hesitate*.

I covered my face and ducked a second before a gunshot exploded through the room. I lowered my arms as his body jerked and staggered onto the balcony. He coughed, reaching for me, blood gurgling from his mouth.

I wouldn't hesitate twice.

I sprinted at him and shoved him as hard as I could. He flipped backward over the wall and tumbled down the rocky cliff. His guttural yells echoed through the mountainside until he hit a crag with a *thud* and landed on the strip of shore below.

Silence descended. Even the alarms became white noise. I'd killed a man. I hadn't thought about it. Just rushed him . . . pushed him . . . murdered him.

I clutched my neck. Something warm and sticky filled my palm. I pulled my hand away—blood. He would've killed me without a second thought. I didn't owe him one, but I peered over the edge anyway. There was just enough moonlight to make out his shadowed figure, arms and legs splayed like a broken action figure. A dark shadow seeped over the sand. "Oh my God."

"He's dead." I whirled to find Jaz's petite frame in the doorway, her gun aimed at me. She raised her voice over the sirens and added, "It's a long way down."

A beat passed as we stared at each other. "Thank you," I said.

She lowered the pistol. "They cut the electricity and killed the generators," she said. "We have to take the stairs to the panic room."

"They?"

"There are more men in the house."

I glanced back over the wall. High tide. The frothy ocean licked at the distorted body on the shore. "He said they're here for us," I told her. "The women. As payback."

"Are you with me?" Jaz asked.

A breeze passed over my half-naked body. "I should—"

"There's no time," she said, turning. "Come on."

She hurried through the room, and I followed as we sprinted down to the second floor. "Wait!" I said at the mouth of the staircase and turned back.

"What are you doing?"

"We have to get Pilar." Keeping my back to the wall, I made my way down the dark hallway to her bedroom, where I hissed her name.

After a second, Pilar slid out from under the bed, her face streaked with tears. "Natalia. *Ay, Dios mío.*"

"Come," I said, squatting to help her up. "Hurry. Are you hurt?"

"N-no." She shook as she got to her feet. Jaz guarded the door, poking her head into the hall before beckoning us over.

Pilar gasped. "You're covered in blood."

"I'm fine."

"Who's doing this?" she asked. "What do they want?"

"Come *on*," Jaz whisper-ordered.

I took Pilar's hand and let Jaz lead us through the dark, trusting her intimate knowledge of the house. When we reached the ground floor, she ushered Pilar and me ahead of her. "Run. I'll watch our backs."

We crossed the main room and slowed as we approached the kitchen, the quickest route to the cellar and panic room. Jaz raised her gun and entered first, her eyes narrowed sharply as she surveyed the room.

"It's clear," she said, nodding at a door that led to the garage. "Through there. You know the way?"

"*Sí*," I answered. "What about you?"

"Right behind you."

I grabbed Pilar's arm and sprinted forward. My bare feet slapped the tile, and we were within reach of the handle when Pilar tripped and pulled me down with her. My head just missed the corner of a table, but my cheekbone smacked the ground. Pain shot through my face, but I quickly forgot it when Pilar screamed.

I looked back and slapped a hand over my mouth. We'd fallen over Rocío, a woman who'd worked alongside Fisker in the kitchen. Blood splattered the ground and cabinets, darkening the floor around her.

"*Shh.*" Jaz yanked Pilar to her feet and, when she didn't quiet, silenced her with a slap across the face. Jaz squatted. Held her fingers to Rocío's neck. Glanced up. "She's dead."

My throat closed. "She—she was going to the panic room, too."

"Maybe." Jaz made the sign of the cross, picked up a gun next to Rocío's body, and nodded toward the refrigerator. "But she went down fighting."

I followed her gaze to what looked like a man's body slumped in one corner. "Is that one of them?"

"He's not one of *us*. Other cartels don't realize that we *always* fight back. Every one of us. We win, or we die trying." Jaz handed Pilar the gun. "But everyone in this house fights."

"I don't know what to do with this," Pilar said, holding out the Glock like it was a ticking time bomb.

"If anyone comes at you, pull the trigger," Jaz said, closing Pilar's hand around it. "You need to watch Natalia's back. She's probably the one they want. And she's going to get you both to the panic room."

"What about you?" I asked.

Jaz's eyes dropped to Rocío. "I told you," she said, swallowing. "I fight."

"No, Jaz." I pulled her arm to get her to face me. "You don't understand. Those men are here for us. They're looking for any woman, and they will kill you."

"I have a job to do. Just like Rocío did."

I still didn't know exactly how Jaz had ended up in the Badlands, but I could piece some of it together. My first morning here, she'd revealed that she'd used sex to survive at some point in her past. Cristiano had said earlier tonight that Jaz hadn't known much kindness. Considering the Badlands had partly been built as a safe haven and rehabilitation center for victims of the pleasure trade, forced labor, and more, Jaz most likely fell into one of those categories. "Maybe they won't kill you," I said. "What if they *take* you instead?"

She froze, fear clearly working through her. "I—I can't hide down there while . . . while the others defend us."

"You're not hiding. You're protecting us." I wanted to yell to get through to her, but I struggled to speak as it was, my throat aching. I gripped her arms and shook her until alarm crossed her face. "We need you. If you don't come with us, then I'm staying here with you."

"No, please," Pilar begged through a sob, her wide eyes fixed on Rocío. "You can't leave me alone."

Jaz shook her head. "If you die, and Cristiano survives—he'll kill me himself."

"So where do you think he'd want his most tenacious fighter?"

"With you." Jaz's jaw firmed. "Fine—let's go."

We all tumbled through the door, into the garage, and down the staircase to the cellar. At the door to the panic room, I was shaking too hard to get my thumb on the fingerprint scanner, so Jaz took over. Within seconds, it lit up green, and the lock clicked open.

I let Pilar and Jaz go in first. After the near complete darkness of the house, the safe room's overhead lights seared my eyes and turned everyone a dull shade of gray. I pushed the door shut, and the slam echoed in the otherwise complete silence. Even Pilar had stopped crying. Locked in the vault, I pressed my forehead against the cool steel door.

*Cristiano.*

Even from a distance, he'd saved me. If it weren't for my self-defense lessons, I wouldn't be standing here. But where was *he*?

*I need you to save yourself and come home to me,* he'd told me once.

I *was* home. I'd saved myself.

Had he?

My breath stuttered.

*"Cristiano is dead. You have nothing to fight for. Go to sleep."*

Taunting words as I'd been held down. No air. Barely enough hope to save myself. My throat constricted as ghost hands wrapped around it.

I made two fists, fighting back sobs that rose fast and overwhelming in my chest. Cristiano hadn't sounded right on the phone earlier. He'd called my name as if in slow motion, from a distance. And there'd been a man in the background. What had he said?

My temples pounded as the back of my throat ached from holding in tears. We'd been talking . . . my heart rate quickening with an unfamiliar and scary kind of excitement.

*Come back.*

*That* was the important thing I'd been trying to find a way to tell him without betraying the person I'd been when I'd arrived here.

If I'd known those were his final moments, I would've just *said it.*

*Come home.*

I turned and leaned back against the door. One of the walls opposite me had been slid open to reveal shelving, like the inside of a large locker. Jaz passed Pilar a blanket and water, even as she held her gun close in her other hand. In a corner, a TV monitor flickered with security footage of the house. Not that there was much to see when it was deathly still and silent.

I opened my mouth to tell Jaz what had happened. Maybe I could connect the upstairs attack with what I'd heard on the phone with Cristiano. But Jaz's words from earlier came back to me.

*If he doesn't make it back,* you *won't make it out.*

She'd warned me nobody in the Badlands would forgive Cristiano risking his life on my behalf. If Cristiano was in danger, *I* was in danger. Jaz had made herself clear not even hours ago.

It would be my fault if he didn't make it home.

The cost of his life would be mine.

Pilar was suddenly in front of me, trying to get me to move away from the door. "You don't look well."

"She hit her head," Jaz said, shifting brown, almond-shaped eyes to me. "Do you feel . . . *¿cómo se dice*? How do you say in English? Sick to the stomach?"

"Nauseous." Pilar twisted her dark hair on top of her head, secured it in a knot, and took my elbow. "You should lie down."

"She should do anything *but* lie down," Jaz said.

"Where's everyone else?" I asked Jaz. Pilar tugged on my arm, but I stayed put. The pounding in my head could wait. "Where's Alejandro?"

Jaz shook her head. "Fighting or dead."

"You saw him?"

"No, but I know. Some cartel thinks it can come in and slaughter us, but nobody who enters will make it out alive. We can defend ourselves, and we will. They can't know that every person in this home will fight to the death for what we've built."

The Badlands wasn't Cristiano's town. It belonged to all of them. And apparently, I wasn't the only one Cristiano had equipped to defend herself—and this place—in the event of his absence.

Pilar returned to the locker, searching the shelves. When the door beeped behind me, I moved, and Alejandro ushered in two women from the staff who ran into Jaz's open arms.

I grabbed Alejandro's elbow. "Have you heard from Cristiano?"

"I've been looking for you." His eyes roamed my face as Jaz and the women talked over each other in Spanish. "What happened?"

"Have you heard from him?" I repeated loudly, and the bunker went silent.

*Cristiano is dead.*

*This is the price.*

Alejandro glanced at the ground. "I have to get back up there. Stay here until I come for you."

"Max?" Jaz asked from across the room. "Daniel?"

Hearing the names of the two men who'd gone with Cristiano on his mission, Alejandro turned his face away. Grease smeared his cheek. "Nothing."

My heart missed a beat as panic rose in me. "*Nothing*?" I asked.

"Nobody's answering my calls."

"Maybe they're not able to," Pilar said. "They could've put their phones down or gone to sleep—"

"They were attacked, too." Alejandro sighed, clearly torn about whether to stay or go back up, and maybe even how much he should say. "And in an emergency like this—danger out in the field, an intruder or attack within the walls—we always check in within ten minutes. No matter what," Alejandro said. "It's a rule."

The air around me constricted. My vision narrowed on a bloody smear on Alejandro's green, long-sleeved shirt. I could still hear Cristiano's deep, *alive* voice over the phone. His hard-earned laugh. His controlled, unnerving command for me to get down to the cellar when the sirens had sounded. There'd been no alarm on his end. Only my name. And the voice in the background.

*"A gift from Belmonte-Ruiz,* cabrón. *You've fucked with us for the last time."*

"Belmonte-Ruiz," I whispered. Mexico's most pervasive human trafficking ring. They wanted Cristiano dead, and with good reason. He'd stolen from them. Evaded their attempts to stop him. Taken pride in hurting them, and in the fact that he was still standing.

It was only a matter of time before it would catch up with him, though. And yet, even knowing it put his home, his people, his wife, and himself in danger—he'd persisted. He wouldn't be deterred from helping those who couldn't help themselves.

I wanted to be mad at him for it, but it only showed the kind of man he was. A man I had doubted and maligned every chance I'd gotten. Some good in this garden of evil. And I hadn't gotten the chance to tell him before they . . .

I choked back a sob. "They tried to kill him."

"They might've succeeded," Alejandro said.

A wave of nausea hit me. I touched the blood-caked gash on my throat. All at once, everything throbbed. My neck. My hand. My forehead where I'd smacked it against the glass, my cheek from hitting the floor.

"Check her head," Alejandro said to Jaz. "She looks too pale."

"I'm fine." I had to be. I needed answers, not more problems. I grabbed Alejandro's rumpled shirt. "You have to find Cristiano. His phone could be broken," I said. "They could've lost signal. Or been forced to leave their things behind. He can't be . . . he needs us."

"I've deployed a team to find them," Alejandro said, a failed attempt to sound reassuring. "According to GPS, Cristiano and

Daniel haven't moved. I think that's good. But Max . . . his phone is offline."

I frowned. "Why?"

"Hell if I know, but he'd answer if he could."

"What happens if you don't hear from them within ten minutes of an emergency?" Pilar asked.

"It's never happened," Jaz answered.

"*Never?*" I looked to Alejandro for confirmation. "In all the years you've known Cristiano, there was never *once* a miscommunication, an accident, a—"

"Never." He checked his watch. "We always find a way to make contact, even if we have to find a phone somehow. It's been over half an hour." Alejo sniffed and grabbed the door handle. "I have to get—"

"That doesn't mean anything," Pilar said, her voice rising as she glared at Alejandro. "Phones fail all the time. And you need to work on your bedside manner."

"I'm just trying to prepare Natalia." Despite his brusque tone, worry etched the lines around Alejo's eyes. "Even putting aside the ten-minute rule, if Cristiano was alive, he never would've let this long pass without checking on Natalia."

*Oh, God.* My limbs weakened, and I grabbed Pilar's arm. Alejo was right. Cristiano's silence spoke louder than anything. He and I had a turbulent history, a marriage that better resembled a battlefield, and we'd been sparring for weeks—but my gut knew. He would've done anything in his power to make sure I was safe.

And even though I'd wished him out my life more times than I could count, I wanted safety for him, too. I wanted him back.

The world began to swim. I slid down a wall and dropped my head between my knees.

If I'd had any doubts, they vanished before my eyes.

Something he'd said at the costume gala came back to me . . .

It had been Cristiano's dying wish to hear me scream.

And the heavens had granted him that.

# CHAPTER 2

# NATALIA

My world shook, and I startled awake. Jaz hunched over me, backlit by the humming white lights that seemed as bright as the sun. "What month is it?" Jaz asked.

"What?" I sat up slowly. I didn't remember lying on the ground or curling up with a blanket.

"Do you know your age?"

"I . . . twenty. Why—"

"Good enough." Jaz stood abruptly and moved back to her side of the room. She sat in a corner, pulled her legs to her chest, and held her gun on the tops of her knees.

I pressed the butt of my palm to my throbbing head to find it bandaged. My hand had been wrapped, too, from the shard of glass. "What happened?"

She kept her eyes on the door. "You passed out."

My vision doubled. Blankets and pillows had been arranged around the room. More women had appeared. Everyone slept except for Jaz.

"How long was I out?" The question came out as a scratchy whisper, my traumatized throat protesting.

"I don't know. A couple hours?" She heaved a sigh. "Alejandro says upstairs is clear, but they're handling the bodies."

"Bodies? Plural? Is there news about . . ." I couldn't bring myself to say his name. *Cristiano*. Even thinking it made my heart sink.

"All the women who survived are in this room." She shifted. "Nothing from Cristiano."

I fought back another wave of nausea. *Nothing* was the worst possible scenario. All signs pointed to his death. I had to believe he was alive, though. That he, like I, had fought back as hard as possible. For all the faith he'd placed in me over my lifetime, I owed him the same.

"No one checked in—not Max, Daniel, or Cristiano. They're dead." Her small, pointed nose twitched. "What are you going to do about it?"

"What?"

"They killed your husband. Not just any man—the leader of a powerful crime syndicate. Our savior. Our protector."

I lifted my head. She expected me to take on Belmonte-Ruiz? *No*. She expected me to cower and fall, or to run away. Maybe that would be wise. If Cristiano de la Rosa couldn't beat them, neither could I. Then again, I'd just taken down an attacker who'd had every advantage against me.

But I couldn't think of something so daunting now. I rubbed my elbows, the newest, but not only, aching spots. "Did you bandage me up?" I asked Jaz, noticing the open first-aid kit by her side.

"I woke you up to make sure you don't have a concussion," she answered. "I don't think you do."

"How do you know?"

"I've done this lots of times for Cristiano and the guys. You'll probably be fine." Jaz pulled her knees more tightly to her chest. "Which is too bad. It would've saved me some trouble. I told you the price of Cristiano's life."

*Mine*.

Pilar sat up from her makeshift bed in the corner, rubbing her eyes. "What does that mean?"

"Your fate is linked to his." Jaz looked to Pilar. "Yours too."

"Cristiano put himself in danger for me," I told Pilar. "According to Jaz, it's my fault if he dies."

Pilar raised her unsteady hands to her mouth. "And they'll kill *us*?"

I had always tried to protect Pilar, but if Cristiano had taught me anything, it was that no weapon could match the truth. The more she knew, the better chance she'd have of making it out of here alive. "They'll try."

I held Jaz's gaze. She didn't scare me. Her threats only came from concern—I knew, because we were both afraid of the same thing.

Losing Cristiano.

And she wanted what I did—his survival.

The question was why I cared? I'd fought Cristiano at every turn. Stripped down, with no indignation to hide behind, only my basic, unadulterated, inexplicable hope remained.

That he'd live.

That he'd come back to me.

That I'd get the chance to tell him I wasn't the same girl who'd arrived here. And that I didn't see him as the same man.

Time passed differently in the vault. I had no concept of how much of it had gone by when Alejandro finally reappeared.

I jumped to my feet, steadying myself on the wall when I got woozy. "Well?" I asked.

"A chopper is inbound. It's not one of ours, but we've made contact." Alejandro looked from Jaz and the women waking up on the floor to me. "Cristiano is on it."

I covered my mouth and released an unexpected sob. "He's alive?"

"*No sé*." Unsure, Alejandro shook his head. "But we've got great doctors on hand to receive him."

I'd get to lay eyes on him. Touch him. Tell him I wanted him to stay. That *I* no longer wanted to leave. "I should be there when he lands," I said, pushing through a sore throat.

Alejandro hesitated. "Respectfully . . . you'd probably be in the way. We have it under control. Might be best if you stay down here."

"Might be best if I *don't*," I shot back.

Alejandro arched an eyebrow. Up until now, I hadn't given him—or anyone—reason to believe I'd want Cristiano to return alive. But despite my best efforts, my feelings for Cristiano had been building. I hadn't wanted to admit it, but now, I had no choice. I had nothing left to hide behind. My soul ached to my core at the thought of losing him, of never hearing his deep, solid voice again, of things left unsaid.

"You said yourself Cristiano will want to know that I'm safe," I said. "Maybe having me there will—will give him hope."

Alejandro nodded behind him. "Come on, then."

Outside the metal box, my chest loosened. I could breathe again. I was taking action. We made our way briskly upstairs to the garage.

Alejandro drew his gun as we entered the house through a back door. "Stay by my side."

Though some of the lights had come back on, my skin crawled with the eerie stillness, as if the house had been deserted for months. Alejandro stayed close to me, his posture stick-straight.

"I thought you said the coast was clear," I whispered.

He didn't respond. According to Cristiano, a hundred percent confidence in anything was a death wish.

We entered a wing of the house I'd rarely had a chance to explore on our way to an elevator I'd only heard mentioned in passing.

Once we were inside, I asked, "Where does this go?"

"To the helipad on the roof."

We exited the elevator and stepped onto an open, brightly lit landing pad. It wasn't even the roof—the top floor of the house was well below us. It was just the endless, black night on the top of a mountain. I had looked up into the same sky earlier and reveled in the array of stars. Now, they were in hiding, drowned out by floodlights.

We walked toward a raised concrete circle outlined in white paint with an "H" in the center. A team of men in jeans and t-shirts waited, hands in their pockets, furrows in their brows.

"Who are they?" I asked.

"The trauma team. Other medical professionals are downstairs tending to the staff." Alejo pointed to the only woman. "She's leading the charge and has worked on Cristiano before."

I bit my thumbnail, looking them over. I'd only ever known sterile hospitals, white lab coats, stethoscopes, high-tech machines. Even when Papá or my grandfather had needed medical attention, the doctors looked professional. And they never would've accepted a female physician at the helm, as senseless as that was.

"Are you sure about this?" I asked. "I could call my father. He'll know where to find the country's most capable people."

"Doctor Sosa is highly regarded. Cristiano trusts her." Alejandro clasped his hands behind his back with an inhalation, searching the sky. "If he's alive when he lands, he'll be in good hands."

With a whir in the distance, we each whipped our gazes behind us. A blinking dot in the skyline came into view. I laced my fingers over my breastbone as it neared.

I just wanted to see his chest rise and fall, his lips and hands warm and pink with life, his long lashes flutter as he opened dark, ruthless eyes that would soften at the sight of me.

Was that so much to ask?

*Please,* I prayed.

I held my hair down as the helicopter hovered in front of us. As soon as the landing skids touched down, the team was moving, opening the door, reaching in, helping out a woman in a short, slinky red dress with legs for days . . .

The unexpected sight of a siren with curled, auburn hair and fire-engine red lips left my mouth hanging open. Freshly applied makeup made it seem as if she'd come straight from a dinner party.

"Who is that?" I asked.

Alejandro followed my line of sight. "If I had to guess . . . could be Natasha."

*Natasha?*

The name set off warning bells. Cristiano had mentioned a Natasha before, but he'd made her sound fleeting, like a one-night stand.

A gurney appeared, transferred quickly from the chopper to the pavement. My heart dropped to my feet seeing the lifeless body strapped to it. Cristiano had never been so still. I didn't remember running toward him, but suddenly he was within arm's reach. Gloved hands restrained me. Men yelled at me to get back. Cristiano's ripped-open dress shirt revealed blood-soaked bandages around a once elegant, now shredded, *always* powerful torso.

Cristiano's body bounced gracelessly on the gurney as they rushed him off the helipad.

Beneath an oxygen mask, his pallor alarmed me. "Is he a-alive?" I heard myself ask.

"You have to step back, *señora*," one of the men said.

Alejandro held the elevator doors for them. I started to board as well, but claws on my elbow tugged me back. "They told you to stay clear."

As the doors closed, I turned to face the sharp, female voice and acrylic nails that had kept me from Cristiano. Had she not been wearing heels tall enough to turn her into a tree in an obscenely short dress, we would've come face to face.

"Who are you?" I asked.

She released my arm. "*I* am the reason Cristiano is alive."

*He's alive*. Was she sure? How did she know? It didn't matter. It was the only answer I'd gotten so far, and I'd take it. I made the sign of the cross and silently thanked Our Lady of Guadalupe.

"You," the woman said over my head to Alejandro. "Are you head of security?"

"At the moment." He hit a button to call the elevator back up. "I'm Alejandro."

"Ah, yes. You spoke to my pilot." She held out a hand. "Natasha Sokolov-Flores. An old friend of Cristiano's."

They shook, and Alejandro tilted his head in my direction. "This is Natalia, Cristiano's wife. She's as much the head of household as I am while Cristiano's incapacitated."

I appreciated the vote of confidence, especially after Jaz's earlier opinions.

Natasha returned her eyes to me. Or to my rings, more specifically. "Is that wise?" she asked. "Cristiano made it seem like this was a marriage of convenience. I'm certain he would not like his business managed by a girl he can barely trust."

"And I'm certain he wouldn't like you speaking to me that way," I said.

I was as surprised as she looked at my response. *Mindset,* Cristiano would remind me. Natasha had the wrong one about me. So did I. Cristiano would expect me to step up in a situation like this.

"Mrs. de la Rosa has many advisors," Alejandro assured her.

Natasha's eyes flitted over me then back to him. "I'm sure you want to know what happened. Is there somewhere we can talk?"

She and Cristiano had been . . . together? Tonight? He hadn't mentioned that on the phone—but why would he? In any case, I couldn't let that bother me now. Cristiano's condition was far more important. "We can talk here," I said. "Now."

The elevator dinged, and we boarded. "Maybe it's better you let us handle the business side of things," Natasha said to me. "It isn't pretty."

I'd own the ivory tower, and I'd rule from it. Cristiano had told me that once our vows had been exchanged. If I didn't believe I could take over in his absence, nobody would. "I need to be included in any discussion."

She looked to Alejandro as if for permission. "Cristiano trusts her," he said. "With all due respect, you're the stranger here, Natasha."

The elevator stopped at the house, and the doors parted to the top floor. "Call me Tasha. Cristiano does," she said, walking out.

I tried to keep up with Alejandro as he strode down the hall to my bedroom—until he stopped abruptly at the doorway and turned back to me with a frown.

"What is it?" I asked.

"You can't let her or anyone intimidate you." He glanced at the ground. "If Cristiano doesn't make it . . . you're in charge. All this is yours. And I don't mean that figuratively—he was adamant that your marriage be legal."

To torture me, I would've once thought. Now, I wondered if Cristiano's reasons ran deeper than that. A need to connect with me on some level when I'd wanted nothing to do with him. An attempt to protect me, even, if something should happen to him.

"You have my loyalty, Natalia," Alejandro said, reading my mind. "Cristiano would've wanted that."

I swallowed, glancing through the doorway. The broken mirror was gone. I assumed the body on the beach had disappeared as well. Alejandro and his team moved fast.

My gaze moved to Cristiano as he was transferred from the gurney to the bed. "We shouldn't speak of him like he's gone. Not yet."

THE TEAM of doctors worked so swiftly, I could hardly keep the four of them straight, much less get closer than a meter from his bed. In no time at all, Cristiano had been hooked up to a heart monitor that'd appeared out of nowhere, irrigated, prodded, and injected. White patches dotted his torso as IVs branched from his chest, arms, and hands.

His dark, disheveled hair had fallen over his clammy forehead, and I resisted the urge to push the strands out of his eyes. "What happened?" I asked anyone who might respond. "Was he shot?"

Tasha turned to me with her slender arms crossed. "Stabbed."

This close, I could see Cristiano's blood had stained her red dress. She'd helped saved his life while I'd been accused of putting it at risk.

If I had the energy, I'd hate her for having information about my husband that I wanted. And for a pointed chin that gave her a markedly heart-shaped face, her sultry, Eastern European features, and a smooth indistinct accent that made her sound exotic.

Alejandro beckoned us toward the fireplace and away from the doctors. "Tell us what happened," he said to Tasha.

"Cristiano pissed off the wrong people with his little operation," she said.

She knew the truth of what went on here in the Badlands, then. She and Cristiano were close—but how close? Enough to have discussed my marriage, but not enough for her to know it wasn't a complete sham.

"Cristiano's operation is anything but little," I said.

She lifted a manicured eyebrow. "You're aware of it?"

"My husband's business? Yes." Across the room, masked doctors convened near Cristiano's head. I spun my diamond around my finger and added, "We're already aware Belmonte-Ruiz is behind this."

"They hit us here, too," Alejandro explained. "You said he's alive because of you?"

"Cristiano's attacker is dead," she said. "I didn't have time to double-check, but my father's men have confirmed it, and they're taking care of the body now."

"I have men en route to look for Max and Daniel." Alejandro glanced at his phone screen. I'd lost count of how many times he'd checked it. "Did you see them at all?"

"Only at the event," she said. "One of them guarded the door while Cristiano and I spoke privately on the balcony." She licked her bottom lip, keeping her eyes on Alejo. "Cristiano left before I did. When I came out, I saw a valet attendant standing over him with a knife. Cristiano had been stabbed several times. The valet was about to finish him off."

"And?" I asked. "Then what?"

Tasha took her time unsnapping her slim, snakeskin clutch. She pulled out a tiny handgun that just fit in her palm. "Elena. Named after my late grandmother. Neither lady has ever let me down."

"You *shot* him?" I asked.

She tossed her chestnut-colored curls over one shoulder. "Wouldn't you, darling?"

My cheeks warmed. Cristiano wouldn't even let me carry a gun. Where was the White Monarch now? Still in his office at *La Madrina*? I had the next best thing. My silver, gold, and pearl wedding ring, modeled after the elegant 9mm, had acted as a weapon hours ago.

"We were talking when it happened," I said. I'd heard his smile through the phone when he'd realized I was calling out of concern. To ask him to abandon such a risky mission. After weeks of resistance on my part, how horrible it must've been for him to think he finally had me on the hook—that the only danger was the usual minefield our conversations presented—only to be met with . . . a *knife*.

"Did you see his phone, Tasha? It's offline," Alejandro said. "Was he holding it?"

"Cristiano was barely conscious, slurring his words, unable to do much more than lie on the ground," she said.

"Slurring?" Alejandro asked. "If he was drugged, it would explain why he didn't fight back, and why he didn't alert us to trouble." Alejandro unlocked his phone and began typing. "See if your men can locate and destroy his cell."

I tried to keep up without getting emotional. On the ground? *Drugged*? Cristiano loomed over everything, and not just physically. At the thought of him unable to defend himself, a lump formed in my throat. "How'd you get him here?" I asked to shift my focus.

"My bodyguards," Tasha said. "I didn't know what else was coming, so we got him into my car. Maksim didn't pick up, and I didn't have anyone else's number, so I called my father. He sent a helicopter for us. We did our best to stem the bleeding."

"He could've died on the way," I said. "He should've gone to a hospital."

Tasha snorted. "Don't be naïve. They'd have sewn him up and turned him over to the authorities."

"Do you think I care as long as he'd lived?" I asked, heat rising up my neck. "It wouldn't matter anyway if he was detained—Cristiano de la Rosa can get himself out of any situation."

"Assuming he survives," she said, taking a compact from her clutch, "he may not be able to much longer."

Alejo paused and looked up from his phone. "What do you mean?"

"If Belmonte-Ruiz is on to Calavera's games, others will be soon, too." She checked her lipstick in the handheld mirror and ran a finger along one corner of her mouth. "Rumor is, Cristiano has stopped supplying arms to those who do business with BR."

"And any syndicate heavily involved with human trafficking of any sort," Alejandro said with a nod. "It's not a rumor."

She glanced sidelong at him and snapped her compact shut. "That's a big enough number to ruffle some feathers."

"It is," Alejandro agreed. "Especially if the truth about the Badlands gets out. But it's what we all decided as a team."

I bit my lip, struggling to keep up, but still following. The truth about the Badlands . . .

Gruesome rumors surrounded the Calavera cartel, a reputation Cristiano and his men had cultivated in order to insulate themselves. Calavera was a top dealer in weaponry worldwide, and that made them nearly untouchable. But would it be enough to protect them if word spread that the Badlands actually acted as a rehabilitation hub for those the other cartels had sold into slavery?

The leaders of this underground world I'd grown up in could justify and support nearly anything. But the disruption of the way things were, theft that dearly cost Cristiano's rivals, and the unraveling of decades' worth of industry . . .

That was business nobody around here would support.

But it wasn't anything I could worry about now. Cristiano's life was on the line.

And I didn't want to think of what could happen to all of this without him.

## CHAPTER 3

# NATALIA

The balcony doors had been shut, and the curtains drawn, but through the sheer white fabric, the night sky lightened to royal blue as dawn began to break.

Doctor Sosa stepped away from Cristiano's bed to make notes on a clipboard. It was the first time she'd separated from the trauma team, and I didn't waste my opportunity to try to get answers. "Doctor Sosa? I'm Natalia," I said as I approached her, and added, "de la Rosa. Cristiano's wife. Is he—will he live?"

She stuck the clipboard under her arm. As she pulled her surgical mask's straps from behind her ears, pieces of her light brown hair fell around her face. Judging by her haphazard bun and the puffiness around her eyes, she'd been asleep when she'd gotten the call. "*Sí.*"

Air rushed out of my chest. I hadn't expected a simple "yes" for an answer. I opened my mouth but couldn't find the words. "He—really?"

"Cristiano was stabbed three times," she said. "Two deep but clean lacerations in his abdomen, and one that just missed his heart."

I covered my mouth. Hearing his brush with death put so bluntly, my chin wobbled.

A hand on my shoulder alerted me to Alejandro. "'Just missed' is a good thing, Natalia," he said.

"Cristiano is very lucky," Doctor Sosa agreed. "Well, either that or the attacker was extremely skilled."

"I . . . what?" I asked. "I'm sorry, it's been a long night. It sounded like you said he was *skilled*."

"I heard the same," Alejandro said. "What does that mean?"

"He didn't hit any vital organs," she explained, pointing to her own abdomen. "With three tries, it's almost as if he was trying *not* to kill him."

"That makes no sense," Alejandro said. "But it sounds like good news?"

She nodded. "He's lost blood, but he's smart—or foolish—in that he banks some before each major trip outside the Badlands. There are matches within the town who are donating, too." She reviewed her clipboard and sighed. "Someone less stubborn likely would've gone into hypovolemic shock by now, but fortunately, we're prepared to do a transfusion. I have to observe the wounds for a bit, then once I'm sure there's no infection, we'll sew him up."

"So he's going to be okay?" I asked slowly.

"It's never wise to make guarantees in this kind of situation, but the outlook is good. There's some tissue and muscle damage, plus the sutures, so I'll need him to stay in bed for a couple weeks or so."

"He won't like that," Alejandro said. "He's been confined to bed in the past—we all have for one reason or another, and I know him. He's too impatient. You remember the last time he was shot."

I frowned. "The *last* time? How many times . . .?"

"He was back in the field soon after," Doctor Sosa answered. "Just remind him that if he makes this worse, it could result in surgery. Or an infection. Keep his wounds clean, make sure he takes his antibiotics, and keep him off his feet for as long as you can. He should be on the road to normal soon."

*Normal.*

Did I want that?

My body answered for me. I didn't even know how to handle the relief flooding me. I hadn't prepared myself for good news. My limbs fatigued as exhaustion set in, but I held myself together. "Thank God," I said. "No—thank *you*, Doctor."

"Of course, but my work isn't done yet."

"Far from it," Alejandro agreed, looking me over. "Would you take a look at Natalia next?"

"I feel fine," I said to the doctor. "Cristiano needs you more."

"My colleagues can handle him for the moment. Come. Sit," she said, guiding me by the elbow toward the couch in front of the fireplace. "I see you have some battle wounds of your own. Headache?"

"A little, yes."

"That's to be expected. But your speech sounds fine, which is good. Let's take a look." She sat me down, unwrapped my bandages, and inspected the cuts. "They look worse than they are," she observed. "Surface wounds, though the neck and this one on your cheek are likely to leave a scar."

I glanced at Alejandro. "At least I'll have proof I defended myself when Cristiano wakes up."

He smiled. "He'll be in need of some good news."

After Doctor Sosa stitched me up, I curled up on the couch, watching them do the same to Cristiano.

FINGERS SIFTED THROUGH MY HAIR. I basked in the comforting touch. *Cristiano*. He was here. He was . . .

*Injured*.

I opened my eyes. Pilar perched on the edge of the sofa in Cristiano's bedroom where I'd fallen asleep in front of the fireplace.

"How do you feel?" she asked, tucking me in with a throw blanket.

"Is Cristiano awake?" I asked, sitting up.

"Not yet."

I glanced over at him. The room had emptied out. Only the heart rate monitor's steady *beep* indicated any life.

Pilar glanced at the bedroom's closed door and whispered, "We could go, you know."

I rubbed the remnants of my headache from my left temple. "What?"

"I . . . about what Jaz said in the panic room . . ." She moved her loose ponytail over one shoulder and curled the ends around her hand. "I know Cristiano is supposed to recover, but anything could happen. You and I could be in serious trouble if he doesn't. Or even if he does. We could run. Now. Before he wakes up."

Had Pilar been paying attention at all? "*Nobody* runs from Cristiano," I said. "Especially me. If that were an option, I would've tried weeks ago."

"It's probably the last thing you want to think about right now, but this may be our only chance. He's unconscious. Two of his best men are missing. And the others are distracted looking for them." She gripped one edge of my blanket. "We can go to your father and Barto. Barto will help us, I know he will."

"Cristiano is as strong as he looks." I shook my head, looking her in the eye. "When he wakes up, and I'm not here, he'll come after me."

With her shirt sleeve, she wiped sweat from her temple. "You could . . . you could *kill* him." She winced and rushed out, "We could find a way—poison, overdose, smothering him in his sleep—and escape before they know it was us."

I bit the inside of my cheek. I understood where Pilar was coming from. In the last twenty-four hours, she'd been kidnapped by Alejandro, ferried to a place rumored to exploit women—run by a man she'd feared ever since childhood, when she'd witnessed him beat up her cousin—and endured an attack that could've easily ended her life.

Since Cristiano's return to town, the man she'd known as *El Polvo* had chased her off the dancefloor at *La Madrina*, made her watch us marry against my will, then ordered her brought here.

But she'd heard the worst of him from me. Pilar had been one of the people I'd turned to after my mother's death.

Cristiano had done unforgivable things. What did it say about me that I had no desire to run? That I wanted to be the first person he saw when he opened his eyes? That I didn't even want to *try* to hide my feelings for him from Pilar—or from Cristiano, from myself? Not anymore.

I didn't *want* to consider what it said about me—because I'd made the mistake of blindly trusting a man before. For Diego, I would've done anything—for him, I *had*. Was this any different? I didn't know.

But the idea of losing Cristiano had shown me I wasn't ready to say good-bye. Despite all we'd been through, he and I were only beginning to learn who the other person was. My attacker's declaration that my husband was dead had spurred me to fight for my own life—so that I could avenge his. I'd sworn Cristiano my loyalty, and whether I'd known it at the time or not, I'd meant it.

Cristiano had done unforgivable things, yes—but he'd done admirable ones as well. He'd put himself at risk to get me closure. Except for my questions surrounding my mother's death, he'd always told me the truth, no matter how brutal. He'd taught me strength in many ways.

And though she didn't know it, he'd helped Pilar from the shadows as well.

"Cristiano didn't just bring you here to make me happy. He did it to protect you from Manu." I took her hand and squeezed it. "Did you know your cousin was the one who molested your half-sister?"

She gasped. "Nessa? Yes, I knew—but that's not supposed to leave my family. How did *you* know?"

"Cristiano told me. That's why he roughed him up so badly years ago. Not just for stealing, but so he wouldn't—*couldn't*—hurt Nessa again."

Pilar opened and closed her mouth a couple times. "I . . . I didn't know. Are you sure?"

"He told me earlier tonight." Earlier tonight, when things had been so different. When I'd been so close to figuring out my rollercoaster of a relationship with Cristiano. "He's not who you think he is. There's a very big heart in there, though he tries to hide it. Stay with me." I gave her an encouraging smile. "Spend time with him. You'll see."

"If you say it's true, I believe you." She bit her thumbnail. "But . . . please don't tell him I suggested we try to kill him."

I pulled her in for a hug. "Will you find out from Alejandro if there's any new information?"

"Of course." She stood and fixed her hair as she left the room.

I got up from the couch and folded the blanket over the side. Grateful for my first moment alone with Cristiano, I crossed the room, lowered myself onto his side of the bed, and fit my palm against his warm one. We'd held hands once before, when we'd been staked out in a car, watching Sandra fight for her life.

Some of the last words he'd said to me rang through my mind.

*"Sleep well. I will, knowing you're one of the protected."*

I'd said nothing back. He slept almost too peacefully now, but there was life in his hands—and blood under his fingernails.

Anxiety tightened my chest at the sight of his wounds. Cristiano had always seemed invincible to me. Even when he'd fled our house to escape my father's wrath, he'd done it unscathed.

The truth was, without Cristiano walking this earth, I wouldn't feel as safe. And I didn't mean *just* in the cartel world.

He was a protector—*my* protector.

I'd thought he was the enemy—but maybe he never had been.

Feelings hadn't been blooming inside me—they'd been planted long ago, taking root without my knowledge.

I couldn't pretend that in my darkest hour, I hadn't fought harder so I could get back to him. Had it been the same for him? Was that how he was still standing?

Because he should've been dead. Alejandro suspected he'd been drugged—I'd forgotten to ask the doctor about it. That would mean the attack hadn't been spontaneous. Belmonte-Ruiz had had Cristiano at their mercy and hadn't even done any serious damage. It made no sense.

"You can't sleep there," I heard from behind me.

I looked over my shoulder. Jaz stood in the doorway with an armful of towels, a green plastic bowl, and a sponge. "He needs to be cleaned up," I said.

She entered the room. "That's why I'm here."

My husband receiving a sponge bath from another woman? That

wasn't going to happen. I rose from the edge of his bed. *Our* bed. "I'll do it."

She set the items on his nightstand and unfolded a towel from the top of the pile. "I've been tending to *señor* de la Rosa for years."'

"That was before," I said.

"Before what?" she asked but kept her eyes on the task in front of her. She knew the answer.

"Before me," I said.

Alejandro had been right earlier—gone were the days of conceding to others. Cristiano needed me to step up now and act as his wife. To care for him as one, and to make decisions in his best interest.

"You care about Cristiano," I noted.

She paused and dropped the towel to her side. "And you've made it clear you don't."

"Things change," I said. "People change."

Jaz shook her head. "People don't change. Circumstances do. I don't trust you alone with him."

"And I didn't trust you, either," I said. "You eavesdropped on my call with him last night, then threatened my life, not for the first time. But you also helped get me and Pilar to safety."

She shrugged and took the bowl and sponge to the bathroom. "I did that for Cristiano," she said over the sound of running water.

"Then we do have something in common," I said. "Our loyalty to him."

She poked her head into the room. "You call feeding outsiders information *loyalty*?"

The cell phone Diego had given me. Jaz had likely helped Cristiano find it. "I never shared information outside these walls," I promised. "It was a mistake to accept the phone. I paid the price. Cristiano has forgiven me."

She turned off the faucet and returned to his bedside with a bowl of soapy water. "He's blind when it comes to you."

Her words echoed the distrust she'd made clear to me the night before. But then there was also that *other* thing she'd said. The one I hadn't remembered until this moment.

*"Even if he doesn't know it yet, he loves you . . ."*

Last night, I hadn't known how to feel about that, but now? Was it possible I felt the same about him and hadn't known it, either?

I went quiet with the startling thought. Then pushed it away, considering Jaz tilted her head as if she could read my mind.

"Nobody can deny you've been good to him," I said. "But you have to make room for me, because if it's one or the other, you know who Cristiano will choose."

Jaz crossed her arms. "You're sure about that?"

I couldn't fathom Cristiano having to pick between the two of us, but he'd worked hard to get me here—and even harder to ensure I couldn't just walk away. I pulled my shoulders back as I nodded. "I am."

"Jaz." Alejandro leaned in the doorway. How long he'd been listening, I wasn't sure. "This is Natalia's job now."

Jaz sighed. "I hope you prove me wrong," she said to me and walked away.

Alejandro winked, then shut the door to give me privacy.

I picked up the sponge.

And I prepared myself to tend to the devil. To fix the monster who'd destroy all other monsters. To bring my husband back to life.

CHAPTER 4

# CRISTIANO

I'd opened my eyes once and seen my dark angel above me, silhouetted by sunlight streaming through the balcony's arched doorways. She wasn't here now. Maybe it'd been a dream, but she was one I hoped to have over and over. And yet, I'd almost died without having her even once.

I ached for her gentle touch, the curled ends of her midnight-black hair brushing my skin as her oval eyes soothed me, even when they were filled with defiance. "Natalia."

"Welcome back to the living." It was Alejandro who stepped up to the bed, crashing through my fantasy with a grin on his face. "You're a little slower to recover in your old age. I had my money on you waking up this morning."

Reality hit with brutal force. I shot into a sitting position, pain searing through my chest and down my side. "Where's Natalia?" The words scraped from my dry-as-fuck throat as the machines around my bed beeped faster, louder. "What happened to her?"

"Don't move." Alejandro laid a hand on my shoulder to try to ease me back down. "Your wife is here, *don* Cristiano. She's sleeping." He nodded backward to where her sock-clad feet stuck out over one arm of the sofa. "She hasn't left your side."

Even my relief was exhausting, hitting like a tidal wave and forcing me back against the bed. "Is she okay?"

"She's fine, but she hasn't slept much in the last thirty-six hours." His voice deepened. "I can wake her, but first, I should debrief you."

"Let her rest," I said, despite my demanding need to look into her eyes and hear her tell me she was all right. "What happened?"

"Belmonte-Ruiz. They've claimed responsibility for your attack and for the one here. They targeted every woman in the house."

My wife's blood-curdling screams echoed through our bedroom. A room where, until recently, I'd never felt anything but safe. Anger roiled through my chest like a Mack truck. "Natalia. Someone put his hands on her?"

"She fought back. She survived. Not everyone was so lucky. I'll fill you in later."

I closed my eyes to steel myself against a pain far worse than some stab wounds. Some of my people had paid the price for what had started as a personal vendetta. It'd grown into much more over the years, and Calavera had the support of everyone in the Badlands—but I'd let them down. "I'm sorry," I said.

"We'll arrange a service for them," Alejo said. "Once you're recovered, that is."

With Natalia's safety established, and my immediate concerns eased, hazy details from the attack at the hotel came into focus. My wounds announced themselves, tight and throbbing. Tension in the bridge of my nose made my head feel on the verge of exploding.

I'd experienced worse, but this particular strike had me on edge. I wasn't sure how many times the attendant had stabbed me, but even once was too many. I hadn't been able to stop it. The assault had seemed to go on forever, delivering me slowly to death's doorstep. What had kept Max and Daniel away?

"Why aren't I dead?" I asked.

"Because your attacker is."

"Max got him?"

Alejandro hesitated. "No."

"Daniel?" I asked. "I think I heard a gunshot, but I was out of it."

Alejandro glanced at the ground, taking too long to respond.

"What?" I asked.

He raised his eyes. "Daniel's dead. Found around the side of the hotel. His body's in transit so we can give him a proper burial with the others."

*Fuck*. My throat constricted. It'd been some time since one of my immediate team had taken a bullet for me. Things had happened so fast, and at the same time, they hadn't. This had been an organized attack. My final moments with Daniel played through my head—him teasing me for being overly protective of Natalia. The insinuation that I was paranoid. And yet, he'd always done exactly as I'd asked, up to his final moments. "And Maksim?"

Alejandro inhaled, his chest expanding. I tried to brace myself for the same news, but there was no preparing for that. Daniel had been a good and loyal man, but Max was more than a comrade. He was as good of a friend as I'd ever find. We'd been together since the start and had defeated many who'd like to have seen us both dead.

Finally, Alejandro exhaled. "They have him."

It took a moment for his words to register. And when they did, the heart rate monitor beside me went haywire. "What?" I asked. "What are you talking about?"

"Belmonte-Ruiz captured Max. The good news is, he's still alive, which means they need him. I've seen proof of life."

Blood rushed in my ears as I sat up. "Then what the fuck are we sitting here for? We have to go after him."

Alejandro's brows furrowed. "We will. But first, we need a plan. And in order to make one, we've got to figure out why they tried—or didn't try, according to Sosa—to kill you and not Max. If he's bait, then they must've known—"

Despite the way my torso protested, I swung my legs over the side of the bed, nearly knocking over the monitor. "If you think I'm going to sit here while Max is in trouble"—I yanked an IV from my inner elbow—"then you don't know jack shit about me, Alejandro—I'd do the same for you."

"*Ay. Tranquilo*. You need rest—"

"Don't tell me to relax."

Alejandro shoved me. Already out of breath, I went down easy, and the resulting pain was enough to remind me I could still make things worse. "I wouldn't ask that of you, and neither would Max," Alejo said. "You're useless to us dead, and that's what you'll be if you go after him at anything less than a hundred percent."

"You underestimate me," I said, failing to control the volume of my voice. My face burned at the thought that Max had been gone for over a day, and we'd done nothing.

"You're a danger to yourself, but also to those who go with you," Alejandro reminded me. "We'll get him. But not today."

"We *don't* leave men behind—"

The air in the room shifted. I looked past Alejandro, and my anger immediately fell away as my gaze landed on Natalia.

Long, dark hair in disarray, breathless and pink-cheeked in a white satin robe, she stared at me as if she'd seen a ghost. "You're—you're awake."

"You're alive."

Natalia drew toward the bed. Did she also feel the magnetic pulse beating between us? She scanned me head to toe. "And you're bleeding." She looked to Alejo. "Why is he bleeding?"

"He's trying to leave the bed," Alejandro said—the fucking snitch.

A dark, red rivulet ran down my forearm. I didn't even feel it. I wanted Natalia in my arms as soon as possible. "Leave us," I told Alejandro. "Stabilize everyone within these walls who can fight. We're going after Max."

"With all due respect, sir—"

"You're too polite, Alejandro. The answer is *no*," Natalia said. Her voice faltered but not with doubt—her vocal cords sounded strained. Her posture lengthened as any sign of distress left her. "You're not stepping foot outside this bedroom until you're fully healed."

I slow-blinked at her. "You're telling me no?"

"She just did, and she's right." Alejandro lifted his chin, no doubt smug that he had backup. "We're not ready. We'd only be leaving ourselves open to another attack here and putting more men at risk. Max knows that—so does Belmonte-Ruiz."

All at once, exhaustion hit—along with the urge to promise Natalia I'd never leave her side again as long as she wanted me there. "Call a meeting," I said. Still woozy from whatever medication had been administered, I could admit I wasn't in the best state of mind to make decisions. But I would be soon. "We'll finish this discussion then."

Alejandro exited the room, leaving me with my shame. My partner was in trouble because of me, and I was doing nothing. And yet, Natalia was here. She was safe.

"Come here," I said, and softened my command with, "*mi amor.*"

"How do you feel?" she asked as she approached slowly. "What can I get you?"

The warble in her voice resounded in my chest. I couldn't go to her. I was still hooked up to more than one machine, and even if I hadn't been, my body didn't move nearly as fast as I needed it to. My weakness was on display.

"Just you." Everything smarted when I reached for her. "Please. Come."

"Lie back, and I will."

Willing to concede to anything in that moment for her touch, I rested against the mound of pillows behind me. "You're losing your voice."

She ignored me and opened the drawer of my nightstand to take out a cloth. "Let me just call the nurse Doctor Sosa arranged for us—"

I stopped her. "Please, Natalia. You are my medicine. Only you can heal me."

Her lip curled as her eyes went foggy. I couldn't tell if she was smiling, grimacing, or trying not to burst into tears. She sat on the edge of the bed, scooting closer until the heat of her body warmed me. The contempt, resentment, and anger that sometimes marred her face when she looked at me had vanished. So I *hadn't* imagined the intimacy of our last phone call, then. The girl who'd once pointed a gun in my face seemed relieved to see me alive.

"Here." She held out a glass of water from the nightstand. "Drink this."

*Damn it, Natalia.* She was just trying to take care of me, but I needed answers more than fluids or nurses. I gulped down the water as quickly as I could while she disappeared into the bathroom.

When she returned, I gave her back the glass, and she pressed the now dampened cloth to my inner arm where the IV had ripped. The wound was the equivalent of a scratch, but I couldn't bring myself to stop her.

"I'm sorry I was asleep when you woke up," she said, wiping the area clean.

I'd seen glimpses of her over me, her hand in mine as I'd drifted in and out of consciousness, her normally violet eyes gray.

My freshly stitched wounds protested as I lifted my arm to touch her cheek, but it was worth the pain when she turned her face into my palm. "I know you've been here," I said. "What happened? Tell me everything."

"One of the valet attendants attacked you. How much do you remember?"

"I don't mean me." I took the cloth from her, discarding it on the floor. It hurt like *fuck* to lift my arm, but I took her chin and turned her head to examine the nasty looking cuts on her forehead and cheek. She had her own stitches. When I spotted a long, scary gash running from under her chin down her neck, my free hand curled into a fist. "Who did this to you? What happened here?"

"Tasha shot him, by the way." She ran her thumb over the red mark on my arm. "The Belmonte-Ruiz member who attacked you. She came on the helicopter, and she's here now."

*Tasha.* So that's why I was still alive. "She's at the house?" I asked.

Natalia nodded solemnly and added, "She . . . she saved your life."

"That's the least of my concerns." Tasha was a good friend, and I owed her, but I didn't care to think of that now. "You were screaming on the phone, Natalia."

"I was scared," she rasped. "For you, and for myself."

My eyes drifted once again along the slash. Bruises darkened her slender neck. I urged her chin up. "What are these marks? The cuts? Your voice—it . . someone . . . were you strangled?"

"I fought back," she said, smiling softly. "And I won. That's what matters."

Pride swelled in my chest. My girl. She'd done well, but a victory was hardly enough to placate me. "Don't protect me, Natalia."

As I tried to sit forward again, she kept me in place with a bandaged hand on my shoulder.

"What happened there?"

"Please. Lie back—"

"Stop telling me to lie back. Give me every detail, or I'll go find someone who will."

She glanced at the heart rate monitor. "I don't want you to get upset."

I caught her wrist and brought her palm to my bare chest so she could feel my pulse. "The physical pain is nothing. I've felt worse," I said. "But every second that ticks by without knowing what happened to you, the ache grows. My anger grows, and my heart—"

"Okay," she said, her voice soothing despite the way her eyes darted over the screen as it picked up my increased heart rate. She scooted closer, keeping her warm hand over my heart. "All right. I'll tell you. Belmonte-Ruiz had a mission. For all the women you took from them, they wanted to repay the favor."

"They targeted you."

"All of us. We fought back," she said quickly. "Not everyone survived, but Jaz, me, Pilar—we're all safe."

That wasn't good enough. One life lost, one scrape, even—it was too much. I shut my eyes. "I swore to you that you were safe here. That I'd be here to protect you. All of you." Jaw clenched, I looked away. "I failed you."

She got even closer. "You *were* here, Cristiano. A man entered the room while I was on the phone with you. He put his hands around my neck and squeezed until I saw stars."

I would tear him limb from limb. I would rain fury on his family, his brothers, anyone he cared about. A hazy film shuttered my vision as I shook with an impending explosion. All I could see was another man in my bedroom.

Threatening my wife.

Touching her.

Hurting her.

Visions crashed across my mind like waves against sharp-edged rocks. "I'll kill the motherfucker."

"I already did," she said, her eyes locked on mine.

*What*? My temper simmered as the words registered. "You . . ."

She nodded slowly, a proud smile forming on her face. "I told you. I fought back, and I won. You *were* here. You taught me." Her expression turned serious again. "I panicked, though. I wasn't in the right mindset, and I couldn't fight him off, and I started to give up. I did everything wrong at first. But he didn't expect me to defend myself, and that was his mistake. I don't think any of them expected that of us."

"He underestimated you," I said. "But you didn't underestimate yourself."

"You gave us . . . you gave *me* the tools to defend myself, and I did."

"How?"

"Jaz helped." She curled her fist against my chest. "I'll tell you all the details later, and you can tell me how to do it better next time."

I shook my head, half-awed, half-wishing I'd seen it with my own eyes. "You did everything you were supposed to. You survived."

"Rule number one—don't die." She took my wrist, dipped her head so I wouldn't have to reach much, and brought my fingers to her stitches. "They're a badge of honor. You warned me I might get hurt, so I was ready for it. You have scars. Now I'll have them, too. And they'll remind me that sometimes . . . things might seem scary and impossible. But that doesn't mean they are."

Was she talking about more than her attack? Everything about me and my life had frightened her when she'd arrived. I hoped this was her telling me that I'd prepared her well, taught her to defend herself, and now she was ready to open herself up to the possibility of scary and impossible things—like *us*.

"The scars are a part of you," I said, "and they represent the second chance you gave yourself." I ran a thumb over her bruised, cut cheek. There was a glaring question I couldn't ignore, though, and I worried the answer could set me off in a way I wouldn't be able to come back from, but I had to know.

"Natalia. Did he touch you . . .? Did he . . . did . . ." I urged myself on. She was my wife. We shared a bed. I'd threatened the universe that no man should come near her. If he'd tried anything with her, it would change everything. How I approached her, touched her, even spoke to her. It would break my heart in two and send me to the depths of a hell I didn't want to even acknowledge, but I had to take care of her before I could worry about myself. "I have to know if he raped you, or even if he tried."

She drew back, shock clear on her face. It was blunt, but it was the only way I could ask. I had to know the fact of it—immediately.

"No. No, no, no." She squeezed my hand with both of hers. "They weren't here for that. They just wanted us dead."

My heart rate steadied as resolution settled over me. "I will find a way to make this right. His brothers, his family, will pay—and I will blow up the Belmonte-Ruiz cartel. What I did before, trying to hinder their business, was nothing. Now I'll come for them."

"But first, you'll rest," she said, drawing the sheet to my chest. She picked up the fallen IV, sliding the metal stand closer to the bedside. "And you won't hurt anyone innocent on my behalf. Take comfort in the fact that no man who entered these walls with ill intentions survived."

"That gives me little comfort. They're just the tail of the snake." I sniffed, though admittedly, I was happy to hear it. "Not even one made it out?"

"Not even one. Hold still." She lifted the edge of a bandage on my torso, examining the wound. "Some came close to escaping, but your men blasted their helicopter out of the sky. You've equipped your staff—your people—well. They're composed in the face of danger, like you. Most of them are alive because of it."

It was hardly the time for praise, but I could see she was trying to comfort me. Her interest in my feelings was new—and very welcome. "They came in through the roof then," I said.

"Alejandro thinks they hacked the security system via the cell phone I snuck in. See, when Diego gave it to me at my dad's house, he wanted me to get info he could pass on to Belmonte-Ruiz." She took a breath, her cheeks pink as her theories spilled out. "They'd then be able to access the cameras around the house to get a lay of the land. They would've needed that to down the system long enough to breach the walls via helicopter, enter through the roof, override the backup generators and security—"

"I get it." I didn't need to hear more.

They'd flooded my home. Hurt my staff. Entered my bedroom. Threatened Natalia's life.

They'd put something in my drink. Cornered Max. Shot Daniel.

Distantly, I heard Natalia call my name. "They'll pay for this."

She forced my fist open, slipping her delicate hand in my bruised and roughened one. "Cristiano, please, calm down. You're in no state to get upset."

"They know I won't sit back and do nothing," I said.

"Which is why you have to," she said. "Nobody knows what's happening yet. It could be a trap, or some kind of diversion, or . . ."

I didn't hear the rest. Just her touch brought my heart rate down to a manageable level.

Natalia sighed as if she carried the weight of the world on her shoulders. "Don't you want to know how *you* are?"

I could tell without hearing from the doctors that my injuries were relatively mild. I'd been stitched up, and no doubt they'd try to keep me in bed for some ridiculous amount of time. I knew from experience, though, that the pain could be worse, and since I was already restless, that I'd be on my feet in no time.

It made no sense, though. I should've been dead. Nobody had ever gotten me on my knees and at their mercy for long enough to stick me—what, three or four times? They'd completely immobilized me. I could've watched him draw a gun and put it to my temple—and done nothing about it.

"Some of the doctors think you were lucky," Natalia said softly. "But I know you make your own luck. The valet didn't hit any vital organs, and he missed your heart completely."

I brought her hand to my mouth, watching her face, asking silent permission as I pressed a kiss to her knuckles, her palm. "That's because I'm no normal man, as I've told you. My organs are impenetrable."

"And your heart?" she asked. "Is it impenetrable, too?"

"No, but it wasn't where he thought it would be," I said. "Because it was here. With you."

"Cristiano," she said on a breath. She pushed some of my hair off my forehead, and it took everything I had not to close my eyes and give in to the feeling of her fingers on my skin. I'd already had her out of my sight too long, though. I wanted to get my fill of her. "The doctor didn't say you hit your head. Are you feeling okay?" she asked. "Has this near-death experience made you . . . romantic?"

"Only reinforced what I already knew—time is precious. I won't waste it anymore by holding back."

"You, hold back?" she asked and ventured a small smile. "Since when?"

I wished she'd crumble once and for all, fall into my arms, and seek safety in me, but still . . . *she* held back. Something had changed—I could feel her giving in, but she wasn't completely there yet.

She moved close enough that we could speak in whispers. "You scared everyone," she said.

"You?"

"Yes. Me. Are you going to tell me why you went?" she asked. "What you were looking for? What was so important that you'd risk your life for it?"

"You'd know the answer if only you'd let yourself see it."

She bit her lip as her eyes roamed over my bandaged body, her raven-colored hair falling around her face.

"You, Natalia," I continued. "I went for *you*. I was looking for *you*. I'd risk my life for *you*."

Her gaze shot up, and she grabbed my cheeks so suddenly, I flinched. She forced me to look her in the eye. "No."

I frowned. "No what?"

"No more searching for closure or proof or whatever it was that took you away. I don't need it, Cristiano de la Rosa. Don't you *ever* go looking for closure for me again."

"But it's not just for you. It's for me, too." I placed my crude, unworthy hands over her soft, injured ones, engulfing them. "There will always be a hint of doubt in your mind about my involvement in Bianca's death, and I won't live that way."

She drew back slightly, surprise playing out on her face. Her brows drew together as she looked sideways, away from me. What was it? Did indecision war inside her? Anything to do with her mother, she wanted answers. But that meant letting me continue down that path.

"Do you know something?" she asked.

"Only suspicions I'm trying to verify."

She inhaled deeply through her nose. If she asked me to go back, I would—just as soon as I had a plan in place to retrieve Max and retaliate against Belmonte-Ruiz.

"Don't go," she said finally. "I want you to stay here. Stay home. Don't go looking for answers, and don't go after Belmonte-Ruiz."

I must've misheard her. She would put my wellbeing above learning more about Bianca's murder? Above revenge? In that moment, all my wounds were healed. The loyalty and the trust of my wife was the salve, the anesthetic, the cure for a lifetime of rejection and loss.

It was, finally, the first indication that she could find a way to love me.

The other night, this was all I'd wanted to hear from her—stay.

But she and I both knew it couldn't be.

I had always been and would always be in this life. In the line of fire. At risk. No guarantee of tomorrow. I wasn't letting anything go, and now that Belmonte-Ruiz had struck against us, I would have to retaliate tenfold. Natalia might not like it, and her concern was almost enough to make me think twice, but I couldn't let Daniel and the others die for nothing. And I couldn't leave Max behind—even if, deep down, I knew what his fate would be.

"Enough business talk." I ran my hand up her forearm and squeezed her biceps. I wanted her to come even closer, but we'd made a lot of progress already tonight, and I didn't want to push my luck. "Did you sleep by my side last night?"

Slowly, she shook her head. "You needed space."

"You swore you'd be in my bed." My tone dropped. "It's the rule, *mi amor*."

"Extenuating circumstances."

"If I'd woken up and you weren't there, I'd have sent everyone out looking for you."

"They wouldn't have had to look far. They would've found me on the couch. Still close—in case you needed anything."

"I *need*, Natalia. I need you like I haven't needed anything in a long time. Maybe ever." I drew her closer by her arm until our faces were centimeters apart. "I won't force you to fill that need, but you should know it runs deep in me."

If one thing had kept me from falling into death's grip, it was the promise of her sweet mouth taking my cock again. I dreamed of it, of the last night we'd spent in the same bed, of the way she'd willingly gotten to her knees, and then of our kiss. Those memories had kept me alive.

And the fact that I owed her the same.

If I thought I could reciprocate with all the vigor I intended, I would've splayed her out in front of me now.

It would be the first thing I did once I was back on my feet—devour that pussy like the piece of candy it was.

Warmth crept up my neck as my hunger for her stirred deep inside me. Fuck trying not to scare her. I'd never let that stop me before. "If I told you to climb on top of me now, what would you say?"

Her lips parted for a breath. "It would probably kill you. The doctor said if you rip your sutures, she'll have to perform surgery."

"Nobody knows the medicine I need. Get on. Put me inside you; it will heal me. And if it doesn't, it will give me something to live for."

The rosy flush of her cheeks pleased me. I looked forward to seeing how she'd demur or lash back when she was so clearly trying to be nice to my injured self.

But then she glanced over her shoulder. Leaned into me. Brushed her mouth along the outer shell of my ear. "Okay."

I nearly choked. "O-*kay*?" I asked, not bothering to keep the surprise from my voice.

She nodded, running soft fingertips along my hairline, then against my scalp.

My eyes fell shut in pure bliss. My beautiful queen would finally give what I had practically begged for. What I'd trade my kingdom for just then.

My heart thumped, its *ba-bump* speeding with the machine's *beep-beep*.

*God, don't let me die from satisfaction before I even truly taste it.*

"I only ask one thing," Natalia whispered in my ear.

I opened my eyes to look into her sparkling ones. "Anything."

"If I climb onto your lap and finally take you inside me . . ."

I salivated, my hand on her arm tightening as need coursed through me. "Yes?"

"Do you promise to lie still so you don't worsen your wounds?"

My hope crushed like a vehicle flattened to a pancake by a compactor. I could've cried if I didn't have the urge to laugh. My temptress knew exactly how I'd answer. God was not merciful.

"*Lie still*?" I asked. "I vowed to prove that your virginity was still intact by utterly destroying it. How can I do that if I don't move?"

"*Ah*. Shame." She wet her lips, blinking lazily at me. Did she want it that bad, too? Or was she teasing me? "You may be willing to risk your life for one night of sex, but I'm not." She kissed my cheek—her touch gentle as my body answered with desire's violent pull. "It won't be tonight. Or tomorrow night. But it *will* be," she said. "Heal, Cristiano—so you can make good on that promise."

*Fuck me*. She was ready, then? Her admission was the sweetest consolation. She was going to give herself to me. I weighed the idea of delivering on my promise now and dying in the process against having to wait even longer, knowing it would *finally* happen, and living to enjoy it.

If I thought I could ruin her tonight without ending up on an operating table, I might've tried. I'd have to be content knowing there was light now where there had only been darkness before.

But if it meant opening my wife's eyes to what we could be, I couldn't help thinking I should've gotten myself nearly killed sooner.

# CHAPTER 5

# NATALIA

In our dimly lit master bathroom, Cristiano stood directly under a soft, warm bulb that shone on him like he was a statue in a museum. From the doorway, I admired him in the mirror. He brushed his teeth wearing only low-slung, black sweatpants that showed off the muscles rippling all the way down to a defined "V" . . . and beyond. His sculpted definition spanned so far south, I wondered if his *size* could be the result of some special kind of workout.

I crossed my arms over my nightgown to hide my nipples as they stood at attention. "You should be in bed."

Gauzy bandages glowed white against his abdomen. His smooth, bronzed skin had been marred and scarred—and not just by this attack. "Doc says I've been healing up nice the past few days," he said.

He put his every effort into hiding a grimace as he bent at the hip to spit into the sink, but I knew better.

"Really?" I asked. "Because I spoke to her this morning, and she wants you off your feet for at *least* another week."

He snorted. "A *week*? No, *mami*. I'll go crazy if I'm bedridden more than a few days. And it's been a few days."

It wasn't the first time we'd been over this. I tried to be understanding of the fact that he'd had a traumatic experience, but I'd had one as well. Cristiano wanted to be back in action. And I . . . I didn't ever want to suffer through the crippling fear of thinking I'd lost him again.

"You can't recover in days," I said. "You—"

"I've done it before. It's far more dangerous for me to be off my feet, Natalia. It leaves us vulnerable." He ran his toothbrush under the faucet. "The best way I know how to heal is to get back to work."

"I forbid it," I said. "I forbid you from leaving our bed."

Cristiano paused, then glanced up at the ceiling. "*Ay, Dios mío,* I've waited a long time to hear you say that. I'm happy to stay in bed for weeks if you join me."

He'd certainly retained his dirty mind and insatiable hunger to take me to bed. "If you have to go into surgery, you'll be off your feet for much longer."

"It would be worth it for a night with you."

Jaz entered with ointment, pill bottles, and the items for his sponge bath. "You're supposed to be in bed, *señor*."

I didn't bother hiding my *told-you-so* smirk.

He slow-blinked at the items in Jaz's hands and shook his head. "I already told you both—I'm perfectly capable of showering."

"*La doctora* said you're not supposed to be moving around yet," she said, setting everything on the counter. "Natalia needs to clean the wounds and change the bandages. I showed her how. It'll take two minutes—just stand there."

"Jaz, in five seconds, I'm going to hop in the shower," he said, undoing the tie of his sweats. "So in three seconds, I'm pulling down my pants."

"You're too unstable. You could fall."

Jaz was right—he could slip and hit his head. He could barely raise his arms without pain, though he tried to hide it. He needed help, but he'd never admit it. "I'll join you," I said.

His eyes glimmered as they met mine in the reflection. "Join me? You mean . . . in the *shower*?" The teasing in his voice almost made me rescind my offer.

"I owe you," I said. Last month, I'd been the one injured in my bathroom as he'd removed glass from my feet. "For helping me after the warehouse fire."

Any hint of jesting vanished from his face. "I'm the reason you were hurt in the first place."

"I haven't forgotten." But he'd come for me. He'd scaled the side of a building about to blow just to help me. Diego, on the other hand, had left me to fend for myself as he'd tried—and failed—to salvage the Maldonados' drugs.

I stepped toward Cristiano, hoping my cheeks wouldn't redden. Flirting with my husband a few nights ago had been a glimmer of fun in a dark time, and we could certainly use some fun. "You cleaned and bandaged my wounds," I said. "Let me do the same."

"Thank you, Jaz," Cristiano said. "You're dismissed."

With a twitch of her lips, she nodded once and left the bathroom. At least this time, she didn't argue. Or else she saw what I was also coming to terms with—things had shifted between Cristiano and me.

I didn't recognize this forward behavior in myself, but I'd seen it before. From the man in front of me looking pleased by my demand to take care of him.

I was staking my claim.

He'd told me many times before—I was his.

And for the first time, a small voice in my head answered back.

He was mine.

CRISTIANO WATCHED in the reflection as I approached him from behind. "Lift your arms a little if you can," I said.

He raised them slowly to give me access to the bandages around his middle.

"Does it hurt?" I asked, as I focused on peeling off the gauze.

"Will you kiss it better?"

*Relentless*. I hid my smile. "No."

"Then no, it doesn't."

I frowned at the clean, red gashes, no longer than a toothpick, but wide enough that they needed thick, dark sutures to close them. After peeling the dressing from his chest, I discarded everything in the trash. I crossed the bathroom to flip on the shower, and when I turned back, he was there, standing in front of me. "Can't shower in these," he said.

My eyes dropped to his pants. "Do you need help?"

"Yes." He cleared the rasp from his voice. "It hurts to bend anywhere."

I had no doubt it *did* hurt, but since he rarely shared when he was in pain, I recognized his ulterior motives. Tonight, though, I'd let him get away with it.

My fingers grazed his skin as I worked the sweats over his muscular ass. I released a breath, grateful to see he wasn't hard. Doctor Sosa had explicitly warned Cristiano about straining himself, but if he got sex on his mind, I wasn't sure he'd heed her warnings.

But the sight of him exposed and in need of my help stirred my desire.

The designation of *husband* had taken on many meanings over the past several weeks. Tormentor. Protector. Teacher. I nearly shivered knowing how it would change again soon. *Lover*. The thought of sex with him had always excited me, even when it scared and shamed me. But as the days passed and Cristiano began to heal, my anticipation to finally submit to his advances grew more urgent.

It couldn't be tonight. He was still far from healed.

But for all the times he'd enjoyed making me squirm, I could finally return the favor.

I held his gaze as I drew my nightgown over my head and dropped it with his pants. His eyes jumped to my breasts. My nipples were still two pebbled points, showing off for him.

I stepped into the shower first and held out my hand to help him.

As he moved under the stream of water, I soaped up a sponge and touched it to his back.

"No wounds back there," he said over his shoulder. "You don't have to be so gentle."

I glided the sponge across the broad expanse, reaching to get his shoulders. I followed a long scar from the right one as it crossed his spine. Other marks on his sides, arms, and back told the story of a violent life.

"This isn't your first brush with a knife," I guessed and ran my thumb over some raised, pink skin under one shoulder blade. "Is this from a bullet?"

"I told you—I've been knocked off my feet before."

I'd read a piece in the newspaper years ago about the infamous, anonymous leader of the Calavera cartel. It'd claimed he'd taken more bullets than drugs in his life. I moved around to Cristiano's front, fascinated by each clue to his past. "What happened?"

"Many things," he said. "I'll tell you one day if you like, but the long scar on my back is the only one with any significance. It started it all—my father's belt."

I froze, raising just my eyes to his. I wished hearing that surprised me more, but it was no secret his father had been abusive. Diego had talked about it now and then, but he'd played it down. Was that because he'd been mostly spared? Had his older brother borne the brunt of it to protect him? Weeks ago, I would've never come to that conclusion, but I was beginning to know Cristiano as that kind of man. One who'd shoulder as much as he could to protect others.

"I hate your father," I said. "And I'm sorry he did that."

"I've come to terms with it, and I've worked through my issues with him," Cristiano said. With effort, he raised a hand and leaned against the tile. "I was rarely surprised by how far he'd go. Diego, on the other hand—I never saw his betrayal coming."

Diego and Cristiano were each other's only remaining immediate family, so back then, of course they'd been close. I could see things more clearly from Cristiano's perspective now, though. Diego had turned on his brother, accusing Cristiano of a brutal crime that could've gotten him killed.

I eyed another bullet wound above his left pec. "You've been through so much I don't even know about."

"It made me who I am," he said. "The rest of these scars, they're barely worth talking about, Natalia, so don't worry about them. The same will be true of my new wounds once they heal. We move forward stronger. *¿Entiendes?*"

"I understand." I moved on to washing his wounds, ensuring they were thoroughly clean—and trying not to fixate on the fact that we were physically very close, and stark naked, and for once, I wasn't scared, anxious, or nervous.

As I silently soaped him, his cock twitched. Once, that would've scared me. Now, it reminded me of our last night together before all of this. Upstairs at his nightclub, *La Madrina*, as I'd advised him to go after what he sought, unaware of the trouble it would bring. And then, as I'd gotten to my knees to comfort him . . .

I turned away as a flush worked its way up my chest and exchanged the sponge for his shampoo. Any movement was an effort for him, but there was no way he'd be able to get his arms above his head. I'd need a damn step stool to even reach his hair, though.

I squirted some shampoo into my palm, went to the opposite end of the shower, and climbed up onto the bench to stand over him. When he just stared at me, I said, "*¿Entonces?* Well?" I raised an eyebrow. "Come here."

I could've sworn he chuckled as he walked toward me. I sank my hands into his hair. There seemed to be even more of it when it was wet—abundantly silky and inky in my hands.

He closed his eyes and dropped his forehead to my stomach as I lathered. He scraped the sensitive spot between my breasts with his stubble, and I bit my lip to keep a moan inside. That would only encourage him, and his control had proven slippery. We had to be good, so I had to be the strong one.

He slid his hands up the outsides of my thighs and rested them on my hips, his fingers splaying over my ass cheeks. "Natalia," he murmured. "*Te extraño.*"

*I miss you*. I was right here, and yet I understood. Between everyone fussing over him the past three days, and Tasha and Alejandro monopolizing his time, plus everything I'd been doing to keep the household running, we hadn't been truly alone since he'd woken up. His drugs knocked him out at night, and I slept on the couch to give him space.

My heart beat in my stomach. Maybe I wasn't only worried about *Cristiano's* control. Stripped bare, with his massive hands on me, and my resistance to him no longer holding me back . . . desire pulled in my depths in a way it hadn't since before he'd left. I'd fought him for so long. I didn't need to anymore. I didn't want to.

When Cristiano had woken up, it had hit me as we'd come face to face—up until that moment, I'd been *terrified* he wouldn't survive. That I'd lost him. That I'd be left on this earth to defend myself against Diego, Belmonte-Ruiz, and even my father. The relief I'd felt had been palpable but equally scary in a different way.

It didn't mean he wasn't still the man who'd forced me into this marriage. Who'd stood over my mother's dead body, and who'd left me, a grieving child, in a dark tunnel for hours. But he'd also once protected my family and had made sure my every need had been met since my arrival here in the Badlands.

On our last call, I'd wanted to ask him to stay but hadn't been able to find the words.

And I'd almost lost him. Time was precious, as he'd said, and it shouldn't be wasted.

Instead of trying to tell him all that, I put my arms around his neck and hugged him to me.

He pressed his lips to my skin, working his mouth up my chest before tilting up his head. "*Por favor,*" he said slowly. "Please—don't deny me anymore."

I could bend and kiss him for the first time since the night he'd left *La Madrina*. And this time, I could admit that I was willing. I wanted that. I wanted him to heal. To have what he needed. That meant I cared. But I had cared for Diego, too. I'd overlooked warning signs and had believed anything he'd said or done. After my horrible judgment, could I trust myself? Could I trust Cristiano?

Suds dripped from his hair into his face, so I reluctantly peeled his arms from around my middle. "You need to rinse."

"You don't know what I need, Natalia."

I sighed as I got down from the bench and led him under the stream of water. He took my face in his hands, staring into my eyes. When I moved closer, his erection pressed against my stomach. I wanted to give in. To soothe him.

Maybe he was right to believe that I was the one thing that could heal him.

"Remember the last time you saw me, before all this?" I asked.

"I was stabbed, not hit over the head." He brushed his thumb over the corner of my mouth. "My memory's as sharp as ever. It was the night I caught you with the cell phone and punished you at the club. Are you still angry with me?"

I shook my head. "That's not the last time you saw me."

"You're right," he said. "You were asleep as I packed a bag."

"I'm not talking about that." I took him in my hand. "I mean when I looked up at you from my knees."

"*Christ*, Natalia." He inhaled a breath, his fingers digging into my cheeks and inspiring a thrill that ended right between my legs. "Be careful talking like that."

Last time, we'd been in the dark. Now, I could see everything. He was nearly as thick as my wrist, even more veiny than his brawny forearm, and his pink velvety skin stretched as he grew against my palm.

His eyes turned anguished as I stroked him, and I'd never had such an urge to chase someone else's demons away.

"We can't kiss—you know where that will lead," I said. "But will this help? You have to promise to stand very still and not strain yourself."

"I could never stay still with your hands on me." Water dripped down the bridge of his nose. He caught my wrist, and I released him as he laced his hand with mine at our sides. "That's not what I need anyway."

"What then?"

He tilted my chin back with his other hand, lowering his face to mine. "Have your feelings changed now that you've almost lost me?"

"Yes." I held his gaze. "But you can't expect our relationship to transform overnight."

"I don't. But if there's anything you want to say, say it now."

As determination entered his voice, a warning alarm sounded in my head. "Why?" I asked, my shoulders tensing.

"I have to go, Natalia." He pressed his lips together. "I can't let Max stay with Belmonte-Ruiz any longer."

*Goddamn it.* Frustration flared in me, and I stepped back to cross my arms. Cristiano had almost been *killed* a few days ago. What would it take to get him to pull back? "I know you can't let them get away with this—it's the nature of this world. But *you* can't go. Make a plan, and send Alejandro and your men after Max."

"I'm the one who put Max in danger." Lines deepened in his forehead with a frown. "I can't send others to do *my* job. I'm done playing games with those *cabrónes* and understand me—I'm going to blow the motherfuckers up."

He couldn't do this. Not now. I was finally letting myself see Cristiano for all he was, and he was going to put himself back in the line of fire. Wasn't this all he'd asked of me the past few weeks—to open myself to the idea of us? To stop fighting him? And now that I was ready, he was going to go back out there when he wasn't even at half capacity and get himself killed? "You're not ready."

"You have to trust me to know what I am and am not capable of."

"You're a fool."

He paused, blinking at me.

Now that I had his attention, I didn't hold back. "You think you're a superhero, but you're not. You're mortal. You can die."

"I never said I couldn't."

"You're acting like it. Physically, you're not even close to healed. If you leave now, you'll come home in a body bag."

"Do you really believe that?" He straightened, bearing down on me. "Or are you provoking me in hopes I'll prove just how capable my body is?"

"You're not ready mentally, either. You've barely given yourself a chance to recover from an attack on your life. You're acting irrationally, from emotion—"

"You don't know me at all if you believe that."

"You don't know *yourself*." I rose to my full height, holding his gaze as it darkened. "You're a man, and you can fall, Cristiano. You have people here depending on you."

"You don't think I know that?" He clenched his jaw and turned his face from me. "It's all I ever think about. All the lives that're endangered when *I'm* in danger. That's why I have to go."

"That's why you *can't* go after Max. In your state, you're more vulnerable than usual, and that puts those around you at risk. Don't be stupid, Cristiano."

He stepped into me. "Brave little girl. You think you can call *me* names?"

"You can try to intimidate me to keep my mouth shut, but when your life is on the line, I won't."

"Why?" he asked.

"You almost *died*."

"I've come closer than that."

I wanted to yell at him to get it into his thick skull that he could be more helpful to Max here than in the field, but that wouldn't get us anywhere. I took a breath and tried to reason with him. He flinched as I placed my palm over his chest wound. "*Escúchame*, Cristiano. Listen to me. You're not weak to rely on your men in a time of need. Can't you see it makes you stronger to know when to stand back and let more capable people help?"

He made a fist. It hurt him that an enemy had succeeded in debilitating him and would keep him from doing everything he could for his comrade.

His hand flexed. Covered mine on his pec. "Every one of your touches comforts me. Heals me. But as you soothe me, the opposite is being done to Max. He's a prisoner, not a guest."

I shut my eyes against the idea, but the image only became clearer in the dark. If Max was still alive, there was no doubt he was being tortured. I tried to fight the vision of him tied up in a dark room, bloody and swollen. "I understand," I said. "I want Max to come home, too. But we need more information. Maybe they took him to bait you."

"Can't bait a dead man."

"Maybe you weren't supposed to die."

After a beat, his eyebrows cinched. "What?"

"I've had a lot of time to think about all of this," I said. "'If you're going to aim, kill.' You taught me that. So why take Max? Why go to the trouble of attacking your home if they'd planned to kill you at the hotel?"

Recognition dawned as Cristiano picked up my line of thinking. "Any message would be pointless if I was dead," he said, his expression easing. "They wanted me to live. And you, too."

"Me?" I shook my head. "My attacker almost choked me to death. He almost slit my throat—"

"Almost," Cristiano said. "He might've had orders to get you out alive. He had a syringe on him."

"*What?*" A hazy memory returned of the man holding up what I'd thought was a blade. "A tranquilizer?"

"You would've been their first target. Why not just shoot you?" He swallowed. "My *worst* fear, as I thought I was dying, was that they'd take you, Natalia."

I refrained from shuddering. This new information changed that night entirely. There'd been more at risk than my life. I could've been in Max's position now, in the grips of a rival cartel with an axe to grind.

I *did* want Max out. Desperately. But Cristiano's life meant more to me, so I spoke to him in a way I knew would get through to him. "Are you going to take me with you to retrieve Max?"

The corners of his mouth drooped. "Why would I?"

"Because you'd be leaving the Badlands unprotected again if you go. You'd be leaving *me* vulnerable. If they want me, they may try again."

Torment marred his features, but it didn't deter me. I needed him to understand what he could lose if he acted recklessly.

"They might be waiting for you to walk—no, *run*—into a trap," I said. "And if they have you, then they have me, too."

He brought my palm to his chest. "I . . . I can't let him sit there and rot, Natalia. And if I can't help him, I've failed him."

I threw my arms around his neck, our wet, naked bodies flush. "*Hay un tiempo señalado para todo*," I whispered, quoting from the bible. "*Un tiempo de matar, y un tiempo de sanar*."

*There's a time for everything. A time to kill, and a time to heal.*

"You didn't make these decisions alone. Max knew what he was getting into," I said. "He can handle it. He would never expect you to save his life at the expense of everyone else's. He's strong."

He shuddered. "What do I do?"

I had one of the most ruthless, foreboding crime lords in my arms, asking for my help. It wasn't the first time. My advice to him in the upstairs bedroom of his nightclub had been wrong. If I hadn't told him to go, maybe he would've stayed and neither of us would've faced death.

Then again, we wouldn't be here now.

He'd returned to me. Not just physically, but emotionally. He came back to me for help.

In the possible event of his death, I'd known I'd have to step up. Why should that change since he'd lived? More than ever, I could be the woman he thought I was. The queen he'd chosen for his bride.

I smoothed my cheek against his bristly chin, while all six-foot-five inches of him stood powerful—and naked. Emboldened by the juxtaposition of his masculinity and vulnerability, I drew back and said, "You make a plan. You assemble a team. But you don't rush. Max is tough and stubborn. He will hold on until your men can get to him."

Cristiano rested his forehead against mine. "We," he said. "We will make a plan. We will assemble a team. *We* will get him out."

I was in it now. I had been for a while. With a few words, Cristiano told me I was no longer here against my will. And I accepted that.

I let Cristiano in. I stepped into the role he'd been pushing me toward. I stood by his side in the ivory tower.

We were Calavera royalty.

# CHAPTER 6

# NATALIA

News of Cristiano's latest brush with death had spread through the Badlands, and in the following week, it became a full-time job receiving well wishes in the forms of home-cooked meals and handmade goods such as pottery, candles, and tequila. It was a celebration of his good fortune rather than what could've been, and I was grateful for the distraction.

But as I came in from the town square one evening, I was reminded that I still had other, more personal matters to deal with. I peeled off gloves dirty with soil from planting trees and left them in the entryway as I followed voices to the dining area.

The last two voices I wanted to hear—Tasha and Cristiano.

Regardless of where in the house Tasha was, she was becoming a more unwelcome presence each day, but more maddening was Cristiano's aversion to rest.

I strode in and found them chatting at the far end of the long table, where nobody ever sat. "Do you have wings now?" I asked, satisfied with how my voice carried and my sandals slapped the tile.

Cristiano stopped mid-sentence to turn his gaze on me. "*¿De qué estás hablando?*"

He wanted to know what I was talking about? *Pfft.* I slapped a cordial smile on my face. "I know you didn't walk downstairs since the doctor explicitly ordered you not to. And the elevator's out of service while it undergoes security upgrades. So did you fly? Or is there a slide from the top floor I'm not aware of?"

"I've been in bed for two fucking weeks," he said.

"It's been eleven days—don't exaggerate."

"Doctor Sosa was just upstairs with us," Tasha said, "and she told us it was fine."

*Us*? I turned my glare on Cristiano. I shouldn't need to forbid him from being alone in our bedroom with a woman who wasn't Jaz or Doctor Sosa, but apparently I did. And to make matters worse, not only had he used the stairs, but he'd gotten dressed—and he looked infuriatingly handsome in a pressed, white dress shirt and charcoal-colored slacks. It was the first time he'd been out of loungewear since he'd been delivered home to me bloody and half-dead. Did he think he was going somewhere?

"Lighten up, Natalia," Tasha added. "Cristiano heals at a superhuman rate."

"No, he doesn't." I walked to stand by his chair. "Because he's *not* superhuman. He's a man, and he was stabbed three times."

"I'm still struggling to understand why you care." Her narrowed eyes stayed trained on me. "What did you call your marriage, Cristiano? An alliance between you and Costa? Nothing more."

I *hated* the idea of Tasha thinking this was all for show. She'd been intimate with Cristiano. She knew what he liked, and—considering they'd been spending time together without me—how to get his ear. Not to mention she was a beautiful woman who likely knew her way around a man as experienced as my husband—where I was still a girl in many ways, especially when it came to sex.

I turned to face Cristiano. "The doctor was here? What'd she say?"

His eyes twinkled. "That I'm cleared for *almost* everything."

A flush made its way up my chest. "I'll have to hear that from her mouth."

"You would've if you'd been by his side," Tasha said behind me. "Where were you?"

*Gardening* suddenly sounded unimpressive, but spending time in the Badlands was much more than that. Without Max, Cristiano, or even Alejandro to talk to, the residents had issues to be resolved, and I heard some of them while helping out around the chapel.

I turned to Tasha. "Handling business. Teresa was showing me some things." I held up my left hand before adding, "She's the goldsmith who made my wedding rings."

Tasha checked her manicure. How it was still perfectly intact after the last couple weeks was beyond me. "*Ten cuidado,* Cristiano. You should be careful," she said. "When a mafioso falls, there are always vultures lying in wait."

Cristiano pushed back from the table, rose, and placed his hands on my shoulders. "Are you suggesting I've fallen?" he asked.

Tasha wet her lips. "You will if you don't take control of this situation. Word is spreading."

She'd indicated something similar before, when she'd first arrived. Before I could ask her to clarify, Alejandro opened the door to the kitchen, holding it for Jaz to pass through.

"How many places should I set for dinner, *señor?*" Jaz asked.

"Set it for five," I answered. "Pilar will be joining us as well. Will you get her, Alejandro?"

"Of course," he said, nearly jogging off in the direction of the library where Pilar had been spending most of her time.

As Jaz distributed silverware and napkins and filled glasses with red wine, Cristiano moved to the head of the table, walking almost as if he was back to normal. That didn't mean he wasn't still in pain, though.

I linked my elbow with his and lowered my voice. "How are you feeling?"

"Better than ever," he said without looking at me.

"Tasha said word is spreading. Does that mean people beyond Belmonte-Ruiz are beginning to learn the truth about the Badlands?"

"We're not discussing this now."

"But—"

"I said *no.*"

Tasha and Jaz quieted, looking at us.

"It's not a topic for dinner." Cristiano grabbed one of the elaborate candelabras from the center of the table and thrust it toward Jaz. "Get rid of this. Nobody can see each other with these *malditas cosas* in the way."

My mouth fell open as he cursed something as stupid as candlesticks. Even though he and I had argued since his return, it was the first time he'd snapped at me. I wasn't even entirely sure what the topic *was*, but it was obviously a sore one.

Pilar's laugh floated in before she did with Alejandro. He'd clearly said something to amuse her, but when her eyes landed on Cristiano, her demeanor shrank.

Cristiano hadn't left our room much since he'd been confined there, which meant . . . this was the first time Pilar had seen him—at least while he was conscious—since our wedding. She wrung her hands in front of her, her nerves palpable, even from across the room. "Wh-where should I sit?"

"Anywhere but in Natalia's seat," Cristiano said, standing behind his chair at the head.

Pilar's eyes darted around. Since we rarely ate at the table, she had no way of knowing whose seat was whose. "Here," I said, holding out a hand for her. I led her to the chair next to mine. "Alejandro, you sit opposite her."

Cristiano pulled out my chair but spoke to Pilar. "I take it you'll be staying with us a while."

Pilar glanced at Alejandro as she tucked a napkin on her lap. "I . . ."

"The fiancé won't be bothering Pilar again," Alejandro replied for her.

"Good," Cristiano said, gesturing for me to sit.

I stayed where I was, feeling suddenly out of the loop. "What are you talking about?"

"Whose fiancé?" Tasha chimed in.

"*Siéntate*." Cristiano ordered me to sit, waiting as beads of sweat formed on his upper lip. Knowing he wouldn't relax until *I* did, I obeyed. He helped scoot me under the table and asked, "What kind of food do you like, Pilar?"

I gave her an encouraging smile.

"Traditional," she said.

"Traditional what?" Cristiano asked, taking his seat at the head. "Traditional Vietnamese? Do you like pho? Indian? Chicken curry?"

"You know what she means," I told Cristiano. What was his problem? Whatever nerve I'd hit earlier, it was obviously still tender. "Most people count their blessings after a near-death experience—you just come out even grumpier."

Pilar shifted her horrified stare to me. In her world, women didn't go around calling dangerous kingpins *grumpy*.

Cristiano paused in the middle of unfurling his napkin into his lap and looked at me. "You haven't seen grumpy yet, *mamacita*."

"She has a point," Alejandro said from across the table. "Maybe it's because you stopped the painkillers."

"When?" I demanded.

Cristiano sat back in his seat, massaging the bridge of his nose with a hefty sigh. "Days ago."

"What's wrong?" I asked. "Is it a headache?"

"It's becoming one, yes," he said.

Pilar giggled, then sucked in a breath when Cristiano looked at her, as if laughter might get her into trouble. She was still scared of him. I didn't blame her—he'd kidnapped both of us—but he wasn't going to hurt her.

Cristiano wasn't going to hurt *me*.

It hit me for the first time—I'd known all along that he wouldn't.

Cristiano would *never* hurt me.

Not back then, as a child, when he'd chilled me to the core with the White Monarch under my chin. Not when he'd had me alone and stripped down in my bathroom at Papá's house, or when I'd been at his mercy in the church. Not when I'd stood before him as his new bride, claimed as his property.

My gut had told me so, but as the full realization passed over me, I peered at him. Perhaps all along, Cristiano had simply been pursuing me at any cost. That didn't make what he'd done okay, but it didn't make him the monster I'd thought he was, either.

As I studied Cristiano, his eyes traveled from Pilar's shoulders, which were practically at her ears, to her hands laced tightly on the table. She wore a long-sleeved dress, but I knew Cristiano was seeing the faded bruises beneath it.

He dropped his hand from his face and gave her a comforting smile. It was clearly forced, but he was making an effort. "I'm sorry I was short with you just now. And I'm sorry about Manu."

She looked down. "It's—I'm fine."

Cristiano had just spent the last several weeks trying to convince me he wasn't a threat—now he'd have to start all over with her.

But then, she lifted her head with a hint of a mischievous smile. "I'm better than Manu at least."

Cristiano released a genuine laugh. "Yesterday went well then?"

"Yesterday?" I asked. "And what's wrong with Manu? If somebody doesn't tell me what happened . . ." I threatened.

Tasha puckered her crimson lips. "Who the hell is Manu?"

"Pilar's ex who got physical with her for the last time," Cristiano explained, then turned to me. "I promised Pilar that she wouldn't be a prisoner here. Yesterday, Alejandro took her home."

I gaped at my friend. How had I missed that? With my time split between caring for Cristiano and handling Badlands business, I hadn't seen much of Pilar lately. She'd only planned to spend a weekend here, for God's sake, and it'd completely slipped my mind to check in with her.

"You went home yesterday?" I asked her.

"*Sí*, and she *chose* to come back," Cristiano said, not bothering to hide his smirk. "Imagine that."

I rolled my eyes. "Let her speak for herself."

He responded with a scolding arch of his eyebrow.

From the short, quick shake of Pilar's head, she didn't *want* to speak, but I urged her on. "You want to stay?"

She nodded slowly, her eyes darting from Alejandro to Cristiano. "On the condition that I can leave anytime I want. I just couldn't see any other way out of my engagement to Manu. I had to tell my parents, though, and pick up some things from home, so Alejandro came with me."

I reached for her hand across the table. "I'm sorry I haven't been here for you."

"You've got plenty to deal with," she said. "I'm settling in now—don't worry about me."

Jaz and the chef came through the kitchen door to deliver salads adorned with peach slices, feta, pecans, and dried cranberries.

Tasha forked a small bite into her mouth and moaned. "*Divine*. Where do you get such perfect peaches?"

Cristiano grinned. "Right here in the Badlands."

"Doesn't Fisker make the best meals?" I asked, smiling at him and then Pilar. She knew food best of all, and I hoped a comfortable subject would help ease the tension in her shoulders. "My husband may not have much going for him, but his food is straight from the ground, and he employs a world-class chef."

Cristiano narrowed his eyes on me. I lifted a corner of my mouth enough to convey I was teasing. He opened his hand on the table to me. It was the perfect chance to show Pilar that I was comfortable around him, so she could be, too.

When I placed my hand in his, he brought it to his lips briefly, then lowered it under the table. "Surely your *husband* has something else going for him," he said.

The sudden masculine power underneath my palm sent memories of our shower together flashing across my mind and a tremor of excitement through my body. Part of it was the anticipation of knowing Cristiano was counting the days until he was healed enough to have me.

"Forgive me for staring at my wife. I so love when she calls me *husband* without sneering." Cristiano moved our hands to my upper leg and leaned over to whisper in my ear. "You want me to stay in bed so I'll heal faster. But remember that the faster I heal, the sooner that tender spot between your legs is mine to devastate."

I released a shaky breath. What once had been a threat was now a delicious promise. Tenderness wouldn't do. Not our first time. And he knew it, biding his time until then, teasing me with his words.

Cristiano didn't wait for my response. As his fingers slipped up my inner thigh, he turned to Alejandro, who was buttering a slice of bread. "How did Manu react?"

Alejo set down his knife. "As you'd expect." He took a bite, chewing as he added, "But I handled it."

"He tried to stand up to Alejandro, but instead, he got knocked on his ass," Pilar said. "It was fun to watch."

I laughed at her uncharacteristically wicked grin, glad to see she was loosening up. After all, who better to take down her greatest threat than the most threatening men she knew? "Alejandro's a good fighter," I said.

"Is he?" Cristiano asked as he slid his hand down my thigh and squeezed my knee in the exact spot that tickled.

I gasped, grabbing his wrist and trying not to laugh. "But Cristiano is better," I added quickly, and his hold on me released.

"Ah, thank you for saying so, *mi amor*." Cristiano winked and turned back to Alejandro. "I assume you did more than knock him down."

Alejo dipped his head marginally. "Not in front of the lady."

"And your parents?" Cristiano asked Pilar.

She nodded. "I said just what Alejandro wanted me to."

My focus faltered with Cristiano's hand still resting on my leg. My mind had begun to register that when it came to sex, Cristiano would always wait for some kind of cue to proceed. With the promise of his fingers so close, my stomach somersaulted.

"What?" I asked, sounding as dazed as I felt. "What did Alejo tell you to say?"

"Alejandro gave me instructions," Pilar offered.

"They came from Cristiano," Alejo said.

Tasha looked back and forth, as if watching a tennis match, and not a very exciting one. Every now and then, she sighed at her plate.

"I told Manu and my parents I wasn't going through with the

marriage," Pilar said, "and that I was coming here to work. For Cristiano. Against my will."

*Against her will.* The lie was for the best. Being here with me was better than the future with Manu she'd been unable to avoid on her own. And it perpetuated the myths surrounding Cristiano and the Badlands. I understood why Cristiano wanted that—but how did he feel that so many people thought he was the same kind of evil he fought against?

Was he able to employ logic to remove his emotion from the situation?

Or did it cut deeply, and he'd gotten good at hiding it?

"I confirmed your marriage was a sham," Pilar continued, glancing from me to Cristiano and back, "and that Cristiano had only done it to forge the alliance with Costa, but that both Natalia and I were unharmed."

Two servers entered and placed steak and baked potatoes in front of us.

"Thank you—for letting me stay," Pilar added, and I could see her trying to be gracious to a man she'd feared for so long. "But my family never let me do anything. Just work in their shop and try to find a husband. I'd like to pull my weight, maybe help around the house, or—"

"We can get you your own place if you like," Cristiano said. "Help you start a business—whatever you want."

"What *do* you want?" I asked her.

She sat back. "*No sé*. I . . . I'm not sure."

That didn't surprise me. I doubted neither her parents nor Manu had ever asked. "You can start over here."

"Can I change my name?" she rushed out.

The four of us just looked at her. It was both a small and enormous request.

One dinner, and Pilar was coming out of her shell. Perhaps she'd believed what I'd been trying to tell her about Cristiano. Or maybe it was Alejandro's presence that comforted her. I was pretty sure they'd been spending some time together—another reason, I suspected, I hadn't seen much of her.

"Well . . . of course," Cristiano answered. "Countless people within these walls have changed their identities."

"Esmeralda," Alejandro said, suddenly laser-focused on cutting his steak. "It's, ah, a good name."

"Yes." I picked up his line of thinking. "For her emerald eyes."

Pilar smiled to herself. "Esmeralda. It's pretty."

"It suits you," I said.

"This is *very* touching," Tasha said, "*pero, por Dios*, is it boring. I don't understand why none of you are discussing what really matters." Her teeth scraped her fork as she took a bite, chewed, and swallowed within seconds. "Almost two weeks have passed, and Max is still missing. You haven't struck back, and it makes you look weak."

"Don't mistake strategy for weakness," I said.

"You've run out of time for strategy. It's time for action," she said, looking from me to Cristiano. "A true crime lord would never let this happen."

"Tasha . . ." Cristiano warned.

"Nobody even knows where Max is," I said. "It's better to strike quietly, when they least expect it, once we're certain of his location."

"That could take months. In fact, you may never know his exact location. And every day that passes, people talk." Tasha dabbed the corners of her mouth with a napkin. "You look even weaker for the fact that the truth is coming out."

Cristiano looked at his plate and didn't deny it.

"Go on," I invited.

"Calavera's ruthless reputation has been enhanced by the mystery shrouding them. But with these attacks, and Cristiano's refusal to arm certain cartels, it's becoming popular gossip that Calavera is working for the wrong side."

"Because he isn't trafficking anyone—he's helping them," I said.

"Right," Tasha said. "How do you think that makes him look? Like a traitor. And not just to Belmonte-Ruiz."

I'd heard it twice from Tasha now. Even Alejandro had seemed to think it was possible. But Cristiano had yet to bring it up to me. "Is this true?" I asked him.

He looked up at me. "Give me a moment with my wife."

Alejandro stood first, picking up his plate. "We'll move to the kitchen."

Pilar followed suit, but Tasha took her time pushing her half-eaten dinner away and rising from her seat. "Ignoring the problem won't make it go away," she said. "And it will get Max killed."

I followed Tasha with my eyes until she'd made her way through the room and disappeared up the staircase.

"Tell me what's going on," I said.

Cristiano sat back in his seat and crossed his arms. I got the sense he hadn't dismissed the others so we could talk candidly. "Don't question me in front of others."

"I didn't."

"Did I not make myself clear earlier?" he asked. "I told you the topic was closed during dinner."

*Ah*. Well. If he didn't want to discuss business, then I didn't mind changing the subject at all. And since he kept insisting he was better, then there was no reason to keep letting him off the hook. I raised my chin. "Then tell me this. Why is Tasha still here? Who is she to you?"

# CHAPTER 7

# NATALIA

Cristiano ate his last bite of steak the way he had all the others—chewing fast and hard before washing it down with a gulp of wine. Injured or not, he held true to his claims that he ate as if someone might take his plate away before he was finished. "*Chin-chin.*" He raised his wineglass. "*Brindis, a mi bella esposa.*"

"Toasting 'your beautiful wife' won't get you out of answering my question," I said. "Why is Tasha still here? And what does it mean that people are learning the truth about your business?"

"Her family has an extensive network here and in Eastern Europe." Sucking his teeth, he set down his glass. "She knows this world well and is good for information, so she's been helping me find things on Belmonte-Ruiz. But ask me to send her away, and I will."

"Send her away."

He paused and tilted his head, clearly unprepared for that answer. "Why?"

How could he even ask? Did he not see the way she looked at him? At me? "She's pressuring you to make rash decisions."

"Nobody pressures me to do anything," he said. "And I'm nothing if not thorough."

"Remember, you were going to charge in guns blazing after Max was taken without even considering it could be a trap. I talked you down. You think you're immune—that you can do no wrong and survive anything."

"This again. I understand your point of view—I have heard it. I have heard Alejandro's." His silverware clattered to his plate. "I've made a decision, and you will stand behind it. Alejandro and his team will leave tomorrow."

"Why? Because Tasha bruised your ego?"

He curled his hand into a fist on the table. "How do you think it looks to have you question me? Argue with me? I told you I didn't want to discuss any of this at the dinner table, yet you and Tasha push me."

"Then let's instead discuss how you told her our marriage means *nothing*—that's none of her business."

"Haven't you discussed our arrangement with Pilar?"

"That's different."

"How?"

"I was confiding in Pilar, not trying to sleep with her."

"Ah." He gripped the arms of his chair and crossed an ankle over one knee, looking amused. "Is that why you think I told Tasha you mean nothing to me?"

"Why else? You were out of town. It would've been the perfect excuse." I shifted in my seat, discomfited over the idea of Cristiano at the political event with another woman on his arm. Especially statuesque, cunning Tasha, a guest in our home. "An arranged, celibate marriage means you wouldn't *technically* be cheating."

"You think Tasha cares if I cheat on my wife? If I wanted to fuck her, I would. Don't I have every right to? My own wife won't even sleep in my bed."

My face warmed at his bluntness. "I've removed any temptation—for your own good."

"We're hardly alone. And when we are, you're always moving around. There are constantly people in my room, and at night, you go to the couch." One eyebrow rose. "Perhaps if you treated me like your husband instead of a pariah, she'd get the message."

"I don't treat you that way." I frowned. "I've been a good wife to you. On one point, I won't back down—your recovery is my priority. I won't allow you to risk your health for Max, or so you can get laid." The hint of a smile on his face only spurred me on. "If that makes me the villain while Tasha treats you like a superhero, then fine. But I want you alive and strong."

He ran one hand down his chin, his eyes unnervingly fixed on me. "Get laid?" He chuckled. "You don't have to sit on my cock to make me feel wanted around here. All I ask is to have you at my dinner table and in my bed."

I inhaled through my nose. It hadn't been my intention to spurn him, only to make things less difficult. As it was, the heat of his stare could conjure all the promises he'd made over the past few weeks—to erase Diego. To show me what it was to have my virginity taken. To wreck me. "I don't . . . I don't trust myself to sleep by your side."

He ran the tip of his tongue over his bottom row of teeth, then wet his lower lip. It glistened in the warm light of the overhead chandelier, full, sexy and tempting. "And why not?"

This went beyond sex, but I hadn't given him much on the emotional front, either. Both topics were scary. I sighed. "When you called me from the political event, I was about to ask you to come home," I said. "I was worried."

"I know," he said. "Had you asked, I would've come running. I'm here now."

"But so is she. I wouldn't have been so daring over the phone if I'd known you were with a woman you've been intimate with. So answer me—did you sleep with her that night, or any time during our marriage?"

"You're jealous." He didn't bother to hide his grin. "My God, it's even more spectacular to witness than I could've ever hoped."

He was enjoying this too much. With a sigh, I started to get up from my seat.

"Tasha's an old friend I met early on in the second part of my life—after I left Costa," he said. "She comes from a very powerful *familia Rusa-Méxicana*."

"I have old friends, too," I said, sitting back down. "If that's your excuse to fool around, I should get the same pass."

He snort-laughed. "Any man who tries with you can't value his own head too much."

When he stood, I looked up at him. "Does that mean I get to decapitate *Natasha*?"

He froze as one corner of his mouth twitched. "During our short marriage, you've accused me of sleeping with Sandra, Jaz, and now Tasha. While I sit here celibate and desperate for release—and no, not the kind of release you've already given me." I moved against the back of my seat as he stepped forward until his feet met the legs of my chair. "Although, I do dream of the moment you'll swallow my cock again."

My cheeks flamed. Well, Cristiano was certainly back to his old self. The vulgar but hot picture he painted made me squirm—and reminded me of what he'd told me about Tasha before all this. "*She* did that for you, too."

"But not like you. Nobody will ever do it for me like you. I don't want to get my dick sucked or handled or anything of the sort." He dragged out my chair, with me in it, and stood over me. "I want. To fuck. My wife."

I was finally ready for it. He wasn't, but by the look in his eyes, I wasn't sure I could stay him any longer. If he was willing to put himself in surgery to have me, he would. I'd tasted the power of unraveling him before, and it was just as sweet now. He only wanted me. At any cost.

"But . . . I can't," Cristiano said finally. "Not how I plan. I don't know what kind of sex Doctor Sosa has, but she'd probably *never* clear me if she had any idea what I've got in store for you."

*Oh, God.* I didn't know what to feel—relief? Disappointment? I wanted him. Having *all* of him, without reservation or an injury to slow him down, scared me. But there'd be no other way with him.

Gripping the edge, he sat back on the table. "You want to know about the women in my life? I'll tell you, and then we're going to drop this bullshit about whether I'd keep a mistress when I have perfection at my fingertips. Understood?"

I chewed the inside of my cheek. Cristiano was a god, and he called *me* perfection? He declared his loyalty to me when I'd fought him tooth and nail up until recently? I agreed more out of curiosity than anything. "Understood."

"Jaz was half-dead when we found her. It has been a long and arduous road to rehabilitate her. It will be a while still before she lets a man touch her, and I'm one of the only people in the world she trusts. Eduardo and Alejo, too. So, no, she's not, and never was, a mistress." He drummed his fingers along the table's wood edge. "She can be scrappy, but when it comes to learning more technical hand-to-hand combat, there are still too many triggers. Sandra, on the other hand, took to it very well. She wants to fight back."

I curled my hands in my lap. I shouldn't have brought Jaz and Sandra into this, but apparently, something about Cristiano with another woman changed the chemistry of my brain—and it had even in the beginning of our marriage. "I'm sorry," I said.

"Sandra—I already told you her aunt sold her into prostitution—she doesn't sleep well, so some nights, we stay up late strategizing how she'll attack the ones who bought her years ago. She's hoping to take down all of them on her own—and then her own family for the way they betrayed her." He cocked his head. "That's why you found her in my office so late at *La Madrina*. We were breaking down her strengths and weaknesses in the fight earlier that night."

I had the infuriating urge to apologize again. It was a strange feeling for me, believing every word Cristiano said. But instinctively, I knew—he wouldn't lie about this. The subject was too raw, and the evidence of his efforts to help was all around me.

He'd only ever shown such undeniable honesty with his kiss and his touch, when we'd each been stripped of anything but primal urges. I had never doubted our chemistry, but I *had* his words. I didn't now.

"None of that changes the fact that you've been intimate with Tasha, and now she's under this roof." I never would've deigned to tell Cristiano how to live before, and even now, I faltered. It was my place, but it would take time to grow into this role. Time, and practice. "I don't care if she saved your life," I said. "It's disrespectful for her to stay."

His eyes scanned my face. "I told her our marriage was simply an arrangement between two families for the same reasons I told Senator Sanchez you're a spoiled brat who doesn't compare to the kind of women I can get."

My face heated. "Then why didn't you steal one of *them*?"

"You know why. Because I wanted *you*." The buzz that came with hearing that never wore off. With Cristiano's knuckles whitening against the table, and his lids lowering, I had to restrain from arching toward him. "Because even though marrying Natasha would've been a better business move," he continued, "it never crossed my mind to marry *anyone* until Diego laid you at my feet. I knew you were bait, and I bit the hook anyway."

Cristiano—hooked. I'd done something no other woman in the world had been able to, and I was sure many had tried. "Why me?" I whispered.

He undid the button at his collar with one hand. "No one else has been able to give me what I want."

"More power?" My eyes dropped to the pulse at the base of his neck, the veins running along the back of his muscular hand. "No," I said, answering my own question. "That's not what you're looking for. There's no lack of powerful families with eligible daughters around here."

"You're not a spoiled brat. Nor did I make our arrangement solely for business reasons. I said those things, and I keep you at arm's length in public, for your protection, Natalia."

He slid one foot forward. His nearness, and his protectiveness, only made me want to be closer to him. I moved my sandal to graze the inner edge of his dress shoe. Making a fist in his lap, he ran the sole up my ankle. I couldn't help my shudder. How could such an innocuous touch send a thrill up the inside of my leg?

"I don't have many attachments." His tone remained firm, but softened at the edges. "My cartel is one, but its people can fend for themselves. As you did when you were forced to. It's why I go overboard with the safety measures. When someone suspects my weaknesses, they attempt to exploit them."

I hadn't forgotten Jaz's words to me—that Cristiano loved me, even if he didn't know it. *Did* he love me? And did he know it now? He'd been ordered to care for my family and me in the past—maybe all this was because he'd never stopped. "*I'm* a weakness of yours."

"Diego knew it before I did."

My heart skipped painfully. Diego had used me; that wasn't news. But Cristiano could easily do the same. I was here because of deals they'd made behind my back—how could I trust Cristiano after all that he'd done, after years of hating him? But the bigger problem was how I could trust myself. I touched my neck. "The last thing I want is to care about someone again—and have him betray me."

"Then hear me." He leaned forward. "I've been trying to tell you this for a while. You are more than a conquest to me. More than an exchange of power. You're Bianca and Costa's daughter." Grabbing the arms of my chair, he dragged it forward until our faces were centimeters apart. "You're the girl I was hired to protect, and would have, if I hadn't been framed for Bianca's murder and forced away. You're my wife." His breath teased my lips, and I resisted from closing the short distance between our mouths. "And if seeing me on my deathbed wasn't reason enough to convince you of that, then I'll have to get creative."

I didn't need more convincing. But his declarations and determination were too good not to indulge. I met his eyes. "Creative how?"

He ran the backs of his knuckles along the length of my throat. With that one touch, my mouth went bone dry, but I got very wet somewhere else—the tender spot Cristiano grew more and more impatient to claim.

"I believe I owe you a debt, Mrs. de la Rosa—and you're about to collect." He took my chin in a gentle touch that contradicted the hardness in his gaze. "You've sworn to be at my dinner table every night." Rising to his full, intimidating height, he looked down on me. "Now I want you *on* it."

# CHAPTER 8

# NATALIA

It was time to collect on a debt Cristiano owed me.

Words I'd never expected to think . . . and especially not in this context.

Dinner was over before it'd begun, and Cristiano stood above me, looking hungrier by the second. "Do I need to repeat myself?" he asked. "I said get on the table so I can make your cunt my next meal."

Butterflies exploded in my stomach. I barely managed to contain my gasp at his vulgarity, but I *couldn't* control the gush of warmth between my legs. "But your wounds—"

"My mouth still works."

I rose from my chair. "The doctor said—"

"Your husband is hungry." With a knuckle under my chin, he raised my face. "I've waited long enough to see how you taste, and you've waited patiently for me to pay my debt. You don't have to tell me you want it—only if you don't." He stepped aside and nodded at the long, sturdy table that seated at least twenty people. "You have until my face is between your legs to object."

Desire coiled in me. At one time, keeping him at arm's length had been the right move, but the best part of resisting him up until now had been giving in. "I can't object once you've started?"

"You can"—he picked me up by my waist and plopped me on the table—"but you won't."

"Maybe I should shower first."

"I'll take you any way, including ripe. *Especially* ripe."

*What?* My mouth fell open. "That doesn't bother you?"

He took my ankle to untie the straps of my leather sandals. "Nah," he said, removing each shoe. "Some other time, I'll make up for it by scrubbing you clean with peppermint soap. Just breathing on your pussy will make it scream."

"Cristiano—"

"Don't pretend you're scandalized." He slid my ass to the edge of the table. "Now, put your feet up and bare yourself to me."

I stared at him for a moment. I *wasn't* pretending. I'd truly never been in the presence of someone like him. The most Diego had ever demanded of me was a kiss. And what had I thought back then? That Diego and I would unleash our passion when the time was right?

It didn't work that way. Heat had been smoldering between Cristiano and me since the start, and each time we struck against each other like flint, we came dangerously close to setting fire to everything around us.

I lay back and lifted my heels to the table. As if he hadn't just affectionately removed my shoes, he tore a hole clean through the crotch of my leggings.

"What—"

"I'll buy you new ones." He kept his eyes on my face as he slid a finger under the fabric of my thong, his knuckle grazing me. Goose bumps exploded over my skin. He snapped the sliver against my clit, and I gasped at the sting. "That's for arguing," he said, "but don't worry—I'm about to make it better."

I bit my bottom lip, not bothering to hide my excitement. "What if someone sees?"

"They won't, I promise you that." He pulled up a chair like he was sitting down to a meal, then spread my legs and pushed his face between them. With the thong between his teeth, he let it snap against me again.

"As much as I enjoy making you squirm," he said, picking up a steak knife, "the underwear has to go."

I inhaled sharply. "What are you doing?"

With the serrated edge, he sliced through the thin strip of fabric. "Unwrapping your candy pussy like I promised so I can lick and suck until I find what I want—your sweet core."

His black eyes bored into mine, beckoning me to the dark side. This was the submission he'd promised I'd enjoy, if only I'd listen to my body and give in. Warmth seeped over me, pulling me under.

Cristiano grew serious. "I understand why your guard is still up, but starting now, it comes down. I want you to think long and hard about the past several weeks, Natalia. To wake up by my side and know without a doubt that I mean it when I say I want you and only you here as my wife. That I've promised to care for you. That I'm trying to protect you and others from things no person should ever witness, much less experience. And in case none of that is a good enough reason for you to accept me once and for all as your husband, then tomorrow morning, you will remember how I ate your pussy so good, you can't imagine a future without sitting on my face whenever you feel like it."

He sank his mouth onto me like I was a juicy steak, obliterating any shock I might've felt over his declarations. Having only ever experienced Diego's gentle tonguing, I wasn't ready for Cristiano's onslaught, the way he gripped my hips and pulled me onto his face so hard I wondered how he could breathe.

Nothing could prepare me for his animal growl vibrating through me.

Or how he thrust his tongue inside me and shredded the last of my willpower to resist him.

My feet jumped to his shoulders. He sucked on my clit. A whimper escaped my open mouth. Pleasure so severe it bordered on painful ripped through me, but it was due to more than a skilled combination of tongue and teeth. It was his voraciousness to devour me that made my spine arch to the point of snapping and my moans echo through the hall.

Consumed, I closed my thighs around his ears, but he pried them right back apart, holding them open. "Don't close your legs again," he said, licking his lips. "I need my hands."

He spread me wider. With the unexpectedness of a long finger inside me, I sucked in a breath. He added another, easing both in as if testing me. He withdrew them, stuck them in his mouth, and grinned wolfishly. "Wanna taste?"

"No," I nearly choked out, horrified at the suggestion.

"More for me."

The faster his fingers slipped in and out, the wetter I got. I hadn't known I could even drip this way. His tongue sucked and explored my clit like it was his new favorite toy, lavishing attention on it until my insides flurried and contracted around his fingers.

*"I understand why your guard is still up, but starting now, it comes down."*

With my surrender, bliss radiated from my core to the tips of my fingers and toes, scorching anything in its path.

He removed his fingers, took a bruising grip on my hips, and burrowed his face between my legs. His tongue invaded like he was mining for gold. His voraciousness brought on my climax, simultaneously spurring it on and easing the raw, agonizing pleasure with groans that vibrated along the waves of my orgasm.

By the end, I was pulling his hair as my thighs quaked. He kissed me gently, his tongue tender on my quivering pussy as he helped me back down to Earth.

He uncurled my hands from his hair and stepped away, taking me in. A satisfied rumble from his chest made me feel as if I'd pleased him.

Even in my haze, I wondered how he seemed as content as I was.

I was almost too shy to look him in the eye. He'd transformed from man to beast, and me?

I'd loved it so much, I'd come as hard as humanly possible.

With a mouth like his, I'd be a fool not to chain myself to him.

If there'd been any question about whether I could learn to follow the devil . . .

I had my answer.

IN OUR BEDROOM, I unbuttoned Cristiano's shirt from my body as he watched from the bed, naked from the waist up. He stuck his arm behind his head. "If you take even one step toward the couch, I will carry you back to this bed—and you wouldn't want to risk me opening my wounds, would you?"

I smirked. Suddenly his condition was a concern of his?

But the truth was, I didn't *want* to sleep apart—I hadn't for a while. I'd chosen the sofa the last week and a half to give him space. Let his body heal. Remove temptation.

And, if I was honest, this part was still new to me in many ways—not just because I'd had only one lover, one time. Cristiano had been right to call me out for having my guard up, but it was more about wading into unfamiliar territory than resistance. About moving past the shame of having fought so hard against him only to give in practically overnight.

"I didn't see you take your antibiotics," I said, holding the dress shirt closed over my naked body.

We'd already undressed his wounds, and now they breathed. I'd gotten used to the sight of them, but my anger still simmered over what they represented. "So give them to me, Nurse Natalia," he said.

I went to the closet to change into a nightgown, discarding his shirt and my destroyed pants in a pile. In the bathroom, I washed my hands for thirty seconds like the doctor had told me to, soaked a gauze pad, and carried his pills, fresh bandages, and antibiotic ointment back to the bed.

"The first night I brought you here," he said as I climbed onto the bed next to him, "I thought you'd instantly see how well we fit together once I got you in my arms. I'd already known from the moment I'd seen you at the costume party that there was an attraction between us. I assumed you'd fight it, resist it, but that once we were alone, you wouldn't have to fear it anymore." His gaze, nearly as potent as his touch, drifted from the hem of my short, slinky slip down my bare legs. “As my wife, you’d have the freedom to give in.”

“You didn’t know me as well as you claimed.”

He shook his head. “I don’t consider myself a naïve man, but when it came to you, I suppose I was.”

He’d never intended to force me. His only mistake had been overestimating his male prowess and underestimating my will to hate him. It made more sense that he’d stormed out of my father’s house after bandaging up my wounds from the warehouse fire. I’d made it clear that morning that I believed he had it in him to rape me. Or how he’d grilled me about whether Diego had been forceful with me by the fountain the night of the costume party.

I sat back on my heels. Ghosting my fingertips around one wound, I asked, “Does it hurt?”

“Much less than it did a moment ago.”

“What was it like?” I asked as I gently touched the wet gauze to his torso. “Were you scared?”

He watched me. “Terrified.”

My eyes jumped to his, surprised by his admission.

“Not for myself,” he added. “For you.”

“Do you regret any of it?”

He paused, digesting the question. “I can’t, Natalia. I never want to put you in danger, but so many lives have been bettered because of everything leading up to the attacks.”

I was glad to hear he’d do it all again. If I hadn’t survived, at least my death would’ve been in the name of something good. “Why?” I asked. “Why is helping these women so important to you?”

“Do I need a reason?”

I smiled sadly as I patted his skin dry. “In this world, yes. Nothing is free. Nobody acts with good intentions.”

After a few silent beats, he reached up and cupped my cheek in his large, warm hand. “You do, don’t you?” His thumb touched the corner of my mouth. “What do you think Bianca would’ve wanted for you?”

How often did anyone bring up my mother to me? Rarely, if ever—as if the topic of her death was off-limits, when really, I relished the chance to talk about her. "I don't know what she'd want for me," I said, "but it wouldn't be to stay in such a dangerous life."

"She was raising a strong woman who wouldn't allow fear or shame to rule her. Bianca would've approved as long as you were honest and unwavering in your choices." He dropped his hand to my thigh and squeezed gently—not playfully this time, or even sexually. Just comforting. "If you truly want out of this life, then go, Natalia. But you'd be running away because wanting it scares you . . . and I think your mother would've made you question that. Confront it. If you want a place by my side, the way she stood by your father, then take it. Own it. Don't feel ashamed that the cartel runs in your blood."

Cartel life was maim, murder, and supplying evil with the means to tempt the good. "It *is* shameful," I said, unscrewing the top of the pill bottle to shake his antibiotics into my palm. "Innocent people pay the price for what we do."

"Was your mother innocent?" he asked. "Was mine? No. But they made no apology for it."

I wished I could believe in my mother's innocence the way I had as a child, but there was no such thing as a bystander in this business. But if my mother had helped Papá make decisions, or even stood by without protest—did that make her as ruthless as him? My father had killed, and so had she. I leaned over to trade the pill bottle for a glass of water on his nightstand. "The women in this world aren't to be underestimated," I said, handing him his meds.

"They're good caretakers, too." He tossed back the antibiotics with a quick sip and set down the glass. "I look forward to the day you finally realize what Diego is, and I pray all your mercy will have been used up by then."

"I already know, Cristiano. He's a coward and a manipulator." Something that resembled pain passed over Cristiano's face—but I hadn't hurt him. His relief had. Perhaps because he wanted so badly to trust that I'd finally come to that conclusion after all his efforts to get me there.

Since Cristiano's return, he'd never wavered in his hatred for his brother. “Diego told me once that you two could never trust each other again,” I said. “And he was right.”

“He blames Costa and me for our family’s demise. And if Diego can’t understand why our father had to die, then I worry what else he can justify.”

“He must’ve aided in the Belmonte-Ruiz attacks,” I said. Up until very recently, I wouldn’t have thought Diego capable of putting me in harm’s way, but I’d had no idea what I was dealing with. He’d already admitted his involvement with Belmonte-Ruiz, but if he’d fed them information, then he’d known I was a target as well as Cristiano.

“It’s . . . it’s my fault,” I said. “I brought the phone into the house.”

“True.” Cristiano rubbed his jaw. “But if that hadn’t worked, they would’ve found another way. Trust me.”

“Then I’m also to blame that the truth about your business is leaking.”

“No, *mi amor*. It was only a matter of time,” he said quietly. “It’s why I’ve formed many powerful partnerships over the years, amassed as much money as possible, and insulated my people. And if I were truly worried, I’d shut down my operation.”

“You’re not going to?” I popped the cap off the ointment and dabbed some on each of his wounds. “Where are the girls you rescued the night I was with you?”

“In a safehouse a few blocks from here. Trained staff helps them work through the stages of recovery. After, we set them up here, or somewhere else if they choose.”

He had an answer for everything. “So, what happens now, Cristiano?”

“I don’t know, but we’re not going to stop. Does that scare you?”

I chewed on my bottom lip. Both Diego and my father had said at different times that I’d be safest with Cristiano. Even California would leave me exposed if someone really wanted to get to me. Cristiano wasn’t trying to hide that I was in danger, and I appreciated that. More, I didn’t have to wonder if I’d risk my safety so Cristiano could help more women, men, and children. “No,” I said. “I’m not scared.”

"I thought by presenting our marriage as no more than a contract, people would be likely to leave you alone. They didn't."

"Maybe you should try the opposite approach," I said.

A corner of his mouth lifted. "Not a bad idea. I said the Badlands were treacherous as well, yet they came for us anyway. So perhaps now I'll make it clear that you belong to me in every sense of the word. And there's no question that the rumors about what I do to those who fuck with my things are true."

The scary way his voice dropped sent a bolt of excitement through me. Cristiano had warned me plenty of times that he was very protective, but it'd never felt truer than in that moment.

I unwrapped a fresh bandage and set my hands in my lap, studying him. "Are you going to tell me why?"

He didn't ask for clarification. He knew what I meant. He'd evaded the question once tonight, but I wasn't going to keep quiet like I had when I'd arrived. His hesitation meant there were reasons behind why he did what he did, and I wanted them. I wanted to know more. To know him.

He scratched under his nose. "I've always had, uh, a physical advantage over most others," he said. "I've used it. And I hope anyone I've killed has deserved it."

"But . . ." I played with the corner of the paper packet. "You deal in weapons, Cristiano. You arm the bad guys and give them an advantage over everyone."

"I'll never be the good guy. I'm sensible. Our country, our people, rely on the production and movement of contraband. Take that away, and we'll fall. That's just how it is."

"In this case, sex is contraband."

"If we fall because I disrupt the sex trade, then we deserve to."

I was equally warmed and horrified by the pride that spread through me. His conviction moved me as I tended to the physical evidence of what had resulted from him advocating for good. Equally scary was how wrong I'd been about him.

"But if it gives you any comfort," he said, "I never armed Belmonte-

Ruiz. And I've stopped selling to anyone who does business with them."

"Tasha and Alejandro told me. That's another reason they're coming after you?"

"*Sí.*" He held out his hand for the last bandage. "*A ver*. Give me that."

"I still need to wrap your chest."

He gestured for me to hand the packet over. When I did, he set it aside and took my forearm, tugging me down to the bed. I let him guide me into the crook of his neck. "When we drove into the Badlands the first time," he said, "what'd you think you'd see?"

I shut my eyes like I had that day, transporting myself back to that moment. "The worst," I admitted. "I thought you were a monster."

With a deep breath, he shifted under me. Whether from physical pain or something else, I wasn't sure. "I am, Natalia. No question there."

I tilted my head to see his face better as I half-whispered, "You're scarier than any monster."

"You remember."

"You said that to me one night after a nightmare, when my mother was still alive. You promised you'd keep the monsters away. But if you're the *good* guy, what does that make everyone else?"

"Not figments of our imaginations, unfortunately. They're bad. So I have to be worse. I've made peace with it, but that doesn't mean I can't also stand for something."

I scooted over on the bed, getting even closer to him. He'd talked of owning my wants and needs. I *wanted* to know him better. I *needed* to know why—why I sat beside him now, why he felt compelled to help, how he'd gotten to this place.

"Is there really no reason you do all this?" I asked.

"Nobody should need a reason to help those people," he said and paused.

"But you have one," I guessed. I slipped my hand into his. He tensed under me but then relaxed. Offering him comfort was new for us.

Or maybe I was the one who needed it.

Getting to know the innerworkings of Cristiano's mind, heart, and soul wasn't a task for the faint-hearted. Wondering what I'd find scared me—but not enough to pull back. Not physically, and not from whatever new emotional territory we were wading into.

"Tell me what happened," I said.

## CHAPTER 9

# NATALIA

With each inhalation, Cristiano's massive chest expanded underneath my cheek, but his arm remained firmly around me. Silence permeated our bedroom. Secured in the crook of his arm, it would've been easy to change the subject back to something safer. Why rock the boat with questions about his past, now that we'd set sail on smoother waters?

But he'd always encouraged me to ask questions, to look closer, to live this life with wide-open eyes—and he hadn't shielded me from the ugly sides of it. So, the longer he remained quiet, the more anxious I became. If Cristiano struggled over opening up about his past, I suspected that meant it was deeply painful for him. Could I be the comfort he needed? Had I made him feel safe?

Was that even possible when I'd only just begun to concern myself with his safety and comfort?

Maybe that was his hesitation. To open up about what haunted him, he'd have to take a leap of faith.

After a while had passed, he shifted. I placed my hand on his chest and raised my eyes to his. He nodded toward the bedroom door. "Growing up, our household had staff, like yours. Like mine does now."

"It's not unusual."

"My dad had groomed me my whole life to help with, and eventually take over, his business. Diego, too, but he was much younger. I was significantly more involved. My father had a warehouse near the border of Juárez and El Paso. He had to hide it from your father and the other families around here. There, my parents trained and housed mules, prostitutes, and slaves. I visited several times before their deaths, and I saw the innerworkings of the sex trade."

"How old were you?"

"Thirteen when it started." He closed his fingers around my hand on his chest, veins protruding from his forearm. "I watched him quietly build that business. Anytime I tried to speak up, he'd beat me. After a growth spurt, I tried to physically interfere with a deal. The next day was the first time he brought Diego to the warehouse. He was only eight."

Cristiano's punishment had been Diego's introduction to the darker side of that life. His father must've known how that would affect Cristiano. I flipped my palm over to squeeze his hand. "I'm sorry."

His dark eyes drifted up to the ceiling. "He tried to get me to see people as commodities. No different than weapons or drugs to be moved across borders for a profit. Same with my mom. They didn't see faces, just dollar signs. And control. Maybe I would've, too, if not for . . . for Angelina."

Just hearing a woman's name, especially since Cristiano struggled to get it out, put my nerves on edge. She had to be the reason. "Who's Angelina?"

He slid his hand up my back, pulling me closer by my shoulders. "It's weird to say her name aloud after this long. She was the daughter of the head of our household staff. I had no time for girls, but she worked around the house a lot and was the kind of beautiful everyone noticed. I had a harmless crush—at least, it was harmless until my father noticed it."

His hand became clammy in mine—or maybe I was the one sweating. I didn't want to ask, afraid I already knew the answer, but I had to. "What happened to her?"

"The last time I stood up to my dad, he didn't beat me, and he didn't involve Diego."

"He beat her?" I guessed.

"I wish he had." The haunted look in his eyes turned the pit in my stomach into a sinking rock of pure dread. "I wish he'd just fucking killed her."

The back of my neck bristled. To hear Cristiano, champion of innocent women, admit *that* of all things . . . it said everything. "How come?"

"He sold her to a Ukrainian man for a couple hundred dollars. I was in the room. My father had me restrained as the man beat her, raped her, then took her. And then my father gave me the money."

I covered my mouth with both hands as bile rose in my throat. I'd heard his parents were malicious from my father, Diego, Cristiano, and others—it was common knowledge, really. But it'd mostly been in the context of their business and plans to overthrow my family.

This, though?

It was a whole new level of evil. Just hearing the horrific words brought tears to my eyes. "I had no idea. I . . ." My chin trembled. "I'm so sorry, Cristiano. Diego never said anything."

"He was young. I used to talk about it with him, so he knows—but he only witnessed the tip of the iceberg in person."

Cristiano pinched the inside corners of his eyes and breathed through whatever was working its way through him.

I brought his palm to my heart. "You don't have to be strong," I said. "You're strong for everyone, all the time, but you don't have to be that way with me."

"I was forced to be," he said. "Our father wanted to make damn sure I understood that there was *no* room for attachments in this world."

"What did you do?" I asked.

"I knew my father wouldn't stop at that. Diego was getting older, and he'd start seeing more. I wanted to protect him from our parents, but also . . . I couldn't live in a world where I knew that was happening. I had to get us out or stop them—and there was no getting out."

I clenched my jaw to stem another wave of tears that heated the backs of my eyes. It broke my heart, after all the strife between the brothers, to hear that Cristiano had once wanted to shield Diego so badly, he'd put himself in harm's way. And that Diego didn't know it, or even the extent of his father's business . . .

"As you know," Cristiano continued, "your father, mine, and some of the other cartels in the area had formed a pact against human trafficking. So my parents would have to take them out in order to expand their business."

"That's why you chose my father to ask for help."

"At that point, I was barely fifteen and had no resources. I used the money from Angelina's buyer to get a gun and transportation to your house. I'd known Costa to be fair, and your grandfather to be ruthless—the right combination for what I needed." Resolve entered his voice as his shoulders drew back. "I figured as soon as they heard what my parents were doing, and that they were planning to overthrow the other cartels to get away with it, they'd be my best shot at stopping them. And I was right—you know the rest."

My heart raced. If there was no more to the story, then it didn't have a happy ending. "But what happened to Angelina?"

He finally lowered his anguish-filled eyes to mine and shook his head.

"You don't know?" I asked.

"I never found her. I've tried. I started in Ukraine and Russia. That's where I met Tasha's grandfather, whose family had built a strong network in both México and Russia over many generations. But even with their help, it'd been eight years since she'd been taken. It was like looking for a needle in a haystack. But it led me to other men and women that society had cast aside and left to fend for themselves. From Eastern Europe, we went on to see more of the world." He took a breath and resolution firmed his jaw. "I'm certain Angelina's dead by now. I hope she is. Some nights I lie awake thinking of everything she endured—all because of me."

"Oh, no. No, no, no." I got up on an elbow and took his chin to force him to look at me—something I'd learned from him. "It was *not* your fault, Cristiano."

"I've done a lot of work to overcome my past with my parents. They have no control over me anymore. But Angelina . . . I cared about her, and that ruined her life." He took my wrist, running my palm along his stubble before he kissed the inside of my hand. "You can see how that has affected me. Why I keep you a secret from the rest of the world."

"Because you . . . care about me."

He frowned. "I've always cared about you, Natalia. Always." He tucked some of my hair behind my ear as I looked down at him. "In a twisted way, every time I've scared you, hurt you, pushed you away—it was to ultimately protect you."

I had the overwhelming urge to lean in and kiss him. To kiss *Cristiano*—willingly. To chase away the sadness in his eyes. But then, they grew distant.

"But there's no guarantee I *can*," he said. "That's why you need to learn to fight for yourself. I couldn't protect Angelina, and I failed your mother—I can't fail you."

"Both situations were outside your control." The last eleven years, he'd been accused of the crimes of his father. Acknowledging that meant admitting I'd been wrong about everything—including my mother's murder. "You really didn't kill her, did you?" I asked through a rasp in my throat.

"No."

I opened my mouth to form some kind of response, but what could I possibly say? I couldn't give him back the years he'd lost. The life he'd known. The family stolen from him. And I'd played a part in it.

"You never had enough evidence—or reason—to believe otherwise," he said, reading my mind.

Moving forward, knowing all I did now, I could help him rebuild. I sat up, swallowing over and over. "We're going to fix you up," I said quietly. Carefully, I taped the last bandage over the gash nearest his heart. "We're going to fix this."

"I don't need fixing, Natalia. With you on my side, I'm a force to be reckoned with."

I shook my head and pressed the tape down, sealing the bandage. "Sit up."

He pushed off the mattress and into a sitting position. I picked up a roll of elastic wrap and moved forward until we were face to face. He stretched his arms as I reached both of mine around his middle to bind him.

As his breath warmed my cheek, I raised my eyes to his full bottom lip and then higher. I wasn't sure what I expected to find in his eyes—sadness, regret, pain. But he seemed perfectly content just to watch me work.

"Do you still look for her?" I asked.

His Adam's apple bobbed. "It's been almost twenty years, Natalia. Maybe I could've saved her back then if I'd had the resources I do now." He spoke quietly, inches from my face. "I'm using what I learned back then to help others. But no, I don't look for her anymore."

I snapped the clips on the bandage tape closed, securing it as my soul wept. That door would never be closed. He'd always wonder what had happened. His parents would forever have that hold on him from their graves. "Are you afraid to love anyone again?"

His expression fell as if I'd sucker punched him. After a moment, he lowered his arms, took my biceps in a firm but gentle grip, and looked me in the eye. "I didn't love her—it was a boyhood crush, but that doesn't lessen the devastation of what happened to her." He paused as if choosing his words carefully. "If it'd been you, I would damn well still be looking."

Was he trying to tell me something? Was it possible that in the last several weeks of darkness, love had bloomed?

"It wouldn't have been me," I said. "Your parents would've murdered my entire family . . . if you hadn't stopped them."

"Then I've done at least one thing right in my life."

"And . . . what about now?" I asked through the lump forming in my throat.

"If someone took you now? They'd better kill me in the process, because I'd never stop until I found you. There'd be nothing left of this earth. And then, I'd keep going in the afterlife."

"Where would you look first?" I asked. "Heaven or Hell?"

"Heaven," he said immediately. "If you stay here by my side, though, that will change. There's only the underworld for people like us. But down here, we don't burn. We rule."

Physically, it would take almost nothing to lean in and kiss him, but it would cost me in other ways. I'd consent to my downfall. To descend with him. To bleed for him as he'd promised I would.

He cupped the back of my head and pressed his lips to my forehead. "I'm not scared to fall in love," he said against my skin. "If anything, I'm scared not to. Your parents set high standards for what a true partnership looks like, but I don't back down from a challenge."

All bandaged up, but not yet healed, he lay back against the pillow and let his eyelids fall shut.

It wasn't the first time Cristiano had referenced my parents' marriage and their love for each other. It was the *everything* he'd been seeking. It had to be. That would answer many of the questions that had surrounded him from the start.

I let my eyes drift over my strong, menacing, yet achingly vulnerable husband. He was right. With me by his side, we'd be a force to be reckoned with.

*We?*

Weeks ago, it might've surprised me that I'd want that, but I didn't think it would've ever truly shocked me. It was why I'd fought all of this so hard.

It felt entirely and alarmingly natural to stay, put on my crown, and descend deeper into the darkness with Cristiano.

But that didn't mean I had any idea what I'd find once everything went black.

# CHAPTER 10

# NATALIA

Flat on my back on the front lawn, I struggled to breathe under Cristiano's considerable weight and brawn. He pinned my wrists over my head in the grass, and with speed a man of his size shouldn't possess, he maneuvered his hips between my legs, wedged his thighs beneath mine, and spread them.

"You're helpless against me, Mrs. de la Rosa," he said with an infuriatingly smug smirk.

I bucked my hips as hard as I could, knowing it would do no good.

"Third time this morning—and *I'm* injured. Have the last several weeks of training been for nothing?"

Between my shorts and his joggers, only thin fabric separated us. "I fought off a real attacker. It's just *you* who's too strong for me."

"What have I told you? A limited mindset will always be your greatest liability." He bent until his face hovered over mine, and his eyes dropped to my mouth. "Once you defeat me, then you'll know you can take on anyone."

I licked my lips to see if I could keep his gaze there. "Cristiano?"

"Hmm?"

The thing about lightweight workout gear designed to fit like a second skin was that it didn't leave much to the imagination. Cristiano had too much happening down south to hide anything. Even when he wasn't hard, I could feel him between my legs, but now, something stirred. "I think you're the one with the wrong . . . mindset."

"Yeah?" he asked.

I shifted my hips, teasing him with a warm home for the thick, ridged monster rising between us. Reminding him that with the baggy openings of my running shorts, he could unfasten, tug, shift, and be inside me in seconds.

His grip loosened as he inhaled. "*Yeah,*" I said.

Flattening my foot against his thigh and using the advice he constantly repeated to me, I put my weight behind my shoulder, pushed off his leg, and rolled out from under him.

"*Oof.*" He flopped onto his back, clutching his abdomen.

I jumped up to straddle him, careful not to sit near his wounds. "Sorry, but I win," I said, smiling down at him. "Did I hurt you?"

"Nothing a few new stitches won't fix."

As I leaned forward, my ponytail hung over my shoulder, the ends brushing his chest. "You left yourself open."

"I did." He seized my biceps, yanking me down until our bodies were flush—and I was back under his control. "But, no, you didn't win. The fight is never over."

His heart pounded against my breasts—or maybe it was mine. Either way, our breath mingled, and our eyes searched each other's faces. In the weeks since we'd kissed, the electricity between us hadn't dimmed. Just the opposite—it'd become even more charged. At one time it'd been exactly what I'd been worried would happen—that a kiss would be powerful enough to make me forget why I hated him.

But I'd already forgotten. Or maybe he'd given me enough reasons to change my *mindset.*

Not for the first time since he'd opened up to me about his past, I didn't just *want* to kiss him. I craved it.

The need in his eyes had been growing even stronger since he'd begun to fully heal, and it betrayed his powerlessness. I could've asked for anything in that moment. Or, I could be the one to initiate, sliding up the hard length of his shaft, controlling my tempo, his orgasm, and mine . . .

I'd been sleeping by his side as I had the first weeks I'd arrived—only now, he'd pull me into his embrace each night, mouth in my hair, my hips nestled into his, our bodies learning how to share a bed. How to have restraint.

He'd woken up this morning ready to spar. And if he could wrestle me to the ground, then I knew what was next. It'd been coming a long time. He'd been waiting even longer. His unwilling bride would ask for it, and he would answer tenfold. With the ache growing stronger between my legs each day, maybe I'd even beg. He'd warned me I would.

"I see you're fully recovered, sir," Alejandro called cheerfully from somewhere far too near.

I shot into a sitting position so quickly, I almost tumbled back into the grass.

Alejo sauntered toward us, not bothering to hide his grin.

Cristiano fixed my shorts and patted my hips to get me to climb off him. "What are you doing back? You're supposed to be in the south."

After our meal with Alejandro, Pilar, and Tasha—which had turned into dinner for one when Cristiano had decided to *eat out* instead—Alejandro had assembled a team and taken them on an attempt to recover Max . . . against my advice. They'd loaded Tasha in a car to return her to wherever she'd come from, and according to Cristiano, they hadn't had much to report since.

In this case, I worried no news wasn't good news. But by the spring in Alejandro's step, it looked as if I was wrong.

"Did you locate Max?" I asked as I stood, brushing grass off my legs.

"Afraid not. Believe me, Cristiano will be the first to know when we do."

When Cristiano moved me in front of him, I didn't have to ask why—the reason pressed into my backside. "You have that look," Cristiano said.

"Which one?" Alejandro asked.

Like a cat who'd caught the canary. I noticed it, too. "You know something," I said.

"I know two things. First, Max's trail went cold again, but we're extremely close to securing a rat within Belmonte-Ruiz."

"Someone's willing to help?" I asked.

"Willing? No. But he agreed when I presented him with an alternative that didn't end well for his family in the States. Now, we put on the pressure until he caves, then wait for the right time to pounce."

"Then why aren't you closing the deal?" Cristiano asked.

"I don't need to be there for that." He widened his stance and crossed his fists under his arms. "I wanted to deliver this next part in person—we were successful in a *different* mission." He winked, and, in a very odd turn of events, he hooted. Like an *owl*.

Cristiano's hands tightened on my shoulders. "*¿El Búho?*"

"*Sí, patrón*. When we took Tasha back to the city, we got more information from her family. Since we've been waiting around a lot while trying to track down Max, we decided to put that intel to good use."

"Fuck," Cristiano said, but there was no anger behind his curse. If anything, he sounded pleased. "You know where the Valverdes are, don't you?"

"The Valverdes?" I asked, the *apellido* a faint echo in the back of my mind. "Why do I know that name?"

Alejandro nodded, and if he'd looked smug earlier, now he looked downright prideful. "They're closer than you think, boss."

"Not in the south?"

"Not anymore."

Cristiano stiffened behind me. "Don't fuck with me, Alejandro."

I glanced back, twisting to look up at Cristiano. "Are they what you left to find?"

"*Sí, mi corazón*," he said, but his attention stayed on Alejandro. "Where are they?"

Alejandro tipped his chin forward. "Downstairs."

I touched the neckline of my tank top. *Downstairs?* The only downstairs I'd seen was the panic room and storage space, and at the opposite end of the house, the subterranean dining room where the party had been held my first night. "Are they eating?" I asked.

Cristiano laughed, and Alejandro joined in before responding, "No. They may not even have a meal left."

Cristiano's chest pressed against my back. "How'd you pull this off?"

"You've had some bad luck, and it has distracted you," Alejandro said. "We thought you needed a win after the past few weeks."

Cristiano slid his hands to rest in the curves of my neck, his fingers stretching over my collarbone. "How many?"

"Four. Once we located the head, the others weren't far behind."

"*Four*?" he asked and released a string of awed curses. "I hoped for one at best."

"One person?" I asked.

"We'll resume our lesson later." Cristiano pressed a kiss to the back of my head and moved his mouth to my ear. "Don't count on me forgetting the position you got me in."

Every day brought more questions, but I was lucky to make it through with even one answer. Who were these people Cristiano had seemingly chased to the ends of the Earth? And what did that family have to do with mine?

"Wait." I turned to face him, grabbing the front of his t-shirt before he could walk away.

He arched an eyebrow at my fist in his shirt, then raised his eyes to me. "Yes?"

"Who are the Valverdes? Why do you need them?"

"I'll tell you everything, but not now." He wiped sweat from his lip and glanced over his shoulder. "First, I need to see what we're dealing with."

I released his shirt and let him walk away. Even though I believed he'd fill me in later, it was still a *no* that transported me back to my first days in the Badlands. I didn't want to return to the moments when my imagination had been left to its own devices, spinning out of control, conjuring up terrible—and ultimately false—theories.

"You said you wanted . . . that we'd do this together," I called after him. "Like my parents."

Cristiano stopped where he was, then turned back. "We *will* do it together."

The drop in his voice registered deep in my stomach, a threat. "Then why can't I come with you?"

"Now?"

"Yes. Now. Show me what's downstairs."

He strolled back to me, his eyes roaming from my ankles to my eyes. "You haven't got the first clue what you're asking to be a part of."

"So tell me."

He massaged his chest. Fisker said Cristiano sometimes got heartburn. He liked his liquor, cigars and cigarettes, and red meat—the constant stress didn't help. I made a mental note to request something light for dinner.

"The Valverdes were around when you were a child," Cristiano said. "Rivals of your father's."

"Some of the old guard, then," I said. Many of my father's original associates had been murdered or demoted, their cartels dissolved, overthrown, or eliminated. My father had mainly survived due to his shift from narcotics into his safer business around shipping logistics.

"Something like that." Cristiano rubbed his temples. "It could be dangerous down there. I'll assess the situation and come upstairs when I know more."

"So you get to pick and choose what I see? How is that a partnership?"

"Partnership? *Mmm*." He wet his lips, giving me a onceover. "I have to say, I like to hear you own it, my love. I like it very much."

A pleasant warmth traveled up my chest. I hadn't even realized that's what I was doing. The word had just come out. But that's what was developing between us. Cristiano had sought me out to be his queen, and every day, it became truer.

Because what life was there for me now that I'd seen all that I had here?

Now that I'd known a man like Cristiano?

California hadn't been home. It'd been a place to escape my fears and responsibilities. And I didn't want that anymore, which was good —because I'd never be able to go back to that.

Choosing this life left no room for hesitation. Either I was in or out, and Cristiano had to know my decision. "I heard what you said the other night about Mamá wanting me to live honestly," I said. "I don't want to be a victim of my fear. I don't want to be a bystander in my life. I choose this. Whatever's in there, I can handle it."

"I know you *can*, but certain things, you can't come back from."

He warned me with haunting words, but I couldn't ignore the one truth that had persisted since I'd stepped foot in the church over a month ago. "I can't go back anyway, can I?"

Alejandro whistled for Cristiano.

Cristiano retreated. "Wait upstairs. I'll come soon."

With him, *soon* could've meant minutes or hours.

He turned and strode around the side of the house where the mountainside had the thickest vegetation. I hadn't explored much in that area. I hadn't thought there was anything there but overgrown trees. Now I wondered how it could possibly have a "downstairs."

I returned to our bedroom, turned on the shower, and started to remove my racerback tank when I caught sight of the new definition in my shoulders and biceps. My body was changing. Strengthening. Just like my emotional and mental state.

I left my top on and leaned over the sink to look in the mirror. My first night here, I'd found myself in the ground floor bathroom staring at the reflection of a terrified, angry, and exhausted girl who thought she was headed upstairs to be proverbially torn limb from limb by her greatest enemy.

How much had changed since then. I'd been willfully naïve. Scared to learn truths I'd assumed would be ugly. The result of a lifetime of being coddled by Papá and Diego.

Would I trade the darkness of Cristiano's world to go back to living blindly if I could?

It didn't matter. I couldn't. At least it was honest here.

Steam curled over the shower door. My ponytail had come loose during our sparring and hung over my shoulder. Scars began to take form, a tiny one on my cheek, and a slash under my chin. My cheeks flushed from my morning workout and the running hot water. My eyes had seen things I couldn't forget.

*"Certain things, you can't come back from."*

What things? I'd already watched Cristiano slit the throats of the men who'd tried to kidnap Sandra. I'd seen the faces of the lost, but not forgotten, taped to a whiteboard, probably no longer waiting for saviors like Calavera. I'd fought off my own attacker. But there was a more horrific side to what Cristiano did. *El Polvo* pouring sand down the throats of his worst enemies. I'd heard of a slow death, but had not witnessed the intricacies and unspoken truths of what it really meant.

Was that what was happening downstairs? A slow death for my father's rivals? An enemy so old and obscure I barely remembered their name? Before the assaults, Cristiano had gone in search of a key to unlock *everything* he wanted. I'd been learning that his unmet need was me. Us. Our partnership. Our marriage. So why had an old guard family stood between Cristiano and me?

My pulse quickened as the puzzle pieces formed a bigger picture. He'd said it had to do with closure. Jaz had said it was proof. And as with everything here, revenge played a part—Cristiano had admitted that our last night alone before he'd left town.

Revenge in my name. In my father's name. Closure for us. Proof. I curled my fists against the counter as the answer formed in my mind.

Papá had told me the morning after the costume party that my mother's *sicario* had been hired by a rival cartel that was no longer in existence.

But maybe they were. And maybe they were *here*.

## CHAPTER 11

# NATALIA

I'd waited almost twelve years for answers about my mother's death, and now, the people responsible were here. Close by. Somewhere under my feet.

Cristiano had asked me to hold on a little longer, but I squirmed at just the *thought* of more puzzle pieces waiting in some cryptic place Alejandro had called "downstairs."

I pushed away from the bathroom counter, turned off the shower, and went to my closet. After zipping a hoodie over my tank top, I tightened my ponytail and headed to the ground floor and around the side of the house where Cristiano had disappeared.

What was I doing? What was I asking for by opening this door that had been locked to me for so long? What if I couldn't handle it?

Cristiano had said I could. But if what I suspected was true, this family was responsible for more than my mother's death. They'd take the blame for the eleven years Cristiano had been on the run. For his poverty and struggle, and the irreparable rift between him and his brother. For bearing the hatred of his mentor and future wife for so long.

And for all of that, they would pay.

Cristiano had exacted torturous death on many an enemy, and there might be no greater foe than the Valverde family.

The farther I walked from the house, the more wooded it became. Dirt began to soften as twigs crunched under my sneakers. Leafy tree tops blocked out the sky. Wings flapped as birds whistled. *Ah, nature—*

With the metal *click* of a gun, I froze.

"*Alto*." Stop.

I looked around for the male voice but saw nothing—until a nearly completely camouflaged Eduardo stepped out from between some trees. "Natalia?"

My shoulders loosened. "*¿Dónde está Cristiano*?" I asked.

If Eduardo knew where Cristiano was, he didn't answer.

"Get him for me," I said with a sigh. "Now—it's urgent."

Eduardo removed the handheld radio attached to his bulletproof vest. "*Jefe*," he said into it. "Natalia's here."

Cristiano responded right away. "Bring her down."

Eduardo led me a few meters through the trees. When we reached the mountainside, he pulled on a rock that wasn't a rock, but a steel cover disguising a keypad. He pressed his thumb to a fingerprint scanner, and part of the mountain in front of us slid open like the entrance to a vault.

*Dios santo*. The door *was* the mountain. I never would've found this on my own.

Eduardo went first, disappearing down a dark stairwell.

My feet wouldn't move, though. Since childhood, I tried not to willingly go down into dark spaces. With the smell of soil, this particular staircase reminded me of the tunnel Cristiano had taken me into.

Unlike that one, though, he wasn't going to leave me down there.

I forced myself to take the first step, then the next, until I stood at the bottom of a stone staircase and before another secure door. Eduardo entered his credentials, and once it opened, he breezed right in without a second thought.

My only company was the sound of my heartbeat. I got the feeling once I stepped inside, I'd come out slightly changed. But I'd learned more during my metamorphosis since I'd arrived than I had years at university, and I took comfort that it was turning out to be for the best—even when it didn't always feel that way.

This was the underbelly of an already gruesome world. I'd spent years running from it, trying to pretend it didn't exist, and distancing myself from my childhood. Yet I was walking into it with eyes wide open now.

It would show Cristiano—and myself—that I was choosing this life. Choosing him. All of him.

And I deserved answers. I deserved the chance to look my mother's murderers in the eyes.

"It's not too late to turn around." Cristiano materialized in the darkness, shadows turning his eyes into sockets.

Awe, and a hint of fear, mingled within me as I stepped into a cool, dimly lit steel room. Little green, yellow, and red lights flashed with the hum of machinery. Not appliances, I realized as my eyes adjusted. Computers and monitors. Combined with the glass cases of books and folders lining the walls, the space looked like a high tech museum.

And nothing like a place to keep prisoners—but how deep did it run?

I walked farther into the temperature-controlled room. Eduardo had vanished. "Is this where you store the body parts?" I asked.

"Huh?"

I turned to Cristiano. "Legend has it you keep something from every person you kill and put it on display."

"*Ay. Señor, dame paciencia.*" He ran his hands over his face as he asked God for patience, then laughed. "Another rumor. What kind of unhinged *cabrón* do you take me for, Natalia? I'm no saint, but I don't keep a souvenir from every kill. For one, I'd need a bigger building."

Cristiano smirked, amused by his signature sick humor. In any other scenario, I'd have laughed. The rumor *was* ridiculous to the point of being comical, and of course I'd stopped believing most of what I'd heard about him a while ago. But in that moment, I couldn't get past my nerves.

"Although, I suppose, in a way, these are proverbial bodies," Cristiano added.

"I don't know what that means."

"They're files and records on every operation. Sometimes we have to act fast and on little intel, but we try to be as prepared and organized as possible." He glanced around. "There's a tunnel that connects to the house, but otherwise, this area is isolated for security purposes, and so we can work in peace. We don't want to . . . disturb anyone."

"Disturb them how?"

He cleared his throat, checked his phone, and replaced it in the pocket of his joggers. "I told you to stay upstairs. Haven't you ever heard that expression, curiosity killed the cat?"

Or, *your curiosity is an affliction*, as my father had said to me many times. This ran deeper than snooping, though.

I had to tell Cristiano I knew. I knew what he was keeping down here. And that I was ready to get my answers, no matter how it would change my life. That was why I'd rushed down here.

Now that I was on the verge, though, the cliff under my feet crumbled more with each step. And since I couldn't see the bottom, I had to assume it was a far drop. In my experience, answers only bred more questions. Retaliation only incited more wars, more death, more revenge. And as Cristiano said—some things, I couldn't unsee.

I swallowed through my dry throat and walked over to a large control panel below a bank of computer screens. Beyond it, a glass window showed a room full of servers. "Is this the security system?"

"One of them, but it's much more than that. Intelligence on organized crime syndicates around the world, everything from narcotics, artillery, black market, prostitution, slavery, money laundering, etcetera." He stepped away, under the dim lights. "We manage data big and small, analyze it for patterns and trends, hoping to tie pieces together, such as how people move, where they start and end up, which mobs are communicating, interactions that seem off. That's just the tip of the iceberg in terms of what's happening out there."

I couldn't keep the awe from my voice. "I had no idea so much went into it."

"Takes a lot of power to reach dark corners. I . . . I don't want to hide these things from you." He pulled on his jaw, something warring in him. He didn't want to keep me out. But he probably struggled with bringing me in, too. "But some of these subjects are closed. *¿Comprendes?*"

Yes, I understood. I recognized resolution in him now. And melancholy. I didn't argue. Things that upset someone like him must scrape the bottom of humanity. I was likely better off not knowing.

My eyes scanned over the shelved and alphabetized binders. Some had people's names, others listed businesses, cartels, or just initials and dates. "Why isn't all of this digitized?"

"Everything is encrypted, but sometimes, nothing is safer than paper. I assure you, the government has its own hackers, and many officials would like to put a stop to what we're doing."

I frowned. "Helping people?"

"We have all kinds of unlawful ventures, Natalia. They're how we fund our more benevolent ones. Arms trafficking has been very good to me, and I need that income to continue." He massaged the back of his neck. "We have a role. We're the bad guys; the government is the good guy. They don't like when we upset the balance. We're not supposed to do their jobs for them."

"They don't want the press finding out," I inferred. "It would make them a laughing stock."

"The press or other world leaders. Wealthy people, too, who'd take out entire towns to keep the information we have sealed. Fortunately, we don't do what we do for press or for anyone else. But arms trafficking, money laundering, narcotics, freighting—they act as a cover and keep our bank accounts full."

I faced him again. He stood still, hands in the pockets of his joggers, tracking me with his eyes. Cristiano had endless patience. I couldn't imagine my father or Diego walking me through all of this so candidly. They preferred to shield me. To put me in a box. Not Cristiano. For him to tell me not to come down here, it must be bad. I owed him the same trust he'd put in me—I had to include him in my decision of whether or not I was ready to face what lie ahead.

"Are the Valverdes here?"

He glanced at my hands as I twisted my ring around my finger. "*Sí.*"

"Where?" I asked. "What else is down here, Cristiano?"

He worked his jaw side to side before answering, "Every kingpin needs a dungeon, Natalia. It's just the way it is. You'll be glad for it, once you've found out what they've done."

"I already know."

His eyes fell shut. "What do you know?"

"I figured it out. They hired the *sicario* who killed my mother, didn't they?"

He made fists in his pockets and opened his eyes, darting them around the room until they landed on a desk. He strode to it, picked up a two-way radio, and paused. Glancing at the floor, he sighed, shook his head, and said into the speaker, "Make them scream."

My stomach dropped with his sinister command, but Cristiano didn't stop there. He tossed the radio down, went to a closet door, and hoisted a blue bucket with both hands to carry it across the room.

I was about to scold him for lifting things that could threaten his health when he dropped the bucket with a *thud* at my feet.

It was full of sand.

*El Polvo*. I touched my throat as it closed, as if I was about to learn firsthand his trademark method of delivering death.

A cacophony of deep, guttural screams sounded from somewhere in the building.

I spun, my pulse jumping as I tried to determine where it was coming from. "What is that?"

"*That* is the part of this world you're about to walk into. Are you sure you're ready?"

The yelling stopped, but it didn't halt the shiver working its way up my spine. I'd known this would happen. I had to stay strong. "You're trying to scare me away again, like you did back then," I said. "It didn't work when I was nine. What makes you think it will now?"

"Because you know better."

I studied the man before me. Sometimes, dark things that terrified me became bearable when I shone a light on them—bearable, and maybe even welcome. That wouldn't be the case here, but shadows weren't shields. They wouldn't keep the truth from creeping out, so why not face it head on, when I could control it? "I want answers, Cristiano. Don't I deserve them?"

"Yes, and you'll get them. But tell me the truth—does *any* part of you, however small, still want the life you had in California?" he asked, nodding behind him. "Or do you want what's behind door number two? You can't have both."

"I don't want that life anymore," I said, and it was the truth. What I didn't wonder aloud was whether I was ready for *this*. But I'd learned at a young age, from the man who stood before me—never hesitate, or *bang*! You're dead.

I tilted my head when something occurred to me. "You're giving me a choice?" I asked. "I can leave this marriage?"

He'd never lifted the threats that my family would lose his protection if *he* lost *me*. Technically, I was still his captive as much as his wife. Was he brave enough to let me choose for myself?

His eyes darkened. "If that's what you want, ask for it. See what my answer is."

His answer, I suspected, was no. But Cristiano had often said he knew me better than I thought he did, and now, that was beginning to hold true for me about him. If I asked for my freedom, Cristiano would say no. And he'd believe it. But I knew better. If I truly wanted to be let go, he'd release me.

"I promise you'll get your answers," he said. "I promise your mother's life will be avenged. But you don't need to watch this part."

My heart faltered. So it was true. "They *are* responsible," I said.

"Yes."

I expected grief to hit, but having guessed it on my own, the shock was dulled. Instead, my fingers twitched as fury burned a path through me. "I want to see them," I demanded.

"You have every right to be angry, but that can cloud your judgment."

I pointed to my chest. "It's my choice to make. Not yours. You taught me that."

He couldn't argue that. He rubbed an eyebrow, debating. "If I can't convince you to wait," he said, and paused, "then you should know more before we go in there."

I nodded him on. "I'm listening."

"One of the first missions I embarked on was locating the *sicario* who killed your mother. When your father pardoned me, that should've been enough, but I knew while I still had questions, I couldn't leave it at that." He cracked his knuckles. "Though he may have pulled the trigger, any hitman would off the Virgin Mary for the right amount of money."

I saw things through Papá's eyes now. He'd called Cristiano "ruthless" and "relentless" in his pursuit of the assassin, and I'd scoffed. But he'd been right. "The *sicario* admitted to being hired by a rival cartel—*¿verdad?*" I asked. "That's what my father told me."

Cristiano nodded. "We learned the hit had been ordered by the Valverdes, but it was common knowledge that they'd been out of the game a while. Unlike other federations that crumbled and eroded over time, the Valverdes vanished practically overnight."

"And that was what tipped you off that there might be more to it."

He clicked his tongue. "If there was a puzzle there, I was going to solve it. Especially having you here as my wife and knowing you still thought I'd had a hand in her assault."

I walked forward. "I don't think you killed her," I said, stopping in front of him. "I told you that, and to stop pursuing it."

"You don't think so, no. But you don't *know*, either. And it's been eating me alive."

"What has?"

He frowned down at me. "That over time, my wife may learn to trust me, and maybe even love me—but always, a small piece of her would question that day and what she'd seen." He looked away from me, but not before pain crossed his normally controlled features. "If I can't answer that question for you once and for all, if I can't give you closure, and the safety to give me your complete and unrelenting trust —then I don't deserve it."

*Oh*. My heart broke for him. From the day I'd arrived, up until recently, I'd been desperately trying to uncover Cristiano's motives for bringing me here. And he'd been showing me them all along. Starting in the church. His proposal, the lasso ceremony, the paperwork to legalize our union, my mother's rosary, the flowers, and his vows—*none* of it had been a mockery. He'd gone about it the wrong way, but that didn't make it less real.

Love and devotion, that he could give and have returned, was the *everything* he sought. The only things he couldn't take, buy, or command. And he didn't think he'd ever truly get those from me until the chapter of my mother's death had been closed. Until he closed it for me.

I stepped into him, placing my hands on his chest. I wanted to take him in my arms and soothe that ache by finally giving myself to him. *Later*. Now, I could only apologize. "*Lo siento,* Cristiano."

"Don't be sorry." He circled my wrists, keeping my hands against his pecs. "You're smart not to trust words, mine or anyone else's." His voice dropped. "You *do* trust actions, though—so I acted."

My scalp prickled. "You brought them here."

"To confess everything. To rid your mind of *any* doubt about me. To assure you that where your mother's death is involved, I'm innocent."

"I know you are. I don't doubt you anymore." I slid my palms higher, relishing the power beneath them. "You never said why they vanished."

"That's what I'm going to find out." He looked away. "You heard them scream, Natalia. You know what I'm about to do. I'll get the information I want, and a confession for you, but it could be days until I do. Be satisfied until then. I'll bring you back when the pigs are ready to squeal."

That was fair. I'd get to hear it from their mouths. But I'd begged for answers so many times. Patience had been forced on me. If I went upstairs, I'd just go back to waiting. And after all these years, I wanted to do something.

"I want to act, too," I said.

Maybe I'd regret it, but my mind had been made up the moment

I'd realized who the Valverdes were.

With a short sigh of resignation, he nodded once. "Wait here."

He left me alone in the dark with the haunting echo of grown men's screams. The idea that I thought I could exist on the surface of my internal darkness sounded so absurd now. That I could step on it, walk along it, and never trip and fall. That I could turn a blind eye to the way I'd grown up and to my father's business—and that I expected Diego to do the same.

California had been a bubble. My father had called it like it was—a life there with Diego would never have happened.

It wouldn't have been enough for either of us.

Maybe diving in head first into darkness was equally foolish. But there didn't seem to be any in-between, and I'd learned through Cristiano that ignorance only left me vulnerable.

I went into the closet from which Cristiano had taken the sand bucket. On the shelves sat chains I'd seen used to tow trucks, with massive hooks at the ends. Braided rope as thick as my forearm. A chainsaw.

With a noise, I turned. Cristiano stood in a doorway opposite me. "*Ándale,*" he said. "Come on."

I went to him. He nodded for me to pass through first. The door closed behind us with a resolute *click*. Walking through the hallway was like taking a tunnel to Hell. Gone were the steel walls and the comforting buzz of justice at work, replaced with the underbelly of the mountain, wood scaffolding, and masculine, muffled grunts.

The air became dank. Musty. My sneakers chewed dirt on the concrete as we made a right, and then another, until Cristiano opened a door and gestured for me to enter.

As my eyes adjusted, blood drained from my face.

Weeks ago, the scene before me would've been enough to send me running, but not before I'd called Cristiano every horrible name in the book. Now, I understood better.

There was more than one way to make the world a better place. Good didn't always prevail.

Sometimes, monsters had to take the reins.

## CHAPTER 12

# NATALIA

Four shirtless men with duct-taped mouths stared back at me. Flanked by Alejandro and Eduardo, they'd been hooked to the low ceiling by their chained wrists, their toes barely grazing the dirt floor.

Four men, when Cristiano had hoped for one at best.

Four lives hanging in the balance.

Three were around my father's age or older, and the last even younger than I was, possibly still a teenager.

Their bodies seemed mostly unharmed, but bruises darkened their faces. Multicolored confetti underneath them was evidence they'd been tasered.

To my embarrassment, I was too shocked to even move. Knowing these things happened, even hearing them from the next room, was entirely different than witnessing them.

As a rivulet of blood slid from the corner of one man's mouth, the contents of my stomach churned.

But I'd promised myself that I could do this. So when Cristiano said, "*Fíjate bien*"—look closer—I did.

"Read their tattoos," Cristiano instructed.

"What tattoos?" I asked.

Only a few decorated the older men, but they were simply faded sketches that meant nothing to me.

Cristiano guided me forward, staying close enough that I felt his heat even through my hoodie. It wasn't until I was standing within arm's reach of the eldest man that I saw it. Faint, nearly erased ink in scrawling Gothic lettering across his chest. The other two older men had the same word. "Valverde," I read.

"They tried to have them removed. Like cowards."

Two of the four men jerked, their chains and muffled cries echoing around us.

"*Silencio.*" Eduardo smacked one in the back with the butt of his AR-15, and they went quiet. The youngest and the eldest of the four both remained still.

"Perhaps they should've cut their names off if they didn't want to be found," Cristiano said, walking toward the men, his back lengthening so he stood at his full height. "They're going to confess their sins. Whatever it takes. I want you to hear it from their fucking mouths."

And if I told Cristiano that I believed, down to my very core, that he was innocent—would he still proceed with whatever he had planned?

I met the pleading eyes of the youngest one. He couldn't have been anything more than a toddler when this had happened.

"What if they didn't do it?" I asked Cristiano.

"I didn't hunt them down to ask *if* they did. I brought them here to find out *why*."

A sense of dread worked through me. For more than eleven years, I'd wished for answers. Now, they'd be granted by the last man on Earth I'd have expected them from. My husband showed me more every day that he made his own destiny, and that I could make mine.

Cristiano paced, pausing in front of each man. "You know why you're here. You ordered a hit on Bianca Cruz. This is her daughter. *My wife.*" He met eyes with one, and the ferocity in Cristiano's gaze made even *my* stomach drop. He shrugged in that menacing way he'd perfected. "The more you cooperate, the faster this will end—but I'm a merciful man," he said in a tone that was anything but compassionate. "I'll let one of you go—the first to confess."

None of them reacted, not that they really could, but their silence got under my skin. The lives of everyone I cared about had been irrevocably changed for the worse because of the men in front of me.

Maybe they needed to be forced to speak.

The thought caught me off guard.

And brought understanding of Cristiano and Diego in a new way. I'd fantasized about justice for my mother's killer, but not in the direct, brutal way that was currently on offer. I'd thought a bullet in the *sicario's* head was a way of evening the score, but that was nothing. It'd been over before I'd even known it was happening, before I'd had a moment to relish the payback.

Cristiano turned to me. "This is where you get off the ride."

That was it? I'd come for more, though I couldn't say what exactly. Was I willing to witness torture? And if so, what holes would it fill within me to watch men crucified for a decade old crime?

Even as their gazes burned into me, Cristiano and I locked eyes—until the eldest of the four shook his chains. Cristiano turned to him. His gray eyes morphed from dull to expressive as he tried to tell us something from behind his gag.

Alejandro and Eduardo exchanged a look. Cristiano nodded once. "Let him speak."

Eduardo ripped the tape off his mouth. The man stretched his jaw but otherwise seemed unfazed. "*Soy Vicente*," he said hoarsely. "I am—"

"Vicente Valverde," Cristiano said. "The patriarch."

"*Sí*. I knew Costa. I can tell you everything you want to know, since I made the cursed deal myself."

At the mention of my father's name, I stepped forward. "What deal?"

"I must say," Cristiano said, taking my elbow to draw me nearer to him, "knowing your reputation, I thought you'd be the last to crack. Not the first."

Vicente grunted. "I'm not getting out of here alive. There's no point trying to save myself." He twisted in his restraints to make eye contact with the other two men his age, and an agreement seemed to pass between them. "I'll tell you the whole truth on one condition."

Eduardo laughed with such exaggeration, he showed off a missing molar. "He's setting conditions, boss. This should be good."

Cristiano cocked his head at Vicente. "Go ahead."

"Kill me quickly once you have what you want—but spare my grandson and brothers. They're the only remaining members of my family."

Eduardo laughed again, and Alejandro joined in.

"Why would I agree to that?" Cristiano asked.

"My family advised against my strategy. They warned me it could fail and backfire—but I was in charge, and I made the call." With a curt nod, Vicente added, "My grandson was just a boy when this happened. He's only seventeen."

*Seventeen*? My palms sweat, but I kept from wiping them on my shorts so I wouldn't appear nervous.

"All his life, he's been forced into hiding and poverty," Vicente said, "and he has potential. Let them live, and they would be indebted to you. They could be great soldiers."

"Fuck you," Cristiano said, his back going rigid. "*Tienes huevos*—you have the nerve to ask for mercy? I spent eleven years of *my* life in hiding, and I started them in poverty, because of you."

The teenager twisted in his chains. I wasn't used to seeing such fright in someone's eyes. Most people in this world had already been inured to this kind of thing, but like me, he was clearly in new territory.

"My grandson is fascinated with this world but has never been allowed to be a part of it." Vicente became more animated as his pride shone through. "Instead, he put his energy into computers. He can't fight, I admit. But he can find things on the Internet."

Cristiano wouldn't kill a teenager who'd done nothing wrong. I wouldn't let him. Would I? As my eyes moved between each of them, I couldn't help seeing the poetic justice in taking from Vicente as he'd taken from me.

Cristiano walked toward the wide-eyed teenager and looked him up and down. "What's his name?"

"Gabriel."

"Tell us everything," Cristiano said, turning back to Vicente, "and my wife may decide Gabriel's fate."

Had I been alone, I would've gulped. I wasn't strong enough for that yet—to pull the trigger when there was gray area, even when it needed to be done. Was that what it meant to stand by Cristiano's side? To deal revenge where it was owed, and make decisions that I may never discover to be right or wrong?

It *was* those things, but maybe it was also about knowing when to pull back. There was strength in walking away, and in forgiveness, too.

For the boy, maybe—but not the others.

"Unchain me," Vicente said.

"Keep his wrists and ankles bound." Cristiano grabbed a lightweight, plastic patio chair from one corner of the room and stuck it in the spot where Vicente had been standing.

The old man eased into it, rolling his neck a few times. "Come closer, Natalia Cruz," he said.

My hands tingled. He said my name like *un abuelo* beckoning his granddaughter, as if he'd always known me. Cristiano returned to my side and put a hand to my upper back to guide me toward the old man.

Vicente peered up, looking between the two of us. "When your parents fell, Cristiano, there was nobody to take over the cartel. You boys were too young. I wanted de la Rosa's territories. But Costa had the same thought. So we went to war over them."

"I remember," Cristiano said.

Cristiano's presence, and his big, warm palm on my back, gave me the security to ask questions. "Who won?"

"It's not so simple," Vicente said. "Costa was more powerful, and he succeeded at first, taking jurisdiction over enough turf to push us out —but with his own business expanding faster than ever, and your grandfather no longer around to help, it became too much for him to handle. He started losing control. We got hungrier, fought harder, and at one point, we held the majority. Then we lost it. Back and forth, this went on. An epic turf war that lasted eight years."

My jaw dropped. "Eight *years*?"

I looked to Cristiano, who confirmed the story with a nod. "You were only one when it started," he told me.

"And nine when it ended," I said quietly. Nine years old when I'd looked up from the floor at blood-splattered boots. When I'd said goodnight to my mother for the last time.

"For eight years, I watched my men die," Vicente said. "First, mules, runners, then *hermanos*, cousins, friends, their parents, their children. It had to end. I was losing too many people. My livelihood suffered."

I shifted feet. "How did it end?"

He glanced at the ground, lifting up and resettling in the chair. "Your father's no saint, you know. He has taken out entire bloodlines."

Cristiano slid his hand up to my shoulder. "Answer her."

Vicente raised his haunted gray eyes to me. "It was business. It wasn't personal. Until, of course, it was."

Chills spread down my bare legs. I stuck my hands in the pockets of my hoodie. "What do you mean?"

"Everyone knew Costa had one weakness, and one weakness only. With my cartel dwindling and on the verge of collapsing, I had to make a bold move and take it all, or we'd die off."

I knew what was coming. Despite craving answers for so long, looking brutal truth in the face proved difficult. I wanted to turn away until Cristiano squeezed my shoulder reassuringly, even as his voice carried threat. "Continue," he ordered.

"We took out the hit on Bianca," Vicente said. "We hired the *sicario*, and we saw it through to the end."

His confession thickened the already dank air in the small, grimy chamber. That was it. The final pieces in the puzzle of her death. Nothing all that remarkable. An explanation too small to do her vibrant life justice. A story I'd heard too many times—a grab at power that resulted in lives lost. I gulped around the lump rising in my throat. "Why?" I asked, hating how my voice cracked. "Why did she have to die?"

"To incapacitate your father," Vicente said simply. "Everyone knew how much he cared for her, and that her death would cripple him. So I formed my plan around that." The chains around his wrists *clinked* as he rested his elbows on his thighs. "Immediately after the hit, we expected Costa to do one of two things. One, he'd fall into a grief so deep, he'd barely notice our invasion until it was complete. And by then, it would be too late."

"And the second?" Cristiano asked.

"Draw him out." Vicente slowly lifted his eyes to my husband, tilting his head as he peered at Cristiano.

When he didn't proceed, Cristiano asked, "Meaning?"

"What would you do if someone took your Natalia from you? How far would you go?" Vicente asked, pausing. "And how easy of a target would you become?"

Cristiano stiffened behind me, taking a moment to respond. "Bianca's assassination would send Costa into a tailspin. He'd lose control," he said slowly, working through it. "React out of passion, not logic—lash out, become vulnerable, and get himself killed."

Vicente nodded. "I admit, I violated an unspoken rule amongst cartels back then—you don't touch a fellow kingpin's family. But I was desperate. I did what I had to do to save my people."

I fisted my hands in my pockets to try to stem the tremble making its way through me. I understood his reasoning better than I should. Being a liability to Cristiano and to my father had almost gotten *me* killed. "Look around," I said. "You didn't save them."

"No. Because Costa *didn't* expose himself to retaliation as we'd hoped. He holed up in his castle to grieve, but he surrounded himself with guards and advisors"—Vicente shifted his eyes to me—"keeping his young daughter close in the aftermath."

Cristiano's hand moved to the back of my neck, under my hairline. I pulled at my collar. Cristiano was sweating, too, but Vicente most of all. "That doesn't explain why you left," Cristiano said.

"Costa's business carried on as usual," Vicente said. "It got even stronger, as you both know. And we grew weaker. We'd missed any opportunity to attack, and going up against him at that point would've been a losing battle. So it made sense to pack up what was left of my family and relocate . . ."

"Relocate." Cristiano snorted. "You disappeared, practically overnight."

He nodded. "Because there was evidence tying me to Bianca's murder."

"That was reason enough to flee?" I asked.

"Think of your husband," he said to me. "Of how he'd react in Costa's shoes. If he'd do all this to avenge your mother, what would he do for you?"

I didn't have to consider it too hard. Cristiano had pursued the *sicario* for a decade so he could bring him to my father's feet to get his head blown off.

"I'd weed through every person I had to, yanking out the rotting roots of the cartel responsible—until they were gone," Cristiano said, and under his breath, added, "as I will do to Belmonte-Ruiz."

Vicente nodded. "When I learned the evidence existed, I knew we had to get out of town as fast as possible. If the truth came out, Costa would hunt me, and every member of my family, until we'd been eradicated." He paused for a hacking cough against his shoulder. "It was the right choice. Especially since I heard, later, that Bianca was raped that day. I'm sorry, Natalia. That was never supposed to happen."

I swayed, or the ground underneath me did. I'd suspected that. Truthfully, deep down, I'd known it. Over time, I'd come to understand her ripped dress and the signs of her struggle for what it was. But nobody had ever said it to me outright.

Cristiano held me up by my biceps and said against my ear, "Stay strong. For that alone, Vicente will die. Today, if he's lucky. Or over time, if you decide he's not."

Vicente glanced over at his brothers. "I've told you all I know. I've answered your questions." He turned his face forward. "So will you meet my condition, Natalia? Spare my family. Please. Gabriel is innocent. My brothers opposed the assassination."

Still reeling from everything I'd just learned, my legs threatened to give out. Mercy? He was in no place to ask for it. I was in no place to give it. I'd gotten what I'd come for. What Cristiano had sought for me. *Closure*. But it didn't feel as if anything had ended. I could finally picture clearly what had happened in my mother's final moments, and it sickened me. The fear she must've felt—it moved through me now, leaving my stomach weak and my head swimming.

A stranger in the bedroom she'd shared with my father.

"I'll take her upstairs," Cristiano said, somewhere in the distance. "We won't decide anything now."

"*Claro*," Alejandro answered.

Cornering her. Violating her.

Before or after he'd raided the safe? And why?

Where had he found her? In her bathroom, by the bed? Had she been in the closet when he'd suddenly appeared from the tunnel . . .?

I let Cristiano guide me toward the exit, unable to see through my haze of mounting questions.

Until . . .

"Wait." I halted before we reached the door, planting my feet where they were. "Wait."

"*¿Qué pasa, mi amor?*" Cristiano asked. "What is it?"

I turned back to face Vicente. Cristiano released me but stayed close. "Only my mother, father, and I knew about the secret passageway the assassin used to enter the bedroom. How did *you* discover it?"

"*Ah*. Well. That part is simple." Vicente's gaze traveled up, over my head, and fixed on Cristiano. "Someone was more than happy to leave the secret door unlocked for us. To carry out the hit, we needed a little help from the inside. And we found it—in a de la Rosa brother."

*No*. Goose bumps started at my scalp and blazed over my skin. *Cristiano*, my mind said. He'd had some of the highest security clearance at the time. For more than eleven years, I'd blamed him for this crime. I'd had no other explanation. It would be easy for me to slot him into the role as guilty. I turned my head over my shoulder to look at him—my husband.

Cristiano stared back at me. He swallowed but didn't deny it. I was learning to read him better. A blank expression that once might've come off as indifference, was now patience for how long it'd taken me to get here. Anguish that I might not. Struggle not to declare his innocence—and belief in me that I'd arrive at the truth on my own.

My parents had trusted him. He'd been loyal to them. He'd brought me all of this to avenge my mother's death. I could make up some of my faithlessness in him by having confidence that he'd never have cooperated with the Valverdes.

But if he hadn't, that left only one answer. And not only did it turn my life into a lie—it called everything about me, as a person, into question. My choices, my feelings, my judgment.

The ache of the truth permeated throughout me, numbing my hands, stiffening my neck as I turned forward again to address Vicente.

I barely heard myself speak the name that I'd once revered, but which continued to fall even further from its long smashed pedestal each day. And now, it seemed, it had finally hit the bottom.

"Diego."

## CHAPTER 13

# NATALIA

In the dark and dank underbelly of the mountain, Vicente Valverde confirmed the truth. "Diego de la Rosa let us into the Cruz compound," he said from a plastic chair that wobbled on an uneven dirt floor. "But then, he turned my plan against me."

"How?" Cristiano's question rumbled through the small room.

"An assassin only works for the highest bidder. He sold your brother proof that I was behind the murder, and Diego threatened to expose me if I didn't leave." He took a rattling breath as his expression darkened, the first flame of anger I'd seen in him yet. "I should've known if the bastard would betray Costa, the man who'd taken him in as a boy, he'd turn on me, too."

"And us," Cristiano said.

Vicente was only another in the long line of those Diego had wronged.

But at least with him, it'd been business. Not for me. This was deeply personal.

"One of the biggest mistakes I've ever made was underestimating Diego de la Rosa," Vicente said. "We spread rumors of our deaths and hid our identities so he'd never come looking for us."

"You were a liability to him," Cristiano said. "If anyone found out Diego had helped . . ."

"Diego's life would be over." After another coughing fit, he turned his head and spit in the dirt. "With Bianca's death, Diego ingratiated himself to Costa," he said and wiped the corner of his mouth with his bare shoulder. "He rose in the ranks of the Cruz cartel. Became a trusted advisor. And wrapped his grip so tightly around Costa's daughter that she'd do anything for him—including turn against her father if he pulled the right strings."

My face heated as all gazes turned to me. I'd happily tangled myself in a snake's grip and had never even felt the squeeze. Everyone in the room knew it, too.

Including Cristiano.

I'd been a fool.

With my mortification, tears heated the backs of my eyes. I couldn't stay in that room any longer without breaking down. And I'd never give the Valverdes the satisfaction.

I'd heard enough anyway.

I turned and walked past Cristiano, hurrying down the underground hallway that too closely resembled a tunnel, through the proverbial museum of body parts, and climbed the stairs.

My fists shook. I didn't think of going anywhere, but my feet carried me toward the house.

How could it be? *How*?

Diego had held my hand at my mother's funeral and many times since. He'd picked out my dress for the service and worked with the state to get paperwork in order. Later, he'd helped Papá with the details of arranging the elaborate mausoleum that would become my mother's final resting place.

Maybe my blindness to his true character could've been excused then, while I'd been grieving.

But for the eleven years after? What excuse did I have for that?

I reached for the door handle to walk in the house. My hand trembled along with the rest of me, the threat of sobs immobilizing me. I fought to hold them in. I couldn't break down here, in front of the staff, and where anyone from the Badlands could come across me. They, and Cristiano, depended on me to be strong.

They were fools to depend on me at all.

If I believed this to be true about Diego, then I had to admit a much scarier truth.

I'd been tricked and manipulated to the point I didn't even know what parts of me were real and what had been molded by Diego.

Hands turned me by my shoulders, and arms surrounded me, pulling me to a strong, sturdy chest. The deep, controlled bass of Cristiano's voice hummed in my ear. "You're okay," he said. "I've got you. I'm here."

Instantly, my body loosened, my tears subsiding. I'd felt this sense of security before, breathed in this same masculine mix of sweat and dirt. Unlikely as it'd been, Cristiano's solid body had acted as comfort in the tunnel. I'd clutched his neck, silently begging him not to let go, not to leave me behind.

But that hadn't been the only time I'd been soothed this way.

Days later, Diego had held me in the safety of his arms as we'd lowered Mamá into the ground.

All the while, he'd been responsible. His comfort had been a lie. Maybe Cristiano's had been back then, too—maybe it was now.

Cristiano guided me up the staircase to the top floor. In our bedroom, he released me to shut the door behind himself. "Natalia—"

"Every *Día de los Muertos*, Diego lit a candle for her," I said. I looked around the foreign room, its quiet fireplace, white gauze curtains, the empty space where the mirror had been, a bar cart where Cristiano sometimes fixed a drink in the evenings. How had I gotten here? I'd been moved into this bedroom like a pawn. "He brought her favorite dessert to the house, and flowers to her as *una ofrenda*." The remoteness of my voice matched my sagging posture, my curled fists. "He listened to me talk about her for hours. He held me as I cried."

"He manipulated you."

Jarred from the memories, I turned to look at Cristiano. "What he did to me weeks ago, he did out of desperation." Even if I found it vile, at least I could understand *why* he'd lied to get me to the church—his life had been on the line. "To trade me for his own safety—that is an act of a desperate man." I turned my body to Cristiano as my voice rose. "But to allow a woman who'd treated him like a son to get *raped* and *murdered* in her own bedroom?" I yelled. "That's not desperation. It's devoid of humanity. Did you know about this?"

Cristiano took my anger without flinching. "I had suspicions—"

"And you didn't tell me?"

"They were baseless," he said. "All I had to go on was the fact that the door had been unlocked. And when I had him alone at *La Madrina,* I could see firsthand how angry he was with Costa—"

"For?"

"For killing our parents."

The answer went down easily, because I'd been over this scenario a million times in my head. Only, it was never kindhearted, gentle Diego who'd been nursing a grudge. It'd been his menacing, ruthless brother.

My body shook so violently, tears almost fell. I bit them back. Vengeance against my father for killing the de la Rosas. I'd been right all along—but I'd never been so wrong.

My limbs weakened with the churn of my stomach. I reached out to steady myself on something, worried I might vomit.

"Come, let me hold you," Cristiano said, stepping forward as he reached for me.

Instinctively, I moved back, my eyes on the ground between us.

I'd once thought him incapable of experiencing pain, but I didn't have to see his face to know I'd hurt him.

He dropped his arm to his side, walked to the bar cart, and poured himself a drink.

Why was I shutting him out? Cristiano was not to blame for this. He was a victim of Diego's machinations, too. I urged myself to go to him. His body, words, and tenderness held comfort.

But so had Diego's. I'd found a home in him more times than I could count, and each time, I was more the fool. Diego was the reason my mother was dead; that made every single touch of his, every word from his mouth, a lie.

My judgment couldn't be trusted.

I'd been emotionally vulnerable when Diego had helped me pick up the pieces of my shattered life following her death. He'd advised my father in his darkest hour and molded me into the girl he'd wanted me to be. Who was to say Cristiano hadn't done the same, purposely severing my relationship with Diego so he could be the one to fill the void it'd left? So he could turn me into his queen, as he often said?

My past had been a lie.

The foundation I'd built my life on had been nothing more than smoke and mirrors.

And it was crumbling under my feet.

My mind replayed one of the few conversations I'd had with Diego about his parents. Maybe the only honest conversation we'd ever had.

*"Did you ever think of taking vengeance for their death?"*

*Diego didn't answer right away. As seconds ticked by, I grew uneasy. There was only one person he would take revenge on. My father.*

*"In my darkest moments, yes," he admitted.*

Diego had played me.

Cristiano was suddenly in front of me, holding out a tumbler with a few swigs of neat, amber liquor. "You're in shock. Drink this. It will help."

I took it from him. Sniffed it. Sipped it, holding it in my mouth. Brandy. I swallowed and handed it back. It would ease the pain for a while, but I didn't want that. I had to feel the mistakes I'd made.

"I know you're hurting. And if it's the last thing I do . . ." He slugged back the liquor and gripped the glass as he said, "Diego will pay for that."

"He said he *loved* me." The words tumbled smoothly over my brandy tongue. "I loved him back."

"If that's all it takes, I will love you too. More than he ever did. More than he ever could."

My heart reached for him. It was incomprehensible how much I wanted that after hating Cristiano for so long. And that after all the ways I'd pushed him away, he was still standing here. "How?" I nearly choked out. How had he not run for the hills yet? "You manipulated me, too. You forced me into this marriage, locked me up in this house, and made me fall for you."

"Natalia. My darling." He took my jaw in his free hand and pulled my face to his. "I fell for you first."

"Then why did you almost die on me?" I gripped his t-shirt to push him away but couldn't bring myself to do it. I'd lost too much already—but with Cristiano, why did it feel as if I had more to lose than ever? I pulled him closer as my chin wobbled. "I hate him. Help me forget. You promised you'd make me forget his name."

Cristiano's expression hardened as he set his jaw and looked away. "And I told you never to come to me again if *he* was the reason. I will not fuck you to make you forget his name."

"Then fuck me so I know *only yours*. I am willing. And I need this, Cristiano."

His chest heaved with an inhale. What was he waiting for? He had his permission. Not that he or anyone needed it. If I could be tricked into sleeping with the man who'd deceived my family in the worst way, and if my mother could be forced by a stranger, then really—what the fuck did any of this matter? What was so special about it?

I took his empty glass, set it on the nightstand, and slipped my hand between us to touch him. My body thrilled when he stirred against my palm. Nothing could soothe me now except this. Except to be taken so hard, I could think of nothing else. "This is what you wanted," I whispered to him. "It's what *I* want."

"I can't," he said, his voice strangled but determined. "Not like this. You're in pain, and you're angry."

"But I'm willing." I fluttered my lashes up at him. "I'm giving you this gift—"

"I won't do it."

Frustration zapped through me. "Then leave me alone!" I screamed as I shoved him. "Get out. ¡*Vete ya*!"

I turned away, fury eating me up inside. How could he turn me away when I needed him?

Did he feel differently now that he realized how badly I'd been played?

I was a traitor to my mother.

But so what? Cristiano had me where he wanted me. Why not take what he'd often proclaimed belonged to him?

When he spoke again, his voice was even calmer against my rage echoing through the room. "You said Diego loved you, but you're wrong, Natalia. Love is *I'd die for you,* not *would you die for me?*" With his pause, his beautiful, unsettling words hung in the air. "Diego had a certain fondness for you, yes, but it wasn't enough. He took your virginity from you after manipulating you into offering it, but I'm going to walk away from you now to show you the difference between his love and mine. To show you that *true love* means putting you first. Always."

His words struck me at my core. Cristiano would do what Diego couldn't—he'd give up what he wanted, what he'd fought for, what would make him more powerful. For me.

"Is that what you need?" I heard the hesitation in his voice. It wasn't easy for him to do nothing when his whole life had been about action. "Space?"

Shamefully, I kept my back to him. I couldn't look at his handsome, pained face and remember that I'd chosen the wrong brother back then—or I'd fall so deep into a black hole of regret, I wasn't sure how I'd get out. "Yes."

"I'll be right downstairs if you need me."

After a moment, the door closed with a soft *click*.

*If you need me*. Deafening silence remained in his wake.

Nineteen years ago, Cristiano had come to my dad for help. That had ended in a bullet in his parents' heads as he and Diego had watched. What had happened in the eight years since? How had that changed them? Who would I have become if Diego hadn't been there?

I'd let him soothe and kiss and touch, when he'd been the villain all along. And Cristiano had been the hero, showing me respect, even when I'd been a pawn.

I trusted him. But I could trust myself *with* him?

I'd accused him of his brother's crimes time and time again. And even now, he'd taken every hit I'd had to give and come back for more. He hadn't struck back or left me to fend for myself.

Pressure in my chest eased as everything I knew about Cristiano finally became clear. From a young age, he'd defended those who couldn't defend themselves. He'd betrayed his family—an even greater sin in our world than bartering with human lives—and joined ours out of a sense of duty. And he'd been punished for it. Accused of a crime he hadn't committed, driven away, and hunted by the true perpetrator.

Cristiano's truth had fallen on deaf ears. And yet he trusted me to heal him.

I couldn't believe in myself just then, but Cristiano understood that. It was the reason he'd walked away. And that was why I *could* believe in him.

I spun, raced through the door, and down the hall to find Cristiano descending the staircase. "Wait," I said.

He turned back instantly, concern etched in the lines of his face. "What is it?"

I stared at him and saw someone else. I saw *him*. My protector as a child, and my protector now—against enemies who made themselves known and the far more dangerous kind. Those who didn't.

Cristiano was my ally. He was aggrieved.

And he was my husband.

"I . . . I don't need you to walk away to prove your love. I need—"

He strode back up the stairs. When he reached the landing, he opened his mouth to speak, but I was done talking. I gripped his cheeks, pulled down his face, and kissed him with everything I had. He yanked me against his body, one arm strong around my waist, and anchored me as he took a handful of my hair at the back of my head. How could I have ever thought him cold? He was everything warm now as his eager mouth, spicy with brandy, lured me in, our tongues lashing. Then he stopped. Drew back. Slowed the kiss with short pecks from his full lips. His fist in my hair eased, massaging my scalp, then cradling my head.

"*Shh*," he said, brushing his mouth over my cheek, which was wet with silent tears I hadn't realized I'd shed.

I pulled back to look into his eyes. The pain in them, the sheer *relief*, hurt me. Diego had broken both of our hearts, and too many times, Cristiano and I had hurt each other. It was enough. My voice faltered as my tears fell faster. "I—I need you."

"I'm not going *anywhere*. Not now, not ever."

In a moment, I was in his arms as he carried me back to the room, laid me on the bed, and removed my sneakers and socks.

I grabbed his hand as he stood. "Don't go."

He leaned forward and cleared hair from my cheek. "I meant what I said. I'm not leaving your side."

He climbed over me, slipped beneath the covers, and hugged me to his chest. The past hour, the only thing I'd been able to control were my sobs. Knowing Cristiano had me, I released them, breaking down into my pillow as he whispered soothingly into my ear, his hold around me never loosening.

"I let her down," I said through my cries. "I chose the enemy."

"*Shh*," he said, nuzzling my ear. "Take comfort in the fact that Bianca loved you more than anything in the world. And that now we'll all get the closure we deserve."

*Closure*. This was what Cristiano had risked his life for. To give me answers, knowing they'd hurt me, when nobody else would.

The boy who'd played with my heart was no match for the man who, I was fairly certain, had loved me for a while.

Tears soaked my pillow, but not all of them came from pain as a thought formed. An utter and painstaking betrayal had given me the greatest gift I hadn't even known possible—the permission to fall in love with my husband.

"Thank you," I whispered.

He squeezed me to him. To anyone else, he was a boss, a leader, a killer. To me, he was just Cristiano. Up until very recently, I hadn't let him be that.

My puffy eyes ached. I closed them, suddenly exhausted. He'd known better than I had what I'd wanted and what I'd needed. Finally, they were the same thing. For years, I'd tried to escape the truth, but I was beginning to see . . .

This was my destiny.

I belonged by Cristiano's side.

He was the man I wanted, and now I knew—he was the one I needed.

## CHAPTER 14

# NATALIA

The emotional wreckage of the day before felt physical. It was all around me—and Cristiano and I were a unit in the middle of it. Sometime in the night, I'd shed my clothing and fallen asleep naked in his arms. His body curled around mine so tightly that we were practically one. His muscular legs trapped my thighs, intertwined with my calves. His arms secured my back to his chest, and our linked fingers unbreakable.

Dawn had broken on a new day, and the room around me wasn't the same.

The blues were richer, whites brighter, and the golds glimmered as if they'd just been polished. A breeze fluttered the curtains and cooled my exposed skin as Cristiano's body heated the rest of me.

Cristiano was not the same.

He'd suffered for me and because of me. He would never be innocent, but he wasn't guilty of the one crime that had kept me from trusting him. From falling into him.

Everything had changed.

There were consequences to be dealt, concessions to be made, and wrongs to right—starting here in a bed I had come to know as my own.

I knew what lay ahead. I knew what I had to do.

*I* wasn't the same.

My decisions were made before I'd even opened my eyes.

I'd fallen asleep in Cristiano's cocoon and had awoken transformed.

"You're up," Cristiano said.

I would've never thought the sound and feel of his voice against my ear could bring such a complete sense of calm and safety. "Stay," I said. "I couldn't say it before, on the phone, but I'm saying it now. Don't leave me. And . . ."

"And what?"

I swallowed. "I'm sorry."

"You have nothing to be sorry for. I do."

That was true, but I'd never expected to hear an apology from his mouth. I shifted under the sheets, and he loosened his grip on me so I could turn and face him. The near-black of his eyes didn't fool me anymore. I saw depth where I'd once seen bleakness. Love where I'd assumed there was hate. And a strength that had always been there. "Why?"

His arms pulled me so close, we barely had to whisper. "I shouldn't have gloated the way I did after I kissed you on our wedding day. I let Diego get to me."

Of all the things he had to be sorry for, that had never even crossed my mind. "You paid the price for it," I reminded him.

"I deserved the slap. The kiss was as real as anything else between us. It should've been our moment, but I let him steal it. I regretted my mistake immediately." He moved a strand of my hair from my cheek. "And the wedding dress. I didn't know it was Bianca's when I ripped it."

"You had it fixed," I said.

"But it will never be the same." Somehow, his gaze darkened even more. "That's all I'm sorry for, though, no matter what kind of monster it makes me. I can't apologize for anything that's led me here. I took you off the course of a life that might've been right for you and brought you down a treacherous road. My dirt road with all its bumps and potholes." He spoke with the satisfaction of a child who'd been caught stealing dessert *after* he'd filled his belly. "I'm not sorry for the things I should regret—the tattoo was fucked up, but every time I see it, I swell with pride to see that you're mine. De la Rosa men are scum, but I have broken you free of one only to chain you to another."

"And you're *not* sorry," I clarified with some amusement.

"To say so would be a lie—I'd do it all over again."

"I have a regret," I said. "Well, I have a few, I think."

He kissed my forehead. "Throw them away," he said against my skin. "They aren't worth voicing."

"I have to say one, then I'll throw it out." Cristiano had demanded one thing of Diego and me before the wedding, and I hadn't given him that. It had to have been important to him. I blinked up at him. "I wish my first time hadn't been with Diego. I thought I wanted it . . . I thought he was worthy."

"I don't give a fuck that he had you first," Cristiano said, shocking me into silence. "It means nothing. *He* means nothing." He ran his tongue along his top row of teeth. "It will be the thing I think of when I finally put a bullet in him, but still, it means nothing."

I couldn't help a small smile. "And if I beat you to it?"

"You have to find him first."

"You don't know where he is?"

He shook his head. "If he's working with Belmonte-Ruiz, then he could be with Max. I hope one leads to the other." His assessing eyes met mine. "But nostalgia is a funny thing, Natalia. If Diego were standing here now, you wouldn't be able to pull the trigger. Too much history there."

Tucking the sheet under my arm, I popped up onto one elbow. "Give me more credit than that. My blinders have been ruthlessly ripped off. I'd laugh in his face if he tried to talk his way out of it."

"And you know he would."

I touched Cristiano's stubbled cheek, running my finger along his square, angular jawline. I'd never denied his beauty, no matter my resentment toward him. Now, I was free to revel in it. I didn't want to wait any longer. "And you know what I'd say to him?"

"Tell me, *mi amor*."

"That his brother fucked me better than he could ever hope to. And that we're sending him to an early grave."

"Then I suppose I'd better fuck you, so as not to make you into a liar . . ." Cristiano bit his full bottom lip, and the small tell of his arousal made my stomach clench. "I've waited a long time for this."

"I know."

"I don't mean sex." He leaned into me until I fell onto my back, and his darkly handsome face looked down on me. He tugged the sheet to my stomach, and I sucked in a breath as cool air caressed my nipples. Licking his lips, he ran a finger between my breasts, eliciting my shudder. "I've waited for you to stop acting like a princess and start thinking like a queen."

"Nothing less would do for my king."

"I wasn't a king until you came along. *Me coronaste*. You crowned me."

I stopped his hand before it dipped underneath the sheets. "You can't just storm the castle walls. You need a strategy."

He moved his hand up to tip back my chin and graze his thumb over my bottom lip. "What should ours be, *mi reina*?"

"Invade, plunder, and destroy until I beg for the king's mercy," I said softly, letting my breath caress his finger. I pushed his chest. He rolled onto his back, and I threw a knee over him to sit astride his hips. "You took me as your prisoner. But you made the mistake of falling in love with me. And when you least expect it, I will claim my throne."

"Nothing would please a peasant like myself more." He gripped my hips and pulled me over his crotch. I inhaled as my naked clit slid along the erection straining his underwear. "But there's more to being a queen than sitting on the king's scepter."

My breasts swayed, and my long hair pooled on his chest. "What then?"

"You have decisions to make. The fate of four men rests in your hands."

I curled my fists on his chest. The whimsy of our dreamy bed and the early morning hours gave way to a brutal reality. Only one man had paid the price for my mother's death. The others awaited my sentence.

What kind of queen would I be? Fair and forgiving or cunning and ruthless?

Cristiano took my right nipple between the tips of his forefinger and thumb. I sucked in a breath when he tugged, and pleasure traveled down my stomach, ending right between my legs. "Even in times of play, you can't forget there are enemies to be dealt with. You're safe with me, but you should never completely drop your guard."

Just like in physical combat, the fight was ongoing.

"Vicente made the call," he said, "but he and his family are nobodies now. They've paid for their mistakes."

I froze, my heartbeat reverberating everywhere from my ears to my pussy. "Are you saying he's not to blame?" I asked, incredulous. "That I should *forgive* him?"

He pushed some of my hair behind my ear, but it fell forward again, curtaining us from the rest of the world—my new favorite thing. "Simply demonstrating that you can rule two ways. With the truth you want or with the facts. And the fact is, you won't gain much satisfaction from killing three old men and an innocent teen."

"So I should let them go?"

"That's up to you. Most men would say kill all four."

"What would you say?"

His eyelids fell as he slid a hand up my spine and applied pressure to my upper back. I leaned in until we were face to face, my breasts smashed into his bare chest, my clit pushing against him at a new angle. "I'm most men."

"No, you aren't. I thought you were the worst of them, but you're fair."

"Is it fair that I'd kill a man for his grandfather's sins?"

*The grandson.* If Vicente was to be believed, his *nieto,* Gabriel, was smart. And he had his whole life ahead of him. "You would?" I asked.

"We'd be fools to ignore history. There's too much at risk to let any of them live. The betrayal festers—look at Diego."

"Look at *you*," I said, threading my fingers in his hair, putting our lips centimeters apart. I wanted retribution—not just for myself, but for my husband, who'd suffered—and it would be so easy to lump Gabriel in with the others. To turn my cheek as he paid for his family's sins. But I'd be ignoring Cristiano's history, which was also *my* history. "You didn't stick by your father out of familial duty likes others would've. You chose good over bad. Maybe Gabriel would too."

"True. But here I am, doing everything in my power to avenge Bianca's death. And I'd do the same for you. The grandson may not feel resentful now, but that doesn't mean he won't." His hand dipped to cup my right ass cheek. A little lower and to the left, and he'd be able to ease the pulsing ache that'd been growing between my legs for longer than I cared to admit. "Being a leader goes far beyond wearing a crown and making demands," he said with a squeeze. "No decision is ever easy. I'll make this one for you if you ask me to, but don't get used to it."

He wanted me to stand on my own two feet and take ownership over this life. If I'd been paying attention, that was what he'd been asking of me all along. But after years of trying to smother my curiosity and stay willingly in the dark, I was done with that. I wouldn't let him decide for me.

I shifted my weight on him. "I've known what I wanted to do since I woke up."

"Yeah?" He tilted his head. "Tell me."

"The grandson can live. If you see fit, he can work here in the Badlands for you." I met his eyes. "The rest can die."

He stilled. "Natalia . . ."

I made a fist in his hair and stared into his eyes so he knew I meant every word. "I don't care how you do it, but finish Vicente and each of his brothers. I want to dump their ashes at the base of my mother's grave so their worthless souls can spend eternity kissing her feet."

I had watched my mother die, and every single person involved was going to pay.

Including, if I had my way, the son-of-a-bitch who'd ruined my life.

## CHAPTER 15

# CRISTIANO

I had never been more aroused in all of my thirty-four years. I deserved a medal for my abstinence since Natalia's arrival. With the way she was grinding against my dick, and with her order that I execute three men in her name—I was on a rocket ship headed for the moon. She was ready for me; I could see it in her eyes as her hair fell around her face, begging to be wrapped up in my fist.

Even through the haze, though, her pain lived strong. That was fine. Last night, she'd been too deep in it, and it would be a while before it subsided. But now that she'd spent the night grieving in my arms, letting me comfort her, I would give her relief and release.

"It would be an honor to avenge you and Bianca," I said.

She slid her hips back and forth, leaving a wet spot on the crotch of my underwear. "Is there anything you wouldn't do for revenge?"

"You know it's more complicated than that. Retribution can be all-consuming." I struggled to organize my thoughts with her pulsing slit growing greedy for me, but this conversation was important. "I'll never let revenge rule my life as my father and Diego did. That's my promise to you. For me—my wife, family, and people come first."

She hovered her juicy, delicious lips above mine. "I want to know how it feels to come first," she whispered.

With a short growl, I slid a hand into her hair, both pulling it and holding her where she was. "It's a path you can't come back from."

I needed her explicit permission, but I wasn't above playing dirty to get it. With my other hand on her hip, I took a handful of her ass and bucked my pelvis up, ramming my shaft against her clit.

Her eyes rolled back into her head. "Do that again."

*Beg. Demand. Tell me to fuck you raw.*

It had to be about me and her and nothing else. She had to want this more than she wanted to resist me or hurt Diego. My erection was turning painful, but I needed her to ask, and for it to be *now*.

With a knock on the door, we both froze. "*¿Señor?*" came Jaz's voice.

I closed my eyes and sighed. God, give me a moment of uninterrupted pleasure in this lifetime. Hadn't I earned the exquisite pleasure of fucking my horny wife for the first time? "*Vete,*" I called out, sending Jaz away.

"*Es importante,*" she replied.

"*Important?*" Natalia scoffed. "No. She has a sixth sense for when you and I are getting close. She wants to come between us. Ignore her."

Whether that was true or not, Jazmín was intuitive enough to know when she was needed and when she should make herself scarce. I took Natalia's ass cheeks in both hands and squeezed hard enough to send the message that this *culo* was mine when I got back—then moved her off my crotch and stood to pull on some sweats. "It could be about Max."

I shoved my hand down my pants and tried to calm my raging hard-on as I crossed the room. I hid it with the door as I leaned my head out. "*¿Qué quieres,* Jaz? It's not a good time."

"Alejandro wants you downstairs immediately."

"*Puta madre,*" I cursed. "What's it about?"

She shrugged. "I'm just supposed to tell you."

"Natalia needs me here. She doesn't want to be alone."

"Of course not. She wants you all to herself, even if others need you."

I frowned at her and warned, "Jazmín."

"I'm sorry, but it's true," she said, turning away. "Alejo's waiting for you."

I sighed and closed the door before heading for my closet. "I'm sorry, *mi amor*."

"What is it?" Natalia asked.

I threw on a t-shirt, moving quickly so I could get this over with. "I'm needed downstairs."

"You're needed *here*," she called from the bed. "You always go when Jaz calls."

"I do not. This is Badlands business." On my way out of the bedroom, I stopped in my tracks. The interruption had taken care of my erection, but suddenly it threatened to return. Natalia sat with her back against the headboard, the thin white sheet tucked under her arms, barely concealing the rosy berries begging to be devoured. Her long disheveled hair fell around her bare arms. I'd resisted her for so long, and now that I had her, I was leaving her naked and wanting in our bed?

"*Qué pendejo*," I muttered about myself.

"What happened to 'this is a path you can't come back from'?" she accused. With the vitriol in her voice, I met her glare. "I guess it includes the clause 'unless Jaz needs me.'"

She was pissed, and I was just close enough to the edge to say *fuck it* and get back into bed. Especially considering Natalia's possessive side alone was sexy enough to get me going again. But if Alejandro's news had anything to do with Max, I had to go. And I had to do it now, before I changed my mind.

"I'll be back as fast as I can. *Te lo prometo*." With my promise, I bent at the hip and pecked her hard and fast, before she—or my dick—could protest. "Don't move an inch."

I DESCENDED the stairs into the dark basement control center to find Alejandro waiting with his arms crossed over his chest.

"This'd better be good," I said. "You've just put me in the doghouse with Natalia. She needs all of my attention right now."

"She'll forgive the dog if he catches her a rat."

I arched an eyebrow at him as we headed down the hall toward where Vicente and his family remained chained and silenced. Instead, he led me to a different room. Seated alone in the middle was Gabriel, Vicente's grandson, with his hands bound in front of him.

Alejandro yanked tape off the boy's mouth and nodded once. "Tell him what you told me."

Gabriel stretched his jaw but kept his eyes down. "I can help you."

I followed his gaze to a pair of broken glasses on the ground. "Look at me, boy," I said.

He raised his fearful eyes, blinking rapidly and squinting. Perhaps he needed those glasses. "I can help you find Max," he said.

I let my eyes drift over the skinny kid. I was certain I'd weighed more than him at eight years old. "How?"

"My grandfather told you I can find things on the Internet—that's like calling Lionel Messi a good *fútbol* player."

"Lionel Messi, eh? You a sports fan?" I asked, aware of how sinister my laugh sounded as I glanced to Alejandro. "You tore me away from my distraught wife for this?"

"Coding, surveillance, dark web," the kid spoke quickly, tripping over his words, as if begging for his life. "I can do all of it. I built my first computer from discarded parts. The Internet is my sandbox . . . and that makes the world my playground."

"My intelligence team is unrivaled," I said. "They come from all over the world. Beijing, Russia, San Francisco—"

"With all due respect, sir, if that were true, you wouldn't have had a major security breach earlier this month when Belmonte-Ruiz attacked your household."

Alejandro seemed pleased—so, this was why he'd called me down here. I, on the other hand, wasn't so delighted. "How the fuck do you know about that?" I asked, stepping forward.

"All my life I've heard of the guts and glory of my grandfather, great uncles, and the cartel they built. Since we were forced into hiding, I've had to be invisible my whole life. Now, I'm better at hiding than anyone, and I know how to get information. On you, on Belmonte-Ruiz . . . even on Diego." He swallowed audibly. "When I learned he'd blackmailed my family into disappearing, I took an interest in him. I've followed him for a long time."

"Do you know where he is?" I asked.

"No, but give me a chance. I can find him."

"Why should I believe you?"

"Your men learned how to hack, but I never knew a life without it; I *am* it. I never went to school. I only know computers. Let me train with your team, and I will become the best hacker in the world," he said. "Give me a chance to prove myself before you kill me. Let me show you what I can achieve—under your guidance."

From the moment I'd heard Gabriel was Vicente's grandson, I'd known he'd have to die. I wouldn't make the same mistake I'd made with Diego. But I thought of what Natalia had said. I was the other half of that equation. I'd been right by Diego's side and had felt no resentment or anger toward Costa for what he'd done—only gratitude and loyalty.

"Why would I trust you? I'm going to kill the rest of your family regardless."

His fidgeting stopped. "I guess I understand why you have to do it. My *abuelo*, I love him, but he has lived a long life considering his odds."

Spoken like a true math whiz. Logic and reason spoke to this kid. One assassination equaled one retribution.

But then he continued, "And I saw Natalia's face in there. I feel bad. I lost my mom in all of this, too."

*Huh*. Either there was a heart in that motherboard or he was trying to manipulate my evident soft side for Natalia. "What do you know about Belmonte-Ruiz?" I asked.

"Not much, but I learn quickly," Gabriel said. "I know more about what you do here in the Badlands."

"It's not such a secret anymore. We have our fingers in many, uh, pies, as they say." My finger *should* have been in the most delicious pie right then—I mentally hurried Gabriel along.

"Arms, freight, money laundering—but you also traffic in people," he said, and added, "just in the wrong direction, most would say."

The hair on the back of my neck stood up. Rumors had been spreading about our operation, and that would ultimately hurt us, but there was no way the truth could've already made it to the impoverished corners of Mexico. "How do you know that?"

"I told you—I'm invisible. Your security is top-of-the-line, but I got through. You need me."

That kind of skill was lethal in the wrong hands. But in the right ones, it was an asset. How could I know who this boy was, though? His true intentions? "And what do you think of our operation?"

"You're the good guys."

"We're not," I said, crossing my arms as the fluorescent lighting overhead buzzed. "We've hurt far more than we've helped. If guts and glory are what you want, look somewhere else. We do what we have to so we survive, and to further our cause. It brings no recognition, only enemies from all sides, and that's about to get worse."

"Then you will need good intel, security, and protection. I can help. There are more and more kids like me coming up in the ranks," Gabriel said. "We know technology better than our own faces. But I have something many don't—I've known the worst of this country, and I'm willing to die before I return to it."

That rounded out his third reason for offering help. Logic, heart, and motivation for a better life. *Ay*, and thwarting death, of course. Looking to Alejandro, I cracked my knuckles. "Diego's not the one we're trying to find right now."

"Max," Gabriel stated. "Alejandro told me."

I rubbed the bridge of my nose. My hands were tied. I had to do whatever necessary to help Max. I'd be a fool to turn down help and a fool to accept it. "You have until my patience runs out to help us find everything you can on Belmonte-Ruiz and Max's current location," I said.

"Yes, sir. Thank you, sir."

I nodded once at Alejandro. "Hand him over to the IT team. Eyes don't leave him for a second. Get him a new pair of glasses. And Alejo?"

"*Dime*," he said, inviting me to continue.

"Don't fucking disturb me again. I don't care if the sky is falling."

Now, I would go fuck my wife.

That was, if I could find her. Because when I returned, she wasn't in the bedroom.

Or the library. Or by the pool.

After I'd been all around the house, I found myself knocking on Pilar's door.

"*Adelante*," came two female voices followed by a bout of giggling, and, "*¡Embrujado*! Jinx!"

I entered the room and found Natalia on the tips of her toes in Pilar's closet, trying to reach a purse on the top shelf—and wearing jeans, socks, and a sweater over her top. Not naked as I'd left her when I'd ordered her to stay put.

I walked in, plucked the bag from the shelf, and handed it to her. "Going somewhere?"

Her fiery eyes met mine a moment before she turned away. "No. We're reorganizing Pilar's closet."

I blinked around the space. It looked as if Pilar had hardly touched a thing since her arrival. "Seems pretty damn organized to me."

"Well, Jaz's method doesn't quite make sense to us," Natalia explained.

"Why not?" I asked.

"Because it doesn't," she snapped.

Pilar's puppy-dog eyes stayed on me, waiting for my reaction—for the explosion. In deference to her history with violent men, I inhaled a breath to control my temper. "I need to speak to you, Natalia."

"After we're finished." Natalia stepped back, pinching her chin as she assessed a row of sandals. "These should really be arranged by heel height."

*Ah*. This wasn't about Pilar's closet. Natalia was punishing me for leaving her in bed. As if it had been easy for me. As if the thought of fucking her wasn't always top of mind.

I needed to clear my head. I needed the space to think straight. I needed to fuck so hard that there was nothing left in my mind but answers. "Excuse me, Pilar," I said, keeping my eyes on Natalia, "but my wife and I were in the middle of something that needs resolving."

"Oh . . ." Natalia looked over her shoulder and winked. "I resolved it on my own."

If her smirk was any indication, I must've looked as dumbfounded as I felt. The thought of her getting herself off in my bed when that was my job . . .

I stepped up behind her, and by the way she stiffened, she knew I was done fucking around. "March your ass upstairs before I do it for you."

"He expects me to come when he calls," she said to Pilar. "The way he goes running whenever Jaz needs him."

I let a short chuckle free, though I was only amused by the prospect of dreaming up ways to punish her for that comment. I scooped her up, threw her over my shoulder, and gave Pilar a friendly smile. "We'll see you when we're finished. Don't wait up."

To Pilar's credit, for once, she didn't look scared. "Have a good time."

# CHAPTER 16

# NATALIA

Cristiano the Brute dropped me on my feet in our bedroom, seemingly oblivious to my fuming. I'd begun to sweat under all this clothing, but that was part of his punishment for leaving me alone, naked, and more aroused than I'd ever been. "*Pendejo*," I said.

"You're awfully brave to call me an asshole," he said. "Considering you were shaking in your *huaraches* when you arrived here."

"I was not. I stood here, in this room, and invited you to fuck me that first night. You're the one who walked away," I accused.

He didn't deserve that; my gratitude for his restraint during that time knew no bounds. Cristiano could've taken what he'd wanted on our wedding night. How many men in his position would've? I shuddered to think. I'd be a different woman if he had, married to a different man.

But enough was enough. I needed him to finish what he'd started and consummate this goddamn marriage.

"I wasn't going to rape you the way my brother did." Cristiano stalked up to me, taking my chin in his large paw of a hand and forcing me to look him in the eyes. "And that *is* what he did, Natalia. He said whatever he had to in order to coerce you into his bed. I wasn't going to do the same, and I never will, so you'd better learn how to ask for what you fucking want."

"I *did*. I told you not to leave this morning, but you didn't hesitate a second before running off when Jaz called." Smug satisfaction settled in me at the way he flinched. I'd offered myself to him twice in twenty-four hours, and he'd turned me down both times. The unrelenting need to be relieved by him and only him pushed me to poke him until he reacted. "My husband turns his back on his wife when another woman needs him. Jaz, Tasha, Sandra—is there anyone I come before?"

"How dare you say I haven't put you first!" He took his hand back, towering over me. "Have you wanted for *anything* since you stepped foot inside these walls?"

*You.*

My desire for him had been simmering since our first dance, I just hadn't wanted to admit it. Now that I could, it overwhelmed me, and I hated that I could be flipped so easily. I trusted Cristiano with my body, but it didn't erase Diego's violation.

"I thought I knew what *you* wanted, but maybe I was wrong," I said, my lips pinched as I dropped my eyes to the bulging crotch of his sweats. "Or maybe I wasn't. There must be some other reason you keep your hands to yourself."

"Watch your mouth, *chiquita*," he warned.

Being referred to as a *little girl* only infuriated me more. I stepped up under his nose. "I think I hear Jaz calling. Perhaps you should run along so I can return to my friend."

"People's lives are on the line. You expect me to laze in bed when they need me and let them fend for themselves?"

"Yes." I was being unfair, but so was he. It wasn't just my heart that had been aching since yesterday, but my body, too. Cristiano had promised to fuck me into oblivion more than once, and he had yet to follow through. Did he expect me to beg for it?

He stepped forward until we were toe to toe, his eyes darkening as his composure fissured. Finally, his anger matched mine. "Heaven's finest symphony is just noise compared to your pleas for me to stay in bed. I couldn't ask for anything more. But understand—you cannot command me. I don't answer to anyone. I have a duty to fulfill."

"You took me, you put me in this role, so, yes—now, you *do* answer to me." I nearly vibrated with rage. "And I won't come second to anyone, especially Jaz. She's trying to come between us."

"Nobody gets between us unless we allow it. And since when do you care?" Heat flashed in his eyes as he tilted his head, provoking me. "Why does my wife suddenly give a fuck where I go and what I do? What could be the reason, hmm?"

"Because . . . because . . ."

*Love*. That was why.

Because I had run out of reasons not to love him. It had bloomed unexpectedly and brutally. The soil for it had been rich, the foundation laid before I knew what it was to love a man. My mother had trusted him, and so had I. Cristiano had been nurturing that seed all along, and the vines had overgrown my heart without my realizing it.

And he knew it.

"You don't need to pick a fight, *mi amor*," he said smugly. "If you need me to fuck you, just ask—and mean it."

I needed it so badly, I ached with it. I grabbed his cheeks and pulled his mouth to mine. For a moment, he seemed too stunned to react, but then he gripped my hair by the root and backed me up against a wall.

"You thought all these clothes could keep me out, eh?" he said.

"It almost worked."

"You have no idea how wrong you are. Say it," he demanded into my mouth, then yanked my cardigan down around my biceps, trapping me with it. "Ask for it."

My breath stuttered along with my pulse. I was too needy, too aching, too far gone to anything but the carnal pull between us. "Please, Cristiano. Please, will you?"

"Will I what?"

"Do as you've promised. Destroy what's yours to destroy. Take my virginity as it should've been done. Please, fuck me. *Please*."

His hands fisted, tightening my sweater around me. "What a way to ask," he said, his chest rumbling with promise. "You've made it worth the wait. And I'll answer in spades, *mamacita*." He tore off my sweater and shoved a hand down the front of my pants, bypassing the fly, then my underwear. His fingertips slipped and glided against my opening but didn't enter. "Have you been wet this whole time?"

"Since the start," I admitted hoarsely.

His free hand gripped the waistband of my jeans and tugged them higher and higher until the seam of the crotch wedged up against my clit. "How's that?"

Open-mouthed, I gasped as he massaged it back and forth. "Oh. *God*."

He cocked his head, assessing me with complete composure as his chest rumbled with a "*Hmm*."

"What?" I panted.

"I'm deciding what to do with you. Based on how you just came at me, claws out, I think what you need more than anything right now is a good, hard fuck."

The prospect of inviting that from someone like Cristiano both thrilled and scared me—just like everything else when it came to my husband. The last few weeks had been building up to this, a passionate dance, each step becoming easier as we'd each given into faith. I trusted him to hurt me in the ways I needed without going too far.

"I deserve to be punished for how I've treated you. How I've spoken to you," I breathed against him. "Make me repent."

He yanked down my pants and underwear and left them in a heap as he lifted me against the wall. My legs wrapped around him instinctively, like a snake with prey, out of my control, squeezing him closer.

"I'll punish you, Natalia Lourdes, and you'll beg for more," he said, holding me up with one hand and reaching into his pants with the other to stroke himself. "Later, I'm going to ask you to put my cock inside you. I'm going to run my tongue along and inside every part of your body I can reach. But right now, I'm going to shove it inside you, and you're going to let me like the good little doll you are. Understand?"

If I hadn't been pinned to the wall, I might've fallen over with need. Instead, I shoved at his chest, moving him only centimeters. "You don't want a doll. You want the girl who pulled a gun on you. The one you're teaching to fight back."

He trapped my wrists and held them over my head. After locking them there with one hand, he pulled himself out of his sweats, lined his head up with my opening, and started to press inside. "Then it's too bad I haven't taught you how to get out of this hold yet, isn't it?" he asked and thrust his hips forward.

He filled me all at once. "*Fuck*," I cried.

"Yeah, *fuck*," he said, rooting himself there. "*Fuck* you and your too-tight cunt. How's it feel to finally be broken wide open?"

My chest heaved. He quenched a thirst that ran deeper than I'd thought possible. I was full, finally, for the first time in my life, physically—but also emotionally bursting with desire and love and everything else I couldn't seem to get a handle on. "It feels . . ." Even the finest words couldn't convey like the language our bodies spoke. "It feels like we should've done this weeks ago."

"No shit. All I've wanted is to watch your face as I claim you." He used both hands this time to fasten my wrists above my head before he drew back and impaled me again. "As your pussy yields for me, then sucks me deeper."

"*Ay, Dios m*—" I cried. "Oh . . . my . . . G—"

"Who are you talking to, *mi vida*?" He took my mouth for a hard, wet kiss as he moved in and out, making sure I felt every ridge and vein of his shaft. Trapping my bottom lip between his teeth, he pinched it until I moaned, then released it. "Nobody's as divine as you," he professed. "You're the goddess in the sky the rest of us appeal to. Who could match you?"

"You."

His tongue ran along my lip to the corner of my mouth as his hips picked up pace. "Does it hurt?"

It was a simple question with myriad answers. Was pain always bad? Could it feel so good that it hurt? Was I allowed to crave physical agony to incarnate my soul-deep yearning for him? "Yes," I said as my pussy contracted around him and my legs pulled him even closer.

He pulled out until I had to engage my thigh muscles to keep from slipping down the wall. "I could be gentler," he said. "Treat you like a real doll. Like you can't handle it."

"I can take it. I want it to hurt, and I want you to make it better." I met his gaze, the evident need in his eyes. Not to push me up against a wall—he could've done that any time. But a need to fill me in ways nobody else could and master this domain. To *finally* have me willing. I freed my wrists from his grip, hugged his neck, and pressed my forehead to his. "I know it hurts you, too."

Something passed over his face. He leaned in, and I drew back, keeping myself just outside his reach. With a growl that reverberated in my chest, he captured my mouth for a punishing kiss, the kind I'd expect of a deadly, passionate, dominant kingpin.

Without disconnecting, he carried me across the room and lowered me until just my upper back hit the mattress. Holding my hips up, he brought them to meet each of his hard and fast thrusts. "Watch how your pussy takes me, Natalia—every inch," he said, reaching out to press his thumb in my mouth. I automatically sucked. "I'd promise that by the time I'm through with you, you'll be ruined for anyone else—but I'll *never* be through with you." He removed his thumb and bent forward to pinch my chin and keep my eyes on him. "And if that scares you—good."

I arched my back as his relentless drives hit me deeper and deeper. Warmth coiled in my core, another aching knot in me that Cristiano had inspired—one only Cristiano could relieve. "I'm not scared," I said.

He slid a hand under the hem of my t-shirt and spread it over my lower tummy as it trembled. His thumb dipped between my folds to my clit. "You were."

"I was."

"But now, you'll take everything I have to give."

"How much more could there be?" I breathed as my muscles quivered around his cock.

"I can get deeper—so much deeper," he promised. "But I need you to come for me first and loosen up your cunt." He took my waist, his grip so tight that his fingertips almost met as he lifted me higher. Pulled me onto each thrust. Fucked me so hard his balls slapped against my ass cheeks. "Give me that nectar only good enough for a god; let an unworthy man into the depths of Heaven."

I shivered with his words. This was what I'd always needed. Not to be coddled and pacified with Diego's flat, emotionless, stupid-as-fuck poetry. I'd take the raw and profane from Cristiano over lifeless prose any day. I'd take his fast and hard screw over Diego's sniveling lovemaking.

I closed my eyes so I could feel every sensation as it washed over me, every nuance of Cristiano's demanding fuck.

"Eyes open, Natalia," he said. "I know you're afraid of the dark, but in my bed, you'll face me."

I flitted my lids open to the beastly devil above me. The monster under my bed that had crawled out and mounted me. The one who knew my deepest fears and conquered them with me.

I shook with the force of a sudden, foundation-splitting orgasm. He held me in the safety of his black eyes as I found rapture—not in the heights of Heaven but in the depths of his hell.

"God. *Fuck.*" He stilled and groaned up to the ceiling. "You're holding onto me so tight, it *might* be enough to keep me out of your ass for a few days."

I released a quivering breath as the aftershock of my orgasm rolled through me. *Now,* I was scared. I had come for the devil and enjoyed every second of it—and now I feared I'd give it to him any way he asked.

He pulled out of me, his cock hard, throbbing, nearly purple between us—and covered in me. Before I could even register it, he leaned forward and ripped open my top. "Flip over," he demanded, urging me onto my stomach faster, discarding the ruined shirt.

His hands spread over the base of my spine and glided to the clasp of my bra. He got it open, smoothing his palms up and down my back. "*Qué buena estas.*"

I wasn't sure I felt *sexy* in that moment, bent over the edge of the bed, my ass in the air, wide open to him. The thought of taking him back there inspired more nerves than excitement.

He slid his slick shaft between my cheeks and the veiny, soft skin rubbed the raw bud of nerves at my opening.

"You got quiet," he said, and I could've sworn I heard a smile in his voice.

He was enjoying this, the way my body had gone as tense as the strings of an over-tuned guitar. With the curtains open and the sun streaming in, fucking like this in broad daylight felt *obscene*. "Not my ass," I said, pressing the side of my face into the mattress. My voice pitched as I said, "I can't . . ."

"Not your ass," he agreed. "It's not ready yet. I want to play with it first. Get to know it. Introduce it to my fingers. My tongue."

I fisted the sheets, glancing back at him as my face flamed with heat. "You wouldn't."

"Oh, I would, *mamacita*. And I will." He drew his t-shirt over his head, stripping down at lightning speed. "But understand one thing. When we do get there, I'll never hurt you that way. Not ever, Natalia. When I take your ass, it will be to send us both to the moon."

I closed my eyes, and instead of fear, satisfaction washed over me. I'd spent so long fighting to distrust every word out of his mouth, especially when it came to the pain he could inflict. I chose to believe him now.

"Your pussy, however," he said, spreading my lips with his thumbs. He slid inside me from behind, his complete, staggering length impaling me slowly, until I'd taken him to the root. "That, I will use until I've filled you up with enough cum to make up for each night I've missed as your husband."

The bluntness of his words cut through my haze. "But I could get pregnant!"

"*Me vale verga*. I don't care. It's too late. It's already leaking out of me. And your sweet, thirsty pussy will swallow everything, won't it?"

I had never wanted anything so badly in my life. I knew no other response except one. "Yes, sir."

"Obedient little bride."

He put one foot on the mattress, held down my hips, and drove into me so deep, I whimpered. "That's it," he said, his voice full of gravel as he hammered me. "I can feel the end of you now, and I'm going to fuck you there until even that gives."

My face flushed. The utter and complete fullness of my pussy, the feeling of being more him than me in that moment, tapped into my basest needs. The pleasure intensified as he drilled away until all I could do was scream. I'd never heard myself do such a thing, but I was too gone to be embarrassed that my cries nearly shook the walls. "Yes!" The only words I could form spilled from me. "*Yes, papi. Por favor*—please."

I wanted his release as much as my own and I even tried to meet his penetrating thrusts as I was pinned down.

Relief came quickly. He ground me against the mattress over and over until I came again.

My fatigued muscles shook as I relaxed into the mattress. Cristiano took me until the very end, until he delivered on his promise and erupted into my wilting body, breathing life back into me.

# CHAPTER 17

# NATALIA

Cristiano sat squarely in front of a large, majestic, burgundy velvet tapestry with golden thread that hung on one wall of the main room. At the head of the dining table, the open floor plan allowed him to see through the house, down the hall, and almost to the entryway. I couldn't help thinking he'd designed it that way.

Remnants of our small feast, prepared in honor of a visit from my father, littered the table. Papá had been quieter than usual since we'd returned from a horseback tour of the Badlands. We'd invited him to stay for a few days so we could introduce him to the business he'd become a part of with our . . . *merger*.

And, in a way, it'd been an introduction for me, too. We'd made our way through the town square where Cristiano had bought my sandals, *click-clacking* down the road on our horses. From the outside, who would've thought the Badlands would have something as quaint as a Main Street? There were also fully functioning farms to keep residents fed—and even a distillery to keep them in good spirits. Doctor Sosa, who'd tended to Cristiano and me after Belmonte-Ruiz's strike, ran a decent-sized medical clinic where she regularly saw patients.

It awed me how well they operated as a society.

I couldn't quite read my father's reaction, though. Today, he'd learned the truth about Cristiano's business—that Calavera was involved in the flesh trade, but instead of trafficking in people, he was saving them.

Seated to Cristiano's right, I took the last bite of chicken *mole* I could possibly stuff into my stomach and deflated against the back of my seat, covering my tummy. "I'm so full."

"It was an excellent meal, Pilar," Papá said from across the table. He always sat at the head, but there had been no confusion over who belonged there in Cristiano's home.

In *our* home. I suspected it would be a while before it really began to feel like mine. I hadn't picked out any of these things, or, like Cristiano, overseen its construction from the ground up. It was the people who felt more like home than the Badlands.

It was him, Cristiano.

"Should I get the dessert?" Pilar asked and dabbed her mouth with a napkin. When she stood, Alejo and Barto did, too. Her face reddened. "Oh, no, don't get up. I can handle it."

The men exchanged an unfriendly glance. Over Pilar? She and Alejandro had become close spending time together here at the house, but Barto had known her for most of her life as my friend. He'd been quieter than usual tonight, his eyes roaming the room and the company. He was obviously uncomfortable as a guest in the Badlands despite Cristiano's invitation.

As Pilar exited the room, Jazmín entered with a tray of tall shot glasses and a liquor bottle that looked more like a piece of art. A pewter mermaid embraced the tequila, her tail gracefully wrapped around a decanter topped with a skeleton.

"This is a two-thousand-dollar bottle of tequila," Papá remarked as Jaz poured each of us a shot.

"It's aged three years in French oak barrels right here in our region—only a hundred bottles were produced," Cristiano said. "*Sirena del Deseo*."

"Mermaid of desire," I translated. Our eyes met. Cristiano and I had snuck down to the strip of beach below our balcony earlier. "*Mi sirenita*," he'd called me—*my little mermaid*—as we'd swum and danced in the ocean, then fucked under the hot Mexican sun.

As Jaz distributed the drinks, Cristiano brought the back of my hand to his mouth for a kiss. "With the decanter, the artist tells the love story of a Mexican warrior who traveled to the very depths of the sea in search of his beloved mermaid."

"How romantic," Pilar said, crossing the room from the kitchen, her hands full with a cake. Behind her, one of the kitchen staff carried in a stack of plates and silverware. She set toothpicks on the table near Cristiano.

"Ah, Pilar's famous *tres leches* cake," my father commented.

She blushed, handing him the serving utensil. "As our guest, you get first slice, *señor* Cruz."

"I don't think the tequila is meant to be romantic," I said, back on the decanter. "The warrior on top is a skeleton."

"It *is* a love story, but a tragic one," Cristiano said, "as he did not survive his quest."

The warmth of his palm against mine did nothing to stem the trail of chills up my arm, nor did the graveness of his frown.

When we all had tequila and cake before us, I asked, "What's the occasion?"

Cristiano's mood lifted with a smile. "Do I need one to celebrate my wife and her family? *Salud*."

We each raised our tequilas with a "¡*Salud*!" and sipped.

"Though, if my calculations are correct," Cristiano added, lowering his glass, "today *does* mark six weeks since we stood in the church and said our vows."

My eyes stayed locked with his. "Six weeks and a lifetime."

"Give your husband a kiss to celebrate," he said.

I pursed my lips, but not for a kiss. Everyone was watching, and Cristiano knew it. "When we're alone."

"No. Now." He leaned over. "Come. *Un beso*."

Drawn to him like a magnet, I inclined forward to meet him, balancing on his thigh as my mouth found his, the full, warm lips all at once new and familiar. I curled my fist against his leg. I knew him intimately and still had so much to discover. But I drew back quickly when I remembered we weren't alone, lowering my eyes to the table as I blushed.

"What happened to your neck?" Barto's abrupt question and hardened tone made my eyes jump to his. "That looks like the beginning of a hypertrophic scar."

I covered the ugly imperfection as Cristiano and I exchanged a glance. I didn't want to lie, but we hadn't broached the subject of Belmonte-Ruiz's strike with my father yet. The scar wasn't overtly noticeable, but had started to become pink and raised. I'd originally put on a turtleneck for dinner, but on such a warm June night, Cristiano had said it looked suspicious—before reminding me to wear the symbol of my survival with pride.

"It's nothing," I said with my first bite of cake.

"She fell into a mirror," Pilar volunteered. "It broke."

Barto snorted, his knuckles whitening around his fork as he turned his glare on Cristiano. "She *fell*? You expect anyone to believe that?"

"Barto," my father warned, then turned to me. "Is that true?"

"She can't be honest," Barto said. "If she is, she may 'fall' again. Or maybe it will be Pilar this time."

His statement hung as eerie silence descended over the room. All eyes drew to Cristiano. He ate a chunk of his cake, chewing slowly before swallowing it down with a gulp of tequila that must've cost thousands of *pesos*. Looking at Barto, he leaned back in his seat. "Fuck you."

Alejandro grabbed Barto's arm as he tried to stand. "*Tranquilo*," Alejo said. "Relax, friend. Cristiano hasn't laid a hand on Natalia, and he never will."

"Why should I believe it?" Barto asked.

Cristiano sucked his teeth. "Natalia and I need to speak to Costa in private."

Alejandro and Pilar stood with their dishes, but Barto stayed where he was. "I'm here to protect and support Costa," Barto said. "You can say anything in front of me."

"That was an order," Alejandro said, looking down at him.

Barto fisted his napkin and rose to his full height, eye to eye with Alejandro. "I don't take orders from him. Or you, *pinche pendejo*."

"Please, stop," Pilar said, touching Barto's forearm and drawing Alejo's gaze there. "Alejandro is not an eff-ing a-hole, and I know you're just being protective, but we're all on the same side. Cristiano has been good to Natalia."

"Thank you, Esmeralda," Alejandro said, and Pilar blushed at her new name.

Barto's brows drew together. "Esmeralda . . .?"

Cristiano addressed my father. "You can fill Barto in on everything later."

Papá nodded once. With the dismissal, Barto threw his napkin on his plate of half-eaten cake and strode from the room with Alejandro and Pilar behind him. The last thing I heard was Alejandro's taunt. "Try to keep up, Barto. Pilar goes by Esmeralda now."

When we were alone, my father licked his fork clean. "Pilar really is a good baker, like her mother." He sighed, setting the utensil on his plate as his expression cleared. "It's a lot to take in, Cristiano, everything you showed me here."

"It's truly remarkable, isn't it, Papá?" I really wanted him to like it here—to be as impressed by Cristiano as I was, and to feel welcome to visit whenever.

"I would feel a little claustrophobic," he said.

"Beyond the walls, you have open desert on three sides and the whole sea behind you," Cristiano pointed out.

"What good is that?" He shrugged. "The ocean traps you in."

"No, *señor*," Cristiano said. "We have a small naval fleet so that makes land, air, and sea wide open to us. The ships are stored inside the mountain, where we've hollowed it out." He winked at me. "Did I mention there are jet skis?"

I suppressed a smile. No, he hadn't. I discovered more of the Badlands' secrets each day and had just learned about the mountainside that afternoon—but there'd been no mention of watersports. Was there anything they hadn't thought of?

"What I love, is that it's self-sustaining," I told my father. "The woman who made my wedding rings, Teresa, is also an electrician thanks to education she received after her arrival. Another couple makes the smoothest tequila from blue agave grown right here."

"*Está buenísimo*," Cristiano agreed. "So good, we keep it on hand here."

"Everyone has been trained in a trade or skill," I said.

"That's intentional." Cristiano spun his tumbler on the table. "It gives me pleasure to see them well-fed, healthy, and happy, but should the Badlands dissolve tomorrow, its people would survive. And if something happens to me, Max knows . . ."

He stopped.

It wasn't the first time Cristiano had referred to Max as if he was still around. And without fail, I'd see the moment Cristiano realized his mistake, pain flashing across his expression. As I'd learned with my mother's death, one way to help ease grief was with memories. Max wasn't dead that we knew of, but I was pretty sure Cristiano believed he wasn't ever coming home. I couldn't personally think of an instance in which a cartel had captured and then released a rival.

I covered Cristiano's hand with mine. "How did you meet Max?"

"Like everyone else," he said, blinking his dim gaze to me. "Each of us, down and out, were looking for a leg up. We made our own leg up and then helped the other. In the early days after I'd left the compound," he said, looking to my father, "I'd gamble. Turn twenty *pesos* into forty, forty into a hundred."

I eased back against my seat with my tequila, content to learn something new about Cristiano's past. "I didn't know that."

With a nod, he continued, "Max was also scraping by. One night, I lost nearly everything. He'd had a winning streak. He let me stay with him until I was back on my feet, and when the tables turned, and he needed me, I was there. It's been that way ever since."

"So how come he wasn't—*isn't* Lord of the Badlands?" I asked.

Finally, I got a smile from Cristiano, albeit a crooked one. "Diplomacy doesn't suit him. He'd rather do what needs to be done."

"*Ay*, and *you're* diplomatic?" I asked.

With a chuckle, he raised his glass. "To Max. Ugliest son-of-a-bitch I ever saw but with a beautiful heart."

The three of us clinked glasses again. "Your camaraderie, your operation—it's like nothing I've ever seen in my lifetime," my father said. "But what's perhaps most impressive of all is that you've managed to keep it a secret."

"The secret's getting out," Cristiano said frankly. I knew it was anything but easy for him to say, but he wasn't one to sugarcoat things. He cleared his throat. "There was . . . an attack."

My father's dark, bushy brows lowered as he set down his shot glass. "Here?"

"*Sí*. And Natalia was a target."

"*¿Qué?*" His voice, which had become more sonorous with age, was the only one I'd heard go deeper and gruffer than Cristiano's. "When was this? Why didn't I know?"

"I'm fine," I said. "Cristiano was the one who got hurt, but we couldn't say anything because nobody outside of here could know he was injured."

Papá leaned over the table, his hands two fists on the wood surface. "When was this?"

"About a month ago," Cristiano said.

"A month! You should've told me as soon as I walked in the door." He slapped the table. "*Sooner*."

"Your blood pressure, Papá," I said.

He drew back. "Eh? What about it?"

I had no idea of my father's vitals, that wasn't something he was inclined to share with me. But it sounded like the right thing to say, and he looked confused enough to forget his anger for a moment.

Apparently, the art of distraction worked in more scenarios than hand-to-hand combat.

"Is that where you got the scar?" he asked me. "You lied to Barto."

"Because I knew how he'd react."

He waved a hand dismissively, sat back in his seat, and pinned us each with a look. I couldn't help feeling like a student in the principal's office. "What happened?"

My father listened silently and unflinchingly as we told him the details of the strike, right up to the aftermath, including how Alejandro and his team had been out in the field, but had come up empty-handed so far.

"Are you asking for my help with an army?" Papá finally asked.

"No—this leads me to other news," Cristiano said. "I mentioned I spoke with Natasha Sokolov-Flores at Senator Sanchez's event. You know how powerful her family is. Together with Alejandro, they were able to find Vicente Valverde."

At the mention of his old enemy, my father's face changed, his only reaction in minutes, aside from asking for clarification or sipping tequila. "Vicente Valverde is *dead*." He looked to Cristiano and laced his fingers on the table. "I would've hunted him down and killed him after what the *sicario* told us, but many confirmed he died of a stroke."

"A stroke of good luck to get away with it so long, perhaps," Cristiano grumbled. "But his luck has run out. Vicente is very much alive and waiting to see you."

He stilled, his wrinkles easing as a frown slowly overtook his face. "What are you talking about?"

"The Valverdes vanished too easily," Cristiano explained. "I wondered why, and simply bringing you a hitman wasn't enough." He extended his arm toward me on the table. "I wanted you both to be able to face those responsible for Bianca's attack, and now I have brought you all but one."

My father's weighty stare shifted from my husband to me and back. "Let's move somewhere private, Cristiano. Bring those Honduran cigars you've been going on about."

Cristiano shifted in his seat. "Natalia already knows everything."

"We shouldn't discuss such violent and traumatic things in front of—"

"I've faced Valverde myself," I said. My father needed to start understanding I wasn't Cristiano's cartel princess. Like my mother, I was learning how to be a partner in this. "I've seen his battered face, heard his vile excuses and admissions—including, for the first time, that my mother was raped. I knew it happened, but nobody ever told me. I had to wonder for years, then hear it from Vicente Valverde."

My father's face paled. "Why would I tell you that? Learning of Bianca's final moments nearly finished me all those years ago. I kept it from you to protect you."

Cristiano flipped up his palm on the table and gestured for mine. I took his hand. "She's tougher than you know, *don* Costa," he said. "Keeping her in the dark does nothing but harm her."

"I defer to you as her husband, but I can't say I agree." Papá stuck both elbows on the table and pinched the bridge of his nose. "No child should hear such things about a parent."

"You didn't shield Bianca from the horrors of this world," Cristiano pointed out.

"And as I've told you," Papá snapped, "look what happened to her."

"It didn't happen because you included her in your business," I said softly. "And it wasn't because you didn't protect her. You couldn't have stopped it."

"You don't know that."

Cristiano and I exchanged a glance, speaking to each other without words. There wasn't much left to say except for the final bit of news I doubted either of us wanted to break.

My father heaved a sigh. "Tell me you've brought me this information about Valverde so I can act on it. Now. Tonight."

"You can act tonight," Cristiano said gravely, nodding slowly. "I'll take you downstairs to them when we're through here."

"Them?" he asked. "How many?"

"Three plus a grandson, Gabriel Valverde. That's all who remain of the family. But we've decided to spare Gabriel's life."

"*Jamás*," Papá said, shaking his head vigorously. "Never. No."

My mouth popped up. "You haven't even heard who he is."

"What's there to know? He's a Valverde. Their bloodline ends now."

I shifted in my seat. "But—"

"The answer is no." His gaze darkened on Cristiano. "If *any* man had *anything* to do with Bianca's murder—"

"He's not a man." I swallowed. My father and Cristiano's presence dwarfed me, but it couldn't mute me. "He's only seventeen. And he was a child when all of this happened."

My father looked to Cristiano "You can't allow it."

Cristiano's gaze drifted to the plate of crumbs before him as he flexed and curled his hand on the table. I could almost hear the wheels of his mind in motion. I'd made myself clear about Gabriel. What was there to think about?

"It's Natalia's call," Cristiano said finally, "and the queen has decided to let him keep his head. I support her completely."

"Natalia is too merciful"—he frowned at me—"I'm sorry, *mi amor,* but this is a man's domain. If you want to be a queen, step up and—"

"I *am* being a queen." With the weight of a proverbial crown, it took a little more effort to sit up straighter, but I did. "We don't kill the innocent. Not every conflict is resolved with vengeance and violence. I learned that from you. *You're* merciful. You're fair. You showed Cristiano mercy when he was a boy, and look who he is now."

"It's a mistake," he warned.

"But it's mine to make."

"The boy is a computer whiz," Cristiano cut in. "He's only been with us a week, but Eduardo reports he's as talented as he claimed. He could have a lot to offer."

I hoped that was true. I wouldn't know if I'd made the right decision until—*unless*—Gabriel betrayed us. I was getting a crash course in the reality that my decisions no longer affected only myself, but my husband, and an entire town, too.

Cristiano's expression soured as if he were about to endure a tooth extraction. "Enough of that." He looked to me. "Tell him."

*Me*? The nape of my neck got clammy. And for a moment, I understood all too well what my father had just been saying. I wanted to protect him from Diego's gutless betrayal, from the news that he'd not only trusted an enemy for so long, but had kept him close.

I could ask Cristiano to tell him for me or have him take Papá into the basement to hear it for himself, the way I had. But Cristiano's gaze challenged me. Showing strength when others needed it was part of my role.

I stood and rounded the table to sit in the seat next to Papá. When I reached out, he opened his hand, took mine, and brought my palm to his lips for a kiss. "*¿Qué, querida?* What's wrong?"

"You warned me about Diego."

He flinched back. "Yes, and finally, he's out of the picture. Why are you bringing him up?"

"I should've listened—but even if I had, it would've been too late." I paused to think of the best way to put it. I could soften the blow with gentle delivery—or, I could make my father hear me by speaking his language. "He fucked us over."

Out of habit, I expected him to comment on my language, but he only gripped my hand more tightly and scowled. "Explain. Now."

"The Valverdes acted out of desperation to salvage their cartel. But they had help. From Diego. And *he* was not a desperate man, but a vengeful one."

My father's eyes bulged in a way I'd never seen. I could always tell his anger by the way his gaze narrowed, overshadowed by his heavy brows. This was something more. "Diego . . . *helped?*"

"He's the one who let the *sicario* into the house, tampered with the compound's security system, and gave him the codes to the safe."

My father had learned the necessary art of hiding his reaction, but it didn't come naturally to him. Currently in safe company, his face turned cherry red as his hand shook holding mine. "I shouldn't believe it so easily." His low, deep voice reverberated through the room. "And that says everything. Bianca warned me."

I squeezed his clammy hand. "He fooled *everyone*. Except maybe her."

"Why?" Beads of sweat formed on his upper lip. He shook his head. "I already know. His parents' execution. Bianca said he harbored resentment over it. And I, always priding myself on being a good judge of character . . ."

"You are," I said. "This doesn't change that."

"He fooled me, too," Cristiano offered, his tone solemn. "And I was his *brother*."

I didn't miss his past tense reference. I glanced to Cristiano, eager to go to him. That Diego had hurt my husband and father so deeply lit embers of rage in me. I wanted to be fair and just, but did that mean I couldn't also be ruthless when the time came? If I had Diego here in this room, would I try to hold Cristiano back, knowing the damage he could do? Or would I let loose the beast?

Part of me wondered not just about Cristiano . . . but also what *I* was capable of in the name of revenge, especially for those I loved.

"Diego's a liar and a coward who'd commit any sin to serve his own best interests," I said. "He killed *mi madre* to avenge his parents, yes—but he also knew it would cripple you and give him the opportunity to stay by your side as you grieved."

I let my father work through the equation on his own until his head bobbed up and down. "To gain my trust. To advise me. To infiltrate the Cruz cartel—so he could someday make it his own to replace the legacy he feels he's owed."

Cristiano stuck a toothpick in his mouth and sat back. "I'll let Valverde fill you in on the rest," he said. "How Diego ruined and exiled them, and how he'd planned to turn Natalia's love against you—until I came along."

"*Qué cabrón*," Papá uttered. "I'd never have allowed that fucking bastard to do it."

I wished I could agree with him and promise my father he would've always known my deepest loyalty. But if Cristiano hadn't returned, I'd still be under Diego's spell. After everything I'd already fallen for, would I have allowed him to eventually oust Papá?

I glanced at my hands. "I thought I loved him, and it blinded me."

"You *did* love him." Cristiano lifted his eyes to me as he struggled to add, "It's okay to say. It was real for you."

For *me*. That made things all the worse. Pretending I'd been tricked into false feelings would be easier than admitting I'd opened my soul to an enemy.

"You see now the man Diego is," Cristiano said. "That's what matters."

"I warned you I'd have to kill him if he broke your heart," my father said.

I nodded. "You did."

One corner of Cristiano's mouth twitched as he suppressed a grin.

"That gives me two reasons to put his head on a stick and send it down Main Street on a parade float," Papá said, rising from his seat and towering over the table. "Now tell me where to find him."

"I wish we could," I said.

"Nowhere is safe for him now. *Barto!*" Papá called.

Barto entered the dining room at once.

As Papá debriefed him, I met Cristiano's searching eyes. His hungry gaze followed me around the table as I went to him. He pulled me into his lap before sliding my cake in front of him. "You didn't finish your dessert."

I put my arms around his neck. "I'm stuffed. I can't eat another thing. If you want it—"

He stabbed his fork in it, picking up nearly half the slice, and shoved it into his mouth.

I blinked at him. "A full-course dinner and dessert wasn't enough?"

"Never turn down food," he said through his chewing.

I hadn't seen him devour anything with such fervor since he'd eaten my *panocha* on this very table. The man was insatiable—and he'd been right about taking my virginity. Anything I'd experienced up until meeting Cristiano's rooster was forgettable.

Papá cleared his throat, and we each turned to him. "I take it the marriage has been consummated."

"*Papá.*" My cheeks flushed as my arms tightened around Cristiano's neck. "That's none of your business."

"It is my business," he responded, his eyes on Cristiano. "I promised I'd make your husband pay if he harmed you."

"Does she look harmed?" Cristiano asked. "I said she'd be loved, treated well, and protected here. I'm doing my best on all fronts."

I was treated well, and I was protected as much as anyone could be in our circumstances. But was I loved? Warmth pooled in my tummy as I studied, up close, Cristiano's dark, angry stubble, the hollow of his cheek, and the fine lines around his devastatingly shrewd eyes.

Was love something he could voice when he felt it, or would he need time?

"Things have obviously changed between you," my father said. I turned back to find him staring at me. "I guess knowing the truth has made a difference in how you view your new husband, *mija*. Yes?"

"*Sí, Papá*," I agreed. "Surely there were better ways to go about making me his wife . . ." Cristiano had the decency to look contrite—even though he'd made it clear he had little to regret. "But I have a lifetime to punish him for it," I added.

Cristiano's mouth slid into a sinister grin. "A sentence I will gladly serve."

"I expect grandchildren soon," my father said in a good-natured tone that made Cristiano and I raise our brows at each other.

I turned my head to Papá. "Why . . .?"

"Do I need a reason?"

A surprised laugh escaped my lips. I tried to stand, but Cristiano's arms tightened around my waist.

"With this news about Diego," my father said, "I can't help but think of family. Of what he cost me. Of how Bianca would've loved a grandchild, especially since it would be from Cristiano, whom she cared for."

With my mother's approval, even from beyond the grave, my heart fluttered. I leaned in and rubbed my cheek against Cristiano's. "It's a nice thought, *Padre*," I said. "One day. We have time."

Cristiano was uncharacteristically silent on the subject. He had only one thing left to say as he patted the outside of my hip. "Go on to bed—I'll be up shortly. Your father and I have business downstairs."

*Business* was all I needed to hear.

The time to eat, drink, and be merry had passed. Now was the time to kill.

## CHAPTER 18

# CRISTIANO

Maybe it was all the time I'd spent on farms today that'd turned me into an animal tonight. Maybe it was weeks of sleeping by Natalia and thinking of nothing but all the ways I wanted to take her. Or years of wondering about her life—if she'd flourished or had resorted to simply existing following Bianca's death, and whether she'd still been blindly devoted to my brother or if it was more nostalgia than anything keeping them together.

It didn't matter. Tonight, I'd embrace the animal. I'd proverbially lain her mother's murderers at my wife's feet. I'd slit three more throats in Bianca's name.

On our bed, gripping Natalia's hips with more strength than I meant, I pounded into her from behind like a dog mounting his bitch. I'd never been more grateful to have soundproofed a room. I must've known I'd end up marrying a screamer.

I wrapped Natalia's long, dark hair around my wrist and pulled so her head drew back. I liked her from this angle, on her hands and knees, but I missed her face. Especially when it was screwed up in pleasure.

"Faster, *harder*," she cried.

Was she serious? I'd never fucked like this in my life. If I went any faster, she'd end up in the next room. If I went any harder, she'd suck up my balls.

I slowed down instead, and after a few deliberate pumps, curved my hand around her behind. "For so long, you treated me like your own personal monster," I threatened, grabbing a fistful of her ass. "Now, while I'm filling you, I want to hear you say you're my wife."

"Or what?"

She wanted to play. So did I. Natalia had poked the beast before, on our wedding night, when I'd bent her over the side of my bed and threatened to wreck her. Her pussy had left a wet spot on the tip of my dick. Maybe a week later, I'd given her a chicken dinner when I'd jammed *El Gallo* down her throat—and she'd cleaned her plate. She possessed a darkness that extended into the bedroom. Lucky for me.

"Say you're my wife, or I'll spank your ass."

She bit her bottom lip and deliberately didn't respond.

I forced myself to withdraw from her, painful as it was to lose her warm, wet heat.

My palm landed with a sharp slap on the outer curve of one cheek, and she gasped. The shock on her face alone was enough to make my dick jump. I kneaded the meat of her ass, then lined up my hand in the same exact spot.

She dropped from her hands to her forearms, pressing her head into the mattress.

"Get back up," I said.

"And if I want more?"

*Beautiful*. I spanked her twice with enough precision and force to make it sting. After a moment, my handprint bloomed on her skin. Maybe *that* was what I should've tattooed on her, because I'd never seen anything so fucking hot.

Or had I?

I lined up my throbbing head to her wet slit and thrust inside her. Her answering moan was almost as sweet as her candy pussy. Now that my cock filled her up, my handprint looked even better.

I took her elbows and pulled her upright. We both groaned at the new angle. I was fucking *deep* now. I kept her arms in a firm hold, using them as leverage to drive into her. "You're trapped now, eh? This greedy little pussy belongs to me. *Say* it."

She arched her back, dropping her head onto my shoulder. "It's so . . ."

"So what?" Buried to the root, I nudged her cervix with a few short thrusts, and her tits bounced toward the ceiling.

"Is it possible to feel it in my stomach?"

I could see her better now. I wanted her mouth, her exquisite eyes on mine, and to see her delicate features shatter with her orgasm. "You're the most perfect thing I've ever laid eyes on." I captured her earlobe between my teeth. "But if you don't call yourself my wife, I'm going to come in you and stay there until there's no question you'll get pregnant."

She shuddered. In so little time, I'd come to known that specific tremor as the first quakes of her climax. "I don't want your baby."

"I don't care." I circled my hands around neck, pulling her back against me. "Look at me and say it."

She could barely turn her head in my grip. I'd never put my hands around a woman's throat this way. I wanted to scare her. I wanted her fear and her orgasm. Her ever-mesmerizing violet eyes found mine, and in them, *I* found clarity. Determination. Devotion. "I'm your wife," she said levelly. "I'm yours. And you're mine, *husband*."

My ears rang with my impending eruption. I was holding her too hard, rutting into her, trying not to bruise her delicate neck as her cervix took a beating. I only loosened my grasp when I heard the word *stop*. I forced myself to slow down long enough to make out what she was saying.

"Don't stop," she cried. "God, *Cristiano*. Please don't stop."

I fucked her to quiet her. She was a screamer up until the final moments, but her orgasms silenced her. When she went mute, she was close. She opened her mouth and gasped for air, dropped her head back against my shoulder, and submitted to her climax.

The moment her pussy gripped me, I was a goner. I released her neck and hugged her close as she milked me until I erupted.

As she went flimsy in my arms, I eased her onto her stomach, propped myself over her, and pumped slowly, keeping my promise. I spurted every last drop into her, and when I was done, I stayed buried inside her, plugging her up.

"We never talked about this," she said quietly.

"What are you referring to?" I asked, even though I knew.

"What do you *think*?" she asked with that bit of sass I loved. "You know I'm not on birth control."

I withdrew and sat on the backs of her thighs, prying apart her sweet pink pussy lips. "You just look so *fucking* good filled to the brim," I said. "You should see how my cum looks inside you."

"You know what happens when you do that, though, don't you?"

I couldn't help my laugh. "I've heard."

I moved off her to lie by her side, brushing her hair off her face. "At your age, you're extremely fertile."

"Are you fertile *at all* at your age, old man?" she asked, batting her lashes at me.

I balked. "Thirty-four? Sorry to break it to you, but I'm in my prime. We could already be pregnant."

"You say that so easily, like you're letting me know you're going out for *conchas* and coffee." She took her gaze from me, looking at nothing on the bed between us. "We just started doing this, Cristiano. Is it a good idea—"

"I love how you say my name," I told her, suddenly unable to think of anything else but kissing her. "Come here."

"I can't move an inch. After horseback riding, plus training to fight off predators during the day and giving into one at night, I'm so sore."

I'd worked her every muscle the past week. I wanted her strong and satisfied at the end of each day. "We'll stop the training," I said, massaging her shoulders with one hand. "If by some crazy chance you *were* pregnant—"

"I don't *want* to stop," she said, closing her eyes with a contented sigh. "I like it. I'd rather be prepared than pregnant."

We should've had this conversation already. I'd just barely stopped to think about it. I wanted to be inside her all the time. To come as deep as I could. To see my child growing in her belly. "Do you not want a baby?"

She opened her eyes to study my face and grimaced as she got up on one elbow. "Not yet. This has all been so . . ."

"So what?" I asked quietly when she didn't continue. "You can be honest."

"So fast. I'm grateful for it, but sometimes I still feel shame." My stomach clenched before she added, "Ashamed at how happy I am. I spent so long viewing cartel life as evil. You're supposed to be the devil. I feel like I'm living someone else's life."

Alarmed, I also got up on my elbow. "What does that mean?"

"Just that everything flipped so quickly. And at the same time, it didn't. I've always felt something strong between us. At first, I thought it was just sexual chemistry. And hatred. A twisted kind, where I also couldn't stop thinking about you." Her eyes darted between mine before she rolled onto her back and looked at the ceiling. "I'd wonder if I was betraying my former self, but after Diego's manipulation I don't even know who *I* am. So what if *none* of this is real?"

It pained me to hear her question herself. Was this what had been running through Natalia's mind since that day with the Valverdes? She'd just assured her father that Diego had fooled all of us, and it didn't diminish Costa's judgment of character.

"I would rid that shame for you if I could." Her hair splayed over the pillow, and I picked up a handful of silky strands to run them through my fingers. "But you will overcome it in time. His betrayal is still raw. In the meantime, I ask that when you can't trust yourself, trust me to know who you are. And you're right where you're meant to be."

She turned her head to me. "How do you know?"

"When I returned home from eleven years away, I saw what you didn't. That Diego was fooling everyone. And that he had you in his grasp. I went to great lengths to get you out, did I not? I knew. Trust in me. The path wasn't clear or easy, but I had faith we'd end up here."

"Here," she repeated. Simply. With no inflection or enthusiasm.

Natalia had given me no indication recently that she wanted to be anywhere else. But if the truth of Diego's deception had her doubting herself—if it had changed something for her . . .

I swallowed, trepidation sinking in along with a question I needed to ask. I'd faced many fears in my life, and I'd always come out stronger. But not since I was a teenager, standing before Costa, had I been confronted with the fear of willfully giving up someone I loved.

"Right before you confronted the Valverdes and learned the truth, you told me you were done with your old life. Has that changed?"

Her answering silence made me sweat. How tragically ironic it would be. I'd fought hard to bring her the Valverdes so she could finally release any doubts about me and let herself fall for me completely. But she'd begun to fall already. What if learning she couldn't trust her judgment would have her doubt us? Doubt *me*?

"I want to be here more than anything, but . . ." she said so slowly, it hurt.

My heart pounded just as hard as it had during sex. I wasn't sure, if faced with the decision, that I could let her go. Now that she'd glimpsed the life she could have with me, the right thing would be to release her and let her decide for herself.

But then, the right thing would've been not to take her in the first place.

"But can you understand why it's hard for me to admit that?" she said. "That I *choose* this?"

*She chooses this*. That was what I needed to hear to assuage my fears —for now.

"Is it possible that even when I didn't trust you, I did, deep down?" she continued.

"Yes. It'd been my job once to watch over your family."

"The day my mother died shook our foundation to the core, but maybe it never broke." She cupped her hand to my cheek, and I leaned into it, rubbing my stubble over her palm. "I love it when you do that," she said. "It makes me feel as if I've tamed a beast."

"You'd call what we just did tame?"

She smiled. And then, "I trust you."

*Ah. There it is.* Because I'd never felt such contentment, I slid my hand under her hair and bent to kiss her. And yet, in the back of my mind, I understood that I was as terrified as I was fulfilled—Natalia and her love came with even greater fears.

The fear of losing her would only grow as our relationship deepened.

"You're the *everything* I went in search of," I said against her lips. "That loyalty and devotion you showed Diego as a nine-year-old girl —I craved it. The love between your parents—you were a true family." I scanned her face closely. I didn't even want to blink. "Once Diego offered all of that to me, I wanted it so fiercely, I was willing to break all my rules to have it. To have you."

"That's why you were so insistent I come to you willingly. You wanted me to choose you. And I do."

"All that I did, I did with the knowledge that I could give you everything you ever desired."

"And if I desire freedom?"

I paused. The one thing I could give her that would destroy it all. "Then ask for it. See what my answer is."

I didn't know my response, but my gut reaction was *never*. If you love someone, set them free—fuck that. I wasn't the type to crush something I coveted before I'd ever let it go—except maybe when it came to her.

Fortunately, she didn't ask.

"My father told me once he wanted me to marry a 'great' man—not a good one." She inhaled audibly. "Now, he demands grandchildren—he must think you're great."

I'd always believed Costa was a great man. To have the sentiment reciprocated after growing up with a snake for a father meant more than Natalia could know.

"I want a family," I said, "and we'll grant Costa his demands—but you're right. It's not the time. I should be more careful, but with you, and only you, I seem to lose control." I ran my knuckles over the goose bumps on her arm. "The time for a child will never be right when everything around us is a threat, but until we've dealt with Diego and Belmonte-Ruiz, we'll wait."

"Agreed." She reached out and touched one of the wounds on my abdomen with a warm, soothing palm. "You didn't hold back anything tonight. Do you feel all right?"

I'd been riding horses, lifting boxes, and riding and lifting my wife any chance I got. "I'm fine."

"You think you're invincible, but you're not, Cristiano." She turned onto her stomach. "If I'm going to stay here with you, then I need you to stick around."

"I'm not going anywhere," I promised as my eyes jumped to the perfect curve of her ass under the white sheet.

She shut her eyes and moved her cheek against the pillow. After a few moments, she said, "Cristiano?"

"*¿Sí, mi amor?*"

"Did you bring your gun to bed?"

*Ah,* the one cocked, loaded, and prodding into her hip. "I don't control when the rooster crows."

"I meant what I said." She heaved a sweet sigh. "You've wrecked me. I literally cannot move."

"You don't have to. In fact, it would be better if you don't."

"Why?" she asked.

I slid the sheet down to her thighs, then linked a leg through one of hers and drew it open. Salivating at the sight of her smooth, taut ass, I said, "I can break you in just as you are now . . ."

She laughed softly. "You're like a dog with a bone."

"Indeed." I slid down in the bed to get closer to her, ran my hand up her back, and whispered in her ear. "I have to get it out of my system. This overwhelming need to fuck you raw. Then we'll make love, I promise."

"Cristiano, my sun, moon, and stars," she said, her eyes still shut. "We have already made love."

"I know. But I mean in a way that changes us each to our cores. I'm holding back so I don't scare you."

Her lids fluttered open. "You already scare me. Don't you see how I reacted to the idea of you putting yourself in danger again? What if I let myself . . . and then I lose you?"

I inhaled and tried not to read too much into what she *hadn't* said. "What if I lose *you* now that I finally have you?" I said. "Does that mean I shouldn't even try?"

"Try what?"

"To love you or anyone. Nobody in my life is safe. Nobody ever will be." I traced the faint tan lines on her ass cheeks from our afternoon at the beach. "Do you think your father regrets loving Bianca? He doesn't."

Her shudder, and the look of satisfaction on her face, nearly set off the gun between us. That was my cue to go.

Slowly, I withdrew from her and stood.

She lifted her head. "Where are you going?"

"I'm going to shower and jerk off, or else I won't be able to sleep."

"What about me?"

"You're sore. And tired—I hear it in your voice. Get some rest. If I wear you out, I may not be able to enjoy you in the morning. I'll finish you off then."

She rested her cheek back on the pillow as I went and flipped on the shower. Seconds from now, in my fantasies, I'd be balls deep in Natalia's asshole.

But as I stepped under the stream of water and took my dick in hand, that wasn't where my mind went. Instead, I saw Natalia pregnant with my child. No question I was a sick fuck for getting hard over that, but *El Gallo* wanted what *El Gallo* wanted. God help her when she really *was* expecting—I already knew I'd be an overprotective mess.

It was everything I wanted.

I flattened a hand against the tile wall and was about to stroke myself to Heaven when a small, tentative hand beat me to it. I looked over my shoulder. Natalia placed her cheek against my biceps and smiled up at me. My body shielded her from the water, but her wet palm glided along my shaft.

"I thought you couldn't move," I said.

She stroked me gently, almost as if offering comfort. "You have already changed me to my core, Cristiano. And I love you."

Something broke loose in my chest. I hadn't expected . . . not yet. Even though I already knew she loved me, there was nothing like hearing it. Even though I'd kept the faith that she one day would, I almost couldn't come to terms with my luck.

Warmth coursed through me. Warmth, and gratitude. I turned and took her face in my hands, suddenly overwhelmed. "You . . . I love you, too, my Natalia."

I couldn't express the magnitude of it with words beyond that, so I told her with my kiss—and she responded, her soft, plush lips taking every firm peck I had to give.

# CHAPTER 19

# NATALIA

As water soaked my hair, Cristiano backed me up against the shower wall and slipped a hand under my thigh to lift my leg. He slid inside me and rooted himself there, stilling as we kissed, becoming a part of me in irrevocable ways. His fingers curled into my hair. With my arms wrapped around his neck, I pulled him closer.

He slid in and out slowly, hitting me in a new spot, one that sent deep, satisfied rumbles of pleasure through me. I was already swollen, sensitive, and throbbing from my last orgasm, raw and aching.

I hadn't known the meaning of lovemaking until this moment—I hadn't known the meaning of *love*. I'd been foolish to think I had. I didn't *want* to love Cristiano. It scared me, especially when I'd so recently feared him. Knowing him this way, when he could be taken from me, was more terrifying, though.

Everything he wanted to accomplish, everything he wanted to protect . . . I admired him for it, but it also put him in danger every day.

And yet, in a world of machismo and courage, Cristiano's words earlier were the bravest I'd ever heard. Not just loving someone he could easily lose, but *wanting* love. Seeking it out.

I wasn't as brave. Something told me that losing him would devastate me. And losing Cristiano was even more likely to happen than falling in love with a man I'd once wholeheartedly hated.

But it was too late now.

Cristiano groaned, moving into me, our slick bodies slipping against the other. He drew back, his expression pained as his eyes met mine, and his thrusts grew hard and firm, instead of fast and fevered like earlier. Water beat down on us, dripping from his nose onto me.

How could I love him so fiercely in so little time? And feel it returned without condition?

Our mouths met, savoring the taste of each other. "Don't come inside me," I said.

"I have to. I want to, Natalia."

"But I want to taste you." I pushed his chest, and he withdrew, his cock at full attention and bobbing between us. I got to my knees, took him in my mouth, and showed him my hunger, my desire to watch him unravel. With a hand in my hair and a groan on his lips, he spilled into my mouth without so much as a warning.

We exited the shower, and after toweling off, I slipped my wedding rings back on as he took his razor from a drawer.

"You're going to shave?" I asked.

"If I don't, it'll be twice the length by the morning. You'll wake up next to a wild animal."

"Imagine," I said sardonically, as if I wasn't at the mercy of one every night. I rose onto the tips of my toes for a quick kiss, then ran a finger over his chin. "Sometime, when I'm not so tired, I'll shave it for you."

"Sometime," he agreed. "When I'm a hundred percent sure I can let you near my throat with a razorblade."

I laughed. "A wise man once told me one-hundred percent confidence is a death wish."

As I turned to leave, he took my forearm, drawing me back in front of himself. He pressed his lips together, hesitation in his eyes.

"Is something wrong?" I asked.

"I want you to make me a promise."

A breeze passed through the room, or perhaps it was just the chill of his grave tone that made my hair stand on end. "What?"

"If anything ever does happen to me, Natalia—and it could—tell me you'll go on to live a full life. If your place is here, you'll take the reins. You will be ruthless and gentle and prevail knowing you have my blessing from beyond. And if you choose another life, you will relentlessly pursue happiness."

"I don't want to think about that." It hit too close to home. *Of course* I knew anything could happen at any time—it had to my mother. Death had almost caught Cristiano and myself. I was raw, physically and emotionally, both fucked and made love to tonight. And I'd conceded any last shred of resistance I might've had so I could love Cristiano with all of myself.

It was the greatest risk I'd ever taken because of how closely death hovered over him, and—

*You will die for him, your love.*

The soothsayer's words shivered through me for the first time in a while. What was Cristiano saying? Why was he bringing this up now?

Because love wasn't just a slippery slope; it was driving with no brakes and trusting you'd be safe at every hill, valley, and sharp turn. And Cristiano wasn't used to being at the mercy of anything.

"You *have* to think of this," he insisted. "It's part of being a ruler. You need to promise me you'd pick up and move on if you had to." He took my hand in both of his, bringing it to his unshaven mouth, scraping my skin as he kissed it with reverence. He put it to his forehead, as if in prayer. "*Por favor,* Natalia. Give me some peace in the afterlife. Tell me you'd continue on, and pursue happiness, if I were gone."

"Fine," I said, irritated that he was pushing this on me when I'd like to live just *one* day without the anxiety that I might lose everything I'd just found. "But give me the same gift of peace. If Belmonte-Ruiz had succeeded in killing me, you would've gone on. You *will* go on."

Calm pervaded him, and his oft-black eyes were closer to melted-chocolate brown just then. "I can't make you that promise," he said, the heavy words landing at our feet.

I balked. "You just made *me* say it. Why can't you?"

"Because I will follow you."

Frowning, I shifted and placed my other hand over his—so we made a fist like a heart. "What do you mean you'll follow me, Cristiano?"

"Into death."

With a sinking feeling, my eyes fell to our grasp on each other. I could barely wrap my head around what he was saying. I squeezed his hand, more out of a need to hold onto something rather than to offer comfort. "Don't say that. You wouldn't . . ."

His chocolate-brown gaze hardened to an opaque, unreachable void. "Nobody would get away with hurting you. I'd raise hell to avenge you, and if that meant risking my life to achieve it, I wouldn't hesitate."

"Cristiano—"

"I wouldn't be allowed in Heaven, but I swear on all that's holy—I'd rattle the gates until they let me have you."

Goose bumps sprang over my skin with a new kind of dread. He *meant* it—and there was no changing his mind. My death would mean Cristiano's.

I *could not* die for my love—or I would take him down with me.

Sometime around dawn, a firm, wooden knock came on our bedroom door. Cristiano left the warmth of our bed, and as I began to drift back to sleep, he roused me.

"Come," he said, a thread of panic in his voice. "Get dressed."

"What?" I opened my eyes and blinked away sleep. "What's wrong?"

"It's Max."

We got dressed in a flash, and I tied my hair up into a bun as Cristiano and I hurried down to the ground floor. He opened the front door for me, and we stepped outside.

Dawn broke on the bruise-colored mountains, the trees lime green as the rising sun hit their leaves. The peaceful vista of the sprawling, sleeping Badlands was disrupted by a revving engine. One of the security vehicles always posted at the Badlands' front gates barreled up the side of the mountain.

I shielded my eyes, squinting ahead. The truck kicked up a dust cloud as we walked down the front steps. When we stopped at the end of the drive, Alejandro, Eduardo, and Barto appeared next to us.

"Is that . . ." Alejandro started.

The car stopped, and one of Cristiano's uniformed gatekeepers jumped out of the driver's side before hurrying around to the side door. "*¡Ayuda*!" he called for help, then wrenched open the door. As the passenger stumbled out, all four men sprinted forward.

The sun peeked out, shining down on the man as if he'd fallen from the skies. Dragging a foot and with a swollen face the color of the purple mountains at his back, he was almost unrecognizable. Except for the glass eye. "Max," I whispered.

He fell to his knees and curled his fingers into the grass. Cristiano reached him first and fell to Max's side.

I glanced over my shoulder. My father stood in the doorway along with half the staff, hands over their mouths. "Call Doctor Sosa."

Max pushed himself off the ground to sit back on his heels. "Water," he pleaded.

As I walked forward, I called back, "*Agua*—now!"

"You escaped?" Cristiano asked as I reached them.

With a grimace, Max shook his head. "They . . . let me go," he rasped.

Cristiano glanced up at me. "But why?"

"Truce," Max said hoarsely.

*Truce*? I was immediately doubtful. That didn't make sense. "Why would they ever call a truce?" I asked.

Max's face contorted as he swallowed and formed fists against the ground. "Leave their business alone."

"Why would I?" Cristiano asked. His anger sent a tremor through the air. "Because they returned a man *they* took? And tortured? I have even more reason to destroy them."

"They'll get out . . ." Max said. "They'll stop."

"Stop what?" I asked.

"Trafficking."

Cristiano froze. He hadn't expected that answer, and neither had I. It was what he'd wanted—to end their business. But could we trust that information? Concern also registered on Cristiano's face.

Jaz delivered a bottle of water and stood back, crossing her thin arms over her stomach. Max drank it down in one go, tossed the empty plastic aside, and tried to get up.

Cristiano rose and helped him. Max struggling to stand on his own two feet was painful to watch, and Cristiano must've felt the same. "There's no truce," he said. "BR will pay for this, my friend. They've done too much damage—"

Max held up a hand to stop him and wiped his mouth on his sleeve before accepting another water bottle. As he cracked open the twist top, he managed, "Diego."

The name sent chills down my spine. Instinctively, I reached for Cristiano as he opened his arm and pulled me to his side. "He had a part in this?" Cristiano asked.

Max started to nod, then coughed and sputtered, turned away, and puked.

Cristiano looked at Alejandro. "Find Diego and execute him. *Now*. Throw him over a cliff for all I care. I no longer need to watch the life drain from him." Cristiano lowered his eyes to mine. "Do you?"

I shook my head. "I just want him gone."

"My wife demands his death," Cristiano said. "So kill him—and make it swift."

Max, panting for breath, cringed as he hunched over, his hands on his knees. "We—we can't kill Diego."

"Why not?" Cristiano ran his tongue back and forth over his front teeth. "Give me one *goddamn* reason I shouldn't—"

With great struggle, Max lifted his head. "He's already dead."

## CHAPTER 20

# NATALIA

Max lay in a dark guest bedroom, freshly bathed and gripping a bottle of painkillers. The nurse Doctor Sosa had arranged for us placed a damp towel over his swollen eyes, careful of his cheeks marred with cuts and bruises. He thanked her.

Clutching my mother's rosary, I fell into a chair and pressed my thumb to the crucifix.

Diego was . . . dead.

What was I supposed to feel about it? Triumph? Pity? He could've had love, and offered forgiveness. Instead, he'd chosen hatred and revenge—and it'd been the wrong path. Nostalgia tinged my relief that he was gone. There'd been good times. Genuine moments of laughter and fondness. Riding the property line on our horses, racing from one end of a fence to the other. In my mother's art studio, turning our yellow-painted handprints into chickens by adding red feathers and beaks to the thumbprint. And taking turns with the telescope, pointing out constellations to each other. I remembered his wide smile, patient eyes, and his concern for my wellbeing whenever we'd spoken on the phone—but was any of it real if it'd all been built on a lie?

It didn't matter anymore. He was out of our lives, and that was the way it had to be. I'd thought maybe I'd want to face him at the end, even taunt him—but I didn't need it. It was enough to know he was gone.

Max removed the cloth and set his pills on the nightstand. The nurse helped him ease into a sitting position, then arranged his pillows against the headboard.

"How do you feel?" I asked.

"Sore," he answered, "but grateful to be alive."

At the rasp in his voice, the nurse refilled his water from a pitcher on the nightstand.

Worry etched lines around Cristiano's eyes as he dismissed her with a nod. "What happened?" he asked when we were alone.

Max looked at me and then picked at a blackened fingernail. "I'll tell you everything later. For now, the thing to know is that Belmonte-Ruiz put Diego in the ground."

"Are you certain, Maksim?"

Even with Max's puffy eyelids and the bloated, Byzantium-purple welts around his lips, I could see his expression tighten. "I saw it with my one good eye. Diego is gone."

"I want to say I'm not surprised," Cristiano said, looking from me to Max. "But I knew, in the church, that when I turned my brother free, he wouldn't make it as long as I had out in the wild. I underestimated him, but in the end, I was right."

"How'd it happen?" I asked.

"When I learned Diego was dead, I said I wouldn't deliver the message to you unless I could be sure. They allowed me to see the body before they disposed of it. Diego was cold and lifeless in a body bag. Involuntary overdose . . ."

The hair on the back of my neck rose, and I crossed myself. Even as my stomach somersaulted at the thought of my childhood best friend's decaying body, I welcomed the confirmation of his death.

Cristiano covered his mouth with his fist. "Reason?"

"An offering to make peace with you and Costa," Max explained, "but there's more to it than that. From what I gathered during my time there, Diego was costing them money, making promises he couldn't keep."

"Like with the Maldonados," Cristiano said. "History repeats itself. Diego never learns. What kinds of promises?"

Max's face contorted as he shifted. I stood to help him fix his pillow. "My guess?" Max said. "Based on what I picked up from the guards and other prisoners—Diego told BR he could get you working *for* them, not against them."

"Why the fuck would I ever work for them? No dollar amount could convince me, nothing on the planet would—" Cristiano ran his hand down his face as he shook his head. He sighed. "Natalia."

"What?" I asked.

Max nodded up at me. "I heard about the security breach here the same night they attacked us at the hotel. Could they have been trying to kidnap you?"

"*Sí*," Cristiano said through his teeth. "They would take my wife. For payback *and* for strategy."

"Strategy?" My palm ached as the ruby and pearl rosary beads dug into it. I looked between the two of them. "To do what with me?"

Cristiano had ensured the world thought I was nothing to him. Only few people understood, from the beginning, that the opposite was true. Diego had been the first. He had set all this in motion.

He had gone to Belmonte-Ruiz and told them what I was worth.

And how to get me.

My nostalgia vanished as I was reminded how conniving Diego had been all along.

My throat closed as I realized the answer to my question was obvious given what their business had been built on. "They would've sold me."

"No," Cristiano said. He paced Max's bedside, massaging his jaw. "That would've only started a war between us, and it wouldn't have benefited Diego at all. He's always thinking of how to come out on top. If I were in his shoes, my need for control would win over pride."

"I don't understand," I said.

"If they were able to hold Max just outside my grasp, they could do the same to you. I'd be forced to cooperate to keep you safe."

"Cooperate . . . how?"

"Our infrastructure when combined with Costa's shipping solutions spans not only the Americas, but Europe, and parts of Asia, too," Max explained. "Working with us could grow their business overnight."

Cristiano nodded and finished Max's thought. "But after the lengths I've gone to just to handicap them, they must've known I'd never agree to partner up—not for any amount of money."

My fingers went cold as I put the pieces together. "They wanted you to traffic people."

Cristiano dropped his arm to his side. "Diego knows there's nothing in the world that could get me to do it."

"Except for the one weakness he's exploited before," Max said.

Me. I was the weakness. The little girl he'd been charged with protecting. And then, when he'd come back to town, I'd become a whole other kind of weakness. Cristiano had confessed more than once that he'd done all this for selfish reasons. Because he wanted love. *My* love. My family. He wanted me.

And he'd been willing to let Diego live in order to have all of it—giving Diego all the ammunition he'd needed. He'd planned to use me as leverage to turn Cristiano's life into a living hell. To force Cristiano to do the one thing he'd sworn never to do. What he'd built a whole life around preventing. And in the process, Diego would have gotten more control, more wealth, and turned the knife in his brother's back—all at the same time. And what would've become of me?

I would never find out, and for that, I thanked God for keeping the devil safe. And I thanked my devil for protecting me.

When I caught Cristiano staring at me, his face etched with pain, I crossed the room to him and cocooned one of his enormous, mighty hands in both of mine. What would it have done to Cristiano to have to decide between me and the lives of many innocent men, women, and children? I recognized the tormented look in his eyes for what it was. He was beating himself up for not knowing what he would've chosen.

I put my mouth against the warm, sinewy back of his hand and swallowed to control the emotion in my voice. "You would never have gone through with it," I assured him. "You're too good of a man. You would've let me go in order to save them, and it would've been the right choice."

"Too good of a man?" he repeated. "You know what I am. I could never let you go, and that makes me the kind of monster I've been fighting against."

I shook my head and clenched my teeth against a wave of tears. It was too horrible to even think of. Cristiano would've done the right thing. "It doesn't matter. You'll never have to make that choice."

He wrapped an arm around my shoulders and pulled me close. I turned my cheek against his chest, and he covered the opposite one, holding me there. "Diego got off easy if he'd promised them he'd deliver me," he said, his voice rumbling against my ear.

"Yes," Max said. "But if you don't stop fucking with Belmonte-Ruiz, they'll always be an enemy."

"I want to believe the possibility that they'd stop," Cristiano said. "But why would they? Their entire business is a trafficking ring."

"They have something going on the narcotic side," Max said. "All I know is what I picked up here and there, but perhaps the informant Alejo uncovered can find out more."

"If it's not trafficking, it doesn't matter," Cristiano said. "Let them have their drugs. They can even get into arms and try to steal my territories for all I care. As long as they move on."

I turned my face into Cristiano's palm and kissed it, grateful for its comforting warmth, before pulling his hand away. Max had to be exhausted. We needed to let him rest. But first, I had to ask. "You'd accept the truce?"

After what Max had been through, I'd have expected him to say no. He had all the reason to want to strike back. But he only narrowed his eyes and said, "It's not my call alone, but if I set aside my own personal vendetta . . . they made two offerings in good faith—taking Diego's life, and sparing mine. If *they* stop because *we* do, then we all get what we want."

Cristiano nodded. "Do you agree, Natalia?"

It felt like the end. Diego was no longer trying to hurt us. Belmonte-Ruiz wanted us off their backs, and in exchange, there would be a little less suffering in the world. That was what Cristiano had aimed for. I nodded. "I think if it's true . . . we should accept."

Diego was gone, and the only regret I felt was that he hadn't been able to overcome his own demons to make something of his life. But if he had, I may never have known the love rooted deep inside me for his brother. I was glad, if it had to be us or him, that Cristiano and I were still standing.

I twisted to wrap my arms around Cristiano's neck. "It's over, *mi rey*," I said with a genuine smile. "My king."

He searched my face with dark, skeptical eyes. Cristiano had spent eleven years waiting for this moment, and it had eluded him more than once.

I gripped his neck, ran my thumbs up the hollows under his cheekbones that always made him look so grim, and reassured him. "It's *over*."

Months of danger and strife had ended. And yet, I wasn't sure it was a history I'd trade for an easier one. It had prepared me. Educated me. Fortified me. And it had brought me Cristiano.

Together, we would walk into the future stronger than ever.

# CHAPTER 21

## FIVE MONTHS LATER

# NATALIA

Cristiano and Papá waited for me downstairs so we could leave for the Day of the Dead parade, but I wanted just a few more moments to myself on the balcony of my old bedroom. The mariachi music seemed fainter now than it had in my childhood. I remembered dancing to it, skipping through the house as I'd hummed to myself, my worn leather sandals clicking on the tile.

I returned to my bedroom and checked my outfit once more in a floor-length mirror. Today, my colorful, off-the-shoulder dress—an explosion of marigold-orange, fuchsia, and rose-red against bone—was a tribute to Mamá as I'd stand by my father while the town honored him with a ride on the final float.

Strong arms slipped around my middle, and I met Cristiano's molten-brown eyes in the reflection. "Even more a symphony than usual in this dress, and music to my ears," he said in my ear. "You look beautiful. You look like *her*."

In a suit and tie, he was handsome as ever. I covered his forearms with mine, lacing our fingers together. "She should be here with us."

"She is." He kissed the back of my head. "Today, we'll go to the *Día de los Muertos* parade and celebrate her life."

"With the whole town," I added.

"They adored her, as they do you," he said, resting his hands on my waist, fingers inched inward . . .

I inhaled and shivered as a chill ran up my spine.

"Cold?" he asked.

No. It wasn't that. Did he know? Could he sense what grew under his fingertips? I adjusted my crown of red roses in the reflection. "With your hands on me? *Jamás*. Never."

It was true. Cold was one thing Cristiano and I would never be. With Cristiano, there was only warmth. Contentment. Even when we fought, fire burned between us.

I wouldn't have it any other way.

Life was as lively as ever at the Badlands, but it'd been relatively peaceful since our truce with Belmonte-Ruiz.

I had everything I could possibly ask for—a community that kept us both on our toes. My husband's and my father's fruitful businesses. My family in good health. A full and promising future.

A loving husband.

And the blessing of his child in my belly.

I'd first suspected I was pregnant last week, after overwhelming nausea three days in a row, but I'd wanted to be certain before telling Cristiano. It was nearly impossible to do anything in the Badlands without him finding out, so I'd snuck away to see Paula at the medical clinic before we'd come, and she'd confirmed it.

We were having a baby.

My heart fluttered thinking of the sonogram tucked away in my purse downstairs. Cristiano would be nothing but thrilled to learn the news, but still, nerves edged my excitement.

Especially on the anniversary of my mother's death.

It wasn't the life I'd imagined for myself. To be a cartel wife, married to a narco king, and a mother by the age of twenty-one. Cartel queens and kings fell all the time, and where did that leave their princes and princesses? Cristiano and I knew all too well—once upon a time, we'd been them.

It was a great responsibility—one neither of us would take lightly. It came with risk. Already, fear bloomed in me in a new way knowing what I did of this life and what emotional attachments could mean. Cristiano and I had both lost parents early on. I didn't want that possibility for my child, but it was the life we led, and that wouldn't change.

And I had the greatest man in the world to lean on. I would be that same support for him.

As he did everything else with unrivaled passion, fervor, and heart —so would he do fatherhood. This child would know the deepest love from both its parents.

"Ready to head over to the parade?" Cristiano asked.

I nodded. First, we would celebrate my mother's life, along with everyone expecting visits from their loved ones on this, the Day of the Dead.

And then we would rejoice in the gift of life growing inside me.

WE RODE through the parade on the last float, the grand finale—a skeleton in a tuxedo with a cigar stuck in one side of its mouth, surrounded by live roses and marigolds. Cristiano and my father each puffed on his own Montecristo as Papá grumbled about the obligation of his presence, even as he waved and smiled. Secretly, he was pleased by the honor.

Sugar skulls in white and black danced around us, while ladies dressed as *La Catrina* twirled in colorful dresses, and masked men on the floats gestured with both hands to get the crowds to cheer.

We crawled along the main road of shops, fruit carts, and *mercados* advertising cigarettes and Coca-Cola.

"I'm going to send the kid to get me a mezcal," my father said as fine, white, cinnamon-scented cigar smoke wafted into the wind.

"Gabe is working," I reminded him.

"He's hopeless with a rifle. Should've been Barto up here."

I glanced down at Gabriel Valverde, his gun at the ready as he rode on the lower tier of the float. Cristiano hadn't protested when I'd been asked to join my father in the parade, but even though things had been peaceful for a while, being out in the open at any time made him anxious.

"I'm trying to build Gabriel's confidence, and Barto has no shortage of that," I said, smiling down at where Gabriel was stationed, out of earshot. "He's improved a lot. Can't you see how much stronger he looks?"

"The kid is a genius." Father had been reluctant to accept a Valverde in his life, and still wouldn't call him anything other than "kid" or "boy," but at least he recognized his talent. "He should be in front of a computer. You need his brain indoors, not splattered all over a *papier-mâché* skeleton."

He had a point.

Both Barto and Cristiano had made the same argument—and even though it'd been the only thing they'd agreed on in a while, I'd put my foot down. The parade was the perfect opportunity to show Gabriel how much I believed in him. With Barto somewhere patrolling the street, every overprotective man in my life was within a fifteen-meter radius. I'd never felt safer.

A cold drink *did* sound pretty good, though, considering my stomach had been so uneasy. "I'll go get you the mezcal," I said. "An iced *horchata* sounds perfect anyway."

"Better than a warm Coca Light?" Cristiano asked. "Since when?"

My cheeks warmed. My body was experiencing new and unusual things. "Just a craving for something different," I said.

"Oh . . .?" He arched an eyebrow. "A *craving*?"

I raised to the balls of my feet and kissed his cheek before he could follow whatever train of thought was forming in his mind. This moment was about Mamá. We'd have ours later. "I'll be right back."

"You stay here." He reached by me to put down his cigar. "I'll go."

"Relax. Enjoy your Cuban," I said and gave him a scolding look. "It'll be the last one you have for a while."

When I'd learned of Cristiano's heartburn, I'd made him stop smoking, limited him to a couple drinks a week, and had been working with Fisker on healthier meal recipes that didn't make Cristiano want to skip straight to dessert.

But it was a special day.

I picked up my purse from where I'd stowed it, put it over my shoulder, and started to walk away when a hand at my elbow drew me back. I turned around to reassure Cristiano I'd be fine, but when I met his eyes, there was only a spark of excitement in them.

He raised them to the sky. "Look."

A small kaleidoscope of monarch butterflies fluttered over our heads. "Papá," I called, and he ambled over to us, following our gazes.

The monarch migration passed through during early November—like now, on All Souls' Day, when the deceased came to visit the living. That was why monarchs were believed to hold the spirits of the departed. It happened every year, but it was never any less special to believe Mamá was with us. On my wedding day, I'd thought her presence a warning. I now knew it had been approval. Today, she returned to bless me and my unborn child.

"*Te extraño mucho, Bianca.*" Telling her he missed her very much, my father smiled, flicked ash from his cigar onto the live marigolds surrounding us, and walked away.

Cristiano took his Montecristo from his mouth, pulled my face to his with one hand, and pecked my lips.

I walked around to the rear of the float, waving back at the throngs of parade-goers. With the *rat-a-tat-tat* of poppers that sounded too close to gunshots, the crowd inhaled a collective gasp. I descended the stairs of the float and hopped off, into the street.

As I made my way through the crowd toward a drink vendor, a dancing skeleton bumped into me so hard, I stumbled in my high heels. Instead of trying to catch my purse as it fell, I covered my stomach. Once I'd righted my footing, it hit me for the first time that my body would change—as would the way I treated it. I'd have to be more careful everywhere I went—and definitely no more training.

I squatted and picked up the envelope with the sonogram first, then bit my lip to hide a smile as I tucked it into a side pocket.

As people walked around me, I shoveled my things back into my handbag. I searched the street for my cell phone, then checked to see if it was still in my purse. Unable to find it, I stood and turned, my gaze landing on a mariachi in the crowd with a familiar pair of eyes.

A piercing gaze that sent a chill straight down my spine, then vanished under a sombrero as the man disappeared back into the crowd.

*Diego.*

*No. Diego is dead.*

I took a deep breath to try to calm my thumping heart. It wasn't possible. My current condition was doing things to my brain, and my emotions were overwrought from being back home on the anniversary of Mamá's death. I rubbed my temples, took a few more steps, and crouched again to try to locate my phone.

Mariachi music started from somewhere. I'd been hearing it on and off all day, but now that Diego was on my mind, it took me back to my parents' room on this same morning twelve years earlier. The haunting echoes of the music through the house. The fan rotating with a breeze from the open windows, casting shadows over Mamá's body on the tile floor. Diego running in, his gun drawn, acting surprised. Cristiano's forearm a bar around my waist as his hand clamped over my mouth.

A bout of nausea hit me. Something didn't feel right. I got back to my feet and started back for the float when I noticed a man in a ski mask walking toward me.

*Fuck.* I willed my breathing to slow so I could think. We had no enemies at the moment, but as Cristiano said—the fight was never over. I couldn't be too careful. I ducked left and hid in a group of dancing women while maneuvering my way back toward the float. They spun, their skirts blending together into reds, greens, and purples.

I surveyed the crowd and sucked in a breath as Diego's face flashed by.

*No*. It wasn't . . . it couldn't . . .

I stepped up onto a curb and furtively searched the throngs of people, but I didn't have to look long—his height set him apart. He removed his sombrero and shook out golden-brown hair. It *couldn't* be him. And yet, Diego's mannerisms were seared into my memory. As long as I lived, I'd never forget the way his long fingers tracked through the strands of his hair. He palmed the sombrero the way he had his cowboy hat at the costume party. As he started to turn toward me, I noticed a bolo tie—but I wouldn't wait to see if it bore the de la Rosa family crest.

I ran, sprinting through the crowd, pushing people aside.

A man in chalky white face paint and blackened eye sockets stepped in my way, and I stopped short. The skeleton that had bumped into me earlier. I whirled to go another way, but the ski mask closed in from another direction.

I had a knife in my purse. I reached in and grabbed it as a voice said in my ear, "If you make a scene, your daddy gets a bullet in the back. Then we start shooting up the crowd, Natalia."

My scalp prickled, air sucking from my lungs. "Who are you?" I asked. "Belmonte-Ruiz?"

He didn't answer.

My palm sweat around the handle of the knife. I needed to fight back—but as of this morning, physical violence had taken on a new meaning for me. Since my arrival at the Badlands, Cristiano had impressed upon me that I couldn't ever be afraid to get hurt. I wasn't. But now that I was carrying his child?

That was different.

I had to protect my body at any cost.

I'd hesitated too long.

He grabbed my handbag and the knife with it as more armed men dressed in black and in face masks appeared all around me, closing in. With a screeching sound, yelling started. A white van barreled toward us, sending people jumping out of the way.

I opened my mouth to scream, and a damp towel covered it, suffocating me with a sickly-sweet reek. I held my breath, fighting not to inhale. I was surrounded. My vision blurred with little bursts of light. Not even the tight hold on me could disguise the feeling of my lungs caving in. Nor could people's screams and mariachi music drown out one single word in my ear as the world around me faded to black.

*"Princesa."*

# CHAPTER 22

# NATALIA

My head lolled somewhere soft, but the backs of my eyeballs throbbed. Lying on my side, my body jostled with the whir and hum of an engine.

*My baby.*

My eyes flew open to dark nothingness. I went to cover my stomach, but my elbows were bound behind my back and had been long enough that I couldn't feel my hands.

"Sleeping Beauty stirs." The voice sounded both muffled and directly above me and its familiarity tugged me from my dull consciousness. Aching shoulders. Burning throat. My cheek scratched against burlap. I was . . . on a lap?

"We didn't even get to the part where the prince kisses you," he added.

*Diego.*

My heart lurched in my chest as my entire body stilled.

On All Souls Day, Diego had risen from the dead. My head pounded with pain and questions. *How* was he still alive? Where had he been the last several months? What did he want with me?

Traces of earthy soil and pungent gasoline mixed with Diego's familiar smell. *Never get in the vehicle.* It was rule number one around here. I had no idea how long we'd even been driving, but a victim in a van was as good as dead.

Then again, it seemed death wasn't always permanent.

"You were . . ." My vocal chords protested from whatever he'd used to knock me out. "You died."

"Not yet. Not without you." The sack lifted, and my skin cooled as I blinked open my eyes to two armed skeletons in face paint across from me. We rode in the back of a gutted, windowless van with a bench along each side panel. The man who'd helped corner me laid his gun on his knee, and it pointed directly at me. One major pothole and I could be done for.

I shifted, turning my face up to see Diego looking down at me. His golden-streaked, cocoa-colored hair fell around high, regal cheekbones. A black shirt with dust on the collar lent masculinity that offset features pretty enough that he could've been a movie star. I saw the same patience and kindness in his mesmerizing green eyes as I had many times before, but now, I could only interpret it as an act to get what he wanted.

I could act, too, though.

He stroked my hair. "I promised I'd come back for you, didn't I? I risked my life to get you away from him."

*Him.*

They could've hurt or taken Cristiano, too. Everything had happened so fast. My throat thickened with emotion. "Where is he?"

"You're free of him now, *muñequita*."

*Muñequita*—his little doll. Fury snuffed out my confusion as a million rebuttals raced through my head. I could never be, and never *wanted* to be, free of Cristiano. He was my husband, my rock, and my future. He was ten times the man Diego would ever be—and he'd never treated me like a helpless doll.

But I had to think straight. To be smart, like the queen Cristiano demanded I be. One worthy of standing at his side.

One thing he'd imparted: if I'd failed to incapacitate a captor, as I had now, I should act compliant, even if it felt unnatural, until I had an escape plan in place.

I couldn't act recklessly or out of emotion. Raging at Diego wouldn't get me anywhere, especially while I was tied up and at his mercy. While I carried our baby, my body was my priority.

There had to be some part of Diego that cared for me; it couldn't have *all* been a performance. Cristiano had called it fondness. Diego had spent day in and day out by my father's side, picking up my calls, and listening to me go on for hours about school, or how I missed him or my mother.

I couldn't be the girl I was with him anymore—even if I wanted to be—but I could act the part. Cristiano had tried to warn me early on that this was a game, and I had to compete.

I steadied my breathing. "Everything hurts," I said softly.

"I'm sorry we had to ambush you like that," Diego said. "I couldn't be sure you wouldn't scream or fight back. I'm sure my desperate brother has tried hard to convince you that you *want* to be in the Badlands."

"I've had to make my life there bearable." The lie soured on my tongue as it came out, but it wasn't hard to sound convincing. After all, before I'd loved Cristiano, I'd fought against anything to do with him. "But that doesn't mean I forgive you for trading me to him."

"I *didn't* trade you. I let him think he had you for a while so I could ensure our survival—and it worked, didn't it? We're both still standing."

That he should live while the heavens had taken Mamá . . .

I inhaled through my nose to control my urge to unleash on Diego the way I'd fantasized. "I'm really uncomfortable," I said. "Will you *please* untie me?"

His eyes roamed from my face down to my breasts, stomach, and thighs. "You look different," he said. "Leaner. Stronger. How do I know you won't try to fight back?"

"Fight *you*? Even if I knew how, I wouldn't do anything that stupid. You can easily overpower me." He'd always treated me like his breakable princess, but he was right—I *was* stronger. And with enough time, I could free my hands from almost any binding. Solomon and I continued to train almost daily, and Cristiano especially liked

Solomon to put me through potentially life-threatening scenarios. It had been a rigorous few months.

At least, up until last week when I'd started faking a wrist injury until I could go see Paula at the clinic for a pregnancy test.

"I didn't do anything at Cristiano's house but ride my horse and play soccer with the staff to keep myself occupied. And anyway," I added, nodding across the aisle of the open van, "I can't exactly fight back with guns trained on me."

Diego clucked at the man with the 9mm on his knee, and he holstered it. "They're overly cautious," Diego explained. "They think this is a kidnapping, not a rescue."

Diego no doubt picked his words carefully, hoping they'd influence my point of view. This wasn't a *rescue*—to him or to me.

Diego wanted me alive for a reason, which meant he needed me.

I was leverage against Cristiano and my father—but to what end? He'd obviously joined forces with some federation, most likely Belmonte-Ruiz. Which meant after five months of silence, they'd broken their truce. If it had ever been real.

Diego took a knife from the leg pocket of his utility pants, flipped it open, and cut the restraints at my elbows. I rolled my shoulders forward, stretching my arms as I sat up slowly.

I could see him in all his glory now. Tall, muscular, with the baby-faced version of Cristiano's brutally beautiful face. It was Cristiano's black hair and eyes, his hollowed cheeks and high cheekbones, that made him too much for the silver screen. The world probably couldn't handle it, sadly for them.

I tried tapping into that attraction for Diego again. "Where have you been?" I asked. "In the church you said you'd come back for me. You didn't."

"That's why I'm here now." He took my hand, bringing it to his mouth. "Poor girl. You've always had someone to rescue you. Me, Barto, Costa, Cristiano. And yet, we've all hurt you, too."

"The Diego I knew would never hurt me." I took back my hand, rolling my wrists with exaggeration, hoping to lean in to the frailty he expected of me.

"I'm not the one who changed. My brother did." He put his knife away. "First, Cristiano took my parents from me. Then he took you and Costa. He made the first move—I'm just playing the game."

Diego believed *he* was the one who'd been wronged. He'd have carried on his parents' gruesome business without hesitation despite all the lives it would ruin.

Max wouldn't have lied to Cristiano. Since his return, he'd been as loyal as ever. If anything, he was *more* protective of us. So there had to be another explanation for Diego's sudden return. "Max saw you in a body bag."

"I know. As I said, I risked my life for you—I almost died that day."

*That day*. I remembered it well—at least, the moments when Max had come stumbling home to us and broken the news. Diego had put Max, Cristiano, my father, my mother, and myself in harm's way too many times. I licked my lips, finding my mouth dry. "How'd you do it?" I asked. "And why?"

"Cristiano would always be a threat to me. I needed him to believe I was dead."

The road turned bumpy, and I steadied myself on the van's side panel, suddenly overwhelmed with nausea. "Why?" I asked.

"So he'd drop his guard while Belmonte-Ruiz and I formed a plan to get you out."

So this *was* the work of Belmonte-Ruiz. "What about their truce with—" I stopped before I could say *us*. I needed to use language to my advantage, too, and separate my interests from Cristiano's. "With Cristiano and his cartel?"

"A ploy to buy us time while we got things in place."

"What things?" I asked.

Diego pushed up the sleeves of his black Henley. I'd told him on many occasions how strong and sexy he looked in the ribbed, long-sleeved shirt. Had he worn it to remind me of that, the same way he carefully chose his words?

"It's complicated," he said, "and not anything you need to worry about. Just cooperate, and you'll be fine."

*Don't worry*. Diego's mantra when it came to me. Diego asked for my trust in him, which meant he believed I was still foolish enough to give it. And why shouldn't he? He couldn't know the woman I was now. How I'd grown. The depth of love I possessed for my husband, and the lengths I'd go to to get home to him.

Was he safe?

The road had smoothed, but my nausea returned.

Had they ambushed him, too? God. Let him be safe.

I put my face between my knees as I had the urge to vomit.

"Is it morning sickness?" Diego asked.

My heart plummeted to my feet. Blood drained from my face as I stared at the muddy floor of the van. My red toenail polish, too happy for the moment, burned my irises. There was no *possible* way he could know I was pregnant. *I* hadn't even known until yesterday, and my stomach was nothing but abs after the workouts Cristiano had put me through.

I raised my head. "What?"

"I saw the sonogram in your purse." He furrowed his brows. "I'm sorry, *princesa*. To think of Cristiano's hands on you . . . it kills me. The things you must've endured with him."

As he spoke, a red film covered my eyes. If Diego knew I was pregnant, he could—*would*—use that against me. Against Cristiano.

*Fucking bastard.*

Diego thought I endured Cristiano's sexual advances instead of welcomed them. He assumed the pregnancy was against my will when it was the happiest news of my life.

It wasn't the truth that mattered, though, but what Diego believed.

I suddenly understood all too well the position Cristiano had been in since our wedding day. Those who knew our weaknesses could exploit them. That was why, early on, he'd let the world think our marriage was only for show.

It was why I couldn't let Diego know I'd do anything possible to save my baby.

I resisted the urge to pull my knees to my chest and sat up instead. "I didn't ask for it," I said simply. "The baby. The world doesn't need more of someone like Cristiano."

Diego tilted his head at me. "You don't want it?"

A pit formed in my stomach. On Our Lady of Guadalupe, I wouldn't wish away my child. I *couldn't*. But as Cristiano had taught me, it could be the best way to protect it.

I glanced at the ground, shaking my head. "No."

"No?" he prompted. "No what?"

"I . . . I don't want the baby."

Diego quieted. My stomach churned even more for the lie as it settled between us. I felt sick. How could I say it?

After a few moments, he replied, "You're lying."

My eyes fell shut. *He* was calling *me* a liar? "It's the truth," I said, but I didn't sound convincing even to my own ears.

He shook his head slowly. "You forget how well I can read you. You want the baby. I have to assume you want Cristiano, too, then—which is a problem for us."

I gripped the edge of the seat.

I didn't want to cooperate or comply. Or malign or dismiss the most important man in my life. Or to pretend as if Diego hadn't betrayed me in the worst possible ways.

I bit my bottom lip until it smarted. I *had* to hold my tongue. Information was power, and I needed to withhold it as much as I needed to get it. I couldn't reveal that I knew his crimes, his scheming, the mask he hid behind, the fact that he'd . . . he'd . . . unlocked the tunnel and as a result, my mother had—*fuck*. Fuck him. *Fuck* him.

"I can see you're upset, Tali. Tell me what's running through your mind—the truth, though. No more lying."

"Yes, I want the baby," I admitted. "I thought you'd think I was a traitor if I admitted it. It doesn't mean I care about Cristiano—"

"Another lie."

I couldn't do it. I couldn't sit here and pretend he hadn't done this, or that I would betray Cristiano. I'd been innocent and naïve with Diego my whole life, and where had it gotten me? *Here*. For months, I'd lamented that I'd never gotten to hear Diego confess. I'd been given a second chance to face the man who was, in my eyes, my mother's true murderer.

I lifted my head. The words tumbled out, leaving a metallic taste in their wake. "I know what you did."

His expression eased. After a few moments of strained silence, he asked, "What are you talking about?"

"Exactly what you think."

Once I revealed what I knew, there was no turning back. It would permanently put us on opposite sides. But I had to do it. For myself. For her.

"I heard it directly from Vicente Valverde," I said, my jaw tingling with disgust and contempt. "You let them in the house, and then ran them out of town. *You're* responsible for my mother's death."

# CHAPTER 23

# NATALIA

At the mention of the Valverdes—a name Diego had probably never expected to hear from my mouth—he went completely still. He didn't blink.

The shift was palpable, and for a moment, I wondered if I'd just sealed my fate. I was no longer the damsel in distress he wanted me to be.

But I'd been holding it in for months with no guilty party to accuse face to face. Now, I'd redeemed some small part of what Diego had stolen from me, from my mother and father, and from Cristiano. He now knew that in my eyes, he'd never be the hero again.

And that there'd never be a greater villain to me than him.

"Why'd you do it?" I asked. I knew why, but he should have to say it.

He looked across the aisle of the van at the two Belmonte-Ruiz men. Their expressions hadn't changed. I doubted they gave one fuck about this conversation.

"Costa owed me two lives for taking my parents," he said. "When the Valverdes came to me, I saw my opportunity. I took it. Bianca paid the price for what Costa did," Diego said slowly, as if carefully choosing his words. "I'm sorry it hurt you, and I'm even sorry she had to die."

"How can you say that when you were the cause of my hurt and her death?"

His forehead wrinkled with concern as he looked at his hands. "I cared for Bianca—as I care for you. Falling in love with you happened both slowly and overnight. It hit me hard. I *still* love you." He splayed his hand to remind me of the tattoos between his fingers—the roses with his family name on one, and on his ring finger, our initials. "I always wanted us to do this together."

I clenched my teeth. *Screw you.*

I wanted to spit at him, headbutt him, kick him in the balls. But I didn't bat an eyelash. "Do what together? What do you want me for?"

"Costa would've lost the Cruz cartel if not for me, Talia. After your grandfather passed, and before I stepped into an advisory role, Costa could barely control what he had—that's why the Valverdes tried to take it." He sighed, propping his elbows on his knees as he rubbed his face. "But under my helm? It *flourished*. It was *mine* to take over one day—it only made sense that you and I would run it."

"What about my father?" I asked.

"Once you and I were married, he'd have understood it was time to step down."

"And if he hadn't?"

"He would've." A threat. "If Cristiano hadn't reentered the picture, that's what would've happened," Diego said. "We took a little detour, but we'll end up in the same place."

As Cristiano had said, Diego would've taken over by any means, and the course he'd have chosen was using my love for him against Papá.

And if Diego still saw me in that role but knew I wouldn't cooperate—what were his plans then?

"Where?" I asked through a swallow. "Where will we end up?"

"At the head of the de la Rosa and Cruz cartels." Diego linked his hands between his knees and glanced over at me. "And now, you'll help me get Calavera, too. Costa still owes me a second life, but I'll take the next best thing—his cartel. His daughter. Cristiano's wife. If you can get past all this, we can do it as a team again—"

"You lied to me. You kept me in the dark." The van jostled as we hit more unpaved road. "That's not a team."

Diego kept his eyes down as he flexed his hands and massaged one palm. "The secrets surrounding Bianca's death always weighed on me. I know my involvement hurts you, but you'll move past it. And when you do, we'll get everything we always wanted. The fortune, the business . . ." He glanced up at me. "Over time, once you forgive me, maybe we'll even get more of the romantic nights like our first."

My stomach roiled. How *dare* he call that night anything but it was —a violation. It made me sick. God willing, I'd never think of that night again and how stupid I'd been to fall for his empty words. "You *stole* my virginity."

"You gave it to me." He reached out to touch my face, but I flinched back, and he dropped his arm. "You're right to be upset. I just couldn't bear the thought of watching you marry him without having *any* piece of you to myself. It meant so much to me, Tali."

Bile rose up my throat, and this time, it had nothing to do with the road. *It means less than nothing to me,* I wanted to tell him. *Cristiano fucks me so much better.*

I would've said it if I was only responsible for myself, but I couldn't risk provoking him.

Diego sighed. "We should arrive soon."

"Where are you taking me?"

"We have some things to figure out."

*Some things.* I had an idea of what he meant. "Cristiano won't cooperate," I said bluntly.

Diego's eyebrows rose. He didn't respond at first, as if deciding whether I actually knew anything.

I might, if his plan was the one Cristiano, Max, and I had pieced together months ago. Belmonte-Ruiz hadn't killed any of us when they'd had the chance—that was no coincidence. Diego had intended to use me as leverage to force Cristiano into helping Belmonte-Ruiz expand their human trafficking ring.

But that would *never* happen.

Cristiano knew my wishes. I would not allow him to put his soul and others' lives at risk for me. Diego was delusional enough to think he could pull this off, and I'd come to learn that Diego's delusions were extremely dangerous—and for Mamá, they'd been fatal.

"My brother has pissed off a lot of people; I'm not the only one who wants to see him dead," Diego said finally. "If anything, my plan is the only thing keeping him alive—at least, for as long as I need him."

The vehicle hit soft ground and slowed to a stop. Diego patted my knee, shrugged into a jacket, and passed me the burlap sack. "Put it on."

He helped me from the van. The sun never hit my face, and the temperature had dropped, but the sack let in enough light that I could tell it was still daytime. We walked up a small hill, and I struggled for breath, as if something sat heavy on my chest. My dress brushed the ground as dense dirt gave under the spikes of my heels.

Once my shoes hit firmer ground, and the fresh air turned stale, Diego said, "You can remove it."

I pulled off the sack. We stood in a sprawling, one-story concrete and brick warehouse, surrounded by wood pallets and a forklift, steel shelving with plastic bins, gas cans, and crates. I searched for any potential weapons. Petrol and wood to burn the place down. Scissors at a workstation near a conveyor belt. If he didn't tie me up, I could sprint for the fire extinguisher against one wall. Incapacitating *him* would require little mobility and even less creativity—but what about the other men?

Diego took me to a windowed office in one corner of the warehouse. He handed me a key and said, "Unlock it."

He didn't want to turn his back to me. With the truth about my mother out there, I'd lost at least some of the trust he might've kept. I took the single key. *I could jam it in his eye.* Slipped it in the lock. *But that's not strategic.*

He definitely had a gun on him—he'd be stupid not to. It was most likely somewhere around his middle.

I held my breath as I opened the door.

Diego took the key and the sack from me and gestured for me to pass through, then at a metal folding chair against the back wall, under a domed floor lamp. "Sit."

He walked to a desk of computers across from the seat. Above it was a bank of monitors—security footage of the inside and perimeter of the warehouse.

"What is this?" I asked, trying to distract him as I noted my surroundings. Empty buckets in one corner. A stack of bricks in another. A file cabinet. Even the lamp and chair could act as defense weapons. Anything that wasn't bolted down. My purse was nowhere in sight.

"We're just going to let my brother know you're safe."

"Why?" I asked as I walked to the chair.

"Hands behind your back."

I held them together in front of me, hoping he wouldn't think anything of it. Easier to escape that way.

Diego eyed me up and down. "I said *behind* you."

"Does it matter?" I said but obeyed, mentally preparing myself for the most difficult restraints. However he bound me, I could get out of it. I'd practiced countless times. But some scenarios were worse than others. For handcuffs, I could try to find a prop on the desk in front of me, but I'd need time alone. All my sneakers at home had Kevlar laces that could cut through zip ties or rope, and some even had universal handcuff keys strung on the laces for this purpose—but of course, I was in heels today.

I'd have to find another way.

When I heard the screech of duct tape, my fraught nerves settled slightly. Of everything he could've chosen, that was on the easier side to escape. I might even be able to do it with him in the room. He had little faith in me and hadn't even bothered to try very hard.

It would be his mistake.

I made two fists to give myself more wiggle room as he taped my wrists good and tight.

But not tight enough.

"I'm sorry if that hurts," he said. "It's partly for show, and partly because I'm not sure I can trust you right now."

A genuine apology. In his voice, I heard the boy I'd once loved. I tried to see Diego the way I had before—as a creative, smart, level-headed man I'd aspired to spend the rest of my life with. He'd said he'd loved me, and I still believed he'd thought he had. Perhaps selfish love was the most he was capable of, but Cristiano's selflessness had taught me love's true meaning.

His words came back to me now.

*Love is, "I'd die for you."*

*Not, "Would you die for me?"*

A lump formed in my throat. Not for myself, but for what Cristiano must be going through. For me to disappear from right under his nose would devastate him. He'd blame himself. He'd suffer.

If *I* could manage to tap into better times during a situation like this, then Diego could, too. "How'd you do it?" I asked as he ripped off the tape and patted it into place.

"Do what?" He came around to stand in front of me, surveying his work. He held up the tape. "I won't bother with your mouth, but don't scream. The only people who'd hear you would enjoy it and might come sniffing around. I'm only one man to defend you."

I refrained from shuddering. Again, his words were intentionally chosen to rattle me. I wouldn't let them. "How'd you look me in the eye every day?" I asked. "You watched us bury her."

He set the roll of tape on the desk and took the small white envelope with my sonogram from his jacket pocket.

My pulse jumped at the sight of it—but I forced myself to school my reaction.

"It's in the past, Tali. No point in reliving it. Just know, I'm sorry it happened the way it did." Diego sighed, as if truly regretful. "And for Cristiano to be accused of violating a woman who'd acted as a mother to him? A man like him, a known rapist? It must've torn him apart. I can't imagine."

My breath caught in my throat. He *could* imagine, and it pleased him. Maybe Diego *had* known his older brother had tried to shield him during his youth from their parents' business. Yet, somehow, he saw that as betrayal. "How can you say it like it's nothing?" I asked. "She was abused because *you* let the *sicario* in."

"There's no way I could've known it would happen that way." Diego stared at me, his green eyes sorrowful. "Bianca didn't deserve it, but your father did. And he deserves what's coming even more."

My throat dried. Diego could easily rip out the hearts of the two men who'd killed his parents—because he had me. "What's coming to him?" I asked so softly, I wasn't sure he'd heard.

He came and squatted in front of me. The fact that he had the nerve to look me in the eye told me that he'd convinced himself he was the hero of this story.

"My problem is only with Cristiano and Costa," he said.

"Then it's with me, too. They're *mi familia*."

"They can't walk away from killing my parents and destroying my family's business," Diego said. "I'm going after what rightfully belongs to me. Can't you understand that?"

I tried with everything I had. If I could not only understand but love Cristiano after years of loathing him, it shouldn't have been difficult to see the point of view of the boy I'd worshipped. My father had made both of them witness their parents' murders as a warning—loyalty would be rewarded, dissention would cost them their lives.

Cristiano and my father had decided Diego's fate for him. Instead of inheriting the legacy his family had built, Diego would forever be a charge, second in command, "just another worker" as he'd once bitterly referred to himself. He'd lost his family and his empire, as had Cristiano—but at least Cristiano'd had a say in it.

But all of that was erased by the deliberate, calculated betrayal that had cost my mother her life. Diego'd made that choice when he could've easily gone to my father and saved her. So no, I couldn't understand.

My jaw ached, molars grinding together. "You should've known, no matter how much I loved you—I would've never stood by your side and played with people's lives."

"You would've. You will," he said resolutely. He held up the small envelope, then tucked it into the neckline of my dress, over my left breast. Close to my heart. "Just remember this if you're tempted to do anything stupid."

I'd been grateful for the duct tape a moment ago, but suddenly, it was excruciating that I couldn't lash out at him or cover my stomach to protect what'd only just begun to grow inside me. "Cristiano won't play your games. He knows I'd rather die than let that happen."

"It's not your choice." He checked his watch, then walked to one of the large windows to look into the warehouse. "Costa, Cristiano, and I each love you, but we've all used you as a pawn."

While his back was to me, I glanced at the surveillance screens. Two men guarded the inside of the warehouse, though I couldn't tell where they were in relation to us. Two more milled out front, while one stood at the gated entrance. *Five*. Numbers six, seven, and eight held assault rifles and walked the perimeter, which was surrounded by large trees.

"Cristiano will comply," Diego said, still looking off into the distance. "He loves you, and he of all people knows that being with me is a fate far better than the hell I could arrange for you."

It took a moment for his threat to sink in. He could sell me. As his father had Angelina. I didn't want to believe he was capable of it, but the truth was, I didn't know the level of depravity I was dealing with. And the worst part was that Diego knew exactly what a threat like that would do to Cristiano. It may even be enough to convince him to cooperate.

With a series of *beeps*, Diego took his phone from his pocket and hit a button to speak into it. "*Bueno*."

"*Listos*," came a man's voice through the speaker.

*Ready*.

Diego returned to the computer beneath the monitors and the security footage flickered off.

My insides twisted. Something was happening. "What are you doing?"

"Don't worry. Cristiano will cooperate to keep you safe." Diego opened a closet and removed a tripod. He set it up behind the desk, in front of the control panel. Next, he took a smartphone with a bulky case out of a desk drawer and swiped his thumb over the screen. "Knowing I have you will torture him. You saw the way he tried to feed me to the Maldonados. I couldn't let that go, Natalia—you know that. Cristiano deliberately provokes his enemies, and he shouldn't be surprised when that comes back around to him."

I couldn't argue that Cristiano was a good man, or even deserving of what he had. He, like Diego, my father, and myself, had committed many sins. But I loved him for who he was, flaws and all. I couldn't ask for a better partner or for a better father to our future child.

When did one become a mother? I wasn't sure, only that I already felt extremely protective. Maybe it had to do with what lay ahead more than anything. Since I'd suspected the pregnancy, I'd started to envision a new life with Cristiano. Our latest adventure—parenthood. Gruff, rough-around-the-edges Cristiano cradling a newborn son in both hands. Me, passing on the lessons I'd learned to a daughter and thereby honoring her grandmother and her father, who'd both taught me strength.

I had to do whatever I could to protect that.

Survival, no matter what.

Red lights flickered on the TV screens directly in front of me. Images flashed on and off.

Diego hummed with satisfaction, screwed the smartphone onto the tripod by its case, and stepped back before he spoke into his own phone. "We're connected. Put them through."

"What is this?" I asked hoarsely, but I wasn't sure I wanted to know.

He aimed a small remote at the smartphone and pushed a button. "We're streaming. Look into the camera and say hello to your husband."

## CHAPTER 24

# CRISTIANO

It took me a moment to register what I was looking at.

A well-lit office. A metal chair in the center. My *wife*.

Blood rushed in my ears. My heart thrashed hard enough to deafen and disorient me.

My team and I had scoured the abandoned parade.

As soon as guns had come out, people had cleared the area quickly, except for a few bodies in the middle of the road who'd possibly tried to stop *them*. Who were *they*? Who'd taken my wife? All anyone could tell me was that men in black, some costumed, had put her into a van and vanished.

*Just like that.*

Costa's and my choppers had been dispatched but had yet to find anything.

I'd trampled fallen crepe streamers, glitter, and plastic plates and forks looking for a clue—*anything*—until we'd received word that her abductors wanted to make contact, and we'd rushed back to the Badlands.

Now, Costa and I stood in the basement control center as Gabriel patched through a live video feed to our security monitors.

*Natalia.*

Her dress, colorful against a gray backdrop, remained intact—*gracias a Dios*. There were no injuries that I could see. Her hands appeared to be bound behind her back, but she wasn't gagged.

"Natalia, *mi amor*," I said, surprised at the even, calm tone of my voice. I may have learned to keep my composure in a threatening situation, but this was something else entirely. This was my entire fucking life. "Can you hear me? Where are you?"

She nodded almost imperceptibly, but her eyes shifted to the side of the camera. She wasn't alone.

I prayed she'd been taken for ransom by some recklessly stupid faction and that Belmonte-Ruiz hadn't broken their truce.

But why should the devil's prayers be answered?

"Brother."

Chills spread over me at the all-too-familiar voice. One I'd never mistake. One I never thought I'd hear again.

A face resembling my own filled the screen, but it might as well have belonged to a stranger. My brother. *Diego.*

*What the* fuck. He was alive. Everything in my body ceased to function. I froze, and it was a good thing. I never wanted Diego to think he'd caught me off guard.

He blocked Natalia as he looked from me to Costa and back. "Good. You're both here."

My hands twitched with the urge to reach through the screen and wrap my hands around his neck, tighten them slowly so he'd experience the crush of every delicate bone, the collapse of his windpipe—

"You don't know what you're doing, boy," Costa said from beside me, his voice reverberating through the room. If he was shocked to see his former charge, he didn't show it. "Let her go. She doesn't have anything to do with this."

"She has *everything* to do with this." Diego retreated until Natalia came back into view. She focused her eyes above the camera lens.

On me?

"Natalia."

She closed her eyes, swallowed, and reopened them. I couldn't miss the fire in them as my own stare bored into her.

*You've got this,* I silently told her. *Be strong. We'll get you out of this.*

"This will be easier for all of us if Talia's alive," Diego said, removing a gun from the inside of his jacket. "I love her and don't want to hurt her. But let's get one thing straight—I will put a bullet in her pretty face if I have to, so don't do anything I don't explicitly instruct you to."

Rage burned up my chest like heartburn of days past. Days *past*—since Natalia had decided to change my lifestyle. She wanted me healthy. That was my fucking wife, taking command of me when I'd never let anyone tell me how to live. Anyone but her. The love of my goddamn life.

My throat closed. I breathed in and out, willing my fury away. Anger would only blind me.

*Focus.*

Diego *had* loved her in his own selfish way. I believed when he said he still did. But she was more than that to him. She was my weakness, and Diego had always known it.

I had to trust Natalia could get herself out of this after all the drills we'd run, the moves she'd perfected, and the countless hours I'd spent punishing her and myself for the fact that a man had come too close to taking her from me months ago.

A roll of duct tape on the desk gave me hope—she'd be able to free herself if that was what he'd used to bind her hands.

And I didn't miss the way Diego *stupidly* turned his back to her.

He trusted her—that was good. But even better—he didn't seem to consider the possibility that she *could* fight back. He'd never seen her as anything other than precious. Breakable. Compliant.

But she was none of those things, and if she ever had been, it'd been a product of her environment.

She could take him on.

She *had* to.

She just needed to free her hands, and *I* needed to keep his eyes on me and off of her.

Reluctantly, I tore my gaze from her and returned it to Diego, who was watching me with a hint of a smile. He knew this was killing me. "What do you want?"

"It wasn't so long ago that I asked you the same thing." Diego put a hand in his pocket and inspected the other, running his thumb along a tattoo on the inside of his ring finger. "You and I stood across from each other in your office as you stripped away my options until there was only one left—submit to the Maldonados and face death."

*Aren't we a little old for story time, Diego?* I bit my tongue. I could think of a thousand responses that would bruise Diego's ego as I slowly worked my way under his skin. I had rattled him before, like that day at *La Madrina*. But Natalia could pay the price for provoking him. I had to grin and bear it.

"You thought you had me," Diego continued. "You should've known not even my death would end this. Aren't you curious how I'm still alive?"

"No," I said. "I don't give two shits about that or any other lie you've spun to justify the way you are." Natalia jerked silently behind him. She was working her hands free. As Diego started to turn, I said, "Why are you doing this?"

There were plenty of things I wanted to say to him for his involvement in Bianca's death, but none of it was more important than holding his attention. Keeping it off Natalia. Keeping her safe. And *finding* her.

Gabriel, Max, and Alejo monitored everything from the next room, searching for clues on the screen that might indicate a geographic location, listening for any valuable information Diego might slip up and reveal. He wasn't stupid enough to make a traceable call, but this connection was all we had.

Diego crossed his arms over his chest. "I've never met a man more willing to betray family—or turn his back on the world he was raised in. Everyone now knows you as a traitor. You continue to bring shame to our name long after our parents' death."

*Good*. I could think of no greater compliment.

"For Cristiano, blood doesn't make family," Costa said, seething beside me. "His loyalty to me has stood the test of time and circumstance. He is *mi familia*."

I put my hand on Costa's elbow to show my gratitude but also to warn him to control his reaction. It was torturous not to look at Natalia every few seconds, but if I did, Diego might, too.

"Costa," Diego said, shifting his attention away from me, "you would've crumbled without me. Your cartel is what it is because of *me*. You were inconsolable after Bianca's death, but I propped you up. After that, you only kept up with demand and the new order because of the technology and fresh ideas I introduced." Diego leveled his unblinking stare on Costa. "*I* oversaw the development of our advanced tunnel system into the States myself," he said simply. "*I* made most of the connections we needed at the border. I know your business better than anyone." He stuck his hands in his pockets and shook his head. "And without so much as a second thought, after twenty years of loyalty, you kicked me out of the home where I'd spent the majority of my childhood."

"Loyalty?" Costa boomed. "*You killed my wife*." Costa barreled toward the camera, gripping it with both hands. "Your betrayal cost us everything, and *me las vas a pagar*—I will rip your balls off for it," he said, spittle covering the lens. "I won't let you take my daughter, too."

Diego ran his tongue along his upper teeth. He'd finally gotten the reaction he'd come for.

"You've only paid half the price for killing *both* my parents, *don* Costa," Diego responded coolly. "An eye for an eye means you owe me a life still."

"Then take mine," Costa said.

"Too easy. I'm willing to negotiate, though. I won't kill Natalia as long as you do what I say." He glanced at me. "I should like to have her by my side in this next venture."

Over my dead and rotting body. My hands throbbed from clenching them, but I couldn't get myself to release my fists. Couldn't let my anger drown out my reason. Revenge blinded Diego to the fact that Natalia was not the weak girl she'd once been. I couldn't let it distract me, too.

She needed my entire focus.

*Keep her safe. Get her the fuck* out.

I glanced over my shoulder as Maksim entered the room. His haggard face turned sheet-white as he crossed himself and uttered something in Russian. "I saw your corpse," he said to Diego.

"You saw what I wanted you to see." Diego cleared his throat. "Get out."

Max and I met eyes briefly. Did he know anything? Not yet, it seemed. He walked out.

"How'd you learn about the tunnel in my home?" Costa asked, his tone level now. "Nobody knew but Bianca, Natalia, and me."

Diego glanced briefly at the ground and back up. "With an abundance of patience. I watched. I waited. I learned the security codes, I learned about your underground secrets. I left the door open for the *sicario* when I knew you'd be out of town."

"What about the safe?" I asked.

Diego smirked. "The valuables and cash in there totaled well over a million dollars. In exchange for the contents, the hitman provided me a weapon, bank account transfer info, and hidden camera footage linking Vicente Valverde to Bianca's murder."

"Which you used to run them out of town," I said. "And Natalia was supposed to be at the parade, but what about me?"

"I was as shocked as both of you when I walked into the bedroom. I knew what was supposed to happen, but seeing her there was still difficult." He paced to one side of the room, glancing through a window into the warehouse, then turned to me. "You found Bianca, Cristiano, and I found you, gun in hand," he said. "It wasn't part of the plan, but it worked out well. I would've killed you if I could've. Either way, I would've been the hero."

Natalia stilled. Her lips twitched. She wanted to speak. To rail. To protect *me* when she was the one in danger.

*Stay calm.* I had to will it to her without looking at her for more than a couple seconds.

It couldn't be easy for her to hear all this, but she needed to keep her mouth shut and focus on escape.

"Get to the point, *rata*," Costa said on a growl. "Why are we here?"

Diego's jaw ticked. He didn't like being called a *rat*, especially by the man who'd murdered his parents. Costa needed to stop poking him. If Diego took his anger out on Natalia, I *would* find a way to get in that room, even if it meant climbing through the camera lens. But his pinched expression quickly returned to neutral.

"You work for me now. Comply, and Natalia will be safe. She's angry with me now—I have you to blame for that, brother." Diego rolled his shoulders. "But once your spell has worn off, we'll return to the way we were. If you care for her, too, you'll accept it, because she'll be happy here. She will be loved—by me." He bit his bottom lip and added, "Every night, to make up for all the time you stole from us."

*No.*

My heart pounded as I fought off the image of them together.

*Don't react.*

This wasn't about me.

I wiped beads of sweat from my upper lip. I had to focus on her, but she seemed so far away. I couldn't see her as well as I wanted. I didn't know if she sweat, too, or if she shivered instead. If her rage heated her, or if icy hatred took over. She needed me. My warmth.

My breathing grew more ragged. *Don't think of Diego's hands on her.*

Did she feel strong? Or did she struggle to separate the person in front of her from the boy she'd known?

"We'll get to her before you ever touch her," Costa said. "I promise you that."

Whether he promised Diego, me, or Natalia, I wasn't sure, but he was leveling threats that could only hurt us. I looked over at him. His corded neck and beet-red face said it all. He was trying to fight off the same images as I was.

"*Tranquilo*," I said to him under my breath to remind him to stay calm, but he kept his eyes laser focused on the screen.

"Is it worth losing Natalia?" Diego asked, his nostrils flaring. "Because if I hear even a whisper that you're trying to find our location, I will take her life, and then you and I will be at all-out war. Your armies together are strong—but Belmonte-Ruiz's is now three times the size it used to be, and it's growing every day as word spreads about how you're working for the wrong side."

I didn't doubt that now. I hadn't blindly trusted Belmonte-Ruiz's truce, but the more time that'd passed, the less concerned I'd become. They'd held up their end of the bargain by moving on to other ventures. Our informant had been killed; we hadn't replaced him. And foolishly . . . I'd wanted to believe we could all live in peace. Because Natalia and I were ready to start a family, but we wouldn't during a war.

I hadn't realized we were still in one. I should've fucking paid closer attention.

"So you want Cristiano's global network and my shipping infrastructure, eh?" Costa said. "To distribute on a larger, more international scale. Is that right?"

"Everyone will benefit, even both of you—which is generous on my part considering the rules of this world."

"Which are?" I asked, even though I knew. Even though I didn't give a *fuck*.

But I asked to keep him talking. Natalia was squirming now, definitely close to freeing herself.

"The rules mandate that I kill you for your sins against my family," Diego said. "But I'm willing to take another form of payment. We're developing a new drug and want to explode onto the market. We can mostly handle North America, but we need both of you in order to take Europe, Asia, the Middle East. Your income will double."

I watched Diego's face closely as Costa grunted. "Then why blackmail us?" he asked. "Make a proposal, and my partner and I will discuss it. I won't do business with you while you've kidnapped my daughter."

"Because Cristiano's answer will be no." Diego strolled backward. "He needs motivation."

My chest locked up as he rounded Natalia's chair and set his hands on her shoulders. Touched her. Massaged her. My body shook with an impending explosion. I finally let myself look at Natalia for more than a few seconds. I tried to draw from the strength in her eyes. *She* was trying to soothe *me* when it needed to be the other way around.

*I love you,* I said with my gaze. *I'm coming for you. No matter what.*

I inhaled through my nose. I needed a level head—and to keep his eyes on me. He stood behind her now, and if he saw her restraints broken or even loose, that could only make things worse.

"Narcotics distribution is what Belmonte-Ruiz demands in exchange for all that you've cost them," Diego explained. "But then there's what I want."

What had Diego desired from the start?

Revenge. Legacy. Power.

And at any cost.

I crossed my arms. "Nothing will bring our parents back to life, Diego."

"You're wrong. Belmonte-Ruiz is the most successful human trafficking syndicate in the country. With their approval, your help, and my guidance, the de la Rosa cartel will scale that business to an international level—like our father would've wanted."

It was as Max, Natalia, and I had guessed several months ago. Diego asked me to play God. To enslave, torture, and break innocent people. To relinquish the code I lived by. He asked of me the *one* thing I couldn't give him. That was why he had Natalia. "I won't do it."

Diego squeezed Natalia's shoulders. "Then Natalia will pay the price," Diego said, "and if you think that means death, it's far too easy."

I stilled. "You care about her too much to sell her."

"That's why, unlike you, I'm trying to keep her safe," he said. "But maybe our father had it right when he sold Angelina."

My chest tightened at the mention of the childhood crush I'd lost. Diego had been too young to be part of the deal my father had made to teach me a lesson and knew only what I'd told him during our time as young adults at Costa's ranch. I'd been vulnerable with him. Revealed how I'd still thought of Angelina and wished I'd had the means to find her.

"Sometimes, if you want to learn to be ruthless, you have to start by ripping out your own heart," Diego said calmly. "I'd rather not do that by giving up Natalia, but I will. You understand." Diego addressed both Costa and me. "You taught me early the dangers of emotional attachments."

My lesson had been Angelina. Diego's had been witnessing not just a father's death, but a mother's, too.

It had changed us both in very different ways.

"Bianca suspected," Costa said. "She had a feeling what you were. *Are*."

"Regardless." Diego shook his head. "You went to extreme lengths to see me suffer, and make no mistake I want that for you, too." Diego slid down the elastic of Natalia's off-the-shoulder dress, rubbing her bare biceps as a rock hardened in my stomach. "We'll grow our business with or without you, but we can do it exponentially faster with your help." He paused. "You'll never have to come face to face with the lives you buy, sell, and trade—they'll always be nameless, faceless strangers. But Natalia?" He glanced at the top of her head then back up. "By tomorrow, she could be on a yacht in the Mediterranean, at the mercy of a sheikh so powerful that nobody, not even you, can touch him. It's your choice which hell you want to live in."

My blood boiled. This was the chance I'd taken when I'd followed two paths that should never cross—angering dangerous people by disrupting their systems . . . and falling in love. I wouldn't trade the impact we'd made or my love for Natalia for anything, but *fuck* Diego for knowing exactly how to manipulate me.

My fury had coiled too tightly. I slammed my fists on the desk under me and sent everything flying. "I should've murdered you when I'd had the chance."

"I don't think anyone would disagree on that point." Diego patted Natalia's arm, smiling at me. "So, do we have a deal, partner?"

Natalia shook her head as she mouthed, "No."

Diego was just demented enough to follow through with his threat against Natalia. I had no choice. Whatever Natalia asked me to do or not do, I wouldn't put her in harm's way if I could help it.

Diego flattened his hand on Natalia's chest and slid it down until it breached the neckline, over her breast.

*No. Motherfucker. No—*

He flicked a white envelope from her dress. "If you need another reason to comply, let this be it." He tore it open and pulled out a black-and-white photograph.

I squinted. *What . . .?*

As the image before me took shape, my throat went bone dry. It couldn't be.

"What is it?" Costa asked, his eyes narrowed.

My mouth moved, but my ears rang so loudly, I never heard myself say it. "A sonogram."

"What?" Costa roared. "*Vete a la chingada.*"

He cursed Diego, while I couldn't even form a word.

News I'd yearned for over the last few months, I suddenly wished away. I should've been elated. Instead, I prayed to the Virgin Mary that it wasn't true. My knees buckled as a fear I'd never known weighed on my shoulders. It couldn't be. If I let myself believe it, I would either rage or crumble, and neither reaction would help Natalia.

They were lies.

Diego had planted the image to unnerve me. To get me to agree to his terms. It wasn't true. There was no baby . . .

I held onto the desk and looked from him to her, the only one who mattered here. I met her anguished eyes. Her lips pressed together hard, bloodless and white—I knew that look. She was doing everything in her power not to cry.

My vision blurred. The ground underneath my feet rolled. It was true.

It would explain why she'd invented a wrist injury last week to stop our training. And why she hadn't fought back when Diego had taken her from the parade.

It was the one mindset I'd never thought to prepare her for.

She was worried for her condition.

I thought I'd done everything I could to equip Natalia, but this was a situation none of us had ever faced. I'd failed her. I wanted to turn away so I wouldn't break down right there, but I couldn't let Natalia think I'd left her alone in this for a second.

We were in it together.

I limbered up my shoulders as if preparing for a boxing match. "Fuck you," I said.

Diego responded as I wanted, coming out from behind Natalia's chair to look at us straight on. "Is that a yes then?"

Natalia's head whipped up. "Don't do it, Cristiano," she said, choking back her tears. "Those people need you. It's everything you've worked for. Don't make the deal."

The thought of betraying those I'd helped, and those I might still help, chilled my insides. It wouldn't be forever; it *couldn't* be. I'd find a way out. But every life mattered. If I didn't believe that, I would never have taken on the thankless, impossible mission to try to make a dent in the sex and forced labor trades.

If I did this, I'd go from savior to enemy.

I couldn't ruin countless lives to save one, could I?

To save *two*.

The fates of my unborn child and my wife were in the hands of a man who'd spent twenty years waiting to see me suffer.

Natalia's eyes pleaded with me not to do it. But didn't she know I could never walk away from the love of my life? From our baby? That I would do *whatever* it took to keep her safe? Even if it meant breaking all my rules and becoming the worst version of myself . . .

My father.

I nodded once. "You have a deal."

CHAPTER 25

# NATALIA

"You have a deal."

Cristiano's words hung in the room.

My heart broke knowing what it had cost him to agree to the arrangement. He'd call into question more than a decade of work. And going forward, every day, he'd die a little inside aiding a true monster—because I was in its grip.

Except I wasn't. I was going to save him—*us*—from that pitch-black future.

While Diego had listed his demands to Cristiano, I'd put everything I'd had into getting out of my restraints—and I'd succeeded.

I'd freed my hands.

Now, I had to free myself—and my husband and baby.

My throat went completely dry. I couldn't lose my nerve now. There was no time to strategize, and yet, one false move could cost me everything.

I had to act before he turned around and saw I'd gotten loose.

He'd replaced his gun inside his jacket. I had to make sure once I was up, he didn't have even a second to reach for it.

My eyes darted around the room and landed on the stack of bricks against one wall. They were the closest thing to me that could do serious damage. It had to be that, and it had to be now, while Diego distracted himself with the logistics of their deal.

"One week?" Cristiano asked in response to something Diego had said. "It's impossible."

"You'll find a way," Diego said.

My heart pounded as I silently removed my high heels.

"I don't do business with traffickers, I need—" Cristiano's voice faltered when I stood, but his eyes stayed trained on Diego. "I need time for my connections to . . . to build me a new network."

"That would take too long," Diego said.

In bare feet, I tip-toed to one corner.

Diego turned his head slightly, and Cristiano said, "Come on, *cabrón*!" so loudly, Diego's head snapped forward again. "Do you want this done sloppy," Cristiano said, "or do you want it done *right*?"

Diego seemed to consider the question. He actually meant to go through with this—to build a new cartel at any cost.

And whether it was Diego's true motive or just icing on the cake—he believed he'd now be the *only* person in the world with any power over Cristiano de la Rosa.

But didn't he know that title belonged to me?

Only I could tame the beast. Today, tomorrow, and forever. Cristiano was *mine*.

I couldn't wait any longer.

I used two hands to pick up a brick from the top of the pile. I tested its weight. Heavy. Solid. I raised my eyes to the back of Diego's head. At least I wouldn't have to look him in the face. My childhood best friend. My first love.

I shut my eyes briefly, opened them, and ran forward.

*Don't hesitate. Don't—*

Diego spun around. I hefted the brick across his face. *Smack*. Blood splattered. His body flew to one side as his guttural shout filled the small space.

My stomach heaved as I froze.

*Tell me you love me, Talia.*

*Tell me you're still my girl.*

"It's not over!" Cristiano's shouting jarred me.

Diego was still on his feet, doubled over as he spit out a tooth. He rushed at me. I stumbled backward, tripped over the lamp's cord, and dropped the brick as I threw my hands back and caught myself before my ass hit the floor. I used my momentum to push off the ground and spring back to my feet.

I *refused* to go down, especially because of Diego.

He came at me again, leaning to one side, struggling to focus his eyes.

I picked up the metal folding chair and raised it over my head. I brought it down as hard as I could, but he blocked my blow, grabbed the seat, and used it as leverage to fling me into a wall.

As my head knocked against concrete, I shook off a bout of dizziness.

"Talia—" Diego coughed, blood streaming from his head as he tried to grab me.

I ducked out of the way, snatched the brick off the ground, and whirled around.

This time, I aimed not for his head but for his *brain*.

The brick *thudded* against his skull. He staggered back, his eyes pleading with me, then fell to his knees. I kicked him onto his back, jumped on top of him, and lifted the slab again.

He was hanging on by a thread.

I just had to do it one more time.

*Don't look at his face.*

He groaned. My eyes jumped up. Covered in blood, his head dropped to one side, eyes half-open. I'd crushed one of the high cheekbones that made him so beautiful, one I used to touch with reverence.

*"When I go, you'll be by my side, okay?" he said. "I'm with you, life or death."*

*"Life or death,"* I'd responded.

I had so much more to live for now, and everything to fight for. It was me or him.

I slammed the brick down. His skull collapsed. His eyes remained open but distant. One socket had caved in.

My chest seized. Breath halted. Throat closed, cutting off my air.

I shook, and my hands loosened around the weapon.

But there was no time to panic. It wasn't over—the fight was *never* over.

I jolted into action, frisking his legs until I had his folding knife. Sticking it between my teeth, I found the gun tucked into his jacket pocket.

I got to my feet holding both weapons. Ears ringing, I turned around. Cristiano's beautiful, ashen face filled the screen.

*Home.*

I stumbled toward him. "Cristiano." My strangled voice sounded far away.

"I know, baby. I know," he said, his jaw set, eyes shrewd as they darted around the room, then refocused on me. "You did good—but you're not done yet."

My heart raced. I willed it to slow and pulled myself together. "There are at least eight men outside with guns."

His eyes quickly scanned my face before he turned his head over his shoulder and called for Gabriel. "I'm coming for you," Cristiano promised me. "Do you know where you are?"

I shook my head. "Some kind of huge warehouse."

"Get out of that room. Find a place to hide until I get there."

"There are too many of them."

"Listen, *mi amor*." The calm in Cristiano's voice settled my nerves. "Turn around and cut Diego's throat so you *know* he's dead. Don't use the gun unless you absolutely have to. Check his body for a different phone, then hide and call me from it so we can try to trace it. If you encounter anyone—fight, Natalia."

I would fight. I *had* already. But me, with a knife, a pistol, and a baby to protect against *all* of them and their rifles?

"I . . ." I held the weapons to my queasy stomach as my voice broke. "The baby. It's true."

Cristiano gritted his teeth and swallowed. His father had warned him young never to form emotional attachments that could be painfully severed. This was the price of love. I couldn't let him regret it.

"Mindset, Natalia," he said firmly. "*You* are the White Monarch. Don't you see that? You're the weapon, the survivor, the killer. You can do this."

I had no other choice. I sucked in an inhale and nodded hard. "I couldn't see anything as we came in—but the air pressure here is low. Thin," I rushed out. I glanced over my shoulder, unnerved by the silence of the warehouse. "It's like a forest. The ground is soft, lots of big trees—"

"What kinds of trees?" Gabe asked, entering the frame behind Cristiano.

"I don't know. Pine? It's dry—except, it almost sounded like it was raining outside. But it definitely wasn't."

Cristiano glanced back at Gabriel. He nodded slowly, his eyes on me, but his thoughts somewhere else. "The monarch butterfly migration," he said finally. "Must be. Their colonies cluster together in certain winter habitats. The oyamel fir only grows in high altitudes. There are so many butterflies, their wings sound like a rain shower."

"God's messengers," I whispered. They were here.

"*Sí*. You're protected," Cristiano said and turned back to Gabriel. "Do you know where she is?"

"These forests are small, and may be designated reserves, but Belmonte-Ruiz's tunnel system runs right underneath that area with an entrance at the nearby Acapulco port." He pinched the bridge of his nose, talking to himself, as if working through it. "It would make sense that they'd managed to build an operational facility there."

"Where?" I asked.

"Under the cover of the Sierra Madre del Sur mountain range." Gabriel met my eyes and nodded. "I know where you are."

ONE MOMENT, Cristiano's beautiful but drawn face looked back at me, and the next, I was alone. Cristiano was on his way. The TV monitors went dark, the warehouse office deafeningly silent. Diego's blood covered my shaking hands. He'd lost, but what had I won? Wanting him dead wasn't the same as committing the act. He was only the second person I'd ever killed, and at one point in time, I'd loved him more than anyone.

I made the sign of the cross, part of me hoping Diego found peace in the afterlife while I also damned him to Hell.

He was dead, and to make sure of it, I would cut his throat.

And then I'd have to prepare for the possibility of defeating a troop of armed men.

I went to the desk, grabbed the computer mouse, and clicked on the CCTV program. A minimized window opened with a grid view of surveillance from different cameras. This time, it didn't broadcast to the overhead monitors. I squinted and quickly re-counted the guards. The two in the warehouse were the greatest threat, but I only spotted one now as he leaned against a metal shelving unit, scrolling through his phone. I leaned forward, searching each display. Where was the other one? And where in relation to the office were—

My forehead slammed against the computer screen, blurring my vision. Something pinched my upper arm. A fist in the back of my hair yanked me to the ground.

On my back, the room spun so fast, I gagged. Diego stood over me, skull bashed in, blood dripping into his eyes, onto my dress.

My head pounded, my eyes crossing as vomit rose up my throat. I forced it back down. *Don't lose consciousness. Stay here.*

He was half-dead. I needed to get up and finish the job, but my limbs suddenly felt as if they weighed hundreds of kilos.

Diego's wobbling legs gave out. He sank to his knees and fell on the ground next to me. My attention drew to pain in my upper arm where I'd felt the pinch just now. It smarted as if I'd been stabbed with a small blade.

I struggled to lift my head. A syringe stuck out of my biceps. And Diego had his thumb on the plunger, pushing down on it, grimacing as if it took all of his effort to empty it into me . . .

Moving in slow motion, I reached over. He was losing consciousness, and I managed to wrestle the syringe from him and yank it out. "Wh-what is that?" I asked, my voice sounding far away.

His eyes drifted to the ceiling. As sweat trickled down his temple, he wheezed in such a painful sounding way that I felt it in my own chest and throat. "You're . . . coming . . . with me," he said and started to convulse.

My lips tingled so strongly that I had to suck in a breath. A strange but not unpleasant prickling sensation moved down my jaw. Arms. Fingers.

Numbing me.

"What . . . what's happening?" My lethargy glued me to the ground. I couldn't even turn my head away, and I was forced to look at him. "What have you done?

Diego stilled. His chest sank. His gaze went distant—as my mother's had in her final moments. Life drained from his eyes as he said, "*Escalera al Cielo.*"

And then he was gone.

*Stairway to Heaven.* The memory came back in pieces. Diego humming Led Zeppelin. His casual reference over Coca Light that Juan Pablo Perez, the chemist from Nogales, was developing a new drug. Puffer fish toxins . . . sedative . . . a slowed heart rate . . .

A round-trip ticket to heaven. The most elusive and euphoric high.

But with the wrong dosage, the stairway home vanished. Heaven became the final destination.

Mustering all my energy, I lifted the syringe in front of my face and tried to focus my blurring vision. Almost . . . *empty*? No. God, no. If he'd overdosed me, I'd die right here on this floor. Tears filled my eyes as fear tremored through me, then fizzled with the onset of such intense happiness, I had the urge to smile.

I needed to turn over. Get up. Crawl if I had to. But my body betrayed me. Exhilaration and satisfaction mingled in my stomach like a groundswell, rolling through each of my limbs, warming my face.

*Hide*, Cristiano had told me. I couldn't lift a limb. I slid on my back toward the desk. My arms and legs became noodles, loose and droopy, fatiguing with the effort.

My nerves vibrated. A pleasant hum took over.

I had to keep going. Escape. Hide. *Fight.*

But I could only sink into the ground, as the sky pulled me up, up, up—and away.

## CHAPTER 26

# CRISTIANO

Max took the forest's rough terrain as rapidly as he could, but every minute that passed felt like an hour, and we might as well have been moving in slow motion. As dusk began to fall, we crawled up an embankment of boulders. I braced myself against the roof of the Humvee to keep from smacking my head.

Alejandro had a map spread out over the center console between the front seats as Gabriel directed us over speakerphone. Alejo removed the flashlight between his teeth and yelled over the scrape of the truck's skid plates against rocks. "Repeat that."

"If my"—Gabriel's voice cut in and out—"are correct, you . . . close." The bouts of static over the line had gotten worse the farther we strayed from civilization. The kid had been directing us along the red-marker line he'd drawn on the map to indicate Belmonte-Ruiz's network of tunnels, but it seemed we were about to lose contact. "Three clicks."

*Three kilometers*? "Until what?" I demanded.

No answer.

Max straightened up. "Are those tire tracks in the mud?"

Could've been that, or nothing at all. "It's getting dark."

"Look for . . ." Gabriel said. "Trees—"

"A spot where trees have been cleared." I pointed through the forest toward a muddy path just big enough for a car to pass through.

Max ramped up his speed, barreling down the makeshift road. I rolled down my window and gestured ahead for Eduardo and the men in the vehicle behind us.

I mashed my teeth together for the thousandth time since we'd left the Badlands. I had to believe there was an explanation for why Natalia had never called from Diego's phone liked I'd instructed her to. Dead battery. Broken phone. No service.

Any moment now, I'd have her back in my arms. She'd survive this. I knew it in my gut.

When I'd returned earlier in the year, I'd watched Diego overlook and manipulate the best thing in his life. And so, I'd taken her from him. And nurtured her, watched her grow and change, from a girl to a woman, from my captive to my wife, and now, the mother of my child. Diego had underestimated Natalia for the last time, and today, she'd prevailed.

She'd finish this. I'd trained her well. I trusted no one more than my men, and together, we'd taught her how to stay alive. She'd hang on until we got there. And then we'd torch the motherfucking place to the ground.

"You have to be close." Gabriel's voice came through clearly. Alejo and I exchanged a look. The static was gone. We were near a cell tower. "This area is super isolated," Gabe said, "and could serve as an entrance or exit to an underground passage."

Max looked over his shoulder. "If you're leading us into a trap, you should know that you wouldn't be the first. You wouldn't be the last, either."

I didn't condemn Max's skepticism. Of all the crazy shit that'd crossed my mind in the past several hours, wondering if Gabe could be setting us up was a mild thought. Gabe had done everything asked of him, though. He enjoyed both being behind the computer *and* his lessons with Solomon. But Diego's patience for revenge had been never-ending, and he'd fooled just about everyone, even me for longer than I cared to admit.

Gabriel was deep enough inside our systems to do serious damage, but Natalia trusted him, and now, he was my only hope. I nodded Max on down the route laid out for us toward a destination none of us were even sure existed.

From the backseat, Alejandro passed Max and me our artillery and loaded himself up next. Maksim accelerated toward a chain-link gate surrounding a brick structure.

"Take it down," I ordered.

The hand of the speedometer flew higher as we rushed the gate and crashed right through.

I waited for gunfire. Warning shots. Bullets to pepper the side panels or shatter the windshield's exterior glass.

Nothing.

*Silence.*

Max didn't screech to a stop until we were meters from the door to what looked like a warehouse.

I opened the door, using it as a shield as I surveyed the area.

"Maybe the tire tracks in the mud were going, not coming," Max said when nothing happened.

Or maybe we were in the wrong place.

*Fuck*. I had to get inside.

Alejandro opened his door. "We've got your back," he said. "Go."

With an assault rifle strapped over my bulletproof vest, I pulled out my .45 and sprinted the short distance to the entrance. I shot the lock. Kicked open the door. Ducked inside.

The expansive, well-lit space stood deathly still. Utterly silent.

Just me. And the pounding of my heart.

What if Natalia wasn't here? What if she'd never been?

*No*. She was here—hiding, like I'd told her. She had to be.

I strode past a conveyor belt toward rows of metal shelving, glancing down each aisle as I called out her name. When I'd made a partial circuit of the perimeter, I started through the stacks. Kicked aside random bins. Concealed the panic in my voice as I said her name so she wouldn't hear my fear.

"Natalia."

*Nothing.*

"Natalia."

*Silence.*

"Natalia! Goddamn it!"

A windowed security room sat ahead in one corner, lit by computer screens. Gun drawn, I strode toward the open door. I was greeted by the gentle hum of equipment.

And a dead body.

*Diego.*

Even with his face smashed in, and blood smeared everywhere, I recognized my brother. Was I supposed to feel something? I couldn't muster anything except relief to find we were in the right place.

But where was Natalia?

Hiding? Taken?

My throat began to close, and I struggled for air.

I turned to resume searching the warehouse when my eyes snagged on a pair of bare feet sticking out from behind the desk.

Toenails the color of the polish Natalia had waved in front of my face two days ago, begging for a pedicure. I hadn't been able to say no. I'd do anything for those toes.

I took a step forward.

Anything for the slender calves I ran my mouth along any chance I got.

For the hips that swayed against me when we danced. That kept my gaze whenever she left a room. That would bear my child.

A buzz started in my ears. My boots grew heavier with each step. Pressure weighed on my chest. No breath entered or left my body as I rounded the corner.

Arteries of black hair over the concrete ground reached from her pale, heart-shaped face. Eyes shut in peaceful rest. Slightly parted lips —pink and smiling that morning, now an alarming, icy blue.

My handgun clattered to the ground. I dropped to my knees and shook her by the shoulders. "Natalia. Wake up, *mi amor*." I'd just held her in my arms as we'd celebrated Bianca's life. She'd been warm. Glowing and beautiful. Growing with life, I now knew.

"We have to go. Get up!" I gripped her hand in mine. Cold. Limp. I held it to my collapsing chest and pressed my other fingers to the pulse under her jawbone.

No heartbeat.

That wasn't possible.

It couldn't be right. I was just too panicked to find her carotid artery.

I forced myself to exhale. Slid a hand under her head. Pulled her delicate frame into my lap, put my ear to her chest. Listened.

But she'd fought. She'd won. I'd seen it with my own eyes.

Natalia would not lose this battle. She was too strong, too good, had too much left to offer.

I waited with my cheek against her chest. And waited. Her body vibrated under me. Her heart or mine? My own beat so strongly, I couldn't hear anything else. Just silence.

Dead silence.

I couldn't breathe. Air became water, thick and slow, drowning me. "Wake *up*, Natalia."

But her body didn't lie. Her chest was a cavern. Mine hollowed out. My ribs caved in as my heart struggled, pounding hard and full of rage. "No," I begged her. "No, no, no."

How? I ripped off my guns and bulletproof vest, kneeled back, and drew her body against me. There was a new gash on her head, but it'd barely even bled. No strangulation marks. No other wounds.

I choked back an angry sob and yanked up her dress but only found smooth, untouched skin everywhere. No gunshot, injury—nothing had killed her. Why wasn't she breathing? Why didn't her heart beat?

The useless muscles I'd built to protect, defend, and support held her up but could do nothing else. Hope drained from my body.

Clenching my aching jaw, I placed her on the ground, put the heels of my hands between her breasts, and pushed on her chest once, twice, three times—over and over, then stopped to check for a pulse. Cupping the top of her head, I tilted back her chin and put my mouth to hers, breathing into her, willing her to life, calling her back from death's doorstep.

I should've never let her leave the float. I'd let my guard down. I'd turned my back, thinking Diego was dead. That Belmonte-Ruiz had moved on. I hadn't trained her how to fight in case she ever got pregnant—why hadn't I thought of it? Why hadn't I gotten here faster? What had happened between our call and now?

"Come on, Natalia." I returned to chest compressions. "You promised to come home to me—"

*Nothing*. No soul left in her. I didn't want to admit it, but I'd known it the moment I'd seen her.

She was gone.

My unborn child gone.

My life . . . gone.

Boots pounded the pavement of the warehouse, drawing closer until they stopped behind me.

"Cristiano," Max said, his voice breaking as his footsteps resumed. "Come on. We can't stay."

I sat back, staring at her. I couldn't move. Couldn't . . . anything. I'd rushed into this warehouse certain I'd come out with Natalia—not in my arms but by my side.

"Cristiano."

I ignored Max. Someone had to pay for this. Now. Today. "Where are they?"

"Belmonte-Ruiz isn't here anymore. They must've found the bodies and left. But they could come back any minute—"

I gritted my teeth. "I want to be here when they do."

"Then you'll leave in a body bag." Max had my shirt in two fists before I knew it, yanking me to my feet. "Put your vest back on." He shook me as his eyes burned with—what? Fear? Anger? Grief? "Pick up your wife and take her home. Give her a proper burial. You owe her that and so much more." He shoved me away. "Do you want them to carry her corpse out of here with yours?"

*Yes.* If it meant avenging her, then yes. I shut my eyes, but I still saw her lying on the ground.

"Look at her, Cristiano," Max ordered. "*Look at your wife.*"

I couldn't. I couldn't face it.

"Will you abandon her here?" he asked.

*Abandon*? Never. No. I couldn't do that to her.

She needed me—even in death. I had to get it together and take her body home, somewhere safe. I called on strength deep within and forced myself to turn back to Natalia.

The starkness of her lifeless frame was no less shocking. My pulse vanished; my blood ceased to flow.

"How'd this happen?" Max said, searching the ground. "She was alive when—"

"I don't know." It didn't matter. I stared at her. All the lives I'd taken, and I'd never seen anyone so still. So unresponsive. Maybe, since Bianca, I'd never cared enough to look.

"Pick her up," he said.

For once, I had no idea what to do—so I listened to Max.

I lifted her body to my chest as I stood and walked out the building, into the dark, to the forest.

I paused at the door to the vehicle as a breeze moved through the leaves of the trees.

Not leaves. Not a breeze.

*Butterflies.*

Overhead, thousands of monarchs covered the firs, fluttering their wings. Natalia had found comfort whenever one was near, thinking it was the departed soul of her mother returned to check on her.

But not me.

I had faith in very few things, and in even less now.

"*Fuck* you." In my arms, Natalia was simultaneously deadweight and light as a sparrow. "Fuck you for taking her from me."

Boots sounded behind me. Max and Alejandro appeared at my side. "Oh, God . . ." Alejo said. "No."

"Get in," Max said. "We're in enemy territory. *Get in.*"

I carried Natalia into the backseat, cradling her against me.

I'd done everything in my power to bring Natalia back into this life. I'd promised her my protection. I had failed her. I should've left her alone. Costa's words about Bianca's death many months ago rang through my ears.

*"I wouldn't wish my pain or guilt on any man."*

I understood now. Bringing Natalia into this world hadn't just risked her life but mine, too. Maybe Costa was strong enough to live without Bianca, but I wasn't without Natalia. If that made me a coward, then I was one to my core.

As we pulled away from the warehouse, I put my face to Natalia's. I kissed the dried tears on her cheeks, her wet lashes and cold lips. A sigh escaped her, and I swallowed it. Even death's rattle came soft and gentle from her sweet mouth.

"Heaven or Hell, I will find you," I whispered to her. "I will make Belmonte-Ruiz pay, and it will be the *last* thing I do before I join you."

A sense of calm fell over me knowing I would be with her again soon.

CHAPTER 27

# CRISTIANO

I stayed at the back of the dark chapel that anchored the Badlands' town square. Somewhere in the hours between midnight and dawn, Max, Alejandro, and Eduardo lit candles and prayed at the altar where Natalia's body had been laid. Already, her father, Barto, and Pilar had been to see with their own eyes. Tomorrow would be the *velorio* before Natalia's burial, but I could not bring myself to celebrate life as was accustomed at our wakes. I would say my good-byes tonight.

Max rose first and put his phone to his ear to answer a call. Even God's house was not exempt from the demands of work. Maksim looked down the aisle at me, nodded, and came in my direction. "*Gracias* for the update," he said, hung up, and addressed me. "We need to speak."

"Not now," I said, my eyes burning as I stared ahead.

"It needs to be now. Lives are at stake. Put your grief aside."

*Impossible.* I would never know another moment without it. To have loved and been loved by Natalia was all I'd ever needed, even when I hadn't known it.

I couldn't bring her back.

"You still have other lives depending you," Max said.

I swallowed and turned my focus to him. "What is it?"

"We always knew there would be a price to pay for what we do," Max said.

My heart lurched, forcing its presence on me even after it had been torn out. I scowled. "I've paid it."

"The lives of your wife and child might've satisfied Diego, but their deaths mean little to Belmonte-Ruiz." He paused as Alejandro and Eduardo approached, then said, "They're coming."

That was to be expected. I was weak now, and I'd derailed yet another of their deals, one they'd spent months preparing for. "How far?" I asked.

"They should be here by dawn."

"Dawn is now," I said.

"Not quite," Max said. "But soon."

"How many?" Alejo asked.

"Enough. Belmonte-Ruiz has enlisted several other federations to join him, trading strategy for a massive army and sheer brute force to storm the Badlands . . . and cut off Calavera's head." He looked to one side as his nostrils flared. "They want the entire country to know you're done."

Diego had once again promised someone more powerful than him things he couldn't deliver. And he'd paid the final price.

But I hadn't.

Belmonte-Ruiz's thirst for blood and vengeance would not be satisfied while I was alive. I had stolen from them. Killed their men. Cost them business and money. I'd made enemies of several cartels by making them look the fool too many times. And I'd gotten away with it.

Until now.

"Someone give me a cigarette."

"You quit," Alejandro said.

"For Natalia. For my future. I have neither now." My palms sweat. I ached to hold Natalia. It would be the last time. How could it be that I wouldn't be able to touch her when I pleased, take comfort in her presence, her love? I turned my back to her body, glowing in the candlelight as it waited for me at the end of the aisle. "Let me kill myself as slowly or as quickly as I see fit. Give me a fucking cigarette."

Eduardo offered one up with a lighter. He'd always been a man of vice. I lit the thing and took a comforting drag.

"You know the exit plan," I said to them.

"It's already in motion," Max replied.

I nodded. For them to begin evacuations without consulting me had to mean it was truly the end. I exhaled a cloud of smoke. "The fleet is ready?"

"We've already sounded the alarms. People are boarding. They'll have food, water, and money—enough to get them on their feet wherever each person settles."

"There's another option," Alejandro said, gripping his cell at his side. "I could call back the heads of every household. They're armed. We can fight."

"Belmonte-Ruiz has spent the past several months galvanizing others that believe us to be traitors. They have the numbers," Max said. "It would be a battle to the death."

"We're prepared for that," I said, holding out my cigarette as I took in the peaceful nave of pews around me. Everything I had built. "But we will lose—if not today, then tomorrow."

"We're prepared to lose as well," Max said.

Alejo and Eduardo exchanged a look, then nodded.

We'd always been prepared to die for this. And for the possibility that there'd come a time to leave the Badlands behind. I'd never doubted my men's loyalty, but to hear them stand up and say they'd run into a losing battle only reinforced that every decision I'd made up until the parade yesterday morning had been the right one.

But I'd taken my eyes off my wife, and now I would pay the price.

We wouldn't fight. I had other plans.

"They won't stop until they get to me," I said, and added with finality, "Get everyone out."

Nobody spoke for a moment. This was where it ended.

"You have served them well," Alejo said. "And you've equipped them. Everyone in these walls will survive outside of them because of you. Many of them are only alive because of you."

I nodded once. "Time's not on our side—go."

"And you?" Max asked.

I looked at the cigarette in my hand. It should've been a cigar enjoyed in celebration of good news. Of my first child on the way. Of the goodwill God had placed upon my wife and me.

Instead, I raised it toward the heavens before ashing it out on a pew. My life had been taken from me. There was nothing more for me here. "Once everyone is out safely, meet me back here," I said to Max. "And bring Barto. Just the two of you. Until then, I'll be alone with my wife."

# CHAPTER 28

# CRISTIANO

Dressed in a white satin nightgown, Natalia glowed at the end of the aisle in the dim chapel. Flickering candles made shadows of her body on the wall behind the altar. I walked toward her and ascended the steps to where she'd been laid on a bed of handmade blankets and cream silk sheets and pillows. The candlelight brought color to her cheeks, creating a painful illusion of warmth and life.

I looked down on her. Hands folded over her stomach. Her dark thicket of hair around her pale face, arranged by Pilar to fall in curls over her slender shoulders.

I touched her cheek. Impossibly soft and smooth. Thumbing the corner of her mouth, I bent over to press my lips to hers—and stayed there. I couldn't bear to pull away.

Wetness dripped from my eyes to her cheeks. What was this? The last time I'd cried, I'd shed one tear for Bianca's death, and then I'd had to run for my life. Now, tears flowed down my cheeks, dropping onto Natalia's lifeless lips.

I gripped the sides of her face, kissing her forehead, the corners of her mouth, remembering how they'd twitched early on when she'd fought her feelings for me. I sat on the makeshift bed and touched her hair. The tattoo on the back of her shoulder. I took her hands from her sides to bring them to my mouth, breathing on them long enough to actually *warm* them.

My mind played tricks on me. I was going mad. Perhaps I'd already gone. There was no question—without her, my mind would surely go.

"I love you, Natalia Lourdes," I said. "*Mariposita.* I'll love you always."

I lowered her hands and kissed the fabric over her stomach. An all-too familiar metallic smell filled my nostrils. I pulled up her dress to find blood between her legs.

*Fuck.* I fisted the satin.

Was it not enough to lose her? I had to witness my dead wife's miscarriage?

I no longer wished for Natalia's life but for my own death. And I couldn't rely on anyone but myself to grant that wish. I buried my head against Natalia's womb, gripping her sides as a sob wracked my body.

There was no God. No Virgin. They would not take my wife from me, and let me glimpse for a moment the family I could've had. They would not show me pure love only to sever it from me so suddenly and viciously—no higher power could be so brutal, not even to punish a man like myself.

Exhausted and emotionally wrung out, I drifted in and out of consciousness.

I wasn't sure how long I'd slept when the *click* of the chapel's heavy front door roused me. Max and Barto stood at the entrance. I rose to meet them halfway down the aisle.

Barto's eyes stayed narrowed on me. "You asked for me?"

"Is everyone out?" I asked Max.

"Every person. Every animal. Only we remain—Alejandro, Eduardo, Pilar, Jaz, and Costa are on the ship waiting for us. Doctor Sosa wanted to stay, too, in case she was needed."

"Pilar should've gone earlier."

"She refused," Barto said. "She's already lost her best friend. She has nobody else and feels safest with us."

I nodded. I wasn't sure *this* was the moment she should finally stand her ground, but there was no other option now. "Gabriel?" I asked.

"Haven't seen him," Max said. "I assume he went already."

"When all this is over, find him if you can. Help him. He's a good kid. He'll be a good man."

Max nodded.

"What's this about? Why am I here?" Barto crossed himself. "To help with Natalia's body?"

I looked to him, my ex-comrade, a man of his word, and someone who, despite our history, I could depend on in my youth and now, when I needed him most. Then to Max, my friend, my confidante, and right-hand man.

"You and I, we've been together a long time, Max." I pinched the inside corners of my tired eyes. "I don't need to tell you how the plan plays out."

"I never truly believed it would come to this," Max said.

I nodded. "But it has."

I was silent a long time. There was only one option, but facing it meant coming to terms with the fact that Natalia was really gone.

I turned to Barto. "Belmonte-Ruiz is here for blood. They won't stop until they get it. Until someone pays—and I will. They'll continue to hunt me. If they don't make an example of me, someone else will. I'm no longer good to anyone—I'll only bring danger wherever I go."

Barto raised his chin. "Are you asking for my help to get you out of the country?"

"No." I paused. "The Badlands is rigged so that in an emergency, it will detonate."

Silence fell over the room. Max closed his eyes briefly but straightened his back.

Barto's expression finally eased. "Smart. Better to perish than be captured."

"Even better if you can take the enemy down with you," I said.

Barto looked between us as my intent registered. "Anyone within the Badlands' walls will go with it."

I nodded. "Belmonte-Ruiz wants me—they'll have to come into the

Badlands and get me. And their entire cartel, plus any other faction that has joined them, will be wiped out. The explosion will completely level the town, the mountain—everything."

My death would stop this. Belmonte-Ruiz could be obliterated, and Costa, Max, Alejandro, and the entire population of the Badlands would be safe from them.

In one fell swoop, I could end this war and make a considerable dent in human trafficking. It wouldn't be forever, but every life held value, and many would be spared during the time it would take to rebuild the operation that would crumble with Belmonte-Ruiz's fall.

Barto looked almost impressed. "You'd give all of this up?"

"To save lives, yes."

Barto shifted feet, nodding slowly. "And Costa?"

"Say he was forced into this arrangement against his will. I had his daughter. He's respected enough that once our partnership is dissolved, he'll be left alone."

"It will be the end of BR and their operation," Barto said. "But it won't finish anything. One leader steps down, and another takes his place. There are others who'd like to see you dead."

"And they will. My life in exchange for many others. It's a sacrifice I've always been willing to make. Only my death will stop this."

Barto glanced at the ceiling, then nodded with pursed lips. "How does it work?"

Max widened his stance and crossed his arms, in full strategy mode. "There are two ways to detonate. From the control center in the basement, or remotely, within half a kilometer."

"If you can push the button from the water, why would you stay?" Barto asked.

I took a breath. Not because I was hesitating—I had no reason to doubt my decision. But because once I said it, the life I'd known would truly be over. "Without Natalia, nothing's keeping me here," I said. "She's gone. I'll die today. You were good to her—" I cleared my throat to keep my voice even. "Even after all we've been through, I consider you a friend."

I offered my hand. Barto looked at it a moment. Perhaps now he finally realized how deep my love for Natalia ran, but whether he did or didn't was no longer important. We shook.

"If you're willing to do this to avenge her," he said, "and to save the rest of us—then the feeling is mutual."

"This is why I asked you here. I appeal to your logic, not your emotion, and Costa would've tried to talk me out of it. I . . ." The next part didn't come easily. I wanted Natalia here with me for the end. It wouldn't make a difference in the afterlife—if there was one, I'd find her. Selfishly, I wanted to hold her until my final breath, but I'd been greedy enough when it came to her. The right thing to do was to give her a peaceful final resting place, not incinerate her with the rest of us.

"Take Natalia with you," I said. "Costa shouldn't go back until things have settled, but I'm counting on you to leave here and take her home. To bury her where she belongs—with her mother."

A hint of despair softened his features. "You have my word."

That was it, then. There was nothing left to say, and time was up. The longer the final ship remained in port, the more everyone on it would be at risk. They were counting on me to be strong.

A deep ache pounded in my stomach, but I ignored it and turned to walk back up the aisle to Natalia. I had to pause at the top of the steps to force breath in and out of my lungs.

There was no other way, though.

Only my wife would be so beautiful in death. I could almost convince myself that her pallor had lifted. That her cheeks had pinked. As I slid my arms underneath her body and lifted her, I felt warmth, not death—self-preservation allowing me to look upon her for the last time as I had always known her.

Beautiful, vivacious, as stubborn in death as she'd been in life.

Butterfly in the sky, monarch in my arms as we'd danced the night of the costume party. She'd buzzed against my body with fear, trepidation, and excitement as our wits had sparred and our feet had tangoed.

Mermaid in the water, showing me how the curves of a woman could soften my hard, sharpened edges.

Owner of my cold, black heart.

I pressed a final kiss against her lips.

*"Mi vida. Mi amor."*

*My life. My love.*

My need for her was so willful, so gripping, that I felt her soft breath caress my lips. I drank in her sweet sigh. My descent into madness had begun, and its timing was perfect. I forced my mouth away from hers and my feet down the stairs.

It was the hardest thing I'd ever do. Even lighting dynamite under my own feet would be easier, I knew.

I handed Natalia's body over to Barto.

Reaching into the holster at my side, I removed the White Monarch I'd brought for her, opened her hand, and curled her fingers around the grip. My tired eyes hallucinated her thumb twitch against the pearl. "Bury her with it. For protection."

Barto nodded once, a promise to see my command through, and took her away.

"*Suerte*. Be prosperous, be good," I told Max. "Don't return to México ever again."

"I hope you'll change your mind," he said as we shook hands. "If you do, I'll be waiting for you."

I wouldn't. I wasn't leaving any chance Belmonte-Ruiz would get to walk away from what they'd done, and what they'd stolen from me.

I took comfort in the fact that eradicating them would save even one life. Every life held value.

But Natalia's life had been worth everything. And in the end, it was worth my own.

# CHAPTER 29

# CRISTIANO

In the moments before dawn broke, I blew out the candles in the chapel, not that it mattered if it burned down. Belmonte-Ruiz would be here any moment, and once they were inside the gates, I'd lay waste to all of this.

The Badlands had been home, but without its people, it was a shell. I made my way toward the house through the empty streets. The quiet brought a sense of peace I could only recognize knowing my pain would end soon, and with purpose. I wound up the mountain path for the final time, across the driveway, and started up the steps to the front door.

At a sound from inside the house, I froze mid-stride.

Hurried footsteps beat against the entryway tile.

Everyone was supposed to be gone.

It could only be one of my men, but I took out my gun anyway and leveled it at the front door as it flew open.

Gabriel Valverde threw both of his hands up. "*Ay*. It's just me."

I holstered the gun. "What the fuck are you still doing here?" I asked, wiping my dusty hands on my pants. "I ordered everyone out of the Badlands. The last boat is leaving if it's not already gone."

"I couldn't leave. Not until I knew everything I could find out about this," he said, opening his hand to show me . . .

"A syringe?" I asked with a frown.

*"Escalera al Cielo."*

*"Stairway to Heaven*? That's a Zeppelin song. You've gone mad," I said, nearly laughing. "Both of us. You're going to die here if—"

"Max picked it up in the warehouse by Natalia's body," he rushed out. "He said you didn't know how she died, so I've been researching all night." As if that fact had only just occurred to him, he blinked hard, removed his glasses with his free hand, and rubbed his red eyes with the back of his fist. "*This* is why Belmonte-Ruiz wanted your help." He replaced his glasses and pinched the barrel between his fingers. "To take this drug to the international market—"

"It doesn't matter anymore, Gabriel."

"It does—just listen. The drug only kills with the wrong dosage, Cristiano. Otherwise, it just puts the user into a trance. This is how Diego faked his death—well, clinically, he *was* dead, but—"

"You've been a better soldier than I gave you credit for." I walked up the front steps and grabbed him by the shoulders. "Run. You may still be able to catch the boat out of here. Get your share of the money and go. Start a new life."

I walked by him into the house.

"You're *staying*?" Gabe asked, panic threading his voice as he followed me through the foyer.

"Another few seconds, and you may have to swim to the boat if you want to catch it."

"Where's Natalia's body?"

*"Gone*!" I snapped over my shoulder, my nerves fraying at the mention of her name. "Get out of here before I—"

"And if she wakes up and you're not there? What then?"

I froze in my tracks, my scalp tingling. I turned around slowly. "What?" My eyes darted between his. "If who wakes up?"

"What I've been trying to tell you," Gabe said, tripping over his words. "I think Diego injected her with this—a tetrodotoxin that could've put her into a cataleptic trance."

I balled my fists. "Speak English."

"Diego used Stairway to Heaven to fake his death. Too much of this could kill her, but the right amount would only put her into a state that *mimics* death. It could take twelve hours, maybe more, until the drug wears off."

My throat dried like my eyes. Couldn't swallow. Blink. Function. Think. It was taking me longer than it should to calculate how much time had passed, but we were definitely somewhere close to that. "You're saying she could still . . ."

He was insane. I'd listened to her chest for a heartbeat. Waited for her breath. I'd felt neither.

"You've really gone mad," I said. "What game are you playing with me? I don't care if you get on the boat, but if you don't get out of my sight—"

"It's no game." I'd seen Gabriel scared shitless before, and he wasn't now. He took a breath. "She could still be alive, Cristiano."

I turned and stalked away. "You're wrong."

"I could be," he admitted. "But what if I'm not?"

It hit me then. She'd stirred in my arms.

It hadn't been an illusion.

My mind hadn't been playing tricks on me.

The ache in my gut hadn't been despair but an instinct I'd ignored. The warmth I'd felt in her lips . . . the final wisps of her breath—they hadn't been final at all. They hadn't been conjured by my mind out of desperation to will her back to life.

"She's . . . she *is* alive," I whispered.

Relief exploded in me, sending pure, unadulterated joy coursing through my veins. I knew the truth without a doubt. "She's alive," I told Gabe.

Gabriel's mouth broke into a grin. "You said yourself the boat might still be here. Go. *Apúrese. ¡Corra!*"

*Hurry. Run.* I could catch her. I would dive into the sea and swim as long and as hard as necessary to do it.

*Heaven or Hell, land, air, or sea, I will find you,* mi amor, *and I will . . .*

*What?*

What would I do? Bring her back here? Go with her?

Dread filled me, planting my feet where they were.

She'd been given a second chance.

As had I.

I'd promised I'd protect her. Since then, there'd been two serious attempts on her life. She'd almost been taken from me more times than that. I hadn't kept her safe. I'd only put her in more danger. I'd risked her life too many times, and this was my opportunity to make it right. Natalia would wake up on the sea, and she would hear it from the people who cared for her most. I was dead. That I had died avenging her and completing the mission I'd set out to do—saving lives. It would be hard, but eventually, she would pick up and move on with her life.

I wasn't going to run into the ocean and call them back when Natalia had already set sail on a better future.

She'd be safe with Barto, Max, Pilar, Alejandro—and her father. It was a new life with them or death with me, and she would choose me if I let her. She'd stay here by my side until the end.

I had a purpose here. I needed to see it through. As soon as I'd decided to stay behind, I'd known it was the right choice, and it still was.

Heaven, hell, or anything in between—I would find her again.

Until we met, wherever it would be, she'd be safe.

"What are you doing?" Gabriel asked. "Let's go."

"*Sal de aquí*," I said, sending him away. "You couldn't find me in time to tell me she was alive, understand? Tell her I died with dignity, and with love for her in my heart."

"Cristiano—"

I charged him, took him by the shirt, and I did for him what I'd once tried to do for Natalia. I scared the shit out of him for his own good. "Get the fuck out of here. *Now*. You can't stay here." My voice threatened to break as I shoved him away. "You still owe Natalia your life. Stay with her. Take care of her. I'm trusting you to do that for me. It's my . . ." I gritted my teeth together. "It's my dying wish."

Gabriel looked as if he'd seen a ghost. He backed away from me and glanced at the floor as he said, "Yes, sir. I promised I'd be a good soldier to you and to her. I will, in life or death. Thank you for—"

"There's no time. Go."

He nodded once, then sprinted away.

I couldn't move, barely able to breathe as it registered. Natalia was *alive*. I couldn't fucking believe it. It changed nothing, and it changed everything.

It was occasion to celebrate.

I made myself a drink, a few fingers of my finest, most expensive mezcal—then filled the tumbler to the top. Might as well finish off the bottle. I took my time cutting and lighting a Honduran Gurkha Black Dragon cigar I'd been saving for a special occasion. The birth of my son or daughter. The wedding I'd tried to convince Natalia we should repeat with as much extravagance as we could. In this case, I'd be celebrating her life, and the fall of Belmonte-Ruiz.

My love, my wife, was alive. I walked through the vacant house, by the patio where Natalia and I had eaten snails, past the dining table where I'd loved her most intimate spot with my mouth the first time, and I made my slow way up the same stairs where she'd called me back to her in her darkest hours after learning the depth of Diego's deception. Where any love she might've had left for him had finally become *mine*.

To our bedroom, where she'd killed a man.

Where I'd held her in my arms after she'd arrived here, where she'd quivered against me.

Where I'd first made love to her.

In the shower, where we'd confessed our love to each other the first time.

The closet, where I'd threatened her with a good time with *El Gallo*.

With my drink and cigar in one hand, I continued on to the closet and removed Natalia's wedding dress from its fancy, padded hanger. She had walked into the church that day tall, with curious, anxious eyes, and jet-black tendrils framing her delicate features and smooth, bronzed skin. The most beautiful thing I'd ever fucking seen, and she'd been mine. I fisted the fine fabric the way I had that day in the church. It had torn so easily and had been mended as close to perfection as it could get.

But it would always be scarred by my hand.

I was doing the right thing.

I folded the dress, set it on the closet island, and went to the balcony for one final glimpse as they sailed away—but there was nothing on the horizon except first light.

I sat in one of the over-sized cushioned patio chairs Natalia had bought for the balcony and tried not to think of her, somewhere out there, alone.

But it was an impossible feat.

She wasn't alone. She had her father. Barto. Alejo, Max, Gabe, Pilar —everyone. Everyone but me.

Natalia was stronger for the past year. She would thrive. *I* had given her that. And she was even more beautiful.

I pinched the expensive Honduran cigar I'd only begun to enjoy between my fingers until I'd nearly halved it.

What would life for her look like without me? It didn't matter; she'd be alive. And wherever I ended up, I'd be watching out for her . . .

I wouldn't risk her life today and allow her to die for me, though there was never any question I'd die for her. She had promised me she'd go on. Live life to the fullest. Pursue happiness.

What more could I ask for? I had a front row seat to one of God's greatest phenomenon—the rise of the sun over the vast ocean. And the knowledge that I'd made the right decision, no matter how fucking badly it hurt. That my Natalia was safe.

I sipped my mezcal and heard bare feet slapping the hallway tile only a second before Natalia came crashing through the bedroom door.

CHAPTER 30

# CRISTIANO

Breathless but breathing, cheeks pink with life, fire ablaze in violet eyes I thought would never reopen—my dead wife stood in front of me with disheveled hair. Furious. "Fuck you, Cristiano de la Rosa."

I dropped my cigar to the ground as I stood. She had to be an apparition. "God in the sky, tell me I'm seeing things," I said, my voice rising as I stepped out from behind the chair. "Tell me I've gone completely fucking mad, and that I'm seeing things, Natalia—" I balled my fists. "*Tell me* you did not come back here!"

She rushed forward and shoved me in the chest. "You think you can send me away while you stay here to die?"

Alejandro appeared in the doorway and didn't look nearly as fearful as he should. He had no idea what I'd do to him for risking her life.

She glanced back at Alejandro. "What, you *pendejos* thought you could make decisions about *my* future? Fuck *all* of you assholes."

I turned my glare on Alejo. "You couldn't handle her? She was *dead* a half hour ago."

"We taught her too well. She fought back when she learned the truth." He wiped his bloody lip. "She has more will to stay than I have to make her leave."

"Then her death will be on *your* shoulders, Alejandro," I snapped, unfair as it was.

"To get back to you, she would've shot me." He nodded at her hand. "I'm certain of it."

She held the White Monarch. I frowned. "Did you shoot someone, Natalia?"

She cleared some hair that'd fallen into her face. "Not yet."

I sighed. "The boat's supposed to be far gone by now."

"We're still docked," Alejo said. "I tried calling."

I took my phone from my pocket. "*No tengo señal.*"

Nothing.

Nothing at all, in fact. I had no service. No signal. No Wi-Fi.

"Belmonte-Ruiz must've turned the area into a dead zone," Alejandro said.

They'd likely blocked the cell towers in an attempt to down our systems and hinder our attempts at escape.

I would've done the same.

And if I hadn't chosen to stay behind, it would've worked. I could no longer detonate anything remotely. I had two options left. Leave with them now and let Belmonte-Ruiz live . . . or implode the Badlands from within the walls.

It was no choice at all.

It would all come down—which meant Natalia couldn't be here. I had to get her back on that ship.

"If they're jamming the signal, that means they're here," Alejo said. "They could be at the gates any moment."

I glanced at him. "*Vete,*" I ordered him out, and he shut the door behind himself.

I put my palms together in front of me. As a man who hardly begged for anything, except only things my wife could give me, I pleaded with Natalia to see the gravity of the situation. "On this, you have to trust me, *mi amor*," I said.

"Don't give me that 'trust me, *mi amor*' bullshit," she shot back through gritted teeth. "Be a man and come out from behind your excuses. Face me."

She struck a match against my anger, and it flared. Did she have any idea how difficult she'd just made this for me? I wanted her here by my side—God, I fucking wanted that more than anything. I had no desire to say good-bye. Not at all. But what kind of man would I be if I put her on my back and took her down with me?

I took her by the biceps. "I ask *one* thing of you." I enunciated every word. "Do as you're told."

"No." She shrugged out of my grip and stepped back to cross her arms. "Alejandro and Max didn't have time to explain. They only said you were planning to take Belmonte-Ruiz down and die in the process."

I pinched the inside corners of my eyes. "It's true. This was always a possibility. I hoped it was a lever I'd never have to pull, but I do." I raised my eyes. "And you can't be here for it."

"I can and I will. I'll stay and fight with you."

"I'm not fighting, Natalia," I said. "None of us are. Everyone's gone but us. We're outnumbered. You're leaving with Costa right now."

Her mouth pressed into a line as it did when she was so angry, she could cry—but wouldn't let herself. Her small hands formed two formidable fists. "And what about you?"

"I have to stay and see this through."

"And then what?"

Now that we were face to face, I couldn't bring myself to lie to her. But I couldn't tell her the truth, either. It would put her in serious danger, whereas ignorance could save her. She wouldn't go, and I had to get her out, whatever the cost. "It's not your job to worry about me. I have things under control—"

"Did you not hear me earlier? I'll repeat myself—fuck *you*, Cristiano." She charged forward and pushed my chest until I was backed up against a wall. Tears filled her eyes. "How could you do this to me? I woke up alone—no husband, no b-baby." Her voice cracked, nearly shredding my resolve. "*Alone.* My own father thought I'd risen from the dead and nearly fainted when he saw me."

"You're not alone," I said quietly. "You have people down there who love you. Who don't want to lose you."

"Without you, I'm alone," she said quietly. "I'd rather be with you. Here."

The tears in her eyes and quiver of her chin told a clear story of her pain. I never wanted to hurt her, but I would to save her. My chest threatened to cave under the weight of the truth—I loved her *too much* to let her stay.

She would be alone, yes—but she would be alive.

"You can't be here for this," I said.

"You would leave me in this world all by myself? You forced me here, you made me fall in love with you, you made me need you as I need air and water"—her voice broke—"and now I'm supposed to walk away?"

She went to shove me again, but I caught her wrists. She was crying too hard to fight me.

"Natalia . . ."

"I already lost my baby," she whispered, looking down as her body shook with more sobs, silent this time. "Wasn't that enough? Why do you continue to push me to be strong if I have nothing to live and fight for?"

I'd thought she'd broken my heart already, but now it shattered. "*Hush*," I said, gathering her in my arms, holding her as tightly as I could. She wailed in a tortured way I'd never heard from her as she crumbled against my chest, and I had to inhale up at the ceiling to stop from shedding my own tears. To stop from breaking down and giving in to her.

"I shouldn't have fought back." Her tears soaked my shirt. "I should've waited for you to come."

"What do you mean?"

"If I-I'd played his game . . . if I'd only kept pretending, at least until you were able to come—"

"You had to fight, Natalia. You *had* to."

"I wished the baby away," she said. "I tried to convince Diego I didn't want it so he wouldn't see it as my weakness—and I lost the baby. The miscarriage was my fault."

*No. No, my love.* She blamed herself for it? No wonder she was inconsolable. I took her arms and shook her gently to rouse her from her grief. She looked up at me, red-rimmed eyes glistening with overflowing tears. "Listen to me," I said. "You did *exactly* what I told you to." I took a breath. "And now you have to do what I say only one more time."

"No," she said. "Please. No."

"Natalia," I said, keeping my tone as even as I could manage. "Everyone is waiting for you."

"So send them away."

Adrenaline coursed through my veins. Fear. Desperation. To keep her here with me. To pick her up and physically carry her downstairs. She was making this impossible, and I was about to lose my temper. I had to be cruel. "You'd be willing to die now, this moment? You're ready to burn alive? Because that's the fate you're asking me to give you." I stared at her. "You're not that goddamn short-sighted—you have a life to live, and it doesn't end today."

I expected her to continue railing at me, but instead, calmness settled over her. "I'm not going anywhere without you, and I don't *want* to. I would rather burn by your side now than spend an eternity in Heaven alone, so good luck trying to convince me otherwise. Now, tell me how this works."

I was wrong—it wasn't calmness. It was resolution. It was the demise of my arguments against her. My demise. Hers. "I'm going to die today—that's how it works," I said.

"Then I will, too," she responded without hesitation. "I asked you not to spare my life at the expense of others, but you did when Diego asked you to make the deal. You were willing to ruin all those lives to keep me safe." Her voice softened. "It's my turn to make a hard decision. Don't take my choice from me. Don't fail me now and treat me as Diego and my father did. I chose you because you're not them."

That wasn't fucking fair. After all the ways I'd pushed her to be her own woman, she knew her autonomy was a plea I couldn't deny.

To lead a life without Natalia would be true hell, but to take her life with mine? That was what I'd be doing.

I thumbed the corners of her mouth as she looked up at me eagerly. I searched her eyes, gripped her face, and gave it my best shot. "You know my love for you spans the world. It trumps time, space, human life. I chose you knowing hundreds would suffer. I could never make a decision that didn't put you above all. Please, Natalia. I beg you. Go."

"Over my dead body. Do you hear me? Alejandro will have to drag my corpse out of here."

I stared my very beautiful, very angry—very much *alive*—wife in the face. If I forced her to go, I'd be making decisions for her as others had.

Her determination would be her downfall. But she'd made it clear—that was her choice.

I told her the truth, start to finish.

# CHAPTER 31

# NATALIA

A breeze from the sea cooled my clammy skin as Cristiano, Alejandro, and I hurried from the house down to the ship. Still docked, our loved ones were at risk—but I had one thing still to do.

I left Cristiano on the deck with Max as Alejandro escorted me onto the modern-day pirate ship. It was only missing flags with skulls and crossbones—but the Calavera presence was everywhere.

We found my father standing at the bow, looking out over a turquoise, horizonless ocean. His tall, imposing frame was no less intimidating against the lifting dawn.

Alejandro turned to face me. "For what it's worth, I think you're doing the right thing. You've always been brave. And don't worry about Pilar, all right?"

With gratitude, and my complete trust in him, I took his hands and squeezed them. "Thank you."

"No need." He kissed the backs of my knuckles. "Until we meet again in Heaven, Natalia."

When he'd left us alone, I walked forward. "Papá," I said.

He turned. "*Mija. Gracias a Dios.* You returned. Gabriel said the death was fake? What the hell happened?"

What had happened was that I'd awoken from a deep sleep of wild dreams so fantastic and realistic, I wasn't entirely sure I *hadn't* visited Heaven. I'd come down floating on a cotton cloud. Things had been fuzzy, and buzzy, my fingers and toes tingling.

As the euphoric hum in my ears had faded, irritation had ripped through me when I suddenly had eyes that tore open and a mouth that gulped air as if it would be my last breath. And I'd woken to a high-pitch whistle, the tip and sway of the sea underneath me, surrounded by men's shouts. With an empty stomach. Blood on my dress. A broken heart. And the White Monarch in my hand.

Had I woken up moments later, I would've lost Cristiano forever.

I swallowed back the horrific, gut-wrenching thought and took my father's hands. "It doesn't matter. Diego lost in the end."

"You can tell me everything on the voyage. I have no clue where we're headed, but Barto is working on it with Max." He heaved a sigh. "*¿Y Cristiano*? Has he come to his senses?"

I looked at our hands. "Yes."

"Good." Papá moved his hands to my waist, and I raised my eyes to meet his sorrowful gaze, lines deepening around his mouth. "I'm sorry to have lost my grandchild. I can't help think I'm partly to blame."

A lump formed in my throat. It wasn't his fault. It wasn't Cristiano's. And it wasn't mine. I'd had a few joyous moments as a mother, and I was grateful for that.

I tried my best to keep my sadness from showing. And I glimpsed —barely—the pain Cristiano must've endured trying to send me away for my own good just now. The doubt that surely plagued him. The deep-seated need to protect me by making the decision for me.

As I'd do for my father now. "None of us knew the depth of Diego's deception."

"Cristiano did. I should've known he wouldn't hurt Bianca, but Diego's complete confidence, and your conviction as a child, convinced me of it."

*"Mija." She fought to keep her eyes open, but they went glassy as her gaze shifted over my head. "Please, Cristiano," she begged, her voice strangled. "Please don't . . ." She shuddered with the effort. "My daughter . . ."*

"I was wrong. I now know her dying words had been pleas to Cristiano to protect me—not her begging him to spare my life," I said. I'd clung to the memory so many times growing up, and now I saw it for what it was . . .

"I should've trusted my gut and brought Cristiano home at once," he said.

"All is well, Papá. We have made things right."

"There will be other grandchildren," he said. "You won't make me wait long to hold them, will you, *mi corazón*?"

How could I lie to my own father, and about something like this? His heart would break with the truth.

I ground my teeth together, almost unable to hold back my tears. But I did—and I committed the same crime against him that he had against me for many years. The one for which I'd persecuted him.

I lied to protect him. "Yes, Papá. You will hold your grandchildren before long."

With a satisfied smile, he looked past me. "Where's Cristiano? We should already be gone."

"I'll go see." I went to kiss his cheek but threw my arms around his neck instead. "I love you."

"*Te amo, mija*."

My resolve nearly broke remembering all the nights Papá had prayed for my mother's soul and cried himself to sleep. The thought of putting him through that again was almost too much to handle.

*Pray for me. I will pray for you.*

All I had to do now was walk away. To say good-bye for good to the man who'd raised me.

"I understand why you ran back for him just now," Papá whispered. "Your mother would've done the same."

Emotion wracked me, threatening to take me down. I pulled back. The pride in his eyes was clear. It meant everything to me. I kissed his cheek and forced myself away before he became suspicious of my tears.

I wanted to say good-bye to Pilar. To see Alejandro's smile light up a room once more. To kiss Barto's cheek and thank him for his service to my family. To assure Gabriel he had the world at his fingertips. But it would be selfish. There was no more time. They needed to leave.

I left my father at the front of the ship and made my way back toward where Cristiano waited on the loading dock. He wore no expression as his dark eyes followed me, but I could read his torment. Maybe he doubted himself, but as painful as this would be—it was the right decision.

He'd made me a queen when others would've had me stay a princess forever. To have the choice to go and live or stay and die meant more to me than he knew. I would remain by my king's side. Now. Always.

Cristiano helped me off the ship. As it prepared to leave, worry crept in, tensing my shoulders.

With a strong arm around me, Cristiano pulled me closer and kissed the top of my head. "They're prepared," he whispered. "They'll be safe, Natalia."

"And everyone else?" I sniffled, slipping my arms around his middle to hug him back. "Teresa and Felix? Jaz, Paula, the Zamora family—"

"They're on to new lives. They'll be okay." The contentment in Cristiano's voice comforted me until he loosened his embrace and looked down. "I have to say this one last time, Natalia. It's not too late. I can call them back. You can still go with them."

I shook my head hard. I was determined, but that didn't mean I wasn't scared.

He smoothed a hand over my hair and down my back. "This is it. Everyone you love and care about is on that ship."

My dear, thick-skulled husband with anguished eyes. I reached up to run my palm along the stubble of his cheek. It was obvious he hadn't shaved since the parade. His scratchiness was comforting in a way. It was real. "There is no possible scenario in which I leave your side. My place is here. With you."

With my husband was where I stayed. Silence fell over us as we stood on our beach for the last time and watched our friends and family go. As we said our final farewell to everyone we cared about, and to this world.

CHAPTER 32

# CRISTIANO

In a black lace dress, Natalia turned in a circle in our closet—the same gown I'd put her in at the church on our wedding day. She lifted the skirt and showed me her sneakers with Kevlar laces.

"In case you need to run in the afterlife?" I asked at the mirror where I fixed the cuff of my dress shirt.

I was perhaps overdressed for death as well—but we weren't going to go down in anything less than the best.

"In case I need to *fight*," she said, holding up *la Monarca Blanca* before placing it in our bag of emergency items.

"That's my girl." I winked and bent my head. "*Un beso*."

She obliged me with a quick kiss.

A hum sounded above our heads, and Natalia looked up. "Helicopters?"

As I nodded, a *bang* echoed through the valley of the Badlands, rumbling like thunder.

"What's that sound?" she asked.

I turned back to the mirror, tightening the knot of my black tie. "Tanks ramming the front gates," I said.

"You know people call them *las puertas del infierno?*" she said.

Of course I did. *The gates of hell.* "For Belmonte-Ruiz, it will be true."

She left the closet and headed for the balcony.

"It's not safe out there in the open," I called.

"I just want one last look."

*My mistake.* If I wanted her to stay indoors, I should've told her to do the opposite.

I stepped out with her and checked the sky to make sure we were alone. When I determined it was safe enough for now, I joined her at the short wall overlooking the water.

In my bespoke suit, Natalia in her black lace evening gown, our hands locked between us, we took in the endless ocean. For those moments, it was calm, but it wouldn't last.

"We'd better get downstairs," she finally said. "Our time is up."

The calm in her voice mildly surprised me. I hoped that was due to her faith in me and the choices we'd made.

I turned, scooped her into my arms, and tipped her back to kiss her with everything I had. We had time for that, at least. There would always be time for that.

I TOOK my wife down into the bowels of the mountain, through the tunnel that connected the house to the control center humming with the data, communication, and files we'd been collecting for years to protect others. Intelligence Belmonte-Ruiz would love to get their hands on for the opposite purpose. The precise reasons we hadn't made it explosion-proof.

We crossed that room, making our way through a maze of hallways, passed two iron-clad security systems where only one fingerprint—mine—would work. Because under any other circumstance, I would've burned, mutilated, or carved off my own flesh to prevent the wrong person from entering this space.

Once inside, I closed the door and sat at the computer system, where I followed the same steps I had a million times—all but the final step, a phase I'd never entered until now.

I put in my credentials, clicked all the systems into place, pressed my thumb to the final fingerprint scan, and waited for the facial recognition software to identify and approve me.

We got the green light.

"Now what?" Natalia asked.

"Now, we wait."

I pulled up security drone feed to monitor the progress of Belmonte-Ruiz and any other faction dumb enough to join them. I wanted as many of these motherfuckers as I could get inside the walls before I hit the button.

Natalia stood behind me, her hand on my shoulder, as the footage filled the screen.

They'd broken through the gates. They flooded the town, teeming into the alleys, filling up the arteries of the Badlands like blood.

"They move like a swarm of lame bees," Natalia muttered.

They drove tanks through abandoned homes, stores and marketplaces, and set fire to structures and farms.

Watching proved difficult. No matter my gratitude for the fact that every human life in my care except Natalia's had made it out, a piece of history would die today.

I chose the present over the past, instead, and stood from the chair to find my true home in Natalia's eyes. I pulled her into my arms. Her heart slammed against her chest. She was scared. I couldn't blame her. I was more terrified than I'd ever been. If I'd miscalculated anything, if the button didn't work, if these fuckers survived—then all of this could be for nothing. It could go fatally, irrevocably wrong.

I tilted Natalia's chin up and pressed my lips to hers. "We were lucky to have you. You have been everything I could've ever hoped for—and so much more."

She slid her arms around my neck, whispering. "I was only getting started. I'm sorry that . . ."

I put my forehead to hers. "What?"

"I'm so sorry you have to watch it all burn, and that your family has been displaced." A frown tugged the corners of Natalia's mouth.

She thought of them during her own imminent end. It *was* sad to know there'd be no rebuilding this tightknit community exactly as it had been—or, most likely, at all. Most of them would never see one another again. "What you did for these people will never be forgotten," she said, "no matter that only ashes will remain."

"None of it means anything without them. Without you." I thumbed the corner of her mouth. "I promised I'd follow you anywhere, and I would've, *mariposa*. I thought you were gone. Forever. And I was right behind you."

She tightened her hold around my neck, rising onto the tips of her toes. "Now we'll go together."

As the horde closed in and more and more of the enemy flooded our home, I took a breath. "What was it like to die?"

She tilted her head as if remembering, then shook her head. "I didn't like it."

"You don't say." I smiled at her. "But I heard the drug was supposed to be pure bliss."

"It's far better to be with you," she said thickly.

*Both* of our hearts were slamming now, but at least it was against the other's chest. I cupped her cheek. "You will be. This is not an ending, but the start of an eternity together. No one else. Just you and me."

"Just you and me," she said, but with less hope in her tone than mine. "I should've told you about the baby the moment I suspected—but I wanted to be sure." She reached into her neckline and pulled out the sonogram. "To show you this and watch your eyes light up."

I took it as my jaw tingled with emotion. "How?"

"Max picked it up with the syringe. He gave it to me on the boat." Her voice faltered. "I'm sorry you didn't get to experience the bliss of fatherhood, even for a little while."

"I'm sorry it was taken from both of us." I tucked the image in my jacket pocket and smoothed back her hair, falling more in love with her for how deeply she felt my pain. "You redeemed your child. Diego murdered our baby, and he paid the price."

"We will carry the loss with us when we go."

"And it is time to go," I said. "Are you ready?"

She bit her bottom lip. "I'm scared."

"I've got you. We fall together."

"We fall together." She nodded, running her hand along my jaw, her thumb over the hollow of my cheekbone, smoothing my eyebrows as if we had all the time in the world. "I'm ready."

I focused on the beautiful violet eyes in front of me. I'd fallen for them at the gala when she'd looked back at me from behind her mask. I'd fought against it. I'd lost.

There was no question I'd won.

Nothing else mattered now. I already knew I wouldn't stay here without her. She didn't want that for herself, either. We'd leave this life together, and I couldn't ask for more than that.

I kissed my Natalia once more. "I love you, my wife. My *mariposita*."

"I love you, *mi esposo*. Cristiano, my husband."

All that remained now was to push the button and detonate. So that's what I did.

A rumble started in the depths of the Badlands, the angry beat of the ground shaking beneath our feet.

The underworld called us home.

# CHAPTER 33

# COSTA CRUZ

"It was the explosion heard round the world—or México, at least. One year ago tomorrow, a mysterious, cartel-run town known as 'the Badlands' imploded, taking out its own residents, plus some of México's most pervasive crime syndicates. But none more famous, or dangerous, than two which have become household names since the explosion.

"One, Belmonte-Ruiz, was known for an extensive sex trafficking ring and the development of a drug rumored to take its users 'as close to Heaven as humanly possible.' The explosion incinerated nine-tenths of their cartel, a large portion of two other factions, and two of the three kingpins the United States government had on the FBI Most Wanted list.

"There are no good guys here, but since its destruction, the Calavera cartel's legend has grown amongst the people. Once feared as an international cartel with an anonymous leader renowned for his merciless ways, *narcocorridos* tell a different story. It's one our station can't confirm, but these ballads canonize the leaders of Calavera cartel for their fight to curb human trafficking in a way the government never could.

"During this *Día de los Muertos,* we remember the innocent lives lost that day—if there were any. But what makes this a tragic tale, and one that has fascinated the public, is the love story between Natalia Cruz, the stunning daughter of Bianca King and businessman Costa Cruz—"

I shut off the television and tossed the remote on my desk. I'd heard enough the past year. It never got any easier. The way they glorified Natalia and Cristiano—didn't the media know they had a grieving father? I respected Cristiano's passion, and if he saw to it to kill himself over principle, fine. But to take my daughter with him . . .

I hadn't yet forgiven it.

"Legend says the explosion shook the earth to its core, changing México's geography forever," I heard behind me.

I turned to Barto as he stood in the doorway. "Legend exaggerates."

But it hadn't exaggerated my daughter's beauty. Nor my son-in-law's determination to do things his way. Determination that would get them both killed.

*Narcocorridos*—Mexican ballads—idolized drug lords, traffickers, and cartels, romanticizing our wins and losses. They told the story right. Natalia and Cristiano had possessed a great love, like mine with Bianca. At one time, it was all I'd wanted for my daughter.

I set my elbows on my desk and put my head in my hands. "Senseless."

"But noble," Barto said, entering the room. "They certainly made a difference in the world, which you know is what they wanted. They're at peace, now, Costa."

I grumbled my agreement. The rest of the year, I could be understanding of the sacrifice they'd made for a better world. But on the anniversary of not just their deaths, but Bianca's, too, I only wanted to grieve.

I was about to tell Barto to leave when the maid knocked at the door of my study.

"Mail, *señor*," she said, handing off a stack of envelopes and catalogues to Barto before she disappeared again.

Barto walked to the desk, sifting through everything until he stopped on the final item—a bulky, padded manila envelope. "What's this?" he asked.

I lifted my head and craned my neck to see better.

Handwriting that looked vaguely familiar. No return address, though.

The only handwriting I knew as well as my own belonged to those who were no longer with me. Bianca and Natalia. Both gone.

"Give it to me," I said.

"It could be dangerous," Barto said, turning over the envelope. "Let me—"

I stood, came around the desk, and took it from him. Danger meant something different these days. It meant nothing. I had little left of importance to lose. I tore open the envelope and a rosary fell out.

Not just any rosary, though. One centered by a polished gilt Sacred Heart and matching crucifix. Red rubies, milky pearls on a gold chain. I'd had it commissioned myself.

I'd know it anywhere.

It had been Bianca's.

"What the . . . *fuck*?" I muttered.

Barto was at my side immediately. "What is it?"

Well-loved, with some scratches in the gold and wear on the gemstones, this wasn't a replica.

I pushed the beads through my fingers as my throat thickened with emotion. "Where did it come from?" I looked at Barto. "Who sent it—and why now?"

Barto's eyes widened as something passed over his face.

Alarm made me straighten. Any reaction was rare with him—especially one of surprise. "I . . ."

"What is it?" I demanded.

Barto met my eyes and slowly shook his head. "I don't know, *don* Costa. I'm sorry." His gaze returned to the precious piece of jewelry clutched in my hand. Barto's tone softened. "Perhaps just a simple sign from God that your wife is at peace, and that . . ." Barto crossed himself. "That your daughter is in good hands."

# EPILOGUE

# NATALIA

*We were warned, and so were you. In the end, death took what it wanted—Cristiano and Natalia de la Rosa. But in their place, Joaquin and Jenny Delgado were born.*

My attacker had no idea who he was dealing with.

I nailed him in the chest with the flat of my bare foot, and my sole landed squarely between his pecs. He grabbed my ankle and twisted until I was forced to rotate around and face the opposite direction. Teetering on one leg, anyone else would've been dangerously close to falling flat on her face.

*Not me.* I lifted my head and met a sea of wide-eyed women, their mouths agape. "A leg grab like this while fighting back is both common and dangerous," I said. My shoulder-length hair fell forward, curtaining my face. "So, in this scenario—"

*Fuck.*

A dark glare pinned me from the back of the room. Cristiano's arms crossed over his wide chest, displaying the massive biceps that had lovingly hugged me just this morning.

With the way his firmed jaw ticked like a time bomb about to blow, he looked more likely to kill me.

He took one step forward into the room.

"Let go, Dimitris," I hissed to the man holding my ankle in a firm grip.

"Huh?"

Poor guy didn't realize his life was on the line. Cristiano took another step.

"Release my leg," I said under my breath so I wouldn't scare the women sitting on the mat in front of us. I was sure they were already horrified enough to see me up here, even though *my* fake last name was on the banner in the registration room. "*Hurry*."

He let go, and I lowered my foot to the ground gracefully to show Cristiano that my body was perfectly within my control. I straightened as I slipped my sandal back on and stepped away, gesturing for Dimitris to continue. "Sorry I interrupted your lesson," I said, retreating. "Go ahead. Continue."

With a funny look, Dimitris turned back to the class.

I gave Cristiano my best puppy-dog eyes since they'd served me well with him in the past. I held a finger to my lips to indicate we shouldn't interrupt. The alternative was that these women, who we'd invited here to learn to defend themselves, would watch me get reamed out.

When I met Cristiano at the door, he placed a hand on my upper back and guided me out of the small, mirrored room and into the office, where he shut the door behind himself.

"Natalia," he started.

"*Lourdes*, my love," I corrected him. Had I not been able to see his anger with my own eyes, my name, loaded with warning, would've been enough to tell me. "Or Jenny, of course—"

"We're alone." His brows lowered. "Don't change the subject."

I tried to look contrite. "I'm sorry," I said. "I was just observing the class before our date, and I get so excited to demonstrate for the girls myself. And I *feel* great—"

"And what if that *pendejo* out there had yanked on your foot and you'd lost your balance?"

I walked to Cristiano, took his hands, and placed them on my thirty-three-weeks-pregnant belly. "Everything's going to be okay, *papi*. We're safe here. Nothing is happening to this baby." I smiled up at him. "I've never been so sure of anything."

His shoulders loosened, if only a little. "I worry, *mi amor*."

I laughed. "That's like saying the Pope prays. It's very obvious."

"I'm not being unreasonable," he cried. "Everyone in that room thought you were crazy. That an eight-month pregnant woman would teach self-defense . . ." He shook his head and uttered a profanity.

His concern didn't bother me; it made him who he was. But it was unnecessary. I squeezed his hands beneath mine. "Can't you feel how strong our *bebita* is?"

As if on cue, she kicked, but her timing wasn't that strange. The baby was always moving around, always telling her mama she was ready to come out and throw some punches. I wanted that, too, considering my uterus had become a punching bag.

Cristiano grunted, smoothing his hands under my blouse and over the warm, tight skin of my stomach. "I can't wait any longer to meet her." His demeanor lightened considerably, as it often did when he spoke of the future. "Do you think she'll come early?"

I nodded. "She's very eager and persistent. Like her father."

He bent forward to place a sweet kiss on my lips. "Don't think you're off the hook. Since day one of this pregnancy, you've been strictly forbidden from teaching self-defense."

"And I have definitely abided by that rule," I said, trying not to squirm from the obvious lie.

As if Cristiano didn't know.

His full lips pressed into a line, displaying his skepticism. "I'm not trying to limit you—you know that." He stepped closer and slipped his hands around the back of my neck to gather my long bob into a loose ponytail. "I've just come too close, too many times, to losing you."

I fought the urge to shut my eyes as his fingers tickled beneath my hairline. "But this last year has been quiet," I reminded him. "Nobody knows we're here but Max. And nobody's losing anybody."

One year ago, Cristiano and I had died.

Incinerated along with the Badlands.

All of Mexico knew it. For months, we'd holed up in tiny apartments throughout Europe, never staying in one place too long, keeping our faces from the public.

The resulting baby was no surprise considering, without much else to do, we'd had sex for days on end.

Officially, we were Joaquin and Jennifer Delgado now. Cristiano hated calling me by a fake name, so sometimes he used Lourdes in public. But always, in private, I was his Natalia.

Fortunately, though we'd been major news in our home country, the story had never really made it outside of Mexico.

And I loved our new life, basking in each other every day, getting to know the very cores of ourselves and of one another. But living a life indoors, under the radar, would never last for us—even if it meant we kept a little danger alive.

Opening a business had been risky. We owned and funded a traveling girls' school that taught self-defense to any and all women—or people—who wanted to attend. Once the course was complete, we'd pick up and change locations so we were never in one place too long.

The little bit of risk suited us. We'd already survived the most dangerous situations possible.

One year ago, we'd descended into the belly of the beast, the mountainside rumbling with its impending explosion. There'd always been a good chance we wouldn't make it out in time, so when I'd told Cristiano I was ready to die by his side, I'd meant it.

But fortunately, it hadn't happened that way.

Cristiano had had every intention of dying the day he'd thought he'd lost me to Heaven's stairway. But my revival had changed his plan back to the one he and Max had originally put into place many years ago in case of an emergency like this—faking his death. Knowing he might not make it out, he'd tried to send me away so he could come for me one day, when the time was right, and he had all of Mexico's underground off his back.

But that hadn't been good enough for me.

I'd die by his side literally, or I'd do it symbolically.

After Cristiano had pushed the button and we'd heard the underground roar, we'd passed through the tunnel system that led out of the Badlands, burrowing down into the mountain and under the ocean. We'd had to run. *Fast.* I'd never moved that quickly in my life, my hand locked in Cristiano's as we'd pulled each other along.

But we'd made it to the end of the tunnel before the explosion could catch us, where a submarine had waited complete with the documents to support our new life and coordinates already programmed into the GPS. Only Max knew the truth. To everyone else, we were nothing more than ashes, gone in the wind.

I thanked Our Lady of Guadalupe every day that my love and I had survived, and that now, we'd finally form a family. And I thanked Cristiano, too, for the devil made his own destiny and crowned his own queen.

DATE NIGHT, my favorite time of week.

Holding hands, Cristiano and I walked through the cobblestone streets of the small town in Greece where we'd chosen to settle for the next little while. Soon, either here or in our next spot, we'd have to stay put to have the baby.

The sun made its way toward the horizon, casting late-afternoon light on the white plaster walls that broke up buildings the colors of blush, pistachio, and melon. We made our lazy way through the labyrinth toward upbeat music in the town center. Every Saturday night, residents gathered for a street fair.

Cristiano bought a bottle of locally distilled single malt and some *baklava*, feeding me a bite before his animalistic appetite possessed him to take a chunk out of it.

We stopped and perched on a short wall to finish our pastries. One man had covered himself head to toe in gold spray-paint and stood still as a statue in front of a bowl for tips. Another played a hauntingly beautiful melody on the violin. A teen girl skulked around the booths in a skull-and-crossbones hoodie.

A cool breeze passed through the square for a perfect November evening.

Cristiano's eyes roamed the area around us, and I knew he was thinking of his people in the Badlands, dispersed around the world now. I had complete faith they'd all made a home somewhere and were thriving, as did he.

I hoped that was true for my friends, Pilar and Alejandro, wherever they were.

For my father, I wished peace, though I knew he struggled with such an empty house. I shouldn't have sent the rosary. Cristiano hadn't wanted me to, but he hadn't stopped me, either. I wasn't sure if Papá would understand, but Cristiano had said Barto definitely would.

I slipped my hand in Cristiano's, and he turned to smile down at me. "More fine, handmade clothing here than we've seen in a while. What do you need?" he asked. "Aren't your pants getting too small?"

"Never ask a woman who can shatter your kneecap with a swift kick whether she can fit into her pants."

"*Ay, pero* you're pregnant, *mi corazón*," he said, as if I needed reminding.

"And do you know what pregnant women like?" I asked.

"Ice cream," he answered.

He knew me so well. Either that, or I'd been milking the cravings too hard. I got my gelato, though. Cristiano bought me a cup with a tiny spoon, and we made our way around the square, stopping to purchase little things we didn't really need, mostly to support the residents, and accepting the occasional gift for our future daughter.

As we stood at one booth admiring wooden jewelry boxes, the hair on the back of my neck rose. The steady tap of nails on glass, over and over, made a simple beat that somehow became chilling.

"Cristiano," I whispered.

He squeezed my hand. "*¿Qué pasa?*"

Slowly, I turned my head over my shoulder and met the dark, cunning eyes of an elderly woman sitting across the way. She drummed her nails on a glass ball centered atop the purple crushed velvet fabric covering her table.

My mouth dried. Shimmering gold headdress. A mélange of rings in silver and gold topped with pearls and gemstones. Veiny, feminine hands.

It had been over a year-and-a-half, but I hadn't forgotten the woman with the slender, wrinkled fingers, haunting eyes, and floral perfume from my father's annual costume gala. And rarely a few days went by that I didn't remember the fortune-teller's words from that night.

*"You will die for him, your love."*

I *had* died. I'd been pronounced dead, my body so devoid of life that it had terminated my first child.

No good could come from this.

I stepped back and hit Cristiano's wall of a body. He squeezed my shoulders. "What is it, Lourdes?" he asked. "Do you need—"

He stopped speaking. I turned around to see why. His gaze was also trained on the old woman staring back at us.

"Who wants to know their future?" she called out in that same craggy voice. Her cackle turned into a hacking cough.

"She gives me a bad feeling," I said.

"And me," he agreed.

"Do you know her?"

He nodded. "I believe we met once."

And had she told Cristiano his future?

This soothsayer had said I'd die for the love of my life, and I had. Not just once, but twice. I'd come clawing back to life for Cristiano, and we were strong and healthy now. I couldn't take any more despair.

I grabbed Cristiano's hand and started to pull him away.

This woman could bring *nothing* but bad news.

# CRISTIANO

"Lovely young couple," the old woman said, slowing us in our tracks as we attempted a getaway. "And with a *chiquita* on the way."

*Clever woman.* She knew the sex of my child. Any other time, I'd have called it a lucky guess. Now? I wasn't sure. I still didn't believe in this kind of hocus pocus. But my fortune *had* been eerily spot on.

Was it premonition that my drink had been drugged at the political event? Or something more?

I soothed my wife with a hand up and down her biceps, bringing her closer to my body. "What did she tell you?" I whispered over Natalia's head.

Her back went rigid. "That I would die," she said and wriggled away from me to march toward the woman's table.

I followed, staying at Natalia's back as she accused, "What do you want, *vieja*? Am I supposed to die a third time? My husband and I are happy. Enough harm has been done."

The woman pressed a hand to the base of her neck. "I simply deliver messages. I'm not so different from your beloved monarch."

All right, that was a bit too far. The monarch was private between Natalia and me. I gripped Natalia's elbow to pull her back. "Let's go."

But she couldn't be moved. "That was just a silly costume," she said.

"And yet you're considering naming your baby after . . ." The woman's eyes traveled up to mine. "Well, I won't spoil it. I'll let you tell your husband the name you've chosen."

Natalia's face drained of blood. I had no idea what the woman meant, though. Had Natalia picked a name and not told me?

"Stay away from us," Natalia said.

The woman sighed. "I don't create anyone's fates. I warned you, didn't I? You should listen next time."

*Next time.*

She *had* warned us—Natalia that she would die, apparently—and me, to get back up when I fell. Moments after I'd seen her, I'd literally fallen to my knees.

And now she was here again.

To give us a warning.

"What is it?" I narrowed my eyes on *la bruja*. "What did you come here to tell us?"

Her sparkling eyes fell to Natalia's stomach. I put my arms around my wife, spreading my hands over her belly, shielding it.

"It's hard to see the future of a dead man. And you are, aren't you?" Her gaze bounced to Natalia as she smiled and squinted. "However . . ."

This didn't mean a damn thing. And yet, I found myself leaning in, my heart thumping against Natalia's back.

"I see nothing."

I released a breath. After a lifetime of non-stop violence and death in the name of revenge, love, and sex, I muttered, "*Nothing* would be *fucking* great. For a while."

"For a while," the sorceress agreed, nodding. "But not forever. I see light and love, too. Well into old age." She lifted up and resettled in her seat, a smile tugging at one corner of her mouth. "And a daughter," she added.

"That we know," Natalia said.

"I'm speaking of the one *after* this."

*Huh*. Two daughters. I was glad for it. I deserved it, and so did Natalia. No girls would be loved more in the world.

The woman sat back with a sigh. "Then again, I've been wrong before." She glanced at her crystal ball. "I can look a little harder if you like? I may see something after all . . ."

"No," Natalia and I answered at the same time.

"Well. I'll be here next weekend, too." She took a pack of cigarettes from somewhere under her table. "Do you have a light?"

"I quit," I said.

"Right."

I put my arm around Natalia and guided her away as she cast a final glance over her shoulder at the woman. "Feel better?" I asked.

"*Me?*" Natalia's brows lifted. "I could've knocked you over with a feather, you were so interested in what she'd say."

I chuckled. "*Nah.* I don't believe in any of that."

"Sure." She rolled her eyes. "So you don't think we'll have a second girl?"

The thought put a smile on my face all the way back to the third-floor apartment we'd temporarily rented.

As Natalia changed, I opened all the windows overlooking a small courtyard. Fresh, cool air breezed in. I turned on the record player, sat on the edge of our bed to remove my shoes, and leaned back on the mattress with an arm behind my head. Something I hadn't gotten to do very much in my old life—sit and listen to music.

I thought of the Badlands often—I couldn't help it. It had been my life for twelve years. But between my childhood with my parents, my service at Costa's compound, and the Calavera cartel, I'd lived several lifetimes. This one, with Natalia, would be just another adventure, and there was nobody I wanted by my side more.

Speaking of the she-devil, she strolled out of the bathroom in a black silk slip with lacy red edges that stopped just below the tops of her thighs. She smoothed her palms over her belly, curving her hands underneath and turning to the side so I could see how far along she was. I liked to watch her grow. To look at her as much as possible and commit these days to memory. Once the baby came, things would be a little more chaotic. Traveling around wouldn't be as easy. I'd have to keep looking over my shoulder everywhere we went, with even more on the line.

But it was a good problem to have. After the life we'd led, I was confident there wasn't anything my wife and I couldn't take on.

She poured me a whisky neat from the bottle we'd picked up during our trip to the square and brought the glass and a lit candle to my bedside. "It's Day of the Dead, and we didn't do anything," she said, sitting on the edge of the bed.

"I think we should be thankful for an uneventful holiday for once." I winked. "But yes, we honor those we've lost. Your mother. Our baby. My men, your father's, too, and our friends."

She nodded and glanced at her purse, where she kept the sonogram she'd received this time last year, and then to her suitcase, which held her mother's wedding dress. They were two of the only things she'd brought from the Badlands.

Along with her White Monarch, of course.

I took her hand, brought it to my mouth and pressed a kiss to the back of it.

With a smile, she passed me my drink. "How is it?"

I took a sip. "Not like the Zamoras' blue agave," I said. "But very nice."

She took the glass from me, set it down on the nightstand, and climbed onto the bed on her hands and knees. The woman acted as if she wasn't pregnant at all. Agile as ever—always down for anything, constantly on the move, participating in hand-to-hand combat despite my explicit prohibition. She was only twenty-two, though. At thirty-six, I probably had more aches and pains *without* carrying a human the size of a cantaloupe.

"You asked earlier if there's anything I need," she said.

"Tell me," I responded. "You know I don't rely on anyone to deliver my wishes to the gods. I make them happen myself. I will grant you anything."

She climbed on top of me. "Just you."

Straddling my waist, she opened my fly. Put me inside her. Rocked on me.

It wasn't the throne I'd once envisioned for my underground queen, but I couldn't complain.

*Bienvenido al infierno. Welcome to Hell, my friends.*

*It happens to look and feel quite a lot like heaven.*

"The fortune-teller said you picked a name. Was she right?" I asked.

Natalia leaned forward, still gyrating on me as her dark hair brushed her shoulders, eyes bright when they met mine. "Mel," she said. "Short for Oyamel."

"The forest where the monarchs make their winter homes," I said. "The one you *died* in. I cursed those butterflies, *mi amor*."

She smiled, her hands curling against my chest. "But I *didn't* die," she said. "They protected me."

I cupped her jaw, touching my thumb to the corner of her mouth. "Every day I think to myself, I've never seen you more beautiful. How is it possible?" I took her hips. "Mel is very nice. Oyamel Cruz de la Rosa."

"But to the rest of the world, she'll be Mel Cristina Delgado."

"Cristina?"

"For her Papá."

"Do I get a say?" I asked. "We should put Bianca somewhere in there, too. Perhaps we pretend it's your *apellido*."

"And curse her with a long, traditional name?" She smiled. "Yes—let's. Oyamel Bianca Cristina Delgado."

". . . De la Rosa," I added. "There won't be any names left for the next girl."

"Angelina," she said at once.

My heart threatened to rupture, overflowing with love. Natalia understood what the name meant to me. Angelina it would be.

Natalia's smile gave way to a moan as she used my chest as leverage to push back on me, her hips sliding faster.

After she'd been at it a while, I put my hands around the back of her neck and held her in place. I took over with a languid, easy rhythm. "Slow down with me. Relax."

Apparently, this was what one did in the afterlife. He ate a good meal, drank fine whisky, and fucked his eight months pregnant wife. Nobody had to die. Nobody depended on us for anything. Nobody cared what we did. Because nobody knew we were still alive.

And nobody ever could.

It was a good life. One I was more grateful for considering I'd almost lost it. I had all I needed in my wife and our child—or children, as the old lady would have it.

*So now you know the truth. It's a lot of responsibility. Don't tell anyone.*

## TITLES BY JESSICA HAWKINS

## LEARN MORE AT WWW.JESSICAHAWKINS.NET

***Right Where I Want You***

"An intelligently written, sexy, feel-good romance that packs an emotional punch..." (*USA Today*'s HEA) A witty workplace romance filled with sexual tension and smart, fun enemies-to-lovers banter.

***Something in the Way Series***

"A tale of forbidden love in epic proportion... Brilliant" (New York Times bestselling author Corinne Michaels) Lake Kaplan falls for a handsome older man — but then her sister sets her sights on him too.

*Something in the Way*

*Somebody Else's Sky*

*Move the Stars*

*Lake + Manning*

***Slip of the Tongue Series***

"Addictive. Painful. Captivating...an authentic, raw, and emotionally gripping must-read." (Angie's Dreamy Reads) Her husband doesn't want her anymore. The man next door would give up everything to have her.

*Slip of the Tongue*

*The First Taste*

*Yours to Bare*

***Explicitly Yours Series***

"Pretty Woman meets Indecent Proposal...a seductive series."—(USA Today Bestselling Author Louise Bay) What if one night isn't enough? A red-hot collection.

*Possession*

*Domination*

*Provocation*

*Obsession*

**The Cityscape Series**

Olivia has the perfect life—but something is missing. Handsome playboy David Dylan awakens a passion that she thought she'd lost a long time ago. Can she keep their combustible lust from spilling over into love?

*Come Undone*

*Come Alive*

*Come Together*

**White Monarch Trilogy**

"Exciting and suspenseful and sexy and breathtaking." (*USA Today* Bestselling Author Lauren Rowe)

*Violent Delights*

*Violent Ends*

*Violent Triumphs*

# ACKNOWLEDGMENTS

Endless thanks to my own personal Badlands, the proverbial village that helped me pull together this series. A thrilling, tasking journey not without its potholes—and payoff.

To my editor (never-let-me-down Maksim), Elizabeth London Editing: you put me through the wringer on this one, but I believe this time, the result were our best yet. Thank you for helping me bring Natalia and Cristiano to the world.

To the people on the ground, my beta Katie at Underline This Editing, proofreader Paige Maroney Smith, sensitivity readers, Chayo Ramón and Maria Dominguez—the foundation of the story was laid, but you helped make it a book.

To my release PA, Serena McDonald for rallying the troops and keeping things moving when I can't.

And special thanks to Najla Qamber Designs, who made my bookshelf look like a piece of art. The pages needed a home, and you gave them the most beautiful ones possible.

# ABOUT THE AUTHOR

Jessica Hawkins is a *USA Today* bestselling author known for her "emotionally gripping" and "off-the-charts hot" romance. Dubbed "queen of angst" by both peers and readers for her smart and provocative work, she's garnered a cult-like following of fans who love to be torn apart...and put back together.

She writes romance both at home in New York City and around the world, a coffee shop traveler who bounces from café to café with just a laptop, headphones, and a coffee cup. She loves to keep in close touch with her readers, mostly via Facebook, Instagram, and her mailing list.

Stay updated:
www.jessicahawkins.net/mailing-list
www.amazon.com/author/jessicahawkins
www.jessicahawkins.net

www.ingramcontent.com/pod-product-compliance
Lightning Source LLC
Chambersburg PA
CBHW020324030826
48979CB00022B/1000

* 9 7 8 1 9 5 0 4 8 8 0 8 7 *